Honors for the first books of

LEGENDS OF THE GUARDIAN-KING

The Light of Eidon

Booklist—*Top 10 Christian Novels 2004*

ForeWord Magazine—*2003 Book of the Year—Silver
Science Fiction*

Christian Fiction Review—*Best of 2003*

Christy Award—2004
Fantasy

The Shadow Within

Borders—*Best of 2004
Religion and Spirituality*

Romantic Times—*Best of 2004 Finalist
Inspirational*

Christian Fiction Review—*Best of 2004*

Christy Award—2005
Visionary

Shadow Over Kiriath

Christian Fiction Review—*Best of 2005*

Christy Award—2006
Visionary

Books by Karen Hancock

Arena

LEGENDS OF THE GUARDIAN-KING
The Light of Eidon
The Shadow Within
Shadow Over Kiriath
Return of the Guardian-King

LEGENDS OF THE GUARDIAN-KING

KAREN HANCOCK

RETURN OF THE
GUARDIAN-KING

BethanyHouse

MINNEAPOLIS, MINNESOTA

Published by Bethany House Publishers
11400 Hampshire Avenue South
Bloomington, Minnesota 55438

Bethany House Publishers is a division of
Baker Publishing Group, Grand Rapids, Michigan.

Printed in the United States of America

ISBN-13:   978-0-7642-2797-4
ISBN-10:   0-7642-2797-1

Library of Congress Cataloging-in-Publication Data

Hancock, Karen.
    Return of the guardian-king / Karen Hancock.
        p.   cm. — (Legends of the guardian-king ; 4)
    ISBN-13: 978-0-7642-2797-4 (pbk.)
    ISBN-10: 0-7642-2797-1 (pbk.)
1. Kings and rulers—Fiction. 2. Coronations—Fiction. I. Title.
    PS3608.A698R48   2007
    813'.6—dc22   2006038410

KAREN HANCOCK has won Christy Awards for each of her first four novels—*Arena* and the first three books in this series, *The Light of Eidon, The Shadow Within,* and *Shadow Over Kiriath*. She graduated from the University of Arizona with bachelor's degrees in biology and wildlife biology. Along with writing, she is a semi-professional watercolorist and has exhibited her work in a number of national juried shows. She and her family reside in Arizona.

For discussion and further information, Karen invites you to visit her Web site at *www.kmhancock.com*.

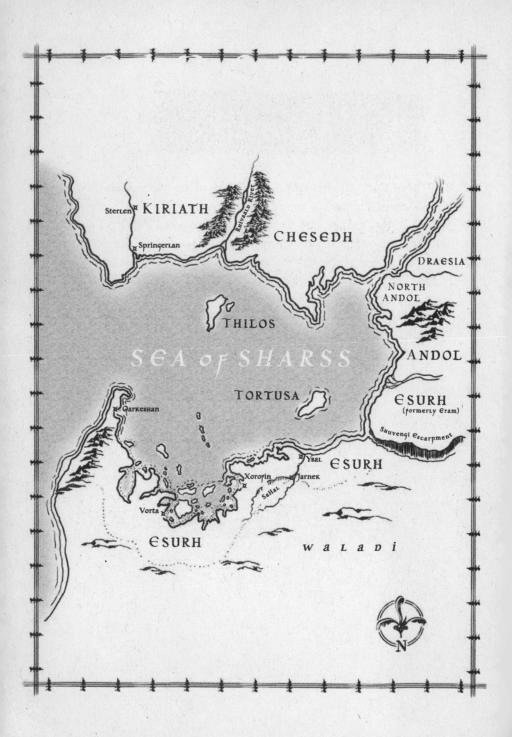

KIRIATH

Sterlen

Springerlan

Kelthalo River

CHESEDH

DRAESIA

NORTH
ANDOL

THILOS

ANDOL

SEA of SHARSS

TORTUSA

ESURH
(formerly Eram)

Qarkeshan

Shuvengi Escarpment

Ysal

Xorofin
Jarnek

ESURH

Sahat

Vorta

ESURH

WALADI

N

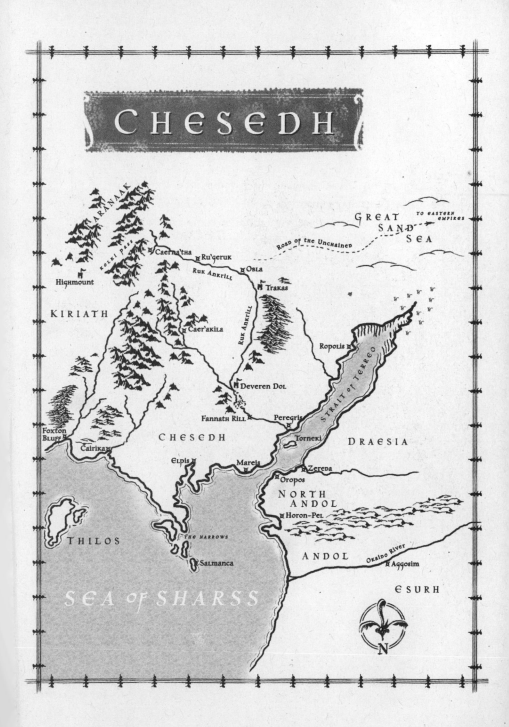

CHESEDH

ARANAAK

Kolki Pass

Highmount

KIRIATH

Caerna'tha

Ru'geruk

Ruk Ankrill

Obla

Ruk Ankrill

Trakas

Caer'akila

Ropolis

Deveren Dol

STRAIT of TERREO

Fannath Rill

Peregris

DRAESIA

CHESEDH

Torneki

Foxton
Bluff

Cairikau

Elpis

Mareis

Zereda

Oropos

NORTH
ANDOL

Horon-Pel

GREAT
SAND
SEA

TO EASTERN
EMPIRES

Road of the Unchained

THILOS

The Narrows

Salmanca

ANDOL

Okaino River

Aggosim

ESURH

SEA of SHARSS

N

"You are my servant. I have chosen you and I will strengthen you to do what I have commanded you. I will provide you with all you need to carry out my plans. And all who come against you will be shamed; they will be as if they never were."

—From the *First Word of Revelation*
Scroll of the Seven Wars

CAERNA'THA

PART ONE

CHAPTER

1

"*I dream of the meadows, green-gold 'neath the sun, sweet with the dew of the morn . . .*"

The bell-toned voice drew Abramm Kalladorne into the sunlight of the open meadow, a yellow butterfly zigzagging ahead of him above a patch of purple lupine. He pressed through the bloom-laden stalks into rippling grass, following the plucked notes of a lirret and a voice as familiar as his own. She must be just beyond that primrose at the meadow's far edge.

Children's laughter echoed in counterpoint to her sweet voice, and his pace quickened. Ian would be over two by now, walking well, maybe even talking in phrases and sentences, while Simon would have left all his toddler-hood behind, a real little boy at last. Then there was Maddie. Abramm ached for her so badly sometimes he could hardly bear it. Now finally, that was behind him. All the worrying about threading the high passes before winter closed them had been for naught. In a moment he would step around that bush and there she'd be, her gray-blue eyes widening with surprise at the sight of him an instant before she'd cast her lirret aside and fling herself into his—

His foot slipped, and he lurched to regain his balance, gripping his walking staff hard as he drove it into the snow. The misstep jolted his entire body as the vision winked out and the dark, icy reality of the blizzard-swept heights filled his senses again. She wasn't here. His boys weren't here. There was no meadow. The passes were not behind him, and winter was very defi-nitely closing in. . . .

Realization slammed him so hard he reeled to a stop, struggling to breathe as he felt again the cold and the exhaustion and the misery. Wind screamed around him, pelting his heavy woolen cloak with slivers of snow and flapping its snow-caked hem about his legs. For a moment the desire to give up was so strong he nearly collapsed.

But he couldn't. Maddie was waiting for him. His boys needed him. And so he drew a deep breath and reached up to dash away the ice that continually froze onto his beard and mustache. Chunks of it clung also to the long hair dangling beside his face, some of them rasping against the inside edge of his cowl, others frozen to his beard. He no longer felt his feet, and his fingers, numb beneath a double layer of glove and mitten, could hardly grip his walking staff.

He squinted down the rocky hill to where a shin-deep trough of footprints angled across the slope through the rapidly accumulating snow. At the end of his pocket of visibility, the last of his companions were starting down the next switchback, obscured by the shifting veils of snow. Shuddering, he started after them, placing steps and stick carefully to avoid any more almost-falls.

Neither he nor anyone else in his party had any real idea where they were going, only that having come through the Kolki Pass they must descend the barren slopes beyond to an ancient Terstan monastery just below the tree line. *"The way will be obvious,"* the men back at Highmount Holding had assured them. Maybe it would be if clouds hadn't swallowed the world and driving snow hadn't made it hard to open one's eyes and the rock cairns that were supposed to be their guides weren't fast disappearing beneath the drifting snow.

It was typical, though, of the bad luck that had plagued them since leaving Kiriath, transforming what should have been a three-week journey through the pass into a six-week trial of endurance. They'd run out of food two days ago and burned the last of their dung-pats in last night's fire. Water had been in short supply for over a week, and they had an old man, a pregnant woman, and a number of children with them. Thinking they'd be in Caerna'tha tonight, they'd left much of their bedding and tents with the wagon when it had irreparably broken down in the pass that morning. Now, with the day three-quarters gone, and the tree line still who knew how far below them, their situation was growing desperate.

For not the first time he sent up a prayer for guidance and protection.

Thus, when the trail rounded a rocky slope to emerge onto a promontory overlooked by a small trailside hut, he should have been elated. His traveling companions certainly were. Many were already picking their way up the steep, narrow stair to the doorway where two men worked to string up a blanket.

At the base of the stair in the slope's lee, the big, blond former black-smith, Rolland Kemp, lifted the pack frame off their one remaining horse. "Ah, Alaric!" he said as Abramm drew up beside him. "I thought maybe we'd lost ye." The wind was lessened there in the slope's lee, but it still made conversation difficult. Rolland tossed the frame onto the ground, then bent to dig through one of the discarded saddlebags. He pulled out a near-empty grain bag and offered the remainder of its contents to the horse. Snow mounded on his shoulders and clung in balls to the fur-lined rim of his hood.

Rolland had become something of a friend on this journey. As the strongest of the men, he and Abramm were most often called upon to search for the lost, unstick the wagon, or carry extra loads—and the shared experience and responsibility had bound them together. Besides, Rolland had an easy temperament, a level head, and a strong sense of loyalty. He was a good man, and a good husband and father. If Abramm couldn't have Trap here with him, he thought Rolland might be the next best thing.

Now Abramm turned to stare over the promontory into the stormy whiteness, relieved they had a place to escape the cold, but uneasy nonetheless. Caerna'tha was supposed to have been but a few hours' hike once they'd left the pass. Wind gusted against his side, ice crystals stinging his cheekbones and making his eyes water as he searched for some sign of the monastery's presence: the glint of a window, the straight line of a wall, even the dark bulk of a mountainside. But swirling white obliterated all beyond the small promontory on which they stood.

"See anything?" Rolland shouted from the other side of the horse.

Abramm shook his head. "It could be right there, for all we know."

"An' we could blunder off the trail and get hopelessly lost b'fore we found it," Rolland said. As with every other man in the party, ice clotted his blond beard and brows, framing a small patch of wind-burned cheekbones beneath deep-set blue eyes. "Ye wanna help me get Pearl here up that stair now?" He slapped the mare's flank, dislodging a mass of accumulated snow.

Abramm glanced back at the hut where the last of the women and children disappeared through the blanketed doorway. His uneasiness remained, but he could think of no reason why it should—other than the fact he was hungry, thirsty, exhausted, and deeply disappointed they'd not reach Caerna'tha after all. He was sick to death of snow and cold and wind and, truth be told, these people and their endless needs. If only he could—

His breath caught and he froze, listening hard. "Did you hear that?"

Rolland regarded him blankly.

"Sounded like someone screaming." But he heard nothing more and clearly Rolland had not noticed it. Probably the wind. Or maybe another hallucination.

Though all the other huts on their journey through the pass had had linked to them a shelter for the animals, this one did not. Since the mare refused to climb the ice-slicked front stair, Abramm suggested they take her back up the trail and try leading her across the slope on a level closer to where the hut sat. But they could get her to go only a little way off the trail before she refused to go another step. Finally they had no choice but to tether her to a pile of rocks back at the foot of the front stair.

"I hate leaving her out here," Rolland said, and Abramm marveled, not for the first time, that a man as big and strong and fearsome looking as Rolland Kemp could be so tenderhearted. He clapped his friend's beefy shoulder. "She'll be all right, Rollie. She's weathered worse up in the pass."

"I suppose . . ." Rolland shook out his own blanket and laid it over the mare as Abramm started up the stairway.

Fatigue was closing in hard on him by the time he gained the top of the slippery steps. He was reaching to push aside the blanket when again he heard the distant scream. Skin crawling, he cast back his cowl. But the sound did not repeat; instead he heard voices arguing inside the hut.

"Well, if yer friend Alaric hadn't insisted on stoppin' early yesterday, we'd have gone on and found the right place t' camp." That was Oakes Trinley, former tanner and city alderman, and the group's self-appointed leader since long before Abramm had met them. "An' if we'd camped in the right place—"

"He didn't insist!" a female voice interrupted him. "You all agreed it was a good idea, so don't go blaming Alaric for what was your decision." Marta Brackleford, the widowed sister of Trinley's wife, Kitrenna, was one of the few who had no compunctions about speaking her mind to him. Once married to a banker, and proprietor of her father's printing business, she'd been an independent woman all her adult life. She'd also taken an unveiled interest in Abramm, which made him as uneasy as it warmed his heart.

Trinley, on the other hand, had disliked him from the moment he'd joined the group at Highmount.

Now, as the former alderman started to reply, Abramm forcefully stomped the snow from his boots, cutting him off. Pushing aside the blanket, Abramm stepped into the close, warm air of the dimly lit chamber beyond.

People sat or curled on the floor between piles of salvaged bedding and gear. A rope net full of murky kelistars hung from the ceiling timber. Others gleamed here and there throughout the company—most of them warm-stars—while in the shadows at the back, old Totten Ashvelt picked his way through a rubble of fallen stones, filling the many chinks in the wall with dried grass from the floor. The three mothers in the group wrapped their crying children into blankets, promising they'd have all the food they wanted tomorrow when they reached the monastery.

For now only snow filled the kettle on the cooking tripod, heated by a fire ring heaped with warmstars. Trinley stood near the doorway, a stocky, broad-shouldered man in an ice-caked leather greatcoat. Marta faced him from the far side of the ring of warmstars, her dark eyes flicking to Abramm as he entered. A blush deepened the pink of her wind-burned cheeks.

Trinley turned to glare at him, but Abramm made no mention of the recently terminated conversation, shrugging out of his rucksack as he informed them of the situation with the mare.

"And Rollie?" Mrs. Kemp inquired from Marta's side. "He's not going to stay down there with the beast all night, is he?"

Abramm smiled. The woman knew her husband well. "He'll be up shortly, ma'am."

She seemed content with that, but Marta gave Trinley a look of alarm.

"We're not below the tree line yet, Marta," the alderman said before she could speak.

Abramm had no idea what that was about and was too tired and discouraged to care. He picked his way through the clutter of people and belongings to a clear spot on the other side of the warmstar ring and settled tailor style before it. As he stripped off his ice-crusted mittens, Marta said quietly, "They told us specifically not to stop after we left the pass. To go straight to Caerna'tha."

"And in good weather that would have been fine," Trinley retorted. "But it's not good weather, and anyway, if Caerna'tha was an easy walk away, why would anyone build this hut? Besides, if the wolves are rhu'ema spawn like they said, they won't be out in this storm anyway. The horse will be fine. Stop worrying."

Wolves . . . rhu'ema spawn . . . Abramm stuffed the wet mittens into his rucksack and conjured his own warmstar to hold directly against his palms,

RETURN OF THE GUARDIAN-KING ‖ 15

thinking he should know what they were talking about but unable to make his mind focus on it. Instead, it wandered off into an exhausted haze that involved another reunion scenario with Maddie and the boys. . . .

The painful tingle of his hands returning to life brought him back to the moment. A sense of being watched and mocked swept over him. Probably with his head bent like this, the others felt freer to stare at him and exchange whispers. They'd all die now, and it would be his fault.

Not my fault. I wanted to move on.

"But you didn't move on, did you? And now you are stuck."

He wasn't sure who had said that. Were they speaking aloud? Why did everything sound so far away? He wanted to look around, but he couldn't seem to lift his head.

"Stuck." Two voices taunted him in unison: *"You didn't think you could escape us, did you, loser?"*

And suddenly he knew who they were. Rhu'ema had dogged him on the journey through the pass, knowing exactly who he was, even if the people he traveled with did not. They'd delighted in harassing him with a stream of subverbal insults and threats. He'd spent many nights maintaining the Lightshield he'd routinely conjured to protect everyone—a duty few of them knew he carried out.

Knowing they'd be forced to ground once the storm hit, the rhu'ema had come ahead to wait for him. And not just to wait . . .

He sensed other minds through theirs—dark, savage minds, full of bloodlust. Human, yet not human at all, feeling the wind and the snow as they ran toward the feast that awaited them in the heights. . . .

"NO!" The shout burst from him as he surged to his feet, drawing the startled gazes of those around him. The room whirled briefly as he stared back, struggling to understand what had just happened. He'd stood up too fast for one thing.

"Sit down, Alaric," Trinley growled. "Ye were only dreamin'."

Dreaming? He glanced around at the rough stone walls bathed with the warmstars' orange glow, and at the back of the chamber he found two other lights—one purple, one green—pressed into the cracks between the stone and the slate roof, hiding from him, even as they laughed at him. For they knew as well as he did that the discovery was not one he could share.

Trinley laid a hand on Abramm's shoulder, giving him a little shake. "Relax, man. We're safe for now."

But were they? Were those other minds he'd touched nothing but dream creatures? His disquiet intensified.

One of the children began to cry. Then Rolland shoved aside the blanket and stepped inside, a giant in the cramped quarters. He shoved back his ice-crusted hood and looked about at them, his expression tense. "I think I just heard wolves," he announced.

Abramm's heart stopped. "Light's grace!" he muttered. "That's what I sensed!" He looked around at the people staring up at him. "This is a trap," he cried loudly. "It's probably not even a real hut."

Trinley shook him again, harder. "Stop it, now! That's enough of yer nightmares."

Abramm turned sharply, knocking the other man's grip loose with his forearm and forcing him back a step. "It *wasn't* a nightmare!"

Trinley gaped at him, his long gray hair straggling over the cast-back fleece-lined hood.

"There are rhu'ema here," Abramm said, scanning the back wall. "Ells. They've worked some sort of spell." An errant draft from the back chilled his face.

In the corner the baby whose crying had been temporarily silenced by Rolland's entrance started up again, while the adults muttered one to another.

Trinley stepped close to Abramm again. "What the plague is wrong with ye, man?" he growled. "Are ye tryin' to set us all apanic?"

"Of course not!"

When Abramm didn't back down, Trinley turned to scowl at the shadows in the drafty rear of the hut. The others followed his lead, twisting round in a rustling of fabric and leather. For a moment the babe cried and the wind shrieked and the rope-slung kelistars rocked gently back and forth in the draft.

Then someone grunted dismissively. "It looks fine to me."

More voices echoed him, and Trinley nodded. "Ye've done a lot for us, Alaric, but ye know ye've been hallucinatin' for days."

"I'm not hallucinating," Abramm said. "If we stay here, we'll die."

Trinley's grizzled brows drew downward. "We can't go blundering out into that storm again. If ye fear t' stay with us, leave. No one'll stop ye. But I'll cock ye on the head m'self if ye don't stop this wild talk."

Abramm quelled a flare of irritation, wondering what would happen if he did leave. Which of the two of them would the others follow? He snorted inwardly. As if there was any doubt. Besides, he knew he wouldn't be able to abandon the children, and anyway, Trinley was right as far as he understood things.

My Lord Eidon . . . they won't follow if they don't believe me. But how can I persuade them to believe me if they can't see the truth? Open their eyes. . . .

More children started to cry, frightened by his mention of the ells. Their mothers assured them there were no ells, and shot angry glances at Abramm while the men glowered at him. Across the ring of warmstars, though, the widowed Marta Brackleford spoke softly to her sister. "Surely if this hut was a safe place, the Highmounters would have mentioned it."

"So d' *you* see these ells o' his, then?" Kitrenna Trinley asked her sourly. She brushed a wet strand of gray hair from her wind-reddened face and glanced at the rafters.

"No," Marta admitted, looking up, as well. "But I sense something here. A crawling up the back of my neck, as if unfriendly eyes are watching us."

Kitrenna huffed. "Stop it, Marti! Ye'll just encourage him."

"What if he's right?"

"What are the ells goin' t' do t' us, anyway?" Kitrenna demanded.

"Hold us until the wolves get here," Abramm answered grimly.

Kitrenna looked up at him. "We don't even know there *are* any wolves."

"Rolland heard them—and so did I, earlier."

"Rhu'ema spawn can't travel through falling snow," Oakes Trinley pointed out.

"I don't think they're rhu'ema spawn," Abramm said. "I think they're something else."

"And how would ye know that?" Kitrenna sniffed disdainfully and turned back to her sister. "He just wants to get t' the monastery as fast as he can so he can lose the rest of us and strike out fer Trakas on his own. Ye heard him the other night—he doesn't care a pin what happens t' us."

The accusation stung precisely because of its element of truth.

"Indeed!?" the ells sniggered. *"You can hardly wait to leave them behind."*

Abramm ignored them and kept his focus on the issue at hand. "How is it you even saw this place?" he asked of Trinley. "Given how far it sits above the trail, hidden by all the snow . . . I'd think we'd all have walked right past it. What drew your eye?"

"What the plague difference does that make?" the stocky alderman snapped. "I happened t' notice it. Ye're not the only one with sharp eyes in this group, ye know." With a snort of disgust he raised his voice and assured everyone they'd be safe here for the night and better able because of it to tackle the forest in the morning.

Abramm glanced back at the two rhu'ema, smug and malevolent in the shadows.

"Ye know, ells bein' here would explain poor Pearl's refusal t' come up here," Rolland mused from where he stood before the blanketed doorway.

As Abramm turned to him, the icy draft from the chamber's rear washed around him again, and with it came inspiration. Wordlessly he wheeled and picked his way across the crowded floor to the back wall. There he bloomed a kelistar into the darkness, making it hard enough he could hold it in one hand while he fingered the wall with the other.

Furious now, the rhu'ema crammed themselves back into their crevices. He touched the cold stone, the rough bristles of grass, then the faint, hair-lifting vibration of the spell. A rush of threats, alternatives, and condemnation flooded his mind from the panicked ells. He ignored it, seeking the Light. . . .

It flared from the shield on his chest and down his arm into the stone veneer of the illusion, shredding it to streamers of mist. A hole big enough to fit two horses through gaped in a wall riddled with holes, many of which had already been chinked with blowing snow or grass. More snow piled up on the threshold as flakes held back by the illusion fluttered through the opening.

At Abramm's back, people gasped and a woman cried, "There's nothing there."

Other exclamations followed the first, the pitch of the voices escalating until in moments Trinley's feared panic was upon them. People raced about, jabbering, grabbing this or that without heed. One woman snatched up her baby and hurried for the doorway without cloak or blanket.

Abramm caught her arm as she went by him and shouted, "Enough! Stop this NOW!" The old kingly imperiousness rang in his voice, and the command produced an immediate and startling effect. Everyone froze and turned toward him. Only the children continued to cry.

"We must go," he said firmly. "And we must hurry. But we must do so in a sensible manner. Eidon has brought us to this point, and he knew we would take this detour."

"Aye, an' now we must pay fer our foolishness," old Totten Ashvelt said fiercely, glaring at Trinley.

"How will we find our way in the dark?" demanded Kitrenna.

Abramm reminded them they had at least an hour of light left.

"Will you lead us, then, Alaric?" This was from young Galen Gault,

Trinley's newly wed nephew. "We all know you see better in the dark than anyone."

"Aye," Trinley said sourly. "Please. Lead us. 'Tis what ye've wanted from the start, isn't it?"

Abramm opened his mouth to deny it, then realized this, too, was a distraction. What's more, he knew it didn't originate with Trinley but with the two glowing forms at the back of the hut. Thus, he gave Trinley a quick nod and set about directing their preparation to leave. Soon, with Pearl repacked and rucksacks redonned, Abramm led them down the trail from the promontory, Rolland on his heels and Trinley bringing up the rear.

The track widened swiftly, and soon the twisted trunks and snow-laden branches of stunted evergreens sprang up along its downward side, further defining the trail, even in the driving snow and gathering gloom. If the wind howled at their backs, it also swept their path relatively clean of snow.

The trees grew in size and number as they descended, the wind lessening, as well. The wolves howled again, and Abramm stopped, tossing his hood back to listen as Rolland, immediately behind him, did likewise. A second scream answered the first, followed by a chorus of strange, sharp squeals, undeniably closer than they'd been before.

"Are those the wolves, Mama?" a small voice asked as the wind lulled.

"Shh, poppet," said the child's mother, Rolland's wife, standing behind her husband.

"Are they coming to eat us?"

"No, son," Rolland said. "Now, hush!"

"They're still down in the valley, where the deep drifts will hamper them," Abramm assured them. "We'll reach Caerna'tha long before they get here."

But a dry voice in his head grimly reminded him that the men at Highmount had said these wolves were like no others. Huge, agile, able to leap twenty feet at a bound, they were not real wolves at all, in fact. But something worse.

We'll make it, he assured himself. *Eidon will see to it*. The wolves screamed again, as if to contest that view, and he quickened his pace.

The snow had been knee-deep for some time when Rolland moved to take over breaking the trail. Stepping aside, Abramm stood gasping back his breath as the others slogged past him, heads down against the storm. With no faces to look at, his eye caught on the lights that glowed in the surrounding tree trunks. Green, blue, red, and gold glimmered from the cracks in the trees' platelike bark—always on the side away from the wind, as if taking refuge from the storm.

"You're not going to get away, you know."

He frowned, realizing that again he was hearing their voices, and irritated he should be able to.

"We've been waiting for you. They've been waiting for you. Especially for you, O great slayer of shadowspawn."

As if on cue, another ululation wailed on the storm winds, closer than ever.

Now Oakes Trinley approached him, trudging at the end of the line, face turned downward like the rest. Only as he came even did he glance up. "Still think we'll make it before dark, Alaric?"

Abramm let him pass without comment. Before long Rolland surrendered the trail-breaking job to Galen, who eventually gave it off to Cedric Ashvelt, and on down the line as the light continued to fail and the wolves' cries drew ever nearer.

Finally, the party rounded a hill and the clouds parted to reveal a wide valley whitened with snowfall and cut through by a dark stream. Out of the near bank rose a great bulk of stone walls and peak-roofed turrets, levels upon levels stairstepping up the jagged outcropping on which it had been built and surrounded by a high, crenellated outer wall. In the dimming light, it stood dismayingly dark, its great mass lit by a mere handful of tiny lights.

A deep ravine spilled riverward out of the draw to their right, their trail running along its near side and finally crossing over it by means of a snow-cloaked stone bridge.

Abramm took back the lead and they switchbacked down a forested slope to the lip of the ravine, then headed back out toward the valley. The wolves felt so close now, Abramm feared his little group wouldn't even break into the open before they were attacked. He urged them repeatedly to hurry, to pick up the children and guard the mare, but they were all too muzzy with fatigue to obey him for longer than a few steps.

As they neared the forest's edge, Abramm rejoiced to see two men tramping through the snow beyond the trees. A thicket of spruce momentarily obscured them, and when Abramm emerged into the open, no one was there. He thought he was hallucinating again until he saw the trail that had been stamped through the snow, paralleling the ravine to the bridge and over it, then up to the monastery, looming on the far side. But where were the men who made it?

The others found the track and burst into excited chatter. Abramm quelled it sharply. "We have no time to dawdle. Our enemies are close."

Trinley took over the lead, and Abramm dropped back to protect the rear. Implicitly reassuming command now that the end was in sight, the alderman called for the lanterns to be broken out and kelistars placed in them. Though Abramm chafed with impatience at the delay, he did not object. The kelistars might have a warding effect, and he feared they'd need all the help they could get.

Finally they were hurrying along again, the wind pressing them up the trail as it pelted their backs with snow. Just as Abramm dared believe they might reach the monastery in time, the wolves burst into loud, triumphant song, sounding as if they were coming up the ravine even now.

Their howls spurred his people to panic, and they ran all out for the dubious safety of the bridge.

2

They'd all crowded onto the length of the stone span by the time Abramm got there, Trinley, Cedric, and Galen at the far end, Rolland and the other men at the near, with the women, children, and mare in between. The wolves' howls and yips still tumbled madly around them, and yet the wolves did not appear.

Abramm stepped away from the glittering path to peer into the gloom-filled valley. And sure enough, there they were—seven dark forms bounding through the deep snow, not nearly as close as they'd sounded, their voices amplified and carried by a trick of the wind.

"They're still a ways away," he said, turning back to the others. They stared at him mutely. His eyes lifted to the tramped-out path beyond them, the kelistars' light reflected in a long ribbon of illumination that stretched up the slope all the way to the monastery gates. It was a straight path, not too steep, not all that far. Most of them could probably make it. . . .

On the bridge, a man cried, "We're trapped! They'll have us for sure!"

"Let's all fall down and pretend to be dead," another suggested. "Maybe they'll leave us alone."

"Aye, there's naught else we can do—"

"SILENCE!" Trinley bellowed from the bridge's far side. When he had it, he rebuked them angrily. "Listen to yerselves! Are ye cowards or men? We didna come all this way t' lie down and die. So put away that woolwash and stiffen yer spines. If they do get us, let's make sure they pay fer it."

"Pay fer it?" his own wife protested. "How about making sure we stay alive, instead? If we take refuge under the bridge, we could defend ourselves easily. Tuck the little ones under it—"

"Have ye even looked under the bridge, woman?" Trinley snarled at her. "The ravine's far too deep to provide shelter, even if we could get t' the bottom of it."

"I didna mean go t' the bottom. There's a ledge just under the bridge. Ye're practically standing on it." She leaned over the edge of the bridge. "There's even a path to it, Oakes. Right there. Don't ye see it?"

The wolves' cries clamored around them. Abramm eyed the path up the hill again, noting how it wasn't filling with snow, though fat flakes were coming down thickly all around them. He glanced toward the portion of the broken trail they'd already come up. Sure enough, it was already losing its definition as the snow gathered upon it. It was also significantly dimmer in reflecting the kelistars' light, especially near the forest's edge where it began.

And there was still no sign of the men who'd made it, though they had to have been out tramping the path until right before Abramm and the others had shown up. Now his glance caught on something else—the trees beyond the trail, all of which glowed with at least one rhu'eman occupant. They'd been more spread out before. Now it was as if they had gathered to watch. . . .

He looked again at the gleaming line of light at the trail's midst, thinking it seemed too bright and too localized to be merely reflected light. What if. . . ?

His heart pounded with sudden excitement. Of course!

"We have to keep going!" he shouted, breaking into the Trinleys' argument.

Again the entire gathering turned to look at him, eyes haunted with fear.

"Have ye lost your mind?" Kitrenna demanded of him.

"I think the path they broke for us here is protected," he explained. "As long as we stay on it, I think we'll be safe." He shoved his way through the clot of women and children on the bridge, and stepped smoothly between Oakes and Kitrenna, pulling the man away from his wife and off the bridge onto the path.

"Look at it," he said. "Can you see the way it sparkles all the way up to the monastery? I believe it's under Eidon's Light."

But from the length of time Trinley looked at the path, the lack of comment he gave, and the troubled expression in his eyes when next he looked at Abramm, Abramm knew he'd seen nothing.

"Just look at the trough itself, then," Abramm pressed. "The way it's not filling up with snow when by all rights it should be. When the part we've already come up is, and if anything, that should be the clearer of the two."

"The wolves will be here any moment," Kitrenna protested. "And ye want t' spread us out before 'em like dainties on a tray?" She turned to her husband. "He's lost his mind, Oakes. Tell him. We need to take shelter on that ledge. Wait 'til daylight when they'll have to seek the shadow."

"If we do that," Abramm said calmly, "some of us will die. Maybe all of us. I believe Eidon has provided us this path, but it's up to us to trust him."

"If it's so safe," Trinley asked him, "why aren't the people in the monastery coming to help us? Why aren't they at least telling us it's safe?"

"Maybe they don't know that it is," Abramm said.

"But if they made it—"

"I don't think they made it. I think the luima made it."

And that damped every further word for a long moment.

"We saw no tracks leading away from it," Abramm said. "And it's too freshly broken for us not to have seen the men who did it heading back up to the monastery. Not to mention the question of why they'd come all the way out here to make it for us and then not wait for us to get to it. In fact, I believe I saw the men who did it, right before we left the trees. But they vanished before we got here."

He fell silent, bearing their incredulous and terrified scrutiny. No one had any answers for him.

With the wolves' howls approaching rapidly now, Abramm backed up the path a bit, then said, "You know I was right about the hut and the wolves. You know sometimes I can see things the rest of you don't. For all those reasons you trusted me to lead you down here; I beg you to trust me on this, as well. If we don't go now . . . it will only get harder."

He eyed the depths of the ravine again, still empty for the moment. . . . He turned his gaze to Rolland, standing on the far side of the bridge and staring back at him in horror. Of all the men here, Rolland was the one Abramm thought he had a chance of convincing first. But it would be hard. The man had three children and a wife, all of whom he'd be putting at risk if he went with Abramm's suggestion. He could see the big man's eyes drop to his wife, who had turned back to face him when she saw where Abramm's gaze had fixed.

In the end, it wasn't Rolland he convinced first.

"I'll go," Marta Brackleford said, stepping forward from the group. Immediately Kitrenna shrieked and threw herself on her sister, forbidding her to do so. Marta pushed her off. "If you wish to spend the night out here shivering to death on that ledge, that is your choice. If you die because of it, it is still your choice. But it is not mine, and I think Alaric is right when he says that trail is Eidon's protection for us."

"You see the light on the trail, too?"

"No. But I believe he can, and I have made my choice." She shook her sister off and started toward Abramm, stopping in front of him a few steps later, since he stood blocking the path. "I'll see if I can get them to open the gate," she told him.

He shook his head in unabashed admiration. "You shame us all with your courage, my lady."

She smiled. "We walk in Eidon's Light, sir. Why should I not be courageous?"

She set off up the path at a brisk walk, boot soles squeaking against the snow.

When Abramm turned back, he saw Rolland had pressed through the gathering to meet his wife midspan. He was speaking to her softly. She looked up at him, eyes wide with fear, her face pale within the ice-clotted edge of her hood. But when he swung his middle son into his arms, then took hold of the shoulder of his eldest and pressed him forward through the group toward Abramm, she followed, clutching the bundle that was their toddler to her chest. The dark-haired shepherd Cedric Ashvelt and his elderly father followed next, then young Galen and Jania Gault, and that was enough to decide the rest of them. Though she held out until the end, even Kitrenna at last bowed to the majority, and soon they were all hastening up the path.

Abramm brought up the rear. He'd gone barely a dozen steps when the volume of the wolves' howls and yips escalated to an ear-piercing din. He turned to see seven dark forms bounding up the drainage's edge, heading for the line of people hurrying toward the monastery. Marta was just reaching the monastery gates, with still no sign of anyone there to open them.

All they needed to do was keep moving, but of course they did not. The wolves' howls coming up on them so rapidly drew them all around, and all stopped to point and shriek. Abramm bellowed for them to stay on the path, but already a handful had blundered off of it in their agitation.

With a curse he charged across the snowy slope, hoping to head the predators off, his staff ablaze with Light.

He heard Rolland, then Trinley, echo his command for the others to stay on the path, then realized with a jolt that he had left its protection himself. As if in tune with his thoughts, the wolves wheeled as a unit and raced toward him. Stopping well within leaping range, they fanned out in a semi-circle before him. The six that looked most like wolves—if abnormally large—kept their heads turned away from the Light of his staff and he knew, without knowing how, that the Light hurt them.

It didn't hurt the seventh, however. But that one was no wolf. Closer in size to a horse, its shimmering fur, silver mottling white, shifted and moved independently of the muscles beneath. A dark, wolflike snout gave way to fine silver scaling that ran to blue across its muzzle and the bridge of its nose, then to purple around the eyes, transforming to coarse fur at the top of the forehead and along the cheeks and neck. Tufted ears dangled silver tassels, and a thick ruff of fur accentuated already humped shoulders that brought images of the morwhol to mind.

The eyes, though, startled him most, for they were human eyes: round pupils in black irises on white, with long curling lashes. They held him riveted, peering straight into his skull, and the essence behind them was neither spawn, nor animal, nor rhu'ema, nor even human—it was all of those and more. And very definitely female.

She advanced beyond the line of her attendants, stopping some five strides away from him, tasseled ears pricked forward, tail curled up, jaws parted around sharp white teeth, almost as if she were smiling. Her breath curled out in a white plume that reached seductively toward him in the suddenly still air.

Her laughter echoed in his head: *"Come out to fight us, have you, O great slayer of shadowspawn? We feared you would lack the courage. Or perhaps the wit."*

A chill crawled up his back. She knew who he was. Suddenly he felt as horribly vulnerable as if he stood here in the snow naked.

She laughed again. *"Come and take me, pup. If you can. . . ."*

In the wind's sudden absence, fat snowflakes fluttered thickly around them, a wonderland of light and movement. Through them came the white tendrils of her exhalation, reaching closer and closer as he stood there watching them with pounding heart but making no move to escape them. Then the first of them wafted into his face. It tasted vaguely sweet and musky. He inhaled convulsively, though he'd meant to hold his breath and turn away. Fear quivered through him, followed by the warmth of unexpected arousal. Then wooziness made the world warp and shift.

Behind him a man said they were all in and Abramm could come back, but the words held no meaning. Never had he seen anything so fascinating as this . . . this . . .

"Tanniym. I am one of the tanniym, handsome one. My name is Tapheina."

Part of his mind reeled in horror with this knowledge. Another, greater part held him where he was. Tanniym were mythical creatures, shape-shifters—part human, part beast—known for their seductive powers, for their great physical strength, and for their brutality. She wanted him for something, and the longer he stood here, the more he fell under her spell, but he could not turn away, for she fascinated him as no other. . . .

Stepping toward him, she blew another plume of her breath across his face. It was sweeter now, tingling on his face. Again the world blurred and shivered. Her eyes were magnificent . . . deep dark pools that recalled to him Shettai, his first love . . . and then his wife, as she looked sometimes in the darkness of the night, lit only by the bedside kelistar when he had

He shut off the thought at once, aghast at how the thing in his mind had pulled it out of his memory—still sought it, in fact—eager to absorb it.

A throaty chuckle echoed in his head, and the insistent prying eased, gave way to a warm, soporific pleasure.

"Alaric?"

That was Rolland. He seemed quite near. What did he want now?

"Can you hear me, Alaric? Everyone's inside the monastery. You can come back to the path."

Irritation ate at the dreamlike lassitude. *Why is Rolland intruding when he must see that I am occupied with important matters?*

"If you want to pass, little pup, you must do so according to the old way, when dragons ruled the skies and only those warriors most worthy in heart and mind and flesh could fight them for the right to pass."

But you are not a dragon, Abramm thought at it.

"Are you sure? Try me and see. Much of my father is in me. How much of yours is in you?"

Her answer befuddled him and she knew it, laughing at the pleasure of his confusion. *"Surely a great warrior-king as you can handle one as lowly as I. Come and meet me. Show my sons your true strength. . . ."*

He was tempted, though he had only a stick. Part of him knew the notion that he could win was ridiculous. Part of him thought it might be his destiny. He carried the Light of Eidon in his heart and flesh, after all, and nothing was stronger than that. Moreover, his command of it was mature now, advanced as few others ever achieved. If anyone could face this creature, it was he. . . .

"*Yes,*" Tapheina said, her voice rough and husky in his mind. "*You are a warrior of the Light who need not be bound by a path prepared for those of lesser status. Come, show me your strength, my beautiful pup. . . .*"

Snow drifted across his boots, powdery and light, and the flakes continued to fall, big and wet and fluttering. The will to close with her mounted. He would take her, rid the valley of her and her offspring, make the way safe for others. . . . He could do it. Had he not slain the morwhol and the kraggin and Beltha'adi himself?

Someone was yelling at him from up the hill. A deep voice, calling his name and harping on that wretched path again. It was Rolland, of course. Why couldn't he see that Abramm had all in hand? Rolland and the others might need the path, but why didn't he understand that Abramm did not?

"*I taste your strength, my king. You are worthy of me, as few of your kind have ever been. Join with me in combat, show them all who you really are. . . .*"

Tapheina stepped closer. Another veil of her breath curled into his mouth and nose.

The dizziness was delicious this time. He could almost see her human form, could almost see the shape of her hips and her—

Someone seized him from behind and jerked him around. He thought to defend himself, but the staff with which he intended to whack his attacker moved with shocking sluggishness. He heard Tapheina's outraged snarl, had a split-second glimpse of Rolland's bearded face before the big man hoisted him onto his shoulder and sprinted through the snow. Behind them the wolves exploded with shrieks of fury, and Abramm felt them leap to attack. Something tugged on his arm, something hard dug into his middle, and suddenly he sprawled facedown in the snow. The wolves closed, snarling viciously. He braced for attack—

It did not come, though he had no idea why, for he felt their outrage and even shared it. She had wanted him, and now someone was stealing him away and he felt bitterly disappointed. A wave of nausea shuddered through him. His head hurt and he had a horrible taste in his mouth. He wanted to sit up or even roll to his side, but he felt so weak. . . .

His stomach cramped again. He almost felt sporesick.

Something shifted in his mind at that, and he realized he'd been enspelled. It was the breath . . . her breath. Revulsion roared through him as he shoved up onto hands and knees, vomiting into the snow. Then, shaking and gasping, without even stopping to consider the advisability of doing a purge under such circumstances, he turned toward the Light, desperate to get all trace of her out of him. White fire rushed through him in an instant of blinding, breathtaking brilliance, cleansing the active spore and driving back the Shadow within him.

He found himself lying on his back at the middle of the broken trail, Rolland bending over him, the wolves snarling hysterically around them. The big man grabbed Abramm's arm and hauled him upright as if he intended to reshoulder him again and carry him up to the monastery.

Abramm stopped him. "I'm all right."

Rolland regarded him suspiciously. "Ye're sure?"

"I'm sure," Abramm said, rolling to one side and gaining his feet. He had a few moments' unsteadiness, during which Rolland clutched his arm and watched him narrowly. Then Abramm shook him off and hurried up the path. In moments he'd gained the ramp leading up to the monastery's gate: a tall, double-paneled portal with a much smaller opening beside. As they drew near, the smaller door squealed open to admit them. Just before he stepped inside, though, Abramm turned back to see that the wolves remained where he'd left them, standing in the penumbra between the light cast by the monastery and the path, and the darkness of the night. Tapheina's eyes gleamed with a golden fire, and he knew it would not be the last time he saw her. . . .

"This storm won't be letting up any time soon, you know," she said. *"If you don't keep moving now, you'll be stuck up here for the winter. It's already been six months. How long do you think she can wait for you?"*

A wild terror wailed up in him. He quenched it savagely, refusing to believe it, refusing to let this creature get to him. Turning his back on her, he stepped through the door into an arched stone tunnel lit with kelistars in wall-mounted wire baskets. At his back, the elderly gatekeeper shut the door with a *whump* and swung the big iron bar down into the holding brackets. And out on the plateau, Tapheina and her sons broke into a chattering of yelps and howls that sounded far too much like laughter.

CHAPTER

3

Madeleine Abigail Clarice Donavan Kalladorne gave the wooden sideboard a mighty heave, sliding it into place against the closed door of their tiny sleeping chamber. In the hallway outside of it, the wolves growled, scratching and pushing to get in, the door shivering with their efforts. Behind her, wind pelted snow crystals against the single second-story window while in the street outside the rest of the wolf pack barked and yelped in eagerness. How their brethren had gotten into the palace, she didn't know, but they had.

Within her massively swollen belly, Maddie's unborn baby kicked hard against her back, and her right leg went out from under her so fast she lurched against the sideboard. One of the creatures outside the door wriggled the latch.

She staggered back and took up the spear, glancing over her shoulder at Simon and Ian cowering together against the wall beside the bed. "Get under the bed, boys," she said to them, trying to keep her voice calm.

Simon dropped to his knees and pulled Ian down with him. "There'll be a bunny hole," he whispered as he fell onto his elbows and wriggled under the bed.

Maddie turned back to the door, which was now banging against the sideboard. Somehow the latch had come undone, and each new hit inched the hulking piece of furniture backward. She tightened her grip on the spear haft, feeling Abramm's presence strongly now and knowing he was on his way.

Just don't look into their eyes.

The door rapped hard against the sideboard, hopping it back another inch. Toothy, foam-flecked muzzles protruded between door and doorjamb.

She pointed the spear's iron head toward them, dismayed to find it wasn't a spear, after all, but a rope with a large knot at its end. She'd been able to hold it rigid only so long as she believed it was a spear. Now that she saw the truth, it collapsed limply to the floor.

She glanced over her shoulder to check on the boys, but they were gone, the bed with them, a small doorway gaping in the empty wall, much too small for her to fit through. *Just as well,* she thought. *Now we don't have to worry about the Esurhites getting them.*

The sideboard shrieked as it slid backward several feet, and she whirled to see the first of the wolves bull its way through the crack and leap onto the chest. The creature towered over her, jaws gaping, black mane swirling around a narrow, gold-scaled face with a serpent's split tongue and eyes like burning coals.

Don't look at their eyes!

Too late. The beast had skewered her gaze with his own and red fire roared around her. *"I have her!"* the creature crowed triumphantly. *"And now nothing of his shall remain."*

She lifted the useless rope and screamed—

The rasping, hoarse croak that came from her throat jarred her from the nightmare, and reality eclipsed the phantom images. She lay gasping in her big canopied bed—alone, save for the maid who stirred on her pallet nearby, rolling over and going still again. The tiny kelistar on her bedside table cast a dim illumination through the great bedchamber. She could just make out the heavy sideboard against the wall to her left, laden with its three bowls of artistically arranged staffid-warding onions amidst sprays of wheat. Outside, a dog moaned a forlorn lament, and the wind chime on her balcony tinkled faintly, touched by an errant breeze. Beyond that she heard nothing. No wolves, no shrieking gale, no snow crystals.

She let out a long, low sigh that held as much regret as relief. It was just a dream. Of course—it rarely snowed in Fannath Rill, and any wolves that had once prowled the surrounding fields and forests had been pushed into the higher lands of the north centuries ago. And while the city had recently seen an influx of jackals on its eastern fringes, that was far from the palace itself.

He wasn't really here. She slid her palm over the modest mound that was her womb, nowhere near the size she'd dreamed it but swelling daily with the seed her husband had sown there six months ago. The only thing she had left of him now.

Her throat tightened with grief and longing, for the sense of him had been so strong it seemed he was in the next room and would any moment burst through the door to take her in his arms. And oh, she wanted to feel those arms so very, very badly, to lay her head against the broad chest and listen to the powerful beat of his heart. . . .

And their boys . . . their beautiful boys . . .

Tears welled in her eyes as the tightening in her throat turned to a painful lump, and she began to weep—as she did so often these days, her dreams tormenting her with hope when she knew better than anyone that her boys were lost to her and her husband wasn't coming back.

The night Abramm had been tortured, both she and Carissa had shared the experience in the fractured way of their linked dreams—that one ending in a terrible wave of agony and defeat, followed by an explosion of blinding light. After that they'd shared no more nighttime adventures, and Carissa was convinced that blaze of light meant he had died. Maddie had found it difficult to disagree, especially when she had no further contact. Nor did it help that she'd suffered from both seasickness and morning sickness on that dreadful journey to Chesedh. And when they'd reached port and learned he had been burned in Execution Square before a crowd of hundreds—including Gillard himself—she'd finally surrendered to the reality of his death. A conclusion that had only been strengthened as the months passed and no word came from Kiriath to challenge it.

Then, about six weeks ago, she'd started dreaming again—intermittently at first, but lately almost every night. Dreams of mist and rock and emptiness, where she wandered aimlessly. The sense of evil was always strong in them. But so had been the sense of her dead husband, as if he was on the verge of bursting into her presence and driving away the evil that threatened her.

Her granny, steeped in the old ways, would have said he was trying to reach her from the grave. Trap was convinced it was something else.

The wolf-thing's crimson eyes flashed in her mind, too vivid for a dream, as if somehow the beast observed her even now. And, perhaps, encouraged her grief. She glanced at the ceiling shadows, wondering if rhu'ema floated there now, watching her. A chill shivered across her shoulders.

She shoved back the covers and padded barefoot into the adjoining chamber. Its wide, windowed doors looked out on the plain from which the palace of Fannath Rill arose, built atop a long rocky outcropping in the midst of the Ruk Ankrill, and as such the highest point in all the Fairiron Plain. Her window and balcony faced northeast to where the far edge of the river gleamed beyond the palace's ancient crenellated battlements. Beyond its stone-worked banks, a sea of tile roofs interspersed with autumn-paled foliage stretched into lavender haze.

The sky glowed in the east, while the rest remained dark and star specked. A flock of geese arrowed south toward their winter feeding grounds. It was a beautiful, quiet dawn. A gift from Eidon she might enjoy, or ignore for the sake of lamenting her losses. . . .

But the dreams always stirred up the grief again, opening the many trails down which her thoughts might travel toward heartache, self-pity, and bitterness. And the smoldering sense of outrage at having been betrayed by Eidon himself.

But that is your Shadow talking, for you have not been betrayed, though that is exactly what your enemies want you to think. They are the ones who did this, hoping to make you turn your back on him. Hoping you will just sink down in your sorrows and never get up again.

Grimly she turned from the window to sidle around the nearby desk and sit before the open volume of the Second Word she'd left there last night. Conjuring a kelistar, she set it on the stand, recalling fiercely that Eidon had given her a beloved husband and beautiful sons in whom she had reveled for five glorious years. Was that not enough? Was that not far more than she had ever dreamed of having? If he had taken them back already, how could she complain?

Barely had she started to read, however, when her eyes strayed to the fold of parchment protruding from the pages. She slid it free and unfolded it. The creases were soft and supple, the paper tearstained. She touched the inked letters scrawled across it, imagining the long-fingered hand that had inscribed its precious words.

The tears returned in force now, and she let them flow until she couldn't see the words. Not that she needed to anymore.

The truest love of all is when a man gives his life for those he loves. This is what I believe Eidon has called me to do. And you must abide it, my heart.

She'd seen the look in Abramm's eyes that day on the mall outside Springerlan's High Court Chamber, the heart-wrenching look of good-bye mingled with grim determination. She knew him well enough, understood the situation well enough to grasp what he'd intended even then, and it had appalled her. The moment she'd exited the coach and seen the galley ship he'd arranged to carry her and the others away, she'd turned to rush back to the city, determined to stop him. Trap had barred her way, his eyes wild with grief. *"He sacrificed all to get you away,"* he'd said fiercely. *"Don't make it be for nothing."*

Shortly after they'd sailed out the mouth of Kalladorne Bay, the galley ship captain had distributed Abramm's letters, one for his First Minister, one for his sister, and the last for his beloved wife. Maddie had read hers in the privacy of the galley ship's stern cabin, her heart breaking on words that erased all doubt of what he'd intended to do.

Abramm had been typically thorough in his arrangements. His wife and sister were each provided a small but comfortable cabin and a lady's maid. Their galley was escorted by three attendant vessels, each loaded, as was their flagship, with trade goods—and ten iron-bound strongboxes of gold, still bearing the mark of the Briarcreek Garrison—to support them in Chesedh.

She suspected Abramm was also the impetus for Trap's startling proposal of marriage to Carissa, and possibly even Carissa's equally startling acceptance. The ship's captain had performed the ceremony on the foredeck two days out from Kiriath, with Maddie, their maids, and the crew as witnesses. Baby Conal had been born a week later.

Abramm had also informed Maddie that he'd assigned Captain Channon to search for their sons, who he'd believed had escaped alive. Though she had long since resigned herself to Ian's death, having seen Simon elude his captors, and knowing that Elayne had escaped in the fracas, as well, she'd clung to the hope Abramm was right. But when they reached Fannath Rill and neither Simon nor Channon were there to meet her, she saw the truth of the matter. If Simon lived at all, he was in the Gadrielites' care, his name and heritage stripped from him as they worked to turn his young mind to their cause. Which was worse by far than believing him dead.

She had ordered Trap, who managed her finances and the personal guard he insisted she keep round her constantly, to send someone to find him, and of course he obliged. But he held little hope for success, and as time passed she'd been forced to accede he was right.

Abramm, Simon, Ian . . . They were all gone. The worst thing that could possibly happen had happened. Despite her desperate appeals, despite her fierce trust that Eidon, in his goodness, would never do such a thing to her . . . he had done it. The one thing she thought she could not live through she had—for each new day dawned and here she was, still alive. All the truth she had ever learned now became her only lifeline. And part of that truth was that those who served the Light would suffer as their Lord had suffered. And as he had endured, so could they, using the same power that had enabled him. When Eidon's servants endured and kept on trusting, it spoke to rhu'ema and luima both, as no outpouring of blessing ever could.

Her husband had already done it. Tortured to recant his faith, he had refused to the point of giving up his life. Her calling was different. It was to bear up under this loss, not to wallow in self-pity nor be consumed by bitterness. To keep recalling what she knew to be true—that Eidon was worthy of her trust—and go on with her life.

And so she had—day by day, step by step—until one morning something had moved in her belly and she realized with a shiver of awe that she'd not had her monthly courses for some time. It was in that moment that she knew beyond any doubt that Eidon loved her. That he had not forgotten nor neglected nor abused her. He had taken away. But he had also given. . . .

And in that she had found her peace, still intermittent, to be sure, but a haven to which she always found her way back.

Outside, the morning had acquired a pinkish cast as fragile fingers of smoke reached for the sky from the ranks of tile roofs across the river. To the east, golden rays of light speared across the pale mauve as the sun's first rays burst through the tattered edge of the cloud bank crouching on the eastern horizon. Not fog, but the Shadow itself, encroaching now on Chesedhan shores as it had not in six hundred years. Her father and brother, neither of whom she'd seen since she'd returned, were there now, leading the effort to hold back the invaders as everyone else prayed for an early advent of the winter winds that would drive back the Shadow for a few months.

"Ah, here you are, ma'am." Jeyanne's voice broke into her thoughts and drew her around. Her Kiriathan chambermaid stood in the bedchamber doorway. "You gave me quite a start when I woke to find your bed empty." The auburn-haired girl stepped through the doorway. "I feared you'd gone for your morning ride and forgotten about breaking your fast with the Princess Ronesca."

"Plagues!" Maddie cried, leaping to her feet. "I *had* forgotten! Oh, bless you, girl! Bad enough I turned down her invitation to that prayer service last night. Being late this morning would really set her off."

"Shall I prepare you a bath, then?"

"That would be good, Jey. Thank you."

But it was hard not to groan. The last thing Maddie felt like doing this morning was breaking her fast with her brother's pious, prissy wife. Especially not after that dream. Especially since Ronesca was sure to bring up the baby, and Abramm's death, and a host of other subjects Maddie was not interested in discussing.

———————

On the other side of the palace, Carissa Kalladorne Meridon, Duchess of Northille and Crown Princess of Kiriath, sat in the chair of her chamber's bay window, six-month-old Conal nursing at her breast as she stared southward across Fannath Rill's interior grounds. A wide promenade stretched away westward between opposing rows of date palms, cutting a swath through the hilly waterpark to either side, all bathed in the morning's golden haze. Beyond it marched the crenellated western wall, shrunken with distance against the gleaming west branch of the Ruk Ankrill and the city's smoke-obscured western sectors.

The multifarious creaking of the waterpark's numerous waterwheels and the rumble of its fountain pumps mingled with the shouted cadence of the morning guard at their drills down in the central square—sounds she'd finally grown accustomed to. As she had grown accustomed to the dank, fishy river smell that permeated every wall and rug and piece of furniture in this great island palace. Today, in fact, she could almost ignore it under the spicy fragrance of the Chesedhans' traditional morning *shae'a*, drifting in from the servants' quarters.

It was a beautiful morning. The sunrise had been glorious and now she felt quietly content, marveling as she often did of late at how thoroughly Eidon had blessed when she so thoroughly did not deserve it. All that angst, all that fury and frustration and hopelessness . . . yet here she was at the end of it all with more than she ever could have imagined, just as Abramm had promised.

It seemed a lifetime ago that Rennalf had cornered her in Whitehill's solarium the first time. He'd held her under Command and raped her very deliberately, chuckling as he did it, and had left her boiling with a fury directed as much at herself as at him, horrified that she'd neither fought nor cried out. The fact that she'd been under Command seemed no excuse. She felt defiled as never before. And ashamed.

It had seemed not to matter that he had done the same many times when she had been his wife. Somehow that time had been different. He had taken her twice more, the last time in her own home in Springerlan. That had been the worst. And when she'd realized five weeks later that his seed had rooted and she was carrying his child, she had tumbled down a dark shaft of depression from which she'd feared she'd never emerge. For what man would ever want her now? Least of all one who was First Minister of Kiriath?

She had tried to rid herself of the child, to no avail. Eidon had decreed her to bear it, though she wept and cursed and railed against him. Why did he always slap her down? Everyone else he blessed. Why was she alone left out?

Foolish, self-absorbed, small-minded questions, she saw now. For eventually Eidon had broken through her darkness in the same way as this morning's sunrise had broken through the gray dawn, beams of light spearing across the heavens, glorious heralds of a new day.

Conal shifted in her arms, drawing her gaze to him. His eyes were closed, long auburn lashes splayed against apple cheeks, his tiny hand resting on the swell of her breast. His thatch of fine auburn hair had shocked them all when he'd been born. Red hair! Who'd have thought? None of her other children, the ones who had died, had had red hair.

She stroked it, smiling as he sucked erratically, falling in and out of sleep. She hadn't expected him to be so beautiful. Hadn't expected her heart to swell with this much love. It still amazed her, especially after all the months she'd spent preparing to hate him. Yet he was as much a victim as the rest of them. More than that, he was *hers*. Strong and healthy and thriving. *"A Kalladorne,"* Abramm had said. *"And bastard or not, he will be raised a Kalladorne. . . ."*

But in the end, even that had been transformed into something greater. For two days after they'd escaped Kiriath, the Duke of Northille had asked her to marry him, and she had astonished herself by agreeing. It was what Abramm had told them he wanted them to do. What he hoped they would want to do, and of course Trap had complied. As he always did.

When Conal was born a week later, Trap had taken him as his own: Conal Abramm Felmen Meridon. Indeed, with his red hair, the only ones who knew for certain he was not Trap's own offspring were his parents.

An act of grace for them all. Now here she sat, safe, comfortable, the child of her dreams in her arms. Sometimes the marvel and the gratitude simply took her breath away.

She heard the door open and close behind her, a sound she'd been awaiting, and her pulse fluttered with anticipation as the familiar footsteps approached. Trap came around the far side of the empty chair beside her and set his tray of jug and cups on the low table before them, his eyes flicking to Conal and away. "Good morning, my lady," he said softly, averting his gaze as he straightened. It was the same every morning. The same greeting, the same ritual, the same strained politeness.

As always, she pulled the blanket up over Conal and her shoulder to cover herself, disappointment bitter in the back of her throat as she said her part: "Good morning, sir. I trust your day has gone well thus far."

"Very well, thank you." He turned to face the window, where he would wait, as he always did, until she finished with Conal.

She was, in fact, finished now, but she made no move to transfer the babe, pleased to sit here, holding him close and looking at the man she'd somehow managed to fall in love with, despite knowing her love was not returned and likely never would be.

Savior and protector, Infidel and First Minister, her dead brother's best and most loyal friend, a man of inestimable integrity and strength, who loved Eidon as few ever did. She loved his soul first, and most fiercely. But lately, she'd found her eyes roving hungrily over his form, as well—whenever she thought he wouldn't see her—taking pleasure in the way the red hair curled on the back of his neck, in how his shoulders filled out the silk doublet so splendidly above a waist still trim despite the approach of middle age, and in the freckled, sword-scarred hands whose tender touch she longed to feel.

Their marriage was one of duty and protection, though, and they had both agreed to it. Except for an occasional peck on the cheek, and the obligatory arm offered in escort, he was careful never to touch her. She'd been happy with that at the start. But she knew now she'd not been thinking clearly. Shocked by grief and terrified of what the future held, she'd planned to hand the child off to Cooper and Elayne to raise. But suddenly Coop was dead and Elayne missing, Abramm was gone forever, and Carissa herself was en route to a country whose people hated her. Who else was there? And so she'd said yes.

She knew now it was a mistake. Not just because he didn't love her and it was unfair to bind him to her like this. Nor because of the ultimate irony to be found in the fact she'd argued against this very thing in Abramm's case, only to enter into it herself. No, the mistake lay in the fact that she'd never expected to feel this fierce, hot longing, this desire for him that shook her to the core and made her hands shake and her heart ache with a physical pain.

She felt Conal sigh and snuggle closer, but still she did not move, savoring both the son in her arms and the man who stood with his back to her only a few strides away, hands clasped behind him, unaware of her admiring gaze and desperate longing. She wondered if she had the same soft-eyed look of hopeless adoration with which Maddie used to gaze at Abramm when she thought she'd never have him.

Maddie had been wrong about that in the end. *Maybe I'm wrong, too. Oh, Father Eidon, let it be so. Please . . .*

But she didn't see any way she could be. She was married to the man, after all. He could have whatever he wanted from her—she'd give it to him eagerly. But after six months of marriage, he'd shown not one hint of interest.

Sighing, she glanced over her shoulder, and Prisina immediately stepped forward to take the babe while Carissa saw to refastening her gown. Trap had the routine timed perfectly. As soon as she finished getting her clothes in order, he turned from the window and set to stirring the pot of cocoa, then poured her a cup.

"Thank you," she said as she took the vessel from him, careful not to touch his fingers.

"My pleasure, ma'am."

"You don't have to do this, you know," she said as she took a sip.

"You enjoy it, do you not?"

"Aye. I enjoy it, but . . ."

"It pleases me, as well." His brown eyes came up to meet hers, dark and soft with affection that triggered a heat of hope and response within her. But he only smiled slightly and turned his gaze to the cup in his hand. "So why should I stop?"

Truthfully, part of her never wanted him to stop. But another part urged her to bring out into the open what they both seemed so intent on ignoring. The selfless part of her, the part that truly loved him, should set him free of this self-imposed bondage.

"You have so much to do."

"And spending a few quiet moments with my wife should be at the bottom of my list?"

She felt the heat rise again, wanting to believe there was something there, reminding herself it was only Trap. Of course he would be gracious. Of course he would be kind. She knew he liked her. She wanted him to love her. *Why can't I ever be satisfied? Why is there always something more that I want?* She sipped her cocoa. "Your sword practice went well?"

"It did." He held his cup in both hands as if warming chilled fingers. "Conal seems to be doing better these days. No more of the crying fits, I understand."

She smiled. "No, thank Eidon. Whatever pained him seems to have faded."

"And you're getting a good night's rest finally. I can see it in your face and the brightness in your eyes."

She blushed and looked at her cup. That she had chosen to reject the wet nurse and see to Conal's feedings herself had not been well received in the Chesedhan court. One more distasteful eccentricity of the Kiriathan barbarians, it would seem, but he was far too precious to her to pass off to some stranger whose dialect was so thick she could hardly understand it. The downside was that she'd been roused from her sleep every night now for months, sometimes for hours at a time when he was fussy.

She looked up at him. "You'll be lunching with Darnley and Hamilton later?"

"I thought to, yes. I also have to drop by the auction house and see if I can pick up the money they still owe me. And then there's the problem of those lost bales."

She smiled at him. "And you wonder if there's something more you could have done to save them. Something more you could do now to make up for it."

His eyes twinkled as he looked up at her. "You know me well, my wife. . . ."

My wife . . . Did he have any idea how those words made her heart melt? She shook her head and smiled again. "You are not so different from my brother."

Which was, she saw at once, the wrong thing to say. The grief rolled across his face like a cloud. Stark and raw. He looked down at the cup in his hand, shielding his face from her as he wrestled his emotions back under control.

She kicked herself for her stupidity and tried to think of something else to say as the silence stretched out between them.

Then, "I miss him," he said. "Sometimes more than others, but today . . ." His voice choked as he blinked several times and turned his face to the window. She saw his Adam's apple move as he swallowed. "Even after all this time it's hard to believe he's really gone."

Her own throat tightened.

"And the boys," he went on. "I had so hoped Channon would come through for us. . . . Now I fear he's been taken, too. Or perhaps there was simply nothing to be found. That more likely, I suppose. We both know what they did to—" His voice cut off then, and he swallowed hard and exhaled a short, hard breath and stood there, thumb and forefinger pinching the bridge of his nose as the nightmarish images of baby Ian being hurled against the cliff wall flashed through Carissa's mind. A moment of silence ensued; then he puffed out another short breath and turned back to her.

"I don't suppose you've heard how Maddie's meeting with Ronesca went?" he asked.

Carissa shook her head. "It would only just be ending now, I'd think." She sipped her cocoa. "I can't imagine it went well."

"No."

Rumors had run wild through the court of late, both of Maddie's unexpected pregnancy and of Ronesca's outrage that her sister-in-law could be six months along and the crown princess not know of it till now. Other uglier rumors speculated on who the father was, and none cited Abramm as a likely candidate. "She never should have tried to hide it," Carissa said. "If she'd announced it immediately, she'd have nipped all the jailer nonsense in the bud."

"Maybe," Trap said. "Or maybe not. I think the Chesedhan court would rather it be a jailer's bastard, actually. I know Ronesca would—easier to get out of the way so they can get Maddie married off to the highest bidder."

Carissa frowned at him, uncomfortably aware that what he said was likely true. "You're aware she's planning to retire early again this evening?" Carissa asked.

"Aye." He paused and she felt a sudden deepening of the tension. Then, in a voice tight and forced, he said, "I was wondering if you might like to take advantage of your night of freedom and have supper with me at that inn on the river I was telling you about."

She looked up sharply, frowning at him. The only inn he'd ever told her about was the one where Maddie had secretly taken employment as a serving girl in a wool-brained scheme to gather information on the war. Both Carissa and Trap had sought to talk her out of it, but there'd been no stopping her. It was by Eidon's grace alone Ronesca had not learned of that yet.

In any case, since Maddie refused to take an escort when she went to "work," Trap had taken it upon himself to follow her, just in case.

"It would do you good to get away from the palace," Trap said, his words coming rushed, as if he had to force himself to get them out. "A change of scene, a change of cooking style . . . no servants sneaking about trying to pry into our business. Well, except for one."

He meant Maddie, and he meant it for a joke, but Carissa had been thrown into such a state of emotional turmoil she could not respond to it, could only stare at him with a feeling that bordered on alarm.

She could hardly believe he would ask her to accompany him, and had no idea why he would. Was he embarrassed by the rumors circulating that their marriage was a sham? That he had married her only to save her reputation? A well of conflicting emotions, the primary of which was terror, boiled up in her, and before she knew it, words were tumbling from her mouth. "Oh no. I can't. I'll have to feed Conal, you know, and I'm just not comfortable leaving the palace yet. But you go ahead. The Gilded Ram is the inn where the rivertraders come up from Peregris, isn't it? I'm sure you'll gather a good measure of news, and you don't want me intruding on that."

She wasn't sure if the look that came into his expression was alarm or horror, but it was only there for a moment. Then his lips tightened and he nodded stiffly. "Of course."

Stagnant silence pooled between them.

"It's all right," she said then. "I don't feel bad that you go without me. And if you wished to spend some time with other . . ." She exhaled suddenly and stared at her lap, her face flaming. "I know this isn't a real marriage. I never expected it would be. You've done so much for me as it is, I'll never be able to repay you. But all this other, the cocoa, the invitations . . . You needn't pretend what we have is anything more than duty. I would feel more comfortable, in fact, if you didn't."

She couldn't bear to look up at him and see the relief in his face, so she continued to study her cup, struggling to breathe, wondering if he might have spoken and she'd not heard him for the thunderous rush in her ears.

The silence was even more awkward now. Just when she thought she could bear it no more, he spoke. "I'm sorry, my lady. I didn't—" He cleared his throat, then said more evenly, "It was never my intent to make you uncomfortable."

He paused, as if waiting for her to speak. When she didn't, he set his cup on the tray between them and said softly, "Well, as you say, I have much to do this morning. If I may have your leave?"

"Of course." She forced herself to look up at him and smile, desperate that he not see how deeply his easy acquiescence had hurt her.

4

The Inn of the Gilded Ram stood at the corner of River and Cantor Streets south of the palace at Fannath Rill. A well-known and respectable establishment, it offered good food, good ale, and a clean, well-ordered environment. A huge stone hearth and multiple levels sporting candle- or kelistar-lit nooks where clients could dine in relative anonymity gave it its distinctive character. So did the cadre of musicians that performed evenings for the inn's customers, mostly well-to-do riverboat traders and their local merchant counterparts, meeting over dinner or mugs of ale to negotiate their deals or exchange the latest gossip.

Fortunately their gossip, unlike that at the palace, dealt more with how the river was flowing through the Silver Cataracts these days, where the price of wool was likely to head that summer, and of course news of the ongoing war to the south. The inn's patrons were only idly interested in the pregnancy of the deposed queen of Kiriath and could care less about the controversy regarding the child's patrimony.

Tonight the place roiled with tales of the recent Esurhite offensive to take the island of Torneki. Lying several leagues off Chesedh's southeastern coast, it was home to some of the richest men and finest villas in all the known world. It was also a key port for the Chesedhan navy, and thus of strategic importance in defending Peregris and the vulnerable mouth of the Ankrill. Maddie's brother, Leyton, had been defending it against repeated Esurhite assaults for months.

Maddie had heard a bit of this up at the palace earlier that day, most of it smothered by the other juicier gossip surrounding her pregnancy and damped by a cultural more that insisted Chesedhan noblewomen were too delicate to endure hearing the details of war and too stupid to comprehend the politics behind it. Here at the inn, ironically, that same belief manifested in a looseness of the tongue before the table maids, as if they weren't even there. With no concern whatever for female sensitivities, the men exchanged gory details of stories that might not even be true. It was the entire reason she had taken up her charade her as a serving girl.

As she set the first of four plates of seared catfish onto the polished oak table, the men seated there were already deep in conversation on that very topic.

Inevitably she finished doling out plates before she'd heard all she wanted to, and had to move on to the adjoining table, where the six men seated there sent her off to the kitchen for tankards of ale and, afterward, slices of bullock with plump dough puddings. When she returned with those, she noted that Trap Meridon, whom she'd been expecting, had come in while she was in the kitchen and had settled himself in a corner booth not far from where she stood. Once she'd set out her current order, she went back to the kitchen, drew a tankard of cider, and returned to his table. He was lounging back against the booth wall, watching the diners at the tables in the lower level, and when she set the tankard before him, he looked up at her.

Weariness etched his freckled face and darkened his brown eyes.

"Alone tonight?" she asked, surprised and disappointed, for she'd expected him to bring Carissa.

"For now," he said, grimly. "Hamilton will be joining me later."

"Hamilton?" She frowned. "Did you even ask her?"

"Aye, " he said shortly. "She didn't want to leave Conal." But from the pain that flared across his face, she guessed there was more to it than that, and knew better than to probe further. Bad enough she'd goaded him as hard as she had into asking. . . .

Usually she twitted him by inquiring if he'd like the mutton stew, though she knew very well he loathed it. Tonight she only asked if it would be the usual, and when he said yes, she headed back to the kitchen for the bullock and an extra helping of the puddings he always ordered.

It seemed the day hadn't been any easier for him than it had been for her. His expression had brought back memories of the hideous breakfast she'd started her morning with. Her brother's wife, Crown Princess Ronesca, had certainly possessed an ulterior motive for her invitation, starting in on all of the things she found wrong with the First Daughter from the moment they'd sat down. Maddie's lack of religious propriety and dedication, her failure to cultivate the proper people socially, her ongoing weakness in continuing to mourn a husband who was dead and gone were becoming inexcusable. Brutally, Ronesca had informed her that Abramm was not coming back and six months of grieving was quite enough time to get over his loss.

She was even worse with regard to the pregnancy, faulting Maddie for not having come to her the moment she'd known of it so they "could have dealt with it efficiently and discreetly." When Maddie had reacted with heated outrage to the crown princess's suggestion of using her physician's special potion to take care of the thing, Ronesca had only shaken her head in exasperation.

"Madeleine, where is your brain? You must know you'll have to remarry if you have any hope of living the sort of life to which you are entitled. I was hoping it would be within a year of your bereavement—we could use the opportunity to strengthen the power and influence of the royal house. And your father's treasury cannot withstand much longer the drain you and your retinue are putting on—"

"Me and my retinue?" Maddie had burst out incredulously. "I have ten people, Your Highness. Are you telling me I have to pay rent? In my own father's house? Fine . . . Or I can find my own residence if you prefer. But I will not be remarrying anytime soon, let alone within the year. And I will *not* be getting rid of my child!"

She'd left on a high hand, so angry she was shaking. For a while she'd stormed about the palace in a fury. She was the First Daughter! How dare Ronesca speak to her like that! How dare she suggest such things as she'd suggested! The woman was not even of royal blood, nor were her precious sons, offspring not of Leyton Donavan but of her first husband, the count of a minor noble house.

Ronesca was, however, born of the House of Harvadan, one of the oldest of the Chesedhan lines, and it was that fact that finally drained off Maddie's anger into uneasiness. Maddie might have supporters in the palace on account of her royal blood, but Harvadan had power in its own right. As well as a longstanding antipathy to all things Kiriathan. A legitimate child of Maddie's—as time would reveal this one to be—would trump any claim Ronesca or her two sons made upon the throne.

What if she decided to take matters into her own hands? A potion could easily be slipped into someone's food or drink to do its work before anyone realized it was there. The pregnancy would be terminated with no one to blame. The thought so spooked Maddie, she ate nothing in the palace all afternoon and had taken her evening meal at the inn just after she'd arrived.

When she returned from the kitchen to set Trap's food before him, he gestured at the empty stools before the hearth on the lower floor. "Where're Kyra and her boys tonight?"

"Entertaining in the back room. Some 'esteemed gentleman' who's fled his villa on Torneki is holding court there. His men came in this afternoon to set things up. They've erected a tent in the big dining hall, and he's brought at least sixteen attendants. The cook staff is all aflutter, and, of course, Serr Penchott is quite pleased to entertain a man of such wealth and nobility. . . ." She trailed off, watching as a glistening brown staffid crawled over the table's far edge and slithered toward Trap's plate.

He killed it without even looking, his Light-thread sending it into convulsions a handspan from his plate as he asked, "Does he have a name, this gentleman?"

"I get the impression he didn't give it." Maddie pulled the folded rag she used to clean up spills from her waistband and wiped up the spawn as if it were no more than the foam off a tankard of ale. "Everyone just calls him 'our esteemed guest' or 'the gentleman from the south.'"

"What's he look like?"

"I don't know. Mace and Lindie are taking the shift."

"What?!" Trap leaned back to regard her with raised brows. "Snoop that you are, I'd have thought you'd be first in line for that duty."

"I would've, but I got here too late—thanks, I might add, to a certain someone who insisted I wait for my 'cousin' to walk me over here!" That had been Lieutenant Whartel, one of her personal guard.

Trap shook his head and sliced into his bullock. "You take your ability to fool people far too seriously, and your safety not seriously enough, my lady."

She frowned at him for the deliberate slip in his mode of address. "And you take everything in the world too seriously, sir." She jerked up her chin. "Anyway, when there's a party like that, it's difficult to argue the other girls out of the kind of coin they're likely to receive. Let alone the notoriety that'll come from serving our esteemed but very mysterious guest."

"Mysterious indeed. I wonder what he's hiding."

"Maybe he'd just like to travel relatively unnoticed—having just been driven from his home and all."

"Generally folk who desire not to be noticed don't travel with sixteen attendants and set up their tents in the dining halls of middle-class inns. He must be Sorian, though, if he's got a tent, so I suppose you wouldn't be able to understand their talk anyway."

She sniffed. "With all the news breaking in here, I'm quite happy where I am, thank you."

Movement at the corner of her eye drew her attention to one of the diners down the row from her, lifting his empty mug at her and wagging his bushy brows. "I've got to go."

In the kitchen Mace and Lindie were arguing over who would bring the platter of bullock kabobs and rice balls, and who would bring the mulled wine. Lindie looked unusually distressed—pale, sweating, and dark around the eyes. Perhaps she was coming down with something. Maddie considered offering to take her place but, recalling what she'd just said to Trap, decided she'd rather hear the latest on the battle at the front. Besides, they were nearly done. As the two went off with platter and tray, she ladled mutton stew into a bowl, balanced a rasher of bread atop it, refilled the tankards from the bushy-browed man's table, and carried it all out into the common room.

She had just delivered the stew and was stopping to hand out the refilled ale mugs when the front door burst open. Three men in heavy greatcoats blew in on a gale of cold wind that ignited shouts of protest from the diners even as the newcomers recaptured the door and slammed it safely shut.

Moments later, the leader among them was recognized as a barge captain just arrived with a load of wounded soldiers from the front, and the place convulsed with excitement. He was ushered immediately to the lower floor, where table and chairs were shoved into the place normally reserved for the musicians, and there he held forth with his news.

"Now, I can't say any of this for sure, since they all had different tales, but the gist is, Crown Prince Leyton is said to have had some sort of talisman that he claimed would clear away the mist so our cannon could fire."

As his words penetrated, Maddie's heart seized. A talisman to drive away the mists?

"He planned to draw the enemy in around Torneki, then use the talisman to drive off the mist while our gunships, waiting hidden on the Chesedhan side of the isle, came round to blast them all to pieces."

Just like on the Gull Islands. As the captain continued with the details, her eyes went inexorably to Trap, who watched the man white-faced and tight-lipped. It had been two years since Leyton visited them in Springerlan. . . . *No! I cannot believe that. I will not believe it. Not until I hear it from his lips. . . .*

Whatever Leyton had, it hadn't worked. The mist hadn't cleared, and the

Esurhite galley commanders, apparently understanding the plan themselves, had slipped around the island and brought their vessels in close under the hulls of the waiting gunships before the Chesedhans even knew what was happening. Southlanders had swarmed like termites across the decks, leaving the Islanders to beat back the horde they themselves had invited in. Leyton and his men had been cut off. Hadrich had taken one of his own galleys to the island to rescue him. And had been wounded in the effort—though not seriously, according to the barge captain.

"Molly!" Her employer's voice hissed into her awareness, her assumed name registering belatedly. "Stop yer gawking and get into the kitchen! They need ye there."

She almost told him to mind his own business and leave her be, but she caught herself and hurried to the kitchen. Lindie now slumped on the bench beside the back door, glassy-eyed and shivering even as she insisted she was fine—she just needed a minute to rest.

"We don't have a minute!" Hulet, head of the serving staff, cried. When she still refused to move, he cursed her vigorously for her weakness, then the esteemed gentleman for his bad timing, and finally the kitchen itself, just because. Then he ordered Maddie to take the sick girl's place.

Irritation washed over her, and again she nearly refused.

"When you've delivered the trays," Hulet said, "don't forget to refill the wine glasses. Mace is already in there." He turned away and spoke to another. "They'll be wanting their coffee soon. How are you coming with that?"

Sighing, Maddie balanced the tray of stuffed dates on one hand, the platter of honeyed pastries on the other, and set off. The esteemed gentleman was set up in the Nobility Room, on the far side of the Gilded Ram's inner courtyard. The servants' entrance was at the back. Balancing her trays, she shouldered the door open and stepped into deep darkness, the air warm and heavy with incense. For a moment she could hardly breathe, for it pressed about her like thick cotton and resisted her attempts to drag it into her lungs. As the door swung shut behind her she felt as if she were falling down a well. Then the air rushed into her lungs and the feeling passed, as did the darkness. With her eyes adjusted, she saw the room was merely dimly lit.

The esteemed gentleman's tent did indeed fill the entire hall. Red and white silk swooped outward from a central stanchion, then draped down in what she surmised to be the six walls customary of an eastern warlord's *deniga*. She couldn't tell for sure because curtains partitioned off a smaller space on the far side of the room. Thick Sorian carpeting covered the floor, and the space had been lit with candles flickering in clear glass pots—some colorless, others tinted amber or scarlet—and arranged in artful groupings around the room, as well as the main table. Small plates of onions stood among them to keep away the staffid.

Kyra was just finishing her song as Maddie entered, the musicians playing out the final few bars. As the sounds faded, one of the musicians plucked the strings of his lirret in a wandering and repetitive melody meant only to fill the silence.

It was immediately clear which of those at the long, linen-clad table was the esteemed gentleman, for he sat at its center, facing the entertainers. He wore a dark silk tunic with a dark robe over, edges stitched with silver and trimmed with small red stones that flashed in the candlelight. Thick dark hair tumbled in loose waves about his shoulders, framing a handsome, angular face, darkened with the closely trimmed beard easterners favored. As dark as the tented chamber was, she was surprised at how clearly she saw his face. In the flickering, multihued candlelight, it glowed like warm gold.

The innkeeper, Serr Penchott, stood just inside the door with one of the Sorites, and Maddie heard the latter asking him if he had any dancers.

"None trained, sir," the innkeeper replied with far too much trembling deference. He suggested Kyra might try it, and Maddie heard the Sorite give a derisive snort as she passed out of earshot and approached the long table. Suddenly the esteemed guest's face turned slightly, light flashing off what looked like gilding on his cheekbones as his dark eyes fixed upon her and his nostrils flared like those of a hound catching a scent. Blushing, she averted her eyes, feeling the intensity of his gaze until she stepped onto the platform and came around behind the men who sat along the table beside him.

From the corner of her eye she saw him turn away to speak to his seatmate. Reaching past the shoulder of the third man from the end, she laid the first of her trays onto the table. Continuing down the line of backs, she deposited the second as Mace laid hers before the esteemed guest himself, and Hulet covered the table's far end.

Free of the tray, Maddie picked up the jug of mulled wine and worked her way down the table, filling the shallow drinking bowls as she went. As she'd expected, the men spoke in Sorian, a language she did not know. Thus, though she could hear them clearly, she had no idea what they were saying. Her time had been better spent in the common room back in the main part of the inn.

Finally she stood at the right shoulder of the esteemed gentleman, reaching past him once to snag the drinking bowl, then again to put it back. She thought he was ignoring her until, as she pulled her hand away from the replaced bowl, he seized her arm with his right hand, the nails of which were long and gilded. The sight of them startled her as much as the fact that he'd seized her, and she froze in sudden alarm. He held her gently, though, as he turned her hand and lifted her wrist to his nose, then closed his eyes and inhaled deeply.

The light flashed upon the fine gold scaling that had indeed been painted—or glued—across his cheekbones, and the delicate skin immediately surrounding his eyes had been stained a pale, cool blue, enhancing their depth and just now the dark length of his lashes. Her heart pounding wildly, she fought the urge to jerk away, and focused on the amber and obsidian signet he wore on his clawed right forefinger. She recognized the jackal as belonging to one of the older, more respected houses on Torneki, but . . . no matter. If he moved his nose upward along her bared arm so much as a hair, she would twist herself free of him and walk away. She was queen of Kiriath and First Daughter of Chesedh, after all. She didn't have to put up with this sort of thing, and if it destroyed her little charade as "Molly," so be it.

He did no more than sniff deeply at her wrist, however. Then his fine lips quirked as he opened his eyes and turned to look up at her. "When will your child be born, miss?"

His grip tightened an instant before her reactive jerk backward, and he held her fast, staring up into her eyes. Chills rushed over her as he smiled disarmingly, perfect white teeth flashing in his swarthy and startlingly hand-some countenance. "I can smell it, you see. Smelled it the moment you entered."

She gaped at him.

He rubbed his thumb gently across her wrist. "How much would you take for it? When the time comes, of course."

"Take for it?" Maddie's voice came out high-pitched and tiny.

"You are wed, with a father to care for it? That is why you work nights at this difficult and demeaning job—one that is surely beneath a flower so lovely as yourself?"

"I—" Her voice choked off as blood rushed hotly into her face. *Flower?* No one had ever called her a flower. Not even Abramm. And though every-thing about this man set her back up, she could not deny the warm pleasure his words and dark gaze provoked in her. She jerked up her chin. "I don't see that's any business of yours, sir." Which of course was the last thing a serving maid should be saying to an esteemed guest. Penchott would have a heart seizure when he heard about it, as he surely would in about half a minute. Mace was already heading toward the door.

The dark brows lifted and the gentleman laughed softly, a marvelous sound that stirred her as she had not been stirred for nearly six months now. "My, but you are high spirited for a serving wench." He turned to his table-mate. "You'd think she was the queen herself. Serr Penchott must really have his hands full with this one."

The others laughed as Maddie's face burned again, her discomfiture so convoluted she couldn't begin to sort out all its sources. And why did she have the feeling that everything he said had a double meaning?

The dark gaze returned to hers. "I mean you no insult, girl. I but offer a solution that will benefit us both. The child would have a good home, far better than what you could provide for him, and I will—"

The meaning in his words slammed into her like a windblown door, and this time when she jerked backward, he let her go.

"My child is not for sale, sir!" she declared.

"Oh, come now. Even here in Chesedh such things are done all the time. Particularly by those in your profession."

"In my *profession*—?" And suddenly she saw what he meant, what he thought she did when she wasn't serving tables. Renewed outrage swept through her, and she glimpsed the beginnings of his smile as she whirled and stalked for the door, mortified, furious, and half afraid he'd call her back or order his men to stop her.

"I like a woman with fire," he commented to one of his companions. "We'll have to come back here."

By then she was stepping into the servants' hall, free of the closeness of that stifling room and finally able to breathe again. Fear nipped at her heels, and she passed through the main room heedless of the barge captain, still going strong. She halted only long enough to glance up to where Trap sat in his upper-level booth. His gaze focused on her instinctively, though he was deep in conversation with his tablemate, Admiral Hamilton, who had arrived in her absence. She gave a thought to telling him she meant to leave, but memory of the Sorite's words roused another wave of mortified indignation and she hurried on toward the kitchen. *He thinks I am a whore! He tried to buy my child!*

Several people spoke to her as she passed, but she had no idea what they said. She found her cloak, told Hulet she had to go home right now and that she didn't know if she'd be back tomorrow or not.

She was out the door before he could answer. His shouted protest followed her into the yard, only to be snatched away by the wind as she hurried up the alley to River Street. Images of the Sorite gentleman sniffing her wrist assailed her. *"I can smell it,"* he'd said. It made her flesh crawl. So did the gilding on his cheekbones and the golden claws on his nails. *He thought I was a whore!* Her emotions ran from mortification to chagrin to outrage as the wind blew ever more strongly, seeming to oppose her every step.

Finally, when an especially strong gust caught her cloak like a sail and nearly dragged her off her feet, she stopped. And realized she had no idea where she was.

The empty street gleamed beneath the kelistar streetlamps, deserted save for several humps she thought were sleeping drunks and a pack of dogs nosing some refuse up near the corner about a stone's throw away. She turned slowly, gazing at closed and boarded-up storefronts, at darkened windows she did not recognize. From this vantage she couldn't even see the palace, the shops' peaked roofs blocking her view. Dried weeds and bits of rope tumbled down the street, driven by a wind that was growing sharp with the scent of rain. Scraps of fabric and leather scurried along; a tin cup clacked along the cobbles, rolled over and over by the wind.

She faced back the way she had come, her wind-driven cloak now enfolding her in great obstructing billows. Nothing looked familiar, and several of the lanterns stood dark up the way, their glass shades broken by the wind, the kelistars in them put out. Nor was there any sign of Trap. *He must not have realized I was leaving,* she thought with dismay. And rightly so, since her shift wouldn't be over for two more hours.

Two new dogs emerged from an alley not far down the street from her and peed on the brick walls at its entrance. These two were large and brown, while the others were smaller and pale. The bigger of the pair sniffed a clump of weeds, then looked up at her, its eyes reflecting the lantern light in eerie copper disks. Then its gaze shifted to the dogs up the street behind her. Its companion's head came up likewise. She turned to look at them again herself, pulling strands of hair from across her face as the cloak now pulled and jerked at her shoulders. A tendril of fear crawled through her.

How could I have been so mindless?

There were six dogs in the first pack up at the bend in the street, three medium sized, two of them larger than she liked, and the sixth she thought was a jackal. As if it felt her eyes upon it, the jackal looked up and froze, staring at her intently. A moment later, one of the larger curs saw her, too. The tendril of fear thickened. Dog packs could be dangerous, even deadly, to a person alone and unarmed. The hot spice mixture she carried in a secret pocket in her cloak would not work in this wind, and the short club looped round her wrist was not nearly enough to deal with so many threats. Best to get away from them as quickly and unobtrusively as she could.

She turned, intending to cross the street on the angle so as to avoid the two dogs who'd come out of the alley, and froze in horror to find two large men standing where the dogs had been but moments before. Her first, irrational hope that they would scare off the dog pack was immediately dashed by the awareness that they were coming straight for her. Recollection of Trap's innumerable warnings about traveling alone through the city at night flashed through her head, and she knew she was in trouble. But she was upwind of the men, and there were only two of them.

Without missing a beat she strode purposefully across the street as the cloak billowed forward around her again. She had to fight to find the pocket she'd sewn into it and the bag of spice.

They crossed the street to cut her off, and when she judged them close enough, she tossed a handful of spices into the nearest man's face, then flicked her wrist to grab the club and smash it against his temple. He reeled backward coughing and sneezing as the wind flung the cloud of cayenne, ginger, and cloves into the face of his companion, and he, too, was overcome with a sneezing fit. She dodged around them, but a jerk on her cloak wrenched her backward. Then a hand gripped her arm and pulled her around. She went with the flow, letting her free right hand come around to fling the bag and the rest of its contents into her assailant's eyes.

As he wilted into a second fit of coughing, she twisted free of him, only to find the other man had recovered enough to lumber toward her—

A shout rang out as a third man stepped out of the alleyway now across the street, the steel of his unsheathed sword gleaming wickedly in the lantern light. She recognized her finance secretary at once, even as her attackers fled up the street, away from the dog pack at her back.

As Trap drew up beside her, she straightened. "I'm all right," she said quickly, turning so the cloak would blow away from her. "They didn't hurt me." She looked about for her spice bag, but the wind had blown it away. He took her arm and steered her back into the alley from which he'd just emerged. With the sudden relative abatement of the wind, they didn't have to shout.

"What are you doing out here, ma'am?" Fury made his voice low and hard.

"I . . . I don't know. I mean . . . I was pretty upset, and I guess I wasn't paying attention to where I was going."

He frowned at her. "Penchott told me you were sent to serve his esteemed guest after all. Is that what got you upset?"

She stared back at him, feeling suddenly and intensely foolish. Yes, the Sorite had called her a whore and tried to buy her child, but what of it? She was pretending to be a serving girl. Ronesca had called her the same thing this morning. Why was she so upset?

Back in the street, framed by the alley's shadow-swathed walls, three dogs stepped into view, sniffing at the spot on the wall where the other pair had recently left their marks. More of the pack ambled up to join them, the jackal last of all.

Trap pushed her around in front of him. "We can talk of it back at the palace," he said firmly.

5

Six days after arriving at Caerna'tha, Abramm awoke to a deep sense of depression and the all-too-familiar howling of the wind in the eaves outside his dormitory cell. Gusting snow granules ticked erratically on the cell's shuttered window, through which filtered the muted light of a new day. He lay on his side on a straw-mattressed cot, his back to the outer wall, clutching heavy fleece coverings to his chin as he stared at the stone-floored chamber before him.

He'd dreamt of Maddie again last night. The details were lost to sleep, but her essence lingered strongly, feeding his sense of loss.

Outside, upward of ten feet of snow had already accumulated, through which they'd had to shovel tunnels just to get to the covered walkways leading to the woodpile, well, stables, and sheepcotes. For several days now he had joined Rolland, Cedric, and Oakes Trinley up on the roofs, battling freezing wind and biting snow to shovel off the new accumulations—a task they'd soon have to repeat for the kitchen, sheepcote, and hay barn. In fact, the latter was so close to collapse they would be shoring up its beams from the inside before anyone would risk stepping onto its outside.

Despite Tapheina's prediction to the contrary, Abramm had for days clung to the hope this was only an early winter flurry and that the mild weather would soon return. Yesterday was the first time he'd seriously considered the possibility he might actually have to spend the winter here. Today, possibility had become certainty, the contemplation of which produced a twisting pain in his chest so sharp he could hardly breathe.

His hope of reuniting with his wife and sons within the month was dead, and Tapheina's parting words haunted him: *"It's already been six months. How long do you think she can wait for you?"*

Bitter frustration tightened his throat. To have come all this way only to have their reunion ripped away from him? How could Eidon do this to him?

It made no sense. With Chesedhan shores under attack by an evil horde bent on eradicating all traces of Eidon's Light and those who worshipped him, Abramm should be down there, helping with the defense. Not up here in the middle of nowhere shoring up beams, shoveling snow, and hauling wood and water. Where even his skills of leadership and decision making were rejected—seen as threatening, in fact—by the people he now lived with. People who disliked him enough as Alaric but would loathe him if they knew who he really was.

Beyond his door the distant clang of the breakfast bell echoed through the monastery: two strikes, a pause, then two more. It was the second bell of the morning, the final call to breakfast. He'd wait a little longer before going down, to give the others time to clear out of the dining hall. He'd listened to quite enough of their insults and, in his present mood, had no desire for more. It would be bad enough working with them in the barn.

He rolled onto his back and stared at the rafters. Had he not suffered enough already? How much more did Eidon intend for him to take? He had given up everything for him, and this was his repayment? Better he should have burned on that stake they'd planned for him in Kiriath. Better maybe he should have just let them cover his stupid mark and renounce his identity as a Terstan.

He wished he had now. If he'd known how things would turn out, he would have.

Moroq's thinking . . .

Suddenly as irritated with himself as he was with everything else, he sat up, gasping at the shock of the cold air on his back, even though he'd slept fully clothed. Shivering violently, his breath pluming about him, he slipped a woolen sweater over his tunic and undershirt, then jammed his feet into his frozen boots. Snatching up the cloak of long-haired fleece he'd used as a supplemental blanket, he stepped from his room into a crooked hall lined with doors and started down the narrow stairway that led to the ground floor.

Like the dormitory, the dining hall had been built to accommodate a crowd. Three long tables ran the chamber's length, a handful of people gathered in small clusters at their far ends near the fire crackling in the great stone hearth. Children raced around playing tag, while a few chickens and dogs foraged for scraps under the tables. As Abramm approached, Rolland's oldest boy, Rollie Jr, came running. The blond-headed lad had taken an inexplicable liking to him over the course of their journey, one that had intensified since they'd arrived in Caerna'tha. "Master Alaric! Good morning, sir. I found some slingstones. D'ye think these would be any good?"

He pulled several rounded oblong stones from the small pouch he'd tied about his waist and held them out for Abramm's inspection. Lacking the heart to put the lad off, Abramm took up the stones, looked them over, then handed them back with a nod. "I think these will do for a start."

"So can we start, then?"

"When the storm's over, Rollie."

The boy's face fell. "That'll take ferever, sir."

Abramm tousled the lad's hair and walked on.

"Ye're late again, Alaric," old Totten Ashvelt commented as Abramm passed him. "The others've already gone down t' the barn."

Clamping down on his irritation, Abramm gave the man a wave and descended the narrow stair into the kitchen, veiled in back-blown smoke. At the room's far end two women stood near the cooking hearth, where the ash and embers of the breakfast blaze had been banked up to one side, and a man was standing in the fireplace. His upper body swallowed by the chimney, he moved the damper inside the flue, the metal squealing as he did. Meanwhile other women worked cleaning up, kneading bread, and preparing a side of mutton for roasting.

Among them were Kitrenna Trinley and dark-haired Marta Brackleford, the latter already approaching him with a covered bowl of the morning's porridge. "Good morning!" she greeted him cheerfully. "I saved this out for you, but I'm afraid it's gotten really thick. . . . I could put some milk in it if you'd like."

He shook his head as he took it. "This is fine. Thanks." He knew he sounded gruff, but her attentiveness grated at him. She reminded him too much of Maddie and, for some inexplicable reason, brought to mind his appalling attraction to the tanniym Tapheina.

He'd learned from Caerna'tha's community of permanent residents that the shapeshifters' breath carried spore that paralyzed the will and dazzled the mind. If they had taken refuge under the bridge as Kitrenna Trinley had wanted, all of them would have died. No one but Rolland knew that Abramm had actually fallen victim to it, and not even Rolland knew to what degree. Abramm understood only that Tapheina had been deliberately seducing him and that, to his shame, part of him had responded.

But he couldn't blame Marta for that—nor for the fact that her presence and solicitous nature reminded him of the wife he'd not be able to see for another six months.

"Are you sure you don't want some milk?" she pressed. "I could water it down. And there's honey, as well."

"I'm fine," Abramm told her more sharply.

His brusqueness only intensified her efforts to please. "An apple might help. How about I chop you an apple to put in it?"

"How about you don't?" he said, shoveling the porridge in as fast as he could.

He saw the hurt flash across her face, but before she could respond, the old man working with the damper gave a shout, fell to his knees, then came scrambling out of the hearth as a dark heronlike bird dropped out of the flue after him. Feyna.

One of the women shrieked and swung a soot-blackened broom at it, but the rhu'ema spawn darted between them, flapping up to the bread table, then the counter, provoking shrieks and ineffectual swats as it did. It bounced off the hearth and soared toward Abramm standing at the far side of the room. He watched it stupidly and, when it was nearly upon him, could only think to throw his mostly empty bowl at it.

The vessel sent it tumbling and flapping across the bread table again, where Marta calmly struck it with a burst of Light from her slender fingertips. It stiffened, jittered briefly, and collapsed on the flour-dusted table in a puff of white.

She picked up the carcass by one of its feet and handed it off to the old man as Abramm realized he had himself just thrown a bowl of porridge at the thing. Embarrassment squirmed in his middle.

"I can't believe there's another of them," the old man said as he headed for the dining room. "There must be a nest or somethin' up there."

Marta grabbed a rag from the dish tub she'd apparently been stationed at before Abramm had entered, and cleaned up the spilled porridge. Then she gathered the spoon and now-emptied bowl and returned to the washtub without comment.

"I'm sorry I snapped at you," he said, following her. "You didn't deserve that."

"No." She concentrated on washing the bowl. "But since you have been doling out foulness to everyone in equal measure these days, I don't feel especially offended."

Doling out foulness to everyone? He'd hardly spoken to a soul since he entered the room. And what did she mean by "these days"?

"Speaking of foulness," she added, dropping the bowl into a tub of rinse water, "as soon as you have a chance, you should make use of the hot springs up the hill. A bath would do you wonders."

"A bath?"

"You've been wearing the same clothes for at least seven weeks, Alaric."

"I don't have any other clothes."

"A fact of which we're all very well aware." She reached for the stack of bowls on the board beside her tub, then hesitated, glancing up at him. "Do you mind?"

He stepped back to give her room, and she transferred the bowls to her tub of soapy water.

"Ye know," Kitrenna Trinley remarked from where she worked at the counter behind them, "the others went down t' the barn some time ago. I'm sure they'd welcome those strong shoulders o' yers, Alaric." She didn't look up from the side of mutton she was seasoning.

"Without a bath?" he asked.

"Ye can bathe once the roof is fixed." Kitrenna tightened her lips as she rubbed salted herbs into the meat. " 'Tis a dangerous job. You should be down there helpin' 'fore someone gets hurt."

Irked anew, he gave her a nod. "By all means, then, I shall hurry down to help." But irony rang sharply in his voice, for they both knew her husband would receive his assistance grudgingly at best.

On his way out the door, he helped himself to an apple from the basket on the sideboard, then stepped out onto a porch completely enclosed by walls of snow. A short, narrow passage had been shoveled through it to the first of the wood-covered walkways leading down to the hay barn.

Things did not improve as the day wore on. In the hay barn, Trinley castigated him for his lateness, for his snobbishness in going off to a private cell rather than sleeping with everyone else in the Great Room, for being obstinate, disrespectful, and foul tempered. Abramm bore it all with increasing frustration until a minor accident sent Trinley ripping into him for his carelessness, and suddenly he found himself facing the man with fists clenched, ready to grab him by the throat and throw him across the room.

Trinley mocked his aggressive stance with an invitation to fight before

Rolland stepped between them. "No one's fightin' anyone. Now, both of ye just calm yerselves down. . . ."

"I have no need o' calmin'," Trinley said. "It's him who's got the fire under him."

Abramm glared at him, the crazy, blind rage slowly subsiding, leaving him trembling in its wake.

Rolland's big hand tightened about Abramm's upper arm as he said, "We're just about done here, Alaric. Great Room woodbox probably needs fillin', though."

A moment more Abramm stood there, wrestling with the wild temper. Then he drew a deep breath and pulled himself out of Rolland's grip, nodding and turning away.

"Well," he heard Cedric say as he stepped out the door, "that was right scary."

Trinley growled a disdainful reply about brigands and brawlers.

Abramm stalked back up the hill to the woodyard, where he spent an hour chopping wood, then brought a load up to the Great Room, the monastery's all-purpose gathering place and communal sleeping chamber for most of the newcomers. Walled in rough-hewn stone with a high ceiling of stripped log beams, it boasted a huge multipaned window at its far end. A red-and-gray wool rug covered the stone floor beneath an array of wooden chairs and worn couches, while overhead a rough-hewn wheel hung on a long cable stretched from the rafters, kelistars burning brightly in the glass-shaded pans dangling around its circumference. A misshapen stuffed elk's head looked down from above the massive fireplace.

Abramm stacked the wood in the hearth box, then went to stand before the great window, beyond which the shifting curtains of snow came down harder than ever. His anger bubbled unevenly, like a cauldron of heated mud. Trinley was insufferable. Arrogant, ignorant, stubborn, and small minded. It was unfair that Abramm should be stuck here the whole winter with him!

Why have you done this to me, my Lord? It makes no sense.

He drew a deep breath and let it out, fogging the windowpane before him.

"I thought you were helping out in the hay barn, Alaric."

Abramm turned to find Arvil Laud standing in the Great Room doorway, regarding him with surprise. Thick, chin-length gray hair framed a narrow, weathered face with a short goatee and an ever-present pipe between his teeth. Once a university professor in Springerlan, Laud had been captured by

Gadrielites over seven years ago and beaten for writing heretical tracts and articles, his right hand chopped off to ensure he never did it again. Now he served as leader and acting kohal to the community of permanent residents at Caerna'tha.

Abramm shrugged. "They were about finished, so I came up to fill the woodboxes."

The kohal arched a gray brow. "Ah."

Abramm turned back to the window, hoping the man would go away. Instead Laud joined him, the sweet aroma of his pipe tobacco overlaying the smoke of the hearth fire.

Together they stared at the storm, the older man puffing silently. "I've only been here six years," he said presently, "but old Wolmer says it's been decades since we've had a storm this heavy so early in the season."

Abramm watched the curtains of snow shift and undulate outside the window and said nothing.

"Did you know," Laud said presently, "that the number of your company is exactly the same as the number of those taken from us in the raid last week?"

Abramm snorted. "How could I not? Your people have been crowing about that from the moment we arrived." Two days before Abramm and his companions reached Caerna'tha, men from the village at the valley's mouth had launched a late-season raid and taken all their able-bodied men, women—even the children—for the slave trade. It had been a bitter blow to those left behind, who, being old and weak, would have been unable to shovel snow off roofs and fix all that would need fixing during the winter. Upon first hearing of it, Abramm had suggested they launch a rescue and was told it was too late. The villagers had already left for the lowlands where they'd sell their captives and spend the winter.

"It puzzles me you cannot find it in yourself to share our joy," Laud said. "Your presence will save our lives this winter season."

"Yours are not the only lives needing to be saved."

The other man puffed on his pipe for a time, a cloud of fragrant smoke rising around him. Then, "You speak of the war to the south."

Abramm turned to him sharply. "A war for the very survival of the Terstan faith! I should be down there helping to win it."

"But instead you are here." Laud shook his head, still staring at the storm. "Eidon simply must not understand how desperately he needs you to defend and protect him."

Abramm frowned, smitten by his mocking words.

"From what your companions have told me of your actions the night of your arrival," Laud went on, "I'd guess you're well skilled in the Light. Rolland says you saw right through the trap that was set for you all in the way station. We at Caerna'tha saw for ourselves how you drew off the tanniym to give your companions time to enter our gates. Your courage is commendable, your strength and skill in the Light impressive." He paused, drawing a puff from his pipe. "But her breath was in your face, Alaric. You must know her spore is in you now."

"I've already purged it."

"Not all of it. And even a little is enough to make you vulnerable. Especially when the Shadow has you."

Abramm stared sulkily at the storm, resenting the man's criticism.

The professor went on. "Do you know how the raiders got in last week?" When Abramm maintained silence, Laud answered for him. "One of our own opened the gate for them. A man who was approached by your tanniym friend on a wood-cutting expedition last fall. And inhaled the spore in her breath."

"I won't be opening the gates for her," Abramm said stiffly. "You have no worry of that."

"You think you're strong enough to resist her?" Laud shook his head, gray hair rasping against his collar. "Your Light skills will be useless if you're living in the Shadow. As you have been for days now, I'd guess. Normally I would not intrude upon a man's privacy this way, but you endanger us all with this ongoing . . . *tantrum* of yours."

Abramm ground his teeth and glared at the window, feeling the blood rush to his face. "You have no idea what I've lost, professor. What I've been through."

Laud snorted softly. "Perhaps not." He sighed. "I do know that I once felt as you do now: bitter, frustrated, angry. As if all my purpose had been stripped away. I had been surfeited with my suffering, and railed at Eidon for what I saw as excess."

Abramm shifted away from the man, discomfited by how close Laud's description was to his own reality.

The professor lifted the leather-bound stump at the end of his right arm. "They took my *hand*, Alaric. Do you know what it is like to go through life without your strong hand? The loss is impossible to forget—everything you try to do brings it back to mind.

"Bad enough that, I thought, but then I had to leave my books behind in the pass when the wagon broke—all I had left of my old life. We, too, came late to the monastery and were trapped for the winter. Suffering upon suffering, I thought. And none of it deserved. He was stripping everything away from me. My worldly possessions, my hand, my writing, my reputation, my job . . ."

Abramm turned to look at him, unnerved by his words. The older man smiled, his eyes blank with remembrance. "Oh yes, I was bitter and angry and wretched. And Eidon let me stay that way for a time. But finally I came to my senses and confessed to him my failings. And when I returned to the place of embracing his will over my own, that's when I recalled that if one wants to know Eidon, one must come to know Tersius. And his sufferings. All of which were undeserved, yet borne without complaint."

He fell silent. Outside the wind whistled, and the snowflakes ticked against the glass. From somewhere outside the Great Room, children's voices echoed in laughter as overhead the roof creaked with its accumulating weight of snow.

"Undeserved, yet borne without complaint. . . ." Laud's words and story shamed Abramm out of his self-pity, truth tearing away the veils his disappointment, frustration, and selfishness had woven about his soul. His sufferings may have been undeserved, but he'd certainly not borne them without complaint. And compared to what Laud had endured, they were nothing. Even less when laid up against what Tersius went through.

So what if things had been difficult and uncomfortable for a time? So what if he would not see his wife as soon as he had hoped? At least he had hope of seeing her. And his sons. At least he had all his limbs..

After a time Laud removed his pipe. "Nothing that happens in this life is beyond Eidon's reach. I'm sure you know that. . . ." He turned now, meeting Abramm's gaze. "The question is, do you live in it?"

Abramm had no answer to that. For Laud was right—though it took effort to admit it. If he lived in what he claimed to believe, then he had no reason for all this misery he was piling upon himself. Even now, he felt the tenuousness of his thoughts—how he could sincerely believe and yet see how, with a simple twisting of perception, he would not. He shook his head. "I want to, though," he whispered.

"The more you learn of him, the more you'll understand him," said Laud. "The more you know and understand, the easier it will be to trust him. In all things." He tilted his head, the spectacles' lenses flashing with reflected light.

"Perhaps that is why you are here: to learn of him."

"Surely I could learn as well in Fannath Rill."

"No. There you would be busy fighting, your mind filled with the distractions of battle. But up here . . ."

Up here Abramm was cut off from everything. He had few responsibilities, no one knew who he was, and even the jobs were menial, allowing plenty of time to think.

"How many times in the old stories do we read of men taken off to a solitary time of learning and preparation before they can fulfill the calling Eidon has placed upon their lives? You are in such a hurry to join in the fighting. But perhaps Eidon has something greater for you, something that can only be carried out with greater knowledge and confidence. . . ."

A current of Light tingled over Abramm's flesh, lifting the hairs on the back of his neck. *Is that what you're doing here, my Lord? Preparing me?* He had only to form the question before he knew the answer. *Yes.*

Apparently Laud noted a change, for he smiled, stuck his pipe back into his mouth, and giving him a nod, turned again to the window. After a moment he added, "You might consider taking advantage of our baths. They're free. And they're quite rejuvenating. If you need some clothes ask Alia. She keeps a supply of 'em clean and mended for folk without a lot of spares, and she'll see your own are washed and mended, as well."

He left Abramm standing at the window, bemused and chastened yet again.

CHAPTER

6

After her fiasco with the esteemed gentleman, Maddie never returned to the Inn of the Gilded Ram, partly for fear of running into the man again, and partly because, after walking out without a word, going back would draw more attention to herself than her little charade as Molly could bear without unraveling entirely.

She'd already done the tavern-girl gambit years ago, at the very same inn, with Serr Penchott's now-senile father. Ignorance, immaturity, and her over-weening delight in becoming the commoners' singing sensation had led to her unmasking. King Hadrich had been so furious he'd sent her to a convent for a year in hopes of instilling some sense of responsibility and decorum in her.

The punishment would be far worse now, with Ronesca part of the triumvirate that commanded her life. And now she had others who relied upon her for their livelihoods, and they would suffer along with her should she bring even more dishonor upon herself than had already come with her pregnancy. It had taken an effort of will for her to stop trying to analyze what had happened and how the eccentric behavior of some Sorian lord she didn't even know could have unhinged her as much as they had, but she was determined to leave it all behind.

So "Molly" had vanished, and Trap was relieved not to have to worry about Maddie walking unescorted through the streets of Fannath Rill after dark anymore.

In any case, the wind that night had brought in the storm clouds, and the next day the rains had begun. It was still raining over a week later when she dreamed of Abramm again.

As always she sensed him nearby, his strong, sustaining presence filling her soul in almost the same way Eidon's Light did. A great storm raged outside, wind howling, snowflakes ticking against roof and shutter as she followed him through dark rooms and twisting drafty corridors, calling for him to wait. But the wind drowned out her voice so he didn't hear her. Time and again she would round one corner only to glimpse him disappearing around the next, until finally she heard a door shut, and the next turn brought her face-to-face with it. When she opened it, she found only a field of white blowing snow and he was gone, never knowing she was there. She'd awakened bereft, consumed by the terrible longing such dreams always birthed in her, and once again the tears came.

After a while, she rolled over, turning her thoughts to Eidon . . . and words flowed into her mind on a haunting melody. Words of sorrow and loss that compelled her to arise and hurry to her music room, where she took up her lirret and began to work out the song. Some time later, Jeyanne interrupted her, reminding her she was to ride with Princess Ronesca to the reception at Tiris ul Sadek's villa, and they were already nearly an hour past the time she'd planned to arise.

"But it's pouring rain," Maddie protested.

"Indeed, and yet Princess Ronesca has just sent over your gown and jewels along with very complex and specific instructions as to how it should all be arranged."

"So she's not canceling," Maddie said.

"I don't think so, Your Highness."

Jeyanne wasn't exaggerating about the specificity of Ronesca's instructions, nor their complexity. Maddie's hair alone took over an hour to work into the jeweled and braided patterns Ronesca wanted. And the gown was a nightmare of buttons and ties and sashes, most of them fastening in the back. The waist was too tight to accommodate her steadily swelling womb, so Jeyanne left some of the buttons undone and covered the breach with an artful rearrangement of scarf and gold-braiding. When all was in place—the hair, the jewels, the cosmetics, and the sashes—Jeyanne floated a white silk veil reminiscent of the Sorian style over Maddie's head and laid a heavy cloak of satin-lined wool over that.

Maddie reached the front foyer shortly before Ronesca and her other attendant for the day, Lady Iolande. Together they stepped out under the covered portico and hurried to the waiting coach as the rain sheeted down beyond the overhang. Gathering her cloak firmly about her, Maddie boarded the coach after her sister-in-law, Iolande entering last. Then the door closed and the coach rolled away. Within moments rain drummed on the vehicle's wooden ceiling and water splashed around the wheels.

The three women sat in silence, swaying in unison as the coach wheeled around the circular drive and started up over the bridge to the mainland. Maddie eyed her sister-in-law covertly.

Ronesca was in her middle thirties, her features sharp and clean, not particularly pretty, but arresting nonetheless. Beneath her cloak's loosely fitting satin hood, her dark hair had been pulled up into an elaborate coiffure of tiny interwoven braids, set off with a sparkling net of rubies and topaz. A single dark curl dangled beside her long, pale neck.

She was intelligent, powerful, and persistent. And she was definitely up to something, for normally she wouldn't·think of going out in her finery on a day like this.

But Draek Tiris ul Sadek was the new sensation in town. His men had arrived months ago to buy the old Portelas villa on the eastern edge of town and had been renovating it ever since. Today was the first time anyone other than workmen had been allowed inside since the renovations began.

He was a high *draek* of one of the old Sorite dynasties, a fabulously wealthy warlord from the east, whose holdings were said to include a palace with archways cast of gold and halls paneled in the same, furnished with plates and goblets and utensils of gold. Even the breastplates of his royal guard were golden. His mythical holdings supposedly lay somewhere out beyond the Mahishi—the harsh, high deserts and the Great Sand Sea few deigned to cross, save on the trade routes which had made men like ul Sadek their fortunes.

In addition to sponsoring the arts, he was also patron of the weak. Having been an orphan himself, he maintained a great orphanage back in his kingdom. He also had armies that numbered in the hundreds of thousands under his command. He would be a valuable ally should Ronesca somehow manage to acquire him.

That she had insisted Maddie attend with her, then taken the trouble to select her gown and accessories for the occasion, complete with meticulous instruction as to how they should be arranged, argued strongly that Maddie was a part of whatever she was planning. And it didn't take too great a leap of logic to guess what that part was.

Since the morning when Maddie had admitted her pregnancy to the woman, they had not spoken of it at all. But Maddie had been careful to attend as many of Ronesca's social functions and religious observances as she could bear—and as did not interfere with her own. Not being concerned with showing up at the Gilded Ram had helped, though for a time she'd refused to eat anything prepared on palace grounds, except that which her own people specifically purchased and prepared. It had, she'd heard, raised a bit of turmoil in the kitchens, but so be it. Ronesca had said nothing, and rumors credited her strange cravings to being with child. Eventually she'd talked herself out of the horrible suspicion, for as much at odds as she was with Ronesca, she couldn't believe the woman would stoop to killing her baby.

"I am pleased to see you have respected my wishes and have adorned yourself properly." Ronesca's prim voice intruded into Maddie's musings.

Maddie met her sister-in-law's gaze. "How could I fail, Your Highness? You were quite specific."

"It wouldn't be the first time my instructions were ignored. Or . . . modified." Her dark, long-lashed eyes dropped to Maddie's waist. "I see there was some of that, regardless. The dress is too tight for you, I presume?" Maddie flushed as Ronesca pursed her small lips. "It's hidden well, though. Don't you think?" She glanced at Lady Iolande, who agreed.

The crown princess's gaze narrowed again on Maddie. "I'd like you to see that it remains so."

"But everyone already knows—"

"They only suspect, my dear. And so long as you say nothing inappropriate, that is the way it will stay. Tell them that you will be moving up to Deveren Dol to stay with the Sisters of the Sacred Graces for a time of spiritual healing and refreshment in the wake of your devastating losses. Certainly you've played the part of grieving widow well enough. When you return, we will have a grand ball to welcome you back and officially introduce you to the court."

Maddie frowned at her. "Sisters of the— I have no interest in going on retreat, Your Highness. And, anyway, what would be the point? It will be obvious I'm not going for spiritual healing."

"Not if you leave within the week. Rumor to the contrary, no one is certain of the truth. And if they don't see you swelling up like an old sow, they will remain uncertain. When the child is born . . . well . . . perhaps Eidon will be gracious and give you a girl, which would solve all of our problems."

"I will not go to Deveren Dol, Your Highness."

Ronesca cocked a shapely brow at her. "You are not queen here, Princess Madeleine. In fact, you are not queen anywhere, so you would do well to stop acting as if you were. I've written to your father about this matter, and he has agreed. You'll go north next week. If your child is determined to be of royal heritage, we will see about procuring him or her a proper sponsor. Otherwise . . ." She let her words trail off meaningfully.

Maddie felt the old anger smoldering within her.

"Say anything to anyone today," Ronesca said before she could speak, "and I'll know of it. In which case you will be leaving considerably sooner."

"My father agreed to this?"

"I have it in writing, my dear." She pulled at the folds of her gray woolen outer cloak. "Of course, if you were to accede to my wishes and promise to properly identify your child with the kirik here in Chesedh, the king might be willing to rethink things. But as it is . . . he is concerned, Madeleine. For you, for your child, and for his realm."

"His realm? My child will be no danger to his realm!"

"Perhaps not at your command, but we have many Kiriathans in Chesedh, unfortunately."

"Helping us fight for our lives."

"Some of them, yes." Ronesca's gloved hands fell still as her gaze came up to meet Maddie's. "But others are simply leeches, noble exiles too good to do any real work. None of us is happy about this, for we all know Kiriathans are not to be trusted. If word were to get out that you had given birth to Abramm's heir, what do you think would happen? They would flock to you, seeking to use the child to regain the throne of Kiriath and throw the usurpers out."

"He would be a babe, incapable of leading any bid to regain the throne."

"Perhaps, but your finance secretary was once First Minister of all the realm. And before that, a military leader. He is also the child's uncle, and at one point his wife was actually Abramm's designated successor."

"That was changed when Simon was born."

"Ah, but Simon is no longer in the way. Nor is your other one. . . . What was his name?"

Maddie stared at her stonily. "His name was Ian."

Ronesca shrugged. "No matter. Neither is an issue any longer, which leaves Meridon as the perfect candidate to serve as regent while your child grows to maturity."

"I can't believe you think these things."

"You deny they are truth?"

"The facts as you've outlined them are all true. Yes, Duke Eltrap would be the logical one to head a regency. But he would never do that. At least not right now. He knows the importance of winning the battle for Chesedh before we can even think about Kiriath again."

"Does he? I'm not so sure. Nor is King Hadrich."

The coach began to slow, then came to a stop, and soon the door creaked open. Maddie stepped out after Iolande into a white silk tent, erected at the villa's entrance alcove to protect guests from the weather. She guessed there must be two layers, for the walls of the inner barely stirred despite the stiff wind gusting outside. The rain was so effectively blocked, the only moisture that dampened the pavement was that carried in by the coaches themselves.

Servants in short white jackets and blousy black trousers guided them to a long, upsloping corridor with a high, arched latticework ceiling of stone and glass. Warmed this chilly, wet day by tall bronze braziers full of coals, its length was lined with other guests making their way up to Tiris ul Sadek's famed Grand Salon.

Ronesca was fashionably late, so the salon was already crowded, the rumble of their conversation competing with the minor key refrains of a cadre of balcony musicians.

Vast sheets of silk draped the great hall, reminding Maddie unnervingly of the night she'd served the Gilded Ram's esteemed guest. Huge orbs hung about the room—not kelistars, but glass filled with swirling, dancing colored lights, mostly in shades of amber and blue. Their illumination reflected off great winged creatures rendered in brushstrokes of silver and gold and sparkling crystal on the silk draperies, benevolent beings watching over the crowd.

A golden fig tree stood at the room's midst, encased in a glass dome, and beyond it a modest dais had been set up for a great gilded chair on which the draek sat to receive the compliments of his guests, the line as long as the room itself. Ronesca and her attendants were immediately escorted to the front, of course, and Maddie was only about ten feet away when she finally got a clear look at their host.

He was a man in his prime—tall, straight-backed, and well-built—in impeccable white robes sashed in gold. A swag of loose gold netting set with jewels and precious stones swept across his chest and a white turban covered his dark hair. A gold ring glittered in his ear against a closely trimmed dark beard. More gold stippled his cheekbones beneath liquid brown eyes lashed in black. It was the eyes that keyed her recognition and drove the breath from her chest. For this was the same man she'd served at the Gilded Ram, the one who'd caught her wrist and smelled it, who'd offered to buy her unborn child. Tiris ul Sadek, gone slumming while he waited for his villa to be prepared. . . .

He stood and stepped off his dais to greet them.

"Draek Tiris." Ronesca dropped a deep curtsey, Madeleine doing likewise at her elbow. "It is a pleasure to finally meet so esteemed a man as yourself."

"The pleasure is all mine, Your Highness."

The dark, liquid eyes fixed upon Maddie and, to her vast relief, showed no sign of recognition. Of course. As many times as she'd experienced the same phenomenon, why had she even doubted?

"May I introduce you to Princess Madeleine, my sister-in-law," Ronesca purred, "the First Daughter of Chesedh, and widow of the slain Kiriathan king, Abramm Kalladorne."

Maddie held out her hand, and ul Sadek took it, the touch of his fingers on hers sending a tremor up her arm. He'd lost the grotesque claws, she noted. "My sincerest condolences on your loss, my queen," he said soberly. She had not noticed how wonderful his voice was when he'd spoken to her in the inn's back room, but now it made her breath catch.

Ronesca frowned, having noted his inappropriate title for Maddie. She didn't dare correct him though, so she diverted his attention back to herself and introduced the Countess Iolande Cheriqual. Ul Sadek greeted her with a cool disinterest that bordered on rudeness, and immediately returned his gaze to Maddie. "Your husband was a great man," he said. "I was shocked to hear he had passed on."

Maddie stared back at him, shocked herself that a great lord and foreigner such as Tiris ul Sadek would have heard of Abramm.

Ronesca was clearly annoyed. It was not often she found herself out-maneuvered in conversation. Now she smiled and intruded again. "Perhaps you have not yet heard the details of his tragic death. I—"

"Rest assured, Highness," ul Sadek said, cutting her off. "All in the south and east have heard by now of the death of the White Pretender. If indeed he is dead." He cocked a dark brow at Maddie, the gold on his cheekbones glittering exotically. "It would not be the first time he has come back from the grave, now, would it?"

"Come back from the grave?" Ronesca tittered nervously. "He was executed before hundreds."

"As hundreds saw him die in the Val'Orda. Or so the song goes. Is that not so, Princess Madeleine?" And he turned again to Maddie, leaving Ronesca in a wordless fluster.

"It is, Your Grace," Maddie replied. "But alas, I fear this time . . ." The words stopped. He stared at her, his dark eyes boring into hers, a slight twitch at the corner of his lip. But she could not make herself go on. Could not make herself say aloud the truth that he was dead and wasn't coming back.

Ronesca did it for her. "This time there will be no miraculous returns. Abramm's death was a great loss to us all."

"I'm sure it was, Your Highness. Thank you so much for coming." Ul Sadek gestured now toward the room at large. "I invite you now to enjoy some of my art collection, mostly sculptures today, but I trust you'll find it as fascinating as it is unusual. And don't miss out on the refreshments." He caught Maddie's eye yet again. "The golden figs have become edible just this week and are especially delicious."

With a nod to each of them, he turned his gaze to the aristocrats waiting behind them, the dismissal again bordering on rudeness.

As soon as they were out of earshot, Maddie expected Ronesca to hiss with outrage. Instead she seemed completely smitten with the man, not even noticing the snub. "Is he not the most charming, gracious, and utterly manly man you have ever seen? I could listen to that voice all day, even if he were just reading figures. And his eyes . . . They look right at you, right into you. He certainly had his eye upon Madeleine, though, didn't you think, Iolande?"

As they made the rounds, Ronesca was unable to talk of anything but Tiris ul Sadek, marveling at the décor, the food, the music, in between blurts of sublime appreciation for his person. Though she showed no interest in the art collection, the food was divine. Before long she was making random comments that gradually evolved into reminders that Maddie had her future to think of, that being unwed at her age was exceedingly eccentric, and though she never came right out and said it, that Tiris ul Sadek would make her a wonderful match.

The notion was so ridiculous—and repellent—Maddie struggled to believe what her eyes and ears were telling her. But that was really what her sister-in-law was suggesting. When Ronesca spotted Tiris moving among his collection of crystalline sculptures and all but shoved Maddie into his path, she was finally convinced—and fully alarmed.

Tiris, of course, was utterly gracious, apologizing for having nearly run her over, while his dark eyes laughed at her obvious befuddlement. With no desire to speak to the man one moment more than she already had, Maddie insisted it was her own clumsiness and glanced about for an excuse to make her escape. But though she's fully expected his other guests to move like water into her place, she was unnerved to discover they had all been drawn away, each person suddenly occupied with the pedestaled artwork or other conversations. Leaving her face to face with her host and no polite way of disengaging.

"You must think I am a dreadful man," he said in that marvelous voice, "sneaking about in back room orgies, trafficking in flesh, buying babies."

The blood rushed to her face, and her mind went blank.

He flashed a glorious smile at her. "I assure you, princess, my intentions were purely honorable, if misguided. Though you can hardly blame me for that. . . ."

It felt as if her cheeks would burst into open flames, but still she could not speak.

He laughed softly and let it go. "I keep an orphanage." With that he offered her his arm. "Walk with me a bit?"

Uncomfortably aware of the amused and speculative glances coming their way, she accepted, and after a few moments of gazing at the crystalline statue of a long-haired, bare-chested man with arms flung wide to the heavens—she couldn't decide if the subject was angry or worshipful—they began to stroll in silence.

"I have heard about the orphanage," she said at length. "That you established it because you were yourself an orphan." She glanced around hopefully, but there was still no one to deliver her. "It appears you have come a long way."

"Oh, I was not a poor orphan. I was an orphan of extreme privilege. Servants, attendants, tutors . . . I simply had no parents. But I understand the hole that leaves in a child's soul. My adopted children grow up fully cared for, educated at the highest level of our culture, with a name and an honored place in society." He paused, eyeing her. "Had you stayed long enough, perhaps I'd have had time to explain that to you. Had you stayed long enough, I might have offered you even more."

She averted her eyes, not sure what he meant by that but not wanting to ask. Instead she concentrated on the sculpture before them, then said, "What is this, exactly?"

He chuckled slightly, shaking his head. "You are a most fitting complement to the White Pretender, my lady."

Which drew her eyes back to him in surprise, wondering at the way his words could please her and cut her to the quick at the same time.

He gazed at the sculpture. "She is a dragon rider. You have never heard of those?"

"From the Sorian myth cycle."

"Virgin riders whose mounts are said to transform into men at certain times of the year and perform their . . . manly duties."

She flushed, as much from his words as from certain physical aspects of the dragon she was only now noticing. "Well, it looks like no dragon I've ever seen."

"And have you seen a dragon, my lady?" He seemed amused, and she thought she had never seen so expressive a mouth.

She shrugged. "In pictures and murals. A few statues. There is a ruins in Kiriath—"

"Tuk-Rhaal."

"You know of it?"

"Of course. Tuk-Rhaal predates Ophir. And they worshipped the dragon there." His eyes glittered keenly. "You have an interest in dragons, then?"

"It's something of a curiosity."

"Ah yes. Your husband was marked with the red dragon brand of Katahn ul Manus, wasn't he?"

"You certainly know a lot about my husband, sir."

"Hmm. I confess I've made him something of a matter for personal study." He led her to another sculpture, this one of a great dragon rising out of the sea in a wonder of form and fury. "They say he gave up his life for his god. . . ."

She nodded slowly. "He did."

"But not for you."

"Oh, it was for me, too. He gave himself up to them so his men could get me free."

"But that wasn't what you wanted, was it? Your freedom without him?"

A chill zinged through her—of surprise and pain and wariness. His question drove too close to the door that would release the deep, dark, angry part of her nature. The part she had refused for so long to let control her. And refused still. She looked him straight in the eye and changed the subject. "So then, have *you* seen a dragon, sir?"

He smiled easily, seeming unaware of the effect his words had wrought in her. "Everyone knows dragons are only a myth."

"And yet," Maddie countered, "every people has such myths. Surely at one time there must have—"

"The Qeptites have no dragons in their stories."

"I am not familiar with the Qeptites."

"They are from the far south. And another millennium."

"So . . ." She dropped her hand from his arm and circled the statue to study its far side more closely, then glanced up at him. "*Have* you seen a dragon, sir?"

He cocked a dark brow, a half smile on his face. "And what would you think if I told you I had?"

"I think I would find that hard to believe."

"Exactly." He started on toward the next piece. "So if you are prepared to believe only one of the possible answers I might give, why ask the question at all?"

"You're saying you have seen one."

"I'm asking why you'd ask me, if you think you already know the answer."

"Confirmation, I suppose. . . ." She gave up then and gestured across at the dragon rider statue they'd left some time ago. "So what sort of dragon is that, then?"

He shrugged. "A Sorite dragon, I would guess."

"You mock me, sir."

He grinned at her. "Forgive me, princess. You provided too tempting an opening."

They walked on to a final sculpted figure, this of a dragon by itself, perched on a rocky crag and clutching an orb in one claw. The ruby that was its eye glittered at her balefully, almost as if it were alive.

"There is another ancient city ruin in the high Waladi—the place you know as the Great Sand Sea," he said. "The city of Chena'ag Tor. They worshipped dragons there, as well."

"And have you been to that one?"

"As it happens, I have." The earring glittered beside the darkness of his short beard, and the light reflected iridescently off his cheekbones. "That is something not very many can say, for it is a hidden city, guarded by the sea of shifting sands, where mist hides the sky and not even the sun can be used to navigate."

"How do the sands shift if there is no wind?"

"How do you know there is no wind?"

"They say once the Shadow mist moves in, the winds die away."

"That is true. In this case, though, there are winds in the sand sea. And sun and heat. But the sands can shift without the wind, and the winds can stir the dust to hide the sky as well as any mist."

"So how is it you alone found this place?"

He smiled. "It is a long tale—one I would enjoy telling you. But . . . as I have other guests today that I must greet, I shall have to decline your request."

His disengagement jolted her, and she realized at once he was playing with her. And also that he was a masterful taleteller. Even though she more than half disbelieved his story of the hidden dragon city, she wanted to hear the rest of it. And he knew it, for now he cocked his head and said, "Have lunch with me next week and I'll tell you my story."

"I fear I'll be leaving for Deveren Dol next week."

"You cannot postpone your trip a day or two?"

"I suppose . . ." If she had a luncheon date with Tiris ul Sadek . . . perhaps Ronesca would relent on her deadline.

"But if you wait too long," he said, a twinkle in his eye, "the purpose for the trip will have been nullified, no?"

She lifted her chin and met his eye directly. "I have no idea what you mean, my lord. Also, I must be honest with you: I have no interest in being courted."

At that he laughed. "You have no interest *yet*, Princess." He paused, then gave her a short bow. "Until next week, my lady."

"Draek Tiris." And she curtsied in return.

CHAPTER

7

Abramm slid the shovel's flat-ended blade under the bank of powdery snow sloping up the kitchen roof before him and flung another bite of it over his shoulder. A glistening veil of fine flakes drifted downward in its wake as he scooped up another bite of snow and flung it likewise. With snow filling the yard to the eaves, he and Galen were in the process of clearing the accumulation from the roof and piling it into a growing ridge along the edge of the newly exposed wood shingles.

The storm had lasted eleven days, and after all the time he'd spent clearing roofs in gale winds and driving snow, it was nice to have a clear sky and bright sun overhead. He could actually feel all his fingers and toes and had even started up a sweat. The work was still backbreaking, however, and when he reached the side edge of the roof, he was glad to stop and take a break.

With a sigh, he straightened, bracing the shovel's flat-bottomed edge against the ice-coated shingling as he rolled and stretched his weary shoulders. His left arm and hand ached fiercely, protesting all the manual labor he had forced upon them these last days. He'd thought it unfair and even a little insulting when Rolland, standing across from him now on the other side of the roof's snow-covered peak, had suggested Abramm and Galen work together on one side, while the blacksmith took the other for himself. Now he had to admit he was grateful he'd acceded to the suggestion. He had more than enough work to challenge him, and Rolland's strength appeared inexhaustible.

Which was a good thing, since, though they each stood a mere three feet from the top, they had wagonloads of weight yet to move.

Shifting his feet to more stable purchase, Abramm lifted his eyes to the stunning scenery that the storm's passing had revealed—the soaring white-clad peaks of the fabled Aranaak Mountains towered on every side, immense and rugged. A flight of crows flapped low overhead, heading toward the snow-filled valley, then turning to follow its now-buried watercourse down-stream to where opposing tumbles of snow-covered ridges came together.

"Looks almost passable today, doesn't it?" Rolland remarked from across the roof peak, apparently noting the direction of Abramm's gaze.

His tone was so wistful Abramm looked round at him in surprise. "You aren't thinking of taking your family out now, are you?"

The big man chuckled. "I have t' admit it tempts me. I hate waitin' around here all winter when we could be gettin' settled into our new lives. . . . My wife's got family there—an uncle. Dunno how welcome we'll be showing up all unexpected, but at least it's something." He fell silent, waiting for Abramm to reciprocate with a tidbit of his own information.

Though Abramm had seriously considered Laud's admonition to be more forthcoming about his past, he'd had no idea how to implement it. Should he reveal everything or continue to live under the guise of Alaric? Mysterious, perhaps, but a commoner like the rest of them. Part of him enjoyed the anonymity, and even the growing easiness developing between himself and the others. All that would vanish once they knew who he really was.

On the other hand, sharing his identity with them would also bind them to him in ways he wasn't sure he wanted to bind them. It would even en-danger them, bringing them again to the attention of his enemies who had attacked them repeatedly coming through the Kolki Pass—because of him. They were simple common folk, not lords nor wise men nor soldiers, not even close to the army he hoped to eventually build. And if they didn't believe him—and they might not—then his revelation would deny him both their camaraderie and their respect.

Thus he'd gone round and round. He'd been so close-mouthed for weeks on all personal details of his life that people had long since stopped asking, and he'd fallen into the assumption that the secret was his to keep or divulge when he wished. Now, out of the blue, an opportunity had arisen, and he found himself paralyzed by his ruminations.

Rolland had never asked him much while they were on the trail, and Abramm sensed that he was only asking now out of simple friendship. So far as Rolland knew, they were just two men working on a roof, of an age and station in life that gave them a natural compatibility. That the blacksmith was relaxed enough to ask, was proof of the ease they now shared. For Abramm not to reply would only hurt him.

But what *could* Abramm say without disrupting everything? His life as king was over. Perhaps all that was needed were the parts Rolland could relate to and understand, bits and pieces that would be enough to satisfy, yet not drive him away—and it surprised Abramm just how much he desired the other man's company and companionship.

"Ye got someone in Chesedh?" Rolland prodded when Abramm said nothing. "Family o' some kind to take ye in? 'Cause if not, ye're welcome t' come with us."

"Thanks, Rolland. I appreciate the offer. But I . . ." Abramm hesitated, touched by the man's generosity. "A wife," he said, finally. "And two sons. They're waiting for me in Fannath Rill." Though his enemies had claimed the boys were killed during the Mataian uprising, he had good reason to suspect otherwise and chose to believe the best: that Captain Channon had fulfilled his mission to find them and had already brought them to their mother in Fannath Rill.

Rolland gave a nod of satisfaction. "I figured as much."

"You did?"

"I see the way ye are with my own boys. With the women, too. And the way ye went so wild t' think we were stuck here fer the winter." He shook his head. "I'd've been wild, too."

Galen had finished his row and, as he moved back toward the center of the roof, called, "Alaric has a *wife*?! Is that what I heard you say?"

Abramm turned to him in consternation. "Is it that difficult to believe I might have a wife, Galen?"

"Well . . ." Galen's dark eyes strayed uncomfortably toward Rolland, and a flush suffused his thin, pale cheeks beneath a baby-fine beard.

"You didn't think brigands would have wives?" Abramm suggested.

"I never said ye was a brigand."

"No, but your uncle Oakes has."

"He has sons, too," Rolland informed Galen. "Waitin' fer him in Fannath Rill." He turned his gaze back to Abramm. "Daesi will be pleased, but poor Marta . . ."

Now it was Abramm's turn to color. "I've never given Marta any reason—"

"I know, my friend. Which is another reason I suspected. How old're yer sons?"

"Two." Abramm hesitated, then, "The eldest is four and a half, his brother . . . a little over two now." And suddenly the sense of loss swept up to seize his throat and throttle off the end of his last word. It tore at him to think how cavalierly he'd headed off for Chesedh to visit Hadrich last winter. And then, not four days after his return, he'd left again, this time to face off with Rennalf, leaving little Simon with that false promise of returning swiftly, when he knew it would be months. And now was already almost a year. . . .

He pushed the thoughts firmly from his mind. Days ago he'd determined the only way to survive the separation was not to think of them. He prayed for them all—and for Trap and Carissa and her baby—every morning, but after that he refused to let himself consider them again. Thanks to the workload, that had been easier than he'd expected.

He saw the sympathy in Rolland's eyes. "Young ones, then. That's rough."

"Why d' ye never tell us?" Galen demanded.

Abramm swallowed the thickening out of his throat as he looked from one to the other of them, marveling that he had just revealed to them he had a wife and two sons who awaited him in the royal city of Fannath Rill, that they could look at his face and see his eyes and the scars that ran from brow to chin—and for all appearances make no connection whatsoever.

"I don't think anyone asked," he said finally.

The cawing of the crows returning up the valley drew his eye. They flew in an uneven flock along the edge of the mist-veiled forest on the far side. On the ground beneath them, snow plumed upward in the wake of the beast that ran with them. The moment he focused on it, though, the creature dodged into the trees.

"So what did ye do . . . before . . . all this?" Rolland asked, gesturing about.

The question dragged his attention back to his companions, and he stared at the big man blankly, the import of Rolland's words dawning slowly. A second chance to reveal the truth of his identity lay before him, and he had even less idea what to do with it than before. It seemed wrong to blurt out, "I was king of Kiriath." Shouldn't they realize it without his having to tell them? And if they didn't, then why should he bother with it? It wasn't as if any of them were eager to put him back on the throne.

They were staring at him, waiting for an answer. Aware of his suddenly pounding heart and dry mouth, Abramm let himself watch the crows as they wheeled from the forest edge and headed now toward the monastery. Then, before he had consciously decided what to do, the words were falling out of him. "I did many things."

"A soldier, I'm guessin'," Rolland said, squinting at him speculatively. "In the king's army, which is why ye've kept so quiet about it. And why Trinley gets under yer skin so much."

"I rather thought it was me who was getting under *his* skin."

Rolland shrugged good-naturedly as Galen exclaimed, "O' course! That's where ye got yer scars as well, wasn't it? In battle."

Abramm said nothing, reminded again that his scars had not gone unnoticed, and marveling how that could be and the truth still not be realized. . . .

"Hey, down there!" Trinley called from the dining hall roof looming above them. "You three gonna get any work done today, or are ye just waitin' fer the sun t' melt it all?"

The crows converged on a huge dark spruce not far from the kitchen, dislodging showers and heavy clumps of snow from its branches as they landed.

About that time Marta ascended through the stepped tunnel they'd dug up from the kitchen porch, shaded her eyes against the sun, and called up for Galen, whose pregnant wife was asking for him. Grumbling good-naturedly, he went down to see what she needed, and Rolland remarked afterward how glad he was not to be in the young man's boots.

"It scared me t' death thinkin' poor little Jania might have to deliver up there in the pass somewhere." He hefted the shovel and drove it under the next increment of snow. "Ye were right to send yers on ahead of ye," he said, lifting it and tossing the snow over his shoulder. "I wish I'd done that now."

"Aye, but then you'd have the worry of not knowing what's become of them. If they're all right, what they're going through, the fact they'd not even know if you were alive." And in his case, since the world had watched his execution and believed him dead, Maddie had particular justification not to know. From her perspective, all his plans would seem to have gone to ash. From her perspective, and that of everyone around her, he was gone and never coming back. With no way to contact her, he'd had only his hope in the mysterious link that bound their souls . . . praying she would know the truth and not give up on him until he returned.

But knowing a thing inside did not persuade others to agree with you.

"*No. It doesn't. . . .*"

His breath hissed as he straightened to scan the forest's edge across the snowfield, right where the crows had turned away. He felt the birds' eyes on the back of his neck as movement stirred among the far trees and the great shaggy bulk of a tanniym stepped into the light. A small human form rode astride it, and he knew who it was the moment he saw her: Tapheina.

"You are a fool to think she will wait," Tapheina's mental voice taunted him. *"A fool to expect a woman pregnant with her dead husband's child—"*

Pregnant?!

"You did not know?"

How could you know that?

"The birds told me. . . ." Tapheina's rich laughter echoed in his mind.

The birds?

"In the spruce behind you. They also told me your sons are dead, killed at your brother's hand."

"Are ye all right, friend?" Rolland asked, his mellow voice breaking into Abramm's thoughts. When Abramm looked at him blankly, he added, "Ye've gone right pale and stiff all of a sudden."

I don't believe you, he thought at the tanniym. *If Gillard had killed them, he'd have shown them to me.*

"What makes you think he didn't find and kill them after *you escaped him?"* She paused, no doubt sensing the dismay those words struck in him. *"It's time you left the past behind, my prince. Time you embraced a higher destiny."*

Get out of my mind!

She laughed again, but when he turned to Eidon and the Light flared through him, the intrusive presence withdrew, leaving him sick and shaken.

Rolland was looking worriedly between him and the view across the valley. "Is it them again? The tanniym?"

Abramm's glance whipped around. "Do you see something?"

"Something, maybe. It's too dark in the shadows to be sure. I thought ye could tell better." He hesitated, watching Abramm keenly. "The professor told me she'd come and try to speak t' ye."

Abramm grimaced at him. "She's not going to get me to open the gate, Rollie. There. See?" He jogged his chin toward the pair of tanniym, rider and beast, now bounding away through the trees, intermittent sprays of the snow tracking their path. "She's leaving."

Rolland stared across the valley as Abramm got back to work.

Not long after that, Abramm's shovel collided with something hard under the covering of snow. It turned out to be a mound of ice that had built up—apparently melting and refreezing repeatedly—over a hole where the chimney met the roof.

"Hey," he said to Rolland, who was just finishing up on the other side of the chimney. "I think I might have found that leak they've been complaining about in the kitchen. . . ." He chipped away at the ice with downward chops of the shovel, and suddenly the ice wall exploded outward in a whirlwind of black flapping wings. *How did the crows get into the chimney?* he wondered as they bumped around him, battering him with their wings and beaks.

The realization that they were not crows but feyna came on him all at once, and momentarily paralyzed him. They were moving too fast for him to actually see them, but he sensed the cold fire of their spore as it burned in the tiny cuts they had made in his hands and face. The smell of roasting almonds filled his head, and he sensed his inner Shadow awaken, then the deeper violet tones of the spore that Tapheina had deposited. In fact, he sensed her watching him from down the valley back in the trees, as other beings, much closer, looked on as well, somehow holding the feyna in a cloud around him, waiting, waiting for the spore to grow bright enough, the Shadow strong enough to seize him—

Aversion exploded in him, and he staggered back with a shout, swinging the shovel as the Light flared out of him, blasting the dark forms away in all directions. It whirled round him and up, chasing the black trail of feyna as they sped away from him and swooped toward the men on the dining hall roof. Shouts of alarm echoed in the morning silence, then the feyna flew off like a cloud of bees, disappearing past the higher buildings of the monastery that tiered up the hill on which Caerna'tha was built.

The perspectives of the rhu'ema and tanniym left Abramm abruptly, and he tumbled briefly through space. Then he felt the canted shingles beneath his feet, the shovel handle hard against his mittened palms. The dark, newly cleared roof and the massive mountains whirled briefly around him, and settled. He swallowed and stared at bearded Rolland, who stared back, blue eyes wide. Then the man's gaze dropped to his feet and frowned.

"What the plague did ye do here, Alaric?"

Abramm blinked back at him, struggling to recall what he had been doing. . . . "I was just trying to get the ice off. . . ."

"No—I mean here." Rolland gestured at the roof, and now Abramm saw the multitude of small feyna bodies littering the shingles around him.

"There's gotta be a score of 'em at least," Rolland said. "Yet ye killed 'em in a single flash."

"They're small," Abramm noted. "Young ones."

"Aye . . ." Rolland was looking at him oddly. "But how did ye kill 'em all so fast?"

"It was the Light, Rollie. I did nothing."

"I've never seen anyone do that before."

Abramm had no answer for him. He had shoveled up the first few bodies of the baby feyna when behind him the crows burst out of the spruce in a thunderous flapping of wings, cawing as they went. They flew an almost perfect circle around him and Rolland, then sped off to the east, following the stream again until they disappeared in the V between the foothills. "Almost as if they were watchin'," Rolland said.

A chill crawled up Abramm's spine. They *were* watching—no question of it. They were the source of the other minds he'd sensed, and now he knew just what they were—rhu'ema who had buried themselves in the birds' bodies so they could travel about in daylight. Not rhu'ema from around here, but creatures from somewhere afar. Like Fannath Rill. Or even Kiriath.

The birds told me, Tapheina had said. They could well have brought information from wherever they had come, spies who would return to those who sent them and report that Abramm was alive. That their compatriots in Kiriath had failed to kill him, as had those in the pass. That he was alive, in Caerna'tha . . . and they would have all winter to plan how they would deal with him.

A ghost of fear rattled through him before he reminded himself whom he served. *Let them plan.* They'd tried with everything they had to kill him and had failed.

But they did succeed in taking away my crown, he thought uneasily. And his way of life. And his loved ones—all of whom were out there somewhere at his enemies' mercy. . . .

He frowned and pushed the thought from his mind, turning back toward the ice blob he'd been struggling to remove. It was gone, and in its place a brick-sized hole gaped in the chimney where it met the roof. "Might as well get this sealed up right now," he said.

After they'd repaired the hole, they went down to the dining hall for the midday meal. The central topic of conversation, not surprisingly, was the startling revelation that the loner Alaric had a wife and sons. Abramm was peppered with eager questions, the answers to which were discussed at length among the others, many of them voicing the very worries Tapheina's vicious lies had ignited in Abramm himself.

"A woman with two young sons in her care and who has every reason to believe her husband is dead?" Kitrenna Trinley asked as they sat at the long center table eating. "Of course she'd be looking to remarry."

"She wouldn't have every reason," Rolland argued. "She doesn't know for sure he *is* dead."

"Aye, but these are difficult times. And she has her children to think of."

Or maybe not, Abramm's treacherous memory supplied. *If her children are dead.*

Galen and Jania jumped into the discussion, but Abramm no longer heard them, consumed with the sudden restless desire to try following the river down out of the mountains after all. How could he spend six months not knowing? And if Maddie was pregnant—

Oh, but you don't know that. So stop thinking about it. . . .

So distracted was he by his own thoughts and fears, he forgot to worry about the others finding out who he was, and so answered many of their questions without any regard for what those answers might reveal. Such as the fact that he had been married for six years, same as King Abramm; that he had lived and worked in Springerlan all that time; that he'd sent his wife out of Kiriath by sea—a very expensive proposition even if one could find a ship's captain willing to take her; that Gadrielites had indeed tortured him; and that after being rescued by the Terstan Underground, he had spent several months recovering from his injuries in a north country hunting lodge. And few commoners, indeed, had access to hunting lodges of any stripe.

Yet for all of that no one seemed to assemble the pieces sufficiently to guess the truth. Except perhaps Professor Laud, who listened to the conversation without comment as he ate and afterward sat back, puffing on his pipe and watching Abramm closely.

When the meal was over, Abramm half expected the man to take him aside and question him privately, but the kohal returned to his study without comment, leaving Abramm to go about his business as usual. They had a couple more roofs to clear, and then he spent a good hour and a half filling the kitchen and Great Room woodboxes.

The work lent itself to contemplation, and as the day wore on he found himself returning again and again to Tapheina's words, each time considering them for a longer period of time than before. And with his contemplation, the pressure to leave mounted.

Yes, he knew that was most likely her intent. And if the crows really had given her the information, it was likely for the same reason: to draw Abramm out of the fortress's protective walls and put him at her mercy. He wondered if they were still around, waiting to see if he'd take the bait. Waiting to see if she could overcome him. He didn't understand the feyna, though. How could they have known he would be on that roof? Did they have that much manipulative control?

He kept to himself at the evening meal and found his concentration sorely compromised during Terstmeet that night, though at one point it seemed to him that Laud was directly addressing his situation. It did, indeed, seem that he was being tempted.

On the other hand, if what the tanniym had told him was true, how could he stay here for the whole winter? Now at least he had the hope of a few days of good weather, maybe even a week or two of a dragon's summer. Laud had speculated he could be to Deveren Dol at the heart of Chesedh within a month. Should he not be willing to take the risk and trust Eidon to get him through it?

Afterward he sat in the Great Room with the others, listening to their banter and to Marta's reading—she'd avoided him scrupulously all afternoon—as Trinley and Rolland played a game of uurka. Eventually the children were put down, then the others took up their customary positions, and soon—from the sounds of the snores and gurgles and deep, regular breathing—everyone was asleep but Abramm.

And still he sat before the fire, watching the flames dance, reluctant to go up to his cell. Being alone would only make the temptation worse. He ached for Maddie's mischievous smile and bright eyes, for her wit and counsel, for the warmth of her embrace, the sweet scented silk of her hair, and right now especially for the way she could look at him and make everything bad disappear. He loosed a long sigh and rubbed his eyes, seeking Eidon in his thoughts.

"Crows are not at all normal for this time of year." Laud's low voice coming close at his shoulder made him jump. "In fact, they're not normal for any time of year this high up the mountain."

He looked around as the professor settled into the chair beside him. "Aye. They came from the south," Abramm said.

"So you know they were probably possessed."

Abramm nodded.

"I'm told they gathered round to watch you open the feyna's nest. As if they knew what was going to happen." From his coat pocket, Laud pulled out his pipe and a wooden holder someone had made for him, setting both on the small table between their chairs.

Abramm nodded. "It did seem so. Though I can't figure out how. The nest was there long before they came. And how did they get me on that side of the roof? They weren't even here when Trinley assigned me my place."

"Perhaps not, but there are others. Permanent residents, you might say."

And Abramm recalled the ells he'd seen taking shelter in the trees the evening they'd arrived.

"Never think they are gone simply because you cannot see them," Laud said. "Never think they are not close and real and watching. . . . Just like *she* is." He inspected the empty bowl of his pipe, blew a bit of ash away, and said, "I suspect she can sense you now from quite some distance away."

No need to say whom he meant. Rolland must have told him about Tapheina's second visit. Abramm shifted uncomfortably and turned his face to the fire. "I thought you'd gone off to study, Professor."

"I got stuck and thought I'd take a break." He set the pipe in the holder and fished a small leather pouch from his pocket. "So what did she say to you?"

Abramm watched the flames leaping and dancing from the last of the logs that had been put on earlier. Answering Laud's question would admit the power the tanniym had over him, something he wasn't eager to do. And yet he also felt the need for counsel. Or at least to have someone to talk about it to.

"She said that my wife is pregnant with our third child and will be unable to wait for me." He hesitated, still staring at the fire, then added, "And that our two sons are dead."

Beside him, Laud sat in silence for a moment. "And you believe her?"

"I don't know. She said the birds told her. I guess it's the possibility she's told the truth that's killing me."

"So you want to go south. Try to beat the weather, maybe."

Now Abramm turned toward him eagerly. "Do you think I could?"

"If it were Eidon's will." Laud fingered open the pouch and poured a measure of fragrant tobacco into the pipe's bowl. "I thought you'd made this decision already."

"I thought I had, too. But now I wonder if I would be remiss if I did not try every possible way to get back to them as soon as I can."

"Why would you wonder that?"

Abramm was momentarily bewildered. "Are they not my responsibility?"

"Did you not see them as your responsibility when you made your decision to stay here a few days ago?"

"Yes, but a few days ago it seemed I had no choice. I had to put them in Eidon's hands because there was nothing else I could do."

"And you accepted the fact that Eidon had brought you here for the winter in order to teach you something."

"Aye, but things are different now."

"What is different? The weather is better. And your enemies have brought you troubling news that may not even be true. Yes, you could try to go south. Sheer common sense says otherwise, but if you believed that was Eidon's course for you, perhaps you might go against it. I don't think that's what you believe. And the circumstances of your arrival coupled with what happened today cannot be overlooked in assessing what's going on here."

Abramm considered that as Laud busied himself with lighting his pipe. Once he'd gotten it going and taken a couple of puffs, he added, "If you're sure your motivation was right, and you were in the Light when you made your decision . . . don't let circumstances—or the enemy's innuendoes—push you into second-guessing yourself. Trust that Eidon made himself clear the first time, and stay the course."

He'd said nothing Abramm hadn't already thought of, but it was good to have his conclusions affirmed. After a time he sighed and gave in. "I guess I'm here for the winter, then."

Laud almost smiled. "Good. Now . . . perhaps you would be willing to aid me."

"Aid you?"

"I don't think I've come down to the Great Room one night since you've arrived and not seen you with a book in your hands. So I'm guessing you know how to read."

Abramm glanced at him sharply, not until that moment considering how much his demonstration of that skill would say about him.

"And if a reader," Laud went on, "I presume you also write."

"Why? Are you looking for a scribe?"

At that the older man laughed outright. "Actually"—he held up his leather-bound stump—"I am. Though I've learned to scratch out the words with my left hand, I have a terrible time reading any of it. If I had someone to write for me, it would help immensely. I'd thought your script might be suitable. It's got to be better than mine."

Abramm stared at him. "You want me to be your *scribe*?"

Laud chuckled again. "I realize it would be a considerable demotion from your former position." His brow cocked in such a way that for a moment Abramm thought the man had guessed who he really was. If he did, though, he didn't pursue it. "My scribe. Yes. And lest you worry about the workload, now that the storm has passed, there won't be quite so much. I was thinking you could do the heavy labor in the morning and help me in the afternoons. . . ."

8

So Tersius left his throne, stripping himself of his position to take on human flesh and be abused by those whom he had made. Thus he paid the penalty Eidon's justice demanded. . . .

Abramm lifted pen from paper and paused, as much to rest his hand as to reflect upon what was being said. It was early afternoon, a week after he'd agreed to become Laud's scribe, and he sat at the smaller desk in the professor's study, copying the man's barely legible scribblings into notes for a future sermon. Outside another storm howled, but inside a crackling fire filled the book-lined chamber with light and warmth. Laud's desk stood nearer the fire, piled with books and deserted by the professor, who'd gone off to Caerna'tha's vast library in search of a special volume.

Having spent the morning clearing snow off the hay barn roof—again— Abramm reveled at being inside, though his hand shook annoyingly in reaction to the hours of gripping the shovel's handle. Laud would no doubt comment on the wobbles in his lines. With a smile he dipped the quill point into the inkpot and began copying the next paragraph.

As Tersius suffered, so must we who have been faithful, counting it an honor to do what the luima cannot: believe that Eidon is good and right, though everything around us seems to say he is not. Will we stand firm and wait for him to keep the promises he has made to us? To restore what has been lost for his sake?

A shiver zinged through him and he paused again. *To restore what has been lost . . .*

For almost a week now, the quiet conviction that he would one day receive back all that he had lost had grown. It was a thought he'd been reluctant to contemplate—easier to accept his losses if he did not think of gaining anything back. Except for wife and children, the rest hardly mattered. And if he were to hang his hopes on that promise . . . what if it were not fulfilled? What pain would he know then?

Yet here it was again. He'd lost count of the times and ways it kept coming up. Almost as if Eidon insisted that he accept it, embrace it, and believe it. It would come in Eidon's time and manner, of course. Abramm had only to wait—though waiting, Laud liked to say, often took more courage than doing. Especially waiting peaceably.

Abramm let his eyes drift about the room. *Am I at peace?* It hardly seemed possible, or even logical, but he had to say that so long as he kept his focus in the moment, he was. Laud had been pleased with his script, and they worked well together. Abramm was even learning some of the Old Tongue in the course of things, determined to master it before he left so he might surprise Maddie.

But that was not all of it. Years ago as a Mataian novice he'd relished the calm quiet of the scriptorium, the smell of the paper and ink, and the way the smooth lines flowed from the tip of his quill. The time it took to write things out ensured protracted concentration upon them, transforming the process into a form of worship, drawing the thoughts into himself to write them out again until they became his own. In the Mataio he had copied the words of Eidon's Revelation. Now he copied those and, in addition, the comparisons and categories and concepts embodied in them, from which sprang not only a greater understanding of Eidon himself, but a deepening sense of contentment. And of promise.

Beyond that, he was warm, well fed, and healthy, and he was with people who, while not exactly friends, were still companions he was growing to appreciate. Most of them, anyway, he reflected wryly, recalling Trinley's antagonism at the recent midday meal. That everyone in Caerna'tha now believed him to have been a member of Abramm's Royal Guard was a misperception he'd still not corrected, largely because the thought that he was Abramm's man had inspired new heights of abuse from the disgruntled alderman. Every day he still considered setting them all straight, and every day backed down, unable to muster enough motivation to overcome the aversion. What difference did it make anyway, whether they knew who he had been or not? He wasn't that man anymore. Certainly not at Caerna'tha.

The hollow thump of footsteps on the wooden stair preceded the appearance of Marta Brackleford, ash pail and broom in hand. She stopped in surprise at the sight of him, and a slow blush crept up her cheeks. She gave him a polite greeting, then went straight to the hearth, shoveling a portion of the excess ash into her pail. He frowned at her, disappointed that the atmosphere had become so strained between them, and knowing it was largely his fault.

"I'm sorry I didn't let on sooner about my wife. I had no intention of—"

"I know." Her voice was clipped and oddly high-pitched. "I'm glad you told us about her." She set aside the shovel and worked a bit with the broom. "So did the Gadrielites take her, too?"

"No. By Eidon's mercy she escaped before then."

"With your sons."

"No, they went with a friend after her. At least that was the plan . . ."

"Oh." She paused, then straightened and picked up her pail. "I'm sure they're safe." She started for the door, then stopped. "Your wife. What's her name?"

Abramm hesitated. Was this the bit of information that would make all fall into place? "Madeleine."

Marta's expression lightened. "Like the queen!"

"Yes."

She was at the door when he asked, "Why did you want to know?"

"So I can pray for her."

The sound of Professor Laud's approach in the hall set her into motion again, and she hurried away before he could say anything, shocked as he was by her admission. And pleased, as well. A moment later, Laud entered in her place, a stack of books balanced along his left arm and chest. He slid them onto the already crowded desk with a sigh.

Abramm cocked a brow at them. "I thought you were going for a single book."

Laud grinned sheepishly. "There are so many interesting titles. In fact, I came across a couple I thought might interest you." He pulled two books from his stack and brought them to Abramm.

One was small and gray, the black symbols of its three-word title rendered in the Old Tongue alphabet. The other, ledger-sized, was bound in an age-stiffened brown leather cover and fastened with a belt and buckle, also titled in the Old Tongue. "Ah, you mean for me to practice," he said, opening the bigger book. Inside were pages of parchment inscribed in the clear, flowing hand of some ancient person, whose words Abramm could not read. A lack of pictures forced him to sound out the title's letters. After a moment, he looked up at Laud in confusion and disbelief. "The Journals of Avramm?" he asked. "Avramm the First? Of Kiriath?"

"I think he is the only Avramm of note." The professor eyed him over slipping spectacles. "I thought the hope of reading the exploits of your king's namesake in his own language might motivate you to learn it faster."

Unwilling to risk speaking further, Abramm turned to the smaller book, hoping Laud wasn't noticing the suddenly increased tremor of his hands. He struggled with the next title, distracted by the welter of thoughts bubbling up in his mind. Once a world-renowned retreat for learned Ophirans desiring rejuvenation for body and mind, Caerna'tha's library had been almost as famous as its baths. But that was over six hundred years ago, and Abramm had assumed most of the ancient collection would have been carried away by now.

The . . . As he pieced together the first word of the little gray book's title, he thrilled to think that Avramm might have written of the regalia—of their creation, of how they worked. He would surely tell of his battles against the Shadow in conquering Kiriath. *Red* . . . Perhaps the secret of the guardstars lay between those pages. Or some insights into the reason a red dragon had been woven into his tapestries. What part had it played in his struggle to bring peace to his realm? Would Avramm's writings give some hint as to how it might figure into Abramm's life, as well? . . . *Dragon.*

His thoughts lurched to a stop. He went through the letters again, heart slamming hard and fast in his chest. Finally he looked up at Laud. *"The Red Dragon."*

Just saying it sent a current of foreboding through him.

"I happened to see it," Laud said, "after I found the other. And, since the red dragon was a part of King Abramm's coat of arms, and as I understand it, you wear the same mark on your own arm . . ." He shrugged and smiled again. "Looks like I guessed right."

Having no idea what to say, Abramm turned his eyes to the book and paged through its yellowed leaves. As with the other, the text was inscrutable, but this one had pictures, rendered in multicolored inks: a scarlet dragon flying over pointy mountain peaks jabbing up through rolling waves; a cow staked out in a meadow, the dragon a silhouette over the trees; a page of varied designs involving dragons; a handsome, dark-eyed man cloaked in golden scales; a dragon soaring above a vast plain filled with armies. . . . Abramm closed the book, unable to breathe, fighting the roaring of his ears. The awareness of Eidon's hand upon his life had never been stronger.

After a moment he realized Laud had spoken again. Abramm stared at him blankly. "I'm . . . sorry?"

The professor arched a smug brow. "I said, Rolland tells me it's a slave's brand. On your arm. That last night you admitted you once fought in the Esurhite games. He says you have the battle scars to prove it, too."

Last night Abramm had, for the first time, been persuaded to visit the hot spring-fed baths up the hill while the others were there, too. Though all had seen his brand and scars, none had realized the truth, proving again the validity of Maddie's claim that people most often saw only what they expected to see. The only thing to come of it was that Rolland, having established that Abramm had fought in the Games, asked if he'd teach them all to fight.

"So . . ." Laud continued. "Are you going to join the queen, then? In Fannath Rill?"

"Why would you think that?"

"That *is* where she's fled, is it not? Along with the First Minister and the king's sister and the little crown prince?" He smiled at Abramm's look of shock. "You are not the first of Abramm's guardsmen to come this way. Many passed through last summer, right after he fell. All of them hurrying to join with the queen and her sons in hopes of forming an army to retake the throne. Of course, there are others who say the sons did not survive. . . . Rumors, of course. But if not them, there is always Princess Carissa."

His words were like fiery darts, each of them piercing Abramm's heart with increasing horror, though, of course, Laud had no idea. What if his sons *were* dead? . . .

He wrenched his mind off that dark path and changed the subject, uncaring if it seemed rude or too revealing. He held up the gray book. "What do you know of this dragon?"

If Laud noted his evasion of the question, he did not pursue it. "The Words refer to the red dragon as one of Moroq's two forms. The beautiful man, a creature of light and wonder, yet able to turn into the cruel and powerful dragon at will."

"So why would *his* symbol be in Abramm's coat of arms?"

The professor shrugged. "The symbol is ubiquitous in Kiriathan heraldry, dating back to the time of Avramm. In his day, it was common to put the sign of a defeated adversary on one's shield. Avramm defeated the tribes of Hasmuluk in establishing his realm, and they worshiped the dragons—hence a dragon in his crest. Since Abramm was named for Avramm, it's only logical his coat of arms would echo that of his namesake."

"Aye, that's the human explanation. But Eidon guided the crest maker in his choice, as he guided Abramm's parents' choice in naming him. Why? Even more, why did he allow Abramm himself to receive that very same mark on his own flesh?"

Laud looked at him oddly. "Is it Abramm you're asking about here, son? Or is it yourself?"

Abramm stared back at him, his thoughts arrested by the ironic ambiguity of that question.

"Abramm, after all," said Laud, "is dead. So whatever meaning the mark had for him will have to be assessed within the boundaries of his life. And I think it's pretty obvious that as Avramm was victorious over the beast's followers and received its sign in his crest, so Abramm was victorious over them in refusing to renounce his shield, even to the point of death."

Except that Abramm isn't dead yet, professor, Abramm thought wryly. He almost uttered the words aloud, but something held his tongue, and instead he found himself saying, "So you don't believe Avramm might have fought a real creature, then?"

The question took Laud entirely aback. "A real dragon? You mean like Moroq himself?"

"The Words say Moroq is the enemy of all who wear the shield."

"Aye, but you can't think he personally confronts each of us. He has his underlings for that." Laud leaned back in the chair, smiling at him in amusement now. "Do not think so highly of yourself, lad, as to concern yourself with having to battle a dragon. You'd do better focusing on the battles you're facing with Oakes Trinley."

And as swiftly as that he had turned the subject to the rift widening between Abramm and the other man, one he judged must be bridged before reconciliation became impossible. It was a familiar subject, and Abramm saw there would be no returning to the subject of the dragon. Likely Laud had given him all he knew, and Abramm doubted the man would agree to read the book aloud to him.

————

Trap Meridon, once the Duke of Northille, now the finance secretary to the Chesedhan First Daughter, strode through the cobbled street of the palace's southeastern service gate, dodging carts, horsemen, and piles of manure as he fought his way upstream through the mass of humanity pouring through the gate. It was early morning, the first clear one in three weeks—

and the servants, groundsmen, and guards were arriving for their shifts along with the service people bringing in their fruits and grains and milk. None gave him more than a passing glance, though his cloak and trousers were considerably finer than most and his boots much shinier.

In Kiriath, a duke would have traveled by horse or carriage. But here, as the finance secretary of a First Daughter out of favor with the ruling princess, and a Kiriathan exile out of favor with everyone, it was difficult to get the grooms at the royal stable to give him either. Even when they promised him something, they took all morning to deliver. It was easier to walk, since his errands were rarely far from the palace. Besides, he liked the exercise and the opportunity to be alone with his thoughts. And since he was no longer sharing cocoa with his wife in the mornings, he certainly had time for it.

He'd taken to living in his office, which was across the palace from the quarters he'd shared with Carissa. Yesterday he'd moved most of his clothing there. It was easier that way. For both of them.

He had thought when he married her he'd be content just to be near her, to give her his name and his protection, and provide for her needs. After all, he had loved her from afar all of his life, and even lived in her house those last three months of her pregnancy. What difference would a public vow-taking and her wearing of a gold ring make?

At first it hadn't. Conal's birth and the journey from Kiriath hadn't left them much time for intimate moments. Moreover, she was a new mother, grieving the loss of her brother, her position, and her land—and was seasick on top of it all. Even had it entered his mind he might eventually want more than simply to provide for her, he would have considered the desire base, selfish, and demeaning to both of them.

At Fannath Rill they'd settled into their apartments and the routine of living as man and wife, and for a time all was well. Then something had changed. Somehow friendship and quiet conversation were no longer enough. Suddenly he could not keep his eyes or his mind from straying places they had no business straying. Erotic dreams jerked him awake in the night, sweat-sheathed and battling a nearly overwhelming desire to go to her room on the opposite side of their apartments and take what was rightfully his as her husband. The only thing that stopped him was the certainty she would be horrified by it, seeing him as no better than Rennalf, who some would argue had also taken only what was rightfully his. . . .

That last morning he'd spent with her was now burned into his memory. How he'd stood before the bay window, staring blindly at the promenade with its flanking rows of date palms, hearing the susurrus of fabric and the creak of a step that told him Carissa was handing Conal off to Prisina. He'd given her a few moments to get her clothing back in order, listening to Prisina's footsteps as she carried the baby away. Then, finally, he heard the sigh that was his signal and turned from the window, catching her looking at him with an expression so sorrowful it tore at his heart. She veiled it swiftly, but not soon enough.

Trapped, he'd realized with profound dismay. *That's how she must feel. Trapped in this marriage she never would have sought had I not pushed it upon her.*

She'd confirmed it soon after with those dreadful words: *"You needn't pretend what we have is anything more than duty."* They still made him shiver with horror. *"I would feel more comfortable, in fact, if you didn't."*

He'd felt as if he'd fallen flat on his face, all the wind knocked out of him. Later he'd berated himself for not protesting right then and there. *"No,"* he should have said. *"I am not pretending."* He should have told her how he felt, how much he wanted her. . . . But that only brought him to the horrified realization that, on account of all he'd done for her, she might feel obliged to service him. Which appalled him even more than his traitorous feelings.

Weirdly it had all boiled up into a bitter anger directed toward Abramm. Why did he have to write those letters? Did he have so little respect for his liegeman that he thought Trap would not see the need himself, not be able to do what needed doing without being told? Worse, did Abramm know his friend so poorly he did not realize Trap would leap at the opportunity to marry Carissa and it would be of his own choice whether she was crown princess or fishmonger, pregnant with another man's bastard or a virgin? It didn't matter to him. It had never mattered.

The only things that had ever stood in his way were her lack of relationship with Eidon and the fact she was a king's daughter and Trap a swordmaster's son. Then she'd taken the Star and had thrown herself into learning of Eidon, living in that knowledge as best as her naturally morose personality allowed. She had made tremendous gains in the face of incredibly difficult pressures. He had stood in awe of her tenacity. No matter what crushing disappointments she faced, or what inner battles raged with a spirit far too inclined toward pessimism and self-pity, she had not given up on Eidon— even in those dark days when Conal still slept in her womb and none of them knew what would come of it all.

Suddenly in the midst of terrible tragedy, the doors had opened and it only made sense that he should marry her. She saw it . . . he did . . . all of them did. But thanks to Abramm's meddling, he'd never had the chance to show her that he asked from his own heart.

Not that it mattered anymore. She'd made her feelings plain enough.

He stepped off the curb, then jerked back to avoid being run over by a horse and carriage barreling down the street. People poured past him into the wake created by its passage, jostling him as he regained his bearings. Then he scowled, realizing he was back in the same thought cycle he'd indulged in for the last three weeks. One he'd sworn he'd not return to.

He stopped at the bakery to buy a nutty bun, refusing the baker's attempt to engage him with the latest gossip about Draek Tiris's obvious interest in Maddie. Their luncheon meeting three days ago had been the talk of the town for two weeks prior—all the speculation as to whether it would happen at all—and now, in its aftermath, the endless analysis of what it meant, even though she was leaving for Deveren Dol tomorrow.

That she was going on a "spiritual retreat" had fooled no one, but even the baker agreed she was better off not bringing her child to term where everyone could see. "Makes it easier for everyone to forget it ever existed."

The man hoped that Tiris would marry her in spite of it, and might even take the jailer's bastard off to his orphanage to free her completely of her shame. "She'd be respectable again," he'd added. "And rich, too. . . ."

Trap left before he throttled the man, his frustration intensified by the fact that the baker was only repeating what everyone else was saying. They were all eager to forget she'd ever been to Kiriath, ever married Abramm, ever been anything but their First Daughter. It was as if all Chesedh was trying to reabsorb her as swiftly as they could, desperate to get her married off to some respectable house and erase the shame she'd brought them.

Which was why her forthcoming trip to Deveren Dol filled him with such dread. Especially since he wouldn't be able to go with her. Her finances were in such straits, he feared if he left them to themselves, there might be nothing when they returned. And though it wasn't his fault—he'd been routinely cheated by Chesedhan merchants, and his every attempt to purchase property on her behalf had ended with the seller's sudden, unexplained withdrawal of the property—he still felt responsible.

From the baker's he walked down to the clearinghouse on the river to get his bales of wool entered in the sale roster today—fine Kiriathan wool, straight from the Heartland, his last bit of treasure—and then on to his appointment with the young son of the shipping magnate whom he was training in the art of the sword. The morning was completed with a frustrating and futile half hour at the Exchange attempting to collect the payment due him from his auction sale of the week before. Then it was off to Arvill Ang's Tavern, where Kiriathan exiles gathered every noonday to exchange the latest gossip and news about Kiriath.

As Trap entered, he nodded to Oswain Nott and his cronies, sitting at his table by the front bay window. The man scowled in response, but Trap only smiled and walked on to his own table, where Temas Darnley, Wade Callums, and Walter Hamilton awaited him, nursing mugs of ale. Respectively an earl, a general, and an admiral, they had become his closest friends among the exiles. While rank-and-file military were welcomed into the Chesedhan army, their leaders were not. Thus the pair had been relegated to business pursuits. Callums played whist for money every night at one of the card houses and lived in a tiny attic on Cheapstreet, and Hamilton worked afternoons as a clerk in a printing house. Darnley, hardly recognizable as the foppish lord he'd once been, had arrived without a stitch of his once renowned wardrobe. Now he tutored a lesser nobleman's children. All three men's clothing was growing undeniably threadbare, and though none would admit it, Trap suspected this was their only real meal of the day. They'd all lost considerable weight.

In the beginning he'd come here hoping to hear news of Channon and the princes, but after more than six months with no word and no sign, he'd finally accepted the fact that Channon was probably dead. Now he wasn't sure why he came.

He'd not been there long when the innkeeper called their attention to a newcomer, Roy Thornycroft, recently arrived from Kiriath with no more than the shirt on his back. He'd been a merchant and a secret Terstan who, upon learning his Mataian wife meant to turn him in, had sailed for Mareis on a business trip and never returned. Living on what he'd been able to sell off in port—including the vessel he'd come on—he'd made his way north to Fannath Rill much the same as the rest of them. And like the rest of them, his once-fine clothes were worn and shabby, his hands stained with the grime of travel and hard living.

The others received him warmly, eager for news of their homeland. The new Keep of the Heartland, he told them, had added yet another wing, the economy was in the gutter, there'd been terrible flooding, and the silt-heavy river emptying into the harbor at Springerlan had made the port too shallow for the big ships to come in very close at all, which everyone was grumbling

RETURN OF THE GUARDIAN-KING || 99

about. There were rumors that Esurhites had already shown up at the palace to offer terms, but so far as he knew that was only rumor. The one thing for sure was that Gillard—or Makepeace, as he was now known—had issued an edict demanding all attend Mataian services and wear a red tongue of flame on their lapel in sign of their allegiance. And it was still illegal to speak Abramm's name. A man had had his tongue cut out for it shortly before Thornycroft left.

He also echoed other reports that Makepeace had regained his former size and strength, allegedly the blessing of Eidon for purging his realm of Terstan apostasy.

When finally the merchant had wound down, the innkeeper prodded him to tell them the latest about Abramm. "It's only rumor," Thornycroft qualified, "but some say he was rescued the night before his execution . . . that it wasn't him they burned but another."

His words died into a silence so profound Trap heard the crack of the fire, the creak of the sign in the wind outside, and the muffled voices of the kitchen help. Then like the bursting of an invisible dam, sound flooded the room, everyone trying to out-shout one another with questions and comments and declarations of disbelief.

When the ruckus had settled enough that one voice could be discerned from another, Hamilton demanded, "Where is he, then? Still in Kiriath plotting his return?"

"I don't know," Thornycroft replied. "Some say he was so badly injured he can no longer walk. Others that he was spirited away to Thilos."

"Why would he go to Thilos?"

"Well, it's not exactly something that can be spoken of freely."

"Where did you hear all this, Master Thornycroft?" asked Nott. "From a tavern drunk?"

The man looked so sheepish, Trap guessed that was exactly where he'd heard it. He felt the group's enthusiasm deflate and took advantage of the lull to ask if Thornycroft had heard anything about the princes. He hadn't. In fact, he seemed surprised to be asked. "They're both dead, aren't they? That's the official report."

"Yes, but Abramm was officially reported dead, too, yet you've come here saying otherwise. Ever see any bodies?"

"No, but . . . I can't see them doing that. The Mataians would call it evil and barbaric."

"They'll torture 'em and kill 'em, but they won't stake out the bodies,"

Callums said. "Aye, they'd not want to be like the barbarians, that's sure."

That led Thornycroft off onto other topics as Trap sagged back into his chair, pushing his empty mug around on the table. He glanced at Darnley, Callums, and Hamilton, all of whom were staring at him thoughtfully. "Do you think, maybe—" Hamilton began.

"No," Trap said flatly. "He's dead, and we do ourselves no favors hoping otherwise."

He stared at the half-eaten food on his plate but found himself suddenly without appetite. "Well, I have books to do this afternoon, so I'd best be off."

As he left, the daily arguments over how they should retake Kiriath were just heating up. Should they use Maddie's unborn child as a claim to the throne? It shouldn't be hard now to build a good army—if she married Tiris, could they count on him to fund it?

Trap moved out of earshot, grateful to leave it all behind. As he walked back to the palace he reflected on the unexpected strength of his reaction to Thornycroft's suggestion that Abramm still lived. Hope had soared within his breast, hot and eager, a wild joy fighting to express itself, even as caution held it in. He of all people understood how one might be delivered from an execution. But common sense argued otherwise. If Abramm lived, surely Trap would know. More than that, Maddie would know. Abramm would never have let things go this long without contacting her.

Besides, Trap had it on good authority that Gillard himself had attended the execution, and Gillard would certainly have known if it weren't Abramm.

No. It was a false alarm, and the reaffirmation of that fact triggered a grief that cut so deeply he could hardly breathe. As his throat seized up in a hard and painful knot, he staggered to a stop, leaning against the brick wall of some building and blinking back the tears as people passed him to and fro, bumping his shoulder erratically. Despair swooped upon him like a curling black breaker.

Why did you take him and leave me here alone? he wailed. *I am little help to his widow, and I've only made a mess of things with his sister. She'd have been better off with a Chesedhan. . . .*

The black wave receded and he came back to himself, struggling to find Eidon's peace as he had never struggled in his life. More and more of late he felt he was losing his way, and repeated pleas for some glimmer of something to reach for were always denied.

"Serr?" A hand clutched his arm, and he opened his eyes to peer into an old woman's wrinkled face.

"Are ya alright, serr?"

"Aye. Thank you." He pushed away from the wall and continued on his way.

Back in his study, he went through the latest receipts, entering them into the account books before turning his attention to the various properties and businesses he was considering for purchase. But he couldn't make himself concentrate. His mind had turned to a block of wood. He read the words and numbers as if they were meaningless symbols, and the sense of depression grew heavier. He knew Eidon had his hand on all of it, knew there would be times of hopelessness, recalled the stories in the First Word, where the people of the shield were over and over led to what seemed a last stand, a dead end, no opening, no hope in sight. And then it came. The mountain opened, the water parted. The winds came and shredded the rocks. . . .

My Lord, I know all this. But my feelings are so dead. What is there for me to do now? With Abramm gone, his sons killed, his wife soon to be taken by another . . . his sister . . . But that thought only made it all a hundredfold worse. *What place for me, Lord?*

The question he'd uttered mentally dissipated into that same old blankness. For a moment there was nothing at all. And then a single thought answered it, a line from the Second Word.

"I see your deeds. I know the heart with which you do them, my son. And I do not forget, nor overlook your faithfulness. Hold fast. Do not grow weary. Your reward is coming."

Do not grow weary. He felt incredibly weary. More weary than he'd ever felt in his life. But he knew that how he felt made no difference. He would claim that promise. No matter how hopeless it all looked, it would all come out right. He *would* believe.

Sighing, he turned back to his accounts.

Less than half an hour later his assistant stuck his head round the door to inform him he had a visitor, and a moment later, in walked Shale Channon.

Trap stared at him, mouth agape. Had he fallen asleep and this a dream?

The man stiffened to military attention and brought a fist to his chest in salute. "Captain Channon, sir, come to report, and sorry it's taken me so long."

Trap leaped up and skirted the desk to embrace his old friend, the man solid and warm and smelling too much of dust and old sweat to be a dream.

"Eidon's mercy, Shale!" he exclaimed. "I thought you must be dead! Where have you been?"

"I figured ye wouldna hold out much hope fer us, odds bein' what they were. We tried t' see the queen, or princess or whatever she is here, but they been puttin' us off, sendin' us here and there all day. Finally someone mentioned ye were here, and . . . I knew I couldna wait. She'd kill me if I did." He cracked a lopsided smile.

Trap stared at him, listening to the soft rhythm of his own breathing. *We? Us?* The floor rocked beneath his feet. "Light's grace, man," he whispered. "You mean to tell me you've not come here alone?"

The smile became an open grin. "Yessir. That's exactly what I mean to tell ye."

9

While Trap was going about his errands in the city, Maddie had spent the morning preparing for her journey to Deveren Dol. Jeyanne helped her, though there really wasn't all that much to pack. She needn't worry about social appearances, and the convent had everything else. Mostly she was bringing warm and comfortable clothes, her books, lirret, and musical compositions in progress.

Ronesca had invited her to lunch, a two-hour ordeal during which the older woman interrogated her about her luncheon with Draek Tiris ul Sadek three days before. Tiris had contrived to present the invitation at the very end of the week, just when Maddie should have been leaving for Deveren Dol and then conveniently—for Maddie, anyway—postponed it to several days later. By now there was no doubt about her pregnancy in the mind of anyone who looked at her, and ul Sadek had definitely looked at her. She pointed this out to Ronesca, arguing that since he was obviously the one Ronesca had her sights set upon as Maddie's future husband, why should Maddie flee to Deveren Dol to hide from him what he already knew? The trip would take over a week, in the cold. . . . She could even go into early labor on the trail.

Despite the logic of Maddie's reasonings, Ronesca remained firm. Maddie would go, spend the rest of winter and early spring there, then at summer's start return to be presented to the court. That was the plan Hadrich had approved, and that was what they would do. And since Maddie had received a letter from her father stating as much in his own hand, there was little more she could say to stop it.

Thus she returned to her chambers, resigned to her fate, and discovered two men waiting in her sitting room in billowing black pants and short white jackets, the typical uniform of Tiris's servants. One of them held a large box wrapped in red silk. As she entered they bowed in perfect unison. Then the shorter one introduced himself and presented the box to her with Tiris ul Sadek's compliments. "There is this, as well," he added, handing her a large ivory-colored envelope sealed with red wax.

She took it without comment. Tiris had already given her a going-away present, an intricately carved wooden box in which she might keep her papers and writing utensils. Nor was it the first gift he'd sent her. She was not officially bound by her acceptance of any of it, but with each one he pulled her closer to him emotionally. And it didn't help that all his gifts had so far been perfect choices.

This one was no different, for inside the box was a fine woolen cloak with ermine-trimmed hood. It was tightly woven to keep out the wind but soft as a dandelion puff and lined with gold silk—perfect for riding through the cold drifts and chilly mornings that undoubtedly lay before her. Even in the rain this would keep its warmth.

The servant helped her don it, and it swirled about her like oil, close enough to keep out drafts, but light and supple for comfort. She ran the back of her hand up the silken lining, marveling at its softness. It took only moments, though, for her to grow warm in it, so she took it off and handed it to Jeyanne to pack for the trip.

"It's wonderful," she told the servants who had brought it. "Tell Draek Tiris I am very pleased."

After they left she stood there toying with the heavy folded note, smiling as she thought again of the luncheon he had hosted for her. It had been far more elaborate than she'd told Ronesca, nor had she mentioned she'd been his only guest. He was an extraordinarily handsome man, and his voice was positively spellbinding. He'd told her the story of his discovery of the ruined dragon city of Chena'ag Tor—or at least *a* story, and an entertaining one, at that. She still wasn't sure if he was telling the truth or playing with her. The part about hearing dragons roaring within its walls had especially strained believability. When the luncheon ended, he returned her to reality, lamenting her upcoming journey, arguing with her as she had with Ronesca that it was purposeless. "And you absolutely must stay the full three months?"

"Alas . . ." She'd smiled at him.

He'd offered to send an escort with her, which she'd declined—Trap had her security on the road well in hand. Thwarted there, Tiris had offered to ride up in a week or so to visit her, but that, too, she had discouraged. Being confined to the convent of the Sisters of the Sacred Graces, she'd not be able to receive him anyway. *"No men allowed."*

He'd liked that no more than Trap had.

She looked down at the card in her hands, fingering the impression his signet had made upon the wax seal. It was the jackal of ul Sadek, one of the oldest of the Sorite noble houses or so he'd said. The image recalled to her the ring itself, and the first time she had seen it that night in the Gilded Ram, when he had seized her arm and put his nose to her wrist, inhaling her scent. The hairs stood up on the back of her neck now as then. He might be the charming luncheon host, but there were deeper things about him she suspected were not so charming. Maybe she wouldn't use his cloak after all. . . .

She was in her music room working on a revision of her ballad chronicling Abramm's life, when a voice broke into her concentration.

"My lady? Duke Eltrap requests audience, ma'am."

She looked up and almost told the man to leave her be. Then the name he'd spoken registered, but even then she was so engaged with her work she thought of putting him off. He probably wanted to go over the books with her one last time, and she'd had more than enough of that lately.

Before she could answer, Trap slipped through the doorway himself, a breach of etiquette she found vaguely annoying. Worse, he'd not even bothered to tidy himself up before making his call—his woolen trousers rumpled and his white blouse badly wrinkled under his vest. She frowned at him. "Why are you here, sir? Didn't my doorman tell you I'm occupied?"

"Aye, ma'am, he did. But . . . I bring important news." His lips twitched, as if he fought to keep his expression neutral.

Sudden concern twisted her heart as she set aside the lirret. "Is it news from the front? Is my father all right?"

"Yes, ma'am, so far as I know." It seemed as if he wanted to smile.

"Leyton?"

"I believe he is well, too, ma'am." Yes, it was definitely a smile.

"Well, then . . ." She fell silent as a child's voice drifted in from the anteroom:

"Where is Mama, Auntie Elayne? You said she would be here."

A woman's low tones responded, but Maddie barely heard her, for the child's voice had ignited every nerve in her body. She leaped to her feet and crossed the room to fling wide the door.

A group of people stood in the sitting room surrounded by her servants:

three men and a gray-haired woman, the latter holding the hand of a small, blond, shaggy-haired boy, all of them coated in the gray dust of travel. Maddie stared at the boy in disbelief, her mind blank with shock, her body thrumming with recognition and wonder. "Simon?"

The lad's head whipped around, and a pair of startlingly blue eyes widened.

"Mama!" he shrieked, letting go the woman's hand and running for Maddie. She bent to catch him, and then the little arms were wrapped tightly about her neck and she was hugging him fiercely. His hair—far too long and shaggy for a crown prince's—smelled of dust and smoke and too many days gone without washing. She didn't care. She had him back, whole, solid, and not likely to disappear into any holes in the wall, or be snatched up by wolves. Eidon had made good on his promise. Abramm had been right to believe. . . .

And suddenly, her cheek pressed to the top of her son's head, tears blurred her eyes. A moment later, the first sob shook her body, and the emotional storm it triggered could not be called back. For a time she held him to her and wept as she had not since this whole nightmare began.

All the while he patted her shoulder and said, "It's all right now, Mama, we're back. It's all right."

"I know, Simon," she said finally, wiping away her tears.

"Then, why are you crying?"

She smoothed his hair back from his face and smiled. "Because I am so very, very happy to see you."

He frowned, plainly doubtful, but after a moment went on to something more understandable. "There really was a bunny hole. Father Eidon showed it to me. And when the bad men went away, Auntie Elayne found me and then we found Ian. He was on a rock crying, and he wasn't even wet. . . ."

The rest of his words were lost as his brother's name registered. Her fingers tightened on his little shoulders. "Did you say you found Ian?" And now the memory she could never bear to call up returned in force, Gillard's man ripping her baby from her arms and hurling him into that cliff, his frantic, terrified screams cutting off at the moment of impact. . . . The bundle drifting downward after, blankets fluttering up around it. . . .

"He's right there." Simon's voice shattered the vicious image as he turned to gesture toward one of the men. "Captain Channon's got him."

Captain Shale Channon, the man Abramm had assigned to find his sons and bring them to their mother. And looking at the man for the first time since she'd entered, she saw he carried a small cloaked form, her baby's pale face peeking out from the hood, a pair of round, deep blue eyes staring at her amidst too-long locks of blond hair. Except he wasn't a baby anymore. . . . *How can he have gotten so big?!*

She straightened from where she'd crouched with Simon, both hands lifting to cover her mouth as it twitched and sagged with renewed emotion. But a moment after he had stared impassively into her eyes, the toddler turned his head away and buried it in Channon's shoulder, squirming in the soldier's arm and whimpering in protest.

"It's all right, wee one," Channon murmured to him. "It's yer mama. She's been waitin' for ye to come to her . . . all these long months." He squatted to set the boy on his own little feet, but the child refused to let him go.

"Ian," Maddie said, her heart nearly breaking with the fear that after all this time and trouble he had forgotten her. . . . "Ian, it's Mama. Don't you remember me, poppet?"

He gave no sign he'd heard her.

Maddie stepped toward him and squatted just behind him. "Ian?"

The boy's head twitched, stilled a moment, then turned just enough that he could look at her, his thumb in his mouth. Maddie held out her arms to him.

Ian stared at her, sucking his thumb, his blue eyes round and wide, their color so exactly that of his father's it twisted her heart with an entirely different sort of anguish.

Just when she thought he was going to turn away from her again, he let go of Channon and, thumb still in his mouth, came hesitantly toward her, suffering her to hold him but not hugging her in return, save for the small hand that plucked erratically at her sleeve.

"Oh, Ian, poppet, I have missed you so much," she whispered in his ear.

But he gave no sign of hearing, just laid his head on her chest and continued to suck on his thumb.

"He hasn't said a word since the day we found him," Elayne said gravely.

Maddie recalled that awful moment when he had collided with the cliff wall. . . . "Is he deaf, do you think?" she ventured, hating even to suggest it.

"Doesn't seem to be." Elayne brushed a hand over Ian's fine, pale hair. "I think he just doesn't want to talk anymore."

"He misses Papa," Simon said gravely.

And that almost set Maddie off all over again. Trap looked little better. Simon seemed unaware, turning now to tug at her skirt. "Mama, is it true that Papa is dead? Auntie Elayne says they burned him up in the Square."

Maddie glanced at Elayne, who frowned at her. In Maddie's arms, Ian made tiny sucking noises around his thumb, his fingers still plucking aimlessly at her sleeve.

"That is what everyone says, Simon," Maddie said. "And I have not heard a word from him in all this time, so it may be they are right."

"But he might have found a bunny hole, too—mightn't he, Mama?"

"He might have, Simon. . . ."

They were delivered, thankfully, by Carissa's arrival, pushing open the sitting room door and stepping among them. "I *thought* I heard a familiar voice," she said with a grin.

Simon's little boy voice shrilled across the room. "Auntie Crissa!" He flew into her arms, and she hugged him fiercely. Ian, however, refused even to look at her, clinging to Maddie now as he had earlier clung to Channon.

"He wouldn't come to me, either," Trap told his wife gently.

"He almost wouldn't come to *me*," Maddie added.

After a moment Carissa gave up, then turned to the gray-haired Elayne and fell into her arms, the two of them mourning their mutual loss in Felmen Cooper, Elayne's husband and Carissa's lifelong retainer.

Maddie recalled then the needs of her guests, informing them they would of course be staying at the palace. When she learned they had not eaten since midmorning, she sent Jeyanne out for cakes, milk, and tea.

"Please, sit down," she told the others, doing so herself, Ian still in her arms. "Jeyanne will get the baths going right away, but while we're waiting, I must hear of your adventures. I can hardly believe you're all here!"

And right then, Elayne Cooper stood and handed over the battered valise she had carried. "I found this for you, as well, ma'am," she said. "I think Felmen threw it into the forest when we were attacked, lest anyone should find it. Leastwise that's where I found it afterward, lying in the midst of a bracklebush."

Holding Ian in her left arm, Maddie opened the case with her free hand, pulled out two pair of child's dungarees and small clothes—and then the Robe of Light, stiff and bulky as it had been when she had wrapped Ian in it that fateful night. The robe had never changed to the suppleness it had when Abramm wore it, but it had saved the life of his son nonetheless. Beneath the robe lay the ring and the orb and, at the bottom, the crown.

Seeing it all made her want to weep again, but she restrained herself, replacing the items and closing the case as she pressed Elayne for the story.

The woman had eluded their attackers that night and slipped into the darkness. She'd seen Simon run away and hurried around to help him, was deep into the forest when she'd heard Maddie's screams abruptly silenced. Torn between the need to keep after Simon and the desire to help the queen, she'd stayed where she was, and in the end that was best.

"By Eidon's covering hand, the searchers missed me, and Simon, as well."

She'd found him hiding in a hollow log and, having heard nothing for a long time, ventured back to the site of the attack. There she found the valise, but no bodies.

"Not even him?" Maddie asked, indicating Ian with a tilt of her chin.

Elayne shook her head. Not knowing what else to do, she'd taken Simon along the path they'd originally been following. It was nearly dawn when they reached the bottom.

"We were crossing that small marshy place there between the rocks, and I heard a noise—like an animal that had been hurt. I don't know why I started toward it, but I'd not gone two steps before I realized it was a child. We found him just as Simon described it. I figured they threw him into the sea, ma'am."

"Yes," Maddie murmured. "Gillard told them to make sure he was dead."

"But the robe saved him somehow, washed him up onto the shore as neatly as if his mama had placed him there, the blankets beneath him. He was crying in the most desperate heart-tearing wail, all alone and scared. But not a scratch on him." She paused. "It was a miracle, my lady. The rock and the bottom wrap were wet, but the inner wrap and the babe himself were completely dry."

Elayne had opened the valise at that point to get some new clothing for him and discovered the ring and crown. It hadn't taken much for her to figure out why Simon's horsey was so bulbous of belly, and later she'd removed the orb from the toy and placed it with the other items. From there they'd walked over the ridge to Stillwater Cove, where she had relatives. News of Abramm's execution had reached her there, and it hit her hard, especially in the wake of Felmen's death during their escape from the palace. At first she'd lost all motivation to go on, having no idea where she would go, anyway. Then some weeks later Channon and Lieutenant Pipping found them.

Armed with Abramm's instructions to bring the boys to their mother in Fannath Rill, and fearful that Gillard's henchmen—also searching for the missing heirs—were right behind them, Channon had insisted they leave immediately. Thus ensued an overland trek that had turned out to be far more dangerous and difficult than any of them anticipated. Not knowing whom they could trust in a land crawling with searchers and informants, they'd had to take the longer, less populated routes, often on foot, and on several occasions had even been forced into hiding for a time. Add to that the weather and the general difficulties of traveling during times of governmental instability and warfare, and it wasn't hard to understand how it had taken them over six months to get to Fannath Rill.

Familiar voices sounded in the anteroom then, and shortly the doorman announced the arrival of their old friends, Darnley, Callums, and Hamilton, along with Oswain Nott. The four had followed Captain Channon's trail to the palace, hoping to see Abramm's sons for themselves. Once they did, they proclaimed little Simon to be Abramm's heir and rightful king of Kiriath, and they would have sworn fealty to him on the spot had not Trap persuaded them otherwise. Given the rumor they'd all heard that day of Abramm's possible survival, it wouldn't hurt to wait and see if the man himself turned up.

This was Maddie's first hearing of the rumor, and it shocked her so profoundly, at first she could hardly grasp what they were saying. When she did, she interrupted their discussion to demand a full report. Their revelation of Roy Thornycroft's arrival and his claim that Abramm had been rescued the morning before his execution left her breathless and light-headed—despite Trap's caution that Thornycroft had gotten the story from a tavern drunk.

She was still struggling to get her mind around it all when her father's First Minister, Temmand Garival, arrived to meet the boys, forcing her to put it aside for a time to attend to him.

In Fannath Rill for the meeting of the Council of Lords, Garival was a man of medium height, with thick, black hair combed back from his brow and tied into a queue at his nape. He had a weathered, clean-shaven face with a prominent nose, and dark, intelligent eyes. As a girl, Maddie had found him somewhat intimidating. Her father, though, had trusted him implicitly. Now he strode across the room to stop before her and her children. He eyed them sternly for a moment, then looked at her. "They certainly are your husband's sons."

His observation startled her, for she kept forgetting that Abramm had been in her homeland, that these people were quite familiar with him. *Abramm . . . could he really be alive?*

"There'll have to be a reception, of course," Garival said. "The court will want to meet them."

She stared at him blankly for a moment, then dragged her thoughts back to the present. "The *king* will want to meet them," she said.

"Indeed, he will, Your Highness." Garival looked briefly troubled, then glanced about and said quietly, "May I speak with you privately, ma'am?"

"Of course. We can talk in the study." She tried to give Ian back over to Captain Channon, but he refused, tightening his little arms about her neck and making small panicked grunts as he buried his face on her shoulder. Deciding now was not the time to press it, she carried him into the study, where Garival awaited her alone.

His dark eyes flicked to Ian in her arms, but he said only, "I wonder if it has occurred to you that, as First Daughter, all of Briellen's holdings are now yours."

Maddie gaped at him. No, it had not occurred to her, though she realized now it should have. Disowned by Hadrich and deported from Kiriath for adultery, Briellen had disappeared into obscurity. Her holdings, however, continued to operate under the supervision of their immediate overseers, and all the revenues they generated now by right belonged to Maddie. She'd been more distracted by her woes than she had guessed, not to have remembered that.

Garival nodded grimly. "I suspected Ronesca might not have brought this to your attention, nor to that of your finance secretary. . . ."

"And I wonder now if she might also be responsible for the failure of all the deals Duke Eltrap has initiated to purchase property on my behalf," Maddie murmured.

"I wouldn't put it past her, Highness. Not out of graft, mind you, but because she desires to bring you into line. Spiritually and politically." He paused. "Was it your idea or hers that you go to Deveren Dol for your lying-in?"

"Hers," Maddie said, startled he'd even ask. "By Father's order, so she said. I have a letter from him, as well."

He grimaced. "I did not read her letter, nor his, so I can't be sure, but I can say your father has not been himself lately."

"Is he ill?"

"We're not sure exactly what the problem is, but his perception is not as clear as it once was. I would suggest you forgo the journey north." He glanced down at her swollen belly and cocked a brow. "I can't see the purpose for it at this late date, anyway. Especially now that your older children have been returned to you." He sobered, his dark eyes meeting hers. "Know, as well, my lady, that there are many who support the House of Donavan—and appreciate what the Kiriathans have done for us. And we do not want to see Harvadan gain any more power than it already has. You have more allies than you know, if you will but cultivate them."

Giving her a nod, he left her to contemplate his words. After a time, she called for Trap to attend her. Ian fell asleep in her arms as she talked with her finance secretary late into the night. When finally she retired to her bedchamber, she found Elayne snoring in a chair by the sideboard, and Simon fast asleep in Maddie's own big bed. She laid his little brother beside him, then stood gazing down on them, overcome with tenderness and wonder that Eidon should have blessed her so magnificently.

Inevitably now, her thoughts returned to the rumor of Abramm's survival. Though Trap had been quick to bring it up in dissuading the Kiriathans from swearing fealty to Simon, he'd been inconsistently churlish about it with her later, reminding her repeatedly that it had sprung from the lips of a tavern drunk and most likely wasn't true.

But the seed of possibility had been sown, and hope had grown from it, despite his words of caution. What if Abramm was alive? As Tiris ul Sadek had pointed out, it wouldn't be the first time her husband was believed dead when he wasn't. Trap himself had been the beneficiary of a secret, early-morning, pre-execution rescue, so they both knew it was possible.

She was just getting into bed herself when she noticed the battered valise sitting on the foot of it. At first she simply stared at it. Then, slowly, she sat on the bed tailor style and turned to face it. Loosing a weary breath, she conjured a kelistar, then opened the valise to remove the robe and orb and set them aside. Now, heart thumping against her breastbone, she withdrew the crown, a shiver of awe running through her. She held it before her, fingering the fine weave of the slick and shimmering strips of metal, this precious object that had once touched the brow of her beloved. She could almost touch him through it. . . .

Then as memory flooded her like a consuming wave, she pressed it to her breast and wept, though whether for joy or grief or longing, she wasn't sure.

Perhaps it was all three.

10

Abramm saw the dragon while it was still afar, soaring beneath the starry night sky and up the canyon of the Ankrill to its headwaters. Spruce trees bowed and shivered in the wind of its passage, and animals large and small fled, terrified, from its presence.

Though it exuded power and majesty, beauty and grace, Abramm watched with growing horror as the creature turned from the Ankrill into a small snowbound valley ringed with massive white peaks. The valley at whose end stood Caerna'tha, where Abramm lay on his cot in his dormitory cell, shivering beneath the fleece cloak.

As the dragon drew near, Abramm's awareness of it changed from sight to sound—sudden rushing of wind outside his window, a few quick wing flaps, then a wave of creaking through ancient roofs and walls as it settled on Caerna'tha's uppermost tower. A moment later, the snow dislodged by the creature's landing fell to the wallwalk beneath with a reverberating thud.

A chill burrowed into Abramm's heart, for he knew the dragon had come for him. He felt it slithering down the roof to the wallwalk, heard the click of its toenails on the stone as it descended through the monastery's dark corridors. . . .

His eyes snapped open, nape prickling, heart pounding fiercely as he blinked at the dense darkness pressing upon him. He must flee . . . but he couldn't move. He gasped a deep, desperate breath, struggling to drag air through a suddenly constricted passageway.

Too late. The door was opening and a tall man entered. He approached Abramm's bedside. He wore a golden breastplate, his head shaved bald around a long, black, braided topknot. The dark recurved line of a longbow loomed over one shoulder and his handsome face gleamed as if, like the breastplate, it too were made of gold. His eyes bored into Abramm's.

"Hello, Alaric." The voice was warm and friendly, yet Abramm trembled all the more.

"Your king is dead, you know," the voice said gently. "You fight a losing battle. No one remembers him now. Not even his wife. . . ."

The man's eyes drew him down into darkness, where he floated briefly before being assailed by blinding light. He stood blinking rapidly, hearing dance music as the brilliance resolved into a lavishly decorated ballroom. Elegantly dressed ladies and gentlemen whirled on the dance floor in a backdrop to a glorious vision of Maddie gowned in gold, her lovely hair caught up in a sparkling jeweled intricacy of tiny braids. He could see the piercing grayblue of her eyes, the flush of warm color in her cheeks and lips. Now she laughed, lifting her chin as she did, his eyes stroking the pale curved column of her neck as a hundred memories ignited.

He could hardly breathe for the thrill of it, shaking violently now, feeling like a man who'd not eaten in months faced with a banquet. He wanted to sweep her into his arms and lose himself in her, but he could not move.

And all the while she paid him no heed, though surely she must see him. He was well within her line of sight.

At last his attention shifted to the man with whom she spoke. Darkbearded, poised, powerful, and handsome, he wore the silks and linens of eastern cut, a gold Sorite ring in his ear, and an expression entirely too predacious for Abramm's comfort. Worse, Maddie seemed as unaware of it as she was of her own attractiveness. . . .

Alarm crashed through him. Suddenly he found himself gasping on his cot again, swathed in darkness, the man in the golden breastplate looming beside him.

"Her husband is dead, you see," the pleasant voice said. "No one remembers him. You should forget him, as well. And her."

"NO!"

But his visitor turned away as if Abramm hadn't spoken.

"I will *not* forget," Abramm said more forcefully. "I won't."

The man was gone. Abramm felt a heaviness lift off the monastery, and then a trumpeting ululation screamed through the stone corridors, jerking him awake with a gasp.

He blinked around a cell not nearly so dark as it had been in the dream.

A dream! That's all it was!

He took another breath and pushed his hand from under the fleece cloak to conjure a kelistar. White light showed only the bare stone walls and wood floor of his cell, his rucksack and stick undisturbed in the far corner. No tracks of snow nor bits of mud marred the floor. The profound chill was hardly unusual, and though he'd never noticed that sharp, musky odor before, he couldn't say it hadn't been there.

He sagged back onto the cot, shivering with the cold air that had rushed in around him. Thoughts of Maddie filled his head, a thousand memories of sight and sound and touch so that he ached for her presence more fiercely than he had in months. He watched her talking to that young lord again, and a horrible fear rose up in him, riding wings of sharp impatience. *"She won't wait,"* Tapheina had said to him. The restless urgency to be off at once swelled in his heart. *"Abramm is dead. No one remembers him . . . not even his wife."*

And then, from out of the night's stillness he heard the tanniym's howl. . . . They were after him again.

Irritation drove him from the cot. Shoving his feet into his boots and wrapping himself in the fleece cloak, he left his cell to prowl the monastery's corridors and pray. Eventually he landed up in Laud's study, building up the fire and settling into the chair before it. Paging through the little gray book Laud had given him, he found the picture he'd remembered: a man with the gold breastplate, long braided topknot, and tall black longbow. It was this, no doubt, that had fueled his nightmare. This and Tapheina's howling combined with what was left of her spore still running through his flesh. There'd been no dragon. No man at his bedside, and that whole scene with Maddie—

But he was better off not thinking of Maddie at all.

Eventually he fell asleep, awakening to daylight and the first of the breakfast bells, the book open in his lap and the nightmare but a vague memory.

Until he stepped into the dining hall and found nearly everyone talking of the dragon's visit, sharing their dreams and trying to figure out if it was real. Old Wolmer had even taken a stroll around the wallwalk and claimed to have found footprints and snow dislodged from the uppermost tower.

The footprints were not a dragon's, however, but a man's, and the snow could have easily dislodged yesterday under the day's bright sun and clear sky. Wolmer was convinced it was the dragon, though. And he, like many of them, said it was looking for someone.

Trinley claimed to have dreamt nothing, and scoffed at them for their foolishness. "Everyone knows dragons no longer exist," he declared.

"Oh, I don't know," Laud said. "Legends say they've lived in the Aranaak for centuries. Driven here when Eidon loosed the great flood that took the plains and overran their cities."

"You speak of the tanniym," Abramm said quietly. He'd not been able to decipher enough of his dragon book to have gained much from it yet, but he knew the legends of the tanniym, whose fathers were said to have been rhu'ema themselves. In those days the rhu'ema were able to manifest in physical bodily form—most often that of the dragon—though, like Moroq, they could appear as men if they chose. It was their union with human women that produced the half-breed tanniym, who were themselves shapeshifters, though on a much lesser scale. Because they were also vicious, violent, and increasingly destructive, Eidon had destroyed them, imprisoned the ones who had made them, and removed the rhu'ema's ability to assume corporeal form.

"Tanniym!?" Trinley exclaimed now, with an incredulous snort. "Ye mean those wolves out there?"

"Did they look like any wolves you've ever seen before?" Laud asked.

"They sure didn't look like dragons," Trinley said disdainfully. "Or men." He shook his head. "Those are Hill People stories, pr'fessor! Surely ye of all people don't b'lieve 'em!"

"You'd be surprised what I believe," said Laud.

Cedric returned them to their original subject: "If the dragon wasn't real, how d'ye explain us all havin' the same dream?"

"Ye didn't all have the same dream," Trinley pointed out. "Some of ye thought it was outside, some of ye heard it, an' only a couple of ye actually saw it. Who was it lookin' fer? Did it find 'im? Eh? It was probably the wolves howling that ye heard. And the wind blowin'."

Some of them glowered at him, while others studied their bowls with creases between their brows.

"Ye're all making something out o' nothin'. Dragons!" He chuckled. I don't believe in dragons anymore 'n I b'lieve in that conquering Esurhite army King Abramm was constantly scarin' us with so he could get hold of our gold."

Abramm wasn't the only one to stare at him open-mouthed. Rolland laughed outright.

"Ye don't b'lieve in dragons, and ye think the Esurhite army don't exist?"

"Not one that means t' conquer Kiriath and all the world!" Trinley declared hotly. He looked around at them, passion rising. "Aye, an' I know plenty others who think the same. Men who've been t' Springerlan. Men who've lived there fer years and never saw sign o' this army, though we were forever sendin' off our gold and goods so our king could build his own army t' fight 'em."

"Daft, is what ye are!" Rolland sputtered. "The heights must've addled yer mind, man."

"Ye think I'm addled? Well, tell me, then. Have any of ye here ever seen this army? This invadin' Esurhite army?"

"*I've* seen it!" Rolland insisted. "Saw 'em try to take Kalladorne Bay with my own eyes six years ago. Saw their purple firebolts destroy the Hall of Kings in the blink of an eye. I even helped put out the fires it started."

"You saw the actual attack?" Abramm asked in astonishment. "You were in Springerlan then?"

Still glaring at Trinley, Rolland said, "I saw the parade on the bay after Abramm took back the Gull Islands, too—all the galleys and soldiers they captured. . . . So don't tell me there's no army."

Trinley scowled at him, suddenly suspicious. "I thought ye said ye were born and raised in Sterlen. That ye'd spent yer whole life there."

Rolland gave a start. "I was . . . and I did . . . mostly. But fer a time we lived in Springerlan." His ire vanished and his gaze dropped uneasily to his big hands, all but engulfing the crockery mug he held.

"Fer a time," Cedric prodded.

"We came down when the kraggin held Kalladorne Bay, jest before Abramm returned t' take the crown. When things were so bad up north. I'd had t' shut down my forge. . . ."

"I can't imagine things would've been better in Springerlan," said Trinley.

"Oh, it worked out well, actually. I couldn't afford to open my own place, but I found work at the . . . at a large stable."

"Pox!" Trinley burst out. "Ye worked fer the king, didn't ye? That's why ye've always been so defensive about him." He pushed back from the table. "Plagues! All this time ye've been a traitor in our midst."

Rolland's blue eyes flashed. "If anyone's the traitor, it's you, Oakes! With all yer ignorant and spiteful faultfinding of a man ye've never even met."

"Oh, and ye have? Workin' down at the stables . . . a lowly blacksmith? Aye, an' I'm sure ye've had many a heart-to-heart talk with His Majesty."

Rolland glanced at Daesi, who gave him a warning look he didn't heed. His expression hardened. "I saw him from time t' time, and he did speak t' me on occasion. Just day-t'-day courtesies, but he always treated me kindly, like I was a person."

Abramm stared at Rolland, aghast. *I spoke to him?* He wracked his brain, trying to recall the man. He'd had more than twenty groomsmen and ten blacksmiths working in his stables, and truth be told, he was as guilty as the next man of not seeing what he supposed did not matter.

"He kept a fine stable, too," Rolland added.

Trinley snorted. "Now, *there's* the measure of a king's quality: He keeps a fine stable!"

"He was a good man, Oakes. He didn't deserve to die like he did."

"No? Then why did Eidon let him fall?"

Rolland frowned at him and said nothing.

"Some say it was so he might be tested," Professor Laud remarked mildly. "So that all might see he did not serve Eidon for what he had received. That no matter what they did to him, he would not break."

"Some say he did break," Trinley said.

"He died with the shield on his chest. Everyone saw it. And they say that a number of the men involved in his torture have since taken the Star themselves."

That was something Abramm had not known. Was old Belmir one of them?

The professor arched his brows at Trinley. "Why do you think men are forbidden to speak Abramm's name in Kiriath these days?"

"'Cause he was cursed by Eidon," Trinley said. "He lied to us, abandoned us, thought more of his foreign wife than of his own people and paid fer it. All that gold we sent t' support his efforts to build his army, yet when the time came we really needed deliverance, where was he? Where were the forces that should've been there to throw back Rennalf and his barbarians? Why didn't our great king at least come with his magical scepter to stop it all?!"

"Because he didn't know," said Rolland fiercely. "Ye've heard the tales as well as I have: He was betrayed. His scepter stolen and replaced by a power-less copy."

And now, for a moment Abramm was back on that knoll outside Springerlan, reliving his hour of greatest need, when he'd swung the scepter over his head and nothing happened. He'd thought first that it was being contrary again, for he had never fully understood how it worked. Only when the Light had illumined all its length and still not stirred the slightest breeze had he stopped to examine it more closely. And realized it was not the real scepter, not made of Light but of gold, with a thick glass orb. The work of man and not of Eidon. Even now in recollection, he found it hard to breathe through that moment of terrible realization.

Trinley was speaking again. ". . . and if he'd never married her, it wouldn't have happened. I say he got exactly what he deserved."

"So then, we're better off without 'im? Better off with *Gillard* and his Mataians?" Rolland shoved to his feet, the bench shrieking backward over the stone floor. "Ye're a fool, Oakes. All caught up in yer bitterness and blame. Ye're not the only one who's lost things, ye know."

He took his leave then. Trinley watched him go without comment, then snorted and fell into a silence no one else was willing to break. After a few moments the group began to disperse, going off to their various morning duties and pursuits. Abramm headed down toward the cleared-out stable where they practiced their stickwork, pondering the ramifications of the breakfast conversation.

His loss of the scepter had been a bitter blow, and for a time during his convalescence he had pondered who might have taken it. Blackwell was a known betrayer and could have taken it virtually any time. But Leyton Donavan had had motive, funds, and opportunity. He had asked to borrow it more than once—and had been refused—and Abramm wouldn't put it past him to take it upon himself to borrow it without asking. He almost hoped it was Leyton, for at least that would mean Gillard didn't have it.

But the mystery of who'd taken his scepter was not one he'd solve anytime soon, and so it did not interest him nearly so much as Rolland's revelation that he had known Abramm when he was king. Never once in their journeys had he shown the slightest indication of recognition. True, Abramm had no recollection of Rolland, either, but he had been the king, and Rolland had obviously been impressed by the few times Abramm had spoken to him. One would think he might recall something—Abramm's voice if nothing else. . . .

"You fight a losing battle. No one remembers him anymore."

Were the rhu'ema somehow blinding these men to who he really was?

When he reached the stable, the big blacksmith was already there faced off with Galen and still grumbling about Trinley.

"Come on, Rollie," Galen said as Abramm hesitated in the doorway. "Ye know how he is."

"Aye. Blind and stubborn and can't even hear how wild he sounds anymore. I could understand some high-hills shepherd holding to such beliefs, but Oakes was an alderman. Why can't he just let it go about Abramm? The man is dead."

"I don't know, but . . . why does it matter? Ye barely knew him."

"He was my king." Rolland stood in silence a moment, then added in an anguished voice, "I watched him die, Galen." He glanced at Abramm. "To my everlasting shame, I stood and watched him burn."

Well, Abramm thought, *that explains a lot. If he saw me die, he sure won't be expecting to find me in Caerna'tha, his traveling companion of many months.*

Rolland pulled himself together and turned more fully to Abramm. "That's why I want t' learn t' fight. Havin' t' stand there and watch it, knowin' I could do nothing but get myself killed if I tried to stop it. I hated that."

"Even if you'd known how, you couldn't have stopped it," Abramm said. "What was happening there was far bigger than one man."

"You were there, too?"

"No."

"Well, maybe I couldn'ta stopped it, but it don't change how I feel. So I thank ye for trainin' us with the sticks. I hope soon ye'll teach us a bit of the sword." He lifted his chin. "When we reach the southland and I get my family settled with Daesi's uncle, I mean to find the queen and give her my allegiance. Or maybe little Prince Simon if he lives."

When Abramm said nothing to this dismaying revelation, Rolland prodded him. "That's what ye're goin' t' do, isn't it?"

And at that Abramm gave a long sigh. "Aye, that's what I've planned. . . ."

"Don't throw rocks at the fish, Simon," Maddie called, watching her firstborn hesitate, small arm raised to send another missile splashing into the moss-lined pool at his feet. It was one of many here in Fannath Rill's renowned waterpark, all of them stocked with Ronesca's prized golden carp. Now Simon looked over his shoulder at his mother, a bright, mischievous grin on his face. Maddie saw the wheels of his mind turning, weighing the tradeoff of inevitable punishment with the pleasure of continuing on his chosen path. Beside him Ian crouched on chubby legs, squealing with excitement and pointing at the huge orange fish as they sidled through the dark water before him.

It was Eidonsday and they'd just finished Terstmeet. A month after the boys had been returned, and now, in the midst of a very rainy winter, they'd taken the opportunity of a clear day to come out for a late morning stroll with Carissa and Conal, the latter asleep in his carriage behind them under Prisina's care. Captain Channon and Lieutenant Pipping also accompanied them as they meandered through the mostly deserted waterpark. Trap had gone off to a meeting in town and the rest of the court was still over in the Great Kirikhal, whose service would not conclude for at least another hour— which was why Maddie had agreed to come out here, being well advanced in her pregnancy now and supposedly confined to her apartments.

Now she stopped in her tracks and frowned at her son. His grin widened, and then he turned and flung the rock, not exactly at the fish but toward the side of the pool. It smacked the stone edge and raised a good splash, which Ian applauded with another squeal and a clapping of his chubby hands.

Carissa snickered as Maddie tightened her lips. With a sigh she waddled to her son's side and seized his arm before he could flee, grunting with the effort of bending over. She felt as big as a river barge, and about as unwieldy.

"What did I just tell you, Simon?" She shook her son's arm.

Unbelievably his grin was still there. "Not to throw rocks at the fish! And I didn't, Mama. I threw it at the moss."

She stared at him, befuddled anew by the fractured logic of a four-and-a-half-year-old. "I don't want you to throw any more rocks at anything at all."

"But Papa throws rocks. Why can't I?"

"Your papa doesn't throw rocks, Simon."

"Yes he does. With his leather strap. He throws the little red stones. Him and Uncle Trap and Great Uncle Simon."

She stared into his big blue eyes, astonished that he would remember that at all. That day when the three of them had taken it upon themselves to have another contest had to be more than a year ago. "Yes, well. Papa threw his stones with a sling, and you do not have a sling. And he did not throw them into your grandfather's ponds or at your Auntie Ronesca's golden fish. She would be very upset if she knew you had done that, Simon. What if you hurt them?"

"I wouldn't hurt them, Mama. They always swim out of the way."

"No more rocks, Simon, or you'll go back to the apartments for a switching. Do you understand?"

Simon nodded contritely.

She turned her attention to Ian, who watched both of them with wide eyes. "And you aren't to throw rocks at anything, either, Ian. Do you understand?" The little boy stared up at her, wordless as always, but finally he nodded.

She hesitated before sending them off, wondering what else she hadn't thought to tell them not to do, then gave up trying. They ran around to one of the bridges and raced across it, back and forth, delighting in the booming echo of their footfalls.

Maddie left Lieutenant Pipping watching over them and strode on with Carissa, Conal's carriage squeaking along behind them.

"See what you have to look forward to?" she muttered to her sister-in-law.

Carissa laughed and shook her head. "Simon is so much like Abramm, it's shocking sometimes."

"I thought Abramm was sickly."

"He was. But in between he was always into something. Never anything you would expect. Never anything anyone had thought to tell him not to do. And he could argue rings around our nannies. Drove them crazy. Especially when he got older."

They circled a great pond where swans glided. Overhead the sun shone down thinly from a clear, winter-blue sky, the air almost mild now at midday. Around them, streams chuckled, fountains sprayed and danced, and the waterwheels and buckets clanked and ground and whooshed as they raised the liquid high so it could flow beguilingly down its manmade courses. Palm trees lined the way, birds squawking and rustling in their fronds.

Maddie still marveled at the return of her sons. Some days she sat in wonder, thanking Eidon with all of her heart for this gift. Others she felt Abramm's loss more keenly than ever, perhaps because so many seemed to think that having regained her sons, she should stop mourning the loss of her husband. In any case, her sons' return had sparked a series of receptions and, more importantly, had moved Ronesca into a much more pleasant and solicitous mood. Maddie suspected Garival had spoken to her, because the very morning after the boys' return, she had arrived at Maddie's chambers, professing relief at catching her before she'd left. "It would not be good to put your sons at risk on yet another journey, especially when they have so recently arrived," she'd said, adding that Maddie could do her lying-in at the palace and she would begin interviewing midwives and wet nurses that very day.

She'd been friendly and helpful ever since, showering the boys with gifts that included a special spiritual tutor with puppets and bright sparklers of

Terstan light. Maddie had sent him away, kindly but firmly, and was astonished when Ronesca had accepted the decision without one word of criticism. But perhaps that was because shortly afterward Ronesca's own sons returned home from the front—the war temporarily shut down by wind and weather and the withdrawal of the Esurhites. The last two weeks had been downright peaceful.

At least on the surface. Maddie continued to fret about her father's condition, which Garival said seemed more an ailment of mind and mood than body. He was erratic, emotional, prone to uncharacteristic fits of temper and sometimes stubbornly and even aggressively irrational. His aides were at their wits' end for how to deal with him. Garival thought it might be the strain of the war, and hoped that a few months at home in Fannath Rill with his daughter and grandsons would help to ease him.

But as the days passed and still no word came of the king's return, Maddie had grown more and more uneasy.

As for Leyton's ill-fated attempt at drawing the Esurhites into a trap on Torneki, Garival claimed there was no talisman so far as he knew, though there had been an attempt to draw the Esurhites into the bay at Torneki. It had gone horribly wrong, but more than that he would not tell her.

"So," Carissa said. "I understand you've received yet another gift from Draek Tiris. A book of nursery rhymes and some figs?"

"Sorite nursery rhymes," Maddie corrected. "And the figs were gold." She lifted her skirts as they started up one of the wooden footbridges. With her monstrous belly hiding all sight of her feet these days, she had to step carefully and hope she didn't trip.

"I thought the golden figs were out of season now," Carissa said.

"For eating, yes. These are solid gold."

"Off the same magic tree that made the edible ones a few months ago?" Skepticism colored her voice.

"Aye. Whether it's true or not, I still have no idea what I should do with them. Would you like one?"

Carissa looked at her in surprise, then shook her head. "Oh no, my lady. I'm sure he meant those just for you. Perhaps you can use them as paperweights."

And they laughed together at the notion.

When Ronesca had informed Maddie that a proper princess needed a coterie of noble ladies-in-waiting, she undoubtedly had in mind some Chesedhan ladies to recommend for the position. Instead Maddie had chosen

Carissa. Besides being her boys' aunt, Carissa needed a position in the court beyond "exiled Kiriathan princess." Though Maddie had not wished to draw her from husband and baby when they'd first arrived, now, with Trap living across the palace from her, and Conal needing her less and less, she'd seemed lonely and at loose ends. Serving Maddie as lady-in-waiting was the perfect solution, and she had called upon her services frequently of late. As a result they'd grown closer than they'd ever been—Carissa's recent pregnancy and Maddie's current one, plus the antics of their boys, providing a wealth of subject matter for discussion. Now, apparently, Tiris ul Sadek was to be added to the mix.

"You two are developing quite the relationship," Carissa remarked as they came down the other side of the bridge.

"I don't know that I'd call it a 'relationship.'"

Her sister-in-law shrugged. "Not a day goes by you don't hear from him. He visits you in person several times a week and showers you with expensive gifts. Exotic fruits and flowers, that amazing cloak, the gold-trimmed lirret with those fancy strings you were so excited about, jeweled books of Sorite music, all those dragon things. . . ." Here she grimaced and uttered a little groan of distaste. "Those, though, are just plain odd. Whoever heard of sending someone a dragon sculpture as a courtship gift?"

"Well, lots of folks say I'm odd, so I guess it fits." She shrugged. "He knows I have an interest in dragons. He knows why, as well."

"Nevertheless he's obviously courting you."

"I have no interest in Tiris ul Sadek, Riss. At least not like that. And I've been entirely forthright about that with him."

Carissa chuckled at her. "Abramm said you were stubborn, and now I see why. Why in the world do you fight it so? Tiris is rich, charming, erudite. And he is a *very* attractive man."

"So was your brother," Maddie said tartly. "In ways Tiris will never be."

For a moment Carissa was silent. Then she sighed wearily. "Maddie, Abramm is gone. Don't let that rumor mess this up for you."

"I'm not. Even if it's false, Abramm has not left my soul. I doubt he ever will."

"Maybe not, but you'll still need someone to support you. And your sons."

Maddie looked at her in surprise. "Didn't Trap tell you? As First Daughter, all Briellen's holdings are mine now. He's been traveling the realm this last month visiting each of them, getting to know those who oversee them, gathering tribute where it's due." Which was almost everywhere.

Carissa stopped in surprise, and when Maddie stopped a step afterward and turned to face her, she said, "You mean he's not even been in Fannath Rill all this time?"

"Doesn't your husband tell you anything?"

Pain flashed across Carissa's aristocratic features, swallowed up by that mask of impassivity the Kalladornes were so good at. She lifted her chin to gaze across the hills and fountains and moving waterwheels. "I haven't seen him in weeks," she said. "And no, he tells me very little." She started walking again.

Maddie fell in beside her, dismayed by this revelation but having no idea what to say. How in the world could things have gone so wrong between those two? After their unexpected marriage, she had hoped to see the promise of love that had always sparkled between them finally grow to fruition. Instead it seemed to have shriveled and died away altogether. Ever since that day she'd pressed Trap into asking Carissa to come with him to the inn and she'd refused. It hadn't been long after that she'd learned he'd moved out of their shared apartments to live in his office across the palace from them. He'd claimed it was Carissa's desire and more convenient for him, and Maddie hadn't pressed him.

Now, feeling she might be partly to blame for it all, she was hesitant to intrude again.

"He's given me his name," Carissa said tightly. "He's taken my son for his own and all the evil talk that goes with it. Is that not enough?"

They walked on in silence, the crunch of their feet on the gravel path overlaying the ever-present trickle of water. When Carissa said nothing more, Maddie decided she couldn't leave the matter without probing further.

"You told me once that you loved him," she said cautiously. "Do you still?"

"That was years ago!" Carissa protested. But she didn't answer the question, lapsing into silence again. Just when Maddie was about to try another tack, she sighed. "I know he doesn't love me, Mad. He is kind and attentive and unfailingly polite, but never anything more. Finally I suggested he shouldn't pretend what he didn't feel, that I would never expect any more from him than he'd already given. That's when he left."

Maddie's stomach dropped to her toes. "Oh, Carissa . . . you actually said that to him?"

"I gave him his freedom and he took it." Carissa wiped a tear from her eye. "I've even heard he's found a mistress, a tavern maid down by the river."

"Well, since he's not been in town for the last month, I find that very hard to believe." She shook her head. "Abramm said Trap's loved you since he was seventeen. I really don't think the problem is that he doesn't care."

"You're saying this is my fault? That I drove him away?" Carissa's ire rose quickly, fueled by her pain. "You didn't see the expression that came over his face when he thought I wasn't looking. Miserable and sad and hopeless."

"Maybe he looked that way because you asked him to leave."

"No. He looked like that before I asked. I know—"

She was interrupted as hurried footfalls on the gravel path behind them brought both women around. One of the royal guardsmen ran up to them.

"Your Highness?" he gasped, bowing sketchily to the First Daughter. "The king has been wounded, my lady. They're bringing him through the city gates as I speak. He should be here shortly."

"Wounded? How can he be wounded when the war is paused?"

"I don't know, my lady. It may be the old wound. I've heard it was inflicted by the Shadow. They feared he'd not reach Fannath Rill alive. As it is, they don't expect him to last much longer."

11

Maddie sent the boys back to their nursery with Channon and went to prepare herself to meet the king. A little over half an hour later, she was striding into the newly opened royal apartments, closed and locked since the monarch had left for Peregris over a year ago.

Hadrich's physician, Dr. Lavek, greeted her in the outer chamber, and so far only he and the servants were there. Ronesca and First Minister Garival were still at the Kirikhal, though Lavek expected them soon.

"I thought my father was healing," Maddie said.

"He'd been up and walking for over a month, the wound fading," Lavek explained. "Then a week ago he collapsed. Spent the next night raving as the fever overtook him, and the wound—"

He broke off as a voice shouted from the chamber behind him, "No! No! I will not see them! Take them away!" Silence followed the words, and then, in a much stronger voice, "I want to see my daughter. Bring Madeleine at once! I must see her NOW."

Lavek frowned. Maddie prodded him. "And the wound?"

"The wound is something you will have to see to understand. But . . . I don't know that you should go in just now."

"I want to."

"My lady, he may not even know you. When Leyton came to see him right before we left to return to Fannath Rill, the old man threw a candlestick at him. And that after he'd been howling for his son to attend to him all night."

"I'll make sure I'm ready to dodge."

Lavek's stern face grew sterner. "It's dark in there, Your Highness. He can't bear the light. We've had to put the kelistars behind screens to have any illumination at all. If you conjure one while you're beside him, the chance is great you'll set him off into a rage."

Madeleine frowned at him, chilled. "The man who fetched me said you suspect shadowspawn."

"Aye, spawn spore has been the issue from the start, though he'd done a purge and we thought him in the clear."

She frowned. *Just as we thought Abramm was after the morwhol.*

Lavek led her through the bedchamber's arched doorway into the darkness and the shocking, stomach-turning stench of vomit, feces, urine, sweat, and something close to rotting flesh, all cloaked in a thin veil of incense. Her gorge rose, and it took all her willpower not to turn and run. Pulling her kerchief from her waistband and holding it over her face, she breathed through her mouth as her eyes adjusted to the darkness.

Kelistars lay behind two dressing screens, out of her father's sight. Others rested in sconces on the wall above his bed, high enough that he apparently didn't notice. The sideboard held a bowl of onions, one of which lay quartered on a plate. Candles, fat and thin, burned before a small altar of stone and evergreen—a nod to the old ways some in Chesedh still practiced and silent testimony to Lavek's desperation to find a cure. Small tables on either side of the canopied bed held pans from which ascended streams of pale, fragrant smoke. On the table nearest her sat a plate of roast game hen, rice and almonds, and a sweet dumpling, picked at but little eaten.

The king lay in the great canopied bed, propped up against a mountain of pillows and covered with a thin linen sheet. As her eyes adjusted to the darkness, what she saw shocked her more than the stench. Her father was but a shadow of himself, his tall frame nothing but bones. Beneath his gold circlet, long, sweat-darkened gray hair frizzed to his shoulders, framing an overgrown beard. Fissures carved his face, and his eyes had sunk so far into his head she saw nothing but shadow beneath his brows.

Able to breathe as long as she did so through her mouth, Maddie withdrew her kerchief and approached the bed. Her father lay unmoving, his bony chest rising and falling erratically beneath his silk bedgown. She caught the vague glint of his Terstan shield through its loose weave. One of his skeletal hands picked absently at a fold in the sheet. The fingernails were long and dirty, the fingers themselves shiny with grease from picking at the food before he'd pushed it aside. Outrage stirred in her that his servants had left him in such a disheveled state. Even traveling, there was no excuse. He was the king. He deserved their respect.

She stopped at the bedside. An empty starstick stood just behind the arrangement of flickering candles, obscured by the ribbon of scented smoke. The incense was stronger here, but so was the stench of death and rot. His eyes, the lashes caked with yellow crust, were slitted, though he had given no sign he was aware of her.

She conjured a small kelistar and held it out to see him better, mindful he might rise up and slap it away. When he did not move, she decided he was indeed asleep. In the increased light his face looked thinner than ever, the bones pressing out against the skin. His large nose and sagging cheeks were netted with tiny red and purple lines where the smallest blood vessels had broken. Dried blood rimmed his nostrils. This close she felt his fever heat and saw that white bandages bound his abdomen beneath his sleeping gown.

She slipped her star onto the starstick, then gingerly perched on the bedside, her throat tightening with grief.

Finally he stirred, the watery blue eyes focusing distractedly upon her, fever-bright, bloodshot, and lined with the narrow ridge of white curd that was the sarotis. Dismay drew her stomach into a knot. *Oh, Papa, not you, too* . . . It was a moment before she could actually look past the curd to the eyes themselves, staring at her now and flicking back and forth in tiny oscillations.

"So," he said. "You've come."

His teeth were huge and yellow, the gums receded so far it was probably a miracle he had teeth at all.

"You've come," he repeated dreamily.

She took his hand, hot and dry beneath her own. "Come to help you heal, Papa."

"No." He shook his head, hair rasping against his pillow. "I will not get better. There are things we must settle between us, you and I."

"Those things can wait."

"They *cannot.*" Sudden strength powered the words, then faded away. "They cannot." He lay panting for a moment. Then his eyes dropped to her swollen womb and pain flashed across the runneled face. "Oh, my poppet. I am so sorry for all that has befallen you. After all that you have lost, why Eidon would choose to lay this final indignity upon you. . . ."

He pulled his hand free of hers to touch her belly, and a jolt zinged through her. The babe recoiled in violent reaction as Maddie herself flinched back. Hadrich seemed not to notice, reaching blindly to touch it again. She made herself take his hot, dry hand and moved it back to the bed.

He shook his head, his red-rimmed eyes tearing up. "I never should have let Leyton press you as I did."

She stared at him uncomprehendingly. "When did you let Leyton press me, Papa? I haven't seen him since I've returned."

"To marry him. I never should have pressed you to marry him. You were dedicated to Eidon, and now . . ."

"I am still dedicated to Eidon, Father. And it wasn't Leyton who moved me to marry Abramm. Regardless of what you said, I'd have married him anyway."

"He was a good man."

"Yes. He . . . was." She'd almost said *is*.

"You loved him? Truly?"

"With all my heart and soul."

He reflected upon that for a bit. Then a frown creased his brow and he shook his head. "No . . . if you had stayed true to Eidon, if I'd not forced your hand, none of this would have happened. I lose my kingdom because of you, you know. And he has been taken from you, and at the last your womb sullied with a commoner's seed."

It was her turn to frown. "Not a commoner, Papa." She laid her hand on the swelling and smiled. "This one is Abramm's, too."

"But they told me—"

"Ronesca refuses to believe me. I wrote you all about it."

"Did you. . . ? I can't recall." He watched his fingers pluck at the sheet, then reached for her belly again. "But this one. You say it is his? You would not lie to me."

She headed off the wobbly gesture and captured his hand again, trying not to be hurt by his fear she'd lie to him. "Of course not, Papa."

"Then it is the true heir to the Kiriathan throne. The last claim to his line." He paused, then added firmly, "You must do away with it."

"What?"

"It will destroy us all. It cannot be allowed to live."

His hand flew out, striking at her belly as she lurched up and back, standing at his bedside, trembling. "You speak madness, Papa!"

His head thrashed about, hand opening and closing as the fire died from his eyes. Tears welled up in them again. "I'm sorry, Poppet. I'm sorry. Please . . . I don't know why I said that. . . . It is the fever. I . . . there has been so much concern. Ever since Abramm was deposed. We've lost the Kiriathans. They're treating with the Esurhites, you know. And they've become mercenaries. Or else just disbanded and fled. This child could bring so much trouble."

He was talking of the Kiriathan troops Abramm had lent him for the fight along the Strait. Troops sworn to Abramm who, when they learned their king had been deposed and executed, had reacted in turmoil. Some had transferred their allegiance to Chesedh, others had abandoned the field altogether, and a few had returned home. Most, however, had remained in Chesedh, gathering with the other exiles as they tried to figure out what to do next. And so far as she knew, the Kiriathans had not treated with the Esurhites, confident in the protective power of their Holy Flames. It would serve no purpose, though, to argue the point with him.

She drew a deep breath and patted his hand, which was once more lying quietly on the folded sheet. "Right now our main concern is Belthre'gar and his armies of the Black Moon."

"Yes . . ." His gaze drifted unseeingly across the room. "My grandson." He sighed. "If only I could live to see him born."

She squeezed his hand. "Don't say such things, Papa. You will live to see him. You will."

"Wish I could have seen the others, too. I should have made the trip when I could . . . but I guess . . . maybe I will see them soon enough now."

"Papa!"

" 'Tis true, daughter. I am passing. Soon the crown will go to Leyton. And I don't think he will hold it long. Then it will come to you."

"NO. You're going to be fine. And as for your grandsons, you *can* see them. This very day in this very room if that is your wish. For Eidon has delivered them from the fires of Kiriath and brought them back to me. They are here in Fannath Rill right now."

The light flickered in his eyes again as his hand twisted to grip hers, hard. "Your sons are here?" The sudden eagerness in his voice roused her uneasiness again.

"I sent you a letter, Papa," she reminded him. "Telling you all about it."

"I . . . don't recall."

She frowned at him, wondering if his forgetfulness was truly a result of his fevers or if he'd actually received any of her letters.

Her father's whispered words drew her attention. "What did you say, Papa?"

"I want to see them before I die."

"Papa, you're not going to die. Stop saying that!"

He grimaced and gestured at his midsection. "Have you looked at my side, lass? 'Twas no mortal shaft that stuck me. I can feel it even now, a coldness creeping across my side." His eyes flashed again, and he bared his teeth as he said, "Why don't you look at it yourself? You've a reputation as a healer."

She went still, then gently drew her hand from his and sat back to glance at Lavek standing a little way behind her.

The physician stepped forward. "Are you sure—"

"Show her!" Hadrich snapped, that uncharacteristic temper once more empowering his voice.

A moment more Lavek hesitated, staring from daughter to father as the latter struggled to move up on his pillows, hiking up his bedgown as he did. The impending revelation of his privates spurred Lavek into action.

"Here, Sire. Let us." He and Hadrich's body servants moved hastily around Maddie to minister to their king as she gladly stepped back and let them work. Shortly they had him readied, the bedgown pulled up to his chest, the linen sheet covering his lower half and only the bandaged area around his waist revealed.

"We'll need to light a kelistar, sir," Lavek said. "So I can cut this away."

Hadrich gave a negligent wave, but Maddie noted that he turned his face from the orb and gritted his teeth. Hadrich's manservant held the star on his open palm as Lavek cut through the blood-and-pus-soaked bandage. As he peeled it back, the odor of rot intensified.

A dark, mottled mass sprawled across the right side of her father's torso, like some sort of griiswurm that had managed to slide itself under his skin. Its uneven edges extended in purple and black fingers of varied lengths, groping across skin as white and thin as writing paper. The surface was slightly raised, and almost shiny, but dry and cold to the touch, despite his fever. At the mass's midst, a small hole oozed bloody pus.

"What is this?" she asked, lifting her gaze to Lavek's.

The doctor shook his head. "No one knows. He said it was an arrow, though we found no shaft. At first it was just a normal puncture wound."

"Use the Light to burn it off," Hadrich growled, his face still turned away.

Lavek frowned. "Sire, you know we've tried that already." He glanced again at Maddie. "As well as bleeding it and salting it. We even had a healer proficient in the Old Ways try his potions and spells. Nothing worked."

"She's got a gift, though," Hadrich growled. "And she's always been strong in the Light. Dedicated to Eidon, she is. Let her try."

Evidently he'd forgotten his earlier declaration that she was also cursed by Eidon for marrying a Kiriathan.

Lavek tried again. "Sire. You know how much the Light hurts you. How much strength it drains from you every time we use it."

"Aye, last time it sent me into blessed unconsciousness. Why should I fear that?"

"Because last time it took you two days to come out of it, and this time you might not come out at all."

"So I'd be walking the high valleys of Eidon's realm. I'd be home safe in his kingdom. Why do you wish to deny me that?" But he was still clenching his teeth and had wound his hands into the top of the sheet that covered his lower body. "Just let me see my grandsons first."

Lavek eased back and said quietly, "I think the only thing that remains is to try to cut it off of him."

"Do you have any idea how deep it goes?"

"Deep," Hadrich grated. "You'll not cut it out of me. Let her try." He swallowed hard and blinked at the side of the room where he still stared. "If she's willing."

"Of course I'm willing, Papa!"

But Lavek looked more worried than ever. His eyes dropped to her swollen belly. "Your Highness . . . we don't know what this thing is. Or what it does. . . ."

"I'll go slowly. I'll be careful. The Light will protect me."

Lavek pressed his lips together. He turned again to Hadrich. "Forgive me, Sire, but I thought you wished to see your grandsons first."

"Yes. Yes. Bring them now. And Ronesca. And Leyton should be here, as well. They all have to go." His head writhed. "Come. They have to come. They have to be here. I have to . . . I have to . . . no." He wrung his hands into the sheets and began to weep again. "No . . . no, no, no . . . I can't. I won't."

"Papa."

"No. Take it away. Take it away. Do not bring them here now. Take this thing away first. You have to. Lavek's right—we don't know what it will do."

She exchanged another glance with the physician, hesitant, for what if he died of this as Lavek feared he might? But only a moment's thought told her that her father was right. She could hardly bear the thought of her sons being in the same room with this thing that had somehow claimed her father's flesh.

She lowered herself once more onto the edge of the bed, then reached toward the darkness sprawling across his side and closed her eyes. *Father Eidon, please, touch his body. Heal him of this blight. . . .*

She felt the Light rise within her, tingling down her arms, into her hands and fingers, then out into the infected flesh beneath them. Only not really. She opened her eyes in time to see the threads of Light skittering over the darkness and dissipating without effect. Frowning, she let loose another burst, stronger this time, willing it deeper and feeling now the resistance of a griis-wurm's aura. She set her jaw as she set her determination, and the Light flashed out of her in a great surge of power that loosed a scream from Hadrich's lips and knocked her backward with its force.

When they had both recovered, sweat sheened on her father's ravaged face, and the skin around the blight had reddened. When she touched the dark mass again, he hissed and recoiled in pain.

"Put that star out!" he growled.

The servant flicked out the orb he still held on his palm.

"And the other, as well," Hadrich added.

The man leaned forward to flick out the star Maddie had set on the bed-side starstick.

"Father, who shot you? Did you see?" Maddie asked.

Hadrich grinned, still looking to the side of them. "I'd hoped it would be Belthre'gar himself, but it wasn't."

"Was it a Broho?"

"I don't know," he said, irritation sharpening his voice. "More like a foreigner—a big fellow, head again taller than those around him. And bald, save for a long black braid coming off the top of his head. And a golden breastplate. He stood afar off with his long black bow and shot his arrow at me. I felt it hit, but low as it was and off to the side, I figured it had just gone through and done little damage. Until that night when I collapsed." He stopped to catch his breath.

Lavek took up the tale. "By then we had no idea where to look for the fallen shaft."

"Even if the field *had* been ours by then," Hadrich muttered. "At least that *speylcur* Belthre'gar won't be able to make me watch him slay my children." He breathed out a long sigh. "Just wish I could've seen my grand-sons before I went."

"Oh, Papa, don't talk like that. I have a friend, more skilled than I. He'll know what to do. You rest and I'll be back later with the boys."

"Yes. The boys," he murmured, his hands loosening their grip on the sheet, his face slackening. "Have to see the boys. Before I die . . ."

She frowned but did not correct him this time, for he had already fallen asleep. Besides, she no longer had the heart for it. The way the mass had repelled her Light filled her with dread. It had him. It was probable that only his own use of the Light against the thing would save him. And he lacked the skill and strength.

Still, she wouldn't give up. Before even leaving his chambers she sent a rider to Ang's Tavern with a summons for Trap.

The meeting of the Kiriathan exiles at Arvill Ang's Tavern, convened by Oswain Nott at eleven in the morning and running through the afternoon, involved a good deal of shouting and arguing, with everyone offering his opinion, as they had for a month now, on what was to be done regarding the survival of Abramm's sons and their duty to retake Kiriath.

Though Thornycroft's tenuous rumor of Abramm's alleged rescue had been thoroughly debunked by now, there remained the concern Maddie might remarry a Chesedhan, which many viewed as intolerable. The boys belonged to Kiriath, not some Chesedhan nobleman—and certainly not some Sorite heathen. They seemed to have forgotten that the boys were Chesedhan as much as Kiriathan. Or perhaps they didn't care. They had a legitimate heir to the Kiriathan throne, and now their planning could begin in earnest.

Trap listened with guarded skepticism, less concerned that the boys should ascend to the throne than that they lived to reach adulthood. Indeed, he found he didn't much care what happened to his homeland any longer. He wanted only to see Simon and Ian safe and happy.

Nott and the others made strong declarations that, as Abramm's son and the rightful king of Kiriath, little Simon must be properly groomed for his destiny, and that such grooming could only be accomplished by a Kiriathan. Darnley was the one who suggested the idea of foster parents, with Kiriath's former First Minister and his wife being the perfect candidates. Trap could even serve as regent.

"We have the power to determine that right here," said Nott.

When they got around to asking Trap what he thought about it all, he told them flatly that he would not take them from their mother, as Abramm would never countenance such an action and it was to Abramm that Trap was sworn, not Simon.

Nott snorted. "Abramm is dead. You can't hold an oath to a dead man."

Hamilton protested, and the argument veered off on the tangent of whether or not an oath made to a dead man need be kept. Eventually, they got back to Trap, whereupon Darnley offered additional support for his suggestion: "Queen Madeleine has no power in Chesedh. Her first loyalty will be to her blood family and then, if it ends up that way, to her new husband. You, however, as you have just stated, are Abramm's sworn liegeman. Regardless of these others, you believe such oaths are binding, and the very fact you've sworn to Abramm means you're bound to little Simon. I don't see it stops you from swearing liege to the boy, as well."

Aversion hardened in Trap. He'd sworn an oath to Abramm to protect his sons, and he would do so. But he would not swear an oath to the son. Not yet, anyway.

And why is that? he asked himself. Because deep down even after eight and a half months of silence, part of him hadn't accepted the fact his dearest friend was gone? On that day last month when Thornycroft had suggested Abramm lived, the realization of his own dividedness had taken Trap by storm. He still fought it—knowing with his mind what was true, waiting for his heart to believe it.

His refusal to go along with their plan launched another lengthy discussion. If Maddie remarried, might she agree to accept Trap as the boys' guardian? Could she even make such an agreement? Her father might not force her to go against her desires, but her father wouldn't live forever.

Everyone was arguing and proclaiming emphatically on this subject when Maddie's messenger appeared at Trap's side and whispered her summons in his ear. Cold with sudden dread, he left immediately, his departure unnoticed in the uproar. Outside he pressed the messenger for details, but the man had none to give.

Trap took his horse, clattering through the streets to the palace, where Maddie awaited him in her quarters, more distraught than he'd ever seen her. Words tumbled out of her willy-nilly, explaining the situation, hoping he would be able to heal the old man where she had not.

He shook his head. "I am no more skilled in the Light than you, madam." Actually he suspected he was less so. "If your Light had no effect—"

"I thought perhaps the two of us. Ronesca has brought in Minirth and a team of clerics. Along with the doctors . . ."

"I don't see what—"

"He is my father, Trap. And he's dying." She drew breath in that sounded more like a sob, and the look of utter desperation in her eyes caught at his heart.

He didn't know exactly how it happened, but somehow she came into his arms and he held her, awkwardly, as she cried upon his shoulder. It was too much for him to bear. He told her finally he would do what he could.

Thankfully she'd already pulled away and was wiping her tears when a servant burst into the room with the typical Chesedhan disregard for privacy.

"My lady, the crown princess bids you present yourself in His Majesty's quarters immediately. The king's had a seizure. Dr. Lavek says this is the end. He's asking for you and your sons. In fact, they're being brought to him now."

Maddie turned to Trap in horror, and they rushed from the room together, Trap ordering Channon to come with him as he took the lead. Hearing little Ian's screaming while they were still crossing the courtyard below the Royal Apartments, he took the steps two at a time and caught up with the guards as they were heading into the king's chambers. Ian saw him and reached toward him over the shoulder of the man who carried him, his screaming escalating to ear-piercing pitch.

In moments Ian was safe in Trap's arms, clinging fiercely to his neck, his terrified screams subsiding to more modulated sobs. As Maddie jogged up the stair into view, Simon pulled free of his own escort and ran to her.

Through the apartment door, an old man shouted for Leyton to attend him, despite the fact the crown prince was, as far as Trap knew, still in Peregris, commanding the army.

The doorman looked simultaneously relieved and worried as they approached. "It's good you're here, Highness. He's getting more agitated by the moment!"

"Where is Madeleine?" Hadrich roared from within. "Where are my grandsons? I want them here now."

A woman's voice sounded in soothing response, her syllables too faint to be distinguished as words.

Maddie stepped around the doorman, holding Simon's hand, and hurried through the arched opening into the darkened bedchamber beyond. Trap followed, carrying Ian, the boy's face buried in his chest.

He had known the king was ill, but nothing could have prepared him for the scene that met his eyes. Princess Ronesca had preceded them and stood ar her father-in-law's bedside, High Kohal Minirth and his clerics lurking in the shadows behind her. Her two grown sons stood in their dress uniforms at the foot of the king's bed, with First Minister Garival in his gold-edged robes of state beside them.

The old man himself lay propped on a pile of pillows, shriveled and gray in the light of the banks of candles on the bedside tables. His sharp, restive eyes flicked to Maddie as she entered, and the raspy voice said with startling strength, "What have you been doing, girl? Didn't they tell you I'm dying?" His gaze fixed next upon Ronesca. "Leyton is still not here?"

"He is in Peregris, Sire."

"He told me he would be following me on the road." The fierce eyes darted to little Simon, still at Maddie's side. "This is your firstborn?"

Maddie edged toward her father, pushing Simon ahead of her. The boy moved unwillingly, back pressed against her skirts. "Yes, Papa. This is Simon." And to her son, "Simon, say hello to your grandpapa."

In Trap's arms, Ian hitched around to watch his brother. Simon looked at the floor and murmured a hesitant hello.

Hadrich frowned. "Is that any way for a crown prince to speak?!" he boomed. "Show some poise, lad! And some manners. Stand straight and look me in the eye when you speak to me!" He glared at Maddie. "Have you taught them *nothing*?!"

Ian pressed his face against Trap's lapel again and whimpered, both movement and sound drawing the old man's attention. His scowl deepened. "That is the younger one? Mewling like a babe and needing to be carried?" He turned his gaze back to his daughter. "What sort of spineless worms are you raising here?"

Ian must have understood, for the whimpering became outright crying, which only irked the old king more. He grimaced fiercely and bared long yellow teeth as his arm waved at Ian. "Stop that crying at once, sir. I'll hear no more of it."

The sudden deepening of the darkness in his eyes sent a chill up Trap's spine, as all the uneasiness he'd felt upon entering crystallized into outright alarm.

The skinny arm waved. "Bring him here. I'll straighten him out."

Ian wailed in terror as Ronesca turned to Trap and hissed, "Get him out of here!"

Trap was already pulling the boy's arms from his neck. He passed him off to Channon, who wheeled for the door. Seeing them leaving, Hadrich lurched up in the bed with a great shriek of *"NO!"* and everything went to chaos.

The king's eyes and mouth turned black, only emptiness where once had been tongue and teeth and lips. The shadow flowed out of his side, a great bloom of darkness soaking the covering sheet beneath his hand as a ragged stream of inky liquid spread down toward the hem and dripped onto the floor.

Trap had never seen anything like it, but its cold malevolence was unmistakable. Yelling at Channon to *"Go! Go!"* he threw himself at Simon, who had pulled back from Maddie to stare down at the oily liquid rising toward his shoe tops. Trap swooped the boy up into his arms as Ronesca screamed and Maddie stared dumbly at her father. The old man's eyes and nose and ears and mouth all ran with the black oil that by then had eaten a hole through sheet and bandage, bubbling up from the wound in his side.

As Simon's arms tightened around his neck and the darkness rose around them, impossibly fast and cold, Trap caught Maddie's arm and jerked her backward.

"They must die," the ancient voice boomed. "They must all die! There can be none left."

He did not know who spoke. It seemed like Hadrich, and yet . . . it did not.

He sought for Eidon, and the white light exploded in his mind, blinding him, driving off the darkness. When it faded he stood with Simon still in his arms, Maddie hugged to his side, and Ronesca clinging to all three of them. They stared at the king, who had fallen back onto his bed. His eyes and mouth were normal again, save that his mouth lolled open and the eyes stared blindly at the ceiling. The black oil had vanished, leaving the sheets gray-stained and riddled with holes.

Lavek sprang to the king's side, searching for pulse or breath. Before he could voice his pronouncement, however, Maddie said quietly, "He's dead."

Ronesca moaned, stepping away from them and shaking her head even when the physician agreed. "He's gone." He stared at her, swallowed once, then went to one knee and bowed his head. "My queen."

A moment after him, the others in the room followed his lead, including Maddie, and finally Trap, still holding Simon.

"Please, get up," Ronesca said, shaking her head at the doctor. "You must be mistaken."

"I am not, madam. He is gone. You are queen."

She wrung her hands, looking from one of them to the other, her face pale and sweat-sheened, her dress blotched with the spore's gray stains. Then her eyes rolled back into her head and she collapsed. At the same moment, Maddie put her hands to her swollen womb with a cry. She looked at Trap in surprise, and her face whitened as she bent over, cradling her distended belly with both hands as she gasped, "No! It's not time yet. It's not time!"

12

"She's out there again, isn't she?" Rolland's quiet statement carried in the wind's lull.

Abramm straightened from where he had just pounded the pivot pin through the knuckles of the barn door's bottom hinge and looked up at his companion. Light from the kelistar lantern hanging on the stone wall beside the gate illumined Rolland's face, his beard and mustache coated with ice. His heavy brow cast his eyes into shadow, but it seemed he was looking down the twilight-filled valley. "You see them?" Abramm asked.

Rolland nodded. "Standing on that knoll out there. She and her offspring, looks like—though I can't make out how many."

"Seven," Abramm said. "Like before."

Rolland shook his head. "Discomforts me how ye can see in the dark like that."

Abramm had felt their approach an hour ago, when he and Rolland had come out here to fix the sheep barn door, torn off its hinges by last week's storm. The light was beginning to fail then, and now, barely four o'clock in the afternoon, night was nearly upon them.

Even so, Abramm saw them as clearly as if it were day: dark, shaggy, hump-shouldered forms standing on the snow-covered knoll on the near side of the stream. The monastery walls were still plenty high to keep them out, even with all the snow, but that wouldn't matter if someone opened one of the outside gates for them. . . .

"I thought Laud said the villagers wouldn't return again until spring," Rolland muttered.

"He did."

The wind kicked up again, whipping at Abramm's fur-lined hood as it carried his breath away in a long feather of white. With mittened hand he knocked away the ice clots from his mustache, then gestured at the top hinge. "You got that set?"

Rolland nodded.

"Let's try it, then." He stepped back and kicked away the block of wood they'd used to support the door's end, and the wooden planking swung back, banging against the frame. Abramm worked it back and forth. "Looks good."

He glanced up as the tanniym howled, and darkness flowed across his vision like a curtain of black oil. It brought with it a deep, breath-seizing, irrational fear for Maddie. He stood rigidly, shivering as the tanniym's howl coursed over his skin. Then it ended and his sight returned, the seven tanniym watching him from the knoll as the hairs on the back of his neck stood upright.

Maddie was in grave danger. Right now. But how could he help her, trapped in this icy prison? Unless he'd been deceived. Maybe there really was an easy way down. Maybe the villagers knew. . . . Maybe—

"Ye alright, friend?" Rolland's voice tore through the web of maybes. Abramm looked at him blankly.

"She was talking t' ye again, wasn't she?" the blacksmith guessed.

"No." Abramm's eyes drifted back to the dark shapes on the knoll. "It was more a feeling." Abruptly he scanned the night sky, fearing the dragon's return, as beside him Rolland did likewise. But the expanse of starry heavens held nothing unusual.

"A feeling," Rolland said.

"Maddie's in danger."

"Maddie? That your wife's name?"

"Aye . . ." Another rise of wind whistled around them, making the gate shudder. Inside the barn, the sheep baaed nervously. Abramm wiped at the ice clots stuck to his mustache again. The fear returned like an incoming tide. She was in danger. The boys, too. He needed to go to them. Maybe one of the villagers would be willing to take him south. . . .

"Ye sure she's not talkin' t' ye? 'Cause ye keep fadin' out on me, like ye're listenin' to something else."

Again, Abramm shook free of the spell, then bent to pick up his tools. "We'd best get on with the feeding."

But even inside the barn, out of the direct line of sight of his enemies, the sense of being watched remained. And the thoughts of Maddie's peril kept coming, anxiety thrumming in his belly.

The sheep continued to baa and mill restlessly, after they were fed, and Abramm wasn't sure whether they sensed his jumpiness or he sensed theirs. He kept hearing things—breathing, a voice—but every time he stopped there was nothing. Only the sounds of the sheep and the rustle of Rolland's pitching straw onto the floor. He noted, too, that the shadows looked especially dark, appearing to flow from place to place, like pools of pitch-black oil. And overhead, where they were the deepest, he glimpsed the glowing colors of several rhu'ema. Which distressed him even more, since it seemed the rhu'ema only came out to watch when something significant was about to happen.

Whatever it was, it didn't take place in the sheep barn. But when they stepped outside, though he could no longer see the tanniym, he felt them out there, waiting.

Terstmeet gave him an hour's respite, but soon after the meeting ended his anxiety returned. And again, it seemed to spread from him to the others. At supper everyone had been cheerful. Now they grew increasingly irritable. Arguments broke out, and the children kept crying—now this one, now that one . . . now the other—their shrill voices grating at Abramm's nerves. Then, around nine o'clock, Jania shrieked and leaped to her feet, both hands pressed to her swollen belly. And when Abramm saw the rush of water that darkened the carpeting beneath her feet, he went cold with sudden, profound terror.

The women hustled her off to a corner of the room—no one was willing to brave the dark corridors of the monastery tonight—while some of the men rigged a screen using ropes and blankets. But blankets couldn't block out her gasps and screams of pain, and these affected Abramm even more profoundly than the crying children. For he had heard Maddie's birth pangs with both Simon and Ian, and could not forget how often—and easily—women died in childbed. It was like that now, his concern as visceral and irrational. As if somehow it were not poor Jania who lay on that bed behind the screen but Maddie herself. He kept seeing her—and Simon, for some reason—swallowed up by a rising tide of blackness.

Finally the intensity of his anxiety was so great he could bear it no longer. "I'm going to the study," he told Rolland. The big man stared at him suspiciously.

"Do you think that's wise, Alaric?" Cedric asked, having overheard. "How do you know what you'll find there?"

"I'll find books, Cedric." Abramm smiled wanly. "I'm not going down to open the gate, if that's what you fear. But if you want to make sure of it, why don't you chain the doors leading out of the kitchen and keep the key in here under guard?"

As Abramm reached the door, Rolland was right behind him. "I'll come with you."

"What good's that gonna do?" Trinley growled. "Better ye both just stay here."

Rolland glanced over his shoulder at the alderman and was about to reply when Jania let loose with another shriek. Abramm flinched so violently he was sure Rolland saw it, even if no one else did. He didn't wait a moment more.

Rolland caught up with him in the anteroom. "You're white as a sheet, man. Didn't you say you have two children?"

"Aye."

"Did you almost lose her with one of them, then?"

"No. It was a hard birth, but they both came out of it fine. This is . . . I told you earlier I feared for her, and now it seems somehow it's her in there." He paused, frowning. "Or maybe not there, but somewhere else. Where I can't do a thing to help her."

"You couldn't do anything anyway, friend. Except pray." He paused, frowning. "Did you send her off to Chesedh with child, then?"

"No. Of course not. I—" His voice died as panic washed over him again. *Oh, my Lord Eidon . . . I didn't, did I?* That last night with her, though—and the four nights previous to it—could certainly have had such a result. How would he ever have known? Yes, the tanniym had told him she was with child, but he'd refused to believe that and had concentrated on not thinking about it at all. Now he counted back in his mind and realized with a growing horror that it was very close to nine months since they'd been together.

"Plagues!" he whispered. "It *is* possible. . . . But how could I know anything about her from here?" He knew the answer before he'd finished his sentence. The mysterious link that had always connected them, even before they'd become man and wife. It was a link through which he'd felt nothing for years now. Not since they'd been on the Gull Islands when she'd been kidnapped by the Esurhites. And been in danger.

His head swam. His stomach churned. For a moment he thought he might pass out.

Rolland clapped his shoulder. "Ye can't, friend," he said in answer to

Abramm's question. "So ye must give her over to Eidon, as ye have been all along." He gripped Abramm's upper arm, leading him toward the hallway. "Come on. It'll be easier out of earshot."

Abramm let himself be walked into the corridor and on to the study, which was deserted, Laud having gone to bed. Memorizing Old Tongue verb forms was not sufficiently distracting, however, and though Rolland was soon snoring in the hearth chair, Abramm could not follow his example. Every time he dozed off, a dark tide of terror rolled in to jerk him awake. Finally, as he snapped upright in the chair yet again, heart pounding in his throat, he heard a cry he could have sworn was Maddie's.

It had him out of the chair and across the room to the door before he caught himself. Where was he going? Back to the common room? The cry was certainly Jania's, and it didn't sound as if she'd had her baby yet. And since first deliveries were often lengthy, she might be crying out for hours yet.

He went back to his desk and his verbs. Moments later a vision of Maddie choking in darkness blotted out sight of his books and papers. When it vanished, he found himself standing in the hallway outside the study. Colored ribbons of light coiled near the ceiling, and a small blond boy stood directly ahead of him.

He frowned in disbelief. "Simon?"

The lad turned, his blue eyes widening as they fixed upon Abramm. "Papa?" Simon shook his head. "You can't be here. You're dead."

"No. I'm just stuck in the mountains waiting for the snow to melt." Abramm crouched down to look his son in the eye.

Simon nodded gravely, then said, "Grandpapa had blackness in him. It spilled on Mama and me."

"Blackness?"

But Simon was shrinking, pulling off into the distance until he was swallowed by the darkness at the hallway's end. The hairs on the back of Abramm's neck stood up. It must have been a dream. . . .

I need to wake up. . . . Blackness spilled on Mama?

He was walking again, trying to figure out what it could mean, even as he argued with himself that it meant nothing. Grandpapa had blackness in him? Hadrich was a Terstan. He could not have blackness in him. Unless it was spawn spore. He would have been in battle. He could have been injured.

I have to get to them. I have to—

He stopped dead, chilled to realize he stood in front of the outer gate, his hand on the bar. The wind rushed strongly outside, blustering and blowing

against the walls, whistling across the crenellations of the wallwalk overhead, rattling the gate beneath his hands. He jerked them away and staggered backward. "Pox!"

The need to go to his family pressed at him insistently. The observation that they weren't out there and this was a ploy to get him to open the gate changed nothing. He could even sense the tanniym waiting for him outside, yet some irrational part of him remained convinced that all he had to do was throw back that bar and wrench open the gate, and there his loved ones would be.

"No!" he cried, taking another step back. "You know it's a lie!"

His voice rang in the darkness, the sound giving strength to the words so he was able to force himself to turn away and stride back up the tunnel. He exited into the gate yard and stopped, his way blocked by a semicircle of five men. He recognized their leader at once.

"Trinley?" he grated. "What the plague are you all doing down here?"

"We'd ask the same o' you, Alaric," Trinley said. "Didn't ye tell us ye'd be in the study?"

A kelistar bloomed into the blackness, its clear light casting weird shadows up Oake's bearded face.

"I was in the study," said Abramm. Red, green, and blue ribbons of light undulated in the shadows around them, watching avidly.

"But now ye're down here, opening the gate."

"I didn't open the gate."

Trinley's brows, drawn down angrily, blazed in the kelistar's light. "Go back and close it, Alaric."

"I didn't open it."

"Fine, then, we'll go and see."

Turning, Abramm strode quickly back down the tunnel to the small gate, the others on his heels. Several strides away he stopped and conjured a star of his own. Its white light washed over the rough wooden portal, shivering and rattling against hinges and bar. "There. It's closed. Satisfied now?"

But Trinley only scowled the more. "Ye knew we were here, didn't ye? That's why ye turned away."

Abramm sighed wearily. "I think we should all go back to the common room."

"You lead," said Trinley.

Abramm returned them quickly to the Great Hall, but he'd barely entered the flagstone anteroom outside it when another of Jania's shrieks stopped him in his tracks. Her deep, rasping gasps grated like metal on slate. "I think I'll go up to my cell."

Trinley laughed outright. "I think ye won't."

"Lock me in, if it'll make you feel better. I can't go in there."

"Ye'd rather be locked in yer cell this night than be in there with the rest of us?" Trinley's voice was both incredulous and disapproving.

"With Jania still screaming like that?" Abramm nodded. "Aye."

Trinley exchanged glances with his companions. "Fine, then."

He sent Cedric to find chains and a lock while the rest of them escorted Abramm to his cell at the top of the stair. He entered it freely and shut the door behind him, the others muttering nervously among themselves outside. How it was poxed odd that Alaric would ask to be chained up in his own cell, that he'd want to be in the cell at all, and that he'd ever chosen to sleep up here in the first place. What was wrong with him, anyway? And did anyone notice how he'd recognized Trinley right off when they were standing in deep darkness?

Cedric's arrival with the lock and chain ended the gossip. As soon as the door was secured, they trooped back down the stairs, leaving Abramm to the wind and the tanniym's howling and the dark fear beating at his soul. For a time he paced restlessly, repeatedly confessing his fears and failure to trust, and seeking Eidon's help to overcome his weaknesses. When that did not work, and the visions of darkness sweeping wife and son away rose up to catch him, too, he dropped to his knees beside the cot and plunged himself into Eidon's Light, beseeching him to deliver his loved ones from whatever it was that held them.

The birth pangs were the most savage Maddie had ever known, as if some giant hand squeezed and pulled at her until she thought her insides would be torn out. How was it she always forgot this? It was the third time and yet was every bit as awful as it had ever been. Worse now, with the spore that had come out of her father, dark and virulently bitter, coursing through her veins. It had gone at once for the child in her womb, and she'd had no time to start a purge, instantly forming the light into a shield around the baby to keep out the dark. A shield inside her own body, not outside, something she'd never done before. Something that in the best of times would have taken all her concentration, yet here she was holding it together by a thread. The upheaval of her body as the contractions grew more and more powerful broke into her thoughts time and again, terror waiting at each interval to seize her. She heard Simon screaming somewhere, terrified and in pain, but she could not go to him, for she could not leave the little girl in her womb lest the darkness take her.

She had thought at first that the shield would be enough. Once stabilized she would let the Light flow out to purge her own body. But this spore was different. Mindful. It shrank back, waiting. Then attacked when she faltered. And too often the pain was so intense it commanded all her attention. Coils of light undulated in the shadows around her, and she sensed other beings watching avidly, hoping for her death. Hoping for the child's death.

No. Not hoping—waiting.

And all the while that horrid voice kept repeating over and over: *"You will all be taken. All . . . nothing of his can remain."*

Then, finally, a prodigious push, the fire of her flesh ripping to give the babe room, and the release of terrible pressure. She lay gasping, head swimming with the pain, blackness clouding her vision . . . and heard a cry. Someone held her daughter up for her to see, blond-haired, pink-skinned, bloody but crying lustily.

"Abrielle," she gasped. "Her name is Abrielle. After her father."

Thank Eidon. No blackness. The spore hadn't gotten to her child. Relief flooded Maddie in a great tingling wave. Then she felt a strange heaviness in her womb, a sudden flash and the sense of something tearing again where it should not be tearing. . . . And now someone was crying out at the foot of the bed about the blood. Too much blood.

She felt it pouring out of her . . . and realized suddenly that it was not the child the spore had been after but Maddie herself. It had congregated on the womb so she would think it wanted her baby, but it didn't. Couldn't have gotten through anyway, for all the water. . . . They just wanted her to think that so she would not defend herself, would not do the purge until it was too late.

"And now you are ours. All that was his must be taken—especially you."

"Why? Why must I be taken?"

She fell into deep darkness, into the nausea and dizziness brought on by the poison of the spore in her veins. Guilt and despair overwhelmed her. She would die now, and who would care for her children? Who would protect them? Why had she been so foolish? Why hadn't she guessed what it was doing?

She deserved to die, wanted to die. . . .

For now at last she would see Abramm.

She felt her life bleeding away, her body growing light and empty.

"*Soon,*" said a warm, friendly voice. "*Come to me, child. See your husband. who has died and waits for you with me.*"

It made no sense that she should mourn that statement. He was dead?

"*And never coming back to this mortal life. But you can come to him.*"

Yes. She could go to him. . . .

But then she heard her husband's voice, and it held her back. He was praying, and she sensed his spirit knit somehow with hers again. She felt his horror at what was happening to her, his anguish at the life fading swiftly now from her flesh, felt his deep, powerful love for her.

Why would he feel anguish if he knew she was coming to him?

Why was he praying?

Though it was like moving a millstone across the floor, she shifted her attention from the friendly voice to the deep, smooth tones of her husband and forced herself to hear the words:

"*Father, open her eyes. Tear away the veil her enemies have woven before them. Remind her of who she is and who you are. That nothing can stand against your might, that she has only to rest in that and stop her striving. Draw her out of this darkness, my Father; don't let them do this. Her children need her. Her realm needs her. And you know how much I need her. . . .*"

The meaning in his words registered slowly, tearing the veils of Shadow and spore from the eyes of her soul as she realized she had been deceived. The warm voice was not that of a friend at all. She didn't have to die. Nor did she want to. And Eidon's Light was right there, waiting for her to call upon it, stronger than any darkness, even this horrible spore. The moment of realization unleashed it.

Blinding, instant heat sizzled away the black oil that had stained both flesh and spirit, and a strong but gentle hand took hers. She looked up into Tersius's eyes. No reproach, no disappointment there at her gullibility. He always knew. He always accepted anyway. *Come, my daughter. I have something to give you.*

He led her up a short stair into a small white room where an even brighter window blazed in the wall at his back. She tried to see through the brightness, but it only blinded her. And when she looked back at him, she could hardly see him for its flashing afterimage.

Slowly she made him out again, smiling down at her, love personified. But as the light faded further, she saw it wasn't Tersius after all but her husband standing before her, holding her hands in his.

His thick blond hair fell about his shoulders, and his beard was long and full—scruffy looking, she'd have termed it once. It didn't diminish his appeal in the slightest. Those incredible blue eyes stared down at her from beneath his level brows, igniting fire in her chest. She ran her fingers down the twin scars on the left side of his face, then over to his lips.

"I'd forgotten how astonishingly handsome you are," she murmured.

He smiled at her, shaking his head as he stroked back her hair, then bent to kiss her. His lips were warm and soft, the length of his body hard against hers as he pressed her to him, the sensation so strong, so solid, she guessed she'd died and entered Eidon's eternal realm of Light after all. . . .

13

It had to be the eternal realm, for it was not like any dream she'd ever had—vivid, intimate, and lasting all night. Drifting in and out of sleep, she felt again and again the sheer delight of his body against hers, warm and strong, the familiar smell of it, the languid warmth of his arms around her, making her feel safe, secure, and loved as only he could.

As the light began to sift through the shuttered window above their cot, she saw her surroundings for the first time: a small, bare, stonewalled cell, with cobwebby wooden rafters and an endlessly blowing wind outside. Not what she'd expected. He shifted beside her and an icy draft chilled her shoulder. She rolled onto her back, not surprised to find him looking at her, propped up on one elbow as he lay beside her.

"I didn't expect Eidon's realm to be so cold," she said. "Or to have all this wind."

Abramm chuckled softly. "That's because we're not in Eidon's realm, my love. We're in Caerna'tha." He stroked the fall of her hair beside her face, then tucked it behind her ear. "Though how you got here I cannot imagine."

"Well, I suppose I've come by coach. . . ."

He lifted a dark brow. "Coach?"

"Lately, it's the only way I've been able to go anywhere since—" She broke off as a new thought struck her, one she was amazed she'd forgotten. "You have a daughter, sir."

"A daughter?"

"Born this very night."

The dark brow lifted again. "And after giving birth, you took a coach to Caerna'tha."

"I must have."

"You've not heard of Caerna'tha, I take it."

"I have, I just . . ."

"We're in the Aranaak, love. In the dead of winter. There's fifteen feet of snow on the ground. You couldn't have come by coach."

"Oh. Well . . . we must be dreaming, then."

"Yes." He smiled. "Though it would be very nice to have a daughter."

"Why are we in the Aranaak?"

"Well, *I'm* here because it's as far as I got before the winter set in. It takes a while when you have to walk everywhere. I guess from the remark about the coach, you've forgotten that. As for why *you're* here—"

The distant thunder of footfalls accompanied by voices broke into the wind-glazed silence. She looked round at the door, which had begun to rattle and clank. "What's that?"

"Oh, they're just unchaining the door."

"Unchaining the door?" She sat up, clutching the blanket to her chest. "You're a prisoner here?"

"No. I suggested it." He sat up behind her, moved the curtain of her hair aside, and kissed the side of her neck. "You have no idea how good you smell. And feel . . ." His hands slid up her arms and she leaned back against him.

"We're just going to sit here? Without anything on? Even in a dream, Abramm—"

"We'll wake up before they see us."

"I don't—" She twisted round to face him, tears rising in her eyes. "Oh, my love, I don't want to wake up."

"You must."

"I don't want to leave you. I don't want to be without you." He silenced her with his mouth. When he pulled away again, she was breathless. And the chain was rattling off whatever loop of metal had held it.

He dropped his forehead against hers. "You have Eidon always and first," he said. "As soon as the passes are clear, I'll come to you."

"Do you even have the power to make that promise?"

"No. But Eidon does. And he has promised me. Wait. I will come."

He kissed her again, a quick, hungry embrace before the door banged open. She turned to it with a gasp, only to find it wasn't a door anymore but a window looking out across a wide, snow-filled valley. She glimpsed ragged, snow-clad peaks looming above it all just before the sun broke through one of the passes and blazed into her eyes, blinding her with its brilliance.

Trap paced back and forth across the green-and-gold carpeting of the First Daughter's sitting chamber. Shale Channon sat on the chair before the fireplace, keeping watch over Simon and Ian asleep on quilted pallets beside him, while over in the corner little Abrielle cried in the cradle where Channon had just placed her. He said she'd been crying ever since Carissa had brought her from the birthing chamber—actually the First Daughter's bedchamber—and thrust her into his arms. *"Her name is Abrielle. Keep her safe,"* she'd said before fleeing back to Maddie and closing the door. But not before Channon had heard the other women's alarmed voices talking about too much blood.

That had been hours ago. Trap, who'd been occupied with his own battles drawing the spore out of little Simon and instituting a purge for both of them, had awakened shortly after Carissa had brought in Abrielle, sometime in the middle of the night. Now the sky was beginning to lighten, yet still no one emerged from Maddie's chamber, and the last sight he'd had of her had been frightening. Lying there on the stretcher, she'd writhed and screamed, turning slowly gray as the dark spore rushed through her body. The child, Abrielle, appeared untainted by it, but Maddie must still be fighting it.

A distant wailing arose from out in the courtyard: a lament for the king's passing. Hadrich's body still lay on his bed, where his personal servants would mourn him with appropriate wailing for several more hours yet. And someone somewhere was playing a dirge on a Chesedhan bladderpipe. He supposed workers had been all night procuring and preparing the marble slab that would sit in the main entrance antechamber of the palace for the next week.

Meanwhile, Ronesca fought her own battles in her own chamber. Channon said the Great Kohal himself, Minirth, and an army of his underlings were ministering to her, the crown princess who was now queen.

He shuddered to think of all that had happened in the last day. How the king of Chesedh had been killed and had nearly taken his daughter, her three children, his daughter-in-law, and her sons with him. Nearly all the contenders for the Chesedhan crown. Or, seen another way . . . all of Abramm's children and his wife. It was, he knew, the product of no human machination but of something far greater and more malevolent.

"Why does she keep screaming like that?" he burst out.

"She wants her mama, I'd say," said Channon. "Probably hungry."

Then, why don't they come and get her? But he did not voice the question, for the answer was too horrifying to contemplate.

And little Abrielle—his heart had turned over when he'd heard her name, when he'd seen her little face—was fair as the boys, with the same blue eyes and long thin body. No jailer's dark-pelted child, that was sure.

As the day wore on, he began to think what would happen to them all if Maddie died. For her, it would be a release and a glorious reunion. She would be with Abramm. But she would leave three children orphaned in a realm that already saw them as a threat. Children whose grandfather had just died in a hideous manner and whose uncle's concern for them was questionable. At best.

He stopped pacing and stood still, eyes shut, seeking to master the rush of grief that threatened to sweep him into an abyss from which he wasn't certain he would escape. Bad enough to lose Abramm—even now he struggled to believe it was so. Even now he found himself asking himself what Abramm would think about their situation or what he would do when he returned . . . only to recall there would be no return.

He drew a deep breath and let it out. The tightness in his throat eased. He drew another and exhaled again.

Then abruptly he went to the bassinette and picked up the infant, whose faint, reedy cry was driving him crazy. He cradled the tiny girl to his chest and continued to pace, more slowly now.

Shortly thereafter a new girl came into the room, stopped, looked around at all of them, then came toward him to drop a tentative curtsey. "I've come for the babe," she said.

He frowned in suspicion. "Why?"

"Lady Iolande said the princess would be needing a wet nurse, sir."

"And you are that?"

"Aye, sir."

"What happened to your own child?"

"Died, sir. Two days ago."

"Died of what?"

She looked up at him, dark eyes wide. "A fall, sir."

· Maddie, he knew, had made no such arrangement because she preferred to nurse her own children, as was the custom in Kiriath. She'd do the same with Abrielle. If she lived. If her milk was not tainted. So what should he say to this poor, poor girl, already eying the babe in his arms with a disconcerting hunger?

The door opened and Carissa stepped out. Seeing the girl, she frowned and came to Trap's side. "Who is this?"

When he told her, her frown deepened. "I'm sorry," she told girl. "There was a mistake. We won't be needing you."

Though the girl looked crestfallen to the point of tears, she bobbed a curtsey and left without a word.

Trap turned to his wife. Her face was pale and haggard, dark circles of her sleepless night cupping her eyes. She smiled gently and touched his hand where he cradled Abrielle. "She's awake. And she's well. More than well, actually. The Light came upon her around midnight. It just lifted."

"It's been on her all night and you didn't tell us?" He made no attempt to hide his outrage.

"I'm sorry," she cried, obviously chagrinned. "I didn't think . . . You were asleep when I came out the first time."

"And you thought I would sleep all night?"

She looked as distressed as the poor spurned nursemaid, but he couldn't seem to corral his anger. "Can I see her now?"

"Yes. She's asking for you, in fact."

Maddie was indeed awake. She sat against a mountain of white pillows, looking weak and tired but healthy. More than healthy: she glowed. He breathed a prayer of thanks and crossed the room to present her with her daughter.

For the first time in hours, Abrielle fell quiet, the two of them staring at each other, tears welling up in the mother's eyes. Maddie stroked the fair hair and fingered the tiny hand, then looked up at Trap. "I need to feed her. Do you mind?"

"Not at all, Highness." He started to leave.

"No. I meant just turn your back for a moment. I . . . need to know what happened."

Who survived? she meant. He glanced at Carissa, who had come in with him and now watched the preparations going on behind his back. "Ian is fine. A bit shook up, but overall the spore didn't get to him. Simon is well, too."

"But he was closer than I was, and has no shield—"

"Nevertheless . . ." He trailed off, listening to the rustle of linens and noting Elayne now, standing quietly by the door.

"You can turn around," Maddie said. "We're covered."

When he turned back she was looking at him very seriously, her gray-blue eyes wide, her fawn-colored hair flowing around her shoulders like a cloak.

"You saved him, didn't you? Purged him of it."

"I did, my lady. He is resting, but truly he is fine."

"And my father?"

He drew a deep breath and released it. "With Eidon now, Your Highness."

Her grief was sharp and swift but not surprised. "Yes. That was how I remembered it. . . . And is the dirge for him alone?"

"It is. Though the queen . . ." His voice faltered a bit on that word and he saw Maddie flinch. "The queen still struggles with the spore." He paused. "They sent a wet nurse up."

"I hope you sent her away."

"Carissa did."

She nodded. "Tell me about the spore."

And so he told her what he had gleaned—that it was virulent, unknown, powerful, and also strangely knowing. "I don't know any other way to put it. It links with the Shadow within and goes for all your worst fears and doubts . . . almost like another mind taking over. . . . And it residualized fast. I'm going to be fighting with it for months, most likely. I suspect you will be, too."

"Oh . . . I don't know . . ." She got a funny little smile on her face, then peeked beneath the blanket with which she had covered Abrielle. "I guess she wore herself out with all the crying."

She sat there awhile, staring at her daughter almost without seeing her, that dreamy smile curving her lips. When finally she looked up, she was still smiling, but incongruously, tears glittered in her eyes. She held out her hand to him and, when he took it, squeezed it in her own, the tears spilling down her cheeks. "I don't know any other way to tell you this than to just come out with it," she murmured. "Abramm's alive, Trap. I've seen him. All last night. He's come through the Aranaak and is snowed in at Caerna'tha. But he's alive and he's coming just as soon as he can."

He stared at her, rocked to his toes by an emotion he could not identify— save that it was closer to shock and horror than to joy.

CHENA'AG TOR

PART TWO

CHAPTER

14

Simon Kalladorne, former Duke of Waverlan and uncle to King Makepeace, stood with his friend Seth Harker in the spectator-packed square on the King's Avenue in Springerlan. It was midday, and all awaited the advent of their newly crowned king on this, the first anniversary of Abramm's supposed execution. Simon had no doubt the correlation was deliberate. At least on the Mataio's part. Gillard had wanted his official coronation to occur six months earlier, but Mataian leaders had demurred. A new crown had to be made after the original had gone missing—popular theory held that Madeleine had stolen it when she'd left the palace and entrusted it to servants who'd not been caught. The new crown was to be forged in the Holy Flames themselves and could not be made until the Keep was repaired of the damages it had suffered during the Purge. Thus the Mataian leaders were able to make sure the process took as long as they desired.

Simon wondered at the wisdom of scheduling the new king's coronation on the anniversary of the former king's death. He knew he wasn't the only person to make the connection, and that meant people were remembering what the Mataians had worked so hard to make them forget: that not so long ago they'd had another king, a better one by far than the one they had now, and they'd rejected him.

Perhaps the Mataians hoped the new event would obliterate the old in people's memory, but with the level of oppression suffered by anyone who dared to challenge the majority viewpoint these days, he wasn't so sure. Abramm's name might have vanished from public discourse, but the Underground had made sure it was far from forgotten. Like today, for example.

In the wee hours of last night, Simon had joined two dozen others hurrying among the spectators camped along the king's route, some staging distractions on one side of the road while their counterparts swiftly painted a stylized version of Abramm's coat of arms on the other—two swipes of the broad flat brush with the yellow paint for the shield and a squiggle of red with the small round for the dragon rampant. It took no more than thirty seconds to complete, and they'd put the device on stone walls, pillars, wooden sidings—anything upright. It didn't even have to be visible from the route itself. They weren't for Gillard or for the Mataians to see, but for the people. And the people had seen them.

It amazed him that none of them had been caught. Seth said it was Eidon protecting them, but Simon thought it more likely that more people secretly agreed with what they stood for than would publicly admit.

The marks were found at first light, and immediately Mataian lackeys hurried to paint over them. But Simon's Terstan friends had done something to the paint so that the Mataians' newly applied pigment refused to stick, leaving the shield-and-dragon devices more eye-catching than ever. Scraping worked best, which they'd eventually figured out, in addition to covering them with panels leaned against the wall, or guards repositioned, or even banners hailing the new king, reslung—lower and out of sight—to hide the offending marks.

Now at midday, Simon and Seth had taken a position several ranks back from the gauntlet down which the king would ride, close enough to see, not so close they might be recognized. Seth was not happy the older Kalladorne had insisted on coming out today, but Simon was determined to see his nephew with his own eyes—the first time in seven years.

Gillard—or Makepeace as he was now known, though Simon refused to call him that—would be coming up from the square's lower southeastern end, hidden now behind the heavy fog that veiled this momentous day. It also hid the ruins of Southdock—burned to the ground during the Purge and never rebuilt—and the bay beyond it, where sailing ships stood becalmed by too many windless months, and smaller oar-powered vessels were the norm.

Behind him a man said, "Can you believe there are still people who would put up his device?" He meant Abramm's device, of course, but dared not speak his name. "What do they think they're accomplishing?"

"They're just stubborn old fools who can't abide the loss of their power," the man's companion grumbled. "Still living in the past."

"We need another purge."

Simon scowled at the people-clogged buildings across from him where figures perched on the roofs and hung out the windows, many of the latter with banners slung between them. Maybe he had overestimated the numbers who supported his viewpoint.

Sometimes the sense of loss and hopelessness gripped him with such strength it all but disemboweled him. It broke his heart to stand amidst all these people, knowing how few of them saw their loss, how few even wanted the better man back. They boasted in the streets of how their purity had delivered them, for the Esurhites still had not approached them. No emissaries, no galley ships. Nothing. It was as if Kiriath did not exist. Maybe, some suggested, they'd be entirely ignored, the Armies of the Black Moon realizing they could never prevail against the Holy Flames of Eidon.

If Abramm came back now, Simon wasn't sure what kind of reception he'd get. Maybe it would be best to simply abandon Kiriath and head over to Chesedh, where they at least had armies engaged in fighting those of the Black Moon. Here it was all purity and sacrifice and trusting the Flames to protect. Here the tyranny was almost as bad as what Belthre'gar would dole out.

A deep susurrus crept in under the mutter of conversation, gradually growing louder until he realized it was the roar of the spectators lining the streets down the hill. Immediately his gut tightened, his mouth went dry, and his heartbeat accelerated. He'd last seen his nephew when Gillard had been imprisoned in the Chancellor's Tower, a shrunken waif buried in the bed linens, his flaxen hair and beard grown long with months of inattention.

Thanks to "Eidon," he had supposedly overcome the effects of the morwhol's spell and regained his former stature, though it came at the price of a strange bone malady that caused him constant pain and had led to an overdependence on laudanum.

The roar swelled around Simon, as the first pair of the king's six flag bearers appeared, riding abreast on black horses. The king appeared next, astride a gray horse—not Abramm's Warbanner, though, thanks to Simon himself, who'd seen the horse spirited out of the realm lest Gillard get his hands on him.

As for Gillard, the tales were true: He was, indeed, big again, as broad-shouldered and powerful-looking as ever, even with that pale womanish hair frothing about his shoulders. He wore the gray robes of his Guardian-King station now, and beneath the rubies and diamonds flashing from his newly-made crown, the gold still glowed with the scarlet of the Holy Flames that had birthed it.

Up the gauntlet he came, waving to the crowd on this side and that, astonishing Simon with his size. Was it truly magic? How could he have submitted to such a thing? Closer now, he looked pale and inexplicably fragile—perhaps a result of his bone malady.

Suddenly the king's pale blue eyes looked right into Simon's own. Their gazes held just long enough to send a flood of panicked heat through Simon's body, and then Gillard's focus tracked on across the crowd and over to the other side of the road as all the while he waved. Simon was shaken enough to pull up his cowl, and none too soon, as the king looked back over his shoulder, scanning the crowd again, this time with intent. Simon turned his face toward the Mataians who were coming up the road in Gillard's wake: High Father Bonafil, Master Eudace, and Master Belmir—the latter living a dangerous double life these days.

From the corner of his eye Simon saw his nephew return to his rote acknowledgment of the people's acclaim as he rode on.

Having seen what he'd come for, Simon edged back out of the crowd. As he and Seth headed down a nearby alley toward their bolthole, he muttered, "I can't believe he *likes* being a Mataian toady. Whoever would have thought he'd come to this."

They reached the stable, and Seth opened the door. They slipped inside, the fragrance of horse and straw filling the air. Once their eyes adjusted to the gloom and they were certain they were alone, Seth nodded. Simon stooped to pull up the loop on the trapdoor, revealing a ladder descending into darkness. Seth dropped in first and Simon followed, pulling the trapdoor shut in their wake as the pale white light of a kelistar illumined the rocky walls beside their shoulders.

Neither spoke as they trod the narrow passage, staffid skittering continuously before them, fleeing the light. Only when they had slipped inside a small chamber some ways along it and closed the heavy door behind them did Seth speak again. "I believe a rhu'ema lives in him." He set the kelistar on a tin starstick and went to rummage through a trunk in the back of the room. "That doesn't happen accidentally," he added. "He had to invite it in."

"To get his size back," Simon guessed.

Seth pulled a canvas bag from the trunk and straightened. "Most likely." He handed the bag to Simon and went back to the trunk. "The bad part is, it's only an illusion."

"An illusion!"

"Laid over the top of what he really is."

"How do you know that?"

"I saw it. Just now." Seth pulled a long cylindrical bag from the box. "I have to admit it's hard to imagine selling oneself into bondage just for the sake of making others think you're bigger than you are. He handed over the second bag. "That should be it. You know where to go."

Simon nodded.

"The others'll be waiting for you. Watch yourself at the Barrie Street intersection. They've been monitoring that lately. You might want to avoid it altogether." He paused, then asked quietly, "Have you heard from him yet?"

He meant Abramm. Simon shook his head.

"The storms *were* awfully bad in the mountains this year," Seth remarked grimly. "He probably got snowed in."

"Aye." Ironically there had been no storms at all in Springerlan, just the endless fog. And now the rising river—flooded, thanks to the unusual volume of snowmelt coming out of the Chesedhan Aranaak. "He said he'd send word once he reached Fannath Rill," Simon added. "With the passes clearing it shouldn't be long now."

"If he doesn't—"

"I know," said Simon. Hopelessness pressed down on him again. With no hope of Abramm returning to beat back the tide of tyranny that oppressed them all . . . what was the point of fighting on? Why risk all for something that would never happen?

———

Abramm's time with Maddie had been a turning point. The blessing of being in her presence was incredible, but it had been more than that. It had been the answer to his prayers for her safety and the reassurance that he would see her again, and that, despite the mysterious bowman's message, she had *not* forgotten him. Even better, she knew he was alive now and would wait. He had no idea if their time together was real or not, but the morning after, the scent of her had clung to his bedding and even his hands.

It had filled him with elation and bolstered his confidence that Eidon was indeed preparing him—for between that, the dragon's visit, and what he'd read in Laud's little gray book, he was convinced the rhu'ema here not only knew him, they feared him. And if they couldn't kill him, they wanted him to stay in Caerna'tha for good. Should he attempt to leave once the snow cleared, they would try to prevent it.

Good. They should fear him, for Eidon was with him and would never abandon him, and their power couldn't even come close to his.

After that he'd thrown himself into his studies with as much vigor as he poured into the menial labors that life at the monastery required of him. For both, he realized, finally, were part of his preparation, and he wanted to be a fit instrument in Eidon's hands when the time came. The next three months flew by, and before he knew it, the time came to leave. Still early in the season, yes, but time, nonetheless.

"Today's the anniversary of King Abramm's death," Rolland said quietly from where he worked at Abramm's side, parceling out bags of mutton jerky. "I expect you knew that."

Abramm tied the strap tight on the bundle he'd just finished packing and straightened, looking at the big blacksmith in surprise. "Aye, I did know."

"I wish we could've left today," Rolland said. "'Twould've made it all more . . ." He trailed off, groping for the word. "More right-seeming, I guess."

Abramm turned his gaze across the bustling hall to the bags of flour and jerky and wheels of cheese. Rolland had no idea. In fact, to Abramm's way of thinking, leaving the day after the anniversary of his "death" was even more significant, for it marked a new year, a new life. . . . At last he was moving again.

You need to tell Laud the truth. He frowned as the nagging thought surfaced yet again. The notion had come to him last night as he'd lain on his cot contemplating the tasks he'd been assigned for the coming day, the last day most of them would spend in Caerna'tha. He'd put it aside as a crazy notion. If Laud hadn't figured out who he was by now, no words were going to change that. And yet, first thing this morning, it had returned: *You need to tell Laud the truth.*

Again he'd set it aside, and again it had returned—during breakfast, during their morning's preparation, again at dinner. Nagging him as persistently as the notion to leave had nagged him when he'd first learned there was an alternate route down the Ankrill Canyon—a high, narrow, little-used trail that snaked along the northeastern canyon wall, exposed to the sun all day at this time of year and thus largely clear of ice and snow.

Professor Laud had mentioned it almost idly one night two weeks ago, never dreaming someone might actually want to travel on it. But the moment Abramm had learned of it, he'd known this was to be his route down the mountain, and furthermore that he was to leave before the Ankrill started to melt. And he'd not wavered once, not even when the community at Caerna'tha had convulsed with alarm and distress when they discovered his intentions. Nor when first Rolland declared that he and his family would come, then Cedric and Totten, and one by one, all the rest of those in the original group, including Oakes Trinley.

Abramm had received them all with as much grace as he could muster— probably not enough, given his chagrin—but accepting that part of Eidon's plan had been easy compared to this persistent request. *Tell him the truth.*

What am I supposed to do? he asked. *Just blurt it out? Why should he believe me now, when the obvious truth has been staring him in the face for the last six months?* Abramm still nursed a bit of annoyance that after all this time no one had guessed the truth about him. Not even Rolland, who had known him before, when he had been king. . . . And why did Laud need to know now, anyway? He wasn't even going with them.

Tell him the truth, Abramm.

Oh, very well. But you're going to have to make me an opening. And it's going to have to be obvious.

About then Trinley and a handful of others came in with the tenting and bedrolls they'd been preparing for the journey, and Cedric arrived with a load of snowshoes, which they would need at least to get down the length of the valley and possibly later, depending on how the trail went. Laud knew little of it, beyond the fact that it existed. In the six years he'd been at Caerna'tha, no one he knew of had taken it, and even Wolmer, who'd been here longest— thirteen years—knew of no one.

Though Abramm had taken Rolland and Cedric on a day-trip down to where the stream flowed into the Ruk Ankrill—still frozen and easily cross-able—and together they'd walked up the first mile or so of the narrow trail, it told them little of what lay ahead. Bridges could be out, parts of the trail could have washed away or been lost as slabs of rock peeled away from the cliff face as a natural part of weathering. The path might even cross back over the river and join with the wider, flatter path—still hidden under six feet of snow—on the southwestern bank.

So they'd take the snowshoes just to be prepared.

They were going through the various sizes, finding the right bindings and adjusting the fit, when Marta Brackleford came through, handing out the scarves and mittens she'd knitted over the winter. When she pressed the soft wool into Abramm's hands, she said, "The professor would like to speak with you. Whenever you can break free of your preparations."

And Abramm felt a chill of portent. *You're going to have to make me a way*.

Well, merely having audience with the man was hardly a way. He'd have to have a conversational opening, and the words to put into it. And Laud obviously had other things on his mind.

"Did he say what about?"

She shook her head.

And so Abramm stalled—getting his boots and bindings in order, inspecting his water bags, and bringing a load of wood up to the kitchen. By then, though, he knew he could put it off no longer, unless he intended to avoid the man altogether before he left, and that he would not do. He owed Laud far too much for that.

As he came up the corridor to the study, he heard a man speaking from within it. Not Laud, but someone else. Someone familiar . . . In fact, it sounded like Everitt Kesrin, who had been his kohal in Springerlan. His pace quickened, and as he jogged up the wooden stair, his certainty increased along with sudden excitement. It was definitely Kesrin! But how had he gotten to Caerna'tha? Surely not through the pass.

He stepped through the door and found Laud sitting alone in the room, a kelistar lying on the desk before him. Abramm stopped and looked all around, yet there was no one but Laud present. Seeing him, the professor flicked the kelistar out of existence.

"You're alone," Abramm said.

"Yes."

"But—"

Laud smiled. "I was listening to the stone." He gestured at the pale green lozenge-shaped stone that had been resting on the desk beneath the kelistar.

When Abramm frowned at him, he conjured a second kelistar and placed it atop the stone. Immediately the object turned white as a tracery of gold threads shivered across the kelistar's surface and a man's voice sounded in the hall—coming, it would seem, directly from the stone and star. It was definitely Kesrin.

"It's an Ophiran speaking stone," Laud said. "I found it here shortly after I arrived, and have used it off and on ever since."

"If it's Ophiran, why does it have Everitt Kesrin's voice?"

Laud's brows arched. "You know Kohal Kesrin?"

"Yes. He was my teacher in Springerlan."

"And mine," Laud confessed. "After I left Springerlan, I heard he went on to teach at the palace. Kohal to the king himself."

And here was a perfect opening, except Abramm could think of no words with which to exploit it.

"So why does an Ophiran stone—"

"I don't know. Nor do I know how the lessons are selected. I suppose it is Eidon who does that. Though I will say that for the last year all of them have been repeats." He paused, then added, "I suspect it means he's dead. . . . The way I understand it, the Gadrielites struck rapidly and in concert so as to catch their victims unsuspecting. Your kohal had to be one of the first taken."

"I have always hoped Eidon intervened."

The other man snorted. "He didn't intervene on the king's behalf; why would he intervene on behalf of his favorites?"

And again Abramm saw the opening, but as before, no words came.

Laud leaned back in his chair, eying Abramm speculatively. "You'll never win Kiriath back, you know. You'd do more good staying here, helping us, learning of Eidon, devoting your life to him."

"My life is already devoted to him."

"Not wholly. Not in the way it would be if you spent it studying." Laud paused. "You are a phenomenal student."

"I am not a kohal."

"I never meant to imply that you were. But you do have the potential to be an extraordinary scholar. Think of the secrets of knowledge you could unearth here. If you gave it enough time. Already you've mastered the Old Tongue—"

"Hardly mastered."

"Your progress has astonished me, frankly. It's a hard language to know."

"My destiny lies elsewhere, sir."

"You realize, of course, that your wife has had no idea if you are alive or dead for what? Months? More than a year?"

Oh, she knows. . . . Abramm suppressed a smile at the memories that thought inspired. Desire for her washed through him, sharp and eager now that it saw hope of being soon fulfilled. "I promised her I would join her—"

Laud snorted. "That is not a promise a man can always keep."

"Perhaps not, but I can try with all that I have to do so."

"She's probably living in peaceful obscurity and your arrival will only bring trouble. For even one of Abramm's trusted guardians would not be welcome in Chesedh at this time."

RETURN OF THE GUARDIAN-KING ‖ 167

And for the third time an opening presented itself. He sighed resignedly. *Oh, very well, then.* . . . "Perhaps not, professor, but I am not one of Abramm's guards."

"No?" Laud blinked up at him. "Who are you, then?"

"Is it not obvious?"

Laud looked at him blankly.

"My left arm is scarred and withered and wears the brand of Katahn ul Manus, an Esurhite Gamer of renown. My chest bears the shieldmark of Eidon himself, who delivered me out of those Games and made me what I became. My face is marked with twin scars, carved there by the claws of a beast no man could slay save the one it was made for. And which, through Eidon's Light, I did slay."

Laud stared at him fixedly.

"I did not die in Execution Square that day, as all the stories say, but was rescued the night before by my uncle and three others. Spirited away to heal in secret, then crossing the highlands on foot to avoid being seen or captured until I had slipped through the Kolki Pass to freedom and another chance."

He fell silent. Laud continued to stare at him, his face devoid of expression.

Finally, after a long silence, the professor spoke. "Are you saying you are Abramm Kalladorne, then? The deposed king of Kiriath. Executed before at least a thousand witnesses, now reborn by Eidon's touch?"

"Not reborn. Delivered."

"I see."

"You don't believe me."

Laud snorted softly and shook his head. "I grant there is the physical resemblance. But too many people saw him die, son. Including his own brother."

"My brother, they say, was addled by the use of painkillers for his bone condition." He shook his head, frowning. "Why would I lie about such a thing, professor?"

"I don't know. Perhaps you see a chance to become something you could never be otherwise. Or perhaps it is vengeance for your own losses. Or even a misguided sense of loyalty. Do you even have a wife and children in Chesedh? Or is it the queen you plan to join?"

Abramm stared at him, shocked by the censure in the man's voice.

"This is an evil plan, Alaric. And I counsel you to abandon it at once." He frowned and added worriedly, "You haven't told the others, have you?"

"No." Abramm snorted. "I figured you would be most likely to believe me."

And at that the old man looked almost hurt. "It pierces me to the core that you would seek to use me like this."

"I am not trying to use you."

"No? You are on the eve of your departure. Why tell me now what you have hidden for six months, except that you need my help for something? Do you hope I'll convince the others where you could not? Though I can't see how it would help you with Trinley."

"I told you because I believed Eidon wanted me to. Because . . ." He trailed off, realizing again that he'd had no idea why Eidon had pushed him into this, and even less of one now. But that it was Eidon's doing he did not doubt, for he'd never have said anything otherwise.

They stood eye to eye for a long moment. Then Laud dropped his gaze to the speaking stone. "I need to get back to this before I lose it all." The kelistar flared to life and the arrested message continued on, Abramm dismissed from the professor's mind.

Abramm stood unmoving, mind whirling. He'd argued with Eidon that this would be the outcome. But now that it had materialized, he realized that against all he'd argued, deep down he truly had thought Eidon would move the other man to see at last. And he hadn't.

It made no sense.

He turned and strode quietly to the door.

Perhaps it was not for him, my son, but for you.

For me? I respect the man, and now he thinks I'm a liar and a lunatic, out to steal a dead king's throne.

Maybe I just wanted you to know that your secret is not yours to divulge.

Abramm stopped on the steps outside the study, a chill washing through him as Kesrin's voice echoed in the narrow hall: "All will betray you . . . prison . . . but you will be delivered, and when the time is full, you will receive back what was taken a hundredfold."

The words were from the last sermon he'd heard old Kesrin teach. Words he'd forgotten until now.

15

Filled with the rituals of mourning for the dead king, followed by the preparations for a double coronation, the winter had passed quickly in the Chesedhan lowlands. Trap was kept busy with the financial concerns of a holding triple the size of what he had previously managed—a task complicated by an across-the-board replacement of staff members in not only the palace but also at the Exchequer and other financial institutions. He had kept long hours, and was repeatedly called out of town—down to Peregris or Mareis or up to Deveren Dol. In the six weeks between Hadrich's entombment and the crowning of the new king and queen, he was home in Fannath Rill maybe a week and a half's time altogether.

What little free time he did have when home, he spent with the Kiriathan exiles, trying to put out the fires started by their increasing intolerance of Chesedhan condescension, prejudice, and unjust dealings. An intolerance that seemed to have been intensified as much by little Simon's return as by Maddie's wild stories that Abramm was on his way.

When she had first told Trap she believed Abramm was alive, he'd feared her difficulties in birthing Abrielle had unhinged her mind, that she had fallen into some grief-inspired delusion and was no longer connected to the real world. When that did not prove to be the case, he ascribed her claim to hallucinations suffered during the birth and her battle with the black spore. He was even prepared to believe she'd actually seen her husband in the eternal realm during her own brush with death, and had tried gently, and then not so gently, to get her to accept those explanations. They had exchanged quite a few angry words on the subject, to the point they no longer discussed it, and she had stuck to her original story unswervingly through it all: Abramm was alive, having come on foot through the Kolki Pass to a place called Caerna'tha, where he had been trapped by the winter but would surely be in Fannath Rill by spring's end.

At her insistence Trap had done some asking around and learned there was indeed such a place as Caerna'tha, an ancient monastery that served as a waystation for Terstan refugees coming in from Kiriath through the Kolki. Since it lined up with Maddie's story, Trap had spoken further with Roy Thornycroft, then put out the word that he was interested in any further reports of Abramm's having survived his execution. That so far no others had surfaced didn't surprise him.

All of which had left him little time for bridging the gap that was daily widening between him and Carissa. Maddie had spoken to him shortly after Hadrich's entombment, asking him bluntly if he loved his wife or not, and insisting that, if he did, he ought to be setting himself to the task of letting her know it. "You can't be a pigeon about this, Trap. You have to be aggressive, or she'll think you don't mean it."

"What makes you so sure she'll be receptive to such attentions?" Trap had protested. "She's never given me any indication—"

"I'm not talking about serving her cocoa and making polite conversation!"

"What, then? Shall I grab her and kiss her right out of the blue?"

Maddie had grinned at him. "If you're moved to do so, that might not be a bad start."

He'd been aghast. "You don't understand how it is with us."

"Perhaps not, but I don't think you do, either. And I'm certain she has no idea."

When still he resisted her advice, she'd made a sour face. "What's the worst that could happen? She might reject you? At least you won't have to wonder for the rest of your life if it might have been something else. It's not like you're going to die."

He'd looked at her skeptically, thinking she was hardly one to talk about not dying in matters of lost loves. He had to admit she was right, though. And how could things get any worse than they were?

But if her words had given him new hope and revived purpose, over time his workload and social obligations—and his own cowardice—defeated both. Not living with his wife anymore, he had to go out of his way to even encounter her, making it far too easy to let another day go by without having acted, promising himself that *tomorrow* he would go to her. Finally the hope and intent had dwindled away into a thickening cloud of doubt and second thoughts.

It was the coronation that brought them together—beginning with a series of pre-coronation socials they attended as husband and wife. At these affairs Carissa was unfailingly polite, serene, and so beautiful he realized one reason he'd made no attempt to spend more time with her was because it hurt too much. He could no longer be with her and not want all of her. Their encounters were cordial, even relaxed and chatty on occasion, and several times he brought himself to the verge of telling her how he felt. But something always intervened.

Then, the day before the coronation itself, he turned from playing with Conal down in the nursery and caught her standing in the nursery doorway looking at him with an expression of such tenderness and longing, it shocked him. For it reminded him of nothing so much as the way Maddie used to moon after Abramm. The expression was swiftly veiled, and she turned away without a word to disappear up the hallway outside. When the shock wore off, he went after her, but as always he was too slow.

He determined then and there that he *would* tell her how he felt the next day, the day of the coronation. They'd be together all day, so he'd have no excuse for lack of opportunity—even if the prospect did scare the breath out of him.

The day dawned clear and mild, and the coronation went off without a hitch. Chesedh's newest royal couple was crowned in the Great Kirikhal at Fannath Rill before a standing-room-only crowd. Afterward Chesedhan custom dictated a grand feast for the invited nobles in the Grand Hall at Fannath Rill, while a reception and buffet were set up in the South Pavilion for those of lesser rank. Queen Ronesca had made up the guest list, and the former Duke of Northille and his wife were most definitely among the lesser category. Trap had no illusions of his own status, but Carissa was true royalty, with a long and noble heritage, and she deserved to be in the Grand Hall with the other nobles. It had angered him when the invitation had first come—late, not surprisingly—and it angered him now as they had to serve themselves finger foods from one of the many tables arranged around the perimeter of the spacious octagonal pavilion.

It also irked him how the courtiers, standing no farther than arm's reach of his position, would lean together and talk about him—nothing he'd not heard before, but at least they could have the decency to do it where his wife didn't have to hear.

". . . only married her a week before their child was born."

"Heard he'd been living with her all the time her brother was away."

"And they have the gall to blame it on the ex-husband! At least he finally married her."

As he finished serving his plate he glanced back at them, then at his wife. The hurt in her face made him even angrier. But as he was determined not to let the foolish words of a few petty people destroy his plans for this evening, he refused to let himself dwell on it any further. Instead he concentrated on eating and chatting with his wife and was pleased when after a time she seemed to relax, laughing and teasing with him as she had not done in months. She even acquiesced to his first invitation to dance, and it was wonderful to hold her in his arms and swirl her around the dance floor. He thought she enjoyed it, as well, so when he asked her a second time, he was surprised when she declined. More so when she declined on a third occasion. He asked twice more, and each time her answer came more quickly, as the warm camaraderie they'd shared cooled into increasing awkwardness.

Finally she commented on her weariness and asked if he might escort her to her apartments. Thus, though the party would continue for hours into the night, he walked her through the orb-lit waterpark, then up the palm-lined promenade, feeling bitterly frustrated as defeat overtook him. He saw no way to evade it, unless he just blurted out his feelings, without any of the romantic preliminaries he had hoped for.

They said not a word all up the long walk. Entering the deserted foyer of the palace's west entrance they approached the stair leading up to her second-floor apartments, where she turned to face him though her gaze was directed toward the floor.

"Thank you, sir. It's been a wonderful day."

He frowned at her, wondering uneasily why she had stopped here when they still had some ways to go before reaching her apartments. "It has been my pleasure, Your Highness. More than you know."

She grimaced, as if he'd said something displeasing. Or maybe it was what she meant to say to him that displeased her. A vague sense of alarm stirred in him.

"I . . ." She swallowed, her gaze still fixed upon the gleaming floor between them. Finally she went on very quietly. "If you would like a divorce . . . I wouldn't refuse you."

He felt as if he'd been kicked in the gut, shocked beyond the ability even to breathe.

"I know I haven't . . . been a proper wife to you," she said to the floor.

"You've been an exemplary wife."

"No . . . I mean . . . there are things . . ." Finally she glanced up at him, her eyes so very blue. "Tendernesses and expressions a husband has a right to expect from his wife."

"I've never expected those things from you."

She blanched, pain flickering across her aristocratic features as he berated himself for his clumsy wording.

"I mean, not that I wouldn't enjoy them—just that I know why you entered into this relationship, and I would never . . ." None of this was turning out right. Why couldn't he just say it? "You needn't feel this way, Carissa," he said desperately. "I took this marriage up of my own choice."

"And all I've brought you is grief. I hate it when I hear the courtiers talk of you as they do. It's so unfair and so false. You've been nothing but honorable, yet they call you an adulterer."

He snorted. "You think I care about them? They're a flock of fools. If they didn't call me an adulterer, they'd call me a vicious Kiriathan heretic. Come to think of it, they do."

She didn't laugh as he had hoped.

"I know you have only done this out of your love for Abramm," she said. "Your sense of duty."

"That is not true, my lady."

And again she looked up at him, smiling bitterly. "You are an honorable man, my lord duke. But you are a very poor liar."

He met her gaze directly and firmly. "I am not lying, Carissa. I married you because I wanted to. Abramm never would have asked me to do it if he hadn't known how I felt. I love you. I have for a very long time."

Her eyes were wide, the expression of skepticism giving way to a blankness he could not read. Startlement? Hope? Alarm at learning that the swordmaster's son was not nearly so selfless as she thought? He wasn't sure. At least she wasn't running away. "Courage," Maddie had counseled. "Be aggressive. Make sure she knows exactly what you feel."

So, his heart hammering wildly against his breastbone, he took hold of her shoulders and bent to kiss her, not on the cheek, as he'd done for so long, but on the lips, as a husband who loved his wife would do. Softly. Gently. Half fearing she would jerk away in revulsion at his touch.

Thus it took him a moment to realize her lips were not stiff and cold but soft and warm and pliant, and that her hand, though it rested trembling upon his chest, did not push him away. The shock of it rolled through him like a thunderclap, unloosing a rush of desire so intense it nearly brought him to his knees. Every inch of his skin felt as if it were ablaze, and by the time he pulled away from her—slowly, gently—he was trembling with the effort to control himself.

She stared up at him, lips quivering, eyes still wide and gleaming with moisture, hand still resting on his chest—a sharp, trembling warmth that fed the wildness in him. It so clouded his thoughts, he felt like a man on a drunken binge, though he'd had but a single glass of wine that night. Mindful of the abuses she'd suffered at the hands of her first husband, and alarmed by the swiftness with which his self-control was crumbling, he forced himself to step back from her and tried to get his mind to work again.

Then the tears that had been building on her lower lashes spilled down her cheeks. He stared at them stupidly. She had responded to his kiss. She had laid her hand on his chest and not pushed him away. Why was she weeping?

"What's wrong?"

"Nothing." She reached up to wipe away the tears. "Everything."

"I don't understand."

"No. I'm sure you don't." She shook her head, tears rolling from her eyes, then turned and fled up the stairs. He reeled in her wake, ears roaring, stomach wrenched into a knot of dismay. *What did I do? What don't I understand?*

At first he had no idea. Then the bitter realization swept over him: She'd not been *responding* to his kiss; she'd been shocked to immobility, horrified the swordmaster's son would be so bold. Light's grace! She'd asked him to divorce her moments before! Did he think she hadn't meant it?

Well, I guess I know how she feels about me. Gratitude, pity, a measure of respect. But not the love he'd hoped for. Never that. He was a swordmaster's son, after all. Hardly worthy of being in her presence, much less . . .

The hall grew bright and whirled around him until he had to brace himself on the curved finial at the end of the stair's railing to stay upright. He had not thought it possible to feel such pain without a physical wound.

When at last he was ready to function again, he went back out the west entrance, where a man immediately stepped from the shadows beside the door into his path and bowed.

"My lord duke."

Trap frowned, embarrassed and irritated to think he and Carissa had been watched. The man wore the blue uniform of the Chesedhan military, but his accent was Kiriathan. He was of medium height, with straight dirty-blond hair, a mustache, and a pink scar that cut diagonally across his right eyebrow. He looked vaguely familiar.

"Do I know you, sir?"

"I am Captain Hanris Brookes, my lord. You knew me as Lieutenant Brookes. Second in command at Graymeer's a few years back."

"Ah yes. Under Commander Weston. You volunteered to serve in Chesedh, as I recall."

"Yes, sir. Got a promotion for it, too." He touched the silver bar on his chest and smiled briefly. "We've been attached to Prince—er, King Leyton's company for the last year. Just got into town."

"I see."

"My lord . . ." He glanced right and left down the hall. "Might there be some place we could speak privately?"

———

Serving in her official capacity as a lady-in-waiting to the queen, Maddie sat in the second chair from Ronesca, between Lady Iolande and Lady Locasia. The ballroom was already warm, though they had thrown open all the doors along the filigreed arcade and a breeze now filtered through the wooden latticework.

As Ronesca was already engaged in conversation with the Baron of Bleveny, Maddie was happy to sit and observe both dancers and spectators. It did not escape her notice that there were no Kiriathans in attendance. Indeed, if the crown princess of that country and the former First Minister had been snubbed, no one else was going to receive an invitation. It irked her. Not least because it was so provincial and foolish. Kiriathans were right now dying to protect Chesedhan lands and homes. Abramm had helped these people repeatedly and given up much to do so.

But no, Ronesca had insisted when Maddie expressed these thoughts two weeks ago, Kiriathans were not to be trusted. . . . Just look at how they had behaved toward little Simon, as if he were their king already and the only one worthy of their allegiance. And this new rumor that Abramm had somehow survived his execution and would return to lead them in retaking their realm was even worse. Especially since every Kiriathan exile Ronesca knew was destitute. Where did they imagine the weapons and materiel to fight a war would come from? Did they think Abramm would bring that, as well? No, it was clear they hoped for Chesedhan aid, when Chesedh had all it could do to save itself.

Besides, Ronesca had insisted, Kiriath was doing nicely for itself since Abramm had been deposed—maybe not economically, but they had managed to keep the Esurhites at bay. What difference did it make which of them sat on the throne, so long as they didn't make trouble for Chesedh?

Giving up on Ronesca, Maddie had tried to take her case to her brother, but he'd put her off until after the coronation—the guest list was Ronesca's domain, and he was much too busy to trouble himself with such trifles.

Tonight Maddie surveyed the crowd and smiled to think of how all would change when Abramm arrived. She smiled at the recollection of his arms about her the night Abby had been born, and of the many balls she had danced with him in years past. Soon she would dance with him again, and revel in the jealous stares of her peers.

"You look lovely tonight, Your Highness," said Lady Iolande. "That rose color suits your complexion magnificently, and I am positively astounded at the way you have regained your figure so swiftly. Must be all that riding you do."

Maddie jerked from her reverie and turned to Iolande. "Actually, I've not been riding much lately. Just walking."

"Well, you are stunning. And everyone has noticed. Especially Draek Tiris." She leaned closer. "I believe they will be starting one of those Sorian pattern dances shortly. If you give him a wink, he might come and ask you to dance it with him."

Maddie could not imagine ever, in all her life, winking at a man. Particularly not one so wise and sophisticated as Draek Tiris. Though he was indeed watching her from across the dance floor with those dark, bottomless eyes of his. Meeting his gaze sent a jolt of energy rushing through her that turned her blood to fire. As it burned hotly up her throat and face, she looked away, embarrassed and unnerved by the unexpected reaction.

It fled as swiftly as it had come, leaving her befuddled and uneasy, so that when young Duke Somebody-or-Other bowed before her and asked for the next dance, she turned him down a bit too abruptly. Hastening to cover her terseness with an apology, she explained that she hadn't had so much excitement in weeks and it was taking its toll.

"Perhaps another time," the duke suggested.

And she smiled gratefully. "I would count it an honor, sir."

He stepped away and suddenly Tiris was there. "Perhaps you would prefer a walk around the arcade," he said in his wonderful voice. "The night is clean and exceedingly pleasant. The fresh air will surely revive you."

"Yes," Iolande agreed. "I was just out there, and the weather is perfect. They've even got the fountain working properly."

Maddie glanced through the open doors to the quadrangle outside, and sure enough the fountain's jets were all arcing in perfect symmetry from its central fluted column.

Tiris dropped a bow and offered his arm. "May I have the privilege of escorting you, madam?"

Having spent the last six weeks trying to convince him she was not interested in being courted, she intended to say no. But before she could speak, Ronesca intruded. "Don't even think of turning him down on my account, Madeleine. I want you to feel free to accept whatever invitations come your way. And you look a little pale. A walk would do you good."

Tiris flashed his gorgeous white smile at the queen first and then at Maddie. When she accepted his invitation, his expression grew unabashedly triumphant. As he tucked her hand between his arm and side and walked her toward the nearest door, he murmured, "The queen, at least, seems to think I still have a chance with you."

"I mean no offense, sir, but she lives in delusion."

Outside, in the spacious courtyard that opened off the ballroom, the breeze had died to a gentle fillip and the night air hung mildly about them, redolent with the fragrance of the jasmine that draped the arcade. Kelistar garlands glittered amidst the white blooms, while larger orbs floated in the fountain at the rectangular court's center.

They walked a round of the quadrangle in companionable silence, and Maddie felt the tension that had wound itself around her begin to dissipate. The air did clear her head, but so did the relative silence and the sense that she was no longer the center of attention. Finally they stopped where a railed balcony overlooked the waterpark and the South Pavilion, aglow beyond it.

She let go of his arm to rest her hands on the stone balustrade. Below, the palms that lined the promenade served as stanchions for the garlands of kelistars that looped along both sides of the walk. More garlands illumined the network of paths meandering amongst the waterpark's streams and ponds, reflecting here and there off the water's surface. "This is nice," she said. "Thank you for suggesting it."

"It is my profound delight, Your Highness."

She huffed softly. "You calling me Highness! I'm sure in your homeland, it would be quite the other way around, hmm?"

He smiled and shrugged. "We aren't in my homeland, though, are we?"

She turned toward the view again and loosed a long, low sigh as she watched the river traffic glide up and down the gleaming Ankrill out beyond the park and crenellated wall, illumined by their deck lights.

"The view is lovely."

"It certainly is."

Something in his tone made her glance at him again. He'd turned his hip toward the railing and now gazed shamelessly at Maddie herself. Her face warmed and she turned back to her view. "It's not polite to stare, Draek Tiris."

"I'm not staring. I'm appreciating. You're fairly glowing tonight, my lady. I don't think I've ever seen you more beautiful."

Her cheeks grew positively hot. Feeling like a little girl wanting to hide behind her mother's skirts, she forced a casual chuckle. "It must be all the dancing."

"Mmm. I'm fair certain it's not the company." He turned to face the railing alongside her, so close his arm just brushed her own. "I've missed you these last six weeks," he said soberly. "Was even beginning to think I'd done something to offend you. You don't answer my notes, refuse all my invitations . . . and I've not even seen your lovely little Abrielle, though everyone says she's beautiful. Blond and blue-eyed as her brothers."

"I can't believe you of all people don't know why."

"You speak of the rumor that you were reunited with your husband in some inexplicable way."

She nodded, disliking how close his tone came to condescension. "I know no one believes me."

"You were in great pain and duress that night—your delivery, your battle with that strange spore. . . ." Seeming to sense her rising annoyance, he trailed off. "I understand Ronesca still struggles with it. That it gives her blinding headaches and strange dreams. Dreams that become waking delusions."

"Of which the most absurd is the idea that I'm going to marry some Chesedhan courtier before the summer's out."

"Are the rumors untrue, then?"

Maddie sighed. "The headaches are real. And the nightmares. It's hard to say about the things she's claimed to see at night."

"Yet you suffered from the same spore—"

"And purged it. The Light was on me. It was real, Tiris. I was with him.

And no matter how much you try to pick at it all, you're not going to shake my confidence. I know what I know."

Memory of her disastrous attempts to convince Trap—and Carissa—that she spoke the truth still filled her with dismay. Both had strongly rejected her claims from the moment she'd spoken them, and it had hurt. A lot. She'd expected them, of all people, to trust and believe her, yet they had been her most resolute skeptics. Trap had gotten so agitated the last time they'd spoken of it, he'd begged permission to retire from her presence and hadn't brought the subject up since.

"So . . ." Tiris began tentatively. "The way it was told me, you believe he came through the Kolki Pass and has been delayed by the winter. Now that the snows are melting, you expect him to arrive at any time."

"And now that I've admitted it all to you, you can tell the tale at your next salon gathering and have much amusement at my expense."

"I would never laugh at you, Your Highness," he said softly. He paused, thought a moment, then gave her a sly look. "But I might encourage others to do so, just to make them all look foolish when you are proven right."

"I would prefer not to make anyone look foolish, Tiris. It only breeds ill will."

He shrugged. "Ill will is bred regardless. By all manner of things—good and bad. You can't avoid it."

They stood in silence for a time as she savored the scent of the jasmine, the chuckle of the fountain at their backs, the low conversations of the others who shared the quadrangle with them, the soft strains of the orchestra float-ing out from the ballroom. . . .

"So . . ." Tiris said presently. "I'm guessing you are working on a ballad of all this?"

She glanced at him, startled. Early on she had discovered they shared an interest in music. He'd known of her ballads before they had met—owing, naturally, to his interest in Abramm—and had even composed a few of his own works. Works he confessed to having performed for his courtiers from time to time, though he found it awkward and unsatisfying. *"They always applaud you, but what else can they do? I can understand why you went out to the taverns to do it anonymously."*

He'd made her blush with that remark, reminding her both of what she'd done as a young girl and what she'd done only months previously. She'd not thought at the time that she might be contemplating another performance quite so soon as she was.

Now she shrugged. "Working on it, yes."

"And perhaps have finished?"

"Perhaps."

"Ah. So it remains merely a matter of when and where to perform it—which lucky inn to select to be visited by Molly the tavern wench." He flashed his brilliant smile at her. "I have a better idea. How about you present it next week when I introduce my Desert Salon?"

"I can't imagine why the great Tiris ul Sadek would be inviting Molly the tavern wench to perform at the opening of his Desert Salon."

"I'm not inviting Molly, I'm inviting the exquisitely voiced First Daughter of the realm. Who, of course, needn't worry about the courtiers giving her false praise, seeing as her talent is completely legitimate."

"As you needn't, either, I'm sure, sir. But it is not proper for the First Daughter to be performing in public."

"Not even if the great Tiris ul Sadek presses her to? I will take all the blame."

"And not receive any of it. Everyone knows I know better."

"Ah, but they'll not be sending you off to a convent this time."

She gaped at him in indignation. "How do you know about that?" The first time she'd played "Molly" she'd been fourteen and had made the mistake of agreeing to sing for the customers. Which had been fine fun . . . until her father had found out.

Again Tiris disarmed her with his smile. "I make it a point to find out about the women I take an interest in."

She pushed away from the railing now to face him outright. "My husband is returning soon, Draek Tiris. Why would you want to herald that to all the court and join me in looking the fool?"

"I told you. It will be fun when they are all proven wrong. I love to see the chickens flustered and clucking."

She looked up at him, head cocked. "You are an evil man, Tiris ul Sadek."

"Yes. I am." And the way his eyes glittered gave her an unexpected chill. Then he smiled, dropped her a short bow, and held out one gloved hand. "I hear a familiar melody coming from the ballroom. Would you join me for one last dance? We'll get them all atwitter with the hope you will accept *my* suit."

She rolled her eyes and shook her head. "Oh, very well. At least it will discourage the others from trying."

"It will be our little secret."

16

The morning after Abramm made his ill-fated confession to Laud, he stood on the hard-packed snow of Caerna'tha's gate yard, rucksack slung over one shoulder and snowshoes in hand. The yard around him roiled with activity as those who would go with him bustled about, putting on their snowshoes, making last-minute additions—or removals—to the loads they carried in their rucksacks, and saying good-bye to the permanent residents of the monastery.

Rolland came up as Abramm stood there. "Looks like we're gonna be ready jest about the time ye guessed." He released a big breath, put his hands on his hips, and frowned. "What's wrong?"

Abramm shook his head, bemused. "I really didn't think they'd all come, when it came right down to it—the route being what it is." He lifted a brow at his friend. "It's your fault, you know."

Rolland's grin widened. "Well, I told ye my plans. And I know as well as ye do that if we wait 'til the snow's gone like Oakes wanted, we wouldna reach Peregris 'til midsummer. The whole war could be over by then."

And not in our favor, Abramm thought.

He dropped his snowshoes on the snow in front of him, then slid off his rucksack and jammed his booted feet into the bindings. Once all was fastened snugly, he stood and redonned his pack, which had somehow grown heavier just from being set down.

Most of what he carried was food—flour, crystallized honey, and a load of shriveled apples from last fall's harvest. That in addition to his meager belongings, which had this morning increased by two more items, courtesy of

Professor Laud. The man had caught him at breakfast, early. He'd said nothing about their conversation the night before but presented Abramm with a
book-shaped parcel wrapped in brown parchment and tied with string, and a
leather drawstring bag. "To remember us by. Perhaps to remember yourself
by, as well," he'd said.

The book he hadn't unwrapped yet, but he guessed that Laud was giving
him the copy of *The Red Dragon*. The bag held the speaking stone he'd seen
the professor using the night before. Since he and the whole group would be
without a kohal for a while, Laud thought they would have greater use for it
than he did.

Now as Rolland handed him his staff, Abramm went over to the gate-
house porch to say his good-byes to the professor. The older man looked
down at him, his expression calm but sad. Abramm thought of offering his
hand but wasn't sure Laud would welcome that. Instead he said stiffly, "I'm
sorry I haven't turned out to be what you'd hoped. But I deeply appreciate
all you have done for me."

Laud allowed himself a small smile. "I'm still hoping you'll reconsider."

"I won't." He paused. "But if it's possible one day, I would like to return."

"With that family of yours?"

"My wife would love this place. I would probably have a hard time pulling her away."

Laud seemed to startle. "Your wife is a scholar?"

"A scholar and a bard."

"That is unusual for a woman."

"Particularly a Chesedhan woman."

Laud frowned at him, and Abramm couldn't help but smile. Best to end
this before things got prickly. "We thank you again for your hospitality,
professor."

"It has been my pleasure. And fair journey to you."

Abramm stepped back, started to turn his snowshoes, one after the other,
when Laud said, "Alaric—" Abramm looked over his shoulder.

"Don't let your ambition or your desire for vengeance get the best of you,
son," the old man advised. "It will only bring you ruin. Whatever Eidon has
for you, it won't be accomplished through deception and trickery."

Abramm regarded him a moment; then he chuckled briefly, shaking his
head. "I know that, sir. Have no fear."

He took up the place Trinley had assigned him—at the end of the line—
and trudged down the slope toward the center of the valley where the stream

gurgled merrily between deep banks of snow. First to freeze, it was also first to respond to the sun's heat, flowing downward to meet the Ankrill.

The day was bright, the sky an inverted blue bowl over their heads, ringed with a crown of white peaks. The group—almost thirty of them with the children—moved down the slope eagerly, following the path Abramm, Rolland, and Cedric had made a week earlier when they'd gone down to investigate the alternate trail. Now the creak of Abramm's snowshoes melded into the collective rustling, clinking, and chattering of those ahead of him, and he couldn't help but pick up their excitement. Finally he was on his way!

Their progress was slow. The women needed to rest, especially Jania, and the children had to be let down to move about and relieve themselves periodically, so it took them half a day to reach the village. At their first sight of it, Abramm blew out a breath of relief to see it largely as he remembered from their scouting expedition the week before—still deserted for the winter, the haphazard circle of huts buried to their eaves. Except for the tracks from the men's previous excursion, the snowfield stood undisturbed. As Abramm had hoped, the villagers had yet to return from their lowland wintering grounds.

Nor had Tapheina and her pack been there. He'd half expected to encounter them when he'd started out from Caerna'tha, even though none of the tanniym had appeared since the night of Jania's child-birthing. Trinley argued that, having failed to get Abramm to open the gate and knowing they'd not have another chance—he'd been locked in his cell every night since—they'd given up and gone away. Abramm had refrained from pointing out that the tanniym preferred to travel in darkness and that their own party had many leagues yet to travel and many nights to spend in the forest.

As had also been the case last week, the canyon downstream of the village, where the more widely used route snaked alongside the river, stood swathed in a veil of mist he knew was not natural.

Trinley and the others crossed the frozen Ankrill and climbed the bank to the flat without incident, but as Abramm started across—last in line—a flock of crows burst out of the mist downstream. They flew straight over him, cawing erratically, and disappeared behind the high bank's brow. Everyone stopped and stared at the sky, but after a few moments, when the birds did not return, they moved on.

Abramm climbed the bank and crossed the snowfield without incident to join the others where they'd congregated at the base of the far canyon wall.

The alternate trail snaked precariously across the steep face of the cliff, and the sight of it had unnerved the group. Already Kitrenna Trinley was pressuring her husband to abandon it for the wider, safer trail down on the river's bank. With the villagers gone, she argued, why risk trying to follow a narrow, rocky trail that could very well end in a cliff when they had a much easier and safer route at hand. Her husband pointed out that it wouldn't be safer with all the snow, that there were ice-glazed cliffs to negotiate where they could as easily fall to their deaths.

Abramm knew better than to enter into the discussion, for Trinley would only see his contribution as an attempt to assume leadership. Sure enough, the alderman asked every man but Abramm his opinion. After too much discussion, Rolland finally pointed out the strong possibility that they'd run into the returning villagers on the lower route—and were also more likely to meet up with tanniym there—and that decided them. They would take the high road as originally planned. Any who didn't feel comfortable with that would go back to Caerna'tha and wait for the snow to melt. As it turned out, no one went back.

The trail, wide enough to have permitted the horse to pass had they brought her, switchbacked up the face of the steep slope, then curved around the sun-drenched cliff face on a southeasterly course. Below them a pillowy layer of mist filled the canyon and hid the bottom of the drainage from view. Across the way, the facing ice-clad walls stood in shadow, constant reaffirmation of the rightness of the travelers' choice. There were places where the trail had fallen away a bit, but never enough to make the passage dangerously narrow. Sometimes melting snow above trickled down the rock face and across their route, but that, too, presented little problem. In fact, their biggest discomfort came from the sun, for they'd not traveled very far before it became hot, and Abramm was not the only one to shed his heavy overcoat and woolen mittens.

The crows returned in late afternoon, flying low over the mist, circling the travelers twice, then heading on down the canyon and out of sight. Taking note of the Kiriathans' position, it would seem, just as night was falling.

Shortly afterward, Kitrenna Trinley's fear of no place to camp was put to rest when they reached a narrow ravine carved into the canyon wall where a grassy flat provided space enough to set up tents and lay out bedrolls. A snowmelt stream tumbled downward toward the river beside it, and a screen of spruce trees blocked the chill wind flowing down the canyon. There was even a ring of soot-stained rocks to hold a fire, kindling piled nearby to start it.

Kitrenna was so amazed and thankful she went so far as to credit Abramm for his most excellent judgment in leading them to such a fine place, which did not make her husband very happy.

As the others bustled about getting settled and starting the fire, Abramm did a quick scout of the area. He'd been thinking all day of how to protect them should the tanniym pay a nighttime visit. Laud had suggested last week that he might conjure a Light shield, and even taught him how, though his success had be sketchy at best, Instead of just making the net and throwing it into place, he had to lay out a ring of kelistars first, using them as a primer from which to build the shield itself. Since any wind at all would send them rolling, or put them out entirely, it was not the best method for outdoor use. Thankfully there wasn't any wind yet. Even better, the terrain was rough and steep, good protection in itself. He saw quickly enough that his best approach would be to lay the kelistars around the outside of the ledge and simply enclose the immediate campsite.

Though he fully intended to climb back up to the ledge and begin, somehow he found himself on the narrow footpath that followed the snowmelt stream down to the river. And it was only when a dense mist closed about him and snow once more blanketed the ground that he came to his senses and stopped. He stood in utter silence, nape crawling with the realization that the tanniym were indeed out there, and thankful he'd had the wit to bring his staff with him.

At that point the cliff face had flattened out into a ledge, thick with leafless, prickly berry bushes, clotted with ice. The path disappeared into their midst, where no doubt his enemies lurked. Now his awareness of them suddenly intensified, as gravel rattled at his back. He whirled, bringing up the staff—

And froze. "Marta! What are you doing down here?"

Marta Brackleford stood on the path behind him, cloaked in fleece, staring at him with mild alarm. "I cam to help you lay the kelistars."

That's right. Laud and suggested she do so and even had her practice with him. "You shouldn't be out here alone," he said.

She cocked a dark brow. "And you should?"

"I'll be all right."

Again the twang of the tanniym's presence stroked him, and it seemed she sensed them, too, from the way she stiffened and focused her gaze on the bramble patch behind him. "You should go back to camp," he said quietly, turning from her to face the patch.

"And you?" she asked.

"I'll be right behind you."

A twig snapped loudly in the silence, and something rustled in the brush downhill.

"Go!" he commanded. And heard the receding scrape and rattle of her footfalls as she compiled.

He brought the stick around. A thought set it flaring with Eidon's Light as slowly he backed up the path. But after a few moments of nothing happening, he relaxed and turned to hurry after Marta.

Only to stop in his tracks again.

A silver-haired woman stood in the path ahead of him, blocking his way. Her figure-hugging leathers seemed immensely inappropriate in the swiftly chilling twilight, but they undeniably revealed her considerable feminine endowments. Her hair was twisted into hundreds of tiny ropelike strands that fell to her shoulders in a constantly shifting tumble. The light from his staff showed black eyes fringed by thick dark lashes and highlighted by glittering gold face paint across cheekbones, brows, and temples.

She stepped toward him like a great cat on the prowl, and he fought the urge to back away, afraid of her and drawn at the same time.

"Who are you?" He paused. "What are you?"

She cocked her head at him, the slender cords of her strange hair rippling distractingly over one another. "You don't know, my handsome, handsome pup?"

His nape prickled. "Tapheina."

"Ah. You do know me." She tossed her hair over her shoulder and stepped closer. "You didn't think I'd let you get away that easily, did you?" Her thin lips quirked in amusement. "We could make such beautiful offspring."

He gaped at her, hoping his disgust was obvious. "No, we could not!"

"You scorn me, yet I feel your interest."

"That doesn't mean I'm interested."

"Mmm." She smiled. "Already she is courting again, you know."

He regarded her uncomprehendingly as the dark eyes bored into him.

"Already there is one who scents her desire and seeks to fulfill it," she said.

"What the plague are you talking about?" he snapped.

"He knows her as you never have," she went on sweetly, "and is even now making her forget all about you. You are dead, after all. What else is she to do?"

Maddie. She's talking about Maddie. The realization stole his breath and set his heart racing with alarm. Courting already? *No. She's just trying to rattle me.*

"Our black-feathered friends have brought new tidings for you," Tapheina said.

The dark eyes snared him, and the forest disappeared. He felt her residualized spore come alive in his flesh as he gazed into the courtyard of some fine residence, kelistars festooning a vine-covered arcade, a lighted globe bobbing in the fountain, and a couple walking together. He recognized his wife at once, and saw that she was again with the same Sorite lord the dragon had shown him.

His gut clenched as the vision dissipated.

"She's alone in the world now," said Tapheina. "And she is First Daughter. They will want her to marry."

Knowing she was goading him didn't stop him from reacting, but he didn't have to stand there and listen. Staff held firmly before him, he started up the path.

"To bolster the war effort," she said, stepping aside.

"She won't." He continued past her.

"And the one they most want her to be with is the one she will most want, as well."

He whirled, swinging the stick in a smooth, expert arc that would have struck her soundly at the side of her head—if she'd not dodged out of reach with a speed that was not human. Leaping from the path to a streamside boulder, she stopped, put her hands on her hips, and threw back her head to laugh, the sound full and throaty and as charged with sensuality as the rest of her.

"You are such a sorry man, *Alaric.*" She laced his assumed name with sarcasm. "Once you ruled a realm. Now you can't even rule that pathetic company of shield-bearers with you. They don't want your rule any more than those in Kiriath wanted it."

She jumped lightly off the boulder and aproached him tauntingly. "But *I* want you—"

"Plagues! I knew it!" barked a sharp male voice. "He's down here. With her, as I said."

Oakes Trinley came barging down the path from their camp to rescue him, his stick alight with Eidon's power as he strode right up to Tapheina. She held ground and transformed back into her wolf form before their eyes. The marvel froze Trinley midstride, his jaw dropping open. Then she exhaled

188 | K A R E N   H A N C O C K

and a white plume of her breath undulated from her mouth. As it drifted up toward Trinley's face, he swung his staff and Light blazed out of him, burning the spore-infused breath to nothing.

Seeing her attack repulsed, Tapheina snarled and bounded down the lower trail into snowy darkness.

Trinley tilted his bearded chin to look down his nose at Abramm. "That's the way you're supposed to do it. Now come on back up to the camp before you get us all killed."

She wasn't gone, of course. Abramm could sense her out there, as he sensed the others, lurking in the shadow. And as he led the way back up the trail, her laughter sounded in his head.

"Lay out your little balls of light and make your shields if you like. . . . I'll have you in Ru'geruk, my handsome pup."

Trap had reported Brookes's startling revelation to Maddie the morning after the coronation ball—"He says the king has Abramm's scepter, madam"—but it was two days before she confronted Leyton with it.

One day to calm down and talk herself into doing it, one day to actually see him. Or rather, to realize she wasn't going to see him if she didn't get pushy about it, for he was consumed with his preparations for returning to the front and believed she had nothing of importance to say to him.

"How could Brookes possibly know it was Abramm's scepter?"

"Because he has seen it before, ma'am. He was at Graymeer's when Abramm used it to drive off the Esurhites after they attacked Springerlan. Prince Leyton was with them, too."

Thus, early in the morning of the third day after the coronation, Maddie marched into the antechamber of the king's apartments and demanded audience. He made her wait an hour, during which time her mind skittered between doubt, outrage, and plain cold fear of how his reaction to her possible overstepping might affect her and her children.

Still, she had to know if the accusation was true. And if it was . . .

Oh, please, Father Eidon, let it not be so.

He received her in his breakfast room, where he dined on poached eggs and pan bread but did not ask if she would like to join him. "Ah, Madeleine. I'm glad you've come. I did want to speak to you before I left. . . ." He made her stand at the table before him watching his big, freckled hands as they dumped the eggs out of their cup onto the crisp-crusted pan bread and smeared the still-liquid yolks around. A long puckered, scab marred the back of his left hand.

He stuffed a bite of bread and egg into his mouth, chewed a bit, and then said around it, "I must say you and Tiris ul Sadek made quite the couple the other night. The entire court is talking about you. There's even a rumor he's set himself to win you."

"Mmm," she said. She'd once thought of her brother as a huge man, and she supposed he was large, but six years of living with Abramm had shrunken him in her eyes.

He stuffed another bite into his mouth, the pan bread crunching between his teeth. His weathered face was red-tanned everywhere except on his forehead where his war helmet had blocked the sun. "You probably know that he commands vast armies of Sorites."

"Why, I had no idea!" she exclaimed in mock surprise. "Does he *really?!*"

Leyton grimaced impatiently. "So you know how sorely we could use vast armies just about now."

Maddie schooled herself to patience. "I didn't come here to talk about Tiris."

Leyton waved his knife at her as he stabbed his fork into the bread and eggs. "You can't evade it forever, you know. Sooner or later you are going to have to remarry. You're First Daughter. It is your duty. To your realm and to your children, for it is not fair they should grow up without a father."

Was there some sort of protocol she was unaware of dictating how one was to speak of this matter to her? Why else did everyone sound like everyone else when they did? At least having heard the same warning so many times had defused its power to annoy her.

"You know there are people who blame you for Father's death, don't you?" he went on blithely, changing the subject with startling swiftness. "They say Eidon is displeased with you for the way you've turned your back on the rightful way of worshipping him to follow the Kiriathans' ritual. Or lack thereof."

She gaped at him, surprised and suddenly wary. The matter of her method of worship had long been a source of contention between her and Ronesca, but so far as she knew, Leyton thought nothing of it. She'd long suspected he only attended Terstmeet as a matter of duty and appearances. So why was he bringing it up now. . . ? "I never took you to be concerned with matters of religion," she said cautiously.

"I'm not. But it looks bad. And it distresses my wife."

"I have been attending Kirikhal faithfully every Eidonsday. What more does she want?"

"She wants you to stop attending Terstmeets multiple times a week in a common house, listening to the uninspired babble of a commoner who is not even a real kohal."

"I thought she would prefer the common house to my inviting them all to the palace."

He glared up at her, then drew a deep breath and let it out in a rush. "I don't have time for this!" And with no more warning than that, he switched subjects again: "Abramm's regalia. Do you have it?"

His words shocked her into blankness. Disparate thoughts tumbled through her mind. How did he know she had them? She must deny it immediately! Did this mean he had taken the scepter? The last one struck and reverberated. She felt her stomach clench and the blood drain out of her face. "Plagues, Leyton! You didn't really take his scepter, did you?"

He smiled. "What if I did? Do you have the other pieces?"

Horror transformed to outrage as his admission registered. "Eidon's mercy, Leyt! You destroyed him!"

Her brother grimaced. "Apparently not, since you seem to think he's still alive. Do you have them?"

And in that moment she realized he hadn't been putting her off by denying her requests—he'd known exactly what she was up to . . . and he'd been playing her. Making her think she had the high ground, making her wait, and in that causing her to grow more and more impatient and outraged, so that when the time came her guard would be down, and he could strike . . .

Wariness flooded her. "Why would you think *I* have them? I was rescued out of prison with nothing but the clothes on my back."

He shrugged, his gray-blue eyes watching her sharply. "I heard that your woman brought them when she came with your sons."

"And she would have gotten them . . . where?"

He ignored her question. "You told us all you believed Ian was dead. Hurled against the cliff wall. Yet here he is alive."

She lifted her chin, fighting to keep her voice steady. "Obviously I was mistaken. Hardly surprising given the pressures of the moment."

"Hardly surprising for anyone but you." His bushy blond brows drew down over his eyes. "If you thought he was dead, dear Maddie, I fully believe he should have been. Yet somehow he is not."

"And you think Abramm's regalia had something to do with that?"

"Did they?"

It was like colliding with a cliff wall herself. How easily she had let him lead their conversation to this point . . . had, in fact, spoken the needed words herself, and her brother had already seen the truth in her eyes.

A moment later, he confirmed it: "So you do have them."

"I don't see why it would concern you if I do or don't."

"No?" He exhaled a short laugh of incredulity. "They could be the key to our victory against the Black Moon. The deliverance of all Chesedh. And Abramm's sure not going to be around to use them."

She lifted her chin, anger blasting through her. "No thanks to you!" she exploded, voice trembling with rage. "You took the scepter! And because of that, he didn't have it when he needed it."

"Madeleine!"

"You took what was given to him by Eidon's own hand and in that you caused him to lose everything!"

"I did not cause that. It was his own fault his people rose up against him. They—"

"You know nothing of what happened. Of what is happening now. You stole what was not yours, and now you have the gall to ask for more. To think that Eidon would ever bless you with any of it!"

He laughed again. "He already has, Mad. How do you think we held Torneki?"

"How do you think you nearly lost it in the first place? I heard you had a big plan, a magical talisman, and it almost got you all killed. It did get Father killed."

Leyton's face turned dark. "You will not lay that at my feet."

"I'll lay it where it belongs. You have seen minor breezes, seasonal winds . . . small victories. Those are nothing. You were at the Gull Islands. You saw what happened there."

"And it will happen again."

She glared at him. "Eidon is giving you the opportunity to admit your error and turn from it."

"Abramm's dead, Maddie. He's not coming back—"

"He *is* coming back, Leyt. And he'll have them all."

"Oh, please!" He threw the yolk-covered knife and fork onto his nearly empty plate with a clatter, then sagged back in his chair. "No one believes you, and you only make yourself sound like a crazy woman! Where are the rest of the items? Are you keeping them in your quarters?"

"You cannot have them, Leyton."

"I am king. I can have whatever I want. Either give them to me, or I'll send my men searching for them."

"Send your men, then, for I'll never give them to you."

He went very still, eyes widening. When finally he spoke, his voice was low. "So. Ronni was right about where your true loyalties lie. I thought . . ." His pale brow furrowed, and his eyes flashed with sudden anger. "I *defended* you, Mad! And here you betray me like this?"

"How the plague can you accuse *me* of betrayal when you—"

He surged to his feet and cut her off: "Captain LaSalle!"

The anteroom door opened, and an officer stepped in—tan, lean, and dimpled. He had not been there when she had come through moments before. "Take four men and search the First Daughter's quarters and the office of her finance secretary," Leyton said. "You are looking for a crown, an orb, a jeweled sword, a signet ring, and a white robe of peculiar fabric. Bring them to me at once. If you do not find them all, bring in more men and search the nursery and the quarters of all the Kiriathans who are staying in the palace. For the moment no Kiriathan, no member of the First Daughter's staff, is to leave the palace grounds. And I want Meridon arrested at once, regardless."

Maddie erupted in outrage. "What! You can't arrest a man for no reason!"

"I have plenty of reason, dear sister." Leyton gave her that infuriating look of condescension he was so good at. Then he turned to LaSalle. "Do you understand, Captain?"

"Yes, sir."

"Nothing but ill will come to you if you do this," Maddie said quietly as the man left. "You will get no help from the scepter, or any of the rest of it."

Leyton turned to her, still looking amused. "So you are a prophet now? I thought you Kiriathan Terstans didn't hold with that sort of thing."

"Don't mock me, Leyton. You are making a terrible mistake."

"Well, I have a terrible responsibility, and not much hope of deliverance elsewhere. . . . Unless you're planning on marrying Tiris ul Sadek." He cocked a bushy brow at her, and when she said nothing, he snorted. "I didn't think so."

With that he strode to the door, told the man on guard to see that she stayed there until he returned, and left.

CHAPTER

17

While Maddie was speaking with the king, Carissa had nursed one-year-old Conal and sent him off to the nursery with Prisina, then forced herself to eat the rest of his small bowl of porridge, the first food she'd consumed since the night of the coronation. Afterward she sat at her breakfast table sipping her last bit of morning shae'a as she read through the Words and prayed for deliverance from the deep melancholy that had seized her.

A mantle of hopelessness combined with a sense of deep inadequacy to sap her strength and ambition. Everything seemed too hard and fraught with the near certainty of failure and disappointment. She felt alone, unwanted, and irrelevant—wondered why she even bothered to get out of bed. Even Conal was needing her less and less these days as he transitioned from mother's milk to solid food. Today she'd deliberately fed him less of the porridge than he would have eaten just to get him to suckle longer.

A silly and futile vanity.

Why did Eidon bless everyone else and never her? Even the good things he gave her he took away; and his promises always expired unfulfilled. Was it because she never really trusted him fully? But how could she when he never seemed to know she was alive?

She'd not sat there very long before a bespectacled clerk in a gray suit arrived with the divorce papers she had requested of Trap. He pulled them out of a leather portfolio and arranged them across the table for her to examine and sign. He would wait while she did so.

She stared up at him, unable to breathe, shocked that Trap had actually done it, even as she'd spent the last two days assuring herself that he would.

She had asked him for this, after all, then fled his presence when he'd sought to persuade her otherwise. What else was he to do?

The little clerk cleared his throat, watching her with birdlike eyes, radiating disapproval. She glanced at the papers, but even that made her throat close up and tears blur her vision. "Can I look them over and get them back to you?" she asked, her voice shaking pitifully.

He exhaled a short burst of annoyance but said only, "Of course," then packed up his portfolio and left.

She wouldn't look over the papers. She couldn't even stand to sit at the same table with them. So she went and sat in her chair before the window, where she could look out on the waterpark and grieve.

How could it all have come to this? Why did she have to make that stupid suggestion? Why couldn't she have left well enough alone?

The night of the ball he had been so gallant, so attentive, so wonderful. Asking her to dance not once but five times. She'd said yes the first time, and could hardly believe it when she found herself in his arms. He'd smiled down at her as if he were truly enjoying himself, and she thought she might burst with happiness.

But then the dance had ended, and she'd heard the whispers, a snatch of snide comment here, a bit of deprecation there, the heads bending together, the eyes watching them. She hated the way everyone faulted him and impugned his character. Thus, as much as she would have loved to have danced with him again, she'd refused the next time, unwilling to put him out there for the world to snicker and sniff at.

Why did Conal's hair have to be red? At least if it were black or brown or even blond, people would have some cause to believe the truth. But Eidon hadn't chosen that, naturally. When had he ever made things easy for her?

Finally she'd asked to go home and saw she'd disappointed him—again. The expression was quickly veiled, and gracious as ever, he'd tucked her hand between his elbow and his side and walked her back to the palace. And all the way there, she'd thought about the divorce and whether she should or shouldn't offer it. It had so distressed her, she didn't think she'd even made a decision until the words were tumbling from her mouth. And then he'd kissed her.

The moment would live in her memory forever. She'd yearned for him to do it for so long, yet it had taken her completely by surprise when he had. It was tantalizing, magical, delicious—everything she'd dreamed it would be. She'd felt him tremble beneath her hand, felt his lips grow hot upon her own, and she'd leaned toward him eagerly, hoping he would take her in his arms and make love to her that very night.

Instead, he'd pulled away, gently but firmly, so grim-looking it seemed he'd needed all his self-control to force himself to kiss her. Confusion and hurt had swirled through her, and the cold hard truth had slammed into her—he'd done it out of kindness and the desire to reassure her he was content with their relationship.

Yes, he'd said he'd loved her, but she knew what he meant. He meant the kind of love Kohal Gentry always spoke about in Terstmeet, the kind of love Terstans were to have for one another and all men. A love that treated others in grace and kindness, regardless of how unattractive they were. A love based not on personal attraction but on duty to Eidon.

But duty couldn't inspire passion, and that was what she wanted from him. And though she had hoped desperately in that gentle embrace that he would take things further . . . she had seen in that moment the truth that he never would. Because he didn't want it. Hadn't he claimed as much only a few minutes prior to kissing her? He'd never expected it nor wanted it. Not from her.

It was that realization that had brought her to tears. And when he'd asked her what was wrong, it had only made things worse. For how could she tell him? And how could she blame him? To him, the idea would be unthinkable. He knew her past better than anyone.

So she'd run from him without explanation to closet herself in her bed-chamber. Sagging against the door as she closed it, she had let the tears flow.

Suddenly she was transported back to the stairwell of her home in Springerlan—her first husband lurching out of the shadows, his hand clapping over her mouth and nose so that she couldn't breathe as he'd thrown her back upon the stairs and shoved up her skirts. . . .

Afterward he'd stood at the foot of the stair, grinning down at her as he'd refastened his trousers. He'd spoken, but she'd not discerned his words, only the mockery in his tone. Then he was gone, leaving her to lie there uncovered, bruised, and weeping. Cooper had found her not long after. Cursing under his breath, he'd fetched Elayne and they'd brought her to her room and cleaned her up. . . . But it hadn't done any good. It never did.

Not then, not the night Trap rejected her, not in the days that followed. No bath could take away the sense of shame and filth she felt, and she knew herself to be soiled in a way that could never be cleaned.

Why would a man like Trap want anything to do with a woman like her?

"Damaged goods," she'd once joked . . . before she really knew what those words meant. No joke anymore.

She'd had another nightmare that very night.

Now she stood before the window and prayed for guidance. Should she sign the papers? She'd asked for them. He'd complied with her wishes and sent them. Why would she want to bind him to her when he didn't really want her? Wouldn't the same sort of love as he'd professed for her dictate she set him free with no regrets?

Leaving the window, she went to her desk and found inkpot and pen, then returned to the table and the hated document. She sat down, uncapped the inkpot, dipped in the quill . . . then sat there, letting the ink drip off its tip onto the creamy paper as the tears flowed once more with a vengeance. Finally she threw the pen down and left the room.

By the time she reached the nursery she had herself under control and spent a mindless hour watching her nephews and little Abby, who never failed to have a smile for her. While the children napped, she sat with Elayne and worked on her embroidery.

After a time Elayne asked quietly if something was troubling her.

Carissa started, and the heat rushed into her face. "No. Not at all."

"Mmm . . . well, forgive me if I overstep, my lady. It's just . . . you're weeping."

Abruptly Carissa realized tears were trickling down her cheeks. She stuck the needle into the taut fabric and touched trembling fingers to the moisture.

When Carissa said nothing more, Elayne added, "You keep too much to yourself, my lady. It's not good to be so fiercely alone all the time."

And still Carissa could not speak. The notion of telling the dear woman what had happened—of telling anyone, for that matter—seemed a harder thing than to strip naked and dance a jig for her.

Elayne's knitting needles clicked in soothing rhythm. "You've been distant and sad-looking ever since the ball. Yet the only thing I've heard about you that night is how splendid you and your husband looked while dancing together and that later he kissed you at the foot of the stairs by the west entrance. Surely that cannot be the cause of all this sorrow."

Carissa focused on her needlework, stitching rapidly for a few moments. Then the vigor of her movements slowed and came to a stop. The designs blurred before her eyes, and a lump filled her throat. Elayne's arms wrapped around her, and in moments she was sobbing outright, like a child in her mother's lap—all the loss and frustration and disappointment she'd kept inside for so long finally bursting out of her.

When it had passed and she had regained her poise, she stayed there, strangely strengthened by the older woman's arms.

And after a while she said, "Trap sent me papers of divorcement today." She felt Elayne's start of surprise and went on miserably. "I asked for them. That's why he kissed me . . . but he didn't mean it. Not the way I wanted him to. . . ."

"He kissed you because you asked him for a divorce?"

"No. He did it to reassure me that he was content with the way things are, not because he loves me. But then, how could he? I keep forgetting what I am."

Elayne's arms dropped away from her and the woman drew back. "Ah, my lady, do not let Rennalf do this to you."

"I cannot help it. He's already done it."

"He's done no more than you allow him."

Carissa watched her fingers track the designs on her embroidery. "You say that, but I don't know how to stop it. It happened. I can't make it go away."

"You can stop going back to it all the time. It wasn't your fault, Carissa. Eidon commands us to leave the past behind us, so why do you keep dredging it up to torture yourself?"

"You don't understand. Trap knows about Rennalf."

"I cannot for one moment believe that Duke Eltrap would ever care about that, nor why in the world you would think he doesn't love you. He's done everything for you. He married you, didn't he?"

"Our marriage has never been consummated, Elayne."

There. The dreadful, shameful truth out in the open at last. Let her say he loved her now. "He's never suggested it." Mortified now by her confessions, she staring fixedly at the needlework in her hands. "Nor has he shown any interest in doing so," she added stiffly.

And again the silence hung heavily between them. Then Elayne sighed. "Oh, my poor girl, if you believe there is no interest on his part, you are sorely mistaken."

Carissa looked up at her in astonishment.

"I have seen the way he looks at you. We all have. And I do not think he spends his days away from you by his own choice."

"I know what I saw that night, when he kissed me."

"A man struggling to control himself? Yes, my lady, he does know about Rennalf. Did you ever think he might have been fearful of coming on too strongly? That you might not welcome such attention from him? Or any man?"

"Wouldn't welcome it?! I burn for him every time I'm in his presence. I stand there trembling, unable to breathe, the awareness of him so great I can hardly speak or think. I yearn for a look, a touch . . . some word of affection. But there is nothing. He is cool, polite, and scrupulously proper."

"And what reason have you to think he might know you feel this way?" Elayne asked, eyes upon her knitting.

"I should think it obvious."

"Obvious?" Elayne looked out over the nursery. "Let's see. From what I've observed, every time he comes near you, you move away. You do not meet his gaze, and speak to him only if you must. You decline all his invitations to dinner, refuse to share cocoa with him in the morning—though he's the only one who can make it to your liking—and four out of five times at the ball you turned down his requests to dance. What is he to take from that but that it is you who finds *him* distasteful?"

Carissa sat there, stunned. She had focused so hard on hiding the truth from him, it had never occurred to her that the consequences of success would be a man careful to respect what she showed him and never trouble her with what he felt himself.

Elayne said it was obvious to everyone that he loved her. Was it? She ran back through her memories, searching for signs it might be true. But even as she did, something in her resisted it, mocking it as wishful thinking on her part, and presumption on the part of others. She'd seen what she'd seen, hadn't she? Surely she could not have been that blind. And what did anyone else know, anyway?

"Carissa." Elayne's age-spotted hand covered her own. "Don't let that part of you that hates yourself blind you to this truth. Eidon has given you this man as a precious gift. He's one of the finest I've ever known, but even he has his limits. Don't let the darkness in you drive him away."

"But it already has. . . . He sent me the papers."

"At your request. You don't have to sign them." She returned to her knitting. "Why not set yourself to show him how you really feel and win him back?"

"Show him how I feel?"

Elayne chuckled. "Surely you've not forgotten how to flirt, my lady?"

"Flirt?" Carissa gulped. "I'm not sure I ever knew," she said. "More than that, I'm not sure I even could. . . ." She thought of Byron Blackwell's sister,

Leona, and Maddie's own Briellen, and distaste welled up within her. Distaste wedded to a deep and powerful dread. "He'd probably think me batty. Or worse, he might laugh. . . ."

"You might shock his shoes off, my lady, but I know he'd never laugh at you. You ought—"

They were interrupted then by the breathless arrival of Maddie's auburn-haired maid, Jeyanne, who skidded to a stop before them as the words poured out of her mouth.

"You're saying," Carissa repeated back when Jeyanne was done, "that the king himself is searching his sister's bedroom?"

"No! He's sent that hideous Captain LaSalle. He rounded up all the servants and locked them in one of the sleeping cells. I was out of the suites when they arrived, or I'd be in there, too."

"They?"

"There were five of them, milady. Ripping everything to pieces. Pulling out drawers, cutting up pillows, tearing down draperies. They were even punching holes in the paneling. . . ."

"What in the world. . . ?" Elayne cried. "Did they say what they were looking for?"

"No, ma'am. The girls were begging them to, so they could help, but they refused."

"The regalia," Carissa murmured. She looked at Elayne. "Maddie went to confront him about having Abramm's scepter. Somehow the conversation must have come round to the rest of the pieces and he guessed she has them."

"How in the world could he have gotten hold of the king's scepter? We didn't have it when we fled the palace. Abramm took it when he went to face Rennalf."

"Did he?" Carissa asked coldly. "Or did he take a copy of it?"

Elayne's eyes widened.

"Trap thinks Leyton stole it when he was in Kiriath for Abramm and Maddie's wedding," Carissa added.

"But that was—"

"Almost six years ago. I know. It also lays much of the blame for Abramm's fall at Leyton's feet. Which is hardly going to endear him to the Kiriathan exiles here. Nor is taking the rest of the regalia for his own."

A man in the uniform of the palace guard stepped into the room and, seeing the women, strode briskly toward them. He dropped a quick bow. "Your Highness," he said to Carissa. "I'm afraid you must return to your quarters at once." He held his hand toward the doorway he'd just come through. "If you will, ma'am?"

At her apartments a quartet of soldiers were already searching through her things. When their leader, whom she recognized as Captain LaSalle, asked where her husband was, she told him he lived in his office near the queen's apartments. Frowning, he bade her sit down and returned to supervising the others. To her surprise, not long after that Trap himself arrived, stepping into the sitting room for the first time in months. He looked grim and angry, and he scrupulously avoided her gaze as he addressed the intruders.

"What are you men doing here?" he demanded.

LaSalle turned to him with obvious satisfaction. "Ah, Lord Meridon. We've been looking for you." He nodded at one of his men, who had come up behind Trap. "Bind this man and escort him to Larochell."

"What?!" Carissa cried indignantly. "You can't arrest him!"

"We're palace guard, my lady. We can do whatever we want." As he spoke, another of his men stepped up to Trap's side, pulling a pair of manacles from his belt and binding the former Kiriathan First Minister's wrists behind his back.

"This is outrageous!" Carissa erupted. "You can't arrest a man for no reason!"

"Oh, we have a reason, my lady. The king would like to borrow your regalia. He will of course return it when he is finished, but he needs all the pieces."

"So," Trap said, his voice quietly furious, "the stories about his stealing Abramm's scepter are true, then."

LaSalle smiled at him. "The First Daughter has given us three of the pieces. Two remain—a robe of unusual fabric and a sword. If you refuse to hand them over, we will have to take unpleasant action."

"We do not have them," Carissa insisted, drawing LaSalle's attention back to herself. "The sword is still in Kiriath, and I have no idea what's become of the robe."

"You refuse to obey a direct order of the king?"

"We're not refusing. We simply don't have what you want."

"No? Well, I notice that your husband is not protesting nearly so much as you are, my lady. Perhaps because he knows exactly where to find them." He smiled again at Trap. "But he will tell us soon enough." He nodded at his men to take him away, and they escorted him from the room.

LaSalle addressed her again. "If you'd like to spare him the pain of an interrogation, simply tell us where they are."

"I told you. They're not here. I have no idea where they are."

"Well, we will make sure of that. Now, if you'll sit here out of the way—"
She pulled away from him. "I'll go with my husband."

"I'm sorry, Highness, but you will not. Please sit down and we'll get this over with as quickly as possible."

CHAPTER

18

Abramm stepped from the shadow of the evergreens into the sun-drenched meadow, following the muddy trail as it curved through the grass toward a stand of new-leafed oak trees. A small white butterfly zigzagged before him, and crescents of still-melting snow arced in the shadows at the meadow's edge, fringed by clumps of flowering daffodils. Water trickled all about him as birds chirped in the trees, and somewhere beyond the spring-green foliage ahead of him, a bell clanged.

Eagerness roiled him as, boots squelching on the muddy path, he crossed the meadow with long strides. Any moment now he would come out on the bluff overlooking the river town of Ru'geruk and the Jardrath Valley beyond it. Finally he was free! He'd said his good-byes to the group this afternoon, when it was clear they should easily be able to reach Ru'geruk by day's end. Trinley had not been happy with his decision, but Abramm no longer cared. They planned to part ways in Ru'geruk anyway, and he had his own concerns. Besides, sooner or later the others would have to fend for themselves. In Ru'geruk he hoped to get work on one of the riverboats, perhaps as a deck-hand or oarsman, and make his way downriver. Given his size and strength, and his rock-solid belief that Eidon had already prepared the way for him, he even had the audacity to think he might be on the river as early as tomorrow morning. After that, from all everyone had told him, he'd be in Fannath Rill within a month. Every time he thought of it he wanted to whoop for joy.

There'd be no more of Trinley's faultfinding and sly insults, no more of his arbitrary assignments, his stubborn insistence on what any sane person could plainly see was the hardest way to do a thing, his constant one-upmanship.

Though Abramm had borne it all in silence, leaving the injustice to Eidon to handle, he felt now like a caged bird set free.

Thanks to the winter's unusually deep snowfall, the Ankrill was running dangerously high, and the others had decided that once they reached Ru'geruk they would take the safer route inland to Caer'akila, a settlement of Kiriathan exiles in the foothills of the Aranaak. It had been hardest for Rolland, who had been so determined to go to the front with Abramm and do battle with the Esurhites. In the end, though, he was not willing to risk his children to the river's raging wiles, and his wife had not wished to travel to Caer'akila without him. So he'd reluctantly given up his plans, promising to find Abramm at the battlefront as soon as he got his family settled.

The blue of sky and hazy distance now showed through the rapidly thinning screen of branches, and shortly Abramm emerged onto the edge of a granite cliff that overlooked the world. To his left the Ankrill roared over the same cliff in a cloud of mist, then tumbled along in a flurry of white-frothed rapids before finally settling into the wide, smooth current of a proper river, brown and murky with all the sediment. At the edge of a cove on its near bank stood the stone-and-wood-built settlement of Ru'geruk. The river had swamped the boat docks and lapped against the sandbags the locals had piled atop the existing stone walls to protect the waterfront buildings. From there it coursed southeastward through a tumble of low hills before heading off toward the vast reddish haze of the deserts on the horizon.

Abramm brought his gaze back to the town and the boats, and his excitement rose another notch. *Soon now, my love,* he thought. And he could not keep himself from grinning as he switchbacked down the muddy trail toward the city.

The footpath emptied into a wide square bounded by a stone trough and a low wall. The yard, a patchwork of grass and mud, stood mostly empty, just a few people standing or crouching in small groups with their horses and mules. The riverfront was another matter—it bustled with activity as men stacked bales of wool, kegs of ale, and bags of grain on the dock behind the low stone retaining wall augmented by stacked sandbags.

Abramm walked the busy boardwalk along the wall, eyeing the single-masted, wide-beamed boats drifting aimlessly over the submerged stone quays. Workers sloshed along the top of those quays, back and forth from land to boats, loading supplies and cargo. In fact, it appeared that trade goods were the cargo of choice.

He had his eye on three vessels with wooden sheds built up against the masts to serve as cabins, the trio glossy with varnish and trimmed with yellow paint. From a distance they were smart-looking boats, but when he stopped on the dock directly before them, he was disappointed. The paint was cracked and peeling in places, and the boats were glazed with a general film of dirt and grime. That could have been from the flooding, he supposed. The other vessels were no better, and most were far worse.

An old deckhand leaned on the near gunwale of the closest vessel, watching him with age-clouded eyes. He was gaunt, hunch-shouldered, and clad in a rumpled grimy tunic over which he wore a bright blue tapestry vest with gold embroidering along the front edges—the castoff of some nobleman. His thin, frizzy white hair was caught in a long queue, and the skin of his face was pale and papery. Abramm looked up at him.

"You own this boat?" he asked.

The old man shook his head.

"I'm looking to work my way downriver," Abramm said.

"River's too high right now," the voice rasped coldly. "No one'll be sailin' passengers for at least a week. Best ya go overland." The white eyes stared at him sullenly.

"Are you the captain of that vessel, then?"

"Na. That'd be Arne Dugla'is. He's the owner, too."

"And where would I find him?"

The deckhand glared at him, then waved a hand downriver. "He be in the Silver Wolf with the rest of 'em, down in the south yard. He won't take ya on, though. None of 'em will. 'Cept maybe old Janner, if he's drunk enough. 'Course, ya wouldn't get very far with him, either." The old sailor wheezed a laugh, then turned away.

Abramm continued down the walkway toward the south yard, which turned out to be considerably more active than the one through which he'd crossed earlier. People, donkeys, and sheep milled with the local dogs and cats around more bales of wool, kegs, boxes, and bags stacked in wagons or in piles on the bare ground. Traders came from the surrounding lowlands to sell their wares to the rivermen, who would take them downriver and sell them again. Two lines of men going in and out of the open doorway in the one two-story building fronting the square drew Abramm's attention, and asking about, he confirmed that this was where he would find Arne Dugla'is.

Inside the tavern the riverboat owners were spread out at different tables, traders lining up at each one. One of them pointed out Dugla'is, a potbellied man at a large table nearest the fire. He wore a leather vest over a white shirt decked with copious lace at cuffs and collar, though he wore the latter unbuttoned and gaping open so all might see his Terstan shield. Surrounded by a sprinkling of dark, wiry chest hairs, it was not a pretty sight. Stringy brown hair fell to his shoulders around a doughy face and a warm smile.

The man ahead of Abramm was a wool trader and was just finishing his transaction when Abramm stepped up to the table. The deal was closed, the papers signed, and Dugla'is's assistant counted out a payment of gold coin, then pushed it across the table toward the trader.

Then it was Abramm's turn. When he stated his business, the man's brows raised in surprise. Then his eyes flicked over Abramm's chest and shoulders and down to his hands, gauging his soundness and strength. "Ya ever worked a riverboat before?"

"No. But I've rowed in a galley ship."

"Have you?" Something about his tone and the sudden speculative look in his brown eyes set Abramm's back up. Then Dugla'is's gaze shifted to something—or someone—at Abramm's back, though when Abramm turned, there were so many men, all going about their business, that he had no idea which one Dugla'is had looked at.

Silence stretched between them as the river captain's eyes turned blank. Then, as suddenly as a flame bursting from pitch, his attention returned and he smiled jovially. "Forgive me if I'm a bit startled, but . . . Eidon be blessed! I don't suppose ya have any idea that I lost one of my best workers last week—broke his arm in a fall. I've been wondering ever since how I was going to get all my cargo stowed and handled on the river, fast and tricky as it is these days. Y'are just what I need. Come down to the docks tomorrow and we'll have a place for ya."

He smiled up at Abramm, obviously expecting him to leave now that his request had been granted. So with a "Thank you" and a "See you tomorrow," he did so.

As he stepped into the bright commotion of the square outside, Abramm waited for excitement and relief to break over him . . . but he only felt a dull sense of unease. Men jostled him as they passed, and he stepped aside out of the flow. A slight breeze washed around him, creaking the signboard that hung over the entrance, and for the first time he saw the silver wolf that had been painted upon the weathered wood.

Either the artist who had rendered it was terribly incompetent or it was no normal wolf. Indeed, the creature's large humped shoulders reminded him eerily of Tapheina, who that first night of their journey had promised to meet him here in Ru'geruk. He'd seen neither her nor her companions for weeks, and had begun to count her promise as no more than idle threat—until the night before last when he'd caught her watching him from the shadows in the forest, a beast again and so shockingly changed he'd hardly recognized her.

Her mottled silver-and-white fur had fallen away in clumps, as if she were shedding, except the skin was sloughing off along with the hair. Huge silvery bald spots stretched unevenly across her side and flanks and down her legs, the latter seeming thicker and squatter without the furry body to balance them. The bald hump was bigger and more bulbous, a grotesque deformity without its hair. Her muzzle had faded to gray, and her eyes were as clouded and milk white as a blind man's.

Even the mind behind the eyes seemed weakened and confused, pulling at him one moment, then backing away into the darker shadows when he stepped toward her. A sense of embarrassment preceded angry and spiteful images of his wife in the arms of that dark-haired eastern lord. *"Better hurry,"* she'd taunted him. *"He's almost won her away from you. . . . But we'll get you in Ru'geruk."* He had no idea what she meant by that last and no time to figure it out.

An owl had swooped out of the darkness then, talons flashing, wings battering her cheeks and ears until she'd whirled and run snarling into the trees.

He had no idea what to make of any of it—except that trouble undoubtedly awaited him in Ru'geruk.

Now as he stared up at the signboard he wondered if this place might be a residence she used when in her human form. Though he'd seen no sign of her inside, neither had he been looking. There'd been rumors along the upper trail that some of the rivermen in Ru'geruk were involved in trading slaves, preying on the groups of exiled Kiriathans who so routinely came through the town every spring and summer. Was Arne Dugla'is one? Yes, he wore a Terstan shield, but it might not be genuine. Maybe he wore it openly—a practice Abramm no longer appreciated—just so people would think him trustworthy.

Still, the man had the best table in the place and the highest stacks of coins. His boats were the best, too. Why would a man who was obviously doing well for himself want to risk something like trafficking in slaves? And what choice did Abramm have? He'd known the likelihood of being hired was slim, and having counted on Eidon to provide for him, why question when the provision was made?

"If you want to go down the river at this time of year, Krele Janner's your man," said a low voice at his back.

Abramm turned to find a man standing behind him, dark haired, with a scarred face and deep eyes. "Krele Janner?" Abramm asked.

"Best driver on the river, north or south. Even drunk he's better than most. Especially when it's flowing high like this."

"What makes you think I want to go down the river?"

"You're Kiriathan, aren't you? You all want to go downriver."

"I've already made arrangements with Captain Dugla'is in there."

"Oh? You might want to rethink that." He paused. "Will he be taking all of you, then?"

"All of us?"

"You're not with the group of Kiriathans that's trickling into the upper yard just now?"

So they'd arrived. That was good to know. "We're not together anymore. Why do you ask?"

The man ignored his question, his gaze snagging Abramm's. "You should stay with them. They're going to need you. And you're going to need them."

Abramm stared at him, completely taken aback. How did this man know him? Or the others? Where had he come from? Why was he saying such things? "Who are you?" he asked.

But the man only gestured along the river southward to the end of the town. "Janner's got a shack down there, just beyond where you see that boat on the blocks. And he needs a bowman right now."

Abramm looked in the direction he had indicated, but when he turned back, the man had wandered off, lost already in the crowd. Then his eyes fell upon the white-eyed deckhand in the blue tapestry vest with the gaudy gold embroidery. The one that worked for Dugla'is. He was looking right at Abramm, despite the blind appearance of his eyes. And he was frowning.

Abramm decided to at least talk to Krele Janner.

Though it was barely midday, the best driver on the river sat on its bank under an oak tree drinking whiskey from a gray ceramic jug. He was an unkempt, red-haired, hill-country man, his beard gilt with gold beneath squinty, pale blue eyes. Muscular arms showed a riot of freckles rather than tanning, and a long, thick scar ran diagonally across one forearm. He received Abramm's interest in filling in as his bowman for a trip downriver with studied indifference.

"Do ya even know what a bowman is?" Drinking or not, his voice carried no slur.

"Not exactly," Abramm admitted.

"Ya have experience on this river?"

"No."

"Any river?"

"No."

Janner huffed. "Least y'are honest. Most men woulda lied."

"You'd see the truth before we got to the bend in the river."

"Aye."

"I do know how to row and steer."

Abramm waited as the man drank from his jug, watching as a mama duck led her brood of ducklings out of the bushes and down to the water's edge.

"I could make it worth your while," he said quietly when the other man said nothing. "I have friends in the south—"

Janner snorted. "That's what ya all say. But then the friends turn out to be just as poor as the rest of ya."

"We all?" Abramm asked.

"You think it's not obvious what ya are? Another poor Kiriathan, hoping for a new life in Chesedh, when we can barely keep ourselves afloat. Leeches is what ya are. What ya oughta do is go down to the strait and start fighting Belthre'gar's armies."

"And I mean to, if I can just get down there."

Janner's lips twitched in a wry smile. "Do ya, now?"

"My friends are Chesedhan. Not Kiriathan. Take me to Fannath Rill, and—"

"My boats stop above the falls at Deveren Dol," Janner interrupted. "And it's more than enough that I'd trust ya for the payment as far as that. But to let ya go off t' Fannath Rill promising to return?" He huffed incredulously. "Do ya think I have wool in m' head?" He took another swig from his jug. "'Sides. The river's too dangerous for passengers. Best go overland toward Caer'akila and down to.Deveren Dol if ya can't wait. How many are you?"

"Just me."

"Well, y'are a big strong fella, so I might consider it if I had a reason to go downriver. But seeing as I have no cargo yet and no prospects of gettin' any, I'd say it would be pointless. . . . Yer promises of wealth to come notwithstanding." He took another swig from the jug. "If ya don't want to wait, take the inland road. It'll be clear by now."

"Actually Arne Dugla'is has already agreed to take me on."

Janner frowned. "Then what the plague're ya comin' here botherin' me for?"

"I don't trust him."

"A nice man like him? With that Terstan shield for all to see and know how honest and good he is?" He eyed Abramm sidelong. "Ya're smarter than ya look."

"So you're saying I'm right not to trust him."

The man looked startled, even a little scared—as if he'd not realized where his words were taking them. "I'm not sayin' anythin'." With that he stoppered the jug, ambled over to the shack, and disappeared into its dark depths.

Abramm walked back along the riverfront to the north end of the town, more conflicted than ever. As expected, he found his friends newly arrived in the north yard. Some were just shrugging out of their rucksacks and refilling their water bags at the trough.

Seeing him, Rolland came over to ask how things had gone, and Abramm told him what had happened. "I'd rather go with Janner, I think. He seems a down-to-earth sort for all his reliance on the spirits. But he won't leave until he has the cargo to justify a trip down. And from what I gather, he's something of a pariah around here."

"Well, you can always come with us." Rolland grinned at him.

"Or wait. Or talk some of you into changing your minds." He grinned back.

"We'll go with you," Cedric said, drawing their eyes and indicating himself and his father. He shrugged. "We're used to rivers . . . it'd be faster, and lots easier. Ridin' instead of walkin'. Pop's gettin' weary o' walkin'."

"I'm not sure two would be enough. I'm afraid I'm just going to have to wait."

About then Oakes Trinley came striding up from the town. With but a single snide expresson of surprise at seeing Abramm again, he announced a change in plans: "I couldna find any horses—least not that anyone wanted t' sell. But I did learn the road t' Caer'akila will be harder to travel than we thought. The snowpack's so high this year we'll not get through 'til midsummer, at least. So I made arrangements fer us t' go down the Ankrill, instead."

Abramm was not the only one to stare at him in astonishment.

Relishing his moment in the limelight, Trinley opened his hands. "None of us wanna stay here fer three months. And when they told me 'twould only take a week t' reach Deveren Dol, while we sit an' watch the scenery go by . . . well, it seemed Eidon was making his will pretty clear."

Abramm frowned. "I heard it would take closer to three or four weeks." More than that, Janner had suggested he take the road if he didn't want to wait, and said nothing about its being snowed in.

Trinley's grin widened. "That's 'cause ye talked t' the wrong man, Alaric. Krele Janner is a drunk and an incompetent. His vessels're constantly going aground, I'm told. Hittin' snags, shoals, rocks."

"How did you know I—" Abramm began.

Trinley overrode him. "An' because he spends so much time at th' bottle, he doesn't keep them up—lets the caulking dry out so thet halfway down the river they start leakin'. Those that have the misfortune of traveling with him spend most of their time bailing. Or sitting on the side of the riverbank waiting for him t' fix the leak." He turned to the others. "The man I chose has an excellent reputation. Captain Dugla'is's vessels are bigger and faster—he's the only one who could take us all, in fact. Of course, as I understand it, Alaric, ye've already made yer own arrangements with yer drunken friend, so I didn't include you in ours. . . ."

"We're not going down the river," Rolland said firmly.

Trinley shrugged. "If that's yer choice, Rollie, fine, but from what they've told me here, Caer'akila is burstin' at the seams with exiles. There's food and water shortages, an' most o' the new folks're staying in tents now. Last fall there were rumors of sickness."

"How do you know this Dugla'is isn't lying about that just to get your business?" Marta asked.

Trinley turned to her as if surprised. "Dugla'is wears the shield, Marta. He wouldn't lie to us."

Abramm snorted. "Anyone can slap on a shield and call himself Terstan. Even if it's real, he can still be in the darkness of his own Shadow."

"I suppose ye'd know all about that," Trinley sneered. "You think I can't tell a trickster when I meet one?"

"If he's a good one, aye." Rolland took up the argument now.

Trinley glared at him.

"Remember that one man who told us to b'ware?" Rolland said. "That some of 'em here are suspected o' tradin' in slaves with the desert folk? We'd make the perfect target. Nobody knows we're comin', nobody knows who we are, and no one will know if we ever arrive at our destination because we don't even know what our destination is.

A coldness settled in Abramm's gut.

"You've met Dugla'is?" Trinley demanded. "Looked into his eyes, felt his grip, talked to him? Well, I have. And anyway, why would he lie? He's got plenty o' business."

Rolland glanced uneasily at Abramm.

"Why are you looking at him?" Trinley snapped. "Dugla'is wouldn't even take him. So he's signed on with a drunkard and a brawler who can barely steer his way around the first bend without running aground. If anyone's involved in slavin' it'd be that fella Janner."

"That's not true," said Abramm. "Dugla'is did offer me a place on his boat. I'm supposed to meet him at the dock in the morning."

"Well, now ye don't have to, since he's told me there won't be room for any extras. We'll have t' do some of the rowing ourselves, in fact." He grinned smugly. "Funny how things've worked out, eh? Fer all yer impatience, Alaric, we're the ones set t' reach Fannath Rill first." He chuckled, then turned to the others. "The vessels are being prepared now. We'll move out in the morning. Right now we need to bring whatever can be stowed to the docks so they can get it loaded. I'll be down at the riverfront if you need anything." With that he picked up his rucksack and walked away.

Abramm stood where he was, chewing on his frustration as he watched the group roll into action, organizing their things into what could be taken now and what would be needed for the night, while others went about gathering wood. It would be a bitter draught to swallow, watching them ride away tomorrow without him, and he supposed he could go back to Dugla'is and ask to be squeezed in. . . .

Rolland and his wife had been arguing quietly behind him ever since Trinley had left. Now they broke off and Rolland went striding down toward the riverfront, and Abramm felt another wave of disappointment.

After a little while, his friend returned, spoke briefly to his wife, received a hug for whatever he said, and then came to where Abramm sat on a low stone wall edging the north end of the square.

"Well, it's all set," Rolland announced. "We'll be sailing on Krele Janner's *Sandpiper* in the morning."

Abramm looked at him sharply, then dropped both his feet to the ground and stood.

"All us Kemps," Rolland went on. "Plus Cedric and Totten and Marta Brackleford. And you, o' course." He was grinning now.

"But—"

"We're payin' a reduced price, an' givin' him all the things we aren't gonna need once we get to Deveren Dol. He only goes as far as Deveren Dol."

"And he's going to let me work for my way?" Abramm asked.

"We have coin, Alaric. We paid your fare."

"You have need of your coin. And I'd just as soon work."

"Aye, and just what do you know about river running?" Rolland laughed at him and shook his head. "You can pay us back once we get to Fannath Rill."

Abramm looked at him sharply, suddenly suspicious. Had Rolland finally guessed who he was?

No. It was just the offer of generosity and trust one would expect from a friend. He sighed gratefully. "Thank you, Rolland. I'll do that."

19

"And you say they walk the entire route without being chained at all?" Maddie asked of her turbaned, white-tunicked host, Draek Tiris ul Sadek.

"The entire route. For forty days," Tiris confirmed.

They were walking together through the walled garden of shoulder-high sand dunes he'd installed at the rear of his villa, following a scrupulously swept path of cream and earth-red tiling—an undeniable eccentricity at a time of year when most people's gardens held beautiful spring flowers. . . .

"Or so the legend says," he added, smiling. A gold hoop glittered in his ear at the edge of his dark beard tonight, reminding her of the first time they'd met. "Of course, even aside from the effects of the road, where would potential escapees have run to? They were surrounded by leagues of waterless dunes, and a good half of them died even when they didn't run."

She shuddered. "It sounds ghastly."

Ahead of them loomed the three-leveled outbuilding to which Tiris was escorting her, its white-plastered walls tinted pink by the setting sun, windows flashing in rectangles of bright orange. The whole was set off to especially stunning effect by the blue-purple darkness gathering on the eastern horizon beyond.

The outbuilding, which Tiris named his Desert Salon, was a recently completed addition of which he was quite proud. Tonight was its official introduction to a small, select group of fellow foreign nationals and exiles. With Ronesca and her courtiers occupied in the Great Kirikhal observing one of her many candlelight vigils for the war effort, foreigners were free to follow their own pursuits. The gathering would be heavily Kiriathan—none of them currently welcome in the palace, though most would have refused to set foot in the residence of "that snake Leyton" even if they were. It wasn't *King Leyton* anymore, nor even *the king,* but always *that snake Leyton.*

Not only were they furious about the regalia but also about Trap's having been imprisoned. It was an outrage, completely undeserved, yet after a full month he was still locked up in Larochell. His quarters were at least in accordance with his rank—Maddie had insisted upon that—but no one could move Ronesca to release him. *"It has to be by Leyton's decree"* was the stock answer. And Leyton had left for the front and might not return until summer's end. Or longer.

Maddie had figured out soon enough why he wanted Trap in jail—of all the Kiriathans here in Chesedh, he was most likely to come after what Leyton had stolen. But every day his imprisonment went on increased the boil of the Fannath Rill Kiriathans' anger. One day they could well stage a riot. Already Maddie had heard the suggestion. She had counseled them to hold their anger in, that Abramm would be here soon and he would handle it.

"I've heard it said that road is still in operation," Carissa said from where she followed Maddie and their host toward the Desert Salon. "That even today slaves are being funneled across it to the southlands where they're put in Esurhite galleys."

As they headed up the incline, Tiris glanced back at her. "I think the original destination was to the east. But the Fermikians have always been secretive. It wouldn't surprise me if their descendents were still working the old routes . . . though surely it would be easier to take their goods south across the marshes into Draesia and not even bother with the road."

They reached the salon's double doors—rich red wood carved with bas-relief birds, dunes, cities, and even a dragon high in the sky. Maddie had no time to examine it, though, for swarthy-faced servants in short white jackets, black trousers, and gold sashes pulled open the doors for them, and they stepped into the sandalwood-scented Gallery of the Great Sand Sea.

The plastered walls were sculpted to resemble the curving humps of sand dunes, above which the glass had been set in slivers leaded together to produce a heat-wave effect, dark now as the sunset faded. Curved frames covered with off-white linen arced about the room in an abstract imitation of the dune garden outside, and even the cream and earth-red pattern of the walkway was mimicked in the rug's weave. On this lowest level of the salon, waist-high pedestals stood about the faux dunes, displaying various works of art.

Ahead and several steps above stood the salon's central and largest section, where pillows and low tables had been arranged for their gathering. On the third level, overlooking all the rest, Tiris's fabulous golden fig tree shimmered in a windowed alcove at the top of a huge rock face. Water rippled down to the middle level's pool.

Many of Tiris's guests had already arrived, including Oswain Nott, Temas Darnley, and Wade Callums, one of Abramm's generals. Former Chesedhan First Minister Garival was there, as well as several of the Chesedhans who had aligned themselves with the First Daughter—anomalies among the foreigners. There were also Draesians, Thilosians, Andolens, and Sorites, among them several female acquaintances who shared Maddie's interests in history, the arts, and politics. A handful of upper-class ladies she did not know were also in attendance, to whom Tiris was quick to introduce her.

It was a bigger crowd than she'd expected, and decidedly less intimate than she'd hoped for. But she supposed Tiris could hardly invite just Kiriathans or he'd be raising eyebrows all across the city, and spurring gossip that he, too, was plotting against the queen.

The evening began with an informal period of mingling, where guests were encouraged to peruse the art objects scattered around the gallery portion of the salon, and of course Tiris was right there to show Maddie his treasures. There were figures of dragons, and of men, mounted on pedestals and carved from some sort of fantastically colored rocks, the likes of which she'd never seen. There were crystals, clever glass vases of multifarious colors, perfect orbs of smoky quartz, and a huge lump of deep yellow amber perched on a pedestal at the center of the display. Tiris claimed to have purchased the latter at an open-air market in Soria on the promise that it would show the future to those sensitive enough to see.

He claimed to have been disappointed, having not seen anything but golden swirls himself, but he urged Maddie to have a go at it.

She jerked up her chin. "I don't believe in such things, sir."

"No? And yet you claim to have seen things not present."

She frowned slightly. "That is different."

"You'll not even try?"

"I'd feel like an idiot," she said firmly. "What is this next thing here. . . ? A dragon eating a woman?" She started toward the statue in question, but something in the amber's golden depths drew her eye, and she stopped. *Just a reflection . . .* she assured herself.

Then the room vanished and the golden light resolved into flickers off the surface of a broad muddy river on which she glided downstream, the wind in her face. It had overspilled its banks, the tips of cattails extending here and there above its rippled surface, while to her left the ragged white walls of an ancient city thrust up from the submerged bank. She recognized the place at once as the ruins at Obla on the north bank of the Ankrill, upriver from the fortress at Trakas. She'd spent a goodly amount of time there in her younger days, exploring its labyrinthine streets.

Now however, her surprise at seeing it was overshadowed by her rising certainty that Abramm sat immediately behind her, that any moment he would speak and put his hand upon her shoulder. Heart pounding, she turned to look at him—

And was abruptly back in the Gallery of the Great Sand Sea, the scent of sandalwood tickling her nostrils. Instead of Abramm's hand upon her shoulder, it was Tiris's.

He stared at her in surprise. "Are you all right? The way you started and swayed, I thought you might—" His dark brows narrowed. "You saw something."

She flushed, aware she had the attention of everyone in her immediate vicinity. "I saw the ruins at Obla. From a boat on the river. A sight I've seen often enough before."

Yet she also knew that Abramm would be coming down that way. And the feel of the wind and of the water's bobbing current, and the river's distinctive odor had been extraordinarily vivid for a random memory.

"Obla?" Tiris said, even more surprised. "That's northwest of the fortress at Trakas. Why would you see that? And didn't you say you knew nothing of the Road of the Unchained?"

"Well, I *had* heard of it—but . . . what does that have to do with Obla?"

"Obla is the beginning of that road," he said. "Or near it, anyway. But if you did not know that . . . then it wasn't our discussion that prompted your vision."

"You don't really think it works, do you?" Temas Darnley asked.

"Why would she see Obla?" Minister Garival asked. "It's in the middle of nowhere."

Tiris looked at Maddie in expectation. "You tell us, Your Highness. Obla is on the Ankrill, after all. Was *he* there, too?"

She knew exactly whom he meant. "I didn't see him."

"But you felt him, didn't you?"

"Are you saying King Abramm is coming down the Ankrill right now?" Darnley asked.

"Perhaps." Tiris's intensity bled away. "It's hard to say. The amber is outside of time and can show the present or the future. Sometimes even the past."

"Well, then, what the plague good is it?" demanded Nott.

Tiris shrugged. "The viewer must make the time determination."

"I don't know," said Maddie. "It was earlier in the day than it is now."

"Why don't you have another look?" Darnley suggested.

But Tiris informed them that wouldn't work. Once the amber had been used, it would not present another vision for several days. Nott insisted Maddie give it another try, anyway, and Tiris was proven correct. They continued the tour then, though with less enthusiasm than previously, and Maddie couldn't help but notice the way guests congregated about the lump of amber, staring into it. Which was just as well because some of the remaining pieces of his collection were so scandalous that as soon as she realized what she was looking at, she flushed bright red and moved on without comment.

Tiris noted her discomfort but said nothing, only gave her a sly, amused smile. Thankfully he did not insist upon stopping to dissect and comment upon the works, and finally he took her up to the third level of the salon and the fabulous golden fig tree. He told the guests he'd been assured it would never die, that it needed very little water, and yet it produced copious quantities of fruit year round. Its golden flowers could only be pollinated by a special kind of wasps that lived their entire lives upon the tree. "The tree actually produces a small version of the fruits to house them," Tiris explained. "Without them the tree would produce no fruit."

"Pollinate the flower? But this tree is made of gold," Darnley said, fingering a leaf.

"Aye, and the fruits are solid gold, as well. . . ."

"Then how can it be alive?"

Tiris grinned and spread his hands. "I don't know. That is why it is such a wonder."

"You're saying this tree grows solid gold fruit?" Maddie asked skeptically.

"Indeed, my lovely queen." Tiris reached up to pluck one from beneath the foliage and handed it to her. As she turned it in her hands, Tiris gestured at the stem. "See, it's obviously a plant . . . but the fruit . . . well, you can feel it for yourself."

"Do they sting?" asked one of the Thilosian ladies. "The wasps?"

He chuckled. "Certainly not, my lady."

"You think he would have stinging wasps in his salon?" her friend asked of her.

"Well, it's all very odd to me," the first lady admitted.

"It is a wonder," Tiris agreed. "Brought all the way from Chena'ag Tor, I'm told. As was the amber."

"That cannot be possible, sir," declared one of the Sorites. "No man has ever gone to Chena'ag Tor. If it even exists."

"No man has ever gone and *returned*. . . ." Tiris corrected. "Or so they say."

The other man snorted. "What's the difference, Draek? If no man can return, how could anyone bring this tree with him? If no man can return, how could anyone know if any of the stories are even true?"

Maddie kept her attention on Tiris, wondering if he was going to tell them of his own journey to the city.

Instead he only smiled at his guests and said, "Indeed, how can one know? The stories are fantastic. They say there are dragons there. A whole colony of them." His dark eyes found Maddie's, laughing at her.

She took the bait, replaying the discussion they'd had months ago when first he'd told her of the place. "Dragons in the middle of the Great Sand Sea, you say?"

"Trapped now for millennia."

"What, then, do they eat?" she asked. "Next you will tell me that in addition to guarding their treasure they keep great flocks of sheep on which to dine."

He cocked a brow at her. "Maybe they don't need to eat."

"Or maybe they eat each other!" one of the Thilosians suggested.

The Sorite remained disgruntled. "How can you trap a dragon in a city?" he sneered. "Does it have a great lid on it, then?"

The others laughed, and Tiris received their amusement with a sheepish spreading of his hands. "I tell you only what I have heard."

After that they returned to the middle tier, and after sufficient time for all the guests to have examined his tree, Tiris began his introduction to the special performance he had promised them. As they assembled on the circle of large floor pillows, he drew all eyes again to the golden tree standing at the head of the waterfall above them and recited an ancient Sorite poem extolling the tree's fruit, which was believed to have once imparted wisdom and understanding beyond the realm of any normal man's abilities—if you could find it in the moments before it turned to solid gold.

As he spoke, Maddie watched the fig wasps flying about the tree, little motes of golden light, and thought what a strange thing it all was. But then, she'd seen many strange things in the gallery. Her thoughts returned to the amber and the strong sense of Abramm sitting behind her on the river. Tiris said she was the one who must determine the time, and she thought perhaps it was today or tomorrow. In any case, he was on the Ankrill, close to Obla. Which meant he truly would be in Fannath Rill before the month was out. Her heart leapt with joy . . . and then a sudden silence intruded into her thoughts, and she realized the group's attention had shifted off of Tiris and onto herself.

He had introduced her, and she'd heard not a word of what he'd said. Perhaps that was just as well. The time had come for her to sing. She took up the lirret, half expecting it to slip from her suddenly trembling fingers, and set it in her lap, careful not to pay too much attention to her audience just yet. Drawing a deep breath, she closed her eyes, sought Eidon's strength, and began. Her fingers danced over the strings in the ballad's opening arpeggio, and she hit the first note perfectly. From there on, as always, the song itself swept her away.

It wasn't long before she knew she was delivering the performance of her life. Her audience sat enrapt. Unshed tears glittered in the most unlikely eyes. But just before the new part, just before the best part, the crescendo when the story took its turn from tragedy to victory, some note brought the wasps fluttering down upon them. Swirling motes of gold flashed above the heads of those gathered, though at first only Maddie seemed to notice. They buzzed around, adding their tiny voices to the song in a distracting dissonance.

Focused as she was on her music, she ignored them for the most part, though when at the end they actually came to rest upon her audience, she felt a chill crawl up her spine and came in on the last chorus half a beat too late. Determinedly she closed her eyes and focused on the song, on bringing out these last notes with perfect pitch and intensity.

Then it was done. He had returned, the battle was won, the people rejoiced.

The last chord faded, and only then did she open her eyes again.

Her audience sat spellbound, covered with tiny golden wasps. She could not tell from their faces what they had thought, but the wasps unnerved her. It got worse the longer no one moved or spoke.

Then Tiris said, "Well, that was a most lovely performance, Your Highness."

Suddenly the wasps lifted off the gathering, a great cloud of them, which at last the people noticed. They leaped up, exclaiming in alarm, and fell to brushing the wasps off one another's backs, knocking them from hair and mustache and shaking out their skirts.

"Please," Tiris called out to them. "Your alarm is unfounded. They are harmless, merely entranced, as we all were, by the lady's performance. Do not hurt them. They will return to the tree in a few moments."

And so they did.

Then, slowly, the gathering returned their focus to Maddie and her performance. Inexplicably concerned that the wasps had negatively impacted their perception of it, she was thrilled to find it was actually the opposite. As on the night when she'd performed the "Legend of the White Pretender" for Abramm and his Kiriathan court, when the people had mobbed her, raving in astonishment over her talent and the beauty of her song, so they did tonight. The Kiriathans came to her with shining eyes, thanking her for restoring their self-respect and asking again and again if she really believed Abramm was coming back. And again and again she assured them that she did.

Afterward she heard them talking amongst themselves. Darnley claimed he'd almost seen Abramm himself when Maddie was singing; and Nott said that her vision in the amber was most convincing, as well. He wanted to return and have a look into it himself in a day or so. Even Minister Garival confessed to being strongly swayed by her obvious confidence in her husband's return, though he seemed more troubled by that prospect than the others.

Alone of them, Carissa remained unconvinced. She never said it blatantly, but Maddie could tell from her reserve and the sad look in her eyes that she considered it all a delusion, born of Maddie's battle with the spore while in the midst of a difficult labor. She'd already warned against proceeding with this course, as had her husband from jail—the two of them unaware they were echoing each other. Both feared the ridicule and censure that would descend on Maddie for daring to make such claims publicly. But even the fact that had not occurred did not mollify Carissa's disapproval.

Overall, though, the evening was a stunning success, and Maddie was almost giddy by the end of it. She, Carissa, and the Kiriathan leaders were just leaving when one of Tiris's servants hurried into the salon and came to speak softly into the draek's ear. He sobered immediately, his dark eyes tracking to Maddie as he listened.

He asked a few quiet questions, then finally turned to his remaining guests and said, "I have just received the grim news that King Leyton has been captured by the Esurhites. He and both his sons."

There followed a shocked silence, then an outpouring of gasping denials and questions.

"And what of our regalia?" demanded Oswain Nott. "Did he lose them, too, along with himself?"

Tiris met his gaze grimly. "I'm afraid so, Lord Oswain. He was caught and all the pieces with him. The queen has closeted herself to seek Eidon's mercy and guidance, and asks us all to do likewise."

Janner's *Sandpiper* glided out of Ru'geruk just as the early morning river mist was lifting—some two hours behind Dugla'is's three yellow-trimmed vessels. The small boat's passengers—the Kemps, the Ashvelts, and Marta—huddled on the thwarts, silent and shivering under their cloaks as they pressed together for warmth. Abramm sat at the prow, oar in hand, ready to do as Janner commanded, while Janner himself, sober but miserable, manned the steering oar at the stern.

Because of their later start, they didn't have to suffer long in the chill of the morning, and soon the sun shone in their eyes and warmed their faces. Janner asked Rolland if he wanted them to overtake the other party. " 'Cause we could do it, easy. This boat is lighter and slimmer—faster through the water than his clunkers."

Rolland looked to Abramm for an answer, and Abramm shook his head. "Just catch up enough for us to keep track of them. I don't want to join them, but I would like to be available if our suspicions prove true."

Janner had scowled and muttered something about not being part of some half-brained rescue operation, and Abramm shared another glance with Rolland. The three of them had been up late last night, discussing the grim possibility that Dugla'is really was in league with the slavers of the eastern deserts. Abramm and Rolland had no idea what they might do should that be the case. There seemed precious little chance of success, especially without Janner's help—and he had declared his resistance very firmly—but Abramm was confident Eidon would help them if and when the time came.

Janner was as testy and arrogant sober as he'd been when drunk, but his skill on the river was all they had been told it was. He knew the Ankrill well, even at flood stage, and guided their craft expertly through the channels and safe lanes, taking the rapids they encountered at just the right angle, avoiding shoals, guessing almost the exact spot where the new buildups of silt would occur and where the old would be eaten away. Though Abramm was supposedly positioned to help him, the man never asked him to do a thing.

They caught up with Dugla'is before noon the first day, then had to deliberately hang back to avoid being spotted. Which meant they could make a leisurely departure each morning, and even stop on the banks occasionally to relieve themselves or stretch their legs. They routinely stopped for lunch, though the same could not be said for the party they followed.

On the third night, Janner—aided by the liberating influence of the spirits he still imbibed every evening—once again talked of the things he'd observed and heard and suspected regarding Dugla'is's involvement in the trading of slaves. Abramm, Cedric, and Rolland sat with him around their small campfire—the children tucked away with Daesi and Marta in the tent, old Totten asleep in his bedroll nearby, lulled by the river's rush and the myriad calls of the frogs and insects that came out at night.

"Never had it proved to my satisfaction," Janner said, his eyes on the tin cup he held in scarred and callused hands. "Never seen anything, never caught him at anything . . . I've talked to some he's transported. Met up with them in Trakas and even Deveren Dol. But I also saw at least two parties leave Ru'geruk with him that no one after the Trakas bend ever heard of." He looked up and met Abramm's eyes. "He claimed the people wanted off upriver at one of the garrisons, intending to head toward Caer'akila. I asked up and down the river and turned up nothing, but that doesn't mean a lot. Folk don't stay there long, even the locals. And folk not planning to stay at all could well have been there only an hour at most."

"Wouldn't they have had to make arrangements for their travel?" Rolland asked. "Get directions, hire a guide, buy some horses or a cart?"

"Could you folk buy horses and a cart if I dropped you off along here?"

The big man frowned but said nothing, nor did Cedric, who appeared shocked by everything the riverman was revealing.

"As for the other," Janner went on, "they'd not need directions because the road is plain. And Dugla'is said they had some Chesedhans among them."

"But you think they never made it," said Abramm.

Janner shook his head and emptied his cup. "Don't think yer friends will make it, either."

Abramm exchanged a glance with Rolland, then asked Janner why he thought that.

"Timing's perfect. No one will be coming upriver on account of the flooding, so he needn't worry about being caught that way. I think he stops at Obla—an old Ophiran ruin. The mist is always thick there, so most think it's cursed and avoid it. But with the mist and all the walls, it's a good place to do bad things. And the landing's on the east bank, so it'd be a good spot to meet up with the Fermikians."

"Fermikians?"

"Men who know the routes through the Great Sand Sea."

"But how would *they* know he was coming?"

Janner snorted. "He probably sent out his birds the night before we left." When Abramm looked surprised, he added, "If Dugla'is is involved in the trade, he's not the only one. Locals don't like all you Kiriathans swarming into our lands. They're inclined to look away should ill befall you. And there are innkeepers and river runners both who wouldn't bat an eye at taking advantage of people like you all."

Again Abramm met Rolland's eyes, but neither of them spoke. Cedric stood from the fire first—without a word—and stooped to spread out his bedroll. Since there wasn't much more to say, the others soon followed his lead.

As they traveled downriver over the next few days, they passed beacon towers, an occasional small garrison, and more and more often, signs of recently raided farms and villages off in the fields to the northeast. Finally, five nights along and only two-thirds of the way to Trakas according to Janner—which effectively nullified Dugla'is's time estimate of reaching Deveren Dol within a week—Abramm first saw the signal lights. They flashed red off the cloud of smoke that hung over a nearby ridge and presumably the neighboring camp. If he had not been away from his own group's campfire seeing to his business, he wouldn't have seen it, but the moment he did, he knew what it was. With the night silence broken only by the sounds of the insects and the night birds and the frogs at the river, he crept over to the ridgetop and settled himself in a good position to see Dugla'is's camp, but by then no one was stirring, and the fire was dying down enough he wondered if he'd imagined it. Or else had seen the fire's reflection and made it something it wasn't.

But when the light show was repeated the next night, and Abramm pointed it out, Janner immediately agreed with his assessment, though he expressed surprise at the acuity of Abramm's sight. "I've never seen 'em myself before," he said, "though now you point it out, it's clear."

Rolland wanted to confront Dugla'is the moment he saw them, but the others talked him out of it. For one thing, Dugla'is would never admit to having generated the signals. "And you think Trinley would believe us over him?" Abramm asked.

"Worse," Janner added, "is that he'll know we're on to him."

"Surely he must know we're behind him."

"He does. In fact, I think he's been deliberately making poor time, hoping we'll go past. Probably even wondering why we don't." Janner squinted up into the night sky, dark now, the scarlet light having long-since vanished.

"We should overtake them, then," Abramm said, "find a place to hide downriver, then let them pass us again without their knowing it."

"The mists in Obla are thick," Janner said, nodding. "And the ruins offer plenty of inlets to hide, especially now with the river so high."

Abramm shook his head. "No. If you think he meets with the slavers in Obla, I want to be behind him again before we get there."

Janner frowned. "There may be a couple of places downstream we might tuck into, but . . ." He trailed off, looking doubtful.

"We'll make it work," Abramm said.

20

They passed Dugla'is's three vessels the next morning, coming up on them slowly, then tracking alongside them, the two groups exchanging playful jibes for a time until the current picked up and Janner's *Sandpiper* swiftly outdistanced the other boats. Abramm left them with the image of the gaunt blue-vested boatman burned into his memory, his white eyes staring at Abramm with an unnerving intensity that seemed somehow familiar.

The remainder of the day they played with the other group, making frequent rest stops so they might wait for Dugla'is's slower vessels to catch up, then sprinting ahead again when they did. That night they estimated the location of the other group's camp, now not far behind them, by the scarlet lights flickering on the campfire smoke again. The next morning they headed down the river early to find a place to hide. And a good thing, too, for Janner was right to be concerned. They had to tuck the *Sandpiper* deep into a flooded willow stand, to the point of running her aground, and even then they were visible from the main current in the river if one knew what to look for.

But Eidon was with them, and Dugla'is's vessels sailed right past without a hint that anyone had seen them. After that it was a matter of keeping far enough back to avoid being spotted, but close enough they'd still get there in time when Dugla'is made his trade.

By midafternoon, they had reached the outskirts of Obla, where as Janner had predicted, the high waters submerged the river grasses that normally lined its banks and stood halfway up the trunks of the trees beyond them, or reached in long fingers through the outlying cotton fields. A thin mist overhung water and field and drifted between trees and the old columns and shards of ancient walls thrusting up from the weeds here and there. The farther south they traveled, the thicker it became, until by day's end it had completely veiled their surroundings.

As twilight deepened around them, they glided along in silence, Abramm seated at *Sandpiper's* prow as they searched for Dugla'is's moorage. Janner followed the contours of the river's edge, its waters having overrun the city's ancient retaining walls to lap against the crumbling remains of old buildings and stairways. Shapes and shadows emerged from the gloom seemingly at the last minute, and time and again they narrowly averted collision. As the riverman had said, it was no natural mist, but the dry, chill fog of Moroq's Shadow.

Finally they came round a bend and Abramm spied three pale shapes in the gloom ahead of them. Hissing for Janner's attention, he pointed them out. Even so, the riverman almost hit them, passing them by less than an oarslength. They were Dugla'is's vessels, snugged up to the city walls and floating there deserted. Which was both blessing and curse. Blessing because it was the only way the rescuers hadn't been spotted. Curse because it meant Dugla'is was probably already making his evil transaction.

No one said a word as they continued down the river and around another bend. There Janner guided his vessel up over a submerged shelf of mortared white stone and tied her to an iron ring set into a white wall. Wading through knee-deep waters to a narrow stairway, they ascended to a weed-grown plaza whose walls loomed vaguely in the mist. There Janner said they would camp.

"But no fire tonight," he cautioned. "Only warmstars for the children inside the tent."

"You think we're in danger?" Abramm asked him quietly.

"I think it's best we not draw attention to ourselves," Janner said, "and hope they still believe we're long gone down the river."

That only intensified the tension that had been building among them all since they'd first seen the signal lights and realized the worst was coming. They carried out the rest of their preparations in silence, Daesi and Marta hurrying the children into the tent as soon as it was up and preparing the meal over the warmstars within.

Meanwhile, Janner led Abramm and Rolland into the city's ancient corridors to try to deliver their friends. But, though Janner had a sword and the other two their staffs, Abramm had no idea what they could do against a full company of Fermikians, whom Janner said went armed everywhere they went. More than that, whatever the situation they encountered this night, they would surely be outnumbered. The only hope of success he saw was if the men in Trinley's party helped them.

"How is it ya see so well in the dark?" Janner asked abruptly as they stepped into a narrow alleyway behind the building where they were camped.

"It's a gift," Abramm said.

"You see through the Shadow, as well."

"And your point is?"

Janner shrugged. "Just unusual. A bit unnerving. Makes me wonder why."

"Makes you wonder if you can trust—" Abramm broke off, listening intently. "What is that noise?"

It was a low rhythmic rumble, though he couldn't place its direction of origin.

They all stopped and listened to what seemed a distant bumping, scraping sound that faded into silence soon after they noted it. The riverman shook his head. They walked on in silence, hearing it several more times as they pressed deeper into the ruined city, but never did its nature grow clearer.

Finally they passed through a short arched tunnel and found themselves emerging onto the midlevel tier of a small amphitheater where Dugla'is had brought his little group to camp. A bonfire of thorn branches danced at the midst of what was once a central stage, its pavement buckled and invaded by grasses and weeds. Two opposing tunnel gateways yawned darkly amidst rising concentric rings of white-granite stairs, one tunnel heading toward the river, the other toward the city's heart. The fire's glow lit the amphitheater all the way up to the highest tier, where fluted decorative columns plunged into a thick ceiling of mist. An acrid odor tinged the air, vaguely familiar.

Though Dugla'is and his company had likely arrived several hours ago, there was no sign of any cooking under way or finishing up, no tents raised, and no bedrolls laid out. Instead, three of Dugla'is's men stood at intervals around the encampment as if on guard, and Dugla'is himself, conspicuous in his lace-cuffed shirt and leather tunic, paced before a fifth man a little way off from the fire—which left two of his men unaccounted for, one of them the white-eyed, blue-vested deckhand who had so unsettled Abramm when they'd passed them on the river the day before.

The Kiriathans stood in two groups, the women and children huddled together on one side of the fire, the men standing in an eerie stillness on the other, staring at Dugla'is.

"Odd the way they're all standin' there," Rolland whispered. "Like they don't know what they're doin'. Or they're asleep 'r something."

"They're drugged," Janner said.

From overhead came the sound of leaves rustling in the wind, though the air stood perfectly still. Abramm glanced upward, confirming the absence of trees or vines, only the mist-swallowed columns.

"Probably put it in the food," Janner said. He shook his head and murmured incredulously, "He really *is* a blood-sucking slave trader."

"What are we gonna do?" Rolland asked.

At that moment, the sixth of Dugla'is's men emerged from the tunnel on the left, the one closest to the river. He strode up to his employer as if to make a report. Dugla'is replied briefly, his motions sharp and tense. The man shook his head and rattled off an elaboration, gesturing back the way he had come. Abramm could hear the mutter of their voices, but nothing discernible as words.

Overhead, the leaves rattled again.

Though Dugla'is questioned his man ever more sternly, the latter shook his head with increasing certainty. Finally he fell silent as Dugla'is turned away, barking a heartfelt blasphemy that carried up the stone tiers quite distinctly. The three men who watched him from the midlevel tunnel withdrew to its concealing darkness.

"He sent that other man back to find us," Janner whispered. "Now Dugla'is wonders if his ploy failed and we passed him again."

"Maybe we should get back to our own camp," Rolland murmured, glancing worriedly at Abramm.

The latter had no answer for him, ideas of what they might do tumbling through his head at breakneck pace. They were four men against seven— eight if the blue-vested man returned or, worse, if the Fermikians whom Dugla'is awaited arrived anytime soon.

Barely had he formed the thought when it became reality and five men emerged from the cityside tunnel, clad in the sand-colored robes and turbans of the desert men. Curved swords hung at their hips, along with shorter blades scabbarded in red or black leather. A long strip of looping gold braid dangled around the neck of the one in front, while two in the rear lugged an obviously heavy wooden chest.

Dugla'is strode to meet the man with the gold braid, speaking sharply, as if the group were late. The newcomer shrugged lazily and turned his gaze to the two docile groups of people standing by the fire. Both men and women watched the Fermikians as if they were simply more of Dugla'is's boatmen.

The leader smiled, said something more to the riverman, then raised a hand. Immediately the two men with the chest advanced to drop it at Dugla'is's feet.

The Chesedhan's second-in-command stepped forward to unlatch the lid and press it back. Gold coin˙ and tableware glinted in the firelight as he shoved a hand deep into the treasure, then nodded up at Dugla'is. Shortly, two of the Chesedhan crewmen lugged the chest into the riverside tunnel, presumably to load it on their vessel.

Now the Fermikians advanced on the Kiriathans, who watched them unconcernedly. And when the gold-braid-decked desert man bid them in heavily accented Kiriathan to "Come this way," they complied as docilely as sheep, Abramm realized two things—one, that they were not the first group to be preyed upon like this, and two, he was not going to stand by and let it happen, regardless of the odds.

The decision seized him suddenly, surprising him as much as it did everyone else. One moment he was a passive observer, and the next he was charging down the steps, staff in hand, bellowing at Trinley and Galen and the others to "Wake up! It's a trap! You're being deceived."

He was halfway to the bottom when he felt a sudden smothering crow of triumph as his arena-trained senses screamed with the awareness of imminent danger. Skidding to a stop, he turned toward the papery sound swooping toward him. Monstrous wings blocked his view of everything but a pair of crested yellow eyes above gaping jaws. A blast of hot, sweetly foul breath caught him square in the face as he hurled himself backward to avoid the talons that came in after the breath, struggling to believe the obvious truth that he was being attacked by a dragon. Not of dream, not of myth, but real flesh and blood and claw.

Stumbling off the edge of the tier, he lost balance and fell, bouncing and slithering down several more tiers before he came to a stop, overwhelmed by the burning in his eyes and the crawling, gagging fire that seared the inside of his mouth and throat. The dragon's breath was like that of the tanniym—caustic, poisonous, spore-filled—but in a far more powerful dose.

A familiar voice spoke in his head: *"Still think I'm not a dragon, pup?"*

Tapheina? Shock paralyzed him. What was she doing here? How had she become a dragon? And where was she now?

Coming for him—that much was sure.

Calling on the Light to burn off the spore, he scrambled upright, vision still blurred by tears and obscured by the brightness. No matter—he had to keep moving, and down was the best option. Charging down the tiers, he felt the wind of her wings and the hot fever of her essence coming in behind him, too fast, too soon. He stepped suddenly out of her line of attack and ducked, holding his staff horizontally before him and then jabbing one end of it up into her side as she dove past him. Light sizzled up the stick's length and toppled the creature sideways. One wing hit the stone tiers hard, and she flipped over, stuttering downward over the steps, screaming furiously. But when she hit the paved stage at the bottom, she'd twisted herself round so as to fling herself back at him, her jaws catching the fabric of his tunic as he dodged their vicious snap.

This time he didn't turn to face her but charged down the last few steps to the central pavement and out into its center. When he turned back, Rolland was between him and the oncoming dragon, swinging his staff like a bat and slamming it into the side of her head, the force of his blow reeling her backward and onto her side. Trusting that Rolland had his back now, Abramm whirled and brained one of Dugla'is's men with his staff, jabbed another in the stomach, and had no sooner thought of what he wanted to do next when a burst of white fire leaped off the staff's end. It hissed through the air toward where the women and children clung together wide-eyed and there formed a dome of light around them.

Rolland's grunt, followed by a heavy thud, turned him back to see his friend rolling away from him an instant before the dragon was on Abramm himself, driving the leading, bony edge of her wing into his temple. Whiteness erupted across the world, and he staggered backward, knees wobbling, fighting to keep conscious, praying for the strength to draw himself together. The amphitheater steadied around him again, but he'd lost his staff. His wooziness vanished as the tanniym came barreling at him from the ground, leaping across the pavement with the speed of a big cat, snapping and hissing and blowing gouts of poisonous breath.

Desperately Abramm dodged and rolled away from her, the Light flickering and flaring within him as the spore invaded his flesh repeatedly. Then he saw that Rolland was up again, stepping between him and his adversary and swinging his staff with a mighty wallop. She was ready for him this time, turning aside so that his blow just glanced her shoulder even as her heavy tail swept his legs out from under him and brought him down a second time.

With nothing to defend himself, Abramm scurried back from her. He stumbled over one of the men he'd downed earlier and tore the sword from the man's nerveless grip. As he leaped up, he found himself shoulder to shoulder with Krele Janner.

His captured friends were fast disappearing into the cityside tunnel now, the Fermikians following after them, swords drawn in a rearguard action even as the dragon took to the air again and exhaled a fine, glistening mist over them all. Abramm was gasping too hard to hold his breath and inhaled the sweet-acrid poison in a great lungful, coughing and wheezing as it seared into his chest, wooziness taking him yet again. They couldn't last much longer. *Please, my Lord Eidon. I need your strength. . . .*

And again the Light flowed through him. Eyes still stinging and full of tears, he brought two hands to the hilt of his stolen sword and braced his feet apart. Behind him the shield of Light around the women and children sizzled as the dragon's breath hit it, and they screamed in terror. From out of the tunnel somewhere in the blur to his right came the shouts of men, angry and fearful. He saw the vague shapes of the Fermikians backing into its darkness—

The dragon hit him hard from behind, and he fell forward onto his knees as fire bit deeply into his left shoulder and spore raced wildly through his bloodstream, setting his old wrist wound and the morwhol-caused scars on his arm and face into flames of their own. He saw his wife, dancing with a tall, handsome, dark-bearded man who smiled down at her with a look of possessiveness that provoked Abramm to a rage of jealousy and frustration. The dark-haired lord looked straight at him now, his dark eyes flashing as he smiled in taunting triumph.

Abramm slammed it all down, forcing the image away and calling on the Light yet again. He bent to retrieve his sword as Rolland stepped protectively in front of him, staff in hand, searching the mist above them, though Abramm knew he couldn't see through the Shadow. "She's clinging to the rightmost columns at the top of the ring," he said. Rolland's head turned in that direction as the dragon's yellow eyes skewered Abramm's own.

Her laughter sounded in his head. *"That one cannot help you, little pup. He is too slow and stupid. . . ."*

The spore raced through him hot and nauseating. His left arm burned as if it were plunged in fire, but he refused to consider it. One of Dugla'is's men stirred, pulling Rolland's gaze away, and Tapheina hurled herself off her column. She was almost on them when Abramm erupted from his crouch, knocking Rolland forward with his shoulder as he drove his sword at the creature's silver-scaled breast. For a heartbeat the tip caught, refusing to penetrate. Then he shoved hard, the Light rushed wildly through him, and steel overcame scale and bone, plunging deep into the dragon's heart.

Fire blasted up his arm into the blade as violet blood coursed down it, burning as it came. He felt the dark blue of this new, stronger spore creeping into skin and muscle but refused to let it have more of him than that. The Light shot through him, a current of energy and warmth and searing illumination. He glimpsed Tersius, hanging between heaven and earth, then robed in white and seated on a throne above a vast floor of gleaming crystal. Heavenly voices swelled in powerful chorus, and a sharp, invigorating fragrance buoyed him as he floated on air. . . .

He awakened to find himself lying on the central stage where he'd fallen, his clothing tattered and stained from the effects of the dragon's blood. Beside him sprawled a dead woman, long silvery ropes of hair splayed about her head, a bloody hole in the front of her bright blue vest. He recognized her at once and, disbelieving, levered himself onto his elbows for a better look.

"It was a shapeshifter." Rolland's voice drew his attention around to his offside, where the big blacksmith crouched, staring at him white-faced. He glanced first at the dead woman, then at Abramm again, his expression compounded of dread and wonder.

"Shifted back to this right after the two of you fell," Janner offered from where he stood at Abramm's head. He, too, stared at Abramm oddly.

"She was Dugla'is's old boatman," Abramm said. "I never guessed."

"Are you all right?" Rolland asked. "Your scars . . . on your face. They're all red."

Abramm sat up all the way and touched the twin tracks where they ran over his cheekbone, newly sensitized from the residual spore in them having been awakened. "It'll fade," he said, rocking forward to stand.

"What just happened to ya?" Janner asked tightly.

"I used the Light to purge the spore she put into me," Abramm said.

"I've never seen anything like it. Can all Terstans do that?"

"If they've cultivated the Light enough to know how to let it work . . ." He glanced at Rolland, nodding at the bloody slices on his shoulder. "Speaking of, you'd better do a purge yourself, my friend."

Abramm bent to pick up the sword, then stood looking down at the dead shapeshifter, dismayed to find in himself something that felt entirely too close to sorrow. She'd tried to kill him, after all. . . . Tanniym. Dragon spawn. They'd fled to the Aranaak when the flood had come and there adapted their creature form to the environment—so Laud had speculated. But when she had come down out of the mountains, she'd drawn nearer her dragon roots. Had that prompted the transformation? He recalled now the hump in her wolf-form's shoulders—wings?—and how the last time he'd seen her she'd been shedding gouts of skin and fur, a white film over her eyes like that over the boatman's. . . .

She'd shed her old form and emerged in the new.

"What was she doing with Dugla'is?" Janner wondered aloud.

Abramm met the riverman's blue eyes grimly. "Using him. She was a tan-niym, first generation. He had little chance against her wiles. And once she'd won him, I'm sure it was easy to push him into working for the Fermikians."

Rolland was staring at him white-faced. "Is this yer . . . Tapheina?"

Abramm nodded uncomfortably, then switched the subject. "You must do your purge now, Rolland."

"But what if they come back?"

"They won't," Abramm said.

"Dugla'is is surely speeding down the river as we speak," said Janner. "Try-ing to distance himself so he can deny it all. And the others . . ." He shrugged. "They have what they came for."

"Aye!" Kitrenna Trinley said sharply from across the circle. The shield around the women had dissipated as the men talked. "Shouldn't ye be going after 'em? The longer ye wait, the harder it'll be to get 'em back."

"Get them back?" Abramm cocked an amused brow. "There's only four of us, Mistress Trinley. Even if we found them, what do you think we could do?"

"Don't count me in that four," Janner cut in. "What's lost is lost, and I'm not risking my own neck for a flock of idiot Kiriathans. They should've had more sense than to trust the likes of Dugla'is."

Kitrenna strode swiftly across the pavement to confront Abramm face-to-face. "I expect such talk from a Chesedhan," she said quietly. "But ye claim to have served our king."

Her glance shifted accusingly to Rolland, standing at Abramm's side. He transferred his weight from one leg to the other. "Blast it, Kit!" he cried. "Ye'd have me abandon my own family to look for yers?"

She only stared at them, and when after a time no one said anything, young Jania began to wail, her baby girl clutched to her breast. "Oh, sweet Eidon. Ye can't just abandon 'em—give 'em over to be slaves! Ye can't!"

Kitrenna's stare hardened into a glare, and she stepped even closer. "Ye would see that poor girl lost in a foreign land with her baby girl and no husband to care for 'em?" she demanded quietly. "Ye would see all of us bereft like this when ye could turn it all around?"

"How?" Abramm demanded. "What would you have us do? Blunder out there without the vaguest idea where we're going or what we face? Not even knowing how badly we'd be outnumbered?"

"Eidon doesn't care about numbers, Alaric!" Kitrenna snapped.

Abramm recoiled before the intensity of her anger.

"If ye will only go after 'em, perhaps *He* will show ye what to do."

It shocked him to be reproved by the likes of Kitrenna Trinley, whom he'd never thought of as being strong in the Light or versed in the Words, but reproved he was. Because as soon as the words left her lips, he knew that she was right. Of course he had to rescue them. And if it meant putting off his anticipated reunion with his own family a little while longer, what did that matter? His friends, his countrymen, his subjects needed rescuing. And wasn't this part of the calling? To put aside one's personal desires for the good of those one ruled? Even if they didn't understand who you were or why you did it? And he of all people knew that Eidon had no need of numbers.

He released a long breath of resignation. "Very well. I'll do what I can."

───────────

Queen Ronesca remained closeted for an entire day with High Kohal Minirth before announcing that she would trust Eidon to deliver her husband and sons, and there would be no escalation of the war efforts Leyton's generals were requesting. In addition, she echoed High Kohal Minirth's call for a purification of the city and its people. All the faithful should join in a week of prayer and vigils, beseeching Eidon to deliver their king from the evil one.

The Kiriathans, meanwhile, had been galvanized to action both by what had befallen Leyton—who had gotten exactly what he deserved, they said—and by Maddie's song. All were utterly convinced now that Abramm was not only alive but would be returning any time. They told everyone the story of Maddie seeing him heading down the Ankrill at Obla—even though they knew as well as Carissa that she'd not actually seen him. Even Nott, who had made good on his desire to return to Tiris's salon and look into the amber himself, had admitted to seeing only the ruins, though he claimed he, too, had felt the king's presence. Since he and Abramm had never been close, Carissa found that hard to believe, but no one was interested in her gloomy refutations. Instead, they believed with all their hearts they would soon see a miracle, and it had emboldened them.

Daily they complained of the unjust imprisonment of Trap Meridon, former First Minister of Kiriath, demanding to know the charges against him, which still had not been announced. They were incensed more than ever that Leyton had taken their regalia, and one speaker after another promised a dire fate at the hands of the Esurhites for the scoundrel, thief, and liar, *that snake Leyton*.

Daily, men—or their wives—came to Carissa urging her to seek Trap's release. She was Crown Princess of Kiriath—she had the right.

She might have the right, but her status was not recognized in Chesedh, and so far not even Maddie had been able to gain his release. Ronesca was perpetually praying or resting or otherwise too busy to see her. Carissa couldn't even persuade the authorities to allow her to visit Trap, though he was her own husband.

Every time she went down to see him, or bring him some clean clothing or soap or some notes from Terstmeet, they took the things but told her she could not see him.

Finally she sought out Temmand Garival, who, having been dismissed from his post in the royal cabinet, had taken Trap's place as Maddie's finance secretary. He assured Carissa it was absolutely her right to see her husband and offered to accompany her on her next visit.

Thus, two weeks after Maddie's performance in Tiris's Desert Salon, Carissa crossed the city for the fifth time to enter the prison and ask to see her husband. As always, the warden gave her egress to the level where her husband was housed, but she was forced to stop at the iron-bound door that guarded the entrance to his cell block. She banged on the door with the ladle that had been looped through the latch, grumbling at Eidon as she did it. For each time she came here it distressed her more and more that Trap should be reduced to this. And more that Eidon would have allowed him to be arrested just when she had come to her senses and was about to make things right between them. *How could you do this to me? And worse, to him?* Sometimes the old bitterness and self-pity seized her with a vengeance, and she wallowed into thoughts of how he never blessed her. . . . Always everyone else—never her. . . .

Today she quenched those thoughts before they got entrenched. She had Conal. Trap had kissed her and insisted he had married her for love, not duty. If that was so—and she was coming to believe it was—she was sure that, if she could explain her ridiculous misconstruing of his actions that night and show him how much she truly loved him, he would understand. He'd forgiven so much else. Why would he not forgive that?

The little metal faceplate grated aside in the top half of the door to reveal the mustached face of the guard on duty beyond. He had to know her by now, but always he asked what she wanted. "I've come to see my husband, Duke Eltrap Meridon."

The man glared at her. "You can't see him."

This time Garival spoke up on her behalf. "She has every right to see the man. He is her husband."

The grate squealed back into place, and they heard the muffled footfalls of the guard. *Please, my Lord. Let them say yes. I have to see him.*

Before long the guard returned: "He says you are not his wife, that he sent you papers of divorcement before he was imprisoned."

"Tell him I did not sign them. That they were lost the day the men came to search the apartment." She paused, considering. "Tell him—"

But the squealing faceplate cut her off and the guard was gone. Again he reappeared shortly. "He says you should have some more papers drawn up, ma'am. Send them to him and he will sign them here in the prison. He also said he would prefer that you not come down here to see him anymore."

The metal door closed in her face, and she stood there staring at it in shock.

Garival touched her shoulder. "Maybe they'll let me talk to him."

So he banged on the door again, the metal hatch squealed open, and the face reappeared. Garival requested audience with the same prisoner.

Again the hatch was closed, but this time, to Carissa's astonishment, the door immediately swung open and Garival was let in. It closed with a clang behind him, leaving her to stand there alone, grappling with the realization that Trap had turned her down cold. That it wasn't the jailers, that it had never been the jailers. He had refused all along to see her.

And as she got her mind around that truth, she felt as if something had been torn loose of her and lost. A gaping hole where for longer than she'd imagined had dwelt hope and light and something more wonderful than she'd ever guessed. Images and memories flashed through her mind—of Trap standing at the window in her sitting room, waiting for her to finish with Conal; sharing the cocoa with her; playing with her son in the nursery as if the boy were his own; the look of joy on his freckled face as he'd whirled her around the ballroom on the night of the coronation; the quiet soberness of his brown eyes as he'd told her he loved her. . . . Each image hurt worse than the one before it, until she sagged against the wall with a low groan and began to weep.

Have I really killed it all for us? With my foolish doubts and pride? Oh, Eidon, please don't let it be. Let Garival say something to change his mind. Please, let him see me.

Would she never be free of the curse of her former husband? Would Rennalf always turn up to ruin everything for her? Would she never—

She cut off the thought train abruptly, knowing exactly where it would lead and determined not to go there. It was time she stopped blaming Rennalf for what was her own doing. *She* was the one who had let what he'd done fill her with insecurity. *She* was the one who'd asked Trap for the divorce. After all he had done for her, *she* was the one who'd pushed him away.

The thought of it wrung another moan from her lips, and she hugged herself miserably, praying Eidon would give her another chance.

She wrestled with her agony for what seemed an eternity before the door clanged open again and Garival rejoined her. The guard did not invite her to enter in his stead, either, but slammed the door shut on his heels and clanged the locking bar into place.

One look at Garival's face told her everything. "He really won't see me."

Maddie's new finance secretary frowned. "He's not well, Carissa. I fear he's struggling with some of that spore he picked up from Hadrich."

"But he said he'd purged that."

"A lot of it residualized before he could. And it is a virulent spore. He knows he's wrestling with it, but . . ." He trailed off.

She stood there, horror piled upon horror. She had not seen old Hadrich herself before he died, but she'd heard the tales. To think of that happening to Trap—

Garival patted her shoulder. "It would not be like with Hadrich. Trap's a strong man, and the spore is not a primary source." He paused, cocking a questioning brow at her. "He said you were the one who requested the divorce."

"Oh, I was, I was." Her voice throttled off as tears welled in her eyes. "But . . . it was foolish," she said when she could talk again. "I didn't know what I was doing. I just want to tell him how wrong I was, how much I love him. . . ."

"Well, he says it is better you have nothing to do with him for now. Given the situation, I'm inclined to agree. He's become something of a lightning rod." He shook his head. "You might want to take his advice about the divorce papers. If the Kiriathans do riot, it could all come back on you."

"Let it, then. For I'll not be sending him any divorce papers," Carissa said firmly.

Garival gave her another thoughtful frown, then rubbed his nose and turned toward the outer door. "This is really outrageous, given who he is. Leyton would have released him long ago, I'm sure. But Ronesca is just too caught up in her own problems and worries to see what is happening. It'll come back to bite her. Mark my words."

21

Abramm lay belly down on the crest of a dune overlooking the oasis where the Fermikians' caravan had arrived yesterday. With swift and practiced ease they'd unpacked their camels and thrown up the black-and-white goatskin tents that now scattered the grassy floor of the palm grove. At their midst gleamed a spring-fed pond fringed with cattails. A hand-cranked waterwheel lifted the water into a series of troughs for the camels, while a smaller secondary trough served the slaves.

With free roam of the oasis and virtually ignored by their masters, the hundred or so captives now sprawled about the grass, resting in the shade of the trees, the tents, and even the camels. Smoke from the fire pits wafted from ventilation holes in the tops of the tents, but the pale blue clouds that hung waist-high around the doorways were from the fermikia pipes. A number of the turbaned Fermikians lay up against the bases of the palms, conscious but stupefied. Those within the tents would be no better, and it was the same every day.

He understood now why that route was called the Road of the Unchained. The captives walked unbound because there was no need to chain them. Surrounded by seas of forbidding dunes and endless sunbaked gravel playas, it would take but moments for one unfamiliar with the area to get lost. Even if one knew the way, the sun and the rocks, the frigid nights, and the bone-dry air could and did claim weaker men. As in the Kolki Pass, the bones of those who'd gone before lined the shoulders of the ancient route.

Lifting his eyes from the shining water and the deep purple shade of the trees, Abramm turned to squint westward, where a ridge of hazy blue

mountains floated above the sea of undulating dunes that now entirely surrounded him. Those mountains were his point of reference, and every day
they grew smaller and fainter while he grew more impatient to win his people
free before they pressed any deeper into the wretched sand sea. Already
they'd been in it a week, which was far longer than he'd ever intended.

Back in Ru'geruk, townspeople had suggested no one could cross this
wasteland and live, but obviously people did. For there lay the road directly
ahead of him, its faded gray and iron-red tiles rising from the oasis on the far
side and plunging eastward between curving slopes of sand.

He returned his gaze to the gleaming water and licked chapped lips with
a dry tongue, looking forward impatiently to Cedric's return with the water
bags.

Rolland crept up beside him. "They're at the upper end—there by th'
cattails."

Abramm looked in that direction, but with all the captives robed and
turbaned like the Fermikians, it was impossible to tell them apart. "Did you
show yourself?"

"Aye. But I dunno if they'll cooperate. The road's influence doesn't seem
to have lifted much."

Abramm glanced at his friend. The big man, like everyone else, wore the
desert men's robes and turbans that they removed from some of the fresher
corpses they'd encountered at the start of their journey. The sun had burned
his face dark brown and had bleached streaks of white into his blond beard.
It made his blue eyes stand out brightly, even squinting as he was in the constant glare. "Maybe it's because they're not really off it out there," Abramm
said, fighting down a squall of dismay.

The road, they'd discovered shortly after they'd started traveling it, was a
construct of shadowspawn. At the outset, Abramm could not walk on it for
more than an hour before suffering the symptoms of spore sickness—headache, nausea, weakness. Worse, he'd also been beset with an unrelenting pall
of anxiety and the sense of some vast, unseen, malevolent being waiting
beyond the dunes to seize and devour him. The road alone, he'd believed—
irrationally—protected him. But after his second bout with spore sickness
confirmed the road as the source of his struggles, he had refused to set foot
on it, and had instead walked beside it the whole way.

It was clear that most men did not react to the spore as he did, though,
and the slaves trod it willingly, afraid to do anything but what their new masters commanded. That those masters felt their own anxiety was obvious. The

road's reputation did not help, for legend said it had a habit of betraying those it did not favor. One might awaken in the morning to find it vanished. Or follow it deep into the desert only to have it plunge over a cliff or into a bed of sand. It was the reason, he believed, every one of the desert men was addicted to the fermikia pipe, and why they spent their nights stupefied by its pleasures.

"Their captors at least know where they are going," Rolland said presently, harkening back to Abramm's prediction.

"I know where we're going, Rollie."

"I know that. And I trust ye." Rolland glanced toward the line of mountains in the west, then shook his head. "But I do na see how we'll convince Trinley and the others when none of us can see those mountains but you."

Abramm felt a familiar frustration. It was an undeniable blessing that Eidon had honed his visual acuity beyond the normal . . . and a cursing that the things he saw were forever being doubted.

The rasp of fabric on sand heralded Cedric's arrival. His narrow face was burned even darker than Rolland's. With his dark brown eyes, he could pass for a slaver and already had performed the role without rousing suspicion.

"I talked to them," Cedric said, handing two newly filled water bags to Abramm. "Told 'em the plan. They might balk, but I think if I hurry them along the road like I'm one of the slavers, they'll do as I say." He paused. "None of them are thinking well. And Galen is doing really poorly."

Abramm eyed the near-motionless camp again. "Eidon will help us," he said firmly. "You best get back to your post, Cedric. We'll do it all as planned."

Cedric slithered off the way he'd come, and Abramm and Rolland backed down the dune. Returning to the makeshift canopy they had constructed in a nearby trough using their staffs and an extra outer robe, they settled down to wait for evening.

Abramm lay back on the warm sand. As Rolland's breathing deepened into rhythmic soughs, he reflected on the fact that Janner and the women should have left Trakas by now. . . .

At Kitrenna's urging, Abramm and the others had gone after the Fermikians in Obla, hoping to free the men they'd taken. The desert men had locked their captives into a barred wooden wagon not far from the amphitheater and rapidly outdistanced those who followed on foot. Wagon tracks led them to the city's edge, where the hard-packed surface of the plains defeated their tracking ability. Janner had speculated their quarry was headed east to an ancient ruin that predated even the Ophiran Obla and from which the Road of the Unchained originated. It wasn't far, he'd told them, and given the fact that the slaves were not bound, along with the strong possibility there'd be a horde of them with relatively few guards, Abramm decided to give the rescue a try.

Before they headed out, since Rolland was loathe to leave his family unprotected in Obla for even a few days, they'd persuaded Janner to take the group on to Trakas and wait for the men to rejoin them there. Almost Abramm had left it at that. Then something had moved him to open the package Laud had given him—it was *The Red Dragon*—write a note on a scrap of the paper wrapping, and tuck the note behind the front cover. Rewrapping the book, he took Marta Brackleford aside and delivered the parcel into her care.

"If I don't return, would you bring this to Queen Madeleine in Fannath Rill?"

Her brows had shot up. "Queen *Madeleine*?" she'd cried in astonishment, defeating all Abramm's attempts at being discreet. "You want me to visit the queen?" She laughed. "You must be out of your mind, Alaric. The queen will never see me."

Noting they now had the complete attention of their companions, he gripped her elbow and steered her around the corner of a ruined wall, out of their view. "She will, for you are her subject and you have a gift for her."

Marta looked down at the wrapped book. "This?"

"It's something her husband would have wanted her to have."

Her head snapped up and her eyes narrowed. Then a knowing light came into them. "Something her husband *would* have wanted? Or something he wants right now?"

He regarded her blankly. Why was she asking him that?

She smiled. "Oh, come, my lord. You were never a member of the king's personal guard, were you?" With that she bowed her head and gave him an almost-curtsey.

He stared at her still, struggling to believe what eyes and ears told him was obvious. "I wasn't?"

"Of course not." She looked at him again and something in her expression changed, as if a wall had gone up between them. "The others don't want to see it. I guess I didn't, either. Admitting it would be too . . . charged with destiny. It is no accident we have fallen in with you." She hesitated, then whispered, "Sire."

Chills rushed madly up his neck now. He shook his head. "I am not a king, my lady. I am only a man you've traveled with along the road."

But she was resolute. "You were always that. And you were never that. And you will not be that much longer."

The chill reached down into his gut and transformed itself to a quiver of something he couldn't name. "No man knows what tomorrow brings," he chided.

"I didn't say tomorrow, sir. Only that you will return. And when you do, all will know who you are."

He cocked a brow. "You are a prophetess now, Marta?"

A moment more she held his gaze, then lowered her eyes. "I've only told you what I believe."

He had nothing to say to that, and so returned to business. "You will take the book?"

"Of course."

"Do not tell anyone you are going to see her. No one—do you understand?"

"You fear the ells will try to prevent me?"

He smiled slightly. "As always you are one step ahead of me. Just like Maddie. You and she should get along well. This"—he tapped the book in her hands—"will give her hope. The ells would try very hard to stop you if they knew."

She nodded and tucked the parcel into her sash. When next she looked up at him, she was almost wistful. "I wish your destiny was otherwise. That your wife . . ." She trailed off. Shook her head. "But that is silly. You and she were made for each other, and everyone knows it."

"Aye. We are." He grinned, recalling his night with her in the cell at Caerna'tha. The quiver in his middle became a tremor of anticipation. *Soon . . .*

"You will be back, sir."

He gave her a solemn nod and they were off. At the ancient city's edge, he took Janner aside and made him promise to transport Marta, and whoever else wished to go, all the way to Deveren Dol and there arrange them reliable passage to Fannath Rill. In exchange, Abramm promised he would be well compensated and had given him a folded parchment with instructions not to lose it. "It will be your proof of identity to my friend who will see you paid."

The river man had unfolded the crinkled parchment and scowled at the foreign symbols scrawled across its face. "What kind of gibberish is this?"

"You're a reader, are you?" Abramm asked.

"I read a bit. But these aren't even rightful letters."

"It's the Old Tongue. My friend will be able to read it, and hopefully few others."

Janner studied the missive a moment longer, then looked up at him narrowly. "This friend of yours in Fannath Rill? She is the queen of Kiriath?"

Well, plainly he heard Marta's outburst, Abramm thought wryly. "Exiled queen," he corrected.

Janner refolded the note. "You told me your friend was Chesedhan."

Abramm grinned. "She is."

And that gave Janner a start. He left the man gazing thoughtfully after him.

There was indeed a slave depot at the midst of Janner's second city, as well as the start of the Road of the Unchained. When they arrived at dawn, the wooden pens and barred carts stood empty, the Fermikians already herding their captives along the ancient road. Fortunately, they did not travel at night, which gave Abramm and his cohorts a chance to catch up, though it still took them three days of sorting through the hundred-odd captives to find their friends, and by then they'd entered the sand sea.

Now, a week later, they were reaching the point of no return. The captives were not doing well. Galen Gault, slight as he was, had suffered most from the sun and the aridity, and this last day had been especially bad. He had stopped beside the road repeatedly to vomit until he had collapsed altogether. From then on his friends had taken turns carrying him, and Abramm had no doubt their masters would force them to leave the young man behind at the oasis tomorrow.

They had to act tonight, and they had to use the road if they hoped ever to return to Trakas. Fortunately, he had a plan. . . .

The air was finally cooling, and shadows had completely engulfed their little gully between the dunes when Abramm and Rolland struck their flimsy shelter and returned to their overlook of the main encampment. A slight breeze stirred the air as the sun dropped completely behind the horizon in a fast-fading blaze of salmon, and twilight deepened over the encampment. The Fermikians remained stupefied at their pipes, but the slaves had gathered in the center of the oasis, clustering around four dung-fed fires. Already many of them were nervously eyeing the surrounding dunes, dreading the new terror evening would bring. Abramm would see they were not disappointed.

The road had laid the foundation for their paranoia, and over the past two nights Abramm had stoked it to a fever pitch. Tonight he hoped to push them into outright panic.

Cedric stood nonchalantly against one of the palms near the camels bedded down by the pool. As they watched, he shifted against the tree trunk and scratched his forehead under the edge of his turban, signaling that he had seen Abramm and all was ready. Four of their friends had been assigned to the dung-fires, one per blaze. The remaining seven clustered closest to Abramm's position, sitting with arms encircling their bent knees—except for Galen, who leaned against his uncle as if he were unconscious.

As the pond frogs began their nightly chorus and darkness gathered around them, Abramm and Rolland withdrew down the side of the dune. At the bottom of the trough, they brought out their staves, laid Cedric's on the sand between them, and began beating it with their own, their small rapid strokes creating a loud *cak-cak-cak* that echoed through the desert silence. The frogs broke off their singing at once.

They stopped beating their sticks, and Rolland snatched up Cedric's staff as Abramm brought along the extra robe. Moving to a new position, they repeated the process until they had circumscribed the entire camp.

The past two nights Fermikians had crept up to the top of the dunes to investigate the disturbance. Tonight not one braved the darkness. After making another half-circuit of the camp and returning to the start, beating their sticks sporadically as they went, Abramm pulled out the hollow reed he had cut on the banks of the Ankrill. He'd practiced with it then, and now he took a deep breath and blew into it.

At first it was only air. Then he got the right feel and the sound rattled out of it, a deep, ululating tone that, when he blew harder at the end, shrieked up the scale to a high-pitched squeal. The sound had not even faded when the first of the shouts from the encampment rang out. From their tones he knew they wouldn't be coming to investigate.

Stretching the extra robe between their two staves so that it fluttered as they ran, Abramm and Rolland burst over the crest of the dune. As they ran down toward the startled slaves, Abramm sent a flare of Light across the rippling fabric and simultaneously up the length of his staff, where it exploded in a gout of flame off the staff's end.

It was a plan that in all respects should have failed when their theatrics were seen immediately for what they were. But, as Abramm had hoped, the road had laid the base of terror they needed. Now, as the campfires all went out together, smothered by the sand his Kiriathan friends had been assigned to dump on them, and when their voices raised in wild yells, the camp erupted into pandemonium. Torchbearers raced to and fro. The camels spooked and ran off when Cedric cut the ropes that should have held them. Tents collapsed as men blundered into them in their attempt to escape the desert monstrosity that had come over the hill for them.

Abramm had instructed his people to meet him at the place where the road cut through the dunes to the west, heading back the way they'd come, but he half expected they'd be swept away by the others' panic. Thus, he was profoundly gratified to find awaiting him over twenty man—at least half again the number he'd sought to rescue.

They fled along the road only until he could no longer hear or see any sign of their camp, and then stepped off it, passing the word for the others to do likewise. A grumbling arose at that, but they complied and he led them swiftly alongside the road. Inevitably his charges began to complain of the difficulties of slogging through loose sand, and when the talk finally turned to how much easier it would be to walk the road again, he stopped and announced they'd rest there for the night and head out at first light.

As reluctantly as they settled down, Abramm was astonished by how fast they fell asleep.

Rolland came up to him as the snores started to echo around them and clapped a hand on his shoulder. "Ye did it, Alaric."

Abramm turned to grin at him in the night. "*We* did it."

"I confess when we first reached that city beyond Obla and I saw all that mass of slaves, I didna see how we'd free 'em. An' that trick with the reed? Brilliant."

"Well, we still have to get out of these dunes."

Rolland shrugged. "Ye've got line of sight. What more do we need?"

Abramm took the first watch, which he spent stargazing, thanking Eidon for their victory and dreaming about Maddie.

When dawn gilded the sky and they'd seen nor heard no sound of pursuit, Abramm's optimism mounted. He'd hoped the Fermikians would account for their missing slaves as the result of the panic and leave them to the desert. It seemed that was precisely what had happened.

But when he slogged to the top of a dune to confirm their position, what he found shocked him so badly he could hardly breathe. His mountains on the wrong side! And the bank of cloud that had lain on the horizon yesterday afternoon, and should have been behind him now, instead loomed directly ahead, closer, higher, and darker than before, the sun rising in a great orange orb from behind it.

Somehow they had gotten completely turned around. They had gathered on the west side of the oasis, had headed west on the road away from it, and had ended up well east of it.

Grimly he slid back down the dune and slogged through the sand toward where the others were gathering in preparation for moving out. As expected, his news was not well received. But after he repeatedly assured them they had merely gotten turned around—however it had occurred—and after he had accepted the full range of abuse that Trinley in particular heaped upon him for it, he got them going again in the right direction. They passed the morning in silence, the temperature rising with the wind coming out of the north, which from the sculpting of the dunes, appeared to be its prevailing flow.

By noon, Abramm was deeply alarmed that they had not yet reached the oasis. Even accounting for the fact that they were no longer fueled by fear and excitement, they should have reached it.

When at length he called a halt and scrambled up yet another dune to check the lay of things, hoping desperately to find everything where it was supposed to be, he trembled at what he saw: The moutains were, impossibly, still on the wrong side, and the brown cloud still loomed before them, higher than ever, and revealed now in its proximity as a great churning mass of dust. Hot wind rushed into his face, tearing at the turban and fluttering his robes, stinging his cheeks with fine particles of dust.

He stared at it, disbelieving, for he knew he had not been too hasty earlier when he had chosen this way. He knew when he had stood on the dune crest this morning exactly where everything was—where the road was, and his men and their camp and the wall of dust.

It's the road, he thought. *It has been moving. It has to have been.*

Fear clenched his vitals, and for a moment he couldn't breathe. *Oh, my Lord Eidon! Where are you?*

"Whatdoye see?" Rolland called up at him.

Abramm glanced down at him. "Dust storm. Heading straight for us. We'll have to ride it out. Get everyone together in the lee of that dune."

With a storm this bad, the dune will surely move. . . . Could it bury us? He didn't know. In all his life he'd heard only vague references to storms like these. *What am I to do, my Lord? They're looking to me.*

"I say we go to the road," Trinley bellowed. And immediately he acted upon his suggestion, the others standing where they were, looking northward.

What do I tell them, Father?

He looked over his shoulder again and saw there was only one thing to say.

"Hurry!" he bellowed at them, turning from the crest and sliding down the scarp as the leading edge of the storm swooped around him.

———

Maddie had been requesting audience with the queen ever since Trap had been arrested and imprisoned—almost three months now. She'd been denied, put off, and turned down so many times that when Ronesca agreed to see her one day, she hardly knew what to say. Worse, she'd long since stopped arriving at the queen's apartments prepared, so when she was immediately ushered into the queen's private study, she had to think quickly.

Ronesca stood before the study's open window fanning herself. Her dark hair was coiled in a long braid atop her head, a halo of flyway wisps around it giving her an uncharacteristically disheveled appearance. Her untidiness was accentuated by the unfastened collar of her blue linen gown and the sheen of sweat on her flushed face. Which struck Maddie as odd, for the summer day was mild, if slightly humid. Perhaps Ronesca suffered from yet another of her spore-induced fevers.

Maddie welcomed the heat, actually, for it was better than having the mist overhead. Reports from Peregris said the Shadow mist had rolled in rapidly after Leyton's capture and now hung thickly about the city, which daily was assaulted by Esurhite forces.

"So I suppose you've come to bargain for the release of your man," Ronesca said abruptly.

Swiftly Maddie gathered her thoughts. "I hadn't exactly thought to bargain, Your Majesty."

Ronesca turned from the window. "Oh, come, Madeleine, you are shrewd in the ways of these things. Of course you did. Though I have to admit you haven't much of a leg to stand on, the way you've constantly gone against me, stirring up all your Kiriathan friends with that silly song and now . . . well, now they grow sullen and surly because the promise hasn't panned out."

She was right. Two months had passed since she'd presented the song, and Abramm still hadn't arrived. Every day that passed, her anxiety and agitation increased, and every night she went to bed praying that tomorrow he would come, or if not, that she'd dream of him and find some reassurance that the promise she'd been given at Abby's birth was true. But neither came.

Her friends' excitement had turned to disappointment. Their confident proc-
lamations of Abramm's returning to repay Leyton for his treachery had been
replaced by bitter recriminations toward Maddie for leading them on with
her grief-inspired imaginings.

"So, all that uproar," Ronesca said, "has been for nothing."

"He'll come."

Ronesca snorted. "If he was in Obla the night of your little performance,
shouldn't he be here by now? It's been two months, more than enough time
to get downriver from Obla. Shouldn't he have sent word by now? A pigeon?
Or if not that, surely we'd have heard of it from others."

Ronesca seemed tired, and a little . . . off. It was hard for Maddie to put
her finger on what was wrong. She was too pale, for one. And she had a
strange smell, somewhat acidic. From time to time tremors shook her, and
there was something different about her eyes. The way she focused . . . or . . .
didn't, exactly.

"The amber is not time specific. It could have shown me the future."

"But you didn't think it was future. You thought it was present. You
thought he would be here by now, didn't you? Or at least that word would
have spread."

Maddie sighed and admitted she had indeed believed that.

Ronesca pursed her small lips and nodded smugly, continuing to fan herself. After a few moments she said, "You know, you have to consider it may
well be a result of the spore that was in your father. We were both exposed,
and I will confess to you, I've had my share of nightmares and strange visions.
Often when I'm praying now, Leyton will stand before me. Or one of my
sons. Pleading with me to rescue them . . ."

"My visions are not from the spore, ma'am. I had them before I was
exposed."

"Spore, grief, the duress of childbirth . . ."

"It was none of those."

Ronesca looked round at Maddie, her expression oddly bland. "What *will*
it take for you to admit and accept that he's not coming back? Three years?
Five years? Ten? How long, Madeleine, will you wait?"

Maddie said nothing.

Ronesca sighed and apparently decided to get down to business. "So
you've come to get your man out of prison?"

"Yes."

"And why should I grant you this boon, when all you've been is trouble to me?"

"He is ill, for one, with the spore. And for another . . ."

Maddie frowned, realizing she'd get nowhere trying to trade on how outrageous it was that a close friend of the First Daughter should have been treated as shoddily as Trap Meridon had. Better to appeal to something practical. "Madam, as you, yourself pointed out, the Kiriathans are growing restless. Talk of riots has come up more and more often. And they are not the only discontents in Fannath Rill these days. If they are not placated, they will draw the other foreigners to them, those who have their own gripes. It would be, overall, to your advantage to release him."

The queen continued to fan herself and stare out the window, where the palm trees waved in the breeze, giving no sign she'd heard anything at all.

"Leyton would not have held him this long, you know," Maddie added. "He only wanted him restrained long enough to get away with the regalia. Now that the plan has fallen to ruin there is no reason to keep Trap locked up."

And still the woman sat, fanning herself and staring. Finally she sighed. "Very well. I'll release him, but he is not to leave the city, and you will have legal responsibility to see he abides by that. I can put you in a prison too, you know. And would have every right to do so should you disobey my command."

She went on. "Because of these limitations, he cannot be your finance secretary. You will have to find something else for him to do."

"I'll put him in charge of my guardsmen," Maddie said.

"I'm not sure I'm comfortable with the idea of your having your own special guard."

"The Kiriathans demand it. So does my station. I am queen of that land, despite your constant attempts to ignore that."

"Queen of a land and people who despise you. Well, whatever you wish. You will have no more than six men in your guard."

She stood there staring out the window and fanning herself. Then she sighed and collapsed into the chair. "I am so tired. It never ends. All the decisions. All the advice. All the terrible problems. No one agreeing. How am I to know what's right?" She looked around at Maddie. "My generals want to launch another offensive. Want to try to break Leyton free. They've received some information. . . . I don't know if it's trustworthy. But . . ."

Maddie frowned. "Are you asking me, madam?"

"Yes."

"I say do it. Don't wait for the emissaries to come with their ultimatums. As they will, you know. Most likely within the month."

"But if it means I might receive back my sons . . ."

"You will not receive back your sons from them. Nor Leyton. They have never once done it; they will not do it with you. They will only toy with you, woo you with honeyed words, then do whatever it is they've planned all along. No matter what you agree to, you're not going to get anything back but bitter sorrow."

Ronesca met her gaze steadily, and for a moment Maddie thought she glimpsed the beginnings of a ridge of sarotis in her left iris. But then the queen turned her gaze to her lap, and when next she looked up her eyes were normal and filled with tears.

"But if I don't, they will grow angry."

"They already want to destroy us, madam. Why should we care if we anger them? They intend to destroy the Kirikhal. Treat with them and ultimately they will forbid you from offering prayers to Eidon and demand you give your allegiance to Khrell. Is that what you want?"

Ronesca blanched but said no more, and not long after that Maddie was dismissed.

She returned to her quarters, feeling uneasy and confused. Ronesca was not at all herself. Was it the spore?

"Ma'am?" Jeyanne's voice broke into her thoughts and she looked around. "Draek Tiris has sent you another present. I put it in on your desk."

A rectangular box wrapped in white velvet and gold ribbon sat beside her notes from Terstmeet, and with it a sealed card written by Tiris himself offering his apologies for having abandoned her. *In fact, I've been out of town—an unexpected difficulty has arisen at my estate in Ropolis. . . . That is no excuse, however. Please accept my apologies for my failure to stand by you, and this treasure as a token of my respect. Perhaps it will give you comfort and strength when you need it most.*

She set the card aside and pulled off ribbon and velvet to find a leather-bound chest within. Lifting the lid, she gasped at the sight of the oblong lump of amber she had first seen sitting on a pillar in Tiris's Great Sand Sea gallery. The amber that allowed one to see the future. Or the past.

Eagerness welled in her. This could show her where he was, why no one had heard anything, how long it would be before he got here. Fear and aversion offered other grimmer possibilities: What if she found him dead? What if she found nothing?

It was not a thing of Eidon's. She knew that for sure. What it was, she hadn't quite figured out. More than that, she wasn't sure Eidon would be pleased with her turning to something from the hand of a man whom she wasn't even sure wore the shield of Light. Besides, how did she know what she saw there was even true? Or, if true, that it had any real relevance? With no place in time to fix the visions, what good were they? And didn't she have enough troubles with her imagination running wild as it was?

No. She would put it back in its box and trust Eidon to bring Abramm when the time was right. And only Eidon would know when that was.

And for a wonder, she did exactly as she intended, setting the chest back into its silken nest, replacing lid and wrapping as they were. For a moment she seriously considered sending it back altogether. But in the end she pushed it to the back of her wardrobe and vowed to forget about it.

And that was her mistake. She should've known better than to believe she would be strong enough to resist its temptation. Even knowing how un-reliable its information was, even knowing it was not a thing of Eidon, still its very presence ate at her. All day long, the thought niggled at her that the knowledge she most yearned to have could well lie in the amber's depths. And what would it hurt to look once more, anyway?

She fought it off, and even that night as she sat on the edge of her big bed, staring at the wardrobe in which the thing was hidden, she withstood temptation. She went to sleep happy with herself, determined to place the gift in the royal treasure house tomorrow so it would be out of her immediate reach.

She hadn't counted on waking in the night, pierced with the desperate, overwhelming need to know what had become of her husband. He should have returned to her long ago. Garival had told her just the other day that when Trap had learned of her original vision in the amber he'd arranged from his prison cell to send a man to Trakas with a cage of pigeons. That had been two months ago. If Abramm had come through Trakas, the man would have sent word.

I have to know, Father . . . I have to.

She tore open the wardrobe and pulled out the box. In minutes she was lifting the chest's lid with a trembling hand, the amber's golden depths glim-mering in the light of the night star on the bed table. Aware of her frantically pounding heart and jittering knees, she sat on the bedside, rested the chest on her knees, and looked into the golden resin—

Choking, blinding dust filled the air, as the wind drove sharp, stinging grains of it into her face. It tore at her clothing and hair, and she could see almost nothing. She struggled forward and stumbled over something in the shifting sand at her feet. Looking down she saw a wind-whipped corner of fabric flapping at the end of the robed form of a man. He lay face down in the sand, rapidly being buried by it. She gasped with horror and choked again as sand burned her throat and chest.

The vision vanished and her bedchamber returned, her skin tingling from the onslaught of sand, ears ringing from the wind's howling. Even the scent of the dust lingered as she reeled with nausea and denial. He'd been on the river. How had he come to be lost in a sandstorm?

But of course, she'd long guessed he must have left the river, and the vision in the amber indicated only one logical conclusion: Slavers traded out of Obla, Tiris had said. They followed the Road of the Unchained through the Great Sand Sea. . . . They must have caught him and taken him into the desert. That's why he hadn't come to her yet.

A low moan escaped her as the room wavered. Why had she done this? Instead of comfort and reassurance, she'd only let more horrible possibilities into her soul. Again she saw the robed form, prostrate in the sand, long blond hair streaming in the wind. . . . Anguish tore at her heart.

Her gaze dropped to the amber still resting on her lap, and sudden hatred seized her. She slammed the lid shut, jammed the chest back into its box, tied it up tightly with its ribbon, and called for Jeyanne. When the girl didn't immediately appear, Maddie stalked around the bed and called again.

The girl sat up groggily on her pallet, rubbing her eyes.

"Jeyanne, wake up!" Maddie cried. And when the girl struggled confusedly to her feet, Maddie thrust the box into her arms and told her to throw it in the river.

Jeyanne's blue eyes widened in astonishment. "Now, my lady?"

"Yes. Take Lieutenant Pipping with you and do precisely as I've said." The girl still looked so befuddled, for a moment Maddie considered throwing the thing into the river herself. But no. She knew she couldn't trust herself to carry through. "Go now," she said, picking up her own heavy night cloak from the chair and draping it over the girl's shoulders. "Return here immediately when you've done what I've asked."

Jeyanne left without another word, and Maddie returned to her bed, struggling still to get the scent of dust out of her nostrils. And to erase the image of Abramm's dead body from her mind.

22

Abramm awoke to the terrifying certainty he'd been buried beneath the sand after all. A monstrous weight pressed upon his back, and he could barely expand his chest enough to draw breath. A uniform pressure held his head and limbs, and all he could think of was how the sands had constantly shifted beneath his feet as he'd climbed and climbed one endless dune, trying desperately to stay atop it. With the wind whipping at his robes and filling his mouth and eyes with sand, he could hardly breathe, much less see where he was going, and could only walk at all when the wind was at his back. He didn't recall stopping, though obviously he had.

Now the wind had died, and he was trapped. Panic surged in him and he flailed his arms in desperation—they came free easily, and he found he was able to push himself up onto hands and knees, sand streaming off of him. Twisting around, he sat down, feeling silly for having transformed a couple of inches of covering sand into the sensation of being buried alive.

He squinted up at the pale salmon-tan crest of sand looming above him. Dust still choked the sky beyond it. Below him, scalloped, knife-edged dunes tiered down the great dune's face to his left and right, a frozen storm-tossed sea of sand plunging away as far as he could see before the haze of dust swallowed all. Dense silence enveloped him, broken only by a trickle of sand disturbed by his movement and the rasp of his own breathing.

He saw no sign of his companions. Had they all been buried alive, as he had? Might some of them lie nearby, unseen? He felt through the sand near where he'd fallen but found only his walking staff and his water bags, one still full of fresh oasis water, the other halfway so. His rucksack was still on his back with its flint, socks, mittens, speaking stone, knife, and the packet of flatbread, figs, and dried mutton Janner had supplied them with—all of it coated in sand. At least he wouldn't die of thirst or hunger right away.

He stood and looked around again but saw nothing that even hinted of his former companions: no movement, no bulges in the sand, not even the corner of someone's robe or the strap of a waterbag. A shouted "Halloooo" produced only a fit of heavy coughing, though he tried several times before working his way up to the dune's crest, probing the sand with his staff as he went. As before, he found nothing. Nor did the higher vantage show him anything new. It was as if the storm had blown his friends off the face of the land. Or perhaps it had blown Abramm himself into some alternate desert world.

For an immeasurable period of time, he walked about probing the sand with his staff and shouting until his throat was raw and his chest ached. Intermittent loud bugles on his reed pipe did no more than trigger brief falls of sand down the slopes around him, and finally he gave up, desperation simmering in his belly. How could they be so completely gone? And the road as well? Surely there would be *something*. . . .

But there was nothing. And he couldn't search the entire desert. He drew a long, calming breath.

"Well, my Lord Eidon," he said aloud, "I don't believe you've brought me all this way just to kill me in this barren place." Memory of Marta's prediction he'd return encouraged him. "You've promised to guide yours who ask, and we both know I am yours. So, please show me what to do. Which way I should go."

He squinted across the mounds and gullies, searching for a flare of light, an anomaly in the sameness, a distinct path, a variation of color or brightness. . . . But there was nothing. Perhaps that meant he should stay where he was for now, wait for the haze to settle out of the sky and show the sun's position. Maybe while he did, someone would happen by. He couldn't be that far off the road. . . . Then he grimaced at the realization that the road could be anywhere. And that wherever it was, it could be somewhere else tomorrow.

He might be days waiting for the dust to settle, and even then he wasn't sure what good knowing the sun's position would do him. It might keep him going in the same direction, but it wouldn't tell him which direction was the right one. And impatience rebelled at the notion of loitering atop this dune using up precious stores of food and water while getting nowhere.

He frowned. "My Lord . . . I have no idea what you want me to do."

But still nothing came. Sighing, he sat down and drank from his water bag. Like everything else, he was covered with sand—his beard, his mouth, his nose, his eyebrows, his hair, his ears. A thick crust gummed his eyelashes, and his eyes still burned from the assault they'd endured under the wind. Grit lodged between his fingers and toes, chafed in his armpits, and had worked its way into every other crack and crevice on his body. And shaking out his robes did little to help.

As hunger gnawed his belly, he dug the flatbread from his bag, brushed it off, and grimaced as his teeth crunched sand with the wheat. The fig was worse. Washing it all down with a couple gulps of water, he decided to walk along the crest of this massive dune and see if its far edge blocked anything significant from his present line of sight.

Sometime later, he was still walking, as the first crest had led to a second and then a third. So much for his plan to sit and wait. He'd prayed for direction, so perhaps his current action was part of the answer to that prayer, even if he didn't have any idea where he was going. Even if he couldn't sense the Light he hoped was guiding him.

The haze did not lighten, the scenery did not vary, and when evening finally came, he felt as if he'd walked in place for hours. With the dust in the sky blotting out the stars, the night was like a dense black fog that even his keen night vision could not penetrate. Eventually it forced him to stop lest he tumble off the edge of an especially steep dune crest and hurt himself.

After the first day he lost all track of time and knew that it passed only because eventually his food ran out and he started on his second water bag. As that, too, grew ominously lighter, he spent hours as he walked debating whether to drink the bag dry and have done with it or continue to ration himself. He was always hungry now, his mouth was always dry, his lips increasingly cracked. The water in his second bag was reduced to a mere mouthful, and every time he drank, he thought he'd come to the end of it. Yet, inevitably the next time he brought the bag to his lips there was just another mouthful. Sooner or later, though, he knew even that would give out.

He'd begun to second-guess himself, wishing he'd stayed where he was in the first place. In retrospect, all the reasons he'd listed for doing so seemed far superior to the path he had chosen. It sure didn't seem that Eidon had any part in the process, though he prayed constantly for answers, for direction, for reassurance . . . for something.

And then, one morning, when his desperation had reached a new low and he was seriously asking himself why he bothered to keep on walking, he saw the pigeon. He nearly stepped on it, in fact, for it was white and almost invisible against the pale sand. It flapped out from under his feet, then returned to the ground a little ahead of him, its beak open and panting, its wings held out from its body and dragging a little as if it were tired. Its feathers were tattered and it looked hard used. Probably a homing pigeon, blown off course by the storm. He strode to pick it up, thinking that he would carry it a bit, but it flew up into the sky when he reached for it and flapped away, disappearing beyond the tops of the dunes. After it was gone, he stood waiting, wishing it would come back, suddenly aware of how alone he felt.

When it didn't come back, he trudged on, half hoping he might find it again on the ground beyond the next dune. But it wasn't there. He fell again into his mindless slogging, so he had no idea how long it had been when suddenly the bird returned, circling over his head and then flapping away over the dunes. He thought little of it, until the bird was back a third time, flying the same pattern, almost as if it were trying to guide him.

Well, why not follow it? He was in the middle of the desert, without water, with no idea where he was going. The bird could see what he could not, might even have already found an oasis. In fact, its presence probably meant he was near to one—or else the edge of the dunes—for even a bird blown off course would not likely be blown that far into the desert. It just might lead him out of the desert. Or at the very least to a source of water.

And so he turned in the direction it had flown and followed it. Every now and then he saw it circling overhead, a tiny white mote, almost indistinguishable from the overcast that hid the sky. It circled and then flew off again, always in the same direction. He doubted it was thinking anything of him, for he knew pigeons often circled when they were trying to get their bearings. But he made his way through the dunes, feeling a rebirth of hope, half expecting at any moment to round a dune and see a cluster of palms around the inviting gleam of water.

Instead he stepped out between two dunes to find a sandy expanse at the midst of which stood the vast ruin of an ancient, mist-hung city. Domes and spires and rectangular buildings peeked tantalizingly above a massive outer wall in which a wide gateway stood atop a broad entrance ramp. A pair of pillars surmounted by winged dragons flanked the opening. Gold gleamed in places on their wings, and overhead the mist hung so low it brushed the building tops.

The pigeon flew another circle over his head, then flapped straight for the city, gliding in under the arch and disappearing.

He stood where he was, staring gape-jawed. Might this be the fabled dragon city of Chena'ag Tor? The one no man had seen and lived to tell about? The one legend said held the treasures of a thousand years of dragon thievery, and their coveted secrets of time and eternity?

At first he didn't even want to approach the place, but curiosity got the best of him and he crossed the sandy flat to the base of the ramp. The height of the walls was immense. Had anyone suggested walls could soar that high, he would have laughed at them. The gateway, which had looked almost normal from a distance, was enlarged in proportion to the walls—wide enough to admit twenty horses abreast and as tall as the Grand Kirikhal in Fannath Rill, the tallest building Abramm had ever seen.

Again he stood and stared, and only gradually began to wonder if he was meant to go inside. He had no doubt he'd been brought here. He just wasn't sure who had brought him. Yes, he'd been asking for Eidon's guidance all along, and had believed, at least some of the time, that he had received it. Had the pigeon been part of that guidance?

If so, it had flown before him into the city, which seemed a strong indication he was supposed to follow it. He knew that sometimes Eidon deliberately led his people into situations they did not understand for reasons they could not comprehend, precisely so they would have the opportunity to trust him for who he was.

"My Lord Eidon, you know my uncertainty. If this is not the way you would have me go, make it evident. I do not mistrust you, only my ability to understand what you would have me to do."

Barely had his words died away than a bright luminescence ribboned out from his feet, up the ramp and past the gargantuan statues. It lay there, bright and clear for only a moment, then faded away.

Well, that was clear enough.

But as he started walking, a tremendous roar echoed out of the city, so loud it shook little bits of sand off the dragons on their pillars. He stopped, listening to its dying echoes, all the hairs on his body standing upright. Whatever that was, it was big. And all he had was a staff. Did he really want to go inside this city? A city of dragons . . . That one had sounded far bigger than little Tapheina. . . .

He drew a long, deep breath and let it out, then started up the ramp.

It felt more like jumping off a cliff.

Maddie jerked awake, heart pounding. The bedchamber lay silent and dark around her, the kelistar on the bed table having gone out. She had dreamt of the desert again, of the form lying prostrate in the storm, slowly being covered with sand. This time it hadn't been Abramm's form she'd seen there, but her own.

She smelled the dust again now. Always the dust. She couldn't seem to rid herself of it. Just like the dreams, which returned almost every night. At first it had been Abramm, then a couple of times now she'd found Ronesca, faceup instead of down, eyes wide and full of darkness. Once she'd even discovered little Simon, grown to manhood. The last few days, though, every time she'd stumbled over the body, she'd known it was her own. The shock of it always awakened her.

Looking into Tiris's amber had been the stupidest thing she had ever done. Especially when Tiris wasn't there to help explain away what she had seen. And he wasn't, still occupied with whatever had arisen at his villa in Ropolis. Now, over a month later, she was paying dearly for her mistake.

Repeatedly she reminded herself that the amber wasn't something Eidon had sent and that what it had shown her might not even be real. Or not the whole picture . . . or . . . It was all visions and imagination, things seen with the mind and heart, not flesh and blood and bone she could feel. Certainly it was no proof he was dead. No proof at all!

Yet, ever since that night, something vital had gone out of her. Whatever spark of belief and confidence and hope she'd nurtured in her heart had died, and she'd been unable to resurrect it. Now she felt cut loose and floating, all she'd thought she knew and understood brought into question, her confidence in Eidon's goodness deeply rattled.

To have believed so completely and to be so wrong . . . If Abramm was never to return, why had Eidon allowed her to be with him that night after Abby's birth? Or had he no more to do with that than with the amber? Maybe it really was just a hallucination born of the combined stresses of her pain and grief—and the spore and what all the midwives agreed was a too-close brush with death.

She lay there, staring at the folds of the bed canopy above her, listening to Jeyanne's slow, soft breathing, the girl asleep on her pallet nearby. Silence pressed around them, broken by the occasional creak of the palace's walls and the distant murmur of voices. She wondered if rhu'ema lurked in the shadows above her, watching her and laughing as she unraveled. Laughing as she realized the pointless futility of her life.

What did she do that was of any value? Who cared about another ballad when the last one had turned out to be such a farce? Her children still welcomed her presence, especially little Abby, with her blond curls, blue eyes, and ready smile. But they had their nurses. . . . The only thing she seemed to do besides visit them these days was counsel Ronesca. And that sure wasn't worth anything.

Day after day, the queen would ask what to do, and Maddie would advise her to send a party south to rescue Leyton and to refuse outright to meet with the Esurhites, who had already asked for audience. Ronesca would listen intently, nod as if she agreed, and the next day they'd repeat the conversation as if it had never happened.

Just yesterday, Maddie learned for the first time that the emissaries not only hadn't been refused, they'd been allowed to travel all the way to Fannath Rill and were due to arrive at the palace shortly. Ronesca had even had the gall to suggest Maddie sit in on the negotiations, which the latter refused in an outpouring of righteous indignation. The outburst had provoked the queen to wrath of her own, and she'd dismissed Maddie out of hand.

The First Daughter had left angry, frustrated, and feeling more alive than she had in weeks. But it faded swiftly, and soon the crushing apathy was back. All the world, it seemed, was crumbling to pieces around her. . . .

The awareness of men talking quietly in the next room intruded again into her thoughts, and she recognized Trap's voice among them. Released from prison as Ronesca had promised, he'd been happy to take the position of captain of the First Daughter's guard, a position he considered himself imminently more suited for than finance secretary. Especially since Garival was doing such a superb job in the latter position. Now a soft knock preceded the door's opening. "Your Highness?" Trap asked from outside the bedroom. "Your Highness, the queen requires your presence. Are you awake?"

Maddie frowned and sat up. "The queen? What time is it?"

"A little after the third hour, ma'am."

"She's summoning me at the third hour?" Maddie pushed back the covers and swung her legs over the edge of the bed as Jeyanne stirred on her pallet. "I told her I would not be part of the negotiations."

"The negotiations have concluded, ma'am. The Esurhites left several hours ago."

Maddie froze there on the bedside, gripped by sudden hope. She'd expected they'd all be haggling for days. "Did she send them away without treating with them, after all?"

"I don't think so, milady. She met with them privately for several hours. Her, Minirth, and her closest advisors. The meeting concluded around midnight, and the Shadow lovers left immediately. They did not seem displeased." He fell silent, and she thought he would say more, but he did not.

"And now she's summoned me," Maddie said, sighing. "Very well."

Trap closed the door. Jeyanne, having awakened fully by now and grasping the situation at once, went to the wardrobe. She returned with an undershift, which she laid on the bed, then stood ready to help Maddie take off her bedgown. But for a moment the First Daughter sat there, shaken with a sudden surge of anger that she should be dragged out of her bed in the middle of the night to endure another of Ronesca's rambling and pointless conversations. It was like some bizarre form of torture.

As usual, the outrage died as quickly as it flared, and suddenly she didn't care. If Ronesca wanted to talk, let her talk. If she wanted Maddie to give advice she wouldn't heed, Maddie would give it. What difference did it make, anyway?

Heaving a sigh, she stood and let Jeyanne remove her bedgown. Half an hour later she was ushered into the queen's private audience chamber.

Ronesca awaited her alone, seated before the fire and dressed in a thick robe of wool and velvet, though the room was quite warm and very dark. She held a cup of tea in her hands, an empty saucer on the table beside her. She did not look well: Shadows cupped her eyes and sweat sheened her pale skin.

Maddie curtsied, and Ronesca received her greeting, waving her into the chair beside her.

When she said nothing, Maddie ventured, "So you've concluded your negotiations?"

"Concluded and sent them off, thank Eidon. I could hardly bear to have them here at all."

"Well, we agree on that, at least," Maddie murmured. "I'm surprised they didn't demand you put them up."

"They wished to return to their commander."

"With your concessions?" Maddie asked.

"With my offer."

"Your offer?"

"I had no choice, Madeleine." Ronesca sipped her tea. "They have my husband and my sons."

Maddie sighed but said nothing.

Ronesca looked at her sharply. "You would turn them away even if the captured king in question was your husband?" The queen set her cup on its saucer. "You can't even accept the fact he's been dead for well over a year and you think I believe you would, of your own choice, give him over to our enemies to torture?"

Maddie shook her head. "The only thing they can be trusted to do is *not* return Leyton and your sons. At least not alive. And as Leyton has no virgin daughters for Belthre'gar's harem, you have nothing to offer them that they might want. They'll surely put him in their games—your sons, as well. They probably already have."

"Which is why I must act swiftly in this. And as it turns out, I *do* have something they want."

"And what is that?"

"A man who betrayed them and came to hide among us."

"Would he not be considered an ally?"

Ronesca ignored the question. "He was a great general who betrayed his command, allowing the Draesians to break through some line. . . ." She waved a dismissive hand. "I couldn't follow the details. It doesn't matter. Besides throwing the battle, he took a large amount of gold and other valuables—jewels, religious treasures, and the like—from the imperial coffers and museums. Belthre'gar has sworn to see him pay. They want him back."

"And they came to you asking for this?"

"Not at all. They didn't even know he was here."

"And he is, in fact, still here?" Her curiosity was piqued.

"We have him in irons already." Ronesca smiled. "Held in secret, of course."

"Who is it?"

"Oh, Maddie, my dear. Surely you've guessed by now. What other foreigner has a mysterious past, uncertain origins, a vast fortune, and a villa full of treasure?"

"Light's grace, Ronesca! You've arrested Draek Tiris?"

"Well, apparently his real name is something else. We'll be taking him down to Peregris to make the exchange in a few days. They will meet us on that little island offshore. With the funny trees." She paused. "I'd like you to come with me."

Maddie could not keep her dismay from showing.

"I know it's a hardship, but . . ." Ronesca put a slender hand to her brow and sighed. "You know how tired I am. How badly I feel. . . . People are coming at me constantly. High Kohal Minirth. Minister Freyaz. The generals. Now I have the Esurhites, as well. And I try to listen to them, but sometimes I just know I'm not really thinking right." She dropped her forehead into her hand. It was several moments before Maddie realized she was weeping. "I want Leyton home and in command. I never wanted to be a queen without a king—when I'm the one who has to make all the decisions. And I want my boys back." Her voice broke apart, and for a moment she wept openly. Finally she lifted her tear-streaked face to Maddie. "Surely you must understand the horror of fearing they might die. . . . You must know what I'm feeling and how awful it is."

Maddie shuddered with sympathy, remembering well how awful it was.

"I know we've had our differences," the queen said softly. "That I've not always treated you as graciously as I should have. I always thought it was for your own good, what Eidon would have me do, even if you didn't understand or appreciate it. I just hope you can put your resentments behind you. We both serve and love Tersius. And . . . he has made me queen. And right now the queen has desperate need of the First Daughter."

Maddie frowned at her, still reluctant but moved by her apparent sincerity and her obvious need. "I'll come," she said finally, "but only if I can take Trap and the rest of my guards with me. And have your permission to hire more to protect my boys while I'm gone."

"Of course. Whatever you need."

"Very well, then," Maddie said. "I'll go with you to Peregris."

Trap was going to have a fit.

23

The oblong-shaped island at the mouth of the Ankrill on which Tiris ul Sadek was to be exchanged for the king of Chesedh was small and uninhabited—once the property of a wealthy Ophiran, it was now the residence only of seabirds. Trap stood on its north side, hands on his hips as he gazed around. Before him the ragged remains of the Ophiran's villa jutted up from the wind-tossed, late-summer grasses. A grove of olive trees encircled the flat, sheared off and stretched out in grotesque, gnarled forms from the prevailing winds that came downriver. Winds that rushed around him now, tossing his cloak and sifting through the short whiskers of his beard, reminding him how close to the river's mouth this site was and that while those winds might habitually keep the island and river free of Shadow, it wouldn't matter much with the coming exchange set to occur after moonset.

The exchanging parties would come in from opposite sides—Esurhites landing on the beach beyond the trees to the south, Chesedhans tying up to the small boat dock on the north. He walked now across the flat, through the deformed trees on the Esurhites' south side, and out onto the sloping beach. To his left a rough spine of dark rock rose out of the sand and plunged into the water some ways out, forming a natural harbor. To his right, two men in a rowboat bobbed in the sea at the base of the twenty-foot-high rock cliff that thrust up from the island's riverside end.

The men would be Brookes and Whartel, whom he'd instructed to row around the cliff. Clearly it was doable, an observation Brookes confirmed a few minutes later when he joined Trap on the beach. "No problem at all, sir," he said.

"You think you could do it in a ship's longboat with a crew of six?"

Brookes shaded his eyes as he looked back toward the head rock, wind tossing locks of his blond hair about a broad forehead. "I don't see why not."

Trap nodded, then turned his gaze toward the bank of mist lowering on the southern sea, far too close for comfort.

Again Brookes spoke Trap's thoughts. "The whole poxed, Shadow-loving navy could be out there for all we know."

"It probably is." This whole affair reeked of deception. He hated every bit of it. The Esurhites weren't giving anything back. Not the king, and not the queen's sons. Leastways not alive. And in just a few hours they would have the only two surviving contenders for the Chesedhan crown standing on this one island. Oh yes, the Chesedhan navy would be standing at anchor not far away, ready to move should anything go amiss. But that was small comfort. Whatever plans he devised to ensure Maddie's safety had to rely solely upon himself and the men he'd brought with him. Thank Eidon, Maddie had talked Ronesca into allowing him more than six.

He turned to his subordinates. "Here's what we'll do." The two men listened attentively as he explained.

When he was done, Brookes frowned. "We'll be sorely outnumbered, sir. What if things don't go down as we expect?"

"Then you'll have to improvise. You know the objective. Do what you need to."

Brookes exchanged a sober glance with Whartel. "What about you, sir?"

"I'll be with her. And if you're having to improvise, there's a good chance I'll be dead, so it'll be up to you to save her." ·

He turned and walked back across the island while Brookes and Whartel came around in their rowboat. As he descended through the olive trees and gorse thickets toward the small stone quay where his own vessel was moored, he glanced toward the river's mouth and the floating breastwork Chesedhan engineers had constructed there to defend it. On the stoneworked banks to either side of it rose the city of Peregris, the white-walled royal residence conspicuous on its north-bank hill overlooking river and harbor both. He didn't know whom he should mistrust more—the Esurhites or Queen Ronesca.

His own suspicions of the Chesedhan queen's real intentions for this night horrified him. And despite all attempts to deny them, dread lay in his gut as heavily as an undigested meal, demanding that he do something. And he had, at least partially. Abby had to stay close to her mother and was in Peregris now, but the very day the Esurhite emissaries had arrived in Fannath Rill, Trap had sent Channon off with Simon and Ian to Deveren Dol, and then Carissa and Conal after them the next day.

His thoughts brushed the latter memory and brought it back hard—how she'd stood before him so awkwardly that day, wanting to say something he was determined not to hear.

When she'd run from him in tears the night of the ball, he'd been devastated. The next morning, he'd immediately gone to have the divorce papers drawn up, vowing she would never hurt him like that again. For too long he had hung his heart on the hopes of something developing between them. He'd been as bad as Maddie in her unwillingness to let go of Abramm. Well, no more. He'd granted her the divorce, and that was to be the end of it.

In some ways he'd been happy to be arrested, for in Larochell he didn't have to answer her questions or rebuff her explanations. But alone in his cell he'd had too much time to brood. It didn't help that the black spore he'd cleansed from Simon still lived in his flesh, and it seemed to latch on to his hurts with a vengeance. Time and again, he found himself reliving that moment when his kiss had driven her tearfully from his presence, after all he'd done for her. It was bitterness, it was resentment, it was self-pity. It was a host of thoughts distasteful to Eidon. He repented of them time and again, but time and again they returned.

It was worst when his jailers continued to come with word she was outside, wanting to visit him. Part of him had rejoiced to think she was remorseful, that she cared for him after all. The other part—the hard, bitter, cynical part—reminded him how much it would hurt to allow himself to believe that. Of course she would be distressed he was imprisoned. She probably feared it would fall back upon her and she might end up in jail with him.

When Ronesca finally released him two months ago and he learned he'd been demoted from finance secretary to captain of Maddie's personal guard, he'd been pleased. Not only because he felt himself more suited to the position, but because as captain he could sleep in the barracks with his men. Since Carissa had not redrawn the divorce papers as he'd asked her to, he'd considered doing it himself, just to be done with her once and for all. But he'd had no time with all the preparations for meeting with the Esurhites, and in the end lacked the heart to go through it all again.

Tears had gleamed in her eyes when he'd told her what he feared was to come of Queen Ronesca's dealings with the southlanders, but he'd refused to let himself be swayed by them, reminding himself that it was Maddie she most feared to lose, not him. Without the First Daughter as patroness, she'd have to support her young son on her own. Taking in sewing or something else she was good at. A harder life than she'd ever known, but life at least.

The notion provoked in him a momentary burst of compassion and regret, but in the end his bitterness overwhelmed all sense of tenderness. He'd said good-bye in a voice whose coldness startled even him.

Now he pushed the memory from his mind, repenting of his angry attitude yet again. It was a product of the Shadow within him he could not afford to indulge tonight. Not when Maddie's life rested on his remaining strong in the Light.

He returned to the mainland and the royal residence, where Maddie and Ronesca would await their two o'clock in the morning meeting with the enemy. Tiris ul Sadek, the man they were allegedly trading for the king, remained secreted away. So secreted, in fact, that Trap had been unable to learn where he was being held, or even how he'd been conveyed to Peregris. When he asked about a secret prisoner, the man they were going to exchange, he got only blank stares and shrugged shoulders. Which was, he argued with himself, as it should be for so delicate an operation. If the Esurhites found him and broke him out themselves, they'd have no need of surrendering Leyton.

Trap spent the afternoon and evening finalizing plans, seeing all the details were in place and even napping a bit before going early to find the First Daughter so he might speak with her one last time before the meeting.

She sat alone, reading, in the main room of her second-story suite. Seeing him, she closed her book with a grimace. "Please tell me you've not come to try to change my mind again, Trap."

"Where's the queen?"

"Praying for the success of our venture, of course. As you knew she would be."

He frowned, paced a turn about the room, then faced her, noting anew how drawn her face was and the dark shadows under her eyes. "Ma'am—"

"I know. You have a bad feeling about it." She grimaced again. "I don't have a very good feeling about it, either. Whatever else he may be, Tiris has been a friend. And from all I hear, our ally."

"It's not Tiris that concerns me. Madam, please! Plead a headache. Plead illness. Plead anything at all. Just don't go out there tonight."

"You know I have no choice."

"You do have a choice. This is madness! Think of your boys! Think of Abby. . . ."

"Didn't our Kiriathan compatriots already settle that? You and Carissa serving as foster parents should I marry someone unacceptable?"

He frowned. "Carissa and I . . ." His voice died. Despite all his efforts to harden himself to the pain, admitting his loss and failure still hurt abominably. He'd wanted so much for things to work out between them, but— *Stop now. Do not go down that road. . . .*

Maddie shook her head. "She loves you, Trap. She truly does. And your refusals to forgive her are killing her. As they are killing you. Do you have any idea why she even did what she did that night?"

He snorted derisively. "I kissed her and she didn't appreciate it. Too much boldness from the swordmaster's son."

"Too bold? You were not bold enough! You kissed her so carefully she thought you didn't mean it!"

He gaped at her. "That's absurd. I wouldn't have kissed her at all if I didn't mean it!"

"Have you talked to her? Have you let her explain herself? No. She's tried over and over, and you shut her out completely." She stood to face him. "You're being a fool about this, Trap Meridon. A petty, self-absorbed fool. And if you can't find it in yourself to bend, you really will lose her. For good."

"I don't *want* her!"

"Yes you do." She stared up at him.

He stared back helplessly, then turned away from her. "Why are you doing this, ma'am?! Why are you bringing this up now? And digging at me like this? I don't—" He broke off in sudden understanding. Swallowed on a dry throat. "Plagues. You know it's going to go sour tonight, don't you?"

"I know nothing." She turned from him and walked to the window, parting the drapes to peer out briefly.

He clenched his fists. "Please, Madeleine. Don't do this. Tell her you cannot go."

"I have to." She let go of the fabric and turned back. "Whatever happens, Eidon will see me through it. I have him always and—" Her voice trembled and broke off as she pressed her fingertips to her lips and looked at the floor.

A wave of anguished grief swept across her face, and she swallowed. He saw her pressing it down, pushing it way, saw the deadness that had been so often in her manner these last few months replace it. He'd heard about Jeyanne's late-night excursion to cast the amber seeing stone into the river. And though Maddie had told no one why she had done it, he could guess easily enough. Because she had looked in it again, and it had shown her something she hadn't wanted to see. Something that had knocked the life out of her as it had convinced her finally that Abramm was gone. She'd not told Trap that in so many words, but he'd seen it in her face, and in the things she *didn't* say these days.

It didn't give him near the peace he'd thought it would.

She stared at him expressionlessly. "The queen claims she needs me, and I think in some ways she's right. She is very fragile right now. But still volatile and more spiteful than ever. If I were to refuse her request, what grounds could I give? That I am ill? She is far more ill than I. That I suspect her of the most heinous treachery imaginable? She'd probably send me off to that convent she's been threatening me with before the evening was over. Take my sons, give them to some Harvadan to raise. . . ."

"At least you'd be alive."

Her face went dead white beneath the scatter of freckles across her nose. "Maybe I'd rather be in Eidon's realm."

He stared at her evenly, refusing even to acknowledge that statement. "And you'd abandon your children? Knowing what they've been through? Knowing how devastating it will be for them to lose you?"

She turned from him and returned to her place in the chair. "I don't believe Ronesca would do the sort of thing you're suggesting. And anyway, what good would *I* be as a trade? My father is dead. Belthre'gar already has Leyton, and everyone knows Ronesca would suffer little grief losing me. I have no value to the Esurhites whatsoever."

"You have value as the White Pretender's woman."

She flinched as if he'd struck her, her face jerking up to meet his.

"You think she'd never do such a thing?" Trap pressed. "How about in exchange for her sons?"

At that she turned her attention to the book in her lap. After a time she drew a breath and said, "So what should we do? Stage a rebellion? All of us? Refuse to obey the queen and run away?"

"If we must!"

"Where would we go? Where *can* we go? Chesedh is our last hope."

He frowned at her, dread and sorrow squeezing his chest like a vise.

Soon after that, the oldest of the queen's pages slipped into the room to tell them it was time. Trap picked up the First Daughter's cloak from where it lay upon the chair, and laid it over Maddie's shoulders. She tied it at her throat, then gave him a smile as she patted his arm. "It'll be all right, my lord duke. I have Eidon always."

He followed her out of the room to the hall where the queen's party was assembling to board the carriages that would take them to the waterfront.

Peregris was an ancient port, predating the Ophiran Empire. The harbor had first been dredged over a thousand years ago, and the banks built up with masonry so the big ships could come right up to the quay. It had never been quite deep enough for the biggest sailing boats with their deeper keels, but Chesedh's galleys could snug up quite comfortably.

It was one of those galleys that the queen and her attendants boarded, and they were immediately escorted to the captain's stern cabin. Though Trap would have preferred a station immediately outside the cabin, that space was occupied by the queen's own guard, forcing him and his six men to find places near the ship's bow.

Barely had they taken up their positions when the ship was cast off from the dock, and shortly the oars were pumping and flashing in unison as they headed out for the island, aglow with torchlight in the deep darkness of the now-moonless night. He stared at it blindly, his anxiety rising as he went through scenario after scenario and what he might do to protect his charge. So deeply was he involved with his thoughts, he didn't even hear the sailor come up behind him until a soft voice said, "Sir?"

Trap turned to find one of the ship's officers bowing and touching his cap. "Cap'n would like a word with you, sir."

"Of course." Trap pushed off the gunwale and followed the man through the ship and up the companion to the quarterdeck. The captain stood at the taffrail, looking back toward Peregris as it receded behind them. The mate and two others attended him.

As Trap drew up, the officer turned to him. "Ah, Captain Meridon. Thank you for coming so swiftly."

"Is something wrong?"

"No. There's just been a change in plans."

Trap glanced at the mate, standing close at the captain's elbow, uneasily aware of the other two men—brawny sailors, both—stepping away from the rail to stand at Trap's sides.

The captain was shaking his head. "I'm sorry, sir, but I'm afraid you'll not be accompanying us to the island."

Trap stared at him. "I am the First Daughter's chosen escort."

"I know, sir. And I really *am* sorry. It's just how it has to be." He seemed far too remorseful for the situation, which put Trap off-balance even as it triggered an unfocused alarm.

The captain's eyes flicked to the man beyond Trap's left shoulder, and Trap was turning toward him when the blade plunged into his back. It entered just under his left shoulder blade, a cold, strange pressure driving through his chest that shocked him emotionally and mentally as much as physically. Before he could even begin to regather himself, his lungs erupted in fire, and when he breathed he felt a liquid gurgling where no liquid should be.

His sword came out of nowhere, drawn by an instinct that circumvented thought, and flashing in the ship's lanterns. Too late. The knife blade twisted deep his chest, and he gasped, then could not draw another breath. Brightness blasted away the night shadows as hard hands gripped his arms and the deck spun away from him. More hands gripped his legs. Something smashed into his hip and the hands released him. For a moment he floated, completely disoriented. Then he plunged into the sea's cold, dark embrace, the shock of contact forcing him to inhale a full breath before he could stop himself. As oblivion took him, his stunned mind churned toward the realization that now he'd never know in this life if Carissa had loved him truly, or not.

———

Maddie's misgivings had never been stronger in her life. Surely, though, Ronesca could not be planning to betray her in such a hideous manner as Trap had suggested. She was a devoted servant of Eidon. Had she not brought High Kohal Minirth with her in this endeavor? How could they both be involved in the giving over of the First Daughter of the royal house to the enemy? It went against all Eidon's commands. Minirth would seriously compromise his standing and create an uproar in a church already fractured by increasing numbers of sects.

Still, there was no denying Ronesca was gravely ill. She'd lost considerable weight, her cheekbones angled sharply now beneath pale skin stretched tautly over them. She hadn't been eating at all that Maddie could see. People said she'd been fasting too much, but she'd not announced it if she was, and she always made a point of announcing it. Her skin had a perpetual sheen of moisture, as if she were fevered. And then there was the smell—acidic, sour, growing stronger by the day. Maddie feared it was the black spore, and if it was, there was no telling what sort of things Ronesca might decide to do.

As they were settled into the captain's cabin and the steward brought tea, Maddie looked around at the small party gathered there and asked about

Draek Tiris. "I thought he would be coming with us once we were on the island."

"Oh, he is, my dear," Ronesca replied. "But he'll stay safely hidden until we make certain our counterparts have kept their part of the bargain."

"He's in the other boat, then?"

Ronesca smiled and patted her hand, her fingers icy even through her gloves and Maddie's. "Don't worry yourself about it, dear. All is in hand."

Minirth cleared his throat. "We should use our time wisely here and beseech the Father of Lights for His grace and mercy on our efforts this day."

Ronesca nodded at once and arose to approach the altar, where she knelt on the low bench before it, crossed her hands upon her heart, and bowed her head. Immediately Lady Iolande and Lady Locasia joined her. As she began to murmur her prayer, Minirth turned to Maddie, who had not moved. "These are serious times, girl. Can you not do your sister-in-law this one small kindness and join her?"

Realizing it made no difference what position she assumed when praying, Maddie complied. If it made Ronesca feel better, what harm was there? She'd barely settled when a loud ripping sounded just outside the stern window followed by a splash of something heavy plunging into the water.

"What was that?" she asked, looking toward the window.

"Probably the anchor, my lady," Minirth said. "We've not much time left."

"But the oars are still pumping."

Minirth scowled at her, but after a moment of appearing to listen, agreed that they were.

"Then it couldn't have been the anchor."

"Oh, Maddie, please," Ronesca burst out. "Do you always have to ruin everything? Can't we just pray? It was surely just some ship's business—nothing to concern ourselves with."

Maddie looked from Minirth, so cold and stern, to Ronesca, obviously hurting and ill, and surrendered. In the end, she was glad she had, for it was freeing to call up all her concerns and uncertainties and fears and lay them at her Father's feet, knowing he knew of them and that his hand governed all. Knowing, more, that he loved her beyond her ability to comprehend and had chosen all of this as part of his perfect intention for her life.

All too soon, though, it was time to stop, the moment of truth and revelation upon them. She heard the booming of the oars being shipped as both Minirth and Ronesca stood. Maddie and the other ladies did likewise, waiting in silence as the gangplank thundered across to the island's small quay and the guardsmen disembarked to prepare the way.

By the time the door swung open, Maddie's pulse raced and her stomach had turned to a nest of skittering crickets. She followed Ronesca and Minirth onto the main deck and glanced at the Chesedhan guards surrounding them.

"Where is Captain Meridon?"

"Oh, I'm sure he's gone ahead, my dear," Ronesca said. "To arrange his men as he feels best to protect you." She made a face of displeasure. "I still don't see why you can't trust our Chesedhan guards to do that duty. It's hurt-ful, you know. To me and to them."

Her tone of veiled antagonism made the crickets in Maddie's stomach leap and twitch all the more.

Ronesca, though thin and frail, moved regally toward the gunwale and through the gap, making her way carefully over the lanternlit plank to the quay. Above, more light glowed from atop the island, turning the sky into a golden backdrop for the dark outlines of the gorsebushes that covered the slope they must climb.

"When this is over," Ronesca said as she started up the path, "I'm thinking we really need to find a proper tutor for your eldest. It's time he start learning his letters."

Since her back was to Maddie, she did not see the look of astonishment and dismay Maddie flashed at her. Why was she talking about Simon now?

Atop the flat, torches affixed to poles stood at intervals along the wide circle of men ringing the villa's ancient pavement. Dark-tunicked Esurhites formed the far half of the circle, while the leather-clad, white-tabarded royal guardsmen formed the near half. None wore sword or dagger, as the agree-ment for this exchange stipulated, but she did not doubt blades abounded in hidden sheaths on both sides of the circle.

She did not see Trap or his men anywhere, but knowing at least some had intended to watch from the shadows, she could not consider this absolute proof of something wrong. She had expected him to stay with her, though, and it bothered her that he had not.

Once the royal party had arrived on the flat, the line of Esurhites opposite opened and the negotiating party emerged—one tall, dark-skinned man in a tunic shot through with gold thread, accompanied by two others. Together the trio advanced toward the circle's center as Ronesca's party did likewise.

The queen, dressed all in white, approached at a regal pace, Minirth at one elbow and Maddie at the other, as she had earlier been instructed. The captain of the queen's guard and his lieutenant followed behind the three-some.

The two groups stopped about six feet apart, and the Esurhite bowed his head in a cursory greeting that fell short of any true deference. He looked vaguely familiar, though Maddie did not recall having seen any of the delegation when it was in Fannath Rill.

"Do you have them?" Ronesca asked.

"We do, Chesedhan queen. Do you have what we agreed upon?" The voice was familiar, too. Where had she encountered this man before?

"You can see that we do," said Ronesca.

Maddie's attention reverted suddenly to the conversation. *Them*? It was only supposed to be Leyton. Why did she say *them*? And what did she mean that he could see they had Tiris? Maddie twisted about to see if the Sorite lord was even now being brought forward. He was not. Nor was he with the men guarding their backs, among whom she saw no Kiriathans. The crickets turned into a cold hard lump of fear.

"I would like to see my sons," Ronesca declared.

Maddie could hardly believe what she had heard. And before she could even grapple herself free of her denial, Captain of the Guard Romney, who stood at her elbow, seized her arm and compelled her forward past the queen toward the Esurhites. Right then the veil lifted—the spell she'd not even realized had been woven—and she knew that Trap's worst scenario was true.

Her sons? She's done all this for her sons?

Stomping on the foot of the man who held her arm, Maddie whirled, dashing a handful of the pepper from her cloak pocket into his face. He cried out and fell into a coughing fit as she jerked free of him and raced toward a gap in the circle. A bellow of Command fell on her like rain on a hot desert day, sizzling away as Light flared toward it.

In the end it was her own people who caught her and brought her back to face both queen and Esurhite. The latter looked amused. Ronesca wore a face of savage hatred.

"You always have to make things as hard and unpleasant as possible, don't you?" the queen asked her bitterly.

"How could you do this?" Maddie demanded.

"How could I do this?" Ronesca barked a derisive laugh, and her eyes flashed with sudden blackness.

Maddie gaped at them. *Oh, mercy! It's true!*

"You have set yourself to be my enemy since the day you returned to

Fannath Rill," Ronesca sneered. "Refused to comply with my requests, flagrantly resisted my authority with your outright disobedience, shamed both our houses with your scandalous behavior, your madness, your recalcitrance. Even Eidon you have scorned. You are a disgrace to your family and to the realm, and it will only get worse. When they asked for you, I jumped at the chance to be rid of you, for I knew it to be Eidon's judgment and Chesedh's deliverance. He will never let the Shadow lovers have us, but he will let them have you."

She turned to the Esurhite and threw her head back regally. "Where are my sons, sir?"

The tall Esurhite gestured toward the men behind him. "They are right here, Your Majesty."

And between the gauntlet of dark forms came two slender men in white shirts and stained britches. Their hands hung unbound at their sides, but dark hoods covered their heads, and a pair of soldiers flanked and guided each. As they walked slowly forward, stumbling over the uneven pavement, one of the Esurhites came to pull Maddie away from the others. She gave thought to struggling again but realized it was futile. The Esurhite commander seemed to guess her conclusion, for he laughed at her. "I knew you would be trouble, and you have not disappointed me, my lady."

His words registered with a shock. *Where do I know him from?*

Then she was passing Ronesca's sons, and the cold, unmistakable presence of raw rhu'eman power washed all other thoughts from her mind. She looked at the young men in alarm and the horrendous stench of death slammed into her, so strong and thick she reeled with it, held up and propelled forward only by the hand of the Esurhite biting into her arm.

Light's grace. It cannot be!

But a few moments later, as she was forced down the beach toward the galley's waiting longboat, Maddie heard Ronesca's shriek of horror.

"No! No no no no. . . . Oh, Eidon!" Her wails echoed over stone and sea, the depth and misery of her grief clutching at even Maddie's heart. "Oh, sweet Father, no! They are not dead. It cannot be. It cannot *be*."

But Maddie had known from the moment she'd passed by them that it was.

24

As Abramm ascended the ramp, the first thing he saw was a huge red-stone statue of a dragon landing on a rocky pillar. It stood at the midst of a wide entrance square directly in line with the gateway, commanding the attention of all who entered. Piles of dust-laden rubble and fallen pillars scattered the yard around it, bounded by decaying multistoried buildings—the only thing intact and perfectly preserved was the dragon.

As Abramm stepped through the gateway, he was hit with a noxious stink, reminiscent of a stable in need of cleaning, only sharper. Not horse or ox or pig. *Dragon, maybe?* he asked himself, staring up at the massive sculpture. Its outstretched wings spanned some thirty feet, and its great, reaching talons would easily enwrap the width of his body. Carved from translucent scarlet stone, every scale and muscle and vein was rendered in such perfect placement and proportion, he half expected it to continue its downward motion until it settled on its rocky pillar. Even the eyes, which appeared to be fashioned from faceted topaz, glowered knowingly.

Drawing a deep breath, he took his eyes from it, noting now the divided thoroughfare that led off the square behind it, flanked by long faces of crumbling masonry as it disappeared in an increasingly thick curtain of mist. Since it headed in the same direction the path of light had started him on, he decided he'd follow it.

As he crossed the square, his nape prickled with the sense of an unfriendly awareness focusing upon him. Small snorts and hisses issued around him, and here and there the paving stones had been pulled up and shoved aside to form shallow depressions in the sand, several of which looked as if they might have something in them. Mounds of very large scat lay everywhere, most of it dried. But not all.

It had to be dragons. And probably not the half-human variety he had thus far encountered. Given the roar he'd heard earlier, and the heavy sense of this city's age, he guessed these might even be the tanniym's progenitors, said to have been imprisoned for seducing and raping the females of a lower creation. Though why Eidon would bring *him* to such a place, he could not imagine.

Before long he'd moved close enough to see that the low wall encircling the dragon's pedestal held a moatlike pond, maybe two feet deep. In fact, the perch itself glistened and trickled with the moisture that apparently supplied the pool. Green algae lined the pond's bottom and floated on its stagnant surface. Thirst-wracked now for days—maybe weeks, for all he knew—Abramm thought it the most enticing sight he had ever seen.

He sat on the wall and was reaching down with cupped palms when his water bag sloshed against his hip and brought him to his senses. This was a dragon city cloaked in Shadow. A place of ancient evil. Possibly even a prison. The water he reached for lay at the feet of the red dragon, a creature he knew to be his mortal enemy. He had no business drinking this water, or taking anything else this place might offer him. He might not know why Eidon had brought him here, but he was near certain it wasn't to give him a drink.

He stood up off the wall and sucked the last mouthful of water from his bag. It wasn't close to being enough, and for a moment, despite his conclusions, which he knew to be correct, he hesitated, staring at the dark liquid in the moat. He felt anew the chapped roughness of his lips, his cottony tongue, the dryness of his throat. Need and desire melded into a terrible craving. Just a few sips. Just enough to get him through whatever Eidon had for him. In fact, maybe he was wrong about Eidon's intent. Couldn't Eidon use anything for his purposes? Maybe he really had directed Abramm to this place in order to refill his bag. It would be cruel to lead him to water only to deny him its taste. . . .

No.

He jerked himself back from the pond again and looked up. The dragon's yellow eyes glittered balefully. *These are not my thoughts.* . . .

The water pulled at him, inviting him to look again, but he turned and forced himself to walk away. As he came around the low wall and headed for the thoroughfare, a great roar thundered from the buildings to his left, and he stopped. The sound shook bits of plaster off the decaying walls and provoked a sudden flurry of snorts from the square around him as, to his horror, a dozen large reptilian heads poked up from the rubble and fallen pillars—not all of which were pillars. As the first roar faded, another answered, then a whole chorus of them, from points all around the square.

The creatures around him rose to their feet, giant lizards whose scales looked dry and cracked and sallow beneath a coating of dust. Most were wingless, but not all—one stretched out green-webbed limbs and pulled itself into the sky. Two downflaps carried it into the misty ceiling and out of sight. The rest stared in the direction of the roar for some time. Then, as they relaxed and looked around, a big salmon-colored beast nearby noticed Abramm and froze, staring at him with glittering ruby eyes as its dark forked tongue flicked in and out between thin-lipped jaws and far too many teeth. Never in his life had Abramm felt so much like prey.

Now, as if their minds were linked, other dragons noticed him, too, and closed in upon him. Heart pounding, he brought his staff horizontal. . . .

And was saved when a huge silver dragon crashed through a gap in the far wall and scuttled across the yard, long tail flicking back and forth to balance the motion of its thick, powerful legs. A blue dragon burst from the same gap in pursuit, a green right behind it. The silver whirled back to face its pursuers. Immediately all the other dragons abandoned Abramm to focus on this new interest.

Some of the silver's scales had been torn free, while others hung loosely from great bloody wounds. The beast's forked tongue flicked in and out, its ribs lifting and falling rapidly. Big as it was, its attackers were bigger.

For a long moment they held position, unmoving save for tongues and heaving sides. Then the silver bugled a challenge, a bright red ruff flaring round its neck. With a roar, the green one charged, slamming into the silver with a heavy thud and bowling it back through the dust and rock.

Then the blue was upon it, as well, dust boiling up around them. They killed their fellow with alarming swiftness and fell to ripping it apart, tossing great gobbets of meat into the air and swallowing them whole. Before Abramm knew it, five others had joined the first two, and the rest of the beasts in the square, all of them smaller, drew near the kill, watching avidly as the others fed.

Seizing his chance, Abramm hurried across the gap to the thoroughfare. When he glanced back, the big dragons were already withdrawing from the near-stripped carcass to flop down in the dust, satiated, while the youngsters crowded in for their turn.

Revolted and unnerved, he turned away and, eyeing the mist-hung thoroughfare before him, wondered again what he was doing there. He hadn't gone two steps when a pleasant voice remarked behind him, "They used to be men."

He whirled to find a lithe young man in a white linen tunic leaning with arms folded in one of the open doorways lining the street. He was clean-shaven and so handsome he was almost pretty. Blond curls tumbled in a gleaming mass about his shoulders, and his long-lashed blue eyes were the sort that set women's hearts aflutter and drove men to valiant deeds.

"Who are you?" Abramm asked suspiciously.

"You can call me Lema," the man said, stepping from the doorway and coming toward him. "And you are?"

"Alaric." Abramm glanced about. "You live here?"

"I do." The blue eyes flicked up and down Abramm's form. "You look like a warrior, Alaric, though somehow that name does not seem proper for you."

"Well, Lema doesn't seem a proper name for you, so I suppose we are even." Abramm stepped away from him. Closer now, he realized the man's proportions were scaled to the city's gargantuan architecture, so he'd not seemed unusually large until they stood face-to-face. Now he towered over Abramm, his broad chest and powerful shoulders almost double the width of Abramm's.

The stranger cocked his head, looking almost pleased. "You don't think Lema suits me? Why not? Too . . . ordinary? Too plain?"

"Too small." Abramm took another step back.

Lema threw back his head and laughed. "Where are you headed, Alaric?" he asked when he had finished.

"I thought I'd follow this road," Abramm said, gesturing vaguely up the street, which was littered with weeds, fallen rocks, and the ever-present piles of scat. Broken-off pillars marched in line along the central divider on his left, while in the tall masonry walls soaring to right and left, the high-placed window holes and remains of stone balconies gave evidence of long-lost upper stories.

"Ah, that'll be the Central Plaza, then." Lema nodded and eyed him with a knowing gleam. "I guess we know what *you're* after."

"And what would that be?"

"The treasure of Chena'ag Tor, of course."

"I don't think so," Abramm said. He started down the thoroughfare.

"Well, you're headed right for it," Lema said, falling into step with him.

Abramm said nothing, wondering suddenly if he might be right. Riches such as Chena'ag Tor was said to hold would certainly build him the kind of army he'd need to take back his homeland and defeat the Esurhites.

"You're not the first to come here looking for the treasure, you know," Lema remarked cheerfully. "In fact, it's the only reason any of your kind ever come here."

"There are more of my kind here?"

Lema waved a dismissive hand. "They're all dead. Last one passed a few years ago, I think. It's hard to keep the time straight anymore. They never seem to last long, but maybe that's just relative since the rest of us have been here so much longer."

"So there are others like you here, then?"

"Oh yes. Many of us, in fact. Most live down near the plaza, where it's nicer." He paused as a loud snort erupted from the shadowed interior of a room beyond the street-level doorway they were passing, then said, as if it were nothing, "You can't take the treasure away, you know. The road will only bring you back." He paused again, then added, "Of course, it would do that even if you didn't have the treasure." And the grin he flashed at Abramm seemed almost a leer, as if he hoped his words might have provoked fear and dismay in his listener.

Abramm shrugged. "Well, since I didn't follow the road here in the first place, I doubt I'll be relying on it to leave."

"When you leave—"

He was cut off by another snort, followed by the sudden appearance of a fat yellow dragon lumbering out of a gap in the wall to their right. It scuttled into their path and stopped when it saw them, as if startled. Topaz eyes fixed upon them as its black tongue tasted the air. It was twice the size of the pair that had killed the silver back in the square.

Lema made a shooing motion at it. "Go on!" he said as if it were a stray dog. The beast ignored him, staring at Abramm as if it were trying to figure out what he was. In that instant something about it looked almost human.

Lema waved his hand again. "Go on! Get out of the way."

The creature flinched, then turned and scuffled across the divider into the adjoining street, where it turned back to watch them.

Abramm stared back at it. "What did you mean earlier when you said they used to be men?"

"Before they were trapped here," Lema said as he tugged Abramm around and forward, "they were men. Well, not 'men' as you take the word.

Ban'astori we call ourselves. The Shining Ones. Like us they were once beautiful and talented and wise. They flew above the clouds, composed odes and poetry, and built many great and wondrous cities." He gestured around. "Like this one."

"Trapped here?" Abramm frowned, remembering the open gateway through which he had entered the city.

"By the Old One's decree. He was angry with us—he was *afraid* of us, because of our dual natures. So he cursed us and put us here." Bitterness laced his voice. "Now some of us"—he gestured at a big dragon lying along the wall—"have been so long in this place, so long frustrated with the injustice of their fate, they have lapsed into the forms you see now and have forgotten how to change back."

Abramm contemplated that for a moment, then asked, "And who is the Old One?"

"Oh, he goes by many names—Eloshin, Sheleft'Ai, the Dying One . . ." Lema turned toward him. "I've heard that more recently his followers are calling him Eidon."

Abramm met his fierce gaze stoically, surprised and yet not, for on some level he'd seen this coming. "You *are* the fathers of the tanniym, then," he murmured. *Oh, my Lord Eidon, what are you doing? Why have you brought me here?*

Lema regarded him narrowly. "All we did was seek the freedom to make our own decisions and live out our lives as we chose. Is that so bad a thing?"

"You raped the wives and daughters of men!"

"Rape?! Is that what he's told you?" Lema shook his head, laughing. "It wasn't that at all. The women *wanted* us. Loved us. Begged us to take them. And we loved them in our turn." The amused expression became a scowl. "But he could not abide that. He had to be center of everything. As if his ideas and ways were the only ones of any worth."

"Well, seeing as he knows the end from the beginning and has made us all—"

Lema snapped around, fast as a dragon, nostrils flaring, blue eyes fierce and cold. "What do you know!" he sneered, cutting Abramm off. His brows drew down and his face flashed with a preternatural fire. "Blind, stupid little termite. The Old One made us all! Ha! If you had the least idea what he *really* was . . ." He had leaned so close Abramm could smell his astringent breath. Now he stopped as if coming to his senses. "Why am I wasting words on you? You'll never understand until it's too late."

He turned and walked away, leaving Abramm to breathe a sigh of relief, happy to be rid of him. But Lema hadn't gone far before he turned back. "Come along. It's not far now." And it was as if a different person spoke. All the dark rage was gone, the man's breezy golden air returned as if it had never left.

Unnerved by the change, knowing for certain now that this man was his enemy, the last thing Abramm wanted to do was come along. But what else could he do? Even if he had been shown another way to go, Lema would undoubtedly follow.

They continued through the city, the mist unveiling new sights ahead as it closed in from behind. Dragons rose and scuttled out of their way, or grunted and stirred behind the open street-level doorways, and it wasn't long before Abramm noticed he and Lema had acquired a procession of reptilian attendants following along after them.

Lema ignored them, taking it upon himself to serve as impromptu tour guide and consumed with his descriptions and explanations.

His great city had once been divided into three distinct regions—the outer two now lost—and was so vast that it had taken a man ten days to traverse and three times that to encircle. Those who could always flew. Common men, such as Abramm, with their short legs and constant need for rest and replenishment, took even longer to cross it.

He delighted in pointing out the ruins of an ancient theater here, a marketplace there, the home of a once-prominent resident, a particularly well-preserved artwork or architectural detail. He waxed eloquently on the Ban'astori's skill and grace in the arts. And even in its present state of decline, Abramm saw signs of wondrous beauty—like the stone fig trees that marched down the divider of the thoroughfare. The sheered-off pillars Abramm had seen near the dragon square were actually beautifully rendered tree stumps, broken by the heedlessness of fighting dragons. As they progressed toward the city's center, more and more trees remained intact and were as amazingly crafted as the dragon statue in the square—accurate down to each twig and leaf, and so cunningly shaped they seemed to quiver in a nonexistent breeze.

Though usually he agreed with Lema that all had been quite magnificent, he once made the mistake of wondering why it had been allowed to fall into such ruin. Lema's tone sharpened as he attributed the decline to the Old One and reverted to complaining of how unjustly he and his people had been trapped here. As he went on and on, Abramm came to understand that not all the dragons in the city were Ban'astori in various states of regression.

Some, like Lema, had retained the full awareness and use of their dual natures. Others, consumed by bitterness and anger, had lived in their dragon aspects so long, the strength of their gentler, more civilized side had wasted away. Now, living only in their lusts of the moment, those poor beings had lost even some of the higher characteristics of the dragon, like their wings and the beauty of their scaling, becoming little more than overgrown lizards.

"It will not always be like this, though," Lema promised. "One day the Chosen One will come to set us free. Some of us think it will be soon." He eyed Abramm speculatively. "With us as his army, he will unite the realms into one and end the divisiveness that has so long plagued the world. We will regain what has always been ours, and the Old One will be exposed for the fraud he is. A drooling, hunchbacked old man, who survives only so long as other foolish men believe in him. Maybe we will save a little bit of the desert just for him and those he has deceived to wander in for the rest of time." He thought for a moment, then chuckled. "Then again, maybe not, since there'd be no one to care enough about him to keep him alive."

Something big flew over their heads, hidden in the mist but for the wind its passage generated.

"We will set forth a new order where men will be cared for properly and no one will go without. Where wisdom and talent will be appreciated, where faith will mean peace not war and worship will become the greatest joy ever known. Where men will know no limits, free to progress beyond anything they can even imagine." He smiled and glanced at Abramm. "What say you to that, friend Alaric? Does that sound like such a dreadful thing?"

Abramm found himself unable to speak. Even aside from Lema's boasting at the demise of Eidon, his glowing description of the new order had made Abramm's skin crawl, for he'd remembered all too clearly how earlier Lema, bristling with hatred and disgust, had called him a termite. As if he were some kind of infestation needing to be removed, not "cared for properly . . ."

And he was more at a loss than ever to explain why he had been brought here.

The crowd of dragons following them continued to grow, both behind and before them, joined now by large men of Lema's kind. They stood at the side of the street, watching silently as the two passed. Lema ignored them all, and Abramm supposed himself to be something of a novelty here, so why wouldn't the locals turn out to have a look at him?

Yet, despite the sense they were about to reach their destination, they walked on and on, until it seemed they'd walked three times the distance he'd walked in the desert. His legs and back and hips ached with fatigue, and he was beginning to wonder if they were walking in circles when the mist dissolved before them to reveal a sudden drop in the city's elevation. Stairs descended to and through a landing from which flat rooftops extended into one long connected network of buildings. These encircled a vast, circular flat that sloped down to a dark central pit from which a gout of mist arose to meet the cloud overhead.

A glut of dragons crowded the flat's near edge, as if they, too, had been awaiting Abramm's arrival. There were giant men, as well, lining the stair and pressed onto the landing below. Not a landing, exactly, but a platform overlook extending out from the stairway, which continued through it to a chamber below.

He eyed the circular expanse, the dark clot of mist, and the dragons, shimmering with exquisite jewel tones as they jostled for position. They bugled and roared and whistled their excitement, and occasionally one would leap up from the mass to fly over Abramm's head and return.

This was the Central Plaza he'd been seeking?

My Lord?

For answer the path of light, which he had not seen since before he had entered the city, now flashed down the stair before him, disappearing into the landing and reappearing on the terrace below it, where it shot across the dragon-filled flat all the way to the smoking pit. It flared for a moment, then faded.

Dismay filled him. None of this made any sense. Maybe he was dreaming. Maybe he'd fallen in the desert and lay dying in the sand. . . .

Things are not always what they seem . . . my son. In fact, they are often not what they seem. I am with you still.

The thought drifted softly into his awareness as the men began to cheer, while the dragons shook the air with their roaring.

"Why are they so excited?" Abramm wondered.

He did not think Lema could hear him over the din, but the Ban'astori leaned close. "They think perhaps you are the Chosen One."

"The Chosen One? I'm a Terstan. I serve Eidon, whom you've been reviling from the moment we met."

"We hope your eyes will be opened."

As they descended the platform, the Ban'astori continued to cheer, and Lema waved and grinned and nodded. Then they descended into the long dim-lit chamber under the platform, and Abramm understood what was happening.

He was surrounded by treasure. Golden shields lined the walls behind full-sized marble figures decked out in breastplates and helms of gold. Velvet-lined boxes held artful arrangements of jeweled necklaces, bracelets, ear and nose rings. Silk-draped tables displayed golden plates and cups and tableware, candlesticks, vases, and silver chests overflowing with jewels. There were basins, lamps, carts, wardrobes, even tables and chairs—all of gold. There was even a collection of golden idols—fat-bellied Khrell, voluptuous Laevian, Aggos with his stern face and prodigious masculine endowments, as well as others he did not know. Jewels sparkled throughout: ruby, diamond, emerald, sapphire, amethyst. Waist-high ceramic jars piled with golden coins of many nations and denominations stood everywhere. Never had he seen such an accumulation of wealth. Never would he have even been able to imagine such a gathering.

The legends were true. And then some.

"I *knew* it was the treasure you sought!" Lema exclaimed. "And this is only the first room of it. Come. Let me show you the rest." He started toward one of two doorways that—Abramm saw as he drew closer—opened into adjoining galleries whose far ends linked to another set and another after that, all filled with more of the same.

The amount of wealth was more than he could comprehend.

"Come," Lema said again. "Let me show you." He stood in the doorway beckoning.

Curiosity niggled at Abramm, but he resisted it. This was far too obvious a temptation, and he'd already seen enough.

"I did not come for the treasure," he said firmly, continuing on toward the daylight opening at the chamber's far end, where the stone terrace overlooked the flat full of dragons.

Lema hurried after him. "If you didn't come for it, then, why are you here?"

Ahead a marble warrior loomed in Abramm's path, backlit by the light from the terrace door. Just as he was about to alter course to go around it, a pink-orange light blazed from the ceiling above and he stopped, stunned by the sight of a golden breastplate above a kilt of gold, armbands of the same, a sword scabbard of scrolled gold, and on the faceless head, a crown—a filigree of rich yellow gold set with diamonds and rubies. Looking at it, he shuddered, for it was the most beautiful thing he'd ever seen.

"I think it is yours," Lema whispered at his side.

Abramm shuddered again, then glanced at Lema. "I thought you said I'd not be able to leave the city with any of this."

"Only if you intended to steal it. But if you are the Chosen One . . ."

"I'm not."

"No one comes to this place save they who have been brought here. And there is only one who could have brought you to us. Our great father . . ."

"Moroq is not my father. He is my enemy."

"Are you sure? For I have seen upon your arm his very mark."

The words drove into Abramm's soul with a jolt of shock—painful truth that spawned a host of doubts and questions.

"You could be the one to return and conquer, Alaric. With all of us at your back. What has Eidon ever done for you save wound and steal from you? With us you could rule the world."

Temptation struck him like a lightning bolt. For a moment he could hardly breathe. Possibilities tumbled through his mind. He could overthrow the Esurhites, drive the Gadrielites out of Kiriath and retake it for his own. Even Chesedh would fall under his sway. He would kill that handsome eastern lord who was lusting for his wife and take her back once and for all. And who could stop him? No one! Not with this kind of wealth. Not with these kinds of warriors.

Lema grinned at him, his eyes bright and cold with that metallic sheen, as if he knew all that went through Abramm's head. Outside the dragons roared and bugled, their voices enflaming his imagination. Lema lifted the crown from off the marble head. "This is yours, my friend. Made for you to wear . . . You will be king of all. . . ."

Yes. King . . . He stared at the gold crown with its jewels. *I will rule the world. There would be no more wars, no more famines, no more persecutions. . . . I will . . .* He stopped. *What am I thinking?! These are horrible ideas. Arrogant ideas. And this creature is lying to me. I would never rule. That is reserved for his master.*

He wrenched his eyes from the crown and looked at Lema. "Your king, you say? Or merely king of the termites?"

Gratified to see the Ban'astori's eyes widen in surprise, he started around the golden armor before his treacherous inner Shadow could get hold of him once more.

"Wait!" Lema gripped his shoulder, and a vision of Gillard kneeling before him filled his mind. He saw himself touch the fine white hair of his brother's head, saw the other man flinch as he did so, felt his brother's fear and shame and remorse. "Consider what we offer you."

"No." Abramm shook free of him. "It will never be like that with Gillard. And I do not want to be king of the termites at the behest of your master."

He strode around the armor and headed for the doorway, where the men on the terrace and the dragons beyond them had fallen silent.

"You cannot go that way," Lema warned. "The dragons will kill you if you try. . . ."

Abramm kept walking, out the door and onto the terrace, following the light path as he recalled it.

"Stupid termite," Lema said at his back. "You could have everything."

He kept going, right for them. The dragons piled upon the stair, watching him come, some half standing on their fellows. They were big as draft horses, with heavy, thick chests, powerful wings, and mighty tails—compared to these, Tapheina was small and feeble. Their teeth were uncountable, white, sharp, dripping with drool. Their eyes, a myriad of metallic gleams, were as cold and hard as any he had ever looked into. Images crowded into his mind of the silver dragon torn asunder.

He glanced down at his feet, but the path of light did not show itself. His knees trembled. Fear congealed in his belly, and the compulsion to turn back pressed him strongly.

When he had drawn within five paces of them, the dragons erupted, screaming and hissing and bellowing, lashing one another with their tails, climbing up one another's backs, filling the air with their roaring. Sheathed with sweat, he looked again at his feet, begging the lane of light to lead him, aghast at how badly he was shaking, trying to quell a terror that would not be quelled. If he could have closed his eyes and still walked, he would have. Already he smelled the acidic odor of their exhalations, which no doubt would be as poisonous and seductive as anything Tapheina had breathed on him. He'd have to hold his breath as far as he could—at the rate he was panting, he wouldn't get very far.

Oh, my Lord, I don't know—

He cut off the thought and, focusing fiercely on the Light within him, held his staff waist-high, at the ready, and stepped among them. The din shook the organs in his chest, and his heart was hammering so fast he didn't see how it could even pump his blood.

He braced for the first of them to seize him, but to his surprise, they drew back, as if he had some margin of personal space they could not penetrate.

So the Light really was with him. This really was the way he was to go. He strode on, confidence rising giddily. It was just another test. How could he ever have doubted?

As soon as he was completely surrounded with no hope of ever fighting his way back to the stairs, they attacked, lunging as if of one mind, jaws snapping, gouts of breath burning into his face and eyes. Reflexively, he flipped the stick down, striking a nose, then up to strike another, whirling to bat this one and that away. They were far too fast for him to get in any solid blows, and far too many for him to keep them at bay. His robe jerked at his left shoulder, then gave way as he whirled, while another pull came at the back hem. A sleeve tore, and then his ragged, poorly wound turban was pulled off. . . . They had him spinning and dodging in an increasing frenzy, and as he saw how helpless he was, he wanted again and again to bolt, as if he could run fast enough to evade any of them.

They are playing with you.

The thought burst into his chaos and brought him to a stop. He let them come at him, and soon saw that they attacked only his clothing, never quite reaching his flesh. It was all a deception. Empty threats. He took a deep breath to calm himself—and realized in dismay that was the last thing he should have done. Not that it mattered, since in his panic he'd long ago forgotten to hold his breath. Now he realized that even so, he'd not felt the least bit sick. It must be a more subtle sort that didn't hurt, didn't sicken. Indeed, now that he sought for it, he felt the faint tingly burn in his nose and throat and brought the Light up to meet it, burning it off, holding it back with every breath.

You must keep going, my son.

And so he settled himself, brought the stick up, set his eyes on the Light within him, and walked forward. Not really sure where he was headed, he just put his head down and walked.

The dragons tugged and tore at his clothing, spit and breathed their poison upon him, roared and screamed with all their might, as if they hoped to slay him with sound. His ears throbbed with the pain of it, but he shut that out. Shut out even the mental voices he realized were shrieking in his head. Again and again he forced his thoughts back to Eidon, releasing the Light through his flesh to purge the spore as he placed one foot after the other. Repeating verses and promises memorized as a Mataian acolyte, he walked and walked and walked. . . .

And then it was over.

The sound cut off abruptly, and the beasts withdrew. Glancing back, he saw them returning to the foot of the stair, snapping and biting at one another sulkily. Then, as if desperate to kill *something*, a black dragon crested with silver seized a smaller blue and scrubbed it along the ground. A gray one jumped in to help and the feeding frenzy began.

Abramm turned away and walked on across the barren slope toward the smoking pit at its midst.

25

As Abramm headed toward the curtain of black mist, he began to feel strangely disoriented. Though his eyes assured him he was heading downward, his feet and lungs kept insisting he was climbing upward. Perhaps it was a result of all his trials—he'd been shaking awfully hard in that gauntlet and had been without food and adequate water for uncounted days.

Barely had he strode into the outer fringes of mist, than it thickened into a dense black fog that stymied even his night sight. He walked on, trusting in Eidon's unseen, unfelt guidance. Gradually a sense of aversion and resistance arose in him—an irrational fear of going forward that reminded him of a griiswurm aura. But after what he'd just endured, a little unfocused anxiety was nothing, and he pressed on.

Ahead, a soft glow suffused the mist, and with each step it grew appreciably brighter. His disorientation increased as he looked at feet angled downward with the terrain and felt as if they flexed up. To say nothing of heart and lungs that labored as if he were climbing one of the peaks back in the Aranaak.

Then, in a single step, he burst free of the darkness into the intense glare of the sun in a clear blue sky, and the brightness nearly knocked him over. Once he was able to see again, he discovered that his sensations had been correct: He stood on a steep, rocky hillside just below a small domed hall of white marble. It perched at the top of the peak, its dark doorway looming directly in his path.

Once he'd caught his breath, he climbed the last bit of slope to the porch, where the doorway's impenetrable darkness gave no hint of what lay behind it. An inscription tumbled across its lintel in the odd squiggly symbols of the Old Tongue: *"No other shall come before me."*

It was from the Second Word. Reassured, he stepped over the threshold into a moist-smelling chamber every bit as black as the cloud he'd just endured, the doorway having vanished as soon as he'd passed through it. The chuckle of running water sounded at his feet, echoing in what seemed a much larger space than should have been possible for a temple as small as this had appeared from the outside.

He conjured a kelistar and gasped in amazement. The chamber in which he stood was bigger than the great rotunda of the library back in Springerlan—save there were no books, no shelves, and only a single pedestal in the room's center surrounded by a great dome of dark walls sprinkled with stars. A trough of running water ran like a moat between the outer walls and the inner floor. To get to the latter he'd have to wade. Which, from the folded towel and small bench that stood on the other side of the channel, he guessed he was intended to do.

He gave thought to stooping and taking a drink, so great was his thirst, but decided it might be improper, so he only bent to unfasten his sandals before wading across. As he sat on the bench drying his feet with the towel, he noticed the cup of water beside him. Hardly enough, he thought at first, but obviously meant to be drunk. And so he did.

The water was cool and sharp, and the cup magically refilled, letting him drink and drink and drink, until thirst and hunger and fatigue slipped away before renewed vitality. Finally, sated, profoundly grateful, and bemused by the never-emptying cup, he set the vessel aside and stood up. The moment he did, light flared from his bare feet across the floor and up the walls, engulfing even the central pedestal, which was revealed now to be more pillar than pedestal.

He stared around in awe, for there was no confusing the light and sense of Eidon's power. As it clarified and brightened he saw that floor and walls alike were covered with a living mural, words and images dancing together: a golden tree, a great forest, ancient fortresses crowned with orbs that looked like guardstars, great armies of giant beautiful men flying in formation over green fields that turned to ash in their wake, a glorious being hovering over a mountain, a man suspended between heaven and earth—bloodied, beaten, and screaming as the darkness took him. . . .

Abramm passed before it, walking slowly, his mind battered with concepts and images from past, present, and future. Snatches of Laud's voice—

or Kesrin's—explained what he was seeing in a mad jumble he couldn't begin
to follow. He wanted to close his eyes, to stop his brain, to sort it out, but it
just kept coming.

He saw himself taking the Star in the cistern of the SaHal, felt again the
shield burn into his chest, then was crowned a king again—but in a hall
greater than Avramm's Mount. The dragon flew overhead, coming after him,
coming for him and all those he loved . . .

Because of Eidon.

Something flickered beyond the wall, a new image forming behind the
others in a second room like this one, with another pedestal. The moment he
shifted his focus from the wall to the room beyond, the wall dissolved. Before
him stood the second pedestal, clear as day, and on it rested a massive lump
of amber, dancing with an inner light that caught and held the eye. Part of
him knew that he stepped toward it and should not, drawn as he'd been
drawn to Lema's promises of limitless wealth and power.

Suddenly the warm light and amorphous shapes drew into forms, dark
and light, hard and soft, scallops of brilliance on a dark sea. A man's body—
startlingly familiar in form—floating facedown, red hair splayed in the water
around his head, blood spreading across the pale tunic on his back as a small
boat approached. It was Trap. In dire straits.

The scene shifted, and he saw his wife, propelled by a tall Esurhite down
a beach toward a galley from which hung the lighted purple banner of the
Black Moon. He felt her fear, her shock of betrayal, her desperate plea for
help.

He jerked back, horrified by the certainty that what he saw was real,
though whether past, present, or future, he did not know. It drew him still,
but he turned from it, seeking the euphoric almost-understanding he'd
known before its intrusion. But whatever train of thought he'd been following, it was lost, for the images on the dome wall were different now. . . .

Annoyed with himself for succumbing to the distraction, he jumped back
into the river of events and information. Again it overwhelmed him, and he
struggled to keep up, his mind stretched to the limit by concepts too high
and deep and wide for a mortal man to ever hold. And yet he kept trying,
feeling as if he stood on the verge of grasping something . . . marvelous.
Something he had lived all his life to understand. Something impossible to
know, and yet . . . The Light flared in him, and for a moment his awareness
expanded beyond anything he'd ever known, and he saw Truth. Saw how it
fit together in all its myriad pieces. Time and space and choice. Saw how

much Eidon loved him, saw the immensity of what Tersius had done for him, saw the evil in Moroq's—and his own—drive to independence. All of the tales in the Words of Revelation came together for him, all of them following the same thread—the power and might of the God he served, the perfect justice and righteousness, and the unfathomable depths of his mercy and grace. But even with his vast comprehension he saw still more he did not understand, new knowledge birthing new questions in a chain that stretched to infinity.

And then it ended. He came back to a form that seemed small and cold, weak and watery, and tinged with terrible darkness. For a moment he writhed at being put back into it, then the resistance gave way to acceptance and he was himself again, standing now before the bench on which he'd first sat, the dirtied towel still draped over it. He stared at it bemusedly, for it did not seem the sort of thing that should have remained in this glorious room.

Why am I here, my Father?

You have been traveling to this place ever since I put my mark upon you, my son. Turn now, and find your symbol on the pillar.

He did as he was bade. Names, symbols, letters he could not read scrawled across the marble, some in the Old Tongue, most of it not. But there. A shield with a tiny dragon upon it.

Why a dragon, my Lord?

Because you were once a slave. And I freed you.

Oh. Of course. . . . Why would he not want to remember that from which he had been delivered? And he understood that Eidon did not refer to his slavery to Katahn, but to the Shadow within him and the corrupted world around him. His eyes moved to the crowns and scepter above the dragon and shield. *What are these?*

They are yours to lose. Touch the shield, my son.

Abramm did so, and the floor zinged beneath his feet, catapulting him forward into the pillar—and through it. He did not think the light could grow any brighter, but it did.

Words echoed around him, a deep, sonorous voice, more beautiful, more compelling, more marvelous than any he had ever heard. It plucked at his heart, captured his mind, abducted his love. . . .

He glimpsed something in the brightness before him—a great space, a raised dais . . . a figure standing before a whiteness that could not be penetrated. He heard the wondrous voice, and only gradually was he able to focus on the words. Which seemed to be a litany of accusation against someone.

"He claims to be your servant yet refuses to believe you and torments himself with worry. Yesterday he spent hours feeling sorry for himself."

Is it me he is accusing? Abramm wondered.

"He has failed in every way, for you sent him to protect his queen and he was so preoccupied with his own concerns he failed to see the danger in time. Now she is lost and he is dying, cursing you as he does."

Not me! Abramm realized. *Trap . . . and Maddie. What I saw in the amber on the other pedestal. . . .* The wondrous voice, beautiful as it was, now grated.

"After all you have done, all he has learned, he has come to this. A bitter disappointment and a failure. I say take him now before he can embarrass you further."

The compelling voice fell silent, and Abramm breathed a prayer of thanks.

Now another voice replied, warm as sunlight, soft as lamb's fleece, but iron firm regardless.

"That is all true, but he is mine, and I have paid for his failures. We no longer hold any of it against him."

"But he curses you. He seeks his own way over yours."

"It is a family matter now and not the purview of this court." Silence fell, and when the accuser said no more, the warmer, richer voice said, "I wonder, though, what you think of Abramm? He has done rather well, wouldn't you say?"

The figure turned—a giant of a man and no man at all. Dark eyes, perfect features, too beautiful to be a man, too full of light and power to be mortal. And yet, he looked inexplicably familiar, and the shock that widened those beautiful dark eyes, then the rage that narrowed them, was all too human.

"What is *he* doing here? He has no right to be here!"

"He has more right than you do, Moroq," the warm voice said dryly.

"Your servant." Moroq sneered. "You are proud of *him?*"

"He has passed through Chena'ag Tor."

"No! I don't believe you. No man passes through Chena'ag Tor."

"Very few, it is true."

Moroq passed over that as if nothing had been said, glaring at Abramm again before turning back to the throne. "This one is *nothing!* You have been too kind to him. Protecting him on every side, giving him hope in the midst of his trials. Let me take all that he loves and see what he does then. He would be just like his friend Meridon."

"You already have taken all he loves. Over and over, pushing me to harm him without cause. Yet he has not forsaken me. And I will reward him for it."

"His loved ones live. His realm remains. I say destroy it all. Burn it barren and see what he does then. You have not been fair with me in this. You are never fair with me."

"Very well, Moroq. Do your worst, then. His reward will only be the greater for it."

The beautiful immortal—could it truly be Moroq?—whirled from the golden throne and stalked away, his face dark with fury. As he moved past, a terrible sense of smallness overcame Abramm. A sense that here was a dangerous and deadly enemy. He trembled as the creature passed by him, and nearly jumped out of his skin when the marvelous voice, distorted now by anger, hissed at his right ear, "You think to stand against me, little man? You don't know pain. Whatever reward you think you've gained, you'll give it over in a heartbeat when I'm done with you. Oh yes, you may have seen it on the pillar. But I will take it from you. I will take it all from you this time, Abramm Kalladorne."

He strode away, and Abramm watched him go, the sense of terror and smallness ebbing like a receding tide. Then the white robes burst into light and the retreating figure vanished in a column of amber and flashing wings.

Abramm staggered and gasped as he found himself back in the domed chamber, the amber corridor immediately in front of him, the white one beside it.

Tersius's voice sounded in his head, quoting from the First Word: *"I place before you life and death, my friend. Do you know which one is which? All that you have learned will tell you, but you must know where you want to go."*

Wherever you send me, Lord.

"Are you sure?"

You know I am.

"The two ways are so close that if you are not sure, if you do not focus, if you do not know, you can be pulled to the wrong one. . . ."

Maddie had been given to the Esurhites and needed Abramm's help; Trap floated wounded in the water, soon to be dead if Abramm did not go to him. He could save them both if he took the amber corridor. Or he could take the other way. Where he saw nothing but light. Felt nothing but light. Had no idea where it would take him. No idea if it would take him anywhere. . . .

But after all he'd come through, all he'd seen, how could there be any decision but one? He stepped toward the white column, and a gust of wind buffeted him so that he staggered toward the amber column shooting up beside it. He felt his wife beseeching him to save her, to save their sons, to save all of Chesedh.

But it was Eidon he must serve and Eidon who did the protecting.

No other shall come before me.

The wind subsided the moment he chose, and he stepped unhindered into the white fire of his Father's will.

ELPIS

PART THREE

26

Maddie was escorted down the beach toward the water where the Esurhite longboat waited just out of reach of the white-lipped waves lapping beyond it in the darkness. Iron manacles were snapped about her wrists, then and she was forced to climb over the gunwale into the vessel. As she sat on a middle thwart, the others arrayed themselves outside the boat and shoved it toward the water, scrambling in as the waves lifted it and the outflow carried it away from the beach. In moments eight oars plied the water, increasing the vessel's speed as it met and bobbed over the next incoming wave.

As they left the susurrus of the breakers tumbling against the shore, Ronesca's wails echoed more loudly around them, cycling between disbelief, desperate grief, and fury. As the galley toward which they headed loomed up in the darkness, the Esurhite commander chuckled where he sat across from Maddie. "She truly didn't see it coming, did she? Of course we'd return them to her dead. What did she think?"

Repelled by his amusement as much as by his willingness to betray his word, Maddie asked abruptly, "And is her husband dead, as well?"

White teeth flashed in the night. "Not yet. Him we're preparing for the Games. I understand he's something of a fighter—nothing like your husband was, I'm sure. You have my condolences on his loss." He paused, then added, "We all mourned his passing."

She stared at him wordlessly. Why on earth would he say such a thing? Did he think she might believe him?

His grin widened. "We wished to see him die at our hands, of course, not chewed upon by the dogs of his own realm." He paused, gazing at her. "You don't remember me, do you? We met on the Island of the Gulls."

Ah yes. That was it: He'd been the commanding officer there. Uumbra. She jerked up her chin. "I'm surprised that incident didn't bring you a demotion, sir."

He laughed, but she heard the note of bitterness in his voice. "It all worked out in the end. I'm here now, am I not? Here to bring you to your new husband, who has come himself to receive you—the Pretender's woman given into his hands." He barked a command in the Tahg to the steersman, then turned back to her. "You will meet him in a few moments, and he will be pleased to ease your grief."

Horror washed over her. *In moments? Oh, Father! Deliver me!*

And Uumbra must have seen her reaction, for he laughed again and said no more.

She watched the galley's narrow prow loom ever higher before them, its banks of oars raised along its sides now, since it was at anchor. Big painted eyes gleamed softly on its dark hull, seeming to watch her as the longboat came alongside and a rope ladder tumbled down from the gunwale.

Maddie thought she might throw up. Or faint. *Oh, Abramm, where are you? Eidon . . . help me.* Yet she could not think from which quarter any help might come. And then the longboat took a sudden sharp dip, and the light that had been creeping round the edges of her vision flared brilliantly across it. She gasped, and instead of falling into blackness as she'd expected, she saw a figure through brightness. A man whose form struck powerful chords of recognition. Tersius? No. Abramm! Gladness rushed through her in a giddy storm. He was coming. Just like before. He would do it.

Then she saw him clearly, and the giddiness subsided.

He stood between two columns of light—the amber one between him and her, the white one beside them both. His face was browned with the sun, his hair flowing well over his shoulders, his beard long as a hermit's. His robe was dusty and tattered, his feet bare, his face gaunt. His eyes, though, shone like beacons of blue as they fixed upon her. She felt his fear for her, his desperate longing to come to her, balanced by something even more powerful— his desire to follow their God. The white column that was Eidon.

"I'm sorry, love. I cannot come now. He has something else for me. . . ."

Both columns vanished, and he was gone, but she felt the pain of terrible regret and also of his iron-hard determination to serve only one. It left her breathless with disappointment and weeping with pride. For she knew he'd been tempted and made the right decision.

Oh, Father . . . I know I have you always. . . . Nothing is beyond your power.

The transfer from longboat to galley-ship deck passed in a blur of darkness, wet rough rope, and hurting shoulders, but finally she stood before her husband's greatest human enemy. The High Priest of Khrell and Supreme Commander of the Armies of the Black Moon: Belthre'gar ul Manus, son of Abramm's dear friend Katahn.

He looked like a bald version of his father, which struck a strange and unnerving blow to Maddie's poise. Like Katahn, his build was short and powerful, and he had the same hatchet face, the same crescent scar on his cheekbone that was the mark of a Brogai lord, the same dark eyes. There the similarity ended, for where Katahn's eyes held lights of kindness and the glow of a deep thinker, his son's were flat and hard and angry. Even now that he had won everything, he still looked hungry.

Back on the island, Ronesca's wild screaming turned to rage again, climbing higher and higher up the scale as she screeched at whoever had the bad fortune to be in her vicinity. Maybe she even cursed Eidon—the words were impossible to pick out. Whatever pity Maddie had felt for her earlier had been consumed by the reality of the situation into which the woman had deliberately placed her. Wife to a man who already had a hundred of them, prize to her husband's most powerful enemy, doomed to be used until her womb bore the desired fruit.

The temptation to hatred was strong, but she put it away, Abramm's example inspiring her now. Whatever wrong Ronesca had committed, it was done against Eidon first. She had paid sorely already. And would continue to pay as she watched her realm torn from her grasp. The Kiriathans would never forgive her for this. They would rebel. The Esurhites would take advantage. . . .

Maddie let out her breath in a long, low sigh and tried to think of something she could do. But there was nothing. Whatever was to be done, Eidon would have to do it.

Suddenly the wail cut off completely, so instantly silent that Maddie wondered if someone had cold-cocked her. Maybe they had. Captain Romney had looked surprised and none too happy with the role he'd played in this affair. Most likely he'd not been told what it would entail.

She stood listening along with the Esurhites, but there was nothing to hear. Even the normal boat sounds had been smothered in the blanket of silence that had fallen upon them. Almost as if the world held its breath, waiting for something.

Then it all came rushing back—the slap of the water against the hull, the ship's constant creaking, the men's thumping footfalls on the deck, the squeak of tackle.

"That was odd," someone muttered.

Commander Uumbra pointed past Belthre'gar. "Look, Your Eminence. You were right. Here they come." And across the glittering sea came the Chesedhan galleys that had been stationed north of the island waiting . . . to rescue her?

"They're taking the bait."

Belthre'gar muttered something in the Tahg, and Uumbra shouted a command to the ship's captain, who repeated it to the men, provoking a furious burst of activity. The oars slipped back into the water with a great thundering belowdecks, and the drummer struck a slow but quickening cadence. Meanwhile amidships the lids were removed from two iron cauldrons bolted on squat pedestals beside what looked like a catapult. Men hurried to scoop purple ooze from the cauldrons into clay jars, which were then placed onto the catapult.

Once the ship started moving, a second round of commands rang out. The starboard-side oars lifted out of the water and held while the portside oars continued to work, turning the ship as she went. The galley's prow slid around, angling away from the shore. As it did, her eye caught on the shimmer of a Light-cloak coming up on them from the north end of the island. It shielded a longboat full of men that looked as if it would catch up with them while they were still turning and the starboard oars were up and out of the way. They must be the men Trap had arranged as backup in case his worst scenario played out. Her heart leaped with hope as the galley continued to turn, and the gunwale blocked sight of her rescuers.

No one else noticed the longboat's approach, for all Esurhite eyes were on the approaching Chesedhan galleys. The Esurhite flagship turned until her portside was presented square to the Chesedhans. At Maddie's side, Belthre'gar laughed and said something to the ship's captain that, from his tone and the captain's pleased response, must have been a compliment.

She looked over her shoulder to see Brookes and young Corporal Henning hauling themselves over the starboard gunwale. A sudden breeze washed into her face, blowing out of the south and hitting the vessel broadside, the ship rocking slightly at its passing.

Then a dark-tunicked soldier appeared at her side to grip her arm and drag her toward the open hatch ten feet away. She fought him, as behind her the sudden shouts of the galley ship's crewmen suggested Brookes and his men had been discovered. Then another gust of wind slammed into them, again from the south, much stronger than the first. The deck tipped sharply, came back to level—and she saw a monstrous wave, higher than the mast-pole, rearing over them, blotting out the star-speckled sky.

It crashed down in a smothering wall of water that tumbled her headlong in its cold embrace. The deck vanished beneath her feet, and she hit something on her side, briefly—the gunwale, perhaps? Then it was gone, too, and all she knew was coldness and tumbling, coughing and sputtering as her face met air one moment, swallowing giant gouts of water as the sea closed over her the next.

She fell into the darkness, shackles hindering her efforts to swim, the weight of her skirts and cloak pulling her down, down, down until she hit the strait's sandy bottom. . . .

The next thing she knew, she lay on her side in the darkness coughing water from her lungs in great phlegmy expulsions of air. Sand lined her mouth, and her lungs, nose, and throat burned. For a time it seemed she'd never stop coughing.

She must have passed out again, for the next time she awoke, it was light and she was no longer alone—someone patted her back and held up her head so she'd not choke on her own expulsions of water. When at last she could stop coughing long enough to look up and blink away the salt and sand in her eyes she recognized Brookes, who knelt at her head, and Corporal Henning, who crouched before them both, watching wide-eyed and pale-faced. He had a lump on his brow, and various small cuts on his face. At first she could not think what they were doing on the beach, then recalled they had been on the galley with her when it capsized.

Her iron manacles sprawled across the wet sand not far away, and she realized they were back on the beach she'd been escorted from not long ago. A clear sky stained gold to pink to mauve arched overhead. She heard the cries of thousands of sea gulls and the susurrus of the waves far down the slope of the beach, along with the occasional distant shouts of men.

With Brookes's help, she sat up and peered at the sea, littered now with shards of wood floating toward the beach. Already a ragged line of debris, which included several bodies, had piled along the upper edge of the waves' reach. Numerous vessels bobbed hull-up out on the sea of wooden shards, Chesedhan three-masters gliding among them on a freshening wind. The longer she looked, the more bodies she saw, drifting amidst the flotsam.

Nearer she saw the beaked prow of Belthre'gar's galley ship, perched atop a stony outcrop at her beach's end, painted eye staring at the sky, the bulk of its hull hidden behind the rocky spine. Her gaze came back to the men beside her.

"What happened?"

"A giant wave, my lady. It came out of nowhere. Bowled over the galley and washed you up here." Brookes shook his head and stared at her in wonder. "The hand of Eidon himself delivered you, ma'am."

She looked from him to the others, then back to the sea and the beached galley ship.

"Looks from here like we've lost a good portion of our navy," Brookes went on, "but the Esurhite's fleet lost more. They're devastated."

"Fleet?"

"There were hundreds of ships waiting out there. They meant to destroy us outright last night, madam. Deception piled upon deception."

Maddie looked up and down the beach, then pulled a wet strand of hair from her mouth and asked, "Have you seen Captain Meridon? He boarded the queen's vessel with me, but he wasn't there when we came ashore. . . ." She trailed off, alarmed by the sober look that came onto Brookes's face.

"No. We've not seen him, Your Highness. But we haven't seen Lieutenant Whartel, either. He was supposed to have commanded a second longboat along with ours. Maybe they're together."

A member of the Chesedhan royal guard appeared at the top of the hill, and as he approached, Maddie recognized Captain Romney, the tall, freckled officer of the queen's guard who had himself handed Maddie to the Esurhites. Seeing her, he stopped in his tracks and stared down at her as a man stricken. "Princess Madeleine?"

Seemingly unaware of anything but her, he started down the slope, but immediately her guardsmen barred his way. He regarded their shining blades in befuddlement, then looked at her again. "You're alive?"

"No thanks to you," growled Brookes.

"Let the captain approach," Maddie said, before things got even uglier.

They lowered their swords to let Romney through, and he fell to his knees before her. "Forgive me, Your Highness. I had no idea it would turn out . . . Oh, plagues, what have we done?"

For a time no one spoke, and Maddie watched as more guardsmen appeared on the hill their captain had just crested. They descended slowly as Romney found his voice again. "The queen has been lost, madam. We found her body caught in one of the olive trees on the other side of the island. Her neck was broken. And the waves carried her sons clean away. We're still looking for their bodies."

"Eidon's vengeance," Brookes said low at Maddie's side. "Struck the witch dead for what she did to Princess Madeleine."

Dead. Maddie struggled to lay hold of the reality, feeling somehow as if she were still caught beneath the water. Everything seemed so dim and far away. How could Ronesca be dead?

Captain Romney looked at the sand, his face red with shame. "Aye, he did," he said softly. "And brought you back to us, though we do not deserve it."

She stared at him blankly, his utterance seeming no more than a string of random words.

How could Ronesca be dead? I want to see the body! I won't believe it until . . .

Her eyes fixed on the corpses piled at the crest of the beach, at the others floating in from the sea. . . .

"It is a fearsome thing to fall into the hands of He Who Lives."

The phrase from the First Word floated into her mind, and she shivered.

Finally Romney said, "Ronesca is dead, Your Highness. And Leyton is captured. That means—" His voice broke again. He had to clear his throat. "That means, as the only surviving member of the royal line, *you* are queen of Chesedh, madam."

He bowed his head and added, "Long live the queen."

Around them the sea gulls called and the wind blew as the men stood stunned before her. Then Captain Brookes followed Romney's lead and dropped to one knee, as well. "Long live the queen," he echoed.

In seconds all the others did likewise, as Maddie stood there, shivering fiercely, nausea and shock churning in her stomach. She had never felt so cold in her life. Nor so lost and terrified.

I cannot be queen of Chesedh! Not without Abramm. Or Papa or Leyton. Oh, Father Eidon, what will I do?

She wanted to run away, to tell them all she was not suited, could not do this . . .

But the words of abdication and refusal would not come, and she knew it was no accident. She'd been sold off to Chesedh's enemies by her sister-in-law, the queen, and now it had all been turned about. Ronesca was dead. A massive wave had decimated the Esurhite fleet. And brought her back with hardly a scratch to this very beach.

Queen of Chesedh. Her scalp crawled, but warmth was slowly returning, and with it, her fear subsided. Eidon had called her to this duty, and he would see that she had whatever she needed to carry it out. *Nor will you leave me to do it alone. You will always be here to guide me, won't you? One moment at a time.*

So she lifted her chin and looked around, trying to think what Abramm would do. The answer came easily: First he would take stock.

The situation was as Brookes had described it: The sudden wave had swamped a third of the Esurhite fleet as well as a good portion of Chesedh's. It had also severely damaged the quays and structures all along the shoreline, the breastwork defense on the river, and about a quarter of the city of Peregris. The damage to the fleet, though, was the most alarming, for they had already been at a numbers disadvantage.

The remnants now limped along, commandeering the swamped Eshurhite vessels if possible, sinking those too damaged to save. As for prisoners . . . They weren't taking any, the reporting admiral had told her.

"You're just letting them drown?" she'd exclaimed in horror.

He'd shrugged. "We're letting all the galley slaves go. As for the others, we don't have a place to keep them, nor food to sustain them . . . and we can't just let them go to fight again."

He had a point, but she couldn't bear it as a policy. "It would make us no better than they. Try to capture as many as you can."

He hadn't liked it, but he'd agreed to it.

The bodies of Queen Ronesca's sons were found that same morning on the shore northeast of the island. They were brought to the palace, where preparations were made for them to lie in state with their mother. Maddie quickly passed the details of that operation off to others.

The burning question of her day was what had happened to Trap. She'd immediately assigned Brookes to find out, and he'd returned shortly with the horrifying news that Meridon had been stabbed in the back and pitched off the stern of the queen's galley after they'd left Peregris. Lieutenant Whartel and his men, were following along just behind when Meridon plunged into the sea before them. They'd picked him up at once, pressed the water out of him, got him breathing again . . . only to discover a knife wound. Seeing their original plan had already gone irrecoverably awry, and sensing that Trap was on the verge of death, Whartel had returned to shore, and two of his men disembarked with Meridon under orders to find the royal physician as soon as they could. None had been heard from since.

She could hardly believe Trap been stabbed in the back and questioned Whartel repeatedly on that point. He stuck to his story. At last she summoned Captain Romney.

When she told him what had befallen her friend, Romney's mouth gaped. Then his jaw firmed and his eyes turned flinty. "Captain Meridon was supposed to accompany you ashore, and we feared he'd make too much trouble for the handoff to go smoothly. Madam said she'd see that he was taken care of." He shook his head. "She was so devout. How could she deliberately order such an act?"

"She hadn't been herself lately," Maddie murmured, recalling with a shudder how hateful she'd been at the last.

It was midafternoon before she finally found Trap. The two soldiers who had brought him ashore had avoided the royal residence on account of not knowing who exactly had tried to kill him. They had taken him, instead, to the home of a prominent physician. Because Trap had been bleeding internally, the physician had to cut him open to sew up the vessels and organs that had been damaged. He finished about the time they all got word that Ronesca was dead and Maddie had been made queen in her stead, and one of the soldiers hurried to the royal residence to tell her what had happened.

In all the chaos, though, it had taken him a while to catch up with her, but when he did, she dropped everything and bade him bring her to the physician's house at once. There the doctor explained what had been done as he escorted her up to the spacious second-story bedchamber in which the captain of her guard was recovering after his surgery.

She entered to find him propped up on pillows, with a white linen bandage wrapped about his chest and a small tube sticking out from it dripping blood in a bowl.

She was surprised to find him awake and aware enough that he recognized and smiled at her. "They didn't get you after all. Or . . ." His eyes lost focus as a frown creased his brow. "Or do they have us both now?"

"No. We're back in Peregris."

"Ronesca . . . you can't trust her."

"She's no longer a concern."

He blinked up at her dazedly.

"Eidon took her," Maddie said softly.

A brief focused intensity came into his gaze; then he nodded and lapsed back into vagueness. She left him then and spoke at length with the physician in the sitting room downstairs. Trap's prognosis was not good. "He's lost a lot of blood. Lungs are still congested . . . and there's the danger of fever."

"What are you saying, sir?"

The man was soberly direct. "I'm saying . . . I don't know how much longer he'll last, ma'am. Maybe a week, if we're lucky. More likely only a couple of days."

She felt as if he'd slammed a door in her face. *A couple of days?*

She wanted to scream and wail. But she was queen now, and she hadn't the luxury of falling apart. Returning to the palace in Peregris, she instructed her newly instituted secretary to send word to Carissa in Deveren Dol. "A pigeon tonight, and another in the morning."

"But, madam, even a post rider would take near a week to get here from Deveren Dol."

"I know," Maddie said grimly. "Tell her to hurry." She paused, then added, "Better send riders to Fannath Rill, too—just to be safe. Tonight and in the morning."

As the man hurried off, she sagged into a chair by the fireplace, dropped her head into her hands, and began to pray.

27

Abramm dropped swiftly through whiteness, the wind rushing by him, tossing his beard up into his face, tugging his hair straight up from his head, and shoving his robes up around his chin. He was falling fast and thought he should be afraid, but he wasn't. Instead he felt euphoric—safe, protected, and given an experience as close to flying as a man would get in a mortal life.

He was not aware of slowing, but he must have, for suddenly he touched down on a hard surface, landing lightly in the bleached-out tableau of a huge chamber. It stretched away from the foot of the dais on which he stood, rows of stone pillars marching away from him beneath a ceiling of intricate vaulting. Though he heard nothing, a great wind whipped his robes and hair while light swooped from the dais into the multitude of shaven-headed priests and black-helmeted guards gathered there and knocked them flat.

Slowly his hearing returned to a distant roar filled with shrieks. The stench of burned flesh and oil and wood filled his nostrils as the brightness faded and he realized he was standing in an Esurhite temple where the only illumination seemed to be coming from his own body.

Men sprawled unmoving on the apronlike dais stair before him, and as the brightness continued to fade, he saw they were badly charred. Most were priests, but a number wore the armor and breastplates of soldiers in the Army of the Black Moon. In fact, beyond the sea of red-robed priests surrounding the dais, the chamber was filled with soldiers, now picking themselves up. The bodies of those closer lay in a long line between the bodies of the priests, and he realized they had been waiting to pass through the corridor he'd just destroyed.

For a moment all was still, the survivors staring up at him, as he tried to figure out where he was. Then, out in the crowd, a tall priest straightened, eyes blazing crimson. Rhu'ema. He pointed at Abramm.

"YOU! What are YOU doing here?"

Other lights flickered in the eyes of the priests around the tall one, and Abramm felt the shock of their recognition, the fear that followed, then the fulminating fire of their hatred—even as he realized he was weaponless, barefoot, and badly outnumbered.

Red fire glowed at the tall priest's throat as the rhu'ema worked his voice and mouth to speak. "He's an Infidel! Seize him!"

Immediately the priests broke ranks and a stream of temple guards burst past them, racing up the aisle. The white glow surrounding him was fading fast, and the angry men racing toward him seemed anything but intimidated. All he could think was that the only combat practice he'd had in over a year was the stickwork at Caerna'tha.

My Lord? I know you didn't send me here to kill me, so—

The floor wrenched under his feet with a roar, and he fell flat on his face, barking elbows and knees on the suddenly heaving marble. A deep roar tore at his ears. He pushed up onto hands and knees and tried to crawl, but the floor leaped and bucked as if intent on flinging him down again. Dust burned his nose and brought tears to his eyes as streams of crumbling rock rained upon him. And all the while the ground roared and shook, on and on and on, until he thought it would never end.

But it did. The floor stilled, the rumble faded, and eventually all he could hear were small streams of still-falling dirt and rocks, and people coughing. He pushed himself up and sat back on his heels. Dust veiled all that lay more than ten feet away from him, glowing now with the light that poured in from above. To his right, the nearest pillar lay half buried by the ceiling and wall debris that had fallen with it. At Abramm's side, the ground had ruptured, one edge of it thrusting four feet higher than the piece upon which he lay. Huge ceiling slabs surrounded him, one having fallen but a handspan from where he had crouched. The floor's displacement had kept them from crushing him. Eidon's doing . . .

As the dust continued to settle he stood and, wiping the tears and grit from his eyes, peered around at the slabs and rocks and piles of rubble covering the temple floor. The multitude of men, who moments ago had been intent on killing him, all lay dead—he saw a triangle of red robe here, a hand there, a bloody foot beyond. Even the coughing he'd heard earlier had ceased.

He considered searching for survivors, but a brief aftershock reminded him the rest of the temple's vaulted ceiling could yet come down. Even if it didn't, the place would soon be crawling with Esurhites. Let them find the survivors. He must seize his opportunity while it was still an option.

As swiftly as he could without shoes, he picked his way through the rubble toward the opening, moving along with a handful of others. Around him silence reigned, broken only by the small sounds of their movement.

The displacement had shattered the porch outside and collapsed its columns, the portico piled in huge chunks around them. Not far from the doorway, vents spewed steam from the barren ground. Between them a stairway switchbacked down to what appeared to have been a large tent camp, though most of the tents lay as piles of canvas. Bright purple banners bearing the silver-limned device of Belthre'gar's black moon hung from canted poles, and tiny black figures in the hundreds, maybe even thousands, massed at the base of the hill.

Beyond the camp, a city sprawled along the bank of a wide gray river beneath a layer of gray clouds. Only above the temple was the sky clear, and that was filling in as he watched.

He squinted at the river and city, at the distant blue mountains behind them. Nothing looked familiar, but from the temple, priests, and soldiers he knew he was somewhere in Esurh. The biggest temples he knew of stood in Aggosim, Oropos, and Xorofin. He'd have recognized the latter two, so maybe this was Aggosim and that river the Okaido. He sure couldn't think of any other river that big in Esurh.

He started down the steps, and his legs wobbled as a wave of dizziness swept him. The aftermath of his trip through the corridor?

Loathe to follow the front stair right into the midst of the enemy's camp, he found a smaller side stair that descended into a ravine beside the temple.

As he did so, his weakness intensified. So did the dizziness. Several times he nearly fell down the stair. His tongue clove again to the roof of his mouth, dry and cottony against suddenly chapped lips. His head throbbed, his ears rang, and his stomach churned.

He had no idea what was wrong with him. *Sporesick?* But when he turned his awareness inward, he found no sign of it. Besides, he'd taken Eidon's route back there in the domed room. He'd made the right choice. So how could he be sporesick? But if not sporesick, what? It was as if he had been utterly drained of life and strength, his body turning in on itself, consuming itself as he walked.

It must have been from going through the corridor. Even if he couldn't tell he was sporesick, he should still do a purge. As soon as he found a suitable hiding place. . . .

He had no idea how he reached the bottom of the stair, but finally he stepped off it into a sandy-floored gully. Nearby he found a rocky overhang behind a screen of gray ratbush and crawled under it, lamenting its proximity to the stair but assuring himself that any searchers wouldn't expect him to stop and sleep this close.

His thoughts wound off into darkness and light and dreams that were much more than dreams. He was back in the Hall of Record with the pillar and wall murals, though this time there was no adjoining room, no corridor of amber. . . . Only the great pillar itself, sometimes stone, sometimes light so pure and dense it seemed like stone.

His problem wasn't sporesickness but profound exhaustion—mental, emotional, and physical. He had gone without food and sufficient water for months, it seemed, for time had been stretched in Chena'ag Tor. . . . And yes, the corridor *had* taken a lot out of him, for it was entirely alien to his flawed and mortal flesh, which did not tolerate it well. Which would not have tolerated it at all, had Eidon not . . .

He wasn't sure what it was Eidon had done. Shielded him in some way he could not really understand. In any case, it would take him days to fully recuperate, days he did not have, and so for now the Light enfolding his flesh and penetrating into his soul and spirit would rejuvenate him enough to do what needed doing.

And what is that, my Lord?

For answer Eidon showed him a pen of men, bedraggled, half clothed, shaggy haired, and bearded, many of them blond, all of them relatively fair skinned, though some appeared to have been burned by the sun. Esurhites stood around them, and behind them gleamed the river. . . . The scene shifted to that of a great army beneath the combined banners of Abramm's own dragon and shield and the Chesedhan white with gold crown.

I will gather you an army with which I will vanquish your enemies and deliver your people. All that was lost will be restored. . . .

Abramm felt the hilt of a sword against his palm and the weight of a crown upon his brow, reached up with his left hand to touch the plaited metal—

A harsh cry shattered the dream like a rock hurled through glass. He grew aware of the sand beneath his cheek again, the hollowness of his belly, and the quivering of the ratbush shielding him from unwanted eyes. Air swirled around him; a brief stirring swiftly settled. The cry came again, earsplitting in its proximity as the bushes stirred anew. He heard the hiss of feathered wings on air, and his skin crawled with alarmed recognition. The priests had sent a veren to search for him.

Rhu'ema spawn made from the bodies of men who were so far gone in their self-willed bondage to Shadow they gave themselves willingly to be transformed into monsters, veren were huge, vulturine birds, renowned for their ability to scent their quarry from miles away. They were even more sensitive to Terstan power. Which meant the creature knew where he was.

Abramm heard the returning whisper of its wingbeats as the air stirred again and the ratbush quivered. Soon it would alert its masters to his location. He couldn't stay here, but he had nothing with which to defend himself, and if he tried to move, the thing would surely attack.

I have the Light, he told himself firmly. *And if Eidon could get me out of that temple filled with priests and soldiers, he can handle one measly veren.*

A second cry followed the first, deeper and more resonant, obviously from a different beast.

Okay, two measly veren. If he didn't want it to be three, he'd best move now.

He stood and, having his wits about him now, saw the reason for the stair he had taken: Beyond the gully lay a practice yard on the shelf that extended out from the mountainside, a great stone barracks looming on its far side. The quake had stove in the barracks' roof and collapsed its sidewall. Though he'd have expected guards to be on duty, or at least men moving about, the place stood eerily unattended.

Cautiously he climbed out of the gully and crept along the base of the slope from which the shelf extended. Passing the struts of a wooden water tower whose tank now lay shattered on the ground at its base, he dashed across the open yard to reach the barracks. Halfway across he felt one of the veren dive through the mist at him and threw himself sideways just when he judged it about to strike. It missed him entirely, and he rolled to his feet in time to see it shoot up into the mist.

Moments later he'd entered the barracks and made his way through piles of rubble interspersed with standing walls and clear spaces. The few men in the building when the earthquake struck lay dead in their beds, half-buried by debris. Their uniforms, which had apparently been hanging on wall hooks nearby, were now mixed with the rubble. Picking through it all, Abramm was able to find for himself a tunic, britches, cloak, and pair of boots. His own clothes, of course, had been shredded by the dragons, but he was surprised to find, caught in the remnants of his ruined rucksack, the speaking stone Laud had given him—his only possession to have escaped Chena'ag Tor and the trip through the corridor intact.

As the veren continued to circle the ruined building, he sought out the armory, belting on the best of the long blades and slinging another to his back. He also fastened a dagger to his hip, strapped another to his leg, and used a third to cut away the beard that had covered his face for well over a year. Its length shocked him, for it did not seem enough time had passed for it to have grown as long as it had. For that matter, his hair was nearly as long as it had been after his eight-year novitiate as a youth.

He had no idea how long he had been in Chena'ag Tor—or the Hall of Record room, for that matter—but clearly, it had been considerably longer than it had seemed.

He scraped his beard off as closely as he could without cutting himself too badly. The job was rough and uneven, but a little grizzle under the present conditions would surely go unremarked—and might even serve to camouflage the scars on his face. His hair he tied into a tail and stuffed down the back of the tunic, trusting the helm and the cloak to conceal its color from those who might note it with suspicion.

From the armory he hurried through the rubble-filled corridors until he found the dining hall and kitchen—happily undamaged—where he provisioned himself with food and water, and even found some fat and soot with which to darken his face. When he was done, however, he smelled so strongly of mutton, he wondered if he'd only traded one problem for another. Hopefully, whoever he encountered would chalk it up to a tunic too long unwashed. And maybe it would confuse the veren.

He'd decided he must go to the city first and find out where he was. If this was Aggosim, as he'd guessed, he had to decide whether to find a boat downriver, or cross over to head for the mountains he'd spotted earlier. First, though, he had to get past the veren.

The moment he left the protection of the barracks' portico, one of them swooped out of the darkness, talons reaching for his face. He was ready, though, and its own momentum impaled it on his blade. As its claws scrabbled at his helmet, he let the Light flare, bursting out up his arms and into the sword and flinging the veren off him as if it were made of rags. As it arced limply through the air, the second veren dropped from the mist in its own dive and ran straight into its fellow. The two tumbled earthward together.

Dashing around the barracks into a second yard, Abramm skirted another heavily damaged stone building and came to a road that appeared to lead down to the city below. Sure enough, it wound through thronetrees and a shallow ravine to emerge on the flat below, where it headed straight into the army's demolished tent camp. From the torches that had been lit, he guessed it was full dark, though for him the light was still more twilight. There were soldiers everywhere.

So, my Father? Abramm thought dryly, *You mean to build me an army of Esurhites?*

He thought he sensed warm laughter and set off briskly toward the encampment. As distracted and frantic as everyone was, he suspected he could pass unhindered, and so he did. Every man he encountered immediately averted his eyes and stepped aside.

He was fast approaching the riverbank when he passed a pen of men: ragged, bearded, long-haired, hunch-shouldered men, many of them blond.

Memory of his recent dream stopped him cold. Though most of these were likely barbarians, there were surely some Kiriathans and Chesedhans among them, en route to the rowing benches of Esurhite galleys waiting at the river's mouth. Without another thought, he turned aside and, as he drew up to the enclosure, saw the prisoners were already being moved out, filing down the sloping riverbank toward a lanternlit barge moored at the end of a short dock. Like sheep they were herded into the vessel's hold, and every man among them wore a Terstan shield upon his chest. Abramm thought that odd until he realized that while other slaves could have been transported through the corridor, the Terstans would either have died in passage or left the corridor irreparably damaged. Or both. They had to be ferried to their posts in the normal way.

He glanced across the river toward the twinkle of lights on the far bank, aware for the first time of all the flotsam that floated downstream—bushes, branches, bodies, even trees, all from the earthquake, no doubt. Faint as the far lights were, he judged it was probably a good four or five hundred strides to the far bank. It had to be the Okaido. The only Esurhite river that wide— the only river south of the Strait of Terreo. Forming the border between Andol and what was formerly Eram, now officially Esurh, it flowed westward into the Salmancan Sea. Where the need for galley slaves would be great.

As the last of the slaves stepped aboard, he hastened down the bank, and again his uniform made the way for him. Seeing him coming, the soldiers held the gate open until he had leaped aboard. No one said a word to him, nor seemed to expect anything from him, and everyone avoided making eye contact.

He couldn't have picked a better disguise. *So I see you have this whole thing well in hand,* he said to Eidon. *But I still don't understand what I'm doing here. Or where I'm going. The few men on this boat are not going to make an army. And besides that, they are in terrible shape. And probably not fighters at all. . . .*

His eye was drawn to the ruined city and the gap-faced temple, lit now by a mass of torches, and he snorted, recalling all he'd been through of late.

Yes, my Lord. I am an idiot. And I will simply look forward with great anticipation to seeing how you pull all this off, since it is obvious that you can.

The barge swept out into the river and the current caught it, hurrying it along beside a leaf-crowned tree floating downstream. He stood at the stern beside several of the soldiers, who stared at the torchlit temple, murmuring to one another. At first he struggled to pick out the words, for he'd not heard the Tahg for years, and these men had an accent he was unaccustomed to. But after a few moments their words grew clearer, especially when he discerned the subject matter.

"They say it was the White Pretender who came through and destroyed the temple."

"That's impossible! The Pretender is dead. And he was never that strong anyway."

"What if he has come back from the dead?" The voice was full of awe.

"Come back from the dead?"

"He served the Dying God. Surely of all the gods, Eidon would know how to restore the dead. It is said he brought back his own son. . . ."

"Gods do not die."

"Well, something came through that corridor. Something that looked like a man, all blazing with white, at first. He was tall and blond, they say, with a gold shield on his chest and a red dragon on his arm."

"Tall, blond Terstans with red dragons are everywhere."

"Tall, blond Terstans are everywhere. The red dragon is increasingly rare."

That stopped the conversation for a moment. Then the first man said, "He destroyed the corridor. They're worried the damage might even have extended out from Aggos through the corridors to the temples at Oropos and Xorofin."

They spoke on, but Abramm pulled away, pleased his conclusions about his location were correct, and even more pleased that his trip through the corridor might have affected the other temples. That would surely cause the Esurhites a major hindrance in their efforts to take Chesedh. Assuming Chesedh still stood, which it must or they wouldn't have been planning to funnel all those soldiers through the corridor.

In any case, now he was heading downriver on the Okaido toward the Sea of Sharss and most likely the Esurhite naval base at Tortusa, which meant he must get himself and the slaves ashore before they arrived. To find the best place for that, he needed to look at a map.

In the wheelhouse, the captain was irritatingly solicitous. Abramm attempted to squelch him with a brusque manner and monosyllabic answers, refusing offers of tea or more light—surely the blaze in the captain's wheelhouse was bright enough!—and finally convincing the man to leave him alone. Perusing the map, he committed to memory the towns, the distances, the streams that fed into the river, and the lay of the land on either side. Eventually they would need to cross the mountains he had seen earlier, but for now, he just had to get his countrymen off this barge and out of Esurhite hands, in the right place, at the right time.

The captain informed him they would arrive at the river town Abramm had selected as a likely point of debarkation around dawn, which gave him the night to prepare. He found a place to settle on a pile of rope foreward of the deckhouse and sat down, watching the poleman at the bow as he considered how he might gain access to the hold full of slaves. But he'd not sat there long before the silence, the fresh air on the river, and the boat's gentle rocking opened the door for his exhaustion—barely dented by his earlier nap—and he dozed off.

Sometime later he jerked awake with the sense of the boat having struck something hard, and found things gravely amiss. It was still night, but four men now stood at the bow, shadowy figures heaving on their long poles as they sought to force the barge out of the current. The north bank loomed as a dark mass not far off the starboard railing. From their shouts, he guessed that more men poled at the vessel's stern, blocked from his view by the boathouse. The moment he stood up, he felt the deck's ominous cant to starboard and realized the vessel was shipping water. And the only place it could be going was into the hold with the slaves.

Would anyone think to free them? He rounded the deckhouse to find the hatch standing open and the Esurhite officer's assistant perched on the hold ladder with a big iron key in his hand. The barge captain and the officer stood beside him arguing, the officer wanting to unchain the slaves lest they drown, the captain refusing to concede the possibility his vessel might actually sink, and unwilling to complicate the efforts of his sailors in bringing her to shore by having a mass of slaves wandering about on deck.

Finally, the officer swore at him in exasperation and ordered his assistant to unlock the chains that bound the slaves to the boat. The captain belayed that instruction, even as something banged deep in the hold, and the screams grew more desperate. Both men turned to look into the hold as the deck shuddered and canted even more sharply, and Abramm seized the moment. Plowing between the two leaders, he sent them sprawling across the deck as he collided with the assistant on the ladder and brought the man with him, banging and slithering down the ladder's rungs into the hold's dank depths.

Abramm's night sight showed him the clear outline of men's bodies, the gleam of their eyes, and the glints of the chains. The setup was painfully familiar: Men lay chained in a line along both hulls, two huge locks at the middle of each line. Snatching the key from the still-addled assistant, Abramm sprang to the starboard line, found the lock that secured the stern-ward half, jammed in the key, and wrenched the hasp open. The rest he left to the captive as he turned to the man's neighbor, and released the lock on the foreward half.

After unlocking the second man, he repeated the process with the port-side line. By then the first of the slaves from the starboard side were struggling up the ladder. Fearful the hatch would be closed upon them at any moment, Abramm shoved his way past them to the deck just in time to stop the two boatmen who were lifting the hatch cover. The captain erupted in outrage, lunging ominously toward him and receiving for it the full force of Abramm's backhand, which knocked him backward over the gunwale.

By then freed slaves crawled out of the hatch like roaches, fear and the sudden promise of freedom providing them new strength and speed. Abramm stood at the hatch hauling them up and over its lip, and soon a big, bare-chested, shaggy-bearded Terstan stopped to help him.

They kept at it until the ship's cant grew sharp enough he could hardly keep his position and still help the men out. He turned to the big man beside him, a hulking shadow in the night. "You've got to go," he said in Kiriathan.

"There's still men below," the man growled.

"I know." Abramm shrugged off his heavy cloak and wadded it into a ball to tuck under his arm. "But this thing is going down, and the backwash will take you with it if you're on the deck when it does." He pulled off his helmet and stuffed the cloak into it. "You've got to jump free. Now."

Stubbornly the big man bent to pull yet another slave out of the hatch, and when he was done, Abramm shoved him off the hatch lip. "Jump free, now! You can do no more here, and those ashore will need you."

He'd already thrown the man too much off balance to recover, though he windmilled his big arms wildly in the attempt. Finally, though, he leaped free, clearing the slowly rising rail and disappearing into the water. Abramm leaped after him, wondering only then if the poor fellow could swim. Well, too late to worry about that now.

They weren't far from shore, which was a good thing, because it was hard to swim wearing a longsword at one's side while clutching a helmet and cloak. At least he didn't have to do it wearing leg irons. In any case he was greatly relieved when his boots touched the mucky river bottom, and shortly he was slogging through a stand of flotsam-clogged cattails and up the soggy shore to solid ground.

Others collapsed on the grassy shore around him, leg irons clinking as a new day began to dawn. After shoving his helmet, cloak, and breastplate under a bush at the base of the undercut bank some ways up from the shore, he hurried back to the water's edge to pull some of the weaker survivors to safety. When there were no more of them, he walked downstream to search for others. The day had fully dawned by the time he returned to their original landing site. Many of the slaves had found a way to remove their leg irons, and a group of them sat on the bank above the river, looking as if they didn't know what to do next. Abramm went to retrieve his armor and cloak, and was just starting up the slope to join them when a lean, dark-haired man with a hideous slash where his left eye should have been stepped out of the under-brush to block his path. Abramm stopped in surprise, for the man wore the rags of a slave, yet brandished a stout plank from out of the flotsam that had washed up on the riverbank.

"We don't need your kind around here," he growled in Kiriathan, his voice laced with a strong Chesedhan lilt. "Traitor to their own blood."

Abramm stared at him, wondering what he was talking about. The sudden sense of an attacker coming at him from the left provoked an instant response, his sword grating from his scabbard as he whirled and stepped backward. An ax head whooshed past his face, and he drove forward reflexively in the safety of the follow-through, his sword tip penetrating his attacker's eye with a practiced accuracy he'd thought he should have lost after so much disuse.

No time to consider that, though, for a host of figures were emerging from the mist around him, armed with daggers, planks, and even stout tree limbs. As his first assailant went down, Abramm turned to a second, using the edge of his cloak to block the latter's sword thrust as his own sword came around automatically, part of a coordinated sequence in the forms he had practiced for years, its tip slashing the side of the man's throat in a fountaining of bright blood. The second man died as swiftly as the first, sagging lifelessly to the ground as Abramm turned to the one-eyed Chesedhan now attacking with his plank. Seeing he no longer had the advantage of surprise, the Chesedhan dropped his weapon and backed off, the others following suit.

By now those on the bank had stood and were shouting back to others who had settled out of his sight.

The one-eyed man gazed at his fallen comrades, lying glassy eyed in a gelatinous pool of blood. "You killed them," he said in disbelief.

"If you come at a man with a bared blade, you should expect you might meet one yourself," Abramm said testily, eyeing his victims, as well. It had been a long time since he'd killed a man. It made him vaguely ill to look at his handiwork. Considering how rusty he was, he was shocked by his reaction—swift, deadly, and without hesitation.

He looked again at the dark-haired man. "Why do you attack me?"

The man's face hardened as his good eye came up to meet Abramm's. "You are a traitor."

"A traitor to whom? I set you free."

"You serve Khrell."

Abramm snorted. "I serve Eidon." And to prove it, he tore open the front of his borrowed tunic, buttons spattering wildly, to reveal the shield on his chest.

The man's eye flicked to the shield and back to his face, his hard expression not wavering.

"Shields can be faked. Or renounced and forsaken."

"Well, mine is none of that."

"Why are you dressed like a temple guard?"

"It was the only way to get out of Aggosim."

"I don't believe you. You are one of the Darian." Darian—northlanders torn from their homeland as children and raised in their enemies' lands. They might be Kiriathan or Chesedhan on the outside, but they were Esurhites in their hearts.

"I set you all free," Abramm repeated.

"He speaks truly, Borlain!" came a deep voice from up the hill. One that sounded unexpectedly familiar. "He's the one who helped me pull the rest of ye out."

They turned toward the big man now pressing through the crowd on the bank, head and shoulders above the rest of them. His blond hair was long and his face bushy with beard, but there was no mistaking the set of those broad shoulders, nor the twinkle of his blue eyes.

Abramm gaped. "Rollie? That was *you* helping?"

His words stopped the big man cold at the bank's edge. His broad face drew into a frown as he stared at Abramm intently. "How d' ye know my name?"

"He serves Khrell, that's how," said Borlain. "The evil ones have told him."

Abramm stepped around him to face his friend. "I had a beard when last you saw me, Rolland Kemp. In the Great Sand Sea some leagues away."

He saw the light of recognition dawn in the blacksmith's eyes. "Alaric?"

A moment later Rolland was skidding down the bank to embrace him, and they pounded each other's backs, though Abramm still gripped his sword unsheathed in his hand. When they parted, Rolland's eyes shone with unshed tears. "Eidon's mercy, Alaric. We thought ye were dead. Lost in the desert . . ." He stepped back farther, looking him up and down. "Ye look awful."

"Well, thank you very much. You don't look so great yourself."

"Ye look like ye've been through torments."

"Well, I was lost in the desert." He glanced around, uneasy with pursuing that subject. "Are any of the others here? Cedric? Galen?"

"Aye, Alaric, we're here," Cedric said, stepping out from the crowd to stand at Rolland's side. Galen stood on his other side. Even Oakes Trinley was with them.

Abramm stared at them in astonishment, the chill of portents so strong he all but reeled. *How can they be here?*

And yet, he knew. Eidon had told him how—and why—months ago.

They will have need of you. And you will have need of them.

He frowned. *But, Lord . . . surely you don't mean these to be my army?*

28

Carissa sat at her husband's bedside in the palace at Peregris, embroidering a length of coiling vine onto a table runner, the design taking shape one leaf at a time. It had been nine days since she'd ridden into Peregris, beside herself with fear for him, about to faint with the prospect of seeing him again, and praying her foolish insecurities had not destroyed his feelings for her beyond resuscitation. She prayed for the courage to say what she needed to say, and that she wouldn't suddenly fall into that pit of sudden terror where the words dammed up in her throat and refused to be uttered.

But it all turned out to be useless worry, for the reality was far worse. He wasn't even conscious when she'd arrived, and at first sight of him she'd wanted to howl with dismay for the way he looked—so pale and gray and weak—and for the way his breath rattled in his chest as he struggled to breathe, the little tube sticking out between his ribs, dripping blood into a bowl.

They'd performed surgery on him to sew up the bleeding, the attendant had informed her, and kept the tube in place in case their efforts were unsuccessful, though he assured her they had been. After that there had been the fever and the horrible gurgling in his lungs as she had prayed for all she was worth. On the fifth night after she'd gotten there, everyone thought it was the end, and she'd knelt with her head resting on the side of his bed, clutching his hands as she prayed and wept all night long.

And in the morning, thank Eidon, he was still breathing.

A few hours later, he had opened his eyes for the first time since she'd arrived, but he'd been groggy from the laudanum they'd been giving him, and she wasn't sure he even knew she was there. He'd fallen back asleep shortly thereafter and had been in and out ever since.

Her thread too short to work anymore, she tied it off and reached into her basket for a new piece, glancing up at her husband as she did. Trap lay swathed in silk sheets, arms resting atop them alongside his body. Ravaged by his two-week struggle to survive, his freckled face was pale and gaunt beneath the red beard. For the first time since she'd arrived, though, his brown eyes were not only open but alert. And watching her.

"Oh," she said, straightening self-consciously. "You're awake."

He flashed a tentative smile. "You look at me . . . speak to me. I hear the rustle of your clothing—it must be that you really are here . . . not a dream, after all."

"Not a dream, my husband," she said, putting aside her work and rising to pour water from the pitcher. "Would you like a drink?"

He accepted the cup, drained it, and handed it back. But he refused her offer of more, focusing upon her once again as she sat on the bed beside him. "How long?" he asked.

"It's been about two weeks since you were injured."

"I meant how long have you been here."

She smiled again. "Almost that long."

"But . . . were you in Deveren Dol? It would take you a week at least . . ."

She felt her cheeks heat but did not look away. "I turned back from Deveren Dol the very morning I set out for it."

The crease deepened between his brows. "You turned back? How can I protect you . . . if you won't do as I tell you? If the Esurhites' plot had worked—" He broke off, frowning in his attempt to recall. "What *did* happen . with that, anyway?"

She smiled, happy to get past the matter of Deveren Dol—happy, too, that he still cared enough to worry about protecting her—and told him what she knew: how Maddie had been turned over to Belthre'gar himself, but the wave had swamped his ship and brought her back. How at least a third of the Esurhite fleet waiting south of the island to attack had been destroyed by the same wave. Which had also drowned Ronesca and left Maddie queen in her place—a turn of events all the army and navy saw as Eidon's doing.

"Queen!" he exclaimed when she had finished. "Well, that is happy news. Who is advising her?"

Carissa shook her head. "I have no idea. She left for Fannath Rill three days ago for the funeral. They'll hold the investiture afterward. I suppose

she's technically regent, seeing as Leyton's still alive, so far as we know. . . ."
She gave him a rueful smile. "That's about all I can tell you. I've spent most
of my time with you, actually." She paused. "I was so afraid I was going to
lose you. . . ." Tears welled in her eyes, and she fell silent. It had been like
this often over the last few days—sudden weeping taking her by storm at the
most unlikely of triggers. Now that he was well and on the mend, she'd
expected the strange emotional vulnerability to end, but apparently it had
not.

His fingers touched the tear track on her cheek, drawing her eyes to his
own.

"Why didn't you go to Deveren Dol?"

"Because I couldn't bear to be that far away from you." She sniffed and
wiped away the tears. "Not the way we parted. Not the way everything was
going. Even Fannath Rill felt too far, but I could think of no reason to go on
to Peregris. . . ." She studied her hands, nested together in her lap. "Then, the
night you were stabbed, I knew something horrible had happened. The way
I used to dream with Abramm . . . Only this time it was you and—" She felt
her cheeks warm again as she looked up to find his sober gaze still upon her.
"I knew I had to come or risk never seeing you again in this life. So I took a
post coach. We got here in a little over twenty hours."

"We?"

"Conal's with me. And Prisina.. They're in the other room."

She fell silent, waiting for his response.

"What about the princes?"

"They are in Deveren Dol."

He snorted. "Well, at least someone listens to me around here."

A tap at the door preceded its squeaky opening, and the royal physician
joined them, pleased to see his patient awake and alert. He questioned
Carissa briefly, then directed his inquiry to Trap, and finally announced that
he would do a thorough examination of his patient. As he started to pull back
the sheets, Trap stopped him with a scandalized expression and glanced
toward Carissa. She stared back at him, feigning incomprehension.

He frowned. "My lady . . . I don't mean to be rude, but . . . isn't there
some other duty you must be performing now?"

She smiled at him. "My duty is wholly to you, my husband."

His frown deepened. He opened his mouth to speak, but no words came
out. So he closed it, glanced at the physician, then at her again and said,
red-faced, "My lady, I have nothing on under this sheeting."

"Oh, you have your bandages," she said sweetly, wondering why she was enjoying his discomfiture as much as she was. He stared at her as if she had said nonsense to him. It was probably the laudanum fuzzing his brain. She took pity on him and explained.

"I've been bathing you, changing your bandages, and helping you use the bedpan for over a week and a half now, sir. I'm afraid I've already seen everything there is to see."

His eyes widened as his face turned intensely scarlet. He flashed a desperate gaze at the doctor. "I thought I was dreaming all that."

"No." *But it was part of my dreams. . . .* She smiled but kept the thought to herself.

Unfortunately, despite her assurances that she had grown quite accustomed to seeing his body unclothed, that was the end of that. He insisted she go down and see about arranging a meal for him and from then on jealously guarded his privacy.

She, on the other hand, set herself to take Elayne's advice to flirt to an extreme she doubted the older woman had intended, and that she herself would never have been able to accomplish even a month earlier. But having come so close to losing this man, she found in herself a total lack of pride when it came to making sure he knew just how she felt about him. In the evenings, she made a point of beginning to unbutton her gown while he was still present, or complaining of the heat while lifting her skirts and fluttering them around. When it was time to nurse Conal, she did not hesitate to do so openly, before her husband's shocked eyes. Sometimes, if he was talking, his voice would strangle off midsentence, and if she glanced up to find him staring, as he always was, he would swallow hard, wrench his eyes away from her, and "go out for some exercise."

She always held her giggle in until he was gone; then wondered at her newfound brazenness and worried a bit that she might be going too far. But since he always came back from his walk, and never complained about what she'd done, she didn't think he minded too much.

Though the physician had warned him to rest, once he was on the mend and able to get up and walk, Trap would have none of it. She accused him of being a worse patient than Abramm had been, but it made no difference. He wanted to be up and moving, walking around, seeing how the repairs were going, seeing how the fleet was shaping up, wanting to hear the latest gossip from the southland. He had no doubt another assault would come soon. Already the Shadow had crept back over the wide blue sea.

Belthre'gar would return, he promised her.

"But not immediately," she pointed out, chiding him gently for his disregard of the doctor's recommendation. He only shrugged and claimed the more he moved, the faster he would heal.

"Doctors don't know everything," he said. And in the end, the only harm his method caused him was to tire him out by day's end.

Since she couldn't fight it, Carissa took advantage of his restlessness by inviting him to walk with her each morning along the garden wall. He always seemed surprised she would make such a request, even when she asked him every day and even when he agreed. It was the best part of her day, as they walked together, enjoying the fresh breeze whether the sky was clear and blue or cool with fog, and talking as they had not since before Rennalf had intruded into their lives. When one day she dared to slide her hand into his and he did not shake her off but clasped his fingers firmly about hers, she all but shouted for joy.

As they walked she often studied him covertly—reveling in the familiar freckled profile with its upturned nose, the red-gold glint of stubble on his cheek above the trimmed-back beard, the curls of russet hair that kissed the top of his ear and brushed the leather collar of his tunic. With the glow of health returned to his face and the sparkle to his eyes, it was sometimes all she could do not to throw herself upon him. Whatever she had felt for him in the past seemed nothing to what she felt now.

"You've changed," he remarked one day, turning to meet her gaze.

She blushed but kept her voice light. "Oh? How so?"

He came to a stop, regarding her thoughtfully. "You're more relaxed, I guess. Softer, somehow. Happier."

She smiled at him. "I am happier. You're alive, you're awake, and you're walking out here beside me."

His expression altered slightly, from thoughtful to vaguely troubled. For a moment she thought he would say something; then a bell rang out in the harbor and the shouts of men drew his attention from her. The moment was lost, but even that couldn't tarnish the golden haze of her pleasure.

More than three weeks after he'd been stabbed, as he complained for what seemed the hundredth time of the soreness and itching on his back, she pressed him—as usual—to let her take the stitches out. His wound was long closed by now, and the doctor had been too busy with other patients to come and remove them. She thought he expected her to do it, and rightly so. Trap was reluctant, by turns saying that it didn't need doing at all, and that the doctor should be the one to do it. But finally she convinced him he was making much out of nothing and would be far more comfortable if he'd just let her do it.

"I'm getting weary of your constant complaining about it," she teased him.

Thus he pulled off his shirt and sat on a stool with his back to her, pointing out as she brought her embroidery scissors to bear that this was not embroidery.

"No," she agreed. "It's not. It's a simple cutting of threads. I'm sure you've done it a hundred times."

"But you haven't."

"Of course I have." She gestured at the hooped fabric with its half-stitched design and told him to stop worrying.

For a time she worked in silence, exquisitely aware of the warmth of his bared back, and from time to time letting her eyes drift over the strong shoulders and the tight, corded muscle. All too soon she pulled the last thread free and dropped it into the pan with the others. She should have stood then and stepped away. Instead she let her fingers travel up the flat plane of his back, tracing the curve of his freckled shoulder up to his neck and the locks of red hair curling at his nape. She toyed with the curls for a moment, her breath held, aware of him holding rigidly still beneath her. Then she slid her palm along the firm ridge of muscle topping the opposite shoulder, and down over the curve of the joint . . .

With a gasp he shot out of the chair, kicking it aside as he whirled to seize her by both arms, a terrible look on his face. He loomed over her, shirtless, and she had never seen his eyes so dark. He seemed angry and desperate and filled with something she couldn't quite read but which held a repressed violence that recalled to her the fact he had fought in the Esurhite Games right alongside her brother. That he had been the mighty Infidel to Abramm's unvanquished Pretender.

"What are you trying to do to me, Carissa?" he choked. "Do you think I am made of stone?"

She gaped at him. Then took a breath and felt the blood rush to her face as a giddy joy soared within her. *He does notice. And he's not unaffected. . . .*

His expression softened. "Do you have any idea how sorely you tempt me, my lady? How much I want to—" He cut off the words, but not before she'd heard the tremble in his voice. Now he released her arms and stepped back. "Why do you do this to me?"

And there it was. The question asked. The moment of truth. Did she have the words and courage to answer? She lifted her chin to meet his gaze, feeling weirdly fluttery, and said, "Because I want to know if things between us can ever be . . . like they're supposed to be between a man and his wife."

When he stared at her uncomprehendingly, more words tumbled nervously from her lips: "The night you kissed me at the coronation ball, I thought maybe it could. . . . But you were so careful, and when you pulled away . . ."

"You thought I didn't mean it," he said.

She must have shown her surprise, for he added, "Maddie told me the night we went to meet the Esurhites. She said I wasn't 'bold' enough. I didn't believe her."

Carissa refused to let herself look away, though embarrassment now pressed her to do so. "Maddie was right," she said sturdily. "What I wanted that night is what I want now. What I've wanted since the day you married me: to be your *wife*, Trap Meridon."

Then it seemed he really did turn to stone, staring down at her with an expression as blank as one of Abramm's best. She held his gaze for a few seconds, then, heart pounding madly against her breastbone, whispered, "And not just in name."

And still he stared at her, unmoving, unbreathing, until finally her courage deserted her and she was gripped by the old familiar conviction that she had read him wrong, that Elayne had misled her and all her worst fears were true. She had let her longings lead her into a place she never should have gone, forcing him now, at last, to tell her baldly and bluntly the horrible, scalding truth that he really *didn't* want her, and—

He seized her by the shoulders and kissed her, and there was nothing polite or proper about it. His lips were hard and hot and urgent, tasting sharply of the wine he had drunk at lunch and cutting through the miasma of her fears to ignite in her a firestorm the likes of which she'd never known. And that afternoon the Duke of Northille made very sure his wife would never again doubt the depth and fire of his love for her.

———

Four weeks after the sea wave demolished Peregris and took Queen Ronesca's life, Fannath Rill was finally settling back to normal—the triple funeral for Ronesca and her sons observed, and the investiture of Madeleine as queen regent completed within days of that. Now, at last, Maddie was able to get back to business.

At midmorning she dismissed the first cabinet meeting she'd been able to hold in a week and departed, grimly aware that once more she had in some way shocked or offended every man among them. They were competent men, and respectful, but they struggled still to accept her as their queen. Or rather, to accept the fact she had ideas of what was to be done that ran contrary to their own and, worse than that, was as liable to act on those ideas as she was to act on theirs. She'd already sent off a team of men to rescue her brother in direct opposition to their counsel, and brought a portion of the army up to Fannath Rill to begin the emplacement of the defensive works she knew would eventually be required. She had also initiated preparations for a siege, despite their unanimous agreement that it was a complete waste of time and resources.

She returned to her quarters for her midday meal, lunching with several of her allies from her days as persecuted First Daughter, then sought out her secretary of appointments to see what awaited her for the afternoon. Lord Umberley was not in his office off her sitting chamber, but the roster of daily supplicants was. She was scanning through it when he returned.

Seeing her, he exclaimed in surprise and directed her to the ledger of her official appointments, which typically held only about a third of the names on the daily roster. She glanced cursorily at the ledger, then to a name on the roster. "Why does this Marta Brackleford keep moving down this list instead of up it? I've noticed her name now for several days."

He peered at the name and sniffed. "Well . . . I imagine because other supplicants' concerns are more urgent, madam."

"Deciding the venue for next summer's Hashnut Festival was an urgent concern?" She referred to a supplicant she'd met with yesterday.

He grimaced and said nothing.

"Brackleford sounds like a Kiriathan name."

"Yes, ma'am." He frowned. "But you know how so many of them are coming these days, hoping to trade on some alleged relationship to your husband. You cannot help them all. And not all of them deserve it."

"No. But I should like to make the decisions as to whom I help for myself. It says here she has a gift. But it doesn't say from whom."

Umberley looked dismayed. "From your husband, I would imagine. That's usually the claim."

"And you have deigned not to inform me?"

"Your Majesty . . ." He sighed and spread his hands helplessly. "So many of them are obvious frauds. And you have so much to do."

"Well, you're right about that." She set down the roster. "But find out what she wants, anyway. And where she's from."

"Yes, ma'am."

He left, and Maddie strolled to the window. She'd inherited the queen's apartments, which included a great semicircular receiving chamber, with a stunning view that overlooked the east branch of the Ankrill and offered perspectives that let her look almost straight down the river toward Peregris or out toward the eastern deserts. She could not gaze upon either aspect without thinking of Abramm, out there somewhere, waiting for Eidon's perfect time.

Since her brief time with the Esurhites, she had thought often of the vision she'd been given. Not a vision, really. Maybe more a glimpse into some other reality, her husband going about their Father's business. And the reports that had been coming out of the southland gave an inkling of what that might be. The wave that had swamped the Esurhite fleet before it could annihilate the Chesedhan navy had been generated by a massive earthquake in Oropos, on the North Andolen coast where the Salmancan Sea flowed into the Strait of Terreo. The Esurhites' great temple of Laevian, site of a huge etherworld corridor and almost continuous troop transfers, had completely collapsed. Stories of damage from tidal waves had come in from the Chesedhan coastline all along the Salmancan Sea, and recently she'd heard there'd also been a quake in Xorofin, though details on that were sketchy. Tortusa was said to have been inundated, but unfortunately, most of the fleet that harbored there was on the open sea—moving in force upon Kiriath.

All three events coming at almost the same time led her to conclude they probably had the same trigger.

And the trigger just might have been Abramm. But if so, there was no word about him, unless she was to believe the stories of yet another tall, blond man with twin facial scars leading a group of rebels out in the northern end of the strait. But she did not. Whatever he was doing, it was bigger than that. She'd given up on his coming down the Ankrill, but she'd not given up on his coming. It would be in Eidon's time and from Eidon's direction, wherever that would be. It was not a thing she chose to share anymore, for she knew it would only resurrect all the doubts about and criticisms of her mental state. Which no one needed right now, least of all her. She knew what she knew. And if no one else believed her, so be it. Perhaps one day things would be different.

Umberley returned. He paused, then added stiffly, "Serra Brackleford's gift is a book, which she will only surrender to you personally." He paused, then added stiffly, "She says she came through the Kolki Pass and spent the winter at Caerna'tha."

Maddie snapped up her head from the list as the floor lurched beneath her. "Caerna'tha?"

"Yes, madam. She said she has come down with a group along the Ankrill through Trakas." Umberley looked thoroughly chagrinned, for it was common knowledge this was the same route Maddie claimed Abramm had traveled last year. He should have questioned Marta Brackleford sufficiently to have discovered this when she'd first requested audience.

Maddie saw no need to reprimand him, though, for he was well aware of his fault. Besides, she was too intent on finding out what Marta Brackleford knew to be distracted by lesser matters. "Trakas," she murmured. Trakas was south of Obla, and just west of the Great Sand Sea.

Dismay tempered her surging excitement as she recalled the terrible storm, and her husband's body lying half buried in sand. Was the vision in the amber real, then? No, he could not be dead. She had seen him afterward. He had sorrowed at not being able to come to her. Then her heart clenched as a new thought occurred: What if she had seen not her living husband but Abramm gone on to the realm of Light? There *had* been light all around him. . . .

Her middle twisted, and panic flapped at the edges of her soul. Then she jerked up her chin and made herself take a deep breath. *Find out what is really happening first,* she counseled herself. *If it's real and true that you will never see him again in this life, then you may fall apart.* She faced Umberley and said calmly, "I will see her now."

Marta Brackleford was a small, purposeful woman, with dark, expressive eyes and black hair caught into a bun on her nape. At once she handed over the book, which was wrapped in worn and wrinkled brown paper tied with string and stained with water spots.

"You claim to have known my husband," Maddie asked, turning it over in her hands.

"Yes, Your Majesty." The woman dropped her gaze respectfully to the floor.

"You will not mind, I hope, if I ask you to describe him."

"He was taller by a head than most of the men in our party, ma'am. Only Rolland stood as tall. His hair was long and blond, and he wore a thick bushy beard, darker than his hair. He has twin scars running down the left side of his face."

"That's a description anyone could give."

Marta nodded, pressed her lips together, and tried again. "His eyes are so blue they make your heart catch. His brows are dark and level, and the way he sometimes cocks one is utterly endearing. His hands are mesmerizing— beautifully shaped, long fingered, and strong, but callused and rough from the work. And his smile, which doesn't come very often, is like the sun parting the clouds after a storm."

"I don't think I much like your second description," Maddie said, somewhat aghast.

Marta smiled. "You're right. I lost my heart to him, even knowing his belonged to another. And still does, I might add. You have no worries there. But I think perhaps from my description you believe me now."

"You have done much to advance your case," Maddie said warily.

The other woman nodded. She gestured at the book, now in Maddie's hands. "He gave me that when he set out into the desert to rescue our friends from slavery. He instructed us to leave immediately for Fannath Rill, but we decided to wait a week, anyway, and then that great sandstorm blew in off the desert. When three weeks later they still had not returned, we headed south. Abramm arranged for a riverman to take us to Deveren Dol, but the man even went so far as to escort us to Fannath Rill. Your husband said you would see him rewarded for his time and generosity, but I fear he has returned to Ru'geruk disgruntled and disillusioned, since it has taken me so very long to finally meet with you."

Maddie raised her eyebrows at this gentle scolding, and Marta flushed. "Not that I expected to be allowed to see you at all, Your Majesty," she added, her flush deepening. When Maddie still said nothing, the woman dropped her gaze to the floor and murmured, "Forgive me, madam. I meant no offense . . . ."

"And I took none, Serra Brackleford. Please, be at ease." Maddie turned her attention to the parcel in her hands, vaguely disappointed now that he'd not sent her something more personal. If it was truly from him.

"It's from the library at Caerna'tha, Your Majesty."

Caerna'tha. Warm memories of Maddie's time there bloomed distract-

332 ‖ KAREN HANCOCK

ingly, and for a moment she forgot she had a guest. Reluctantly she shook it off.

"We were snowed in all winter," Marta was saying. "And when he wasn't working, your husband—we called him Alaric—spent much time there."

"Alaric! So he's going by that name again."

And when Marta looked at her in puzzlement, she added, "It's his second name. Abramm Alaric Kesrin Galbrath . . . He's used it before when he didn't want anyone to know he was king." She paused, realizing he'd probably started using it to get out of Kiriath undiscovered, and by then had cemented his alternate identity with the people he traveled with. "One last question . . . Where did my husband sleep in Caerna'tha?"

"Where did he sleep?" Marta's dark brows arched at this odd question. "He chose one of the unheated dormitory rooms rather than stay with the rest of us in the Great Room. For which he was gossiped about relentlessly. No one could quite figure out what he was about. He was always standoffish, except maybe with Rolland and Laud at the end. But given who he was, I understand it now."

"And the others. . . ? They didn't know who he was?"

Marta shook her head. "He was supposed to be dead, after all, and in many ways he seemed a normal man." She nodded at the book in Maddie's hands. "I saw him write a note and slip it under the front cover before he wrapped it up."

A letter . . . With suddenly trembling hands, Maddie pulled off the string and unfolded the wrapping from around the leather-bound book. Its title, inscribed in the Old Tongue, caught her eye at once: *The Red Dragon*.

She nearly gasped. Even without the letter, she would have known by this that Marta's tale was true. For who but Abramm would select such a title for her? The book was obviously very old, a treasure that would normally make her tremble with awe. Today she cared only for the wrinkled rectangle of brown paper she found behind its cover. That it was filled with the script of the Old Tongue gave her a start. *He's learned to write the Old Tongue now. . . ?*

She closed the book and laid the note flat against its cover to read:

My heart, my life, my dearest love—
    Marta will have told you why you are reading this note and not feeling my arms about you, though the latter is what I most long to do. I do not know why Eidon is taking so long to bring me back to you, but it has become clear to me that he is not in nearly so much of a hurry as I am. The one advantage of staying in Caerna'tha through the winter you've

already seen. I have learned to read the Old Tongue. There were many wonderful books there to learn it with, and I have gleaned much about the regalia and the guardstars and what is going on in realms we cannot see. You would love it, though I think I would become insanely jealous with such an unending line of ink and paper suitors clamoring for your attention. You will have heard about my promise to Krele Janner, the boatman who brought us down. Reward him well. He was a faithful servant. And I hope you can give Marta a position on your staff. She is a good woman. A widow, thanks to the Gadrielites. I believe you can trust her. Finally, I do not know by what route Eidon will bring me back to you, only that he will. Have faith, my love. I will come. He has promised me that.

I remain forever yours,

Abramm

Tears blurred her vision by the time she got to the end, having no doubt now that he had written it. She read it again, then set both book and letter on her desk and broke down completely. Tears ran down her face as she wept into her hands for want of him. Sometime in the midst of it, Marta came and put her arms around her, and the queen of Chesedh wept against her shoulder as if they had known each other all their lives.

CHAPTER

29

Abramm and his companions left the banks of the Okaido River the same morning as the barge sank, eager to escape the scene of their deliverance and any Esurhites who might happen down the river. They'd come ashore east of the town Abramm had selected, which had been flattened by the earthquake. Finding no survivors, the northerners helped themselves to what weapons and provisions they could find—including six live chickens and a kettle to cook them in—and moved on. Trinley, of course, had to debate and dispute everything Abramm said, demanding the most silly and time-wasting things be done, but Abramm held his tongue and let it go. It wouldn't matter in the end.

The map he'd taken from the wheelhouse showed that the road running north out of the town eventually cut through mountains into North Andol. Following it was a gamble, since, being the only one on the map, there was a good chance the road would be used by other travelers. Worse, the map indicated that near the mountains, the road wound past a location marked with an Andolen beehive crown—possibly a former monarch's residence—which could be problematic if they had to pass too near it.

They were a troop of eighteen men, on foot, most of them blond or brunette and half naked, none of them Esurhite. Back at the river they had stripped the Esurhite uniforms from three drowned soldiers and gave them to the men they best fit: Galen, Cedric, and Borlain. Even so, they were sure to draw the notice of anyone they passed, particularly soldiers. And palatial residences tended to have many of those around. But in this land of mist-veiled sun, they would surely get lost without the road, so Abramm insisted, despite Trinley's vigorous objections, that they should keep to it. All the possibilities for disaster he would leave in Eidon's hands.

Of course, once Abramm determined what he would do, Trinley sought to undermine his leadership by trying to get the others to return to the river. When that failed, he wanted to lead the troop himself, a demand Abramm dismissed with the observation that Trinley did not speak the Tahg and thus was ill suited to conversing with anyone they might meet. Abramm, on the other hand, was fluent in the local language and could easily be taken as one of the Darian, who often held positions in the Esurhite army. Defeated and sulking, Trinley dropped back to the middle of their procession and said no more.

Once on the road, Abramm eased their pace and was finally able to learn what had befallen his friends since last he'd seen them—a heart-dropping four and a half months ago by their reckoning. After the sandstorm, they had found their way out of the dunes to a small southern-edge settlement, where they'd run afoul of a friendly innkeeper who offered them food, drink, and beds, only to drug them and sell them back into slavery. Passing from master to master, they'd finally arrived in Aggosim, where the Esurhites bought them for galley slaves.

Of Abramm's own journey, he said only that he had found an ancient ruin where he'd stayed for a much longer time than it had seemed. . . . At which point he'd changed the subject, still rattled by the realization that he'd been in Chena'ag Tor over four months.

Regarding Borlain, the one-eyed Chesedhan who'd led the attack on him after the sinking of the barge, his friends knew little, though all had noticed how intently he watched Abramm. He appeared to be the leader of the Chesedhans in their party, and from the way his men treated him, Abramm guessed they were captured soldiers.

That evening, after they'd made camp a little way off the road and the chickens had been cut up and were cooking in a big kettle, Abramm drew the Chesedhan leader away from his friends.

"Those men I killed were yours, I'm guessing," he said, stopping at the edge of the ring of firelight.

The one-eyed man seemed surprised but didn't deny it. "My best. Good fighters. Good friends."

"I'm sorry." *More sorry than you know.*

Borlain shrugged. "As you said, come at a man with a bared blade, you have to expect to meet some steel yourself." He paused. "I underestimated you."

"I'd take it back if I could."

Again the Chesedhan shrugged. "It was their time. We all have one. It comes, and the world moves on." His one eye came up to catch Abramm's gaze. "I've never seen anyone wield a blade as well as you do."

"I've had a lot of practice."

Borlain's eye drifted to the men laughing now where they sat and sprawled around the fire. "These others, though, your friends. They're not soldiers."

"No," Abramm agreed, looking at them. "Not yet, anyway." He glanced again at Borlain. "I really do wish I could take back what I did."

"Ah. But then perhaps *you* would be the one dead." The man flashed a gap-toothed grin. "And if I had acted less rashly, waited to learn more of what was going on, then maybe . . ." He trailed off and shook his head. "What's done is done, and it serves no purpose to chase after 'what if.' I don't hold it against you, Alaric, if that's what you fear. We're soldiers, you and I. That's how it is."

Abramm had nothing to say to that, and soon they returned to the fire, where the chicken stewed with rice and beans that had also come from the town was doled out into the men's scavenged cups and bowls. Then, as they ate, Abramm asked Borlain how he and his companions had been enslaved. Thus they all learned of King Leyton's ill-fated attempt to win back the island of Tornecki using the Kiriathan regalia his sister, former queen of Kiriath, had given him.

"She *gave* him the regalia?" Abramm exclaimed.

Borlain swore she had, but Abramm didn't believe him. Having long suspected his Chesedhan brother-in-law of stealing his scepter, Abramm had no reason to think the man wouldn't similarly violate Maddie—his own sister and subject—if it meant getting his hands on the rest of the regalia. That none of it had aided him and instead had only gotten him captured by his enemies was only just.

In any case, Borlain had seen the king in enemy hands himself—seen him mocked, beaten, spat upon, and humiliated before all the jeering Esurhite soldiers who had participated in his capture. Belthre'gar had personally taken the regalia from the king and secreted them away.

"That was just at the beginning of last summer."

"They will have put him in the Games by now," Abramm said, scooping more stew and a chicken leg into his wooden bowl.

"Aye. And now that we've been freed deep behind enemy lines, we're thinking maybe we're supposed to rescue him."

"Awful big order for seven men," Abramm said.

"We were thinking you and yours might want to help."

"Help that lying, thieving Chesedhan?" Trinley erupted. "I knew Madeleine wasn't to be trusted! First chance she gets, what does she do? Gives away our regalia."

"Stow it, Oakes!" Abramm barked. "She's the queen of Kiriath. She'd never have given them up freely." He turned his attention back to Borlain. "I don't think you'll find us much interested in helping Leyton."

"I do like the idea of trying to get the regalia back, though," Cedric mused.

Trinley agreed. "They probably took them to Xorofin. If we went back to the river, we could follow it to the coast and then south."

Abramm smiled to himself at the thought of these men trying to travel south through Esurh without being caught. He pulled the chicken leg out of his bowl and chewed off the soft meat as the others offered support for and elaboration of Trinley's idea.

As they came to a lull in their plotting, he said, "Suppose they are in Xorofin. . . . And suppose somehow you were to rescue them. . . . And then further suppose you could escape. . . . All of which are highly doubtful—"

"Not if Eidon is with us!" Trinley protested. "And it's so clear he is. It cannot be coincidence that we have been brought all this way only to be set free. And then to run into you here, as well? Our one real soldier? It is a clear sign."

"Aye, it is that, indeed." Abramm smiled slightly. "But humor me. Supposing all of what I said happened . . . and we got away free with them . . . what would you do with them? Bring them to Gillard?"

"No!" Trinley flashed him a disgusted look. "Bring'em t' Simon, o' course."

"Simon." *My uncle?* It made a certain amount of sense. "Is anyone sure Duke Simon still lives?"

"Simon Alaric," Trinley corrected. "The crown prince. Borlain here was tellin' us earlier he and his little brother were smuggled out by the nanny."

Hearing his son's name spoken by someone other than himself for the first time since he'd left Kiriath hit Abramm like a kick in the chest. His heart seemed to turn itself inside out, twisting with a pain he could not identify. It took all his self-control to keep his voice stable and audible. "So they both do live?"

"Didn't I just say that?" Trinley asked witheringly.

Abramm hardly heard him. *So it wasn't my imagination conjuring Simon up that night in Caerna'tha. Oh, my Father . . . you did hold them. You knew all the time. . . .* Emotion welled up so strongly he thought he might burst with it, and as tears stung his eyes he had to stand and walk away.

He heard the men's puzzled voices in his wake but could not discern their words. It was as if his inner landscape was being shaken as violently as the outer landscape of the Temple of Aggos had been yesterday. Once alone, he fell to his knees in the darkness and wept in gratitude and longing and a tangle of other emotions too deep to be identified. He had come so far, lost so much, waited so long. The experiences in Chena'ag Tor had stretched and drained him to the limit of his endurance. But though it had ended in glorious assurance, now that he was back in the world, the memory of it had faded rapidly until it seemed as unreal as his encounter with little Simon in that dark hallway the night Maddie had come to him in Caerna'tha. Though he'd been sure of what he'd experienced with his wife, he'd never been totally convinced that Simon had been anything more than a figment of his imagination.

To hear the boy's name spoken in the real world, to hear others affirming that his boys lived had unlocked a cascade of assurances that Eidon would deliver what he had promised. And that the deliverance was even now beginning.

The rustle of another's approach roused him from his thoughts moments before Rolland spoke cautiously from behind. "Alaric? Are ye well?"

"Aye, Rolland. I'm fine." He rolled his weight back squarely onto his feet and stood.

Rolland watched him in the light of a kelistar. "Trinley's got 'em all talked into heading back t' the river tomorrow. I thought ye'd want to know."

"Heading back to the river?" Abramm struggled to put meaning in the words.

"He's convinced them we should go after the regalia. That seeking them must be why Eidon brought us down here. I tried t' argue him out of it, but . . . he always talks rings around me."

"So you're going with him, too, then?"

"I'm going with ye."

Abramm said nothing for a moment as he considered. Then, "I don't think I'll be going after the regalia, Rollie."

"Doesn't matter." Rolland was staring at him with a strange expression. "Ye look different without the beard and yer hair tied back like that."

"So you've said."

"Familiar somehow. Like maybe I did know ye before. From the palace, maybe."

"Maybe." He waited, wondering if the time had finally come. . . .

The other man looked almost pained. "But ye don't remember me, do ye?"

"No, Rollie. I really don't. I'm sorry." Abramm sighed wearily and started back to the campfire before Rolland could ask him what he was doing out here, squirming to think the man had heard him weeping. He felt strangely detached from the others and had no interest in discussing their plans for the regalia. Maybe it was just more of the exhaustion left over from his time in the desert, or maybe it was something else he didn't understand. All he knew was that he'd barely rolled himself up in his cloak and stretched out beside the fire before he was asleep.

In the morning the other Kiriathans were all afroth with their plans to rescue the regalia. Trinley, finally back in his element, gave orders freely about when they would leave, what they would do if they encountered anyone, who would carry what, and what order they would travel in. He had Abramm's and Rolland's loads all planned out for them—the heaviest of the lot, as usual—and the possibility they might not share his vision still hadn't occurred to him.

Thus when Abramm finally told him that he and Rolland were not going south with the other Kiriathans, the former alderman was genuinely shocked. "But . . . but . . ." he stammered as all around them other conversations trickled to a halt.

"Did ye just say ye're not goin' with us?" Cedric asked, rucksack already slung over his one shoulder.

"That's right," Abramm said. "We're not."

"But ye were Abramm's man," Trinley protested. "I'd think you above all of us would want t' see his regalia returned to his heir."

Abramm let his gaze slide over the men around him, familiar faces many of them, men he'd grown attached to. "Actually, I wasn't Abramm's man," he said. "And my destiny does not lie to the south."

Their reactions to that were comical: amused indignation, consternation, a little bit of irritation at his hubris.

"Yer *destiny*?" Trinley sputtered. "Who the plague d' ye think ye are, anyway, Alaric?"

Abramm shook his head. "You still have no idea, do you?"

They looked at him blankly.

"I will not seek the regalia. They will come to me."

With that, he picked up his Esurhite armor and started northward on the road, Rolland at his side. The Chesedhans followed them wordlessly. As they climbed back onto the road, Rolland said, "That was awful strange talk, Alaric. What the plague did ye mean, the regalia will come to ye?"

But Abramm did not answer him. No one spoke to him for the entire morning, but when they stopped to rest around midday, Cedric and Galen and a couple others caught up with them. They said nothing to Abramm but favored him with puzzled looks and spoke among themselves of his strange words. "Sounded like someone else talking there for a time," he overheard one of them say. The rest of the Kiriathans, including an obviously disgruntled Trinley, rejoined them by evening. But again no one said a word to him.

In the days that followed, the others continued to give him his space, as if they were afraid of him. Perhaps they thought he had lost his mind. Even Rolland, who didn't exactly avoid him, kept his distance and his silence, though often Abramm caught the other man eyeing him thoughtfully.

Abramm had made the statement about the regalia seeking him without realizing he'd spoken it aloud. The thought had impressed itself upon him as if from another source, even as the words had fallen from his lips. Once they had, it had been too late to retract them, and he'd realized then that it was Eidon working through him, that the hour of revelation was coming.

―――――

More than two weeks later, with the mountains now towering ahead of them and the road winding through grassy foothills and copses of oaks turning yellow with the fall, they passed the estate noted on Abramm's map. The whitewashed plaster of the wall running along the road was cracked and peeling, the fields beyond it long since gone to weeds, and the gateway arch at the estate's entrance lay in ruin, collapsed upon the drive and half buried in dirt—silent testimony to how long it had been since anyone of any means had passed this way.

Which explained how they could have traveled so many days and met no one else. Not far up the road a small town also stood deserted, and he began to wonder why. Was the pass no longer crossable? Would they ascend the mountain only to discover the way was blocked?

So engrossed was he with his speculations and so accustomed to their solitude, he didn't hear the Esurhite troop until it was upon them, trotting around a bend in the road which had, until then, obscured them behind a screen of oak trees. Though Abramm had established a plan in which, should such a thing occur, the last ten men of their troop were supposed to disappear into the roadside vegetation, this troop was on them so quickly he doubted anyone remembered what they were to do. Rather than look surprised or fearful, or turn around to see, he proceeded onward as if nothing were amiss.

The troop's captain pulled up in a cloud of dust, his big gray gelding reminding Abramm of Warbanner. He demanded to know what Abramm was doing here, but Abramm faced him down boldly, aware that he wore the superior rank of a temple guard. The corridor in the Temple of Aggos had been destroyed, he informed the man, so he and his troop were escorting these slaves north over the mountain to the front.

The captain asked why Abramm was on foot. He said his horse had gone lame and he'd had to leave it behind. A brief exchange ensued, during which Abramm learned that the road ahead was closed at the old fortress— unnamed on his map but marked by a solid square at what seemed a pass through the mountains. The earthquake had filled a place called the Slot with rock, and they would all have to go back. The Esurhite captain and his men, who'd been sent to investigate the damage, would escort them to the river. At that point Abramm decided to act upon the ideas that had been percolating in his brain ever since the troop had arrived. Borlain had gotten into position after all—he could see him out of the corner of his eye, hiding in the brush at the side of the road. Hopefully, he'd see what needed doing.

Abramm smiled and said he would welcome an escort, but that one of the captain's men must surrender to him his mount because it was unseemly for him to walk when others of lesser rank rode.

"In fact," he said, letting his smile broaden a hair as he took hold of the reins under the horse's chin, "this animal will do nicely."

Shock preceded outrage on the captain's face. Scowling, he kicked the horse forward. Abramm released the reins and stepped to meet him, grabbing the Esurhite's lower leg as the horse went by. The other man's momentum helped Abramm to pull his booted foot free of the stirrup, then flip him up and over the horse's far side. Meanwhile, Borlain and his men were erupting from the bushes to attack the captain's subordinates, while from somewhere at Abramm's back came the hard thunks and clacks of sticks on sword and bone. Braced against the gray's flank, Abramm pulled his sword and turned to the rider behind him. The man was still fumbling to get his own blade free of his scabbard when Abramm ran him through the armpit.

It was over in moments. Five Esurhites lay dead in the dirt, and the sixth, who had been last in line, stared in horror as Rolland advanced upon him, then shrieked something in the Tahg and flung himself off his horse to crash away into the underbrush.

Trinley, who was closest to his line of flight, started after him, but Abramm called him back. As they all caught their breaths and then came together to take stock, Rolland asked, "What does *rashawin* mean?"

"It means pretender," said Borlain, eyeing him speculatively. "He must've thought you were the White Pretender."

"Aye." Abramm nodded. "You're about the right size and coloring."

Rolland looked embarrassed. "I've never heard any tales about the Pretender attacking anyone with a stick," he grumbled.

"It wasn't his weapon of choice," Abramm agreed.

"Why the plague did you let him go?" Trinley demanded as he stalked up to them. "He'll tell everyone we're here and bring back that army you're so afraid of."

"The Pretender is dead, Trinley."

"Still . . . we don't want to draw attention to ourselves."

"We're a few escaped slaves among a multitude. This earthquake has shaken the whole realm apart. They aren't going to go chasing up some impassable road on the word of a scared young soldier claiming to have faced the White Pretender. They'll think he's just trying to save face. I'm sure he won't be the only one."

"Aye," Borlain agreed. "I heard talk back in Aggosim that some believe it was the Pretender who destroyed the temple."

"I heard that, too," Abramm said. He cocked his head at Borlain. "You didn't tell me you spoke the Tahg."

The Chesedhan shrugged. "I can pick out words here and there. But I understand more than I can speak."

In the course of stripping the bodies of their uniforms and weapons, they found a mail pouch on one of the men, filled with letters in the Tahg along with a detailed map of the area on both sides of the pass. Abramm kept the pouch himself, and as those without uniforms decided who would get the black tunics and helms they'd just acquired, he helped Rolland and Borlain drag the bodies off the road.

Four days later they had followed the road up the side of a steep, rocky canyon to a narrow slot of a pass, filled with fallen slabs of granite. Overlooking it was the blasted-out hulk of an old fortress whose distinctive towers and spiraling stonework marked it as Andolen, probably abandoned since the Esurhites had captured it some ten years ago. Considering how long the villa they'd passed earlier had lain in ruin, Abramm suspected some of the damage to the pass itself had come through that action, but that only with the earthquake had it become blocked completely.

When it became apparent they'd have to go back, Trinley began to complain bitterly over Abramm's stubbornness in keeping on when he'd known there was no passage. Why hadn't he listened to the Esurhites? Now they'd wasted much time and these uniforms would serve them nothing.

Abramm finally told him, bluntly, to take his griping elsewhere. They set up camp at the mouth of the slab-filled slot. In the morning, Abramm was up early, determined to do a thorough daylight investigation before abandoning the place altogether. He'd been confident of Eidon's direction in following this route, and he didn't want to miss whatever might be here for him.

It was young Galen who drew his attention to the game trail that cut away from the slot along the cliff face opposite the road they'd come up. Nearly as wide as the road when they started on it, it narrowed quickly, turning out to be suitable only for the goats that had made it. When the trail disintegrated into a series of rock-to-rock jumps, Abramm gave it up and turned around.

And on the way back down they found the illusion that had been woven over part of the cliff face, just at the point where the path began to narrow. Behind it, a long, crooked crack spilled them into a bowl-shaped valley fringed with yellow-leaved oaks. A corral stood to the right of them, near a number of stone buildings and a now-empty trough that had apparently been spring fed at one time. Beyond this deserted settlement, an ancient stair crawled up a rocky slope to the fortress, which was much larger than it had appeared from the road.

"Plagues!" Galen said as they stood looking about at the site. "It's like it was made fer us."

"I think it was," Abramm said, clapping him on the shoulder. "Let's go get the others."

The first thing they did was bring the horses up, for if they couldn't get the beasts to pass through the illusion, the place would be useless to them. Rolland came up with the trick of blindfolding them and startling them through the spell one by one. It took all afternoon, but finally they had them all through—Abramm's big gray being the last. As he rode the animal through the long, sloping entrance slot, he marveled anew at Eidon's provision. Whoever would have imagined such a thing as this awaited them when they'd left the river?

Once in the valley, he trotted down the incline to where Rolland stood with Cedric and Galen, dismounted, and handed the reins to the blacksmith, hardly realizing what he was doing. It was an action born of habit mixed with preoccupation, an action he had done countless times in the Springerlan stables as Abramm, but never before as Alaric. He'd already started walking away, wanting to check out the spring Borlain had told him about earlier, when he heard Rolland's strangled, "Eidon's mercy!"

He turned back to find the blacksmith staring at him, stricken. "What's wrong?"

"Ye look like . . . like King Abramm! That's the memory I've been chasin' after all this time. Why ye seem familiar to me. Ye . . . look like . . ." He seemed to be having trouble getting his breath. "Ye look like . . . him."

"I know," Abramm said quietly, stepping round fully to face him. And just like that, the moment had come.

Around him the other men had all gone still and alert, looking from Rolland to him in puzzlement. None of the rest had ever seen him as Abramm.

He kept his gaze on the blacksmith, watching the man shuffling the facts alongside his observations and the experiences they'd shared for more than a year. "Dragon and shield . . ." he murmured.

The change came like a huge wave rising up inevitably and unavoidably within him, until the crest finally curled, broke, and tumbled down, rushing over him in a fierce burn of comprehension.

No way to turn it or deny it now. Rolland had seen the truth. At long last.

His rugged face turned white, his mouth sagged open, and his blue eyes widened. "I saw ye die," he breathed.

"You saw someone else," Abramm said calmly, though his ears had started to roar. "I was rescued before the execution took place. I spent three months recovering—"

". . . in a hunting lodge at the headwaters of the Snowsong River," Rolland took over, repeating what Abramm had told them months ago in Caerna'tha, "an' then walked up t' Highmount Holding alone."

Borlain and Trinley had joined the others now, all eyes riveted on Abramm and the blacksmith.

Rolland shook his head, his gaze running again over Abramm's face and form. "How could I have been so blind?"

"It wasn't time for you to see."

Rolland regarded him steadily for a moment, then dropped to one knee and bowed his head. "My lord . . ." he said, voice trembling. And by that action he received a flurry of shocked looks from the others.

"What the plague?" Trinley exclaimed. "Ye're calling him *lord* now, Rollie?"

"My lord . . . and my king," Rolland said gravely. As he recited the age-old words of fealty, the others' eyes flicked back to Abramm, who stood before him, accepting his vows without protest. Their brows furrowed, and they looked nervously at one another, not truly understanding until Rolland came to the end of his speech and Abramm began his own, using his real and rightful name: "I, Abramm Alaric Kesrin Galbrath Kalladorne . . ."

As he spoke the words of his own promise, he saw the realization of truth sweep through the others, forced upon them as they considered the brand on his arm, the shield on his chest, the scars on his face, and what the last few weeks had brought them to.

When he had finished, Borlain said, "You're the one who destroyed the temple, aren't you?"

"Yes."

"Plagues!" Cedric cried. "I remember thinking back in Caerna'tha how ye had all the traits they said belonged to Abramm—the scars, the shield and dragon. But to think ye really are him . . . King of Kiriath. . . ."

"And you're going to take it back, aren't you?" Galen said, eyes shining. "Kiriath, I mean. That's why you're heading north."

"That's why *we're* heading north," Abramm said. "And if any of you don't want to be part of this"—he fixed his gaze on Trinley—"feel free to move on."

It was as if the Light itself moved through them—perhaps it did—erasing the years of hardship and loss and despair and replacing it with new hope and pride and purpose. The change in their attitude was so profound it raised gooseflesh across Abramm's shoulders.

As the Chesedhans looked on, Cedric knelt and uttered the oath of fealty, followed by Galen and—except for Oakes Trinley—all the rest of the Kiriathans. Abramm looked each man in the eye to receive his oath and give his own in return.

When it was done, he had the first troop of his army.

30

For two months Abramm and his men stayed in the hidden valley behind the ruined fortress, living off the land and learning how to fight. Abramm, with the one-eyed Borlain's help, instructed them in the use of sword and shield, and the basic rules of combat. He worked them hard, and they didn't complain; in fact, except for Trinley, they complied eagerly.

Their discovery of his true identity and the Kiriathans' swearing of fealty to him had not only infused them all with new purpose—it had finally given him unquestioned command of the group. Rolland had gone around in a daze for a week, refusing to advance any opinion save one that agreed with Abramm's, and erecting a barrier of awkward distance between them. *Besotted*, was how Trinley put it, though not in front of Abramm.

He was right, though. They were besotted. And to some degree, they had to stay that way. In all his longings to have his name and authority restored, he'd forgotten the inevitable loneliness that came with leadership.

By the time the last yellow leaves of autumn had fluttered to the ground and the chill of winter's advent gripped the mountain air, Abramm judged the men were as ready for combat as any new trainees, and it was time to move on. Originally he'd hoped to cross North Andol through its sparsely populated eastern plains, heading north to the Strait of Terreo and on to Chesedh. But the mountains they were in rose up gradually from the south and ended in a line of impassable cliffs on the north, so that, except for the road they'd followed up, the only way down was a narrow trail heading westward along the ridge. Which meant, instead of the deserted plains, they'd have to cross the populous western coastal region.

Using the horses, uniforms, and weapons they'd acquired so far, he'd planned to disguise them all as a patrol rounding up runaway slaves in the earthquake's aftermath. With the coastlands crawling with Esurhite soldiers, his plan remained viable, though it would surely be put to a far greater test than he had hoped.

Going west, of course, also increased the potential for encountering Leyton—assuming he still lived—and the possibility of rescuing him. Borlain and his Chesedhans were certain they would, convinced it was why they had been brought here, even as the Kiriathans believed they'd been sent to rescue Abramm's regalia. None of them had given any thought to how all that might be accomplished—in a hostile environment, crawling with enemy soldiers. They were just certain Eidon would make them a way.

In any case, almost two months to the day from when they'd arrived, Abramm announced it was time to leave. They spent three days packing and preparing, and on the morning of their projected departure gathered in the valley's yard. Abramm, who had gone up to the fortress's watchtower to be alone with Eidon for a time, was returning down the narrow stair to the valley floor when he came upon Rolland and Trinley in quiet conversation.

The only one of the Kiriathans who had refused to honor Abramm with his fealty, Trinley had continued to be a problem. Though he no longer openly criticized Abramm's decisions, he continued to nurse his bitterness and find fault behind Abramm's back. On occasion, Abramm had heard Rolland and Cedric talk about it, but he had deliberately not intruded to give them the chance to deal with it on their own.

"We've all lost much, Oakes," Rolland said now in a low voice. "Plagues, Abramm's lost the most."

"Aye. Sure he has." Trinley's voice was mocking. "I can't b'lieve the way ye're all scrapin' an' bowin' to a man who's nothin' more than any of us. Ye're such a poor, gullible fool, Rollie!"

Rolland sighed wearily. "How can ye still claim ye don't believe he's Abramm, Oakes?"

"B'cause Abramm is dead. Ye saw him die yerself, and if this fella really *is* him, why'd it take a year fer ye t' figure it out?" When Rolland had no answer for him, he added, "Even if he was Abramm, I'd not give him my fealty. He doesn't deserve it."

"Blaming him fer what yer daughter did t' ye isn't fair. And it won't bring anythin' back. Only eat away at ye until yer soul is dark and bitter."

Trinley snorted. "What do ye know about bitterness, Rollie? What d' ye know about loss? Nothin'."

For a moment Rolland was silent. When he finally did speak, irritation sharpened his voice. "Maybe I don't know as much as ye do, but he's our king, and whether ye believe that or not, ye'd better start treating him like it. 'Cause if ye don't stop yer criticizin' and mockery, I swear by Eidon's throne, I'll leave ye along the road with nothing but yer clothes and yer waterskin."

"Ye wouldn't do—"

"I would. An' I will," Rolland said firmly. "We'll be headin' down among the Esurhites here soon, and I'll not let ye drag the rest of us down. Nor put our king in danger."

"Yer king," Trinley sneered. "Maybe I'll just leave on my own."

"Maybe ye should."

Rolland walked off, and soon after, Trinley followed him. Abramm went round another way, so they'd not guess he'd heard them, and as much as Rolland's actions pleased him, it sobered him to think that after all this time, all Abramm had done and Trinley had seen, his heart seemed only to grow harder and more bitter toward Abramm. Rather like Gillard's had. And like Gillard, there didn't seem to be anything anyone could do to change it.

They set out shortly after that, eighteen of them, six mounted, the other twelve on foot, most of them excited and filled with anticipation for what their future held. Two alone were sober: Trinley on foot and sullen as he brought up the rear, and Abramm astride the big gray he'd named New-banner at the head. For Trinley's unrelenting hostility had reminded him that he faced another enemy, one who was not only far more hostile but far more powerful: Moroq.

For the dragon was out there, somewhere, waiting to do his worst. And the last time Abramm had seen his wife, he'd chosen to abandon her to the care of Eidon. For all he knew she might be dead now. And Trap, as well. He'd been able to put such thoughts aside for the last two months, knowing he'd not have them answered, anyway, and refusing to torment himself with wondering. But now—very soon, perhaps—he would find out if either still lived.

He would not take back his decision, but it was hard not to dread learning the outcome. Because at some deep level he was pretty sure what it was going to be and was still preparing himself to receive it with acceptance and thanks-giving. And the will to go on without his loved ones. For in the domed Hall of Records above Chena'ag Tor, the pillar showed his kingdom restored to him, but not necessarily his wife and friends. And even the kingdom was only potential—a future he could lose if he did not stay the course, if he allowed the Shadow to overcome him and forgot that central command scrawled across the hall's entrance:

No other shall come before me.

Three months after Maddie became queen, Peregris's defenses were still not even close to being restored. The walls that protected the palace and the city from invasion by both sea and hostile forces remained rife with gaps, only a quarter of the demolished retaining walls and quays had been replaced, and the breastwork that protected the mouth of the Ankrill was still less than half finished.

Eidon's grace had kept the winds active through the fall. Without them, the southlanders' galleys would have been up the Ankrill to Fannath Rill in days. As it was, the Chesedhan gunships had had to scramble to guard both city and river, but so far they had succeeded. And now that the winter rainy season had come, they would have a few months' reprieve from the war. Or so she hoped.

But one didn't have to venture far from the coast to find the winds dying, the rains drying up, and the seas lying calm beneath a thick, woolly layer of Shadow. Torneki still lay enfolded in it, and despite Chesedhan attempts to retake it over the last three months, the Esurhites had resisted their efforts. Chesedhan gunships were useless, and Chesedhan galleys were nowhere near as effective as those of the Esurhite forces. With thousands of years of experience in both constructing and sailing galleys, if it came down to a war at sea, the Esurhites would win.

And war was coming. Chesedhan spies reported that the Esurhites had set up a corridor on occupied Torneki and were bringing in men and boats at a prodigious rate. More were being brought in at the Draesian capital of Zereda, due south across the strait from Peregris. Twin assaults would be launched against the Chesedhan coast. Most likely right after the winter rains ended some six weeks from now.

Looking at the preparations her people had made thus far was disheartening, and she knew they needed help. Knew what form everyone thought that help should take, too: Tiris ul Sadek.

She stopped now before the wide window of her Peregris apartments and stared again at the dozen sleek white galleys that had arrived in her harbor overnight. Standing at anchor behind a silvery curtain of rain, they were arrayed in ranks of four. Their prows were shaped in a rough backward semi-circle, the bottom of which ended in a forward-pointing, iron-tipped ram designed to puncture the hulls of the enemy ships below the waterline. The forward line curved back from the ram and up into a crest that gleamed with gold gilt. Large open eyes had been painted on their hulls just beyond the ram, reminding her uneasily of Belthre'gar's vessel and the night she nearly became his wife. Each vessel's two square sails had been reefed, but the plat-forms that formed their upper decks had been rigged with canvas awnings so that the sailors might escape the rain.

Tiris had brought them from Ropolis as a gift, presented to her in a formal ceremony a couple of hours ago.

"Remarkable ships, madam," her Grand Admiral had called them, beside himself with the prospect of adding them to his forces. "They have three tiers of oars, so they move like lightning through the water. And each has a full complement of sailors who know what they're doing. With these we just might hold the river another summer after all!"

The galleys were but a taste of the forces Tiris had at his disposal, and though he'd never be so blatant and uncultured as to offer them as an exchange for marrying Queen Madeleine, he'd dropped enough hints that everyone knew what they would gain should she accept his suit. It was the talk of all the salons and taverns and council meetings. In fact, yesterday her own cabinet had presented her with a resolution they had drawn up and signed, already approving any marriage offer he made her. It was, proclaimed her First Minister, a matter of national survival that they accept him. Even Trap, now instated in her cabinet as Special Counsel to the Queen, had signed. It had broken her heart to see his name there with the others.

As the queen, it was her duty to sacrifice herself for the good of her realm, though all insisted that union with such a man as Tiris could hardly be con-sidered a sacrifice. He was young, handsome, charming, and vastly powerful. What sane woman would turn down such a suitor?

Yet all she felt was stubborn resistance. Even in the face of the almost irrefutable evidence Marta Brackleford had brought that Abramm was, indeed, dead. That he'd been on the Ankrill at Obla, had gone out from there into the desert and been swallowed by the great sandstorm. In both instances, precisely as the amber had shown. So maybe Maddie wasn't sane. Maybe the grief and refusal to accept his loss really had unhinged her mind. Maybe it *was* time to let go of him and move on.

She turned from the window to regard her two ladies-in-waiting sitting across the room from her, Carissa with her embroidery, Marta with her knitting. "You both think I'm crazy, then, don't you?"

"Abramm's dead, Maddie," said Carissa. She'd long since made it clear she supported her husband's signing of the cabinet's resolution.

Maddie turned to the other woman. "You think so, too, Marta?"

Marta glanced at Carissa, then sighed. "Ma'am, I feel certain if Abramm were alive, you would know it by now. He would have sent some word. He would know what we would think, the way he disappeared into the desert like that. The sandstorm and all."

"So you think I should marry Tiris."

Carissa answered first. "He dotes on you, Mad. Even knowing your heart still belongs to Abramm. He would be a safe harbor in this storm, maybe the salvation of us all."

"Marta?"

Marta frowned, drew breath to speak, but said nothing.

"You don't think he would be a safe harbor?"

Dark-haired Marta looked down at her half-knitted sweater. "I cannot say, ma'am," she said finally. "He is all everyone says, and more. And he does dote on you." She fell silent.

"But?" Maddie prodded.

"Please, madam, do not ask me what I think. My heart breaks for you, but I do not know the future, and there are so many other things that must be considered. I fear Eidon is the only one who can tell you what you want to know."

"And if I say yes to Tiris tonight? Will you still stand by me?"

Marta looked stricken. But after a moment she said, "You know I will stand by you, madam. As your lady, as your subject, and as your friend."

Maddie sighed and said no more. After a time she dismissed them both and went to sit at her desk, where she pulled out the slim gray volume with the swirling letters of the Old Tongue glinting on its cover. She'd had no time to read more than snippets here and there, and that reading cursory at best. There'd simply been too much to do. It didn't help that every time she sat down to do so, she read first the two letters Abramm had written her, which she kept behind its cover—the one he'd written in Springerlan before he'd given himself over to the Gadrielites to save her, and the one he'd written in Obla before he'd gone into the desert to rescue his friends.

Oh, Abramm . . . are you really out there? Then why have you sent no word?

What am I to do? I know you promised, but you are only a man. . . . And I don't know what I saw that night before the wave. . . . You were so very sad. Was it truly the end?

"I don't know what to do," she whispered, staring blindly out the window. "I don't know what to do. . . ."

"Madam?" Jeyanne's voice broke gently into her thoughts. "Will you be preparing for your dinner engagement?"

Maddie drew a deep breath of resignation and stood up. "Yes, of course."

Dinner with Tiris was, as always, a delightful affair. The man was fascinating. His mind was quick, sharp, and deeply penetrating. He was darkly attractive in a feral sort of way; not as tall as Abramm, but he possessed the same litheness and grace of movement. His long-lashed dark eyes mesmerized her almost as much as his conversation, which was, as always, intelligent, witty, and even biting at times. He had a way of flattering her without being obvious about it, and when she was in his presence she felt strangely alive, but in a way that was different from how Abramm made her feel. And not necessarily in a good way.

After dinner they bundled up—she wore the fine woolen cloak he had given her for her untaken journey to Deveren Dol—and strolled along the palace wallwalk overlooking the harbor. The night was chill and damp but rainless, and thus pleasant in its own way. It wasn't long before he spoke again of his proposal. "Consider how much better your realm will be for it, madam. It takes humility to recognize one's weakness and seek help."

She sighed and nodded and watched the boats bobbing in the harbor, marked out by their deck lights.

"You still believe Abramm will return." His voice held no expression.

"You know I do. You, more than anyone, know why."

She heard him release a soft breath. "I have never sought to gainsay you in this, my flower. I know your belief is strong and sincere . . . but . . . you do realize that both of the instances you claim as proof and evidence of his being alive occurred when you were under duress. The first when you were touched by the dark spore. The second when you had just been betrayed to the Esurhites and were about to meet the Supreme Commander. And perhaps even more than that, for strange powers were at work that night. I still wonder if that earthquake was not the product of some new experiment in power gone wrong."

All true. She had no words to offer, only this dead and dreary sense of inevitable disaster.

When she did not speak, he pressed his case. "Yes, I'll grant, the first vision you had of him seems to have been borne out as legitimate. But that doesn't make anything of the second or third visions. Your second amber vision showed him dead. Your vision on the longboat showed him surrounded by light." He paused. "Have you considered the possibility that the third one actually supports the second? That what you were seeing somehow was a glimpse of him in the eternal realm?"

"Oh yes, of course I have. That's why this is so abominably hard!"

Beneath the cloak she hugged herself, trying to regain control of emotions that threatened to spiral out of control. For a time they strolled in silence, footsteps crisp on the damp stones beneath their feet, bells clanging down on the dock at the foot of the wall where they walked. Out on the harbor, the deck lamps of his twelve galleys illumined their forms and gleamed off the water. She drew and released a shaky breath, wishing she didn't have to decide, knowing that she must.

Finally Tiris cleared his throat and spoke, treading carefully. "Let's say for the sake of argument that he did survive the desert. From which direction do you believe he will come? And how will he do so without your hearing of it? I know that your friend the duke has ears out everywhere and that so far all reports are of imposters. . . . Last of all, if he comes in secret he can't be bringing an army, and we know the regalia are lost. . . . So what good can you imagine he will do you?

She had no response to that. There *was* no response. All that he said was true, much as she wished to deny it.

They reached the stair to the courtyard garden and descended, strolling through the damp greenery in silence, then returning to her chambers, where they sat before the fire sipping mulled wine and making small talk. Finally Tiris's patience gave out.

"I know your cabinet has drawn up a resolution to accept my suit should I offer it," he said. "But I will not be publicly embarrassed. I will make no official offer until I have your personal guarantee of acceptance." He paused. "Marry me, Madeleine. Become my queen, co-ruler of the three realms. Let your children become my official heirs. Simon will inherit all my holdings. Ian will be a great scholar, unlocking secrets of the ancients; or perhaps a warrior, a leader of men like his father. And as for beautiful Abrielle, she will be the princess of three realms, the apple of her father's eye, and only the finest of men will dare to even ask for her hand. . . ." He chuckled. "I might even have to reinstate a trial-by-dragon ritual again."

She smiled, knowing he was trying to lift her spirits, but the horrible oppression only weighed more heavily. It was as if all her emotions had become flat and dull, to the point where she almost didn't care.

"You think I would not love you?" he asked gently.

"Honestly?" She looked up at him. "I fear it is I who would not love you."

She saw the flash of disappointment in his eyes. "Abramm still holds your heart that tightly. . . ?"

She could not answer, for her throat had swollen and she was teary-eyed again.

He drew a deep breath and let it out. "Well, I am a patient man, and I believe time changes many things. I can wait for the fires of your love to kindle."

They fell silent for a time, until finally he stood to take his leave. She arose to see him off, but he hesitated, gazing down at her. And though he was willing to wait for the fires of her love to kindle, he was not willing to wait for her answer to the question of his suit and brought it up now one last time.

"What say you, my iblis flower? Will you accept me?"

She looked up at him, wondering why this was so hard when she felt so vague.

He stroked her cheek and a tingle swept through her. She let her eyes drift over his face, noting the long lashes, the gold scaling on the cheekbones, the strong jawline beneath his short-cropped beard. The bewitching dark eyes, the gold in his ear and on his fingers, the fresh white linen of his well-made tunic . . . the power in his voice and presence. He was more than any woman could ever hope to have. He could save her realm. He could save her children. He could save her—and he wished to on all counts.

If she were honest with herself, part of her—a very strong part—wanted to let him.

Except for the dwindling hope of Abramm's return, what reason did she have for refusing? None save the undeniable sense that she would be betraying her husband's memory. But would Abramm really have wanted her to go on with the rest of her life, raising his children alone? Would he not have wished her to take advantage of this offer?

She dropped her eyes to the line of buttons that closed his tunic. "Will you show me your shield, Tiris?" she asked.

He smiled, and the long graceful fingers at once began to unfasten the buttons. When he had undone the tunic nearly to his waist he pulled the edges apart, and there gleaming beneath his inner shirt of silk was the golden shield of Eidon that marked him as one who carried the Light.

She felt mildly surprised, for in some part of her thoughts she had not really believed he was marked. Even now, she reached out to touch it, wishing it was not covered by the silk so that she might pick at the edge to be sure it was not of paper or those newer ones of pure gold. But to do so he'd have to disrobe completely, and she couldn't ask him to go that far. So she let go a faint spark of the Light, felt an echo in return.

He smiled at her. "Satisfied?"

"Yes."

"So . . . will you marry me, Madeleine?"

Her resistance to the idea weakened with each moment, as if his dark gaze were pulling it out of her. She felt as if she were sliding down a long hole. *Yes, say yes* . . . The word formed upon her lips. The only word she could give him, the one that would save everyone and everything . . . *yes* . . . *yes* . . .

"Yes." She blinked, staring up at him in astonishment. *I said yes.*

His eyes glowed with pleasure. "We'll announce it tomorrow, then? Together?"

"Yes."

He lifted her hand to his lips and kissed the backs of her fingers, his dark eyes never leaving her own. "You will not regret this, my flower. I promise you. . . ." He turned her hand over and kissed her palm, then pressed his nose to her wrist and, closing his eyes, inhaled deeply, a languorous smile curving his lips. Strangely, the action that had so repelled her the first time he had done it now sent ripples of pleasure up her arm and across her chest.

He opened his eyes, snaring her gaze again, and the power of her attraction to him dizzied her. When he bent to kiss her, she let him, his lips soft upon her own, his beard tickling her face. He smelled faintly of sandalwood, the scent filling all her head and mind so that when he pulled away it made her dizzy. He smiled. "I will make you forget all about him, my flower. You will see. . . ."

He left her then, and she stood at the entrance to her apartments, watching him go, waiting until he had disappeared from view at the end of the long hall. But by the time she had returned to her bedchamber, all the warm pleasure she'd derived from his company had faded and she felt inexplicably dirty. As if something precious had been defiled.

And that night, she cried herself to sleep for thinking of what she had done.

31

Stuck in the long line of people waiting on the road outside the gates of Horon-Pel in hopes of being granted entrance, Abramm brushed yet another sluggish fly off his stubbled jaw. He let Newbanner's reins slide through his gloved fingers as the horse tossed his head and sidled impatiently in place; then he regathered the slack. It was the gruesome reminders of the fate awaiting those who transgressed Esurhite law—human heads staked on poles alongside the road—that had brought so many flies, even this late in the season. The nearest was blond, relatively fresh, and already eyeless, thanks in part to the gull perched on its crown.

Grimacing, he brushed more flies away again and turned his gaze toward the stone anchor posts of Horon-Pel's iron drawbridge looming in a gathering mist ahead of him. Between the posts stood the fancy gold-scrolled coach that had earlier pushed past everyone else on the road to take the head of the line. Its occupant was still arguing with the guards stationed there to question each traveler before allowing them entrance—or, more often, the closer it got to dusk, turning them away. And with every passing moment, Abramm's chances of getting himself and his party into the city that night diminished.

He glanced at Cedric, mounted and dressed in Esurhite black beside him, looking undeniably ill at ease in his bronze helmet. He dared not say a word, for fear of giving his true nationality away. Likewise for Trinley, driving the cart behind them. Galen, who sat beside him, had picked up a surprising amount of the language just listening to Abramm as he'd tutored Borlain, while the latter's command of it had increased dramatically over the last few months. But they were the only three of the group who had even a thread of comprehension, though for most of the men it didn't matter since they were supposed to be slaves.

Their cart they'd found in a deserted, earthquake-devastated settlement on their way down the mountain. Most of the men rode on it now, slaves being brought to the galleys in Horon-Pel, as Borlain and three others brought up the rear on horseback. The multitudes lining the road had ogled them repeatedly for two days now, especially tall, blond, powerful Rolland. Time and again, Abramm had fielded—and refused—offers to buy them before they ever reached the city.

The earthquake that had blocked the pass and devastated the towns across North Andol had combined with the economic drain of supplying a war to drive most of the populace toward the western cities. Now a sea of humanity camped in the flat, muddy fields beside the road. Small domed tents and makeshift lean-tos crowded around the bow-topped wagons of the east plain nomads as far as he could see. In the gathering twilight cook fires gleamed brightly, adding their smoke to air already heavy with the Shadow's mist and the stench of too many people crushed too close together.

They were families who had come looking for work, for food, and for new lives in the wake of the earthquake's devastation. They were also merchants of all kinds, slave traders, goatherds, fishermen, a few farmers selling last season's crops, and water vendors. Earlier many of them had stood along the way offering their goods to those still on the road—for a stiff price, of course.

And many among them had avidly eyed the men in Abramm's cart as it had trundled by. With Leyton's rise to the top of the Esurhite Games, Kiriathan slaves had become a valuable commodity, sought by the Game masters to play the role of the defrauded and vengeful King Abramm. The slave who brought Leyton down would win a lot of money, enriching his owner substantially. With Leyton scheduled to fight in Horon-Pel's arena tomorrow, this fact was especially on the minds of those camped outside the city's gates, and Abramm believed few around him were above stealing a few slaves if it meant their family's survival.

Last night had been bad enough. If they had to spend another in this mass of desperate people, he wasn't sure how many of his men would be with him come morning.

He batted another sluggish fly off his face and shifted restlessly in the saddle, trying to ease the stiffness and chill of his legs and bottom. Would that man from the coach ever stop arguing and accept his fate? Already some on the road were yelling at him to do so.

It wouldn't have been so bad, he thought, if it was just Leyton's appearance and general desperation that had brought people to Horon-Pel, but there was more. Along the route, he'd learned that the blast that had destroyed the temple corridor at Aggosim had indeed also destroyed the corridor in Oropos, triggering a second earthquake that had destroyed much of that city, as well. As a result, new corridors had been set up in the smaller temples in various cities along the coast, including Horon-Pel. The latter's temple was situated outside the city walls, so he'd seen that one in action today, proving the rumors true.

Ahead, the finely dressed citizen was reboarding his carriage, the guards stepping back, their black tunics blurred in the gathering mist. Abramm couldn't even see the entrance tunnel anymore, but two soldiers were jamming lit torches into brackets on the side of the anchor posts. Despite all the arguing—or perhaps because of it—the fancy carriage was turned away, forced to execute a jerky Y-turn before plunging back through the line the way it had come, moving more rapidly and with less concern than ever for whom it hit. At least, once it passed, the line moved on again.

Soon Abramm pulled Newbanner to a halt before the guards, explaining his assignment as the gatemen scowled. One muttered something about not many slaves for all the soldiers he had with him, did a cursory inspection of the property in question, then waved him through with directions to the army slave quarters by the harbor. Directions Abramm would recall only for the purpose of avoiding that area at all costs.

Inside, they plowed into a crowd even more closely packed than the one outside. People filled the gate yard and crammed the narrow lanes beyond, hemmed in by the tall, age-stained plastered walls of the city's buildings. Garlands of colorful fish-bladder lanterns hung across the streets, suspended between facing windows above the crowd. Here and there, jugglers and musicians clad in bright silks performed, as the people danced—or swayed—and the scents of fried bread, spice tea, and grilled meat filled the air. Many people carried cheering sticks, some bearing the old crescent moons of the White Pretender, the others carrying images of the gold crown that Leyton was defending. It was a bright, festive atmosphere, but the moment he emerged from the entrance tunnel, Abramm knew his plan of finding a deserted alley in which they might change into the civilian clothes they'd picked up along their journey would be more difficult than he'd hoped. Still, he gave it a try.

But each time they turned off, they only ended up in cramped, crowded dead ends, where they had to struggle to turn about. And though their Esurhite uniforms protected them from heckling, still Abramm saw the resentment in the eyes of those around them. He'd seen it on the road outside the city and even before then as they'd traveled through a land stripped of its resources. With the men gone, there'd been no one to work the fields, so most stood fallow. Veiled, empty-eyed women, stick-legged children, and skinny old men were the only inhabitants, along with a few skeletal goats. The rare storage barns that held anything at all were usually in the process of being emptied by a troop of black-tunicked soldiers who packed the last bushels of corn, beans, or tubers onto their carts and drove away.

If it was this bad in Andol, he could imagine how bad it must be in Esurh.

When they were forced to return to the main thoroughfare for the third time, Abramm abandoned his first plan and went to his second: He'd head for the amphitheater and see if anyone was interested in purchasing some slaves for cheap. This plan was far less thought-out than the first had been, in part because he had to know where he was going and have some potential for contacts, and he had neither. The "plan" amounted to little more than going in the general direction of the amphitheater and hoping something useful turned up.

They proceeded along what he hoped was the main road, though as narrow, winding, and crowded as it was, he couldn't be sure. It didn't help that the thick mist overhanging the buildings had confused whatever sense of direction he'd had when they'd entered, so he could do little more than let the tide of people carry him and his companions along.

Having experienced Eidon's providence time and time again, however, he was not surprised when that tide bore them up a hilly street and into the plaza that surrounded the city's gaming amphitheater. A medium-sized venue, its outer walls bore the scallops and engravings typical of Andolen architecture. From the lights in its gateways and the windows at plaza level, he guessed the warrens were open for viewing but saw little point in going over there. The plaza itself was more packed than the street, with people camped out to get good seats for tomorrow's Games, and he'd not likely find a buyer there anyway. Better to look in some sort of eating or drinking house . . .

As he looked back toward one he remembered passing, his eye caught on a face in the crowd—a man who seemed to have been staring at him but turned away the moment Abramm's gaze fixed upon him. Though Abramm had only a glimpse, familiarity rocked him: The dark, hatchet profile, the crescent cheekbone scar, and a flash of gold honor rings reminded him sharply of his old friend Katahn.

Already off his horse in pursuit, Abramm pushed aggressively through the crowd, even as rationality argued against his impulsive conclusion. Why would Katahn be *here*, of all places?

It took only seconds to lose the man in the crowd, even with Abramm's height advantage. As his excitement ebbed, he had to admit he'd not seen enough of the man to know more than that he was Esurhite and wore a rank of honor rings—which Katahn had not worn for years. And how often of late had he seen familiar faces only to have them turn out to belong to strangers?

Sighing, he glanced again at the brightly lit teahouse on the corner, then returned to his men. Giving Borlain command of the troop, he left Newbanner's reins with Cedric and headed back for the teahouse.

It was a larger establishment than it appeared from the outside, but it was about to burst with its clientele that night, which were mostly civilians, gamers—as he'd hoped—and their people. The tea's strong, spicy scent filled the air, overlying the aroma of meat and curry—and beneath it all, the faint, acrid odor of fermikia, illegal under Esurhite rule. The house was furnished with the usual pillows and low tables preferred by the southlanders, scattered throughout a honeycomb of dark, smoky spaces marked out by draperies, wooden screens, and beaded curtains. Several larger spaces were positioned amidst them, with communal tables and pillows arranged for those who sought company as they ate and drank.

Taking a seat on one of the nearest open pillows, Abramm deliberately put himself in a conspicuous spot. Even if Katahn didn't come into the teahouse, Abramm would be able to gather much information in a short time at the communal table. In fact, he'd made it a practice in each town they passed through to seek out the place of local gossip and linger, nursing his tea and eavesdropping on the conversations around him.

Now, as he settled onto the pillow and took off his helmet, he saw the dark eyes of the men around him flick toward him in surprise, saw them note his blond hair, the scars on his face, and the width of his shoulders. Several sized him up and made their way over to speak to him. At first he feared they had recognized him. But it wasn't long into the conversation before he learned they only regarded him as one of many who'd taken on the guise of the avenging King Abramm, returned from the dead to take back his regalia from the thief, Leyton. It was a coveted role for which likely candidates had to compete and be willing, if they won, to have their faces sliced in imitation of the man they pretended to be. In fact, there were a series of qualifying matches that had been played out before Leyton even arrived. The winner had already been determined and ritually cut at the end of his match—and would face the Chesedhan king tomorrow.

Since Abramm had toyed with the notion of entering the arena as a competitor himself, that news effectively ended such speculation. Besides, as one man told him, he wasn't even scarred on the correct side. Everyone knew the Pretender's scars were on the right side of his face not the left, so they'd have refused him outright.

A serving man brought him hot, syrupy, very spicy tea in a small, thick glass cup and, taking his coin, hurried away. Abramm nursed it slowly—the only way he could drink the potent stuff even after weeks of trying—and listened to the men on his right argue over whether it would really be Leyton Donavan who appeared tomorrow or a substitute, and then whether it was fair to pit Leyton, middle-aged as he was, against the younger contenders, especially since Abramm, had he lived, would be older, too.

"Aye, but come back from the dead, Abramm would be young again," another countered, and they fell to arguing the increasingly esoteric points of a mortal fighting an immortal. Abramm's interest waned, then fastened with sudden intensity on the utterance of a single name in the conversation unfolding on his left side: Madeleine.

The Pretender's woman and queen of Chesedh had remarried, they said, yoking herself to a powerful Sorite lord who could give her troops and galleys for the protection of her land. The new alliance was received with open chagrin and much worried speculation about how much longer the war would last because of it. As the conversation drifted to the Sorite himself, Abramm found himself increasingly agitated. The first time he'd heard this rumor he'd laughed it off as absurd. But when in every town it was repeated, built up, and embroidered upon, he was finding it less and less easy to dismiss. With all the furor surrounding Leyton's arrival, he'd hardly expected to find anyone talking of Maddie, yet here they were. And after what he'd seen today— Kiriathan soldiers marching out of the temple and into Horon-Pel under the banner of the Black Moon, literally under his nose—it was obvious Chesedh needed an ally. And if it was considered the duty of the First Daughter to make alliances for her people, as he knew it was, how much more would it be considered the duty of a widowed queen?

Movement in the shadows on the far side of the room drew Abramm's eye to a tall man in a white tunic sashed with gold, standing in the shadow of a long hallway. He had the shaved head and long braided topknot of a Sorite warrior, with the gold-scaled cheekbones of a high-ranking noble, and as Abramm looked at him, the other's gaze snared his own. Dark, long-lashed eyes, exotically shaped, and seemingly bottomless above the scaling, held him riveted with familiarity. Then the stranger smiled and a chill rippled up Abramm's back.

Just then a party of revelers came trooping across the main room toward the hallway, swallowing up the Sorite. When they had moved into the shadowed corridor, he was gone, but the image of his face remained. It was the man from Abramm's dream in Caerna'tha. The one where the dragon had come to visit.

Sudden fear clenched his stomach and dried his mouth.

"I will take it all from you. . . ."

Moroq was here. Now. Had been waiting for him, and wanted him to know it. . . .

"So, you look like you've been in a few Games yourself, friend," a voice said at his shoulder, startling him so badly he jumped.

Looking around, he found a short, heavyset Esurhite settling onto the pillow beside him.

"Aye." He hardly knew what he was saying. Terror still clouded his mind, along with images of the throne room and the great pillar in the Hall of Records. Moroq could do nothing Eidon did not allow. But Eidon had given him free rein.

"Do your worst, then. . . ."

The man nodded, eyeing Abramm's hair and scars. He said something that seemed to require a response, but Abramm had no idea what it was. Desperately he wrenched his thoughts back to the here and now. "I'm sorry?"

"I said, your face is scarred on the wrong side. The Pretender's scars were on the right."

"Oh. Aye . . ." Abramm grimaced. If Eidon had allowed Moroq free rein, it meant Abramm could handle whatever came. *"His reward will only be greater for it. . . ."* It would all be for the best. He had only to trust. And after all he had seen, all he had been through, how could he not?

The panic subsided and his rattled thoughts ordered themselves again. As he finally truly focused on the man at his side he realized the other had sought him out. But had Katahn sent him? Or Moroq?

"I'm looking for a Gamer, actually," Abramm said, plunging onward. "I've slaves to sell tonight."

The man lifted his thick glass in long, swarthy fingers and sipped his syrupy tea. "I have a friend who might be interested. He doesn't buy from just anyone, though."

Abramm snorted. "I'm sure your friend has already seen me and what I have to offer, or you'd not be here."

The man smiled, sipped again, then set down his tea glass and said, "Come with me."

He led Abramm from the common room into the same hallway where Moroq had disappeared, then along a series of narrow, plaster-walled corridors. They passed numerous closed carved-wood doors from which the fermikia smoke clouded so thickly it made him dizzy just walking through it.

Finally they crossed a quiet courtyard, descended a short span of steps, and the man pushed open a heavy door to lead him into a large, dark chamber that smelled like the stable. A tin lantern with a spiraling top hung from a rafter in the middle of the room, the light of its kelistar turning the chamber into a puzzle of pooled shadow and dim light. In the corner, horses shifted and snorted, and all around him he sensed men watching him.

His guide abandoned him there, stepping back through the door and closing it behind him. Abramm waited, knowing he was being scrutinized. Was the shaven-headed Sorite out there somewhere, drawing that long black bow of his as he prepared to put an arrow into Abramm's heart?

"So you've come looking to sell some slaves, have you?" said a voice from the shadows beyond the lantern.

"I have," said Abramm, turning toward the speaker and hoping his start of surprise hadn't been noticeable.

For another long moment they all stood there, Abramm in the lantern light, the unseen others breathing softly around him. Then a man stepped from the shadow into the light—short, broad shouldered, that familiar hatchet face now adorned by a gray goatee, which matched the hair in the warrior's knot on his nape. He wore a dark tunic, a rank of combat honor rings in the margin of his left ear, and a broad grin on his swarthy face.

"Khrell's fire!" Katahn ul Manus cried as he came forward to catch Abramm in a rough embrace. "Will you *never* stay dead?"

Abramm laughed as they stepped apart. "I *thought* it was you I saw in the street."

"No one was more surprised than I," Katahn countered. "What were a pack of Esurhites doing up here this early in the night? I thought. And with a cart of slaves, no less. Then something caught my eye. There's no missing the way you move, old friend. Even if you are supposed to be dead." He paused, then shook his head. "What *are* you doing here?"

"That is a very long and complicated story. I am more interested in why *you* are here. Though I have my suspicions."

Katahn's eyes narrowed. "You were the one who destroyed the temple at Aggosim, weren't you?"

Abramm cocked a brow at him. "Why would you guess that? Aggosim is hundreds of leagues away."

"Aye, and it's been four months since it happened. Rumor said the Pretender had come back from the dead through its temple corridor, destroying it in the process. The blast went through the links to Oropos and Xorofin, destroying those as well and triggering earthquakes in all three places. I have to admit the stories perplexed me. I knew you were dead, but who else could do such things? I thought maybe it was Meridon." He shook his head again. "It really was you."

"Actually, Eidon did it. I just went along for the ride."

"Eidon seems to take you on quite a few rides," Katahn said dryly. He shook his head. "Destiny swirls around you still, my friend."

Before they went any farther, Abramm asked if they might bring in the men he'd left outside before some of the locals decided to make trouble. Soon, all seventeen of them had been brought into the stable, the street gates closed securely behind them. It turned out Katahn had come to Horon-Pel as leader of the group Maddie had sent to rescue her brother, and when Borlain and his Chesedhan countrymen met those who'd come with Katahn, a second reunion ensued.

Eventually, though, they all settled down, and Katahn was ready to plot. As the others scattered about the stable, taking seats on barrels, boxes, and kegs, he told Abramm that the man who would fight tomorrow was indeed Leyton Donavan. "I've seen him with my own eyes. And Belthre'gar is here, as well." He flashed Abramm a sharp look at that point. "Though you don't seem very surprised."

Abramm smiled. "I would never have come to Horon-Pel if it had been up to me. My plan was to head north from the pass to Zereda on the strait. But the earthquake closed the pass, and the only other road led here. Eidon would not have brought me to this place on practically the same day Leyton is supposed to appear if it weren't really him."

"Or at least," Katahn added with cocked brow, "if it weren't really your regalia he's got. He has two of the pieces that we know of. The scepter and the crown. They paraded him around this afternoon. Of course, both could be fakes."

Abramm said nothing to that, and after a moment Katahn went on outlining his plan. He'd brought along a man from Chesedh to play the part of Abramm and had entered him into the qualifying rounds for that position last week. The man had fought his way through all the rounds, winning at last the right to have his face cut in imitation of Abramm's scars. Only to have one of the minor cuts he'd sustained in a previous match suddenly suppurate so aggressively that twenty-four hours later he was weak and thrashing with fever, unable even to stand, let alone fight.

"We've been praying he'd recover and are trying every treatment we can think of," Katahn said, "but nothing's helped. This afternoon I told my friend, the one you met in the teahouse, to be on the lookout for anyone newly arrived who might have slaves to sell, but I didn't really expect he'd find anyone." He paused and shook his head. "And now here you are."

"Aye. Here I am."

"Perfect in every regard." Katahn grinned. "Except for your scars being on the wrong side of your face."

And at that they both laughed.

"Wait a minute," Borlain said now, looking from one to the other. "You're thinking of Abramm taking your champion's place?"

Katahn still had his eye on Abramm. "I don't know. Are you ready to get back into the ring, then, Pretender? Think you still have all the old moves?"

"You know I don't, old fox," Abramm said with a chuckle, lifting the arm the morwhol had maimed.

At that point Rolland could no longer contain his horror. "Sire, you cannot be serious!"

"Do you see anyone else here more suited to play me than me?"

"Let me go, sir. I'm the right size and have the right coloring!"

"Rollie, we'd have to cut your face."

"I know that." Though his voice trembled, Rolland stood firm. "I am more than willing to suffer what you already have if it will keep you out of there."

Abramm stared at him, moved to muteness by the man's offer.

Katahn snorted. "So, then, you think you could do better in the ring than the White Pretender, Large One?"

Rolland's eyes widened as he turned to the Esurhite.

"Even at half what he was," said Katahn, "he is still a formidable foe."

"That he is," Borlain offered grimly.

"Not that it matters," Abramm intruded. "Since I'm not expecting to fight him anyway. What I'll bring is shock. When Belthre'gar sees me out there, he'll burst a blood vessel, most likely. Start yelling to have me killed or seized, especially if either of the regalia are real. In their panic and haste, they'll open the gates themselves for the rest of you to come in."

"Don't think Leyton won't fight you," Katahn warned. "He won't have a choice. And last time you faced him, remember—"

"He beat me. Aye. But with you all rushing in to rescue us, surely he'll be distracted enough I can elude defeat this time."

"So it's true, then, sir?" Galen asked out of the blue, staring at him. "You really *were* a slave in these Games? Really were sold off to them by your own brother?"

"I was sold by a man who shares my parentage," Abramm replied grimly. "I have a hard time thinking of him as my brother anymore. Especially after what we saw today."

He spoke of the temple outside Horon-Pel, where today they'd been forced to wait on the road while troops of Sorites, Irianni, and Kiriathans had marched through its gates and onto the road before them. Five score of his countrymen marched by wearing tabards marked with a flame-and-crown device he'd not recognized. If he'd not seen it with his own eyes, he'd never have believed it. When Rolland had yelled to them from the slave cart, asking whom they marched under, the answer was "Makepeace! Long may he reign."

The words had nearly knocked Abramm off his horse.

"They say he's gone mad," Katahn said now, speaking of Gillard. "Obsessed with you. Even cut his own face to look like you."

"Surely that's just a crazy tale."

"I don't think so, my friend. He serves the Bright Ones now. And they are obsessed with you, as well. Do you know how many men bear the same scars as you do? How many men they've sent, pretending to be you?"

Bright Ones . . . He'd forgotten that was one of the Esurhite names for rhu'ema. Bright Ones . . . Shining Ones . . . the Ban'astori . . .

"See?" Galen said quietly to his uncle Oakes. "He really is King Abramm."

Trinley only scowled at the straw-covered floor and said nothing.

Not long after that they got around to planning out the details of the rescue operation. Katahn and his men had already scouted the narrow runs of the city as they extended from the amphitheater's ring-shaped plaza. In addition, just as in the Val'Orda, Horon-Pel's amphitheater had the underground works associated with the arena productions—the elevators, the drainage tubes, the chutes through which the animals were driven. Besides that, it turned out that many of the people who lived in the city had long made their livelihood raiding the nearby tombs of their distant ancestors, and there was a veritable network of underground passages beneath their simple dwellings. Katahn knew of several in particular that he could use.

They would go early tomorrow morning, as Katahn had already arranged: himself, Abramm, well cloaked, and a handful of men to serve as his guards and handlers. Once checked in and approved—as early as possible to avoid the potential of running into someone who might recognize either of them— Abramm and his handlers would be left in a holding cell to await the contest. Meanwhile the others would be infiltrating from the tunnels, garbed in Esurhite black. . . .

It was late when they finally finished outlining all the specifics, memorizing maps and parceling out positions and assignments. As the others settled down to sleep there in the stable, Katahn took Abramm to the spacious chamber he was renting from the teahouse proprietor. There, over small glasses of tea mellowed with the brandylike Andolen *saria*, they indulged in some private conversation, and it wasn't long before Abramm found himself asking about the rumors of Maddie remarrying.

A frown creased the old Gamer's brow as he looked at his glass and shrugged it off as "only a rumor."

"Katahn . . ."

The Esurhite drew and released a quick breath. "I know nothing for certain, for I've not been to Peregris since she sent us off. I can say the man was courting her at that time, but she was holding out for your return. Admittedly, she was alone in that belief and her courtiers and advisors were pressing her hard to accept him. He had them all charmed—handsome, smart, rich, completely devoted to her."

Something in Abramm's chest seized up as Katahn said these things, forming a hard, painful knot.

"It wasn't until we got here that we heard she'd accepted his suit," Katahn finished.

"A man tonight said she'd already married him."

Katahn sighed. Sipped from his tea glass. "You know how these things are, Abramm. This far away, behind enemy lines . . . the truth could be anything. For all we know Maddie put out the tale to buy herself time. The wave decimated the Chesedhan navy and the breastwork on the river, you know. And you must have noticed how nervous it makes the Esurhites to think of Tirus ul Sadek joining the Chesedhans."

"Yes. I noticed . . . and that's another thing. Why do they know of him—and fear him so—when I've never heard of him?"

Katahn smiled grimly. "Oh, the House of the Dragon is well known in Esurh, for our dealings with it go way back. . . ."

He spoke on, but Abramm heard not a word, his attention riveted on that single word: *dragon*. The knot in his chest hardened into stone, squeezing the air from his lungs as the room spun. He'd readied himself to hear of his wife's death and abide it. He was not at all ready to hear of her life with another man. Let alone one said to be of the house of the dragon.

Surely it couldn't be Moroq she had married! He swayed in the chair and pressed his forearms hard against the table, sweat popping out upon his flesh. No. She would know better. She was too smart, too strong in the Light. . . .

"Abramm . . ." Katahn's hand tightened on his forearm, drawing his attention. His dark eyes were crinkled with worry. "Don't trouble yourself over what might not even be true. You have more than enough to think about right now."

But as Abramm stared at him, all he saw was the white blaze of the throne room, the beautiful, vicious voice of his worst and truest enemy echoing in his head: *"I will take it all. . . ."*

32

Carissa Kalladorne Meridon, Duchess of Northille and wife to the man who was Special Counsel to the Queen, stood at the bay window of the spacious apartments she shared with her husband and gazed across the promenade of palms cutting through the waterpark at Fannath Rill. She had weaned Conal almost four months ago now—though he'd nearly weaned himself by then—so there were no more morning nursing sessions. It was hard to believe he was almost two years old. And that it had been that long since Abramm's death.

And here come the tears again. . . . She frowned and wiped them from her lashes, annoyed with herself for being so weepy. This was to be a day of rejoicing, and here she was with one of her horrible moods again.

Though the dawn had earlier turned the ceiling of cloud to blood—it was what had roused her from her bed—that had faded, leaving the flat gray overcast that had obscured the sky for months. Below, scurrying like ants along the promenade, workers swept, pruned, carted in potted orange trees, and set up brightly colored pavilions and flags and garlands of fresh spring flowers for the wedding celebration to come. Today Queen Madeleine of Chesedh was to wed Draek Tiris ul Sadek of Soria, and Tiris had promised the party would last for days. Already the smell of roasting meat filled the palace.

No need to worry about the Esurhites interrupting the ceremony. One hundred of Tiris's galleys stood at anchor in the Peregris harbor, and a hundred thousand of his armed soldiers were garrisoned along Chesedh's southern shores, guarding the strait. No need to worry about rain ruining the festivities, either, for the rainy season had ended early this year. There'd been not a drizzle for at least six weeks. The wedding should go off without a hitch.

All those in power were ecstatic. Ever since Tiris had arrived last month to make his final preparations, he'd been feted by every noble house in Chesedh, one after the other. Thanked for his provision and welcomed to the realm.

They were saved, and it was his doing. Chesedh was gaining a new king, Maddie's children would have a new father, and Maddie herself, after nearly two years of mourning, was finally moving on to a new relationship. Tiris seemed the perfect replacement.

So why is there such heaviness in my heart? Carissa asked of Eidon. *Why do I feel I'm attending a funeral instead of a wedding?*

She heard the door open and close behind her, the clink of the cups jiggling on their saucers as the familiar footsteps approached, sounds she'd been awaiting. Her pulse fluttered, and already her skin tingled at the anticipation of his touch. She and her husband had reinstated their tradition of sharing cocoa the morning after they'd been truly married that afternoon in Peregris. Now each day Trap got up early for his sword practice, then picked up the cocoa from the kitchen on his way back to the apartment.

He set the tray on the table at her back and came to rest his hands on her shoulders as he buried his face in her hair, flowing long and loose down her back. He inhaled deeply. "Good morning, my lovely wife. I've missed you."

She giggled and leaned back against him. "All of two hours?"

"I cannot get enough of you. . . ." He moved the curtain of her hair aside and laid a whiskery kiss on her shoulder, just beyond the neckline of her dressing gown. Then he dropped his hands to her waist and slid them forward to cradle her womb, which soon would be showing the new life he had planted there. A deep and powerful emotion welled in her—contentment as she'd never known it, gratitude so strong it could bring her to her knees, and love. She had not thought it possible to fall more in love with this man than she'd already been, but she had. There was also a strong thread of guilt and piercing sadness. And now here came the tears again.

She wiped them away and pressed her lips together, chasing off the weeping spate before it could get started.

"The darkness is upon you again," he murmured. It was not a question.

She sighed. "The realm is saved. Maddie is moving on. I should be rejoicing." She tilted her head back against his shoulder, her forehead against his bearded jaw. "Instead I stand here hoping she doesn't go through with it.

Though I myself advised her to marry him, and I see what a good match he is for her . . . I just want to bury myself back into my bed and let this day pass without me. The prospect of standing on that stage and hearing her say marriage vows to anyone but Abramm—" Her voice broke, and this time she couldn't stop the tears.

He turned her gently toward him and wrapped his arms around her as she pressed her face to his chest in misery. And when the wave of weeping had passed, he said softly, "She held on to him for so long, believing so resolutely that he was out there somewhere, I think it kept a spark alive in us, too. Now she's come at last to accept the truth. He really is gone. He really isn't coming back. And we have to accept it just as she does."

He fell silent while she wept against his chest as she had not since they'd first left Kiriath. She'd been wrong about Tiris being a suitable replacement. No one would ever replace her brother.

When the storm had passed he eased back enough to cradle her face in his palms, his brown eyes full of warmth and sadness and infinite wisdom. "He is with Eidon now. But we go on, my beautiful wife." He kissed her gently. Then again, not so gently, and as sorrow slowly transformed into a different kind of passion, they returned to their bedchamber to comfort each other as only they could do.

Later, as they lay side by side in utter contentment, the bright morning sun pouring through the veils of silk that draped their canopied bed, she marveled at the change he was able to work in her moods. She still felt the grief at losing Abramm, but it was lighter now, softer. An old grief, really, being superseded, day by day, with the wonders of the new life Eidon had given her. She turned her head to look at her husband, stretched out beside her, and smiled at him. "I still can't get over how I thought for all those months that you didn't care, and now . . ."

He turned toward her and pushed up onto one elbow as he reached out to toy with the heavy lock of golden hair trailing across her shoulder. "I told you," he said, bringing the lock of hair up to his nose and lips, "it'll be a long time before I get my fill of you. Probably take all of my life."

"But I am morose. Melancholic. The woman full of blackness, as they say."

He nodded soberly, though his eyes twinkled. "Yes. You are."

"How can you stand it?"

"I see around it. I know it is your curse. But the Light can overcome it. I've seen that, as well."

"And now it is your curse."

"I knew what I was getting into."

"Did you, truly?"

"No." He sobered then, dropping her hair to trail his fingers softly along the side of her face, and over to her lips. "It's been far more wonderful than I ever imagined."

She shook her head and laid a hand to the side of his face, tears of gratitude pricking her eyes. "I swear, Trap Meridon, you are the living proof of Eidon's grace! How you can say such things, after all I—wait!" She giggled and captured his hand, which had wandered downward from her face. "We can't . . . we'll be late as it is."

"Mmm." He rocked away from her, then flopped onto his back. "I'd rather stay here."

But they were part of the wedding party and could not stay. Even so, they lay there, staring at the ceiling. After a time his hand crept over to take hold of hers.

The thought came to her out of the blue: "He told her she was attending Terstmeet too much," she said. "Did you know that?"

A stillness came over the bed. "Tiris said that?" he asked quietly.

"He said her first duty was to attend the Kirikhal, where the people could be comforted and strengthened by her presence. That the Terstmeets were an unnecessary drain on her time and resources."

"What did she say to that?"

"That she didn't consider them unnecessary, nor a drain."

"And he said no more about it?"

"I guess not."

He was silent for a long time. Finally she asked, "So what are you thinking now?"

"That I wish we didn't have a hundred thousand Sorite soldiers on our soil, and one hundred of their galleys in the Peregris harbor. . . ."

———

Abramm heard the Taleteller's booming voice resound through the heavy doors separating his cell from the arena outside. At the crowd's answering roar, he stood up, adjusting the dark ankle-length cloak that hid his costume—provided once again by Katahn—and checked the draw of his rapier from its scabbard, glad the moment of action was finally upon him.

The past eight hours had been horrendous. He'd spent a sleepless night on the couch Katahn had provided him in the villa, tossing and turning as the horrible images of Maddie married to Moroq himself assailed him. He knew it couldn't be true, but the doubts had grown too thick and thorny to be ignored, or pushed free of. They tormented him all night, and on into the day after they'd come to the arena and he'd been left here alone to await his contest.

For a while he'd run through the old sword forms, so ingrained he'd never forget them, so demanding of mental discipline, he could not think of anything else while he performed them. . . . But when he finished, the evil thoughts came rushing back. Finally, just as when he'd walked the dragon gauntlet, he was reduced to repeating passages from the Words of Revelation, memorized in his youth. The only difference now was that he wasn't moving. Which made it harder.

But finally, at last, the waiting was over. He gave thanks he wasn't facing a real match, though, for he felt as tired as if he'd already fought ten of them, and about as mentally unfocused as he'd ever been in his life. He could only cast it all on Eidon and go forward. Again.

The Taleteller's voice boomed once more, and he recognized his name, the Kiriathan form of it twisted and warped by the Tahg accent, the Esurhite moniker clear and compelling: *"Rashawin!"* The Pretender.

The gate rumbled back on its track, generating another spate of memories, just as his initial entrance into the warrens had done hours ago. The sound alone triggered the wild rush of adrenaline he had so often known in these contests. Waiting for his next cue, he stood on the threshold, still out of the lights, and gazed about the arena, its multitude of faces steeped in darkness. To his right, Belthre'gar sat in his red ringside box, talking with one of his attendants, his disinterest obvious. And rightly so, Abramm supposed. The Supreme Commander had no doubt seen this contest many times.

Abramm turned his gaze to the arena itself, its sandy floor mostly hidden beneath the bright image of a northern palace's throne room—the gleaming stretch of marble floor, the gilded walls, the blazing chandelier, the tall golden throne atop its dais on the far side. Leyton stood at its foot—alone, dressed in kingly finery, the sword in his hand. He didn't appear to have the scepter, but the moment Abramm saw the wreath of plaited metal on his brow, he knew it was his crown.

And that surprised him, for he'd not thought they'd let Leyton fight with the real thing. Then again, why not, if they believed the man it belonged to— the only one who could really use it—was dead?

The Taleteller came to the end of his introduction and presented Leyton,

King of Chesedh, keeper of the Kiriathan crown by reason of his superior skill at the sword, and challenged anew by the man who'd lost them to him, King Abramm of Kiriath, returned from the grave to win them back. The audience did not roar as it had in the heyday of the Pretender, but at least a good percentage of it cheered.

He drew a deep breath to calm the wild energy surging through him, pulled his sword from its sheath, and stepped from the metal-and-wood track onto the soft sand advancing upon his opponent. As he walked, he untied the dark cloak and pulled it off with his left hand, revealing the white of his garments underneath, exactly as the ringmaster had instructed. The crowd remained distracted and indifferent—

Until he stepped upon the illusory marble floor and all of it—floor, walls, throne, chandelier—vanished in an eyeblink. Suddenly silence filled the arena as every eye fixed upon the two men within it. Leyton, who had jumped the moment the tile turned to sand beneath his boots, now looked up at Abramm, frowning. Abramm hadn't expected that to happen, either, but he advanced without missing a beat, his sword glimmering with just a bit more light than was natural. Abruptly Leyton's frown gave way to wide-eyed astonishment, his mouth falling open, the tip of his sword dropping to the sand.

And then, over in the stands, Belthre'gar erupted in outraged alarm, as Abramm had predicted, leaping and gesticulating wildly. "Who let *him* in here?" he shouted. "Why wasn't I informed! It's the Pretender, you fools!" The man beside him must have said something, for a moment of silence ensued before the Supreme Commander bellowed, "Of course it's the real one! You think I wouldn't know? Kill him! Kill him *now*!"

A bolt of purple fire flashed out of the stands and crashed into Abramm's shoulder, the Light in him flaring toward it as instinctively as if he'd parried an incoming sword thrust. He had no idea how he did it, only that he did. The need was there, and somehow it was met. And he wasn't going to worry about it anymore.

It happened several more times, always with the same result, until the purple bolts switched targets, converging on the ground at Leyton's feet and tumbling him backward in a fountain of sand. The next bolt landed behind him, sending him skittering forward for the sword he'd dropped.

Desperate to live, he seized the blade and leaped up as Abramm reached him, his eyes betraying his certainty that Abramm meant to kill him as surely as his Esurhite masters did.

But instead of striking, Abramm cried, "I'm here to rescue you, Leyton. Don't fight me!"

Leyton either wasn't listening or didn't believe him. Abramm saw the decision to attack an instant before Leyton lunged at him, the movement strong but reckless, driven by fear and desperation. Abramm parried, and the man struck again, then came in with the dagger. Catching and entangling the short blade in his cloak, Abramm jerked it free of Leyton's hand and cast both across the sand. The Chesedhan lunged again; Abramm parried again, then drove the point of his own blade into the other man's exposed thigh, sliding it into the muscle alongside the kneecap.

Bright blood bloomed on his pale trousers, as Leyton staggered back with a gasp, then regrouped to strike again. And again, Abramm knocked the descending blade aside, yelling at Leyton to desist and wondering irritably why their rescuers hadn't yet entered the arena. A third lunge from the Chesedhan caught Abramm's sleeve and etched a cut along his forearm as another flurry of purple bolts rained around them. In dodging that, Leyton's injured knee suddenly buckled and he went down, turning as he did so to keep his front toward Abramm. A futile attempt to prolong the conflict, which Abramm ended decisively a moment later by driving the point of his rapier through the hilt of the other man's sword and flicking it out of his hand.

When Leyton looked up at him, Abramm was shocked to find tears streaking his face. "I'm sorry," he gasped, shaking his head. "I never should've taken it."

Abramm said nothing. Reaching forward, he lifted the crown one-handed from the other's head. Leyton didn't even try to stop him.

"I never dreamed you would have such need of it," Leyton continued, speaking of the scepter. "That things would end as they did."

"They haven't ended," Abramm said grimly.

Finally the doors in the arena wall nearest them trundled open and a group of armored men raced out. Abramm stepped again toward the fallen man. "Come on. We're going."

"What?"

Abramm clapped the crown onto his own head, then leaned forward to take Leyton's arm and drag him upright. As they turned, another purple bolt sizzled in, and the Light flared, shattering it into a cloud of purple droplets. The audience was roaring, Belthre'gar was still screaming and waving his arms, and now, lined up at the front of his box, a rank of soldiers raised their bows. Among them, his black longbow at full draw, arrow nocked and aimed at Abramm, stood the Sorite warrior. Moroq.

"You're too late, little man," the familiar voice whispered in his head.

The dark eyes drew him in, and the arena vanished. Maddie stood before him without seeing him, gowned in bridal white and crowned with flowers, her face aglow with love and excitement. The great Kirikhal in Fannath Rill eclipsed her, its arched entranceway decorated with white ribbons and white flowers, surrounded by a roaring crowd. A couple in white stood at the top of the steps, facing them. . . . And then the images shifted again, and he saw the dark-haired Sorite take Maddie into his arms and kiss her hungrily.

No!

The pain was monumental.

It's not true. . . . It can't be true!

Suddenly the arena enfolded him again as the Sorite warrior loosed his arrow. Surrounded by a well of perfect, preternatural silence, Abramm watched the arrow approach in slow motion, a sliver of night, fletched in Shadow. Saw it slam into his side and dissolve as it slid into his flesh, extending outward from the point of entry like a black-tentacled griiswurm. The headache was blinding, the nausea violent. The world spun as the spore raced through his veins, black and hot and more virulent than any he'd ever known. He'd touched it once before in Maddie, but that was third-hand and nothing like this. It residualized with startling speed, even as it spun the images through his mind—Maddie in her wedding dress, the dark-haired Sorite taking her into his arms. . . .

"It is true and now you have seen it for yourself, little man. I told you I would take everything."

Oh, Maddie . . . why didn't you wait?

The grief was suffocating. There were men all around him now, tugging at his arm, yelling things at him he could not hear.

Why didn't you wait. . . ? I was coming. . . .

He glimpsed Leyton kneeling in the sand, a red-fletched shaft protruding from his midsection, looking up at him with a puzzled expression. A dark-armored man bent over him, hauling him to his feet as a second arrow sprouted from his chest.

A purge . . . I have to do a purge. Leyton spun away as Abramm toppled. A huge man helmed and armored in black grabbed his arm before he fell, nearly pulling his arm from its socket. Then he was flipped over the giant's shoulder like a sack of grain as the Light finally took him.

33

Abramm did not regain consciousness until that evening, long after all the excitement was over. He awoke to find himself lying in the bunk of the captain's cabin in Katahn's galley ship, attended by Rolland. A kelistar rolled back and forth in its glassed holder on the desk. From the thump of the drum and the oars' corresponding squeak, drip, and splash, as well as the slight rhythmic forward surging of the ship, he judged they were at sea. The portholes were open wide, as was the ceiling hatch, but the room still reeked of vomit and something rotten.

He didn't feel too badly himself. His side ached, and he had a bit of a headache, but overall, considering what happened . . . He frowned as he realized he didn't recall what had happened. They'd entered the arena to rescue Leyton and something had gone wrong.

"Ah," Rolland said, sitting up stiffly. "Ye're awake at last! How d' ye feel? Would you like somethin' t' eat?"

Abramm shook his head and tried to rise onto his elbows, but Rolland pushed him down again.

"Not too fast, Sire. They shot ye with somethin' . . . some kinda spore. No one here's ever seen the like of it, including yer friend Katahn, but it made ye powerful sick."

"Spore . . . does that to me." He did feel very weak. "What happened? I remember going into the amphitheater. . . . Is Leyton here? Did we succeed?"

Rolland's crestfallen expression and the sudden averting of his eyes told the story without a word. "He died b'fore we could get him out of the arena. Five arrows stickin' out of his chest by then. I had ye and couldn't carry him, too. There were too many of them after us. We had to leave 'im." He glanced toward the desk. "We couldn't find the scepter, either."

"I don't think he had it," Abramm said, recalling bits and pieces of the event now as Rolland's words triggered his memories. The mention of arrows sticking out of Leyton's chest had sprung loose a host of them. That look on his face, his tears of remorse . . .

According to Rolland they'd escaped the amphitheater by following the underground passages all the way to the harbor, where they'd boarded the two galleys Katahn had brought and set off. The creative use of a fire ship set loose in the harbor produced a confusion of milling ships and dense smoke that effectively cut off any pursuit. Now they were heading up the coast toward where the Salmancan Sea met the Strait of Terreo at a place called the Neck. Rolland said Katahn thought it would take them a week or two, for they'd have to find places to go ashore periodically for water. And to rest the men.

"Why are we heading that way?" Abramm asked. "It'll be a worse nest of Esurhite galleys than what we've left."

"Katahn thinks they might've dumped the scepter there. He's heard a rumor, anyway. And he says the thing can float."

"At times. . . ." Abramm lay on his back, thinking through it all, feeling a profound regret that they'd not managed to bring Leyton out. There was more, too, something else that had gone wrong. *Something in my side?* "So our efforts have ended in failure all round, then," he murmured.

"We got yer crown back, sir." Rolland gestured again at the desk.

Now as Abramm again pressed up in the bed he saw the ring of plaited gold resting on a scarlet pillow beyond the kelistar lamp. And the moment he focused on it, a flood of memories overtook him—chief among them, Maddie in her wedding dress, wrapped in the Sorite lord's embrace. That's right— she'd married another man. Because he hadn't gotten back in time.

The wound in his side began to throb.

"Sir, are ye all right?" Rolland leaned toward him, looking alarmed. "Ye've turned all white."

Abramm supposed he should feel some terrible grief or pain or shock . . . something, anyway. In fact, he thought the first time those images had assailed him he had. Now he felt as if he were a shell of skin and nothing more. As if it couldn't matter less that the love of his life had married someone else. . . .

Maybe I'll just go back and kill him, he thought, rubbing absently at his side. The wound was tender to the touch, and it felt as if there was something in it. He looked round at Rolland. "Did the shaft break off? Is the arrowhead still inside me?"

Rolland gaped at him. "We saw no shaft, sir. It went right through you."

"No. I saw it go in. . . ."

"Maybe the spore is back. I can check, if ye—"

"No." Abramm lay back and stared at the planking overhead, still rubbing his side. "It's my wife, Rollie. She married the Sorite."

Rolland's chair squeaked as he sat back. "Sir, ye've known of that rumor for weeks—"

"It's no rumor. I've seen the truth for myself." The images, he realized now, had come upon him right after he'd taken the crown from Leyton and placed it on his own head. Just as when he'd been crowned, it had enabled him to see things from afar.

"Let me take it all. . . ."

Something strange was happening in his chest, as if all his organs were breaking down, liquefying into a mass of gelatin. The air had grown so thick and hot, he could hardly force it into his lungs, and the light in the cabin was growing brighter and brighter. Rolland sat there staring at him, the sorrow far too plain upon his face.

Abramm looked away and wondered how his hands could shake as badly as they did while he felt nothing at all. He clenched them into fists and pressed them against the mattress to either side of him.

"Well," he said in a voice that showed not the slightest tremor, "I guess we don't need to go back to Chesedh, then. We'll just pick up the scepter and head on to Kiriath."

And to his everlasting mortification, he started to weep right there in front of his liegeman.

———

The next three days he spent in a cocoon of blithe indifference as they sailed northward along the coast, in tandem with their Chesedhan sister ship, disguised, as was Katahn's, to look like an Esurhite vessel. It was as if Abramm had lost nothing. He ate, drank, talked, and joked with the men, listened to their story of how they'd gotten him out of the arena, and expressed his gratitude for their loyalty and that all had survived and were with him now. All except Oakes Trinley, that is. He, Galen admitted uncomfortably, had not fallen in battle but had simply walked away when the opportunity arose. For some reason, that thought angered Abramm more than seemed reasonable, especially since the rest of the men counted Trinley an implacable troublemaker they were glad to be rid of. Still it irked him, for it was foolish and ignorant. How could the man be so stubborn and blind? Every time the subject came up, it set him off again, and it frustrated him further that no one seemed to understand why it did.

Then Katahn came to him one afternoon as he leaned against the gunwale watching the sea and asked if he had any idea of useful landmarks that might aid their search for the scepter. Suddenly Abramm was unable to speak, beset with a pain so physically intense he thought he would die on the spot.

How could she have married someone else?!

Rationality supplied all the reasons: She had no reason to believe Abramm was still alive, she had children who needed a father, and a country that would not survive without outside help. She'd had no choice. He had taken too long.

But it still felt like the worst kind of betrayal, and not just one but two. For Eidon had kept him away long enough for it to happen—that hurt above all else. He was vaguely aware of Katahn leaving him to himself, his question unanswered, but Abramm didn't care. All the days he'd spent blocking this matter from his mind and heart seemed to give it a particularly vicious intensity now that it had finally gained his attention.

After all he had done, all he had gone through, all the ways he'd trusted . . . It wasn't fair. It wasn't right. Maybe Lema told the truth after all. . . .

Bitterness simmered and frothed in his belly, and he began to think he understood just how Trinley felt: It wasn't Abramm he'd hated so much; it was Eidon. . . .

I trusted you! Gave up everything for you! And this is how you repay me? You know how much she meant to me! If you wanted to take her into eternity, you know I'd never have begrudged that. But to let him *have her?! How could you do that to me?*

His hands gripped the gunwale as anger burned up in him, the pain sharp and throbbing in his side. Suddenly something snapped and he decided he couldn't bear it any longer. Who was he fooling? All those dreams of the kingdom restored to him? They were naught but empty promises. He'd no doubt been hallucinating in the dragon city, and nothing more.

He was done, taken all he was going to take.

Shoving himself off the gunwale, he strode back to his cabin, flinging the door open so hard it rebounded off the wall and shut itself in his wake. Snatching the crown from its scarlet pillow, he stood clenching it with fingers gone white from the force of his hold. Finally he turned, jerked open the door again, and strode out onto the deck.

Rolland—never far away—saw him at once and started toward him.

Abramm flashed him a grin and held up the crown. "Might as well put it with the scepter, don't you think?"

The big man's jaw dropped. "What?!"

Before Abramm could get to the railing, Rolland sprang to stop him. "My lord, no!"

But Abramm swung the crown up hard, catching him on the chin with it and knocking him back into the gunwale, even as he loosed his fingers from the plaited metal on the follow-through. The circlet sailed out over the gray swells, plopped onto one, and sank, disappearing into the depths of the sea.

Rolland stared after it, stunned to immobility.

Abramm left him there and returned to the cabin, where he stayed for the remainder of the day, brooding and sulking.

He stayed in the cabin the next day, as well, eating nothing, saying nothing. After that, he came on deck to spend hours at the prow staring across the heaving gray seas beneath their cover of mist. Sometimes he would note a galley in the distance, a dark blot against the gray humps of the land, but never sounded the alarm. None of it mattered anymore. He cared about Kiriath no more than Chesedh. Both lands had turned him out, so why should he be concerned with them?

Maybe he'd have Katahn put in at Mareis and let the men off so they could all go home, and then he could take Abramm off to the Narrows. Or Thilos. Or the Western Isles.

Or maybe Abramm would get off at Mareis, too, and go kill Maddie's new husband. . . .

No, that was wild thinking. And it wouldn't do any good, anyway, because the damage was already done. By that simple decision she was lost to him. Forever. He didn't care about her, anyway.

But he still hurt an awful lot for someone who didn't care.

Sometimes he amused himself with the notion of finding someone else, maybe Marta. She'd been interested. But after a few moments the amusement left him and disgust took its place.

He suspected from time to time that not all these thoughts were his own. Despite several attempts at purging it, the thing in his side was growing. Not obviously, but he could feel it in some strange way, and often he was fevered and nauseated for no good reason. And the dark thoughts held a strange power to release him from his pain, even though they didn't really. It was just easier to be angry and bitter and nasty than it was to hurt. Easier to find fault and criticize. . . .

Rolland had the speaking stone and once tried to get him to listen to a Terstmeet message, but he refused and went to stand alone at the vessel's prow, where the waves blocked out the sound, until the message was done. After that, Rolland didn't ask him anymore.

As they approached the Neck between the Strait of Terreo and the Salmancan Sea, the number of Esurhite galleys around them increased dramatically. Soon it became apparent some major operation was under way. Clearly they continued to be regarded by the vessels around them as just one more in the great armada heading north. It wasn't until they turned into the western end of the Neck toward Mareis that they realized a good number of the Esurhites were heading that way, too.

It didn't take Abramm long to figure out that if they intended to launch a double-pronged attack upon Peregris—or Fannath Rill, for that matter— Mareis would be the appropriate point of debarkation. He took a sort of bitter pleasure in wondering where all the great Sorite galleys were that were supposed to be protecting the realm . . . but never got beyond his bitterness to explore possible reasons for their absence. And when his suspicions were borne out about Mareis being a point of debarkation for their enemies, he decided not to go there, after all.

"In fact," he told his men, assembled before him one day on the deck, "I've decided to go down through the Narrows and on to the Western Isles."

The three men who stood with him on the quarterdeck exchanged startled glances. Then Katahn said, "You're just going to abandon these poor people?"

"How can I abandon them? I'm dead. Besides, they have their Sorites to help them. As for Kiriath, they can stew in what they've wrought for themselves. I've never been to the Western Isles."

Rolland stared at him as if he'd acquired three heads. "You can't just throw your destiny to the winds like this, sir!"

"And what is my destiny, Rolland? More than that, can a dead man even *have* a destiny? I just want to live my life somewhere where I'm no one. Where the biggest decisions I have to make are when to move the sheep to a new pasture or what crops to plant in the fields." *And I never have to think of her again. . . .*

"And you think you'll find that at the-Western Isles?" asked Katahn.

"Maybe."

They fell silent.

Then Rolland said, "What is wrong with you, sir? You are not at all your-self these days."

"Well, you might not be yourself, either, Rollie, if you return home to find that Daesi has married someone else."

"I would be upset, yes, but not like this. This is something else. And you haven't been eating, either. . . . How is that arrow wound in your side? Is it healing?"

"Not that it's any of your business, but yes, it's healing." A blatant lie. How easy it had been to tell it, too. That was not like him, either, but he didn't need Rolland nosing around in all that. And what could Rolland do about it, anyway? Abramm had tried to purge it many times, without success.

"We'll go through the Narrows," he said. "Unless, of course, you want to rush back to Chesedh and see if you can all kill yourselves there."

"We have sworn our lives to you, sir. We will go with you."

Abramm stared at them all, wanting to lash out at them so that he could make them all go away. Except he knew it wouldn't work. Which made him angrier than ever. So he went back to his cabin and sat there alone for most of the night, rubbing at the pain in his side.

———————

Two months after she was supposed to have married Tiris ul Sadek, Queen Madeleine and her retainers arrived late one night at the palace in Fannath Rill, having fled the royal residence in Peregris just as Esurhite battering rams were crashing through its front gates. Now, after twenty-four hours straight in the saddle, they were safe, but exhausted—and still in a communal state of shock. No one spoke as the guards escorted the queen and her ladies to the royal apartments, where she dismissed them and sent Marta off to her own quarters, as well. She let Jeyanne take her smoke-impregnated travel cloak and gloves but waved aside any further ministrations and strolled to the great, multi-paneled window in her receiving chamber.

The eastern sectors of Fannath Rill sprawled before her, the dark lines of roofs and walls and trees limned by the twinkle of the kelistar streetlamps.

Most of its citizens were asleep at this hour, and it was quiet, peaceful, and safe. But for how long?

Tired as she was, she was too agitated to even consider sleeping. And too sore. Her back, legs, and seat ached from having spent nearly all that time in the saddle—no comfortable coach for her. Even if they could have found one there at the end, it wouldn't have been fast enough.

Peregris has fallen! It seemed impossible to believe. And yet the images of the city's burning docks and houses had been seared upon her memory, the flames leaping out the windows of the royal residence, smoke billowing skyward. It still clung to her clothes and hair, reminding her with every breath she took of the price she'd paid for refusing to marry Tiris ul Sadek.

The only thing that kept her sane was the absolute certainty it would have been worse had she not, and last week's betrayal had shown her that beyond all doubt.

The very night before the wedding, she'd called him to her quarters and told him she wouldn't marry him, despite her promise, despite the humiliation he would endure, despite the shock and anger she knew her decision would provoke amongst her own people. She'd trembled as she'd told him, fearing his reaction, but he'd received her decision with his customary poise.

He'd nodded, smiled ruefully, and confessed he'd suspected she might back out on him. Then he'd given her a gentle warning: *"You've thrown your lot with Abramm, then. I hope for your sake he really is out there and will return in time to save you. . . ."* With that he had taken his leave. In the morning, he was gone, his villa abandoned. But in the harbor at Peregris, twenty galley ships had remained to help defend the realm from the coming Esurhite plague—a gift of parting and affection, he'd claimed.

It was a gift that had filled her with terrible anguish and second thoughts at the time, making her doubt her own sanity more than ever.

Not long after that, the Esurhites had sent in their emissaries, and when she'd refused to receive them, they had launched their first attack on Peregris. For two months the Chesedhan navy had resisted them, helped immeasurably by Tiris's galley ships. The skill, bravery, and tactical experience of their crews had made them the foundation of the Chesedhan commanders' defensive strategy. But then, just when they were most needed, as the Esurhites prepared to launch their biggest assault yet, the galleys disappeared in the night without a word. Their former allies were left unprepared, out of position, and devastatingly vulnerable. Chesedh lost more than half her fleet the next morning.

Six days later the enemy's battering ram had stove in gates at the royal residence in Peregris, even as Maddie and her company were fleeing north.

Having foreseen the inevitable, her generals had sent many of the troops northward, to establish defensive positions up the river and at other points along the southern edge of the Fairiron Plain, most notably at the locks on the Silver Cascades. They might have as much as a month before the enemy broke through there. But she didn't want to think that far ahead. What point in that if it never happened? *Surely Abramm will have returned by then.*

The whisper of footsteps behind her alerted her to Lord Garival's arrival. She'd been expecting him and turned from the window to face him.

Seeing her, he stopped. "So," he said. "Peregris has fallen."

"Yes."

"And Tiris's ships abandoned you."

"At the worst possible time. I believe it was deliberate."

Garival snorted and came farther into the room. "Could you expect any differently after what you did to him?"

"For a man who professed to love me? Yes. He knew my struggles."

"Abramm is not coming back, madam," Garival said flatly.

She stared at him, refusing to engage, a flush of anger rising in her breast.

He shook his head. "I can only give thanks you told him the night before the ceremony rather than leaving him to stand alone at the altar in front of everyone."

His expression still bore traces of the hurt and confusion he and all the other courtiers had felt when the news had come out that day. The Kirikhal swathed in its ribbons and flowers, the people who had camped in the streets overnight for a good spot all standing there as the most minor members of the wedding party proceeded up the route . . . and that was all. Guards had ridden behind them to announce there would be no wedding after all and everyone should go home.

No one understood. Even now, almost two months later.

No one but herself. And Tiris.

The desertion by Tiris's ships had shocked and dismayed her, but not nearly so much as it had the Chesedhan generals who were counting on him. They had believed him true to the core and that Maddie was a fool for turning him down. Even now they wanted to blame it all on her, not seeing that he'd never been true. Not even close to guessing what she feared he really was.

A far greater enemy even than Belthre'gar.

"I'm surprised he didn't fire on us himself," Garival said after a few moments of silence.

Maddie sighed and began to strip off her gloves. "We've been through this, sir. You have expressed your disappointment in my decision with splendid clarity—as has everyone else of note—and I do not need to hear it again."

"I fear he will retaliate, madam."

"I feared it, too, sir. But now I think he's left the Esurhites to do the work for him."

He grimaced. "You should head up to Deveren Dol, madam. With your sons. Before they come."

"We have some time yet. And it will be hard to besiege Fannath Rill with the river providing a constant water source. Call a cabinet meeting for tomorrow morning. Late. We'll discuss what can be done then."

"Yes, madam."

He left her. After a time she went and sat in the chair beside her travel bags, piled where the servants had left them, and pulled from them the small gray book of the Red Dragon, Abramm's beloved letters behind its cover. The night she'd agreed to marry Tiris, she had cried herself to sleep, certain she had made the worst mistake of her life, but having no idea how she might get out of it. And no real reason why she should, except for want of Abramm. The next morning she sought out the gray book for the letter it contained, and for no reason she could clearly recall, she had finally begun to read it. As the days passed, her conviction that marrying Tiris would be a mistake had only deepened, like a suppurating wound buried within her, turning all her life sick with its poisons. . . .

The Red Dragon, she learned, was one of the forms Moroq chose when he went about the earth. And a beautiful form it was—lean, lithe, covered with gleaming scarlet scales that reflected the light in a glory of iridescence. It was powerful beyond imagining, keen-eyed, its sense of smell so sensitive it could detect prey leagues away. And though its breath could spew poison or fire, its conversation was the most dangerous thing about it. For like its brother the serpent, the dragon could be quiet and slippery and subtle. It could wait for long periods to get whatever it wanted, could beguile and befuddle and bewitch. . . .

It wasn't until she saw the picture of the warrior with the breastplate and the long black braid that she thought about Tiris. For the man in the picture looked very much like him. From then on, she had begun to think of just how much the dragon motif permeated Tiris's home and life. And when, one day in a cabinet meeting, Duke Elsingor happened to mention that the name "ul Sadek" had at one time meant "the dragon," she had reverberated at the statement as if she were one of the great bells in the Kirikhal. It had not let her go, and she had returned to her chambers and read the rest of the book—about the dragon's wiles, about the way he sought out power, and how he so many times came at the man through his woman. More than that, when he appeared as a man, he was—as he had been created—the most beautiful, the most talented, the most intelligent and charming of all Eidon's creatures. Once he had been Tersius's trusted retainer, his closest friend, his most reliable defender. . . . And in the world he could still walk about as that, if he chose. . . .

By the time she was done she could hardly breathe, horrified by the conclusions that were forcing themselves upon her.

But the next day she reviled herself as a fanatic, told herself she was just making up wild stories to justify her reluctance to marry the man when the real reason was that she wanted to wait for Abramm, as crazy and irresponsible as that was. Then Tiris had told her she was spending too much time in Terstmeet. . . .

That one remark had been the turning point, though it was not until the eve of their wedding that she'd gathered the courage to call him to her audience chamber and inform him she would not marry him after all. And in that, unleashed disaster upon her people.

Now she held the book with its precious letters to her breast and let the tears blur the room around her. *Where are you, my love? Why have we not heard? Why have you not returned? You must know what desperate straits we are in.* . . .

It hit her then that if he did not know—or if he did know but had not yet returned—it could only be because he was in desperate straits himself. For if the rhu'ema were her enemies, how much more were they his? And how much would they oppose his return?

The compulsion to pray for him swept over her, and she fell to her knees, pleading for his protection, for his safety, for his healing—at that thought she recalled the dark thing that had lived in her father's side, and a terrible fear overtook her. What if Abramm had been shot by the same sort of arrow that had killed her father? For a moment she almost fainted at the horror of it. Then she fought her way free, and took that to Eidon, as well. *Open his eyes, my Father. Remind him of who you are, and who he is in you. Remind him of all you have done and have yet to do. Of how much you care for him and us all.*

Help him to see whatever it is he needs to see to be victorious. . . .

The words ran out, but she continued on, praying now for herself, for her children and those she loved, for all who wore the Terstan shield, and for the very freedom of her land and her people.

She felt the evil one's approach before she saw it. The cold sense of it intruded into her prayers, until she lifted her head and went to the window. In the darkened city below, kelistar streetlamps gleamed amidst the yellow glow of homefires through the myriad windows of homes and inns—not so many of them now as once. A good portion of Fannath Rill's population had already fled to the northern plateau, though soon there would be an influx of refugees as the Esurhite army moved inland.

Her eye caught on something out above the plain, a great bird, only not a bird. A veren? No. It was too big, and the wings were long, flexible . . . and featherless. She gasped. It was a dragon! Solid black, without any flicker of reflection, as if it were made of empty space winging its way to consume the entire city. She stood slowly, her mouth open behind her hands as she watched it approach, and the terror grew. So huge it was! She was but a worm before it. A helpless grub, worthy only to serve and grovel at such glory.

Though everything in her wanted to cringe back against the floor, something held her upright. The Light within her, the renewed hope that Abramm *was* out there somewhere, and the knowledge that nothing in this world was stronger than the one she served. . . .

It had something in its talons, which she did not notice until it was nearly upon her, flying low now, coming in at her at eye level. It let go its small burden as it swooped over the yard below her, where the soldiers all stood in a group staring up in silence. The burden was a man, dressed all in white, his arms and legs flailing as he fell, and she let out a cry as the great beast came right at her, the golden eyes catching her own. *"You should have gone with me when you had the chance, my little iblis. . . ."*

The wings flapped downward hard, lifting the creature's bulk up over the tower and away. She stood there, hands clenched, shocked to her toes as the wind of its passage rushed against the window.

Tiris.

For a moment she thought she might throw up as the realization gripped her of how close she had come to wedding him.

The ultimate betrayal. In all ways. Abramm and Eidon, both. Oh, thank you, my Lord, that you did not let me do that. . . .

Her eyes fixed upon the men in the yard below, the soldiers clustered about the body where it had sprawled, hardly visible as white upon the white tiles. They shouted to one another in alarm, and as the torchlight glinted off the fallen man's blond hair, new terror overtook her.

She whirled from the window and fled through her apartments and down the stairs. The squad sent to alert her to the body's presence met her as she crossed the Grand Salon on the ground floor, and when they told her it was Leyton—not Abramm—her first reaction was a shameful rush of thanksgiving.

He wasn't dressed in white. He wasn't dressed in anything, and his body had been sorely abused. Five broken-off arrow shafts buried in his chest showed the means of his death, after which his corpse had apparently been dragged about, and the eyes put out. Seeing her brother's empty eye sockets filled her with a horror she had to swallow whole, lest it amplify the distress that already vibrated in the men around her.

Belthre'gar had already promised her this would be her own end . . . after she had watched her children die. That, however, was not going to happen. Even if she had to send them up to Caerna'tha—and she was seriously considering it—there was no way the Esurhites would get their hands on her children.

She straightened and pulled her gaze from her brother's corpse. "Bind it up right here. I don't want anyone seeing this. He only means to distress us by it, and I refuse to give him that advantage. We'll entomb Leyton tomorrow in his place beside my father. With as many of the honors due him as we can muster."

The squad's commanding officer nodded, but the moment two of his men took hold of the body's legs to straighten them out, a red light flowed from empty eyes and mouth and they jumped back. The light spiraled upward and hung there, turning like a tree bauble in the wind. Except there was no wind. In fact, somehow they had all come to be enfolded in a dark mist.

The rhu'ema now spoke, the sound of its voice sending the men cowering to the ground.

"King Leyton was killed in the arena," it said to Maddie, "seeking to defend the regalia which he stole. Alas, he lost . . . slain by a common slave— one tall and blond with twin scars on his face."

Maddie stared at the thing, gritting her teeth with revulsion.

"The slave is dead now, too, at Belthre'gar's hand, and they threw the crown into the sea. Now they are searching for men to play the part of Queen

Madeleine—to demonstrate how she will die, as well. . . ."

She conjured a kelistar, and the thing shriveled into itself, then shot up into the sky and away.

The men stood around her, staring upward, then at her, open fear in their faces. "It is gone," she said abruptly. "Now see to my brother's body. And do not spread this tale around. It was sent for one reason only—to frighten and demoralize us. But it needs our mouths and tongues to do that. Which means if you gossip about this, you will be helping them. Do you understand?"

"Yes, madam," the commanding officer assured her.

She nodded and took her leave of them.

Trap came to her a little later, already informed about the dragon and the rhu'ema. "They say you will not talk of it, though."

"I think . . . the dragon was Tiris," she said softly, still shaken by that revelation herself.

He stared at her, struck speechless. "You're saying Tiris is a dragon?" he asked when he found his tongue.

"Or at any rate it was Tiris's voice I heard when it flew over."

"Maybe he was riding it."

"I don't think so, Trap."

34

For weeks Abramm and his liegemen rowed westward along the coast of Chesedh. Their Chesedhan companions went with them only as far as the mouth of the Elpis inlet, where they split off, heading for the fortress of the same name at the inlet's head. Alone, the Kiriathans continued on, eventually turning southward along the Chenen Peninsula toward the Narrows. Day after day their vessel cut through smooth, heavy swells beneath an unchanging ceiling of flat cloud cover, their rate of travel slowed dramatically as they fought the prevailing current. A slight breeze stirred the air from time to time, but there was no wind, no rain. Nor were there sun or stars to guide by. With the compass befuddled by the mist, they had to stay close enough to shore to navigate—as well as to put in to land from time to time for fresh food and water.

On the first day of the sixth week they rounded the end of the Chenen Peninsula and entered the Narrows, a network of channels threading their way through the archipelago that remained from the sinking of the Heartland centuries ago. Most of the islands were little more than rocky sentinels, but a few were large enough that people had settled on them—fishermen and traders mostly, for the Narrows was the quickest path from eastern Chesedh to both Thilos and Kiriath.

It was early afternoon as they turned into a wide bay encircled by humps of land, not an Esurhite galley in sight. Of course, there hadn't been for weeks now, and all aboard knew why: The Esurhites were occupied elsewhere, and the rocky, cliff-lined Narrows offered few places to land—none that would be practical for the disembarkation of an army.

As they glided across the bay's leaden surface, Abramm stood at the vessel's prow, watching the rocky humps loom incrementally larger on their horizon. He stood there often these days, especially since he'd had to stop rowing. The captain's cabin, which he'd made his own, was too stuffy and stifling to bear for very long. It stank, as well. Out here, even the small breeze that blew over the vessel's prow helped to clear his head and cool his fever, and the hiss and slap of the waves parting before the bow soothed his agitation. If an attack of nausea came, he was standing right at the rail, no need for a pan that Rolland would have to empty. And out here he was free of the haunting images.

Of course, there were days the brightness and the sight of the waters passing alongside the ship were too much to bear. There were days he was too weak or sick to make it out of bed, but it was getting better. *I'm out here now,* he told himself. *We just need to get through the Narrows, away from it all, away from him. And then his power over me will be less. . . .*

He frowned at the humps before him, for though they were still a good ways off, they were disappearing behind a gathering gloom. He hadn't thought it was that late yet . . . but perhaps he'd stood here longer than he knew. . . . That happened a lot. He'd come out at midday and would barely seem to get settled before Rolland was asking him to come in to supper. Which of course he never ate, so he didn't know why Rolland kept asking him.

He watched the once clearly delineated channels disappear into the gloom and reflected how like his life that was—once well lit and clearly defined, now lost in gloom. He didn't want to think about that, though, because thinking only made him hurt more than he already did. Whether it was the past or the future, nothing could be considered without pain. He'd come out on the prow to forget.

The swells were growing more pronounced, along with the increasing mist. That was odd, since usually the sea calmed as the mist dropped. In any case the boat had acquired a dismaying corkscrew roll that was not at all kind to the nausea simmering in his gut. And though he had been hot earlier, now he shivered with a sudden chill. Soon he was engaged in a serious debate over whether to stay here or return to his cabin. He wasn't sure he could make it back before he needed the bedpan. On the other hand, the longer he stood in place the more pronounced his shivering became, and soon the ever-attentive Rolland, leaning now on the gunwale amidships, would be coming to ask if he was all right.

It annoyed him no end the way everyone was always asking how he was.

When it started to sprinkle and the tiny drops burned his skin so fiercely he expected them to sizzle, he hurried back to his cabin. He barely made it through the door before he began to retch. Only bile came up now, for he had nothing in his stomach. It burned his throat and nostrils, and when he was done, even repeated sips of water would not clean the burning away. As always the retching opened the wound in his side, the stench of it worse than that of the vomit. Shaking, weak and dizzy, he collapsed on his bunk, lying on his back and staring at the deck supports.

After a time, when he had regained his strength, he pulled up his shirt. Sure enough, the stained bandage had yet another dark spot at its midst as fresh spore leaked out of him. He sat up and unwound the long strips from around his midriff to reveal the black starfish living and growing under his flesh. If he didn't get it out of his body soon, he knew he would die. But repeated purges hadn't worked, and lately they'd left him so weak and drained, he'd given them up altogether. Now he probed gently about the edges and thought again about cutting it out.

He'd have to do it alone. Couldn't ask anyone to help him and risk getting the blackness into them. More than that it shamed him that he should be so weak he'd not been able to remove this thing on his own. He was the White Pretender! He was the Guardian-King. He was the man who walked with Eidon. . . .

But Eidon had deserted him.

He swung his legs over the side of the bed. When the cabin stopped spinning about him, he stood and pulled his dagger from its sheath, where it hung with his sword belt from a peg on the wall. Then he sat again on the side of his bunk, knife in hand, fingers probing at the corruption as he wondered how deep the thing might go.

And all the while some part of his mind was shrieking at him. *You cannot do this! You will kill yourself.*

I'm already dead.

This is not Eidon's will for you.

I don't care about Eidon's will for me.

Yes, you do. . . .

He set his jaw and clenched his fist about the knife, but then his vision blurred and he had to wait for that to pass. When it had, and he was again nerving himself to plunge the end of the knife into his flesh, the door burst open. He looked up. Rollie stood in the opening, staring at him in horror. An instant later, the big man had crossed the deck and snatched the blade from his hand, Abramm too weak to resist him.

"Eidon's mercy, sir! *What* are ye doing?" He stepped back from Abramm as he spoke, disgust on his face, his eyes on the growth in Abramm's side.

"It has to be cut out, so I'm cutting it out," Abramm told him.

"Are ye out of your mind?" But then, apparently, he could bear the stench no more for he turned and disappeared through the doorway, taking the knife with him.

Gone to get someone else, Abramm guessed. *Now they'll all know of it. . . .* Shame gripped him hard, and he bent over the pain in his middle. *Eidon, where are you? Where have you gone?*

Suddenly the bed lurched out from under him and he sprawled forward, hitting the deck hard on his uninjured side. He heard the rush of a sudden wind outside, and the deck shot up, then twisted in a sickening roll that brought the nausea back with a vengeance. And was that rain drumming on the deck overhead?

How could that be? They were under Shadow. There was neither wind nor rain under Shadow. . . .

Again the planking dropped out from under him, and he tumbled after it. His head slammed into something hard, and the next thing he knew he was waking up, wedged between the table and the bulkhead; the floor canted at a forty-five-degree angle and an awful roaring filled his ears. Then as he watched, the deck straightened out, only to rise up the other way before swooping back down again.

He shoved himself to his feet and dragged himself from table to bulkhead to doorpost, out of the cabin and into the storm.

Rain slanted past him in diagonal sheets and drove like daggers into his flesh as white-capped waves towered above the canted deck. Katahn came slithering down the companionway to grip his arm and shout, "We've got to get out of the bay. Every way we turn, the waves are driving us straight into rocks. Already the wind has broken the mast and we've lost several of the oars. Much more of this and we'll be helpless before it. At least in the open sea we'll have a chance."

"How can there be rocks?" Abramm demanded. "We're miles off from them. You must be seeing things, old friend."

Katahn's expression became one of disbelief. Abramm pushed past him and made his way to the prow, where he peered into the steadily darkening storm. The wind tore at him, lashing his hair across his face, and driving the rain into his eyes. Before the water had burned, but now it felt good. So did the wind.

And there *were* the rocks, just as Katahn had said—dark, ragged teeth stabbing upward from a froth of white, waiting to rip apart the unwary and unfortunate. They couldn't possibly be there, though, so they must be illusion. And if Katahn just turned the prow a hair, the wind and waves would carry them on by. . . .

He blinked water out of his eyes. Rolland was gripping his arm, shouting in his ear that they must turn back to the open sea or they'd be shipwrecked. Abramm listened to him with gritted teeth, annoyed now because he could see that his earlier hopes would not come to pass: They would not miss the rocks after all.

"It's just an illusion!" Abramm yelled back. "We'll go right through it!"

Rolland gaped at him in horror.

Abramm turned to squint again at the rocks. Yes, he saw them wavering, solid one moment, insubstantial as mist the next. "I've been here before. Don't worry."

He gripped the gunwale and grinned at the approaching rocks, which looked more substantial than ever. Suddenly doubt assailed him. What was he talking about? He'd not been here before. This wasn't the Gull Islands, it was the Narrows. Nothing was the same. He wasn't in the Light—couldn't even find the Light these days. His time-sense was so unreliable they very well could have come across the bay, for all he knew. And the rocks looked awfully real and solid.

Yet the desire to keep going would not let him say the words to turn them back.

There was a man standing on the rocks. Abramm blinked water and brushed hair from his eyes and stared hard.

No. Not standing. Sitting on a great golden throne.

Tersius?

"*If you do not turn back, Abramm Kalladorne, you will die on these rocks. Many of these men will die with you, but our Father will let you go no farther with this. Is that truly what you want?*"

He stood there, staring hard as the words battered at his heart and the water in his eyes turned to tears. Then, *You want everything, don't you? Just like Lema said. You want me to keep nothing for myself. It's not fair!*

And for the first time in weeks, his angry thoughts received an answer.

"Not fair? I gave up everything for you, held nothing back for your sake, though you were my enemy. . . ."

The image of Tersius suspended on that pole for the darkness to consume eclipsed that of the monarch on his throne, and Abramm saw that all the vicious, selfish, pride-driven thoughts and feelings he had entertained since leaving Horon-Pel—thoughts and feelings that should have earned for him instant destruction—had gone to Eidon's son instead. Every one of them. There was nothing more he owed. Nothing more he'd ever owe, no matter how vicious and selfish he might become. . . .

A flash of light ripped through the darkness that had wound itself about his soul, and he saw again the purity and perfection he had witnessed in the throne room, the glorious promises on the walls, and his own callous, arrogant disregard for all of it. He was a worm, helpless, insignificant, disgusting in himself, and yet . . . loved. Even now. Even in the face of the greatest failure of his life. . . .

And at that moment, the hard, angry stone that had been his heart cracked into a thousand pieces, and he stood there stunned to tears by the magnitude of Eidon's mercy. As the wind howled and the deck swooped up, blocking sight of the rocks for a moment, then crashed down again, a rush of alarm swept through him and he turned to Rolland. "Aye, head back for the open sea! Now!"

Instantly Rolland turned to bellow the command sternward.

By then the waves were huge, making the turnabout a terrible gamble, lest they be caught sideways and swamped. But the moment Katahn gave the order for the starboard oars to lift and rest and the portside oars to pull, the rain stopped and the waves began to subside. By the time they had completed the maneuver, all was calm again—and daylight had returned.

They left the bay on flat gray seas beneath flat gray skies, gliding forward on nothing but their momentum. In the rowing gallery below, the men shipped their oars and slumped in exhaustion over the handles while those on deck stared at sea and sky—and the rocky island behind them, in a silence born of awe and fear.

They stared at Abramm, too, as he made his way back toward his cabin. For the first time since he'd left Horon-Pel he saw himself as they must: a man driven mad by grief, consumed by the Shadow within him. The black thing in his side had colored everything. When he passed Katahn and Rolland, he asked them to join him in the cabin, and there he showed them the wound that wouldn't heal.

Rolland had already seen it briefly, of course. But even so, his reaction was, if anything, stronger than Katahn's—they gagged and turned away as the dreadful stench hit them. When they had recovered sufficiently to approach his bedside to examine him, their faces still turned various shades of gray and green.

"Why have ye hidden this from us?" Rolland asked finally.

"I believed it would get better on its own." Abramm thought a moment, then shook his head. "No, the truth is, I was ashamed."

"I'm assuming you've at least *tried* to purge it," Katahn said.

"Many times. And each time it takes more out of me. I'm not sure I could even do it anymore."

"Maybe . . ." Katahn glanced at Rolland. "Maybe we could try."

"Go ahead. But I don't think it will work."

They tried. The spore fought them off and punished Abramm for letting them do it.

Afterward, the two men stood beside his bed, staring at the dark thing on his side. Then Rolland left without a word and returned shortly with the speaking stone.

"Will ye listen?"

Abramm almost refused, but then he recalled those moments on the prow in the storm and nodded.

Laud's voice arose from the stone, teaching about destiny, and a chill crawled up Abramm's back as he realized it. There was no way to control what the stone spoke, so he knew Rolland had not set this up deliberately. It was Eidon who spoke to him now. . . . "A man who's born a king will always be a king. Even if he abdicates or his realm is taken from him. If he abdicates, it's his choice to do so, but it doesn't change what's in his blood, what was his heritage, nor the promise that lay before him of what he could have been. And if his realm is taken, even then he is what he is. Not in power, perhaps. Not even recognized, perhaps. But still a king."

In the crystalline globe that blazed above the stone a man appeared, face scarred but familiar, dark eyes warm and wise. The same man Abramm had seen earlier on the rocks outside, enwrapped in glory on his throne: Tersius. Though Rolland and Katahn both listened intently to the lesson, they did not seem to see him, nor did they give any sign when he spoke:

"I did not remove your realm from you for discipline, Abramm. You know that. I have made you a king, and you will always be a king. I promised you even

as you left that you would have it back. And already you have seen the beginnings
of that restoration."

I know that, Lord.

"The dark spore turned your heart . . . but it did not have to. I would not
have let him come against you with it, otherwise."

And yet . . . you know my weakness for her.

"A weakness you could have overcome. One, in fact, you already had."

But a weakness you knew I would not overcome.

"But only because you chose not to."

Abramm held his gaze for a moment, then sighed and conceded. *You are*
right: It was my choice. I wanted what I wanted, not what you had given me.
Like a boy throwing a tantrum. I still don't understand, though. You led me into
that arena, knowing what would happen. Knowing I would fail.

"Knowing you would fail and fall and finally get back up again, and from the
failure understand that it doesn't matter. You are mine. I have bought you, and
no matter what you do, you will always be mine. I do not see your failures,
Abramm. I see only the man you will become."

The lesson ended, and the bubble of light extinguished, the stone lying
quiescent on the desk where Rolland had first set it. His two companions sat
in their chairs, watching him, as if waiting for him to break the silence.

Eidon's voice sounded in his head: *"They can help you remove the spore.*
They want to help you. And you need them to."

You know we've tried.

"Try again. It will be different now. You are different now."

And now Abramm heard the sounds of the ship creaking around him
again, and the men's soft breathing, as if a cloud of silence had lifted off him.
He turned his head to look at them.

Rolland leaned toward him. "Is it better at all, sir? Did the lesson do
anything?"

Abramm smiled at him. "Yes, actually. It did a lot. And if you are still
willing, I would very much appreciate your help in getting rid of this thing in
my side."

They looked at each other sharply; then Katahn stood and approached
the bedside. "Tell us what do to."

Rolland stood beside him. "Should we put our hands on it er somethin'?"

Abramm considered a moment. "No. I think it's at the stage it'll want to
spread."

He had them lay a cloth over it, and then they pulled up their chairs and sat beside him, and though Abramm did not tell them to, Rolland laid a hand on his forearm while Katahn rested one on his knee. They closed their eyes, and he saw the Light flare around them, then draw down toward the thing in his side, which lurched and writhed. The pain was horrible. His scream broke their concentration and they jerked back, breaking contact.

He frowned at them, panting and frustrated. "Do it again. I'll try not to scream this time." As they complied, he closed his eyes and focused on Eidon . . . seeking to add his own Light to theirs. The moment he did, a black cloud reared up in his soul, a twisting dragon shape with a hatefully familiar face. He saw then how it had linked to the Shadow within him, feeding, giving it strength, the shadow in turn allowing the spore to multiply. And he'd let it do so for too long.

His own Light had grown thin and feeble from being ignored. But when he used it to seek out that in the others, their strength drew it into them, then rushed back to him on the same connection, illumining a multitude of rooms in his soul that had for too long been locked in darkness. Old memories and long-cherished knowledge stirred to life, forgotten truths and principles building upon one another in a wild, intoxicating whirlwind of understanding. He had no control anymore. His thoughts and power ran everywhere, but the others' focus brought him back.

Suddenly the fire seared in his side, a sensation worsened by the violent writhing of a mass that shouldn't be there. The pressure built, the pain increased, and it seemed he could hear the thing screaming within him. His focus wavered, but his friends held him to them—strong, purposeful, sure of what they did. He clenched his teeth, tried again to focus, and suddenly the dark thing burst—black spore and mist fountaining out of him into the cloth he'd put over the wound, sizzling and smoking as their combined strength consumed it.

Then the Light took him completely, and he was no longer in the stuffy, stinking stern cabin but in the throne room again, surrounded by the wonderful light, freed momentarily from the darkness of his fallen flesh. Again he experienced that moment of understanding that had come to him in the Hall of Records. What had been done and why, what his place in it was, what remained for him to do . . .

He opened his eyes, and for the first time in months, he felt good. The heavy weight he'd been carrying around unknowing had lifted. He felt alive again, almost hungry and filled with energy. The cabin looked brighter and cleaner, and even Rolland, slumped and snoring in the chair at his bedside, was better looking than Abramm remembered him.

As he drew a deep, half-yawning breath, Rolland started awake. "Ye're back, sir!" The big man's blue eyes widened and then he grinned. "Oh, and ye look *much* better." They pulled the spore-stained cloth and bandages away to find Abramm's side whole and healthy once more, only a small crescent-shaped scar revealing there had ever been a wound at all. But though it looked fine now, he knew his ordeal was not quite over. Parts of the spore had residualized the moment the Light had begun to burn and would on some future day flare back to life if he did not take the proper steps to prevent it.

Rolland went out and returned with Katahn, who was even more astonished by his dramatic improvement. He'd been in a holding pattern over the last day, waiting for Abramm to wake up to know where they would go. "We head north along the coast," Abramm told him immediately. "Back the way we came. We'll make port at Elpis and advance on Fannath Rill from there."

They made much better time heading north than they had south, for they had the currents' help, but it still took them almost three weeks. During that time, Abramm listened to the speaking stone twice a day and spent the interim hours regaining his strength and fighting skills. Appalled by the squalor into which he'd let his person fall while the spore had him, he'd trimmed his hair and beard back to the much shorter, tidier lengths he'd worn as king, and rifled through Katahn's clothing stores for cleaner, sounder shirts and trousers than what he'd been wearing. It wasn't long before he felt more his old self than he had since he'd left Kiriath.

Though speculation was rife aboard ship as to what the conditions in Chesedh were, he mostly stayed away from that subject. He'd already gotten himself into enough trouble dabbling in unfounded and evil speculations—he wasn't eager to start again. But given his observations of the Esurhites' activities in the Neck when they'd crossed it weeks ago—and the absence of any Sorite galleys—he'd guessed that Peregris had fallen. If Chesedh's leaders had not been taken there but fled to Fannath Rill, then it was likely the invaders had pressed north after them. Of all potential scenarios, the best was that they had the city under siege. Because from the devastation Abramm had seen in North Andol, he knew Belthre'gar couldn't keep a siege going for long.

Elpis was one of Chesedh's oldest fortress cities, dating back to Ophiran times. Long home to a strong contingent of Kiriathan exiles, Abramm hoped to find allies here, both Kiriathan and Chesedhan. Along with Mareis, to the east, Elpis was home to the fleets that kept the Esurhites at bay in the Salmancan Sea. Defensive fortifications bristled atop the cliffs that lined the narrow inlet, each with its own set of docks. Though Abramm's vessel was neither challenged nor fired upon as it sailed up that long gauntlet, at every new fortification men stood along the walls to watch it pass. By the time the newcomers reached Elpis itself, tiering up the notch at the inlet's end, the locals were fully informed. The Elpian navy had been mustered, and a group of men in merchant's robes and military tunics had gathered at the end of the newly built dock at the base of the notch.

It undoubtedly helped that from Katahn's collection of sailing banners, Abramm had pulled out his old flag with the dragon and shield used during the action in the Gull Islands. With that on the jury-rigged mast and Abramm standing on the quarterdeck with big, blond Rolland at his side, they had at least avoided being sunk or driven off out of hand.

As they dropped anchor in the harbor's midst and let down their ship's boat, Abramm eyed the men awaiting them on the docks and watching on the vessels that surrounded them. He'd thought originally to make some kind of grand arrival as Abramm, King of Kiriath, complete with all the regalia. Or at least scepter and crown. Now, thanks to his own mule-headedness, that wouldn't happen. Still, he hoped to win at least some supporters here.

Once ashore, they strode down the dock and stopped at the end of it, facing the city's leaders, who didn't seem to be welcoming him so much as confronting him. For a moment no one said anything as overhead the gulls circled and squawked. He was about to draw breath to open negotiations when the crowd shifted and a familiar dark-haired figure stepped between them, one eye covered with a leather patch.

"So you've come back," Borlain said, approaching to meet them, the others following him raggedly. He looked Abramm up and down. "I didn't recognize you from the walls up there. Only Rolland." He gave the blacksmith a nod, then returned his attention to Abramm. "You're looking much better than when I saw you last, sir."

Abramm released a long sigh as he realized what was probably behind the coolness of this reception. "I am better."

"The spore is gone, then?"

"As much as any spore is gone. Yes."

Borlain nodded, then glanced at the big-bellied, auburn-bearded man beside him, clad in a gray military sort of tunic. "This is the one I told you about, Aender. You can see he does bear strong resemblance to Abramm."

Aender, whose blond brows were as bushy as his beard and wild hair, scowled at Abramm. "D' ye know how many like ye have come through here these past months? Commoners claiming to be Abramm reborn, wantin' t' lead us out of our fortress on some woolbrained scheme of defeatin' the Shadow lovers. It'll take more than idle claims and a couple scars t' convince us."

Abramm nodded. "I understand that, and I'm not claiming Abramm's crown—that is Eidon's to bestow. You can call me Alaric, though no matter what you call me, I mean to head for Fannath Rill. Along with these men who've accompanied me, and as many of you as have the courage to go."

Aender scowled at him, then glanced again at Borlain. "We have enough task just protecting our own place. We can't go ridin' off to look after others. Let them fight their own battles." Behind him the other men muttered and nodded, scowling at Abramm as if he had insulted them with his suggestion.

"And when all of Chesedh falls," Abramm asked, pitching his voice louder so that more of those who watched might hear him, "then what will you do? They will not let you sit up here in your hideaway. Once they've taken the rest, then they'll turn their attention to rooting out pockets of rebels like you."

"Let 'em try!" shouted a man from the back of the crowd. "They'll not succeed."

Abramm regarded them calmly, trying to gauge their mettle. Was it worth the attempt to persuade, or should he abandon them now?

Shouts echoed in the growing dusk, and a sudden stirring in the crowd to his right drew all eyes to where an old man in a shabby tunic struggled to get through the line of soldiers and spectators. Some of them were, in fact, holding him back. "He's King Abramm, fer sure," the man said. "I have t' see him."

"He's jest another slave imposter, ye crazy ol' man," a woman shrilled at him.

"I have t' give 'im his things back."

The onlookers laughed. "A brass rod and some miscellaneous flotsam? Even if he was King Abramm, he wouldn't want yer old junk. Now, get back to yer boat and stop trying to shame us all with yer craziness."

Abramm glanced at Aender and Borlain. "Who is that?"

"Just an old, addled fisherman," Aender explained. "He's been goin' on about that stuff for weeks."

"How does he know who I am?"

Borlain, Abramm noted, had gone rigid, his eyes upon the old man as the others shoved him back behind them.

"Your Majesty, please!" The old fisherman's voice rang off water and rock in the twilight.

"Wait!" Abramm cried. "I want to see what he has."

Shortly the old man was before him—weathered face, gnarled hands, white hair tied in a queue. He limped forward as if his hips pained him and, after a moment of seeing that he really had been granted audience, settled awkwardly to his knees. "Yer Majesty."

Men snickered around them. Abramm ignored them and focused on the old man. "You know me?"

"Ye are King Abramm, returned at last." By his accent the man was Kiriathan, which probably accounted for both his poor reputation and his obvious poverty. "And Eidon has given me something for ye, sir." He began to untie the thong about his bag. "I caught them in my nets last month. Right after that big storm. I knew the moment I saw them what they were."

The old man reached into his bag, pulled out the Coronation Ring, and set it on the dock's wooden planking. The translucent Orb of Tersius followed, then a very tarnished Scepter of Rule, and finally the plaited metal wreath of Avramm's Crown—the latter's appearance eliciting a hiss of astonishment from Rolland and the other men of Abramm's party.

The fisherman looked around at them and, realizing that he was finally being taken seriously, rocked back on his heels with a smile.

"Light's grace, sir!" Rolland choked at Abramm's side. "You said they'd come to you, way back in Aggosim. And so they have."

Abramm was overwhelmed, his chest so full of emotion he felt it might burst apart. But instead of taking the offered regalia, he bade the old man to stand, and then dropped to his own knee before him. "I cannot crown myself. That is for you to do."

A susurrus of astonished and indignant muttering arose from the men of Elpis, who looked on without comprehension.

The fisherman blanched before him. "But, sir, I am only a common fisherman."

"Do not think yourself unworthy because of that. Eidon himself has chosen you for this."

And so the old man, with trembling hands, held out the scepter and laid it in Abramm's arms. And when the orblight at its head flickered with a faint light, it provoked yet another rush of exclamation. Then the fisherman picked up the crown from where he'd laid it atop the bag on the ground and straightened, holding it with both hands. Abramm dropped his chin a little, listening to the grit of the man's sandals on the wood and the rustle of his clothing. The fishy odor grew abruptly stronger, almost choking, but then he forgot about that as he sensed the tingle of the crown's proximity. A moment later, the plaited circlet settled into place as if it were alive. The Light rolled through him with a warm, familiar sense of rightness.

The old man gasped and jerked back, and from the way his eyes widened as he looked upon it, Abramm guessed the crown was glowing. Already it was warming and softening against his brow, no longer a heavy, hard weight but almost unnoticeable.

And now their audience gasped likewise, swearing and shouting in their agitation. Some even drew swords, and it took several moments for the ruckus to die down.

Abramm stood then and looked at them calmly, though inside he wanted to shout for joy, more astonished than any of them. Borlain stood wide-eyed, mouth agape, and Rolland was actually weeping.

"As I said," he told them, pitching his voice loudly enough for all to hear, "I am going to Fannath Rill. To meet the armies of the Black Moon and destroy them once and for all. Anyone who wishes to come with me is welcome." He thought of Trinley and added, "So long as he obeys my command." He glanced again at the fisherman. "That includes you, Master Fisherman. Ever thought you might want to be a king's aide?"

FANNATH RILL

PART FOUR

35

It was after midnight. Queen Madeleine stood alone on the railed roof deck of the royal apartments overlooking the city of her youth and wept, hating what this night must bring, knowing she had no other choice. The hulks of burned and half-sunken galleys lay out in the river, just south of the palace island—remnants of the first battle ever fought within the city's walls. As had been the case for over five months now, a ceiling of mist obscured the stars and, in the east, reflected back the emerald glow of the etherworld corridor that had been erected there. The dark flapping forms of veren, as well as smaller dragons, showed briefly in the green-lit overcast, out where an army that numbered in the hundreds of thousands still gathered.

She wrapped her arms about herself and shivered, for though it was still late summer, the air was chilly. At least it was free of the stench of sewage and sickness and death. Only the faint scent of smoke wafted up here, drifting in from the plain where the Esurhites were busy burning the land to charcoal.

When the invasion had begun last spring, her countrymen had fled to the city of Fannath Rill, whose massive outer walls marked the first line of defense against attackers. Hundreds of people with their animals and belongings had crowded into its streets and parks and squares and halls—and it was worse now. Even the palace grounds and halls thronged with refugees. The waterpark had become a great encampment from which the thin threads of campfires arose every morning. Had Maddie not ordered siege preparations begun months before, they'd never have been able to support them all for as long as they had.

By now, though, most of the livestock had been slaughtered and eaten, and other food supplies were dwindling rapidly. Worse, the Esurhites had begun throwing their own dead soldiers into the river upstream of the city, fouling Fannath Rill's only water source. Even after boiling their water, people got sick by the thousands. The existing graveyards were now filled to capacity, and being unable to access the land outside the walls, they were forced to burn the accumulating dead. Fannath Rill was hanging by a thread and couldn't last much longer.

Their only hope lay in the fact that the Esurhites were struggling, as well. Men had to have a reason to stay away from their families and livelihoods for long periods of time, to put up with field conditions, boredom, tension, poor food, lack of good water. And the recent outbreak of disease in the camp, as evidenced by the bodies fouling the river, would only put more pressure on them. Every day that the Chesedhans held out in Fannath Rill was one more day the Esurhites had to hold their own resolve together.

For a while it had looked as if the Chesedhans might win. But then the Shadow lovers had erected one of their despicable corridors in the remains of a ruin east of the city, and now each night its green fires glared off the eastern cloud cover as new soldiers streamed to the battlefield—Esurhites, Andolens, Draesians, Sorites, and most recently, Kiriathans.

Many of her councilmen believed the corridor's advent betrayed Belthre'gar's desperation as much as it did his impatience and frustration. He'd promised his men victory and plunder, and every day that passed left less plunder and an increasingly meager victory. The more men he had, her counselors suggested, the quicker he could overwhelm the walls and bring it all to a close. And indeed the number of scaling ladders, battering rams, catapults, and wall-tapping crews had grown alarmingly in the last month, along with the number of troops, augmented by veren, Broho, and hundreds of crows, which harassed the city dwellers constantly.

Her military advisors believed he meant to launch a full-scale attack soon. And rather than simply wait, they had devised a plan. Their spies said, Belthre'gar considered Maddie to be his property and was furious she'd been snatched from him by the great sea wave. Even more enraging was her con-·tinued refusal to surrender to him. He'd become obsessed with her, they said, maniacally intent on capturing her and her children, so as to slay them in as hideous and public a manner as he could devise. Recent rumors claimed he'd even agreed to ally with Tiris ul Sadek, a startling concession for a man who never allied with anyone, least of all a "dog from the eastern deserts."

Her advisors suggested that if she and her children could be delivered safely to Deveren Dol, those left behind might open the gates in surrender just as Belthre'gar's assault began. Finding she had fled, he might well abandon the city entirely in his frustration at losing her and chase north in pursuit. Yes, many would die, but not all. And if she succeeded in drawing him up to Deveren Dol, she could be absolutely certain of outlasting him in a second siege. One of the oldest fortresses in all of Chesedh, Deveren Dol's foundations and some of its towers dated back to Ophiran times. It was virtually impregnable, built upon a permanent water source that outsiders couldn't foul. And it had been preparing for siege for months.

They were counting on the fact that Belthre'gar's men would rebel and desert should she escape to Deveren Dol. To ensure that, and also to provide distraction while the queen and her party escaped, a group of men would simultaneously venture out to destroy the corridor. Success would not only stop the continued arrival of new soldiers and supplies, it would demoralize those already in Chesedh when they saw the access to their homelands cut off.

It was not a perfect plan by any means. Not one that had much chance of succeeding, nor one she liked at all, and she'd fought them on it fiercely. A queen should stay with her subjects to the end, she'd declared.

But she'd be with her subjects in Deveren Dol, her counselors had argued. And how much better to win the victory and force the invaders to give up even as they preserved not only the queen of Chesedh but also little Simon, rightful king of Kiriath. Such a victory would breathe new life and hope into all those who fought the Shadow.

And anyway, Trap had asked her—brutally—if she stayed and the city fell, could she sit behind her palace walls while Belthre'gar systematically killed every last person in the outer city trying to get her to surrender herself and her children? Better for them to flee and draw him away. . . .

Ultimately she'd agreed, and tonight she was to leave in utter secrecy, smuggled out of the city to the north along with her children, Carissa and Conal, and their combined retinue of retainers. Trap and a handful of men, meantime, would leave by a different route to destroy the corridor.

She walked slowly along the railing, eyes drifting across the sparkling kelistar lamps of her city—lit each night by her express order—intermingled with the red glow of innumerable refugee campfires. Anxiety simmered in her belly as the green on the eastern cloud flared brightly with another arrival of troops. So many threats, so many things to go wrong, so little potential for success . . .

Father Eidon, you are our only hope for victory. Please give those who remain behind the wisdom and resolve to stay this course we have devised. Recall to their minds—to all our minds—what we know of you, and do not let your enemies prevail against us. I know when it is darkest, that is the time for true faith . . . but, Father . . . Her thoughts stuttered and veered off to the one thing that had twisted at the core of her being for months now: *Where is he? You promised. He promised. . . .*

She felt her pent-up emotion start to heave and shift, and she turned sharply from that line of thought before it swept her away. Tonight she must keep her head about her, and her emotions firmly in check, though it seemed she had been doing that for so very, very long. . . .

"Ma'am?" Jeyanne's voice intruded into her thoughts. "Duke Eltrap is here."

"Thank you, Jeyanne."

She stopped, hand on the rail, eyes on the green flicker, and prayed for Trap, as well. And then for what she was about to do in the next few moments. *If this is not your will, Father Eidon . . . make it plain to me. But he will need something, and if Abramm is not here . . .*

As always, the conviction of what she was to do remained. With a sigh, she descended the stair to her apartments and entered her study. Trap stood beside the fireplace, clad in the dark woolen tunic of a soldier in the army of the Black Moon. Sword and dagger both hung at his hips, and he carried a rucksack in one hand. His expression was one of puzzlement and curiosity that she should have brought him here so late, when she'd be seeing him down in the wine cellar only half an hour hence.

"You're sure you want to go through with this, Trap?"

He frowned slightly. "You've heard all the arguments, ma'am. All the reasons it must be done. All the reasons why I'm the one who has to do it." Having helped Abramm on three separate occasions, he was the only one who had even a scrap of experience in carrying out such a mission.

"I know all the reasons." She stopped beside the desk, laid her hand on Elayne's old scratched valise where it sat beside her pile of books, then lifted her head to meet his gaze directly. "I also know you may not succeed. And your wife, sir, is but days from delivering your firstborn. You would desert her at a time like this?"

"He is not my firstborn, ma'am," Trap corrected her gently. "My firstborn is Conal."

"Of course. I didn't mean . . ." She brushed her hand across the handle of the valise. "I know you'll love both equally. But the fact remains—"

"The fact remains, madam," he insisted, "they won't let me into the birthing chamber, so there's nothing I could do but fret, anyway."

"What if she delivers on the road?"

At that his freckles came into sharp relief, betraying his concern about that very misfortune. She watched him shake it off and go on. "Elayne will be there. You will be there. Marta, too. And better she deliver the child on the road out in the fresh air than in this cesspool of sickness and death. Whatever happens, I must leave it in Eidon's hands. Which I would have to do, anyway." Some of the color came back into his face now and his brown eyes twinkled. "Who knows? If all goes well I might reach Deveren Dol before you do."

She stood there staring at him for some time before finally turning to the valise. "Very well, then." She opened the latch and pulled out the stiff, wiry, white fabric of Abramm's Robe of Light. "I want you to take this."

His eyes widened, then moved from the glistening fabric in her fingers to her gaze. "Your Majesty, I can't—"

"It saved Ian. You were Abramm's best and closest friend. It might save you, as well . . . and even help you in the bargain."

He was still shaking his head. "I can't take it. It's his, not mine. I'd be just like Leyton, and what he took didn't help him."

"Leyton stole the regalia for his own use. You are not stealing anything." She paused. "Don't you think Abramm would want you to take it?"

He considered her words with a frown that turned to an expression of open pain as he whispered, "Madam, what if the stories out of Elpis are true?"

Stories that said Abramm had come ashore there in an Esurhite galley, with Kiriathans at his side. That the vessel's captain was an aged warrior of the Brogai caste. That barely had he arrived when an old fisherman came to him, having found the lost regalia in his nets—crown, orb, ring, and scepter— and that Abramm knelt before him. When the old man set the crown upon his head, it had blazed with light. . . .

It was a lovely story that had resonated with truth the moment she'd heard it. But that had been months ago. If it had truly been Abramm, if he'd had the scepter . . . why had he not yet come? Why had they still not heard from him?

"Your faith in his return has kept us all, my lady," Trap said softly. "You would abandon it now?"

"I am not abandoning it," she said sharply. "The simple fact is, he's not here right now. And I must make a decision: Should I take this with me to Deveren Dol, or should I give it to you? For several days now I've believed I should give it to you. And after all my prayers for direction, that conviction has not changed." She lifted a brow and smiled slightly. "Who knows? Maybe he's out there trying to shut down that corridor himself and you'll run into him, having just what he needs to complete the task." She held out the robe with a smile.

Reluctantly he took it, then lifted his rucksack to the desk and stowed the garment inside. "It's not very flexible."

"Well, it wasn't for Ian, either, but it worked."

He refastened the rucksack's straps, then stood before her awkwardly. Impulsively, she stepped forward and embraced him. "You were his dearest friend, Trap Meridon," she whispered in his ear. "And you are mine, as well. I know you will not disappoint us."

She stepped back then. And looking grim but resolved, he gave her a short bow. "Stay safe, then, madam. I will see you in Deveren Dol."

And for the first time he cracked her a smile. With that she dismissed him and went to finish her own preparations.

After leaving the queen, Trap went directly to the wine cellar where the others were waiting and kissed his wife good-bye, horrified anew by how very pregnant she was but refusing to torment himself with all the dire possibilities they faced. He did, however, pray for her safety and deliverance. Again.

From there he was rowed across the river to make his way alone through Fannath Rill's crowded streets to the bolthole located midway between the river and the wall. Between the veren, the dragons, and the ubiquitous crows, he took great care not to be seen. A bolthole used to escape the city could also be used to enter it. Only once he was safely inside the tunnel did he relax.

He'd told neither Carissa nor Maddie that he was going into the Esurhites' encampment alone, for it would only have distressed them and started another argument. But he'd long since decided he'd have an easier time of this on his own. For one thing, he was the only one who spoke the Tahg fluently and was also a warrior. And one man was easier to conceal than two.

For the first leg of his journey he walked with an exquisite awareness of what he carried in the rucksack on his back, amazed and unnerved that Maddie should have given it to him. On the one hand he was thrilled to have it. When Leyton's men had come to take the regalia, Maddie said it must have made itself invisible somehow, for she had watched the man open the valise and rummage around in it without ever pulling the garment out. Afterward, she'd inspected the bag herself, surprised to find nothing there. Later Elayne had brought the bag back to her, astonished when the robe had reappeared in it. None of them had any explanation for its disappearance.

Now, whether it helped him destroy the corridor or not, he was honored to wear it as a fitting salute to the greatness of his dearest friend.

But he couldn't stop thinking of those stories out of Elpis. Maddie herself had sent Katahn ul Manus to the southlands to rescue her brother and the regalia when she'd become queen. It was not unthinkable that he and Abramm might have converged on the Chesedhan king where he'd been the star of the Games in North Andol. Though the rhu'ema that had come with Leyton's body when it had been delivered claimed he'd been killed by a common slave masquerading as King Abramm, it was very possible the thing had lied. What if the "slave" was Abramm? Then the two of them might reasonably have come ashore in Chesedh together, with the regalia in their possession. . . .

One thing was sure: Whoever he was, the man had been able to raise a sizeable army in a very short period of time. It had moved across Chesedh to Fannath Rill seemingly unchallenged, and according to recent reports it had harassed the western flanks of Belthre'gar's great army for weeks. And harassment tactics certainly fell in line with Abramm's preferred method of conducting a war: Cut off the logistics, irritate, annoy, befuddle, and intimidate without ever really confronting, and you would drive your enemy mad enough that when you finally did confront him, he would be too rattled to put up a proper fight.

According to the spies who had come in from among the Esurhites, Belthre'gar, at least, truly believed it was the real Abramm out there. Some said the reason Belthre'gar was so obsessed with Maddie was because he couldn't get hold of her husband. . . .

But if it was Abramm . . . why had he not sent word? More important—as Maddie had pointed out—why had he not used the scepter? Why waste months cutting tent stays and spooking horses when he could drive them all off and be done with it?

On the other hand, that, too, echoed Abramm's tactics. *"Never let the enemy know your position or your intent until the time is right."* But if he was waiting for the right moment, Trap feared he'd waited too long.

Emerging from the bolthole tunnel into a narrow gully, Trap soon found himself surrounded by Esurhites. Still cloaked and cowled, he had the darkness on his side—and the fact that most of the men sprawled snoring on the ground. As he walked by, one of the sentries asked how far he'd gone toward the wall.

"All the way," he said in the Tahg. "They're all asleep up there."

The man laughed, and Trap walked on into the thick of them, praying Eidon would continue to blind their eyes. He estimated he'd have to walk about a league and a half through the encampment before he reached his destination, which should take him about an hour. It seemed, though, that he walked all night before the dark hulks of the ruin walls reared up against the brilliant green column of the corridor itself—a massive one, as it had to be. Its emerald glow bathed everything around him in green so bright it seemed like day.

Not surprisingly, the closer he got to it, the more soldiers he had to contend with—Esurhites, yes, but also Thilosians, Draesians, Andolens, and men from beyond the eastern deserts . . . the shaven-headed, pigtailed Sorites and slope-eyed men the likes of which Trap had never seen before. There were also Broho prowling solitarily among the tents and sleeping men. He always turned aside the moment he saw one of those, veering off his course so they might not pass too closely, careful never to look one in the eye.

Slowly he advanced upon the corridor, which he now saw rose from a depression in the terrain. Only the top portion of an ancient, decaying archway silhouetted against the green showed above the top of the rise ahead of him, but the unseen corona of the corridor's power field crawled over his skin with increasing strength, confirming his fear that it was bigger even than the one on the Gull Islands.

Only when he finally reached the hilltop could he see the column's entire length, shooting up from a weed-lined circular pavement at the center of a once-elaborate arcade built at the low point of a wide, shallow depression. The crumbling remains of the arcade sported a foremost arch still largely intact and framing the cadre of bald-headed priests standing within, chanting their incantations as they channeled their power toward the corridor. An ancient paved walkway wound up the long slope away from it, and all around sprawled scores of bodies, men sleeping off the drugged stupor they'd been put under to survive the trip sane.

A group of men were coming up that weed-grown lane now, heading straight toward him, their unsteady gaits marking them as recent arrivals.

About three-quarters of the way up the slope, a voice commanded them in Kiriathan to stop and settle. Trap was close enough to hear them grumbling about how badly they felt. Some collapsed where they stood, while others broke from the ranks and staggered away as the dry heaves took them. The majority settled without incident and fell immediately to sleep.

The commander, who wore the trappings of a high-ranking nobleman, continued walking with his attending lieutenants up the hill toward Trap. He was a tall, muscular fellow, if somewhat soft looking, with white blond hair that flowed about his shoulders like a cape. He wore a beard similar to Abramm's and also had two ragged pink scars slashing down the left side of his face. In fact, except for the hair and the soft look, he resembled Abramm a good deal. Deliberately, it would seem.

They were ten strides apart when the Kiriathan looked straight into Trap's eyes, and the latter's heart stopped. It was Gillard Kalladorne, false king of Kiriath. Shock turned swiftly to alarm with Trap's awareness that his own face was clearly visible, the cowl of his cloak useless since he was directly in line with the corridor's green light. Though he saw no sign of recognition in the other's eyes, he turned sharply aside to skirt the bowl's perimeter, waiting for the uproar to begin.

When no one shouted after him, he began to breathe again. Gillard had clearly come through without aid of any drugs, which meant he had to be indwelt by a rhu'ema—but that wouldn't account for his failure to recognize Trap. Was he just so preoccupied with his own affairs he hadn't seen what by all rights shouldn't have been there anyway? Or perhaps it had something to do with the treasure Trap carried in the rucksack on his back. . . ?

Not wanting to test his theories, he continued around the bowl's perimeter, widening the distance between himself and the Kiriathans as his mind erupted with new questions. What was Gillard—or Makepeace, or whatever the plague his name was now—doing here? Didn't he have weak bones? Or was that eased when he was made big again? Which was another thing. He looked as big as he'd always been. Yes, Trap had heard the rumors of his restoration, but he'd also seen the wasted waif Gillard had become after his encounter with the morwhol. It had to be rhu'eman magic, which meant the king of Kiriath was unquestionably in the Shadow's grip now.

North of the corridor's basin, the land was cluttered with the random remains of an ancient complex of rooms. Walls rose out of the grass, ran along a ways, then ended. Others formed a grid of roofless chambers in which a few soldiers had laid out their bedrolls but which mostly stood empty, perhaps owing to the fact the place was infested with staffid. Beyond it, the terrain stepped up in a series of rocky ledges and steep slopes to the head of a long, low ridge heading north and east.

Having put enough distance between himself and Gillard, and not wanting to stray too far from his objective, Trap turned down a narrow lane back through the ruin toward the corridor, turning into one of the roofless chambers at the last—

And finding his way blocked by the dark form of a man. He looked up into a pair of pale eyes in a face limned with green and sensed the knife flashing low between them more than he saw it. As he twisted backward and blocked the blow, white light flared from their contact, brilliantly illuminating the wall, the big man before him, and two others.

Simultaneously, the corridor in the basin below them stuttered and flared. Cries of alarm issued from the priests surrounding the corridor, all of which brought the combatants to a startled halt. Then a veren shrieked and they fled for cover. The big man grabbed Trap by the shoulder. As they fled for cover, Trap had enough sense not to fight him. He was almost certain these men were Abramm's—or whoever the newly arrived field commander was.

He was funneled down a narrow passage, then shoved forward on his belly and forced through a crawlway into a hollowed-out chamber not quite tall enough for him to stand up in, and impossible for the bigger man who'd brought him here. They sat in the dust and confronted him.

"Ye're Terstan, then? From Fannath Rill?" the big man asked him quietly.

"From the queen," Trap confirmed. "Are you some of Abramm's men?"

The big man frowned. "Why'd ye think that? Ever'one knows Abramm's workin' out t' the west."

"No," Trap said. "We don't know it's Abramm for sure. There've been many stories. Many imposters." He paused as a sudden thought hit him. "If he's out there, though, I have a message for him. From his wife."

The big man frowned at him, then glanced at one of the others, plainly doubtful.

"We don't have time fer this," one of them said.

The big man grimaced. "Gag him and tie him up fer now."

"No!" Trap said in sudden alarm, aghast to realize if he didn't destroy the corridor, the queen would not have her distraction. "I need—" Caution stayed his words. He didn't, in fact, know for sure who these men were. Best not reveal too much, especially not anything about Maddie. "I need to see him now," Trap said as the men at his back seized him and bound his wrists securely.

"Well, ye're not gonna," the big man told him. "Fer all we know ye're one o' those that just came through the corridor with ol' King Makepeace."

"I'd be in a stupor if that were—" He was cut off as the gag wrapped around his mouth.

"What d' ya suppose is in that rucksack?" one of the other men asked, plucking at it.

Oh, Eidon, please. Don't let them open it here.

"I dunno," the big man said. "We'll look later. Put 'im here between us, where he can't cause any harm." He patted Trap's arm. "If what ye're sayin' is true, we'll let ye go in good time. Fer now, though, we've got work t' do, and ye can't be interruptin'."

"Here comes another batch of 'em," said one of the others as the annoying tingle of the corridor's power field intensified and the green light flared all around them.

36

That night, lying between the two men, gagged and bound, Trap endured some of the most frustrating hours of his existence. He had to lift his head back at an uncomfortable angle to see anything, and he spent most of the time with his cheek to the smoke-tainted ground, staring at the small, dark-haired man beside him. And moment by moment his opportunity to destroy the corridor slipped away. He could only pray Maddie and the others had escaped despite the loss of his distraction—and try not to think about the effect his apparent failure would have upon his wife.

At least no one had mentioned looking into his rucksack again, though the thought of that, too, weighed upon him. Now that he'd had time to think, he couldn't imagine why he had let these men take him. The slimmest promise that they might bring him to Abramm had clouded his mind. Now here he was, completely taken out of action because of something that probably wouldn't even pan out. He'd compromised the queen's escape and worse, for eventually someone would open the rucksack. And then . . .

Another thought that didn't bear pursuing.

From their position on the side of the basin they could see the great throng of robed, bald priests around the corridor, their red robes turned brown in the green light. They had chanted and hummed and moaned all night long, bringing in troop after troop of men, interspersed with yet another catapult or battering ram or load of food—tubers and grain, half cooked by their journey.

Trap dozed in and out of sleep, awakened finally when the corridor's tooth-gritting buzz softened and lowered its pitch. Looking up, he found the column of emerald light had shrunk, the priests collapsing where they stood. Burly men in dark uniforms carried them away as new priests replaced them, though in a quarter of the original number.

"Looks like they're finishin' up," said the big man. From his conversations with the others, Trap had figured out his name was Rollie. "Prob'bly brought a thousand men through tonight."

"Aye, but they're havin' t' drug 'em more," said the small, dark-haired one. "Look how fast they're fallin' now after they come through an' how long it takes 'em to wake up again. The king's right. Things are breakin' down."

Rollie turned Trap over then and freed him of bindings and gag. "Ye want to deliver yer message t' the king, friend," he warned, "ye'd best keep silent and move along with us. If ye do anythin' else, we'll kill ye where ye stand."

They stole out of the camp in the same manner as Trap had entered it— they simply walked, four out of a multitude of soldiers. There were so many different races and languages, had anyone stopped them they'd only need claim to be looking for their home company and they'd have been left alone.

Eventually they strode away through the loosely guarded rear line and up the low, rocky rise beyond, the overcast already lightening with the dawn. Once out of sight of the camp, they stopped to discuss whether Trap should be blindfolded—the two subordinates for, Rollie against. "It'll take too much time to lead him along blind. If he's lyin', Abramm'll deal with him."

The name spoken sent a tingle up Trap's spine, for it was the first admission from these men that they were indeed Abramm's. Not that the man they called Abramm was necessarily the real thing, but Trap was eager to meet him, nevertheless. Maybe tonight hadn't been as much of a disaster as he'd feared.

From a distance, the Fairiron Plain looked flat as a board, but on foot, especially as it approached the Deveren Rim to the northwest, one learned it abounded with deep, steep-walled channels and rocky outcroppings, many of them riddled with caves. It was here that the harassing army had encamped, virtually unseen until one was in the middle of it.

Abramm—or whoever he was—was not where Rollie expected him to be, but the men he talked to sent him out of the cave that appeared to be their command center and along a second steep-walled gully to a sketchy path switchbacking up a rocky, weed-grown slope. They came out on a broad shelf extending from the slope's side, forty feet above the plain now.

At the shelf's far end, one man had squatted to draw in the dust with a stick as a group of others clustered about him, watching. Telling Trap to wait where he was, Rollie strode rapidly across the flat to join the others.

After a moment the man who'd been squatting stood up, head and shoulders taller than the rest with shaggy blond hair, a honey-colored beard, and a plaited crown of white gold resting on his brow. One look and Trap felt the ground lurch beneath his feet. He stared hard at the hawkish profile, the dark brows, those familiar scars, not pink as marks recently made would have been, but white and thin and almost unnoticeable from a distance. He had to admit, the man looked and moved an awful lot like Abramm.

The king spoke to his men for some time, turning toward the plain and the army and the besieged city stretching away from them, gesturing right and left as they discussed their battle plans. Only when that came to an end did Rollie finally approach him. The two spoke at length, presumably about the corridor, but Trap saw the moment he himself was mentioned. The king's head drew up sharply, and he stepped around the blacksmith to look at Trap.

Then he was striding across the hummocked ground to meet him.

Trap watched him come in a state of shock and lingering disbelief. But when his old friend finally stood before him, and it was well and truly Abramm, who had died in Trap's heart and now came to life again, all the shock and pain and disbelief fell away like an old skin and he laughed aloud as they embraced. *Oh, Maddie, you were right all along! And soon now, if Eidon allows, your faith will be rewarded.*

"Is she in Fannath Rill, then?" Abramm asked as they pulled apart.

No need to say whom he meant. "I expect not, if she kept her promise," Trap said. He explained their plan as his eyes roamed across his friend's face, noting the lines around his blue eyes and the white hair at his temples, though he was still only thirty-five. He was all lean, hard, chiseled muscle, too, his skin burned dark from months of living in the field, aged by his trials, perhaps, but stronger and more alive than ever.

"Rolland said you have a message for me," he said when Trap had finished. Behind him, his men had approached curiously, listening in on the conversation. Abramm didn't seem to mind.

Trap flashed a sheepish grin at Rolland. "No. I just . . . didn't want him to kill me." He paused, remembering. "Gillard's out there, Abramm. With a troop of Kiriathans. More than one troop, probably. I ran into them just after they'd come through the corridor."

Abramm shrugged. "I'm not surprised. And at least this way all my enemies will be in one place." He returned to the original topic. "You say Maddie should reach Deveren Dol in three or four days?"

"Barring any unforeseen disasters." Like Carissa suddenly going into labor. . . . *Don't think of that!* "Her counselors plan to open the city gates and offer their surrender in three days."

Abramm nodded. "And what if Belthre'gar attacks first?"

"They'll hold on that long, at least. They have to. If she doesn't get away, it'll all be for naught. . . ." He trailed off.

Abramm gazed now across the plain, thinking. Finally he straightened and said, "You're right about Belthre'gar's position deteriorating. His more seasoned soldiers are already starting to desert. He can't hold out much longer. But at the same time, he'll have to wait a couple of days for the new arrivals to be recovered enough to fight."

He turned to Rollie and another man with a pocked face, an eye patch, and a Chesedhan lilt to his speech, asking them about the degree of preparation in some area of a pre-existing plan Trap knew nothing about. When they responded favorably, Abramm made his decision. "We'll assume the queen's gotten away clean. I want us ready to attack in three days. See the word is passed."

As his two commanding officers hurried off, Abramm glanced at his former First Minister. "If he moves before then, we'll just wait and let him wear out his men before we go wading in." With a grin, he turned and led the way down the slope.

As they skidded to the wash bottom, Trap suddenly recalled what he carried on his back and stopped in his tracks with a startled "Oh!"

Abramm turned toward him questioningly.

"I just remembered," Trap said. "Maddie might not have given me a message for you, but she did give me something." He shrugged out of the rucksack and handed it over. "It's the Robe of Light, sir. She gave it to me just before I left. In case I happened to run into you."

"So she *did* know I was here," Abramm said with satisfaction, unfastening the buckles.

"Not exactly, sir. She said it somewhat in jest. She'd intended me to use it in destroying the corridor, and I was arguing with her—"

"As you always do," Abramm said, grinning.

Trap frowned at him. "It is your regalia, sir. And we've already seen what happened to Leyton for trying to use what was not his."

"I know." Abramm was still grinning and now reached out to clap Trap's shoulder. "You have no idea how happy I am to have you back with me— arguing and all." He returned his attention to the rucksack, pulled back the flap, then drew out a bit of the bright, suddenly supple fabric.

For a moment he stood there staring down at it, and Trap thought he saw tears shining in his eyes. Then he shook it off, shoved the fabric back into the rucksack, and turned to one of the two young men who had followed him. "Galen, take this to Fisher. Tell him to put it with the others. He'll know what it is."

Galen apparently knew what it was, too, for he looked at Trap with awe and took the rucksack as if it were a priceless treasure.

"You have need of the robe, then?" Trap said as Galen hurried away with it.

Abramm snorted softly. "Believe it or not, I do." He shook his head. "It's all coming back to me, Trap. Just as Eidon promised: the regalia, the army, Warbanner, now you."

"Warbanner?"

"One of Rollie's friends brought him down a few months ago. Simon had him sent to Chesedh to keep him out of Gillard's hands. He's been on a farm in the western hills all this time. When they got word I had returned to call up an army, they brought him down." He shook his head, marveling, then turned up the wash and said, "Come, walk with me now. There is much I want to know."

First Abramm questioned him closely about Maddie and his own children, then moved on to congratulate Trap on finally marrying Carissa, delighted to learn they were expecting a second child. When Trap expressed concern for having left her on her own to travel up to Deveren Dol, Abramm assured him he'd made the right decision. Maddie wouldn't have entrusted the robe to anyone else, and it needed to be delivered.

As they walked through the tents, lean-tos, and bedrolls scattering the wash bottom and sides, he said, "If all goes as I hope, this battle will be the last we'll have to fight for many, many years." He turned to Trap with a grin. "You wouldn't have wanted to miss that, would you?"

And Trap admitted he would not. They moved on, the questions focusing now on political and logistical matters. Trap marveled anew at Abramm's command and knowledge of the situation—and more than that, his confidence. Abramm had a new ease of command, as if it were indeed the thing he'd been born to do. There was more to it than that, though. He had a depth and complexity that manifested itself in an indefinable calm, and an unexpected combination of gentleness and iron resolve. Being with him, Trap sensed Eidon's own person in a way he'd never experienced before. It filled him with something that felt almost like exultation and the unshakable awareness that all was well. . . .

Even though, by human standards, all was definitely not well. Belthre'gar had brought in some three hundred seventy-five thousand men, while Abramm had mustered a mere twenty thousand—the bulk of those deployed outside the city's western walls, not here on the east side. When Trap expressed consternation at both deployment pattern and odds, Abramm only grinned and reminded him that Eidon cared nothing about odds.

As they returned to the cave Abramm had made his headquarters, they found a breakfast of bread and mutton pottage awaiting both of them. And finally Trap was able to ask some questions of his own. Abramm's answers confirmed much of what he'd guessed, but though his friend spoke easily of all that had befallen him, he also tended to summarize and gloss over events that Trap suspected were far more important than he made them out to be— particularly his time in the dragon city. It would probably take years to learn all that his friend had endured.

They were finishing up the meal when Abramm broached the subject of Tiris ul Sadek, and for the first time since they'd been reunited, a sudden tension sharpened his tone.

"He was a dragon," Trap said gravely.

"I know."

Trap could only imagine the degree of pain Abramm had known when he'd been told she'd remarried. Pain that probably wouldn't be totally eased until he had her in his arms again. As Abramm toyed with the crust of his bread, Trap considered how best to say what must be said without making more of it than it was.

"He courted her from the beginning," he said at length. "Though she told him bluntly and often that she wasn't interested. Still he pushed her, pressed her, offered her everything she might want. Not another woman in the court would have refused him, and no one could understand Maddie's reluctance. Then the wave came, and you must have heard how bad it was. Tiris offered her galleys to defend the southern shores, and troops to guard the river and the palace. No one had any hope of your return, and she was laughed at and mocked for hers."

"Marta did not come with the book and letter I sent?"

"Oh, she came. But Tiris conspired to make it seem as if you had died in the desert after she'd left you." When Trap told him about Maddie's visions in the amber, he seemed startled but said nothing.

"Everything and everyone pressed her to leave your memory behind and move on." He paused, shame washing over him as he recalled his own part in this. "Her cabinet drew up a resolution to approve a marriage between them." He paused again, then sighed wearily. "I'm sorry to say I signed the thing myself. And finally she agreed to do as we wished, as seemed best for the land. But Carissa told me she cried herself to sleep the night she finally accepted Tiris's proposal. And for many nights thereafter, as well." He summarized the rest of the story—how she'd told Tiris she'd changed her mind and that he'd taken the news civilly and had left the galleys, and how their sudden disappearance led to the fall of Peregris, a loss Maddie was still being held responsible for by many.

"She's taken so much abuse, and stood firm before it. You would not believe how resolute she has been. How strong her love for you is. In the face of all that, she did not give up on you. Even though you sent us no word and we were inundated with false tales of scar-faced imposters coming to rescue us, stories that made her hope a mockery." He hesitated, heard the pain in his own voice as he asked, "Why did you not send word when you reached Elpis, Abramm? It would have made all the difference."

He learned then that Abramm *had* sent word. But all his riders were killed before they reached her. He'd sent out pigeons by the score, and they too were slain, some slaughtered as soon as they left the coop. After that, he'd figured he was supposed to surprise everyone. "I thought you, at least, would recognize my hand in what was going on out here."

Trap nodded. "I have to admit the tactics did appear to be yours. But . . . you said earlier that the regalia are coming back to you. . . . Are you still missing the scepter, then?"

"No. I have it." His lips quirked. "And you want to know why I've not used it."

Trap nodded.

"Because I've realized my true enemy is not Belthre'gar. It is Moroq, whom you know as Tiris ul Sadek. We're not going to kill the dragon himself—Tersius will take care of him when the time is right—so even if Belthre'gar dies, Moroq will only find another puppet and start all over again, as he did after Beltha'adi. I can't just drive them all out of Chesedh; I have to destroy them completely. The army, the priests, all of it." He leaned toward Trap, almost fierce in his intensity. "I've seen Aggosim and ridden through North Andol. He's stripped the land bare. No crops, no livestock. These men will go home to nothing. And the longer we wait, the more men he brings here, the harder they're all going to fall . . . and the longer it'll take before they'll rebuild the resources—or the will—to follow another tyrant bent on conquering the world."

And looking at him, sitting there leaning over the table, it seemed his blue eyes flashed with a blaze of white, sending a chill up the back of Trap's neck.

In the predawn hours of the day of attack, Abramm sat atop Warbanner under a large and very old oak tree on a long, low ridge overlooking the field of battle. Trap and Rolland sat on dark horses to either side of him, the trio ignored by Belthre'gar's army below them. Any threat was expected to come from the front of their lines, not the rear.

Abramm wore the crown on his brow and the Robe of Light hung as fluid silk over his leather cuirass. The scepter rode in its scabbard on his back, and all was covered by a dark woolen cloak and cowl. Likewise Warbanner wore a full caparison quilted of white fabric with chain mail layered in. That, too, was hidden under a thin covering of dark silk. It was a covering that—owing to the slit made along the neck crest and the pull tie at the headstall between the ears—could be as easily shed as Abramm's own cloak. As both would be when the time came.

For now they sat watching and waiting. Belthre'gar's army filled the plain before and slightly below them all the way to the city's outer walls, a distance of three leagues. It stretched to either side as far as he could see, both on this side of the Ankrill and the other—tents, campfires, bedrolls, picket lines, catapults, battering rams, wagons, horses, and all the other accoutrements of a great army engaged at siege.

During the last day the massive gathering had reorganized itself, drawing order out of the earlier chaos. Now its various companies had formed up into recognizable ranks, each under the banner of the realm they represented. Scaling ladders, siege towers, battering rams, and the covering panels that would enable the wall sappers to work stood at regular intervals throughout the multitude, shreds of mist drifting around them, fuzzing the glow of the purple orbs burning here and there to maintain Command. From time to time he even glimpsed the gleaming shaven heads of the Broho who moved among them. All of it beneath a glowering ceiling of mist dyed orange by the campfires and the torches—save to the north, where the hue changed to the green of the still operational corridor.

It had been much quieter over the last two days, though, as those who'd most recently come through it recovered before they had to fight. The lull was as good a signal as any that Belthre'gar was about to storm the great city of Fannath Rill and seize the plum at her heart—the palace on its island where Queen Madeleine would take her stand.

From his position, Abramm could just see the palace's upper towers peeking above the city's immense outer walls, but to those on the battlefield, it would be entirely hidden by those same walls. Walls atop which torches now blazed, illuminating the white banners of surrender that had, in the last hour, been unrolled down the faces flanking the east entrance gate.

His gaze dropped from the banners to the observation platform standing midway through the ranks before that same gate, from whence Belthre'gar would observe and conduct his battle. He stood on his platform surrounded by his newly acquired contingent of Sorite archers. Five of them, with their shaven heads, black topknot braids, and bronze breastplates. All carried long-bows taller than themselves and fat quivers of arrows. The tallest was a magnificently muscled man, whose gold breastplate proclaimed him the leader. Sorite archers being renowned for their accuracy, Belthre'gar could be completely confident that any assassins or assault parties would be eliminated long before they reached his presence. Even so, he'd also retained a squadron of Broho, who now stood in ranks around the platform's base, extending perhaps thirty strides out from it on all sides.

Between the platform and the city stood a vanguard of a hundred men pointed toward the gate. At the vanguard's head, a huge battering ram hung from a covered wooden framework—put in place the day before and ready for action in case the queen changed her mind about surrendering.

After the white banners appeared, a man had emerged from the city to parlay. Abramm had no idea what was said, but Trap told him the plan was to plead for mercy, since the people were starving, low on water, and dying of sickness. What Trap didn't know was whether or not the queen's council had decided to actually go through with the surrender or use it as a ruse to draw the Esurhites in so their military might strike a more significant blow than they could otherwise.

Abramm hoped it was the latter, but he was ready for either outcome. For weeks, his people had been secretly moving in their own catapults, then hiding them in barns or caves or gullies under brush piles. Throughout the night, the machines had been rolled from those hiding places and into position, not far behind the Esurhites' loosely guarded rear lines and still hidden by the predawn darkness. Abramm's plan was a bold one, relying heavily for its success on the shock and fear that surprise would cause but also not far off being a suicide run, as his closest subordinates had repeatedly pointed out. Even so, of all the plans he'd considered, he believed this one had the best chance of success—a belief significantly strengthened by the fact that Eidon had seen fit to deliver the Robe of Light precisely at the moment of his great need for it.

A stirring broke out on the city's wallwalks immediately flanking the gates. Belthre'gar turned from talking to his aides and faced toward the point of interest. His Sorite bodyguards kept their bows on their backs, but throughout the gathered host, men stood up, and a rustling mutter arose from them.

A great squeal echoed over the field, followed by the telltale clacking of the chain gears as the gates swung slowly outward. Abramm uttered a quiet "Now" and nudged Warbanner forward as Trap and Rolland moved out in tandem ahead of him. They trotted in formation down the gentle slope toward the ragged unguarded rear lines. Dressed in dark colors as they were, they approached unnoticed. Or if noticed, then ignored, since what could be threatening about three lone horsemen riding slowly into a camp of hundreds of thousands?

They entered the encampment unopposed, trotting easily along a broad lane between two companies of Esurhites, heading deeper and deeper into the southlander army, straight for the golden platform on which its leader stood.

The gap between gates had widened enough to admit three men riding abreast when Belthre'gar gave the command to attack. As multiple lesser commands rang out, the army roared and soldiers rushed for the opening— only to be shot down from the line of bowmen now appearing on the wallwalk. *It was a ruse!* Abramm thought, delighted. *Perfect!*

Swiftly, he untied his cloak and cast it off, then loosed the tie on Warbanner's headstall, so that the silk covering fluttered away. Then he drew his sword and shouted the word as Rolland and Trap, who'd also drawn their weapons, kicked their horses into a gallop. Together they plunged up the lane, noticed at last, but far too late. Trap and Rolland hit the wall of Broho defenders first, running the first few of them down and sending others flying out of their paths as they carved a path for Abramm, who galloped behind them on Warbanner, sword blazing with Eidon's Light.

As his lead men grappled with the defenders, they moved apart to create a gap, which Abramm raced through, Light flaring like a spear before him. He was nearly to the platform when the tallest Sorite turned. Abramm recognized him at once, not at all surprised it was Moroq. In the blink of an eye, the Sorite flipped his bow over his head and released his first dark arrow. The Light swallowed it half a nose ahead of Warbanner. More came, and the Light consumed then all.

He saw blades slashing toward him as Warbanner was forced to stop, and he met them with his own—steel crashing into steel as he pulled the horse around. Light gleamed off bald heads and shredding mist as purple fire blazed in darkness. The din was horrendous. The terrible stench of blood and spilling guts filled the air. Belthre'gar turned finally, his eyes widening as he saw Abramm. Then Moroq hauled him off the far side of the platform and out of sight.

Abramm wheeled Warbanner full circle amidst a closing line of Broho, all facing him with blades drawn, eyes blazing with purple fire. He was one sword against them all. Purple flame leaped from their mouths, but the Light blasted every bolt of it to droplets. They followed flame with the fearspell, but Abramm used his sword to turn it back upon them, and they fled.

It occurred to him then that while he might be invulnerable, the men who served under him were not. That recalled to him the scepter. He jerked it left-handed from its scabbard and swung it over his head. Lightning flashed down from the sky . . . or did it go up from the scepter? Wind whirled around him, tearing at his hair as he saw Belthre'gar again, riding in a chariot pulled by two black horses, charging north across the battlefield. Toward the corridor.

Abramm jammed the scepter back into its scabbard and took off after the Supreme Commander, determined he should not get away. He had no idea what had become of Trap and Rolland, nor if anyone was following him. Around him increasing daylight illumined chaos— men fighting and fallen, swords flashing—and he realized with a shock Belthre'gar's forces were fighting one another. Different tabards, different armies . . . confused by the darkness? Arrows rained upon them as rocks and pitch pots thrown by catapults from both sides crashed continually on every side.

Warbanner ran like a horse years younger. They dodged wagons, leaped ditches, and scrambled down inclines, blowing over those unlucky enough to be in their way as they closed the gap. The corridor loomed ahead, its green light a brilliant counterpoint to the gray morning. Wind tore around him, moving northward, tearing up the Shadow as it did, though not nearly as fast as he'd have liked.

The chariot bounced ahead of him now, tipping wildly this way and that. Moroq drove it, his great muscled arms tensed with the effort of holding the reins, his legs braced widely to keep the cart from overturning as Belthre'gar clung to the other side. They barreled down the slope and through the arch, where Moroq pulled up and shoved the Supreme Commander from the chariot. Belthre'gar rolled, stood up, saw Abramm coming, and scrambled for his sword. It was only half drawn when Abramm's blade sliced his throat. As Abramm rode on past, hauling Warbanner to a stop, the image of the man's widening eyes above scarlet jets of spurting blood came with him. He wheeled his horse around just in time to see the Esurhite leader collapse, the rhu'ema that lived within him flowing out his eyes, nose, and mouth. It coiled above the fallen man a moment, then drove into the corridor and was gone.

Abramm sat atop his warhorse, sword dripping blood, adversary's body before him, and realized he'd raced in unthinking. Now he was cut off, surrounded by his enemies. Sheer numbers could easily kill his horse, then rip the robe from his shoulders. And he saw little indication anyone had come with him. Out beyond the brow of the basin in which the corridor stood, the arrows still flew and the catapults still heaved. In the distance scaling ladders now propped against Fannath Rill's walls, black-tunicked invaders scrambling over their tops. Rocks and arrows and flaming pitch rained down everywhere. Worse, the winds had stopped, and the Shadow was regathering.

Movement drew his eye to the Sorite giant, bow flexed, black arrow aimed at him. The string twanged, the arrow flew, and Abramm's sword came up—too late. The shaft hit him square in the breast . . . but fell to the stone, where it vanished.

Moroq roared in a way that wasn't remotely human. His eyes flashed into gold fire as he flung aside his bow and leaped forward. The air fluttered around him with a shifting of light and shadow, of red and black and gold . . . and the man shape vanished into a huge narrow face, leathery wings, and golden talons.

Warbanner erupted beneath him, squealing in terror as he reared and turned and tried to run all at the same time. The ruins tilted crazily; Abramm glimpsed talons and wings and the ground coming up fast. A great wind buffeted him as he hit the pavement, the blow knocking the sword from his grasp. He rolled away, barely evading Warbanner's flailing hooves as the horse scrambled wildly upright, a great bloody gash in his neck. A moment later he bolted into the mass of men surrounding them, but no one tried to stop him. They were too busy staring at the dragon as it circled the ruin, its scales flashing like fresh blood in the early morning light.

Abramm leaped to his feet, eyeing the dragon as well. He'd lost his sword.

Warbanner must have kicked it somewhere in his thrashing to get up. The army that surrounded him had fallen silent. He heard the faint hum of the corridor behind him as the dragon circled, enjoying the attention. Then it dropped low over the host of Esurhites and exhaled an orange-scarlet mist. As it settled upon the men, their faces twisted with fury and they screamed as one, charging with an eerie unity of mind and purpose that could have no other source than the creature circling above them. Abramm could almost hear its words: *Kill him! Kill him now!*

No time to find his sword, so he reached for the only thing he had—the scepter, still riding in its scabbard on his back. The moment he pulled it free, the Light exploded through him. He gripped it with both hands and brained the first of his attackers with the blazing jewel at its end.

Then there was no time to know or plan or even think. He swung and whirled and ducked and hit, again and again and again. Yet still they came. Men grabbed him, tried to pull the robe off him, but he drove them away and kept swinging. He heard the dragon roaring, and the men roaring likewise as the scepter blazed, streaming sparks, smashing heads and shoulders and backs, breaking bones and crushing flesh. They came on and on, opposing him like madmen, and he fought them off with a strength he knew was not his own, until the bodies piled up around him, and he had to climb up onto them to keep the high ground.

Then, finally, it stopped.

Despite the slaughter, enemy soldiers still filled the basin outside the ancient arcade, whipped by a gale wind he hadn't noticed until now. It had torn loose the warrior's knots on their necks, their hair streaming from their heads like black banners. Dust and leaves, branches and boards, bits of fabric and all manner of other things sailed and tumbled by. Gradually the red light in the men's eyes faded, and they slowed and stopped, staring now at the great pile of bodies atop which Abramm stood. Then three Broho stepped forth from the crowd and sent a black cloud of fear at him.

He swung the scepter into it with hardly a thought, the movement easy and confident. He'd been swinging and swinging for who knew how long at whatever threat came to him—what was one more?

As the scepter's head hit it, the cloud burst into a plume of dark motes, caught by the wind and blown back over the men—not just the three Broho, but the score of soldiers behind them. Fear gripped them as swiftly as the bloodlust had earlier. They screamed, dropped their weapons, and fled, only to be cut off by the dragon, who roared its frustration and this time exhaled fire, incinerating them as they ran.

That was the drop that burst the dam. Panic seized the field and pandemonium ensued. The dragon flew over them, burning men as it went, then circled up into the sky, breathtaking in its size and gracefulness and the way the new-risen sun sparkled off its scarlet scales. It had to be at least a quarter mile away, but Abramm saw its eyes, and heard its thoughts, which were just for him:

"You may have won here, but you'll still lose all that you really care about." The creature winged over his head, then circled to the north. *"Try to save them if you can. . . ."*

An image of the corridor behind him flashed into his mind.

The dragon's wings flapped languidly, and then the mists, driven northward by the scepter's winds, swallowed the beast from view.

37

Abramm strode toward the corridor, scepter in hand. The prickling inten-sified as he stepped into its aura—and stopped as he saw Maddie and the others riding up the switchbacks to the top of the cliff on which Deveren Dol perched. Close, but not close enough. Urgency prodded him as he realized he was seeing her through the dragon's eyes. Which meant the creature would be there well before she reached the fortress.

The image was overlaid by a view of the Ankrill bending around the base of a castle, the scene framed by stone pillars. At first he had no idea what he was seeing, then realized it was also near Deveren Dol, but atop the falls now, looking out of some temple across the river at the castle. Somehow he sensed it was an opening this corridor linked to. He could be there any moment, step through the gateway, and get there in time to save his family. *Yes!*

No! What was he thinking? He had no business trying to use a corridor to solve his problems.

Maybe Eidon wanted him to use it, though. His passage might destroy it, and he could be where he was needed, as well. It made perfect sense.

No!

Why not? He had the scepter and the crown. What did he need to fear? And if he did not act soon, it would be too late. Maddie would die, and it would be his fault. Impatience roiled in his middle. *Just do it. Do it now before it's too late! What are you waiting for?*

His weight shifted. He almost took another step, then put his foot down again. Moroq had driven Belthre'gar to the corridor, and more or less cast him before Abramm's blade to kill. He'd attacked Abramm with the dark arrows, when he had to have known they'd be ineffective. Had he known Abramm would be able to fight off the hordes of soldiers empowered by dragon-enflamed bloodlust? He might have. Then he'd flamed his own forces and flown away. . . . Because he'd lost, yes. But was it ever that simple?

Dragon vision showed him his wife and—was that his daughter?!—on the second horse from the lead, buffeted by the wind as she came up over the top of the cliff and turned to look south toward him. And the approaching dragon. Did she see it yet?

Fear tore at him as the wind tore at her. He needed to go. Now.

No.

Father, I know I have no business using this thing. Help me to destroy it!

The moment his motivation turned, so did the temptation. Suddenly it was not Maddie he saw, nor even the destination near Deveren Dol, but dozens of others—he was startled to recognize Tuk-Rhaal in Kiriath among them. And there was the domed room in Chena'ag Tor, and a vast hall with the red dragon on the wall above a golden throne . . . Moroq's Throne of Power.

Abramm could go there, to the very center of Moroq's unseen empire, and destroy it. He had the scepter and the crown and the robe, and with them he wielded a power that could wipe out his greatest enemy!

Visions of what a victory that would be swelled in his head. No more Shadow. No more evil. His realm free from pain and suffering at last. Why shouldn't he do it? He had the power. He had the opportunity. How many men would ever face such an opportunity? He would never face it again, he was sure. And if he did not take it, he would have only himself to blame when troubles returned to his land . . . as they inevitably would. It might take a long time for the enemy to rebuild its forces, but eventually they would come again. With this corridor, he could make his victory final.

He leaned toward the nexus of connections, heady with the possibilities before him, and as before, something held him back. A weak and tenuous thread, one that could easily be broken . . . A still, small voice of warning at the back of his head.

The downfall of the victor is that he lets the victory go to his head.

Suddenly he grew aware of his own hubris. What was he thinking? Even with robe and crown and scepter—he could never claim the final victory. He still had Shadow in him, and it was not his place to tangle with Shadow. Not that way.

Tersius would be the one to destroy the Throne of Power. The only one.

And if Abramm tried to take upon himself that which was not his task . . . he would die. As would his wife and his children. It all came down to this one moment. This one decision.

And it appalled him that even after he had seen the truth and come to the clear conclusion, a part of him still wanted to try the corridor.

He stepped back, out of its green aura. "I will not do it, my Lord."

As the words left his mouth something hit him from behind, forcing him to stagger forward, deeper into the field. The pavement wavered beneath him as a small, ratlike man scurried past him, white hair streaming in his wake.

The man vanished, the corridor vanished, and again he saw Maddie, on the ferry now, halfway across the river above the falls. She still held Abrielle. Captain Channon stood beside her holding Ian, Simon clutching his free hand. They were before and below him, far too close for comfort, zooming by beneath him: dragon sight again. It had reached them and was banking against the clouds for another pass. The initial temptation to go to them resurged.

Then he was pulled after the small man, hurtling through the column of green light, and crying out to Eidon as he went.

Queen Madeleine and her party reached the top of the Deveren cliffs three days after they'd fled Fannath Rill through the western bolthole. Passed from guide to guide through a series of wagons, barns, carriages, and ditches, they had escaped the city cleanly and met up with their grooms and horses in the foothills separating the plain from the escarpment. From then on they had made much better time.

Now, as they started up the last of the switchbacks scaling the face of the great cliff, Maddie eyed their destination eagerly. Deveren Dol loomed from the opposite bank, overlooking the Ankrill as it roared over the cliff's edge in the magnificent Royal Falls. The castle followed the old-style architecture, all thick stone walls and windowless towers. Its few openings were high and narrow, made primarily for defense. Its highest towers stood atop a great upthrust of rock overlooking the plain below, the rest of it stairstepping down the incline toward the river that curled round its base before tumbling over the cliff. At one time those towers held a commanding view of the Fairiron Plain; now their tops plunged into the ceiling of mist that had blotted out the sky for months.

Seeing the fortress energized her. Once they reached the top of the cliff, they had only to ride down to the ferry, cross the river, and they'd be safe. Or as safe as they could be until Abramm returned.

They traveled on horseback, Ian riding with Captain Channon, and Simon with Lieutenant Pipping. Maddie carried Abrielle in a sling against her chest, and Elayne held Conal, since Carissa had enough to manage with her massive belly. They had hardly stopped since they'd left Fannath Rill, halting only briefly in a glen at the base of the cliff to sleep last night—until Maddie had been awakened by a bad dream and the overwhelming sense that they must leave.

As they approached the top of the cliff, the Light surged within her, and she looked instinctively across the plain to where the day was beginning to break, the clouds stained red on the horizon. Fannath Rill lay like a dark stain on the landscape, cut through by the gleaming silver of the Ankrill. The city walls showed up as thin white lines encircling darkness, even as darkness raged outside them. Motes of bright orange swirled above it—flaming pitch pots flung from the catapults of both sides. The battle had begun.

As she watched, the blood-red light on the distant horizon spread toward her, and her heart leaped as she realized the continuous cover was breaking up—for the first time in months. And there, north of the city, a white star appeared amidst the corridor's green glow. A star that flickered, then strengthened, growing brighter and brighter.

Wonder swept through her, just before the first stirring of wind hit her. As she rounded the last switchback, she turned quickly in the saddle, reversing position so as not to miss anything. Shafts of sunlight poured through the widening rents, illumining a battlefield that looked like a mound of angry ants. The wind intensified, yanking at her cloak and pressing her and the horse toward the side of the trail as bushes bent flat before it.

"It's Abramm!" she shouted at Carissa, who rode right behind her. She gestured toward the plain as her sister-in-law turned to look. "I told you he was out there! And sure as anything, Trap's with him!" *Why else would I have sent him out there with that robe?*

She reined in her horse and turned it back to watch more easily as, beside her, Carissa did the same, and the others moved by them on the trail.

When Trap had not succeeded in destroying the corridor that first night, they had both teetered on the edge of soul-wrenching grief and despair, struggling not to believe the worst, when it seemed that was the only thing they could believe. Then she'd recalled giving him the robe and comforted Carissa with that information—for she did not believe it had been random or without purpose, and just because Trap had not done what he'd set out to do did not mean he was captured or killed. It could, in fact, mean he'd run into Abramm.

As she watched the dawn light spread and the clouds shred, exultation rose in her breast. Then a small, winged form dropped out of the misty ceiling far in the distance and soared low over the battling armies on the ground, looking as if it were spraying them with fire. A *dragon*. It vanished behind a gout of smoke, then burst into view a moment later, circling back for another pass, bright flame engulfing the field in its wake.

At first she focused on the small white light still bright and clear in the corridor's green. Then she realized the dragon had banked away from the city to head north. Directly toward her. Abramm had won! The dragon had been defeated! Driven off. And now the only thing left to it was to come after Abramm's loved ones.

Sick with sudden fear, she clutched Abby closer and faced forward in the saddle, yelling, "It's coming for us! Hurry!"

Everyone else had seen it by now, and whipped their horses up the last switchback to burst over the top of the cliff and race toward the ferry. A mass of people from the town opposite the castle crowded the bank, and Maddie wondered how they could know of the dragon when she'd just seen it herself. Then someone answered her question: The Esurhites had taken Trakas several days ago and were headed downriver toward Deveren Dol.

The mist drifted around them as they forced their horses through the crowd and onto the landing, Channon shouting for the others to "make way for the queen!" When it finally registered that the queen was indeed among them, the townspeople backed away, shocked and flustered, and she dismounted. They left the horses there on the landing and hurried aboard the flat-bottomed craft, crowding on with as many of the others as could fit. There were still far too many on the landing. "Go back!" Maddie called to them as the gate came down. "Get out of sight; take cover if you can. There's a dragon coming!"

They looked at her with incomprehension as the gate shut and the ferry moved out into the river.

"A dragon," she yelled back at them. "A dragon is coming. Take cover."

The ferry lurched as the current gripped it, pulling at its guide rope, as the water urged it toward the falls. They were more than halfway across when the dragon burst over the cliff top, flying so low over the river its wingtips touched the water on the downflap. As it passed over them, it lashed down with its tail, splintering the ferry's forward railing as if it were straw, and sparking unrestrained hysterics on both boat and shore.

Screaming in full-blown panic, people dove into the river after the ferry, while others raced back toward the town buildings. Maddie kept her eyes on the dragon as it reached the bend in the river and flapped upward into the churning, shifting mist. Those around her jibbered in terror. Some threw themselves overboard to swim ashore, forgetting the current, which promptly seized them and carried them over the falls. Ian clutched Captain Channon's neck, his face buried in the man's shoulder, and she thought he was crying, but it was hard to tell with all the other shrieking. Lieutenant Pipping held Simon now, the boy pale-faced but stoic, looking more like his father than ever.

They were almost to the far bank when a raft of mist obscured it completely. Other shreds sailed past them, all moving in the same direction, and as she noticed the wind had lessened and shifted, she looked around to find the dragon hovering above the bend in the river. Facing southward, it flapped its great wings in powerful, deliberate movements, holding its place as it watched her. Even from a distance, its golden eyes pierced her, and she felt its hatred, sensing some of what it meant to do to her. Fear rolled into her, and she turned her back on the beast, determined not to give in to it, and even more determined not to show the slightest quiver of distress. Eidon was with them, the Light was in them, and Abramm was coming. That was what she would focus on.

Suddenly the ferry was bumping against the opposite landing, where its gate was torn from its hinges in the people's haste to get away. She hurried along with them, the castle's arched entrance gate appearing out of the mist ahead of them. Carissa disappeared into it first, then Elayne and Conal, Pipping and Simon, and then she stepped beneath the stonework, Channon close on her heels. The moment she did, a deafening roar exploded above them. Channon flung her, Abby, and Ian against the wall, covering all of them with his own body, as flame enveloped the ferry and its dock, severing the ropes that worked it. Even if those on the far bank could work up the courage to try, there would be no more crossings this day.

As Channon pulled himself off her she felt his trembling, heard the quick in and out of his breath as he stood back and faced the flaming boat and dock while burning embers rained upon them. Ian lifted his head, face tear-streaked, and stared wide-eyed at the destruction. Carissa returned to gather Abby in her arms. And as Maddie watched her sister-in-law hurry through the entrance gate with her children, she touched Channon's arm and, catching his eye, gave him a small smile.

"I'd like you to note, Captain, that its attack came only after we were safe. It really cannot touch us. Not here, anyway. Not so long as we are in the Light."

The townspeople who had earlier made the trip across the river packed the fortress's main keep and halls. Many were children, crying as they caught their parents' fear, which in the last half hour had increased dramatically. Few of them had actually seen the dragon, but the rumors were as bad as the reality.

Anger welled up in her that the thing would do this, but she squelched that, too. In the dragon's eyes, anger was almost as good as fear. It was better, knowing his strategy, simply to ignore him for the impotent threat she knew him to be. To show no fear, no concern, no complaint, but rather to wait in confidence, knowing he had already been defeated. And that soon Abramm would arrive to drive him off for good.

Eager to see what was happening on the plain below, she went up at once to one of the lookout towers, despite Channon's plea that she stay below out of the dragon's range. "If it's going to flame the fortress, you'd be right in the line of fire."

"It won't," she said. "It can't."

He didn't believe her, but she didn't care. She went up anyway, thinking she'd stop at the first arrow slit she came to, but the mist was thicker than ever, and even at the lowest level, her view was obscured. The winds had died almost completely, just enough to keep the Shadow mist moving past the slit. She closed her eyes and sought Eidon, praying for protection and for deliverance and for understanding. She prayed for Abramm and felt him, somehow, out there, suddenly confused and in inexplicable danger, some great force of evil pulling at him, tempting him. She prayed for him to be strengthened. . . .

The Light swelled within her; then a bright flash seemed to shoot out from the plain and wash over her. A moment later the fortress shook so hard she clutched the ledge of the slit to stay upright. And as the shivering passed away, she rejoiced, for she knew exactly what it meant: He had destroyed the corridor. Any doubt she'd had that Abramm was down there evaporated.

But to her consternation and considerable annoyance, when she went back down to tell the others, they were all screaming and weeping and holding to one another as if something terrible had happened.

"What is wrong with them?" she asked of Channon as they stood on the walled landing at the top of the stair leading down into the Great Room.

He turned to look at her in astonishment. "What is wrong with them? Madam, we have a dragon outside breathing fire at us, the Esurhite army fast on its way, and a massive earthquake has nearly brought the walls of our sanctuary down upon us."

"But it didn't," she said. "We are safe here."

"Well, ma'am, I'm sorry to say that you are the only one among us who believes that."

She frowned down at the terrified throng and was just about to clap for their attention when her eyes fixed upon a tall, dark-haired man moving among them, touching now this one, now that—just a hand on the shoulder, a brush of the hand, a tap of the finger. He seemed to feel her eyes upon him, for he glanced up at her, and she saw the gold scaling flash across his cheekbones, and as his dark eyes met hers, they turned golden, the pupils elongating into draconian slits.

Outrage burned in her, and she started down the stairs to confront him, stopping only a few steps later as she realized that was precisely what he wished her to do. She'd confront him; then he would use those honeyed words, that marvelous voice, lace some truth into his lies, use his undeniable appeal to guide the people even more firmly into their fear, make her look stupid, and probably leave her confused and doubting, to boot. And he would love her outrage. To know that he had succeeded in provoking her . . . that would be his victory.

No. You had it right before, she told herself. *Just ignore him. They will not change their minds even if you stand up and tell them.*

So she went back up the stairs, stepped to the edge of the platform, and called the people to listen to her. "I've come to tell you that King Abramm has returned and that he has won. The Shadow is breaking up over the plain and soon will be blown away from Deveren Dol, as well. The beast that is outside"—and here she looked directly at Tiris where he stood among her people—"cannot harm us unless we allow it to. Its greatest weapon is the fear it seeks to build in us. But I tell you now, it is the last desperate ploy of the defeated. King Abramm has returned. Right and good have won. We are free even now."

Tiris smiled up at her, but she sensed the ire behind it. Then his eyes flared like gold disks, and he moved among the people, who now began to speak to one another, quietly at first but with growing emphasis and ire.

Snatches of their words emerged from the general incoherent rumble:

"She's insane!"

"The strain has driven her mad."

"Abramm's *dead*! When will she finally believe that?"

"Belthre'gar is swarming up the river! Nothing can stop him. Look at all this mist."

Finally a stout, red-faced woman stepped forth from Tiris's side and cried angrily, "O Queen, I think you lie to us. There is no victory! Fannath Rill has fallen, or you'd not have fled. And now that it has, it's only a matter of time before they come here. And because of you, they'll kill us all."

Tiris glanced casually over his shoulder and smiled at Maddie. Behind him a blond man stepped up beside the woman and took up her complaint. "Aye, why didn't you stay there and meet your death with dignity? Why did you have to drag all the rest of us down with you?"

"No one has been dragged down," she said. "The battle of Fannath Rill has been won. As the dragon's presence here proves."

"Oh, I don't know," said Tiris himself now. "Why would you think that? It seems to me the dragon's presence proves exactly the opposite. If Abramm has won—and how you would know he was even fighting is a mystery— wouldn't the dragon be dead?"

She stared at him and felt his laughter, for she'd fallen into exactly what she had intended to avoid—she'd started talking to him, and already he was twisting everything around. *Eidon, please, get him out of here. I can ignore him, but these others cannot. I am not great enough to stand against him, but you are. So, please—*

Turn and walk away, my daughter. Leave him to me . . . .

Father Eidon?

The thought did not come again, nor did she ask, she merely gave Tiris a little smile and turned away, heading for the tower stair at the back of the landing. She'd not even reached the archway when the air fluttered about her as with an upheaval in the warp and woof of reality. Behind her the room erupted, people shrieking and scrambling to get away as a burst of wind whooshed around her and something came to rest at the landing's edge directly behind her. At her side, her guards were backed against the walls framing the archway, staring at it in abject terror. Even Captain Channon, ever so mindful of his duty, had forgotten it in his distress.

Tiris, it seemed, had shown his true form at last.

She felt his immensity in a strange displacement of space, and in the way great whooshes of foul breath washed rhythmically around her with his every exhalation, hot on the back of her neck, blowing tendrils of hair around her face. He wanted her to turn and look at him, but she would not.

"You see?" she said to Channon after a time. "If he could flame me now, he would have."

"Do not confuse forebearance with inability, my flower!"

She ignored him. "But he can't. We are covered by the Light, we are covered by the promises of Abramm and Eidon, and we will stay in our fortress until Abramm comes."

"If Abramm is coming, why is the Shadow still here?" asked Channon.

She looked at her guardsman and was struck by the image of dragons hovering northeast of the castle, flapping their wings as if they were fanning a flame. Or was it the Shadow they fought to keep from slipping away?

She smiled as she realized that was exactly what they were doing. Trying to keep it here, trying to hold it here just long enough. Oh yes, he was definitely coming.

Excitement welled up within her, and she laughed aloud.

Behind her, the dragon snorted.

"Turn and face me, woman. I command it."

She ignored him and laughed again. "You see? He cannot do a thing."

Suddenly the beast behind her let loose a blast of hot air so fierce it sent her staggering. The ululation of its cry was deafening as it launched itself off the balcony and shot upward through the Great Room's wooden roof, burning it away with a burst of flame as it went.

38

Abramm's headlong tumble slowed. Something pressed against his feet, and he found himself standing on another weed-grown plaza ringed by broken-off columns of stone in a grassy mountain valley that looked like Seven Peaks. The little man, having exited the corridor ahead of him, turned now to look over his shoulder. His pale eyes fixed on Abramm and widened as he turned to face him fully.

It was Gillard. As he'd been since the morwhol had taken most of his life and substance. Except for the two scars running down the left side of his face. . . . He looked at Abramm as if he couldn't believe his eyes. Then his mouth opened in a soundless wail and he fell to his knees, his face as full of grief as of fear.

The ground lurched under Abramm's feet and the ragged columns waved like stalks of grass. Then darkness flooded around him as great blocks of stone tumbled down on every side, crashing into a massive pan of scarlet flames that appeared out of nowhere. So did the white-robed guardians running hither and thither in the chaos. Abramm's eyes fixed on those of an old man hung on a whipping rack before him. Simon? The man and the pan did not seem to be in the same place exactly, but near each other.

The man stared back at him, eyes blank with pain. Then he blinked and frowned with recognition as above them a domed ceiling collapsed. Abramm escaped on emerald winds shot through more and more with white, until it was all white, all Light, all Eidon himself.

The light faded. Pressure bore against his soles again, and he stood once more in the ruin outside Fannath Rill. Nothing remained of the green corridor but a smoldering black spot on the uneven, grass-invaded pavement. The arcade's remains lay flat, splayed outward across the grassy basin as if an explosion had emanated from the corridor. In every direction up the basin's gradual slopes, pillars, wagons, tents—even men—sprawled in the same outward-pointing array. And as Abramm extended his senses outward he caught up with the great wind ripping over the land, tearing away the darkness as it went. He saw the dragon, flipped head over tail, wings tangling awkwardly around it, all grip on the air lost. It was blown northward, it and all its subordinates, hurled out of the realm like autumn leaves.

He sensed his wife turning toward him, blooming with the delight of recognition. He smiled. *Soon, my love . . .*

"Sire?"

Trap and Rolland approached him, picking their way through the tangle of bodies, their clothing torn and stained with dirt and blood, and pocked with tiny burn holes. They still gripped their bared, blood-soaked blades, eyes startlingly white in faces darkened with soot and marred with cuts and bruises and blisters from the falling embers. As they stopped before him he saw their exhaustion and realized they had not deserted him after all, but had been covering his back as much as they could, though in the chaos he'd never seen them. He felt a surge of gratitude and affection for both of them.

"Are you all right?" Rolland asked, his eyes drawing away from Abramm to survey the bodies piled around them.

"Yes," Abramm said. He glanced at Trap, who was staring at the darkened disk where the corridor had been. Its diameter was easily the length of a horse.

His friend's gaze came back to his. "I thought for sure it was a trap he'd set for you."

"It was," Abramm said. He moved from the center of the ruin, treading carefully between the bodies across the smoking battlefield back toward the city gate, now a ragged, soot-stained hole in the wall. Behind it bright flames leaped beneath billows of black smoke. More of the dragon's work. . . .

By then news of his presence had spread, and men came toward him from all directions—his men. The soldiers he had gathered as he'd come across the realm: exhausted, bleeding, and filthy, but glowing with triumph. A man on a bay horse picked his way among them, leading a tall gray stallion behind him. Warbanner . . . whose neck had not been slashed after all, merely stained with Belthre'gar's blood. People emerged from the city in a weary stream to crowd around Abramm in rising jubilation.

It was Borlain who brought him Warbanner, and he came with news of how after the dragon had killed half his own soldiers, the rest had either turned on themselves or fled. Most of the Broho had fled even earlier and could not be found. He feared they had slipped into the city to do more mischief when folk least expected it.

The stream of people emerging from the city had doubled, and it included a cadre of mounted noblemen. As Abramm swung onto Warbanner's back and surveyed the field of victory, his heart fell. For he saw there was much work to be done in Fannath Rill—work that required a king's presence—and seeing as Chesedh had no king right now, it was a role he would have to play. So, once again, he could not go to her just yet. But he had learned nothing in these last two years if not how to accept Eidon's will with grace, and he contented himself with the pleasure of knowing that eventually their reunion would happen.

Gillard fell spinning and tumbling, closing his eyes and sinking into that place of semiconsciousness as he'd been taught, feeling the Other rise up to enclose him. He sensed its satisfaction with something, and then through it, his brother coming after him. He had drawn Abramm into the corridor after him, and that was good, for the Other meant to kill him, to take him where he did not want to go. To—

He didn't know what it would do. The notions tumbled too swiftly through his brain to hold on to any of them. Finally he stopped falling as solid stone pressed beneath his feet and he stepped out of the corridor into the central plaza of Tuk-Rhaal, where he had started. The great crowd of Kiriathan soldiers that had been here two days ago was gone, transported like him to the Fairiron Plain outside Fannath Rill. Most were likely dead now.

One of the shaven-headed priests who supported and maintained the corridor and who had been kneeling nearby now stood and started toward him. At the same moment something hissed from the corridor behind him, and he leaped forward, his skin puckering with alarm. Embarrassed to have startled right in front of the priest, he made himself stop and turn back, and was horrified to see the emerald column now shot through with streaks of white. A figure had taken shape in it, one about to step out of the light and into the reality of this place. A figure he recognized.

Abramm.

The green cleared and the white light illumined his brother's face—the blue eyes, the level brows, the hawkish features so like those of their father and their long-dead brothers, and those white scars raking down the side of his cheek. Fear mingled with a strange grief as he looked into Abramm's eyes. His only living brother. The man with whom he had more in common than any other in all the world. Come back to him at last.

Come back to kill him.

He fell to his knees, weeping. They could have been friends. They could have been as the brothers they were. They could have ruled together. Abramm as his counselor . . . but he'd never understood that. Never wanted to take the second position. Now he would kill Gillard with his own hand. Because of that wretched shield on his chest. Because of that monstrous orb that put it there. Because of the dying, useless, vicious god he served.

The grief was overwhelming. Why couldn't they have had what they were meant to have? It wasn't fair. It wasn't right—

Suddenly the emerald light flared back across his brother's face, and Gillard realized that Abramm was receding, fading. . . . And then a blast of white light splintered the green and knocked him backward. He tumbled over and fell facedown as a terrible wind swooped upon him, so powerful it shoved him along the pavement as if he were an old cloak—shoved him and turned him and fetched him up against one of the ancient pillars. Barely had it died away when a loud rumble broke the silence and the ground heaved. He covered his head with his hands and tried to make himself one with the pavement, but it bucked him off. He rolled down a slope where moments before all had been flat, and saw the pillars waving madly against the shredding mist. Then before his eyes, they came apart—huge cylindrical pieces breaking off and slamming to the ground. As he stared, one broke off right above him and plummeted straight down.

At the last moment he rolled away, covering his head again. The huge stone missile hit the ground with a crash and a thud so deep it vibrated the stones beneath his chest, so close to his arm that it scraped the skin and tore his sleeve. Other chunks followed it in a continuous rain of rock. He lay there jittering and quivering, certain every moment would be his last.

Then the deadly rain ended, and the ground quit bucking. Finally he dared to look around. The piece of column beside him was three times his size. It had trapped his sleeve under it, and he had to tear himself free, his flesh throbbing from all the hits he'd sustained as the wind had tumbled him about. His left arm, collarbone, and a few ribs were surely broken. Soon the pain would be white-hot and he'd have to struggle to function at all.

He pushed himself up, sneezing and coughing on the dust that veiled the air. The corridor was gone, the remains of the temple flattened. The priests that had been in attendance lay unmoving beneath various pieces of rock, white with the falling dust. Slowly Gillard turned. Except for a couple of distant horses, the valley lay still and empty, the priests' tents flattened from the quake.

Stormcroft still stood across the grassy hummocks, but it would be a long walk for one in such pain. Perhaps he should sit here and wait. Surely if someone had survived in Stormcroft, they'd come out to see what had happened.

He leaned against the stump of a pillar and slid to the ground, sitting with his back against it, staring at a burn hole that was all that remained of the corridor. Most of his army, what remained of it after the Mataians had forced him to disband it, had been destroyed in Chesedh. Or at any rate were now in Chesedh, with no way to get back to Kiriath anytime soon.

Abramm had taken Fannath Rill, killed Belthre'gar, and driven away the dragon. He had delivered the Chesedhans. And he had the crown, the scepter, the robe, and most likely the orb and ring, as well. The only thing he didn't have—

Gillard stiffened and looked around. He thought he'd brought the sword of state through when he'd come; he'd had it in his hand before he'd charged into Abramm. Had he lost it in the earthquake . . . or in the shock of the pain of colliding with his brother? New misery enwrapped him, for he was suddenly sure that he had dropped it before he'd come through. Leaving it there for Abramm to find. After which he would return to Kiriath to claim the rest of what belonged to him.

It was Belmir who came to unlock Simon's shackles, picking his way through the bodies and the debris to where Simon hung in a secret chamber under the Holy Keep's sacred Sanctum. With the collapse of two of its walls, Simon supposed it was not secret anymore, though there were precious few around to see that.

Belmir confirmed Simon's observation. "All dead," he said, bending to slide his key into the manacles around Simon's feet. "Crushed or burned . . ." He paused and added, "Well, probably not all of them, because not all of them were around, but all that I could see. And those closest are charred beyond recognition. . . ." The manacle came free and he turned to the other.

In a moment both Simon's feet dangled freely, and Belmir backed away to shove one of the rectangular stones from the fallen walls under them. Then he turned to free Simon's arms.

"You were right here in the heart of it all," Belmir said, "and you're not even singed. Want to tell me why?"

"I have no idea." When his chamber's walls had collapsed, Simon had found himself facing the etherworld corridor he'd long known the Mataians operated deep in the Holy Keep. Swollen and shot through with streaks of white, the thing had sparked and flickered as if it were broken. Then a man appeared at its midst, clothes and hair and eyes all white. A man with twin scars down the left side of his face. The light had dimmed and Simon saw the eyes were not white but piercing blue. He'd said his nephew's name aloud, so great was his surprise. But the word had come out a faint croak. Abramm held the scepter; he wore the crown. And he had looked straight into Simon's eyes. Moments later the corridor had exploded and the keep had rained down around him.

"Abramm's alive," he rasped.

Belmir, who was busy lifting Simon's swollen and bloodied arm over his own shoulder, paused. "They told you that?"

"I saw him. In the corridor. Just before it blew. He destroyed it, old friend. And he's coming back."

Belmir said something, but Simon must have passed out, because the next thing he knew, he lay in bed, swathed in bandages. He stared stupidly at the brocade canopy above him, then turned his head—his muscles protesting keenly that simple movement—to inspect the room. Dark wainscoting paneled the lower portion of the walls. A multipaned window looked out on tree branches through which poured . . . was that really *sunlight*? A man sat in a chair against the wall, and looking up now at the sounds of Simon's movement, he broke into a grin. "My lord! You have awakened!"

Before Simon could say a word, the man had run out of the room.

Moments later Belmir appeared in the doorway, followed by Seth Harker, Philip Meridon, and then half a dozen others from the Underground. But there were also the embattled speaker of the Table of Lords and several others from that body. Most of whom, if he recalled correctly, had been in prison. From them he learned most of the details of the destruction of not only the Holy Keep in Springerlan but also of the Keep of the Heartland—both the result of some great explosion from within. The corridor up in the Valley of the Seven Peaks had also been destroyed, and Underground forces had captured Gillard in the ruins of Tuk-Rhaal.

Simon snorted softly. "I thought he'd gone to Chesedh."

"They think he did. They found him close to the remains of the corridor." Harker paused. "Sir, they say he's not spoken but a handful of recognizable words. That he laughs continuously and, if allowed, keeps trying to cut his face again. He's utterly mad."

"Yes, well, he's been in that state for some time now."

"But this is worse. They're bringing him down to present him to the Table, but I seriously doubt he is going to be accepted. Even if he can string a sentence or two together." He hesitated, then glanced at the other men. "Simon, we need a king. And you're the last of the line."

Simon huffed gruffly. "No I'm not."

"The boy . . . is just a boy."

Simon glared at the man. "I'm not talking about my grandnephew. I'm talking about his father."

The men looked at one another, clearly understanding what he meant but wondering if they should believe him.

"Yes," he said when no one else spoke. "I'm talking about Abramm." And oh, did it feel good to just come out and say the name. "He's alive. He was not executed. I know because I helped rescue him. As did Master Belmir and young Philip here."

The others glanced at the two men he cited, and they nodded confirmation.

The former speaker of the Table of Lords said, "So you're saying the stories out of Chesedh . . ."

"Are true," Simon finished for him. "At least some of them. In particular the one about him regaining the regalia, since I saw him with the crown and scepter."

"From a fisherman's nets?" The gray-haired speaker frowned. "Come, Simon. That's a bit hard to swallow. And anyway, if you rescued him, where has he been the last two-plus years?"

"I don't know. I only know he's back. I saw him when the corridor blew, and he was wearing the regalia."

The men looked at one another again.

"He's coming back," Simon said. "I expect he's finally defeated Belthre'gar. We'll probably hear of it soon."

"But we don't know that, Simon," said Seth Harker. "And we need a leader now."

448 || K A R E N   H A N C O C K

"Then I'll be regent for him until we do know."

That seemed to satisfy them. After a bit more talk they took their leave, and Simon was glad of it, for he hurt all over and was very tired. Then he noticed that Belmir had hung back and was now pulling a small velvet bag from his pocket. He held it out to Simon. "You asked me to keep this for you, remember?"

"Thank you." He toyed with the string and smiled bitterly. "You were right, of course. I would have been better off not to have parted with it."

"Well, now you have it back." Belmir gave him a nod and left.

As silence closed about him, Simon relaxed back into the pillows, weary beyond belief, in body. But not in mind. His thoughts brushed lightly over all the things that had gnawed at him so doggedly these last years—the ache, the unrelenting sense of purposelessness. Even saving Kiriath had not come about by anything he had done. And death still lay ahead of him, closer now than ever. Was that to be the end of him, then?

Belmir said not. Belmir said—no, the Words of *Eidon* said that he was already on his way to a place of torment worse than anything he'd experienced at the hands of the Mataians. That the only deliverance from it was to accept the payment that had been made on his behalf. Payment for a mind and will and soul that lived in opposition to the perfect good that Eidon was.

Did he believe any of that? He wasn't sure. It was hard to take hold of something he'd rejected all his life. Even though the very rejection was part of what had been paid for. Yes, he had been a good man, so far as men went, but he hadn't made his own flesh, nor given himself life, nor even kept himself alive. Another did that. One who had fashioned him with the very brain and mouth he'd used to deny and reject. One who not only put up with the rejection and denial but allowed his son to take the punishment for it. . . .

"Religious claptrap," he grumbled as he loosened the bag's drawstring.

But in his mind he saw Abramm again—the white hair and eyes and robe. Not Abramm there at the first, and not Abramm at the last . . . someone else. Someone shining through Abramm. Someone who knew Simon very well.

"I could never wear a shield on my chest," he said gruffly. "It's not who I am."

He upended the bag and dumped the orb into his callused palm. It lay there, shining almost as brightly as the eyes of the man he'd seen in the corridor just before it had exploded.

39

Maddie was more nervous than she'd been on her wedding day. Her husband was coming, and she had a thousand things to do before he arrived. The whole world, it seemed, had crowded into Deveren Dol to welcome him, and she was so excited she could hardly think straight.

It had been three weeks since the victory at Fannath Rill and the dragon had been chased off. Abramm had sent Trap and a small force of soldiers up to Deveren Dol to deal with the Esurhites who had come down the Ankrill. Carissa had delivered their second child the day after he'd chased them off, and as he'd predicted there was nothing he could do but fret in the sitting room. She'd produced another healthy, red-haired boy, whom they'd named Peregrine, in remembrance of their time in Peregris. Maddie had never seen either of them happier, and it only amplified her own expectations for a similar reunion.

For Trap had brought with him another letter—the first of a rash of exchanges between the king and queen—detailing how much Abramm wanted to come to her and that he would. But there was such disorder in Fannath Rill, and everyone was coming to him for guidance.

Some of them are even suggesting I should be their king, he'd written. *And not simply by marriage. They're still using the combined banner we devised for the campaign. You've probably seen it by now—the red dragon on a gold shield under a crown? The dragon was their idea, but in the end I think it's right.*

She had seen the combined banner—Trap had ridden in under it—and she'd also seen the degree of worship the men held for her husband. If it was in any way reflective of what was going on down on the plain—and Trap said it wasn't even close—she could understand why they'd want him for their king. It made her heart swell with joy and pride and wonder to think of all that Eidon had done.

She'd have gone down to Fannath Rill herself, and taken the children, but he'd asked her not to. It was still too unsettled. Just getting the city government back up and running had been a huge chore, and there was much left to be done. Besides the disposition of the bodies, there was the city to repair and rebuild, and the palace was in ruins. *We're all living in tents here, love.* And packs of Broho and other Esurhite renegades—who seemed intent on killing as many of their enemies as they could before they died themselves—needed to be dug out of their hiding spots. Worst of all, they were battling an outbreak of dysentery, and another illness the physicians hadn't yet identified and he couldn't bear to risk any of them to that.

And it wasn't as if there was nothing for her to do in Deveren Dol, anyway. They had their own ranks of wounded to be tended, bodies to bury or burn, and destruction to repair.

But finally things were falling into place, and Abramm had decided he'd waited long enough. He would stay in Deveren Dol for a week, then return to Fannath Rill with his wife and children. Then they would see about his becoming king of Chesedh for real.

It was a four-day ride up from Fannath Rill, and people had come from all over the highlands and the plain to line the way and cheer.

During those four long days, Maddie at times felt nothing but sheer delight in the anticipation, a joy that quickly crescendoed into unbearable impatience for the moment to finally arrive. At others, she was hit with waves of inexplicable anxiety. He had been gone so long and, from what Trap had told her, been through so much, she worried he wouldn't delight in her as he used to, worried that while he had changed, she had not, and they would have lost that easiness, that way of knowing what the other was thinking even before the words were spoken. She worried about the children. Ian still wasn't speaking to anyone and was unlikely to be receptive toward the father he'd not seen in more than two long years. Even Simon had recently developed an inexplicable aversion to seeing his papa. The two of them were so closed and hostile, she feared Abramm's happy homecoming could turn into a trial and an embarrassment for all of them.

But there was so much to be done in preparation, she rarely had time to stop and think it all through, and could only trust Eidon to make it right.

Indeed, after all he had done, it irked her that she could even entertain a moment's worth of doubt.

The day of the king's scheduled arrival, the queen was up before dawn—making sure the preparations for the feast were started and that all they would need was at hand, seeing to the guest list once more, consulting with the steward as to the final decision on the arrangement of the tables and benches, seeing that the musicians were ready and that a new lirret was found for one who had damaged his en route, ensuring that the newly constructed rooms in the fortress's upper stories were swept and ready for their visitors to stay in, and a hundred other little things people couldn't seem to decide without her counsel.

And besides all that, she had herself and the children to get ready.

With space at a premium, they were sharing the small room she had claimed for herself. Naturally, Ian had been cranky and obstinate all morning, and even Simon was being difficult, back to his whining about not wanting to be there when Abramm arrived. "I don't care about seeing Papa!" he said. "I want to go fishing with Ian and Uncle Trap."

As Maddie laid Abby on the bed and attempted to pull her plain morning gown over her head, she pointed out that Uncle Trap was not going fishing today. "Because, unlike you, he does want to see your papa."

"I don't want to see Papa! I want to go fishing!" He started to wail.

She turned from Abby and said sharply, "Enough of that, Simon!" And when he stopped, she demanded, "What is wrong with you? Yesterday you were dancing all around to think you would see your papa today."

"I don't want to see Papa."

"Well, you are going to. And you will not use that tone with me. Do you need a switching to remind you of your manners?"

"No, Mama."

"Now, we must get ready. He'll be here very soon." She glanced over her shoulder as Elayne stepped in with the newly pressed suit that Simon was to wear. But as the older woman came forward and took Simon by the hand, he started to cry in earnest. "I don't want to see Papa."

"Oh, for goodness' sake, Simon!" Elayne scolded. "What are you so afraid of? Your papa loves you. He will be greatly excited to see you. Why do you not want to see him?"

"They said he is just like Grandpapa."

"Like Grandpapa?!" Maddie said, turning from Abby again to look sharply at him.

"Grandpapa was mean. He was bad."

"Grandpapa was ill, Simon. He didn't know what he was doing. The bad thing the Esurhites put inside him made him like that."

"And Papa has a bad thing in him, too. Just like Grandpapa. I heard Uncle Trap telling Auntie Crissa it was so."

Maddie exchanged a glance with Elayne, then came to Simon and squatted before him. "Yes, Simon, that was so, but your papa knows Father Eidon well enough to let him take it all away. Grandpapa did not know how to do that."

"Father Eidon took it away?"

"Yes, Simon. Papa could not have come back to chase away the dragon if he had the bad thing growing in him as Grandpapa did."

Simon stared at her with his big blue eyes, considering what she had said. Then the crossness came into his face. "I still don't want to see him. I want to go fishing."

"Well, perhaps he will want to go fishing, too, and might even take you with him tomorrow if you ask him nicely."

"I want to go today," he said sulkily.

Maddie exhaled in resignation, shook her head, and returned her attention to little Abby.

Finally they were all ready, and she went with Carissa, Trap, and Channon to the upper towers to watch him come up over the cliff and head down the river road toward the ferry—boat, ropes, and both landings all brand-new and decorated with garlands of evergreen. The first sight of him, still a distant dot atop the white shape of his horse, gave her such a burst of excitement she could hardly bear it, torn between wanting to snatch up the spyglass for a better look, and waiting until he was close enough she'd not torment herself. She watched him until he was halfway across the river, then hurried with the others down to the fortress's front door, where a walled landing and side stair overlooked the entrance yard and the opening of the tunnel gate. Like the ferry, the yard was decorated in evergreen boughs, brightly colored ribbons, and broad white banners bearing his new device—red dragon on a gold shield surmounted by a crown.

She tracked his position by the roaring of the crowd, her heart pounding madly in her chest the closer he got. Soon the leading riders of his party came through the gate, and the crowd in the yard erupted. They filed out to either side, and she counted them, knowing finally that the next man to appear would be her husband.

When he emerged from the shadows into the bright sun of the inner courtyard, her heart leaped and tears quickly blurred the image. She was vaguely aware of Simon squealing and that he had let go her hand. Moments later she spied him racing across the yard toward Abramm, who bent down from the back of Warbanner and swooped him up into the saddle before him. Her little boy, who had been so adamant about not wanting to see his papa, flung both arms about the monarch's neck—her own father would have been aghast at such an undisciplined display of affection—as if he weren't a king at all but just a little boy's papa.

She watched her husband grinning at their son as the latter bobbed excitedly on the saddle's pommel, jabbering away, pointing now at Maddie, who still stood on the landing. Abramm looked up at her then, and as their eyes met, a shudder shook her body so violently she had to lean against the warm stone to keep from falling. For a moment all the breath left her as light flared at the edges of her vision and he became the only person in the world. A warm tingle started at her toes and swept up her body to the top of her head, and then a wild, hot energy charged through her, so that she pushed off the wall and flew down the sidestair, around the walled corner and out into the yard, where she stopped as soon as she had stepped into the sun.

He was still across the yard from her, still sitting on Warbanner, his eyes fixed upon her. Letting go the reins, he swung one leg forward over the horse's neck and dropped lightly to the ground, Simon still in his arms. Then, his gaze never leaving hers, he stooped to set his son on his own two feet and started toward her. She stood there, breathless, reveling in the sight of him— the broadness of his shoulders, his powerful build, the easy grace with which he walked, and every small exquisite detail of his beloved face. . . . The strong brow, those blue eyes that always made her heart catch. They had crow's-feet at their corners now, and the hair at his temples carried a frosting of white. She could see in the other lines and the look on his face that he was not the man she'd known two and a half years ago. He was a better one, refined by fire.

He'd crossed half the distance between them when she flew to meet him, throwing her arms about his neck as he crushed her to him and kissed her, and she thought that not even Eidon's realm of eternal bliss could hold more joy for her than this one spectacular moment.

Not until they broke apart did she remember they were not alone. The crowd was whistling, screaming, and cheering all about them. Abramm released her, and she stepped back, under his arm, as he acknowledged the onlookers. Simon had caught up with them and was holding to his cloak.

And then Elayne appeared in the archway where the stairs ended—Abrielle in one arm, Ian clutching the other hand and trying to hide behind the woman's skirts.

"Ian doesn't warm up to anyone quickly," Maddie warned Abramm. "And he still speaks to no one but Simon."

"Yes. Trap told me. Given what he's gone through, I can't blame him."

He strode forward to greet them, marveling at his daughter first, and getting a grin out of her with his extravagant words. Ian, of course, would have nothing to do with him, and it broke Maddie's heart to see it. Her husband finally stood again, his expression placid and relaxed, as if he really did understand, as if it wasn't breaking his heart at all.

"He'll come to me when he's ready to forgive me," he said.

"Forgive you?"

"For leaving him when I did . . . for not coming back as soon as I'd hoped. For all the terrible things that have happened to him."

"Those weren't your fault."

"In his eyes they are. I was supposed to protect him, and I didn't. But perhaps he will grow to understand. And I have learned nothing if not how to wait during these last two years."

He smiled down at her and she lost her breath again for love of him.

Then Abby laughed and held her hands out to him, and he took her into his arms with an answering grin. Ian peeped round Elayne's skirts, his thumb still in his mouth as he watched his father swinging his little sister over his head while she squealed with delight.

Another spectacle old Hadrich would have found abhorrent.

Maddie, on the other hand, loved every moment of it. And so, she judged, did the crowd. Carissa and Trap had come down the stairs after Elayne with both their boys, and he greeted them all with great affection. Then he turned to the big blond man who'd ridden in just before him and gestured for him to dismount and approach. Thus Maddie was introduced to Rolland Kemp, the man who'd stood at her husband's side from the day he'd left Kiriath, who had saved his life more than once, and who had become not only one of his most trusted subordinates but a dear friend.

After that, they entered the great room where the tables had been set up and roast bullock filled the air with its savory aroma.

It was a day filled with celebration. Maddie sat beside Abramm and marveled at the stream of people who came to congratulate him, to thank him, to tell him the specifics of what he had done for them. Among them was Krele Janner, for Maddie herself had summoned him to the celebration when she'd sent a man to Ru'geruk with his payment. He was sober and rough around the edges but clearly awestruck at the notion that Alaric not only had survived but really had turned out to be a king.

Abramm received him and all the others with a relaxed graciousness that she had never seen in him before. Though he had always interacted with his subjects kindly and respectfully, this was different. She couldn't put her finger on it, but it was one more subtle change in him for the better.

The party went on into the night, but the king and queen left early and retired to the bedchamber that had been prepared for them. As soon as the door was shut he took her into his arms and kissed her in a long, tender embrace that felt to her like drinking from a well of sweet water too long denied her.

After a while they pulled apart and she stood looking up at him, delighting in the blue of his eyes, the level brows she loved so much. Truly he was the most handsome man in the world, and time and hard use had only made him more so. She trailed her fingers down the slender scars, and then he kissed her again, hungrily this time. It wasn't long before they'd left their clothing strewn across the floor as they retired to their big, silk-veiled bed, and lost themselves in the glory of their love for each other.

Abramm was officially crowned king of Chesedh two months later in Fannath Rill. They did not use the crown of the Chesedhan regalia but that of Avramm I, which Abramm had received from the fisherman in Elpis and worn when he had delivered the realm from Belthre'gar and the Shadow of Moroq. The Kiriathan robe, scepter, and orb were also used in the ceremony—and again the orb exploded in plumes of tiny Stars of Life to float out over the crowd who had gathered to watch. And for the Robe of Sovereignty, a new garment was sewn of purple and gold, and trimmed with white ermine, a combination of the two realms.

It was an odd ceremony all around, in Abramm's view; the Chesedhans' acceptance of the Kiriathan regalia—and of himself as their king—contrasted ironically with the fact that Kiriath itself had driven him out.

But then Philip Meridon arrived as emissary from Kiriath, his own wife and baby girl at his side, come to see their uncle, aunt, and cousins, and bearing a letter for Abramm. The words were written in a shaky hand by Simon

Kalladorne himself, asking formally for Abramm to return and take his rightful place on the throne of that land, as well. He named himself regent serving in Abramm's stead, waiting only for him to return and take up what was his.

They need you, Abramm. My health is not good anymore, and I do not think I am long for this world. If you do not come, they will bring Gillard out of his prison and put him back on the throne. He is quite mad now. A wreck of what he was. If they do that, he will ruin us. All that's been gained here because of what you did in Chesedh will be lost. We want you back, Abramm. Some of us never wanted you to leave. . . .

Abramm's heart was moved as he read the letter, for he felt his uncle's anguish and understood his position. It shocked him to think that Simon might be ailing, for he had always been robust of health. Philip told them that the Gadrielites had caught him in the act of helping free convicted heretics, and that he'd been tried and convicted of treason himself. When he'd refused to swear allegiance to their Flames, he'd disappeared into the Holy Keep, where he'd been beaten and deliberately starved for over a year. The abuse was more than his aged body could take, and he had not recovered.

"He's been bedridden for months now, sir."

And so Abramm considered the request, asking Eidon's counsel even before he went to the men on his cabinet. They spent the day in sometimes-heated discussion, but by evening all were agreed that a union of the two realms would be acceptable.

The next day he went walking with his eldest son and daughter—Ian still refused to have anything to do with him—along the beach at the end of Fannath Rill's island, where a small park had been built.

"You are going to leave again, aren't you?" Simon asked reproachfully as they looked for slingstones from among the polished rocks on the beach.

Abramm regarded him with surprise. "I haven't decided yet, Simon. Though I think perhaps I might have to."

"I don't want you to go."

"And I don't want to leave you either, my little man. Nor your brother and sister." *Nor your mother, most of all. . . .* "But I think it is what I am supposed to do."

Simon said nothing, head down, eyes on the ground. Behind him, little Abby toddled along a stretch of sand as a barge slid by on the current beyond the swell of the island behind her.

"Do you remember Kiriath at all?" he asked Simon. "It is where I was born. Where you and Ian were born. . . ."

"I remember my pony," Simon said.

"Ah yes, little Warbanner."

His son stopped and looked up at him, the river breeze lifting the straight blond hair that fell over his forehead. "Do you think he's still there?"

"I don't know. But I can look for him." He bent down and picked up a white rock from among the gleaming tumble of stones, brushed away a few grains of sand, then held it out for Simon to examine. "This one would be good, don't you think?"

His son rubbed a stubby, sand-encrusted finger along it, then looked up at him and nodded. "A perfect one, Papa."

"I think Ian might like it, don't you?"

Simon looked uncertain for a moment, and Abramm saw that he might like it himself, despite the fact Abramm had already given him an entire bag of perfect stones. But in the end his face cleared and he nodded with confidence. "Yes, I think he would."

But when they returned to the nursery and Abramm presented the stone to his younger son, Ian would have none of it. Standing up against the play table with his thumb in his mouth, he only looked at the floor. So Abramm left it on the table, read a story to Abby and Simon, then took his leave. Just as he passed through the door, though, he saw Ian snatch the stone from off the table and run to the other side of the room to examine it.

Abramm closed the door and headed back to his own apartments feeling bittersweet. His heart leapt at the knowledge that Ian had taken the gift. But now here he was thinking about leaving again, and that would surely kill any seedlings of trust and warmth for him that might be sprouting finally in the boy's heart.

When at last all the decisions and preparations had been made and the morning came for him to depart, his family gathered at the dock to see him off. He faced Simon, told him to be strong, to take care of his mother and his siblings, and shook the boy's hand. Simon bore it stoically, reminding him weirdly of himself at that age. Then he squatted down before Ian, who for a wonder was no longer trying to hide from him behind someone else. He stood there and looked into his father's eyes expressionlessly, his thumb in his mouth, as always.

Abramm set a gentle hand on his son's shoulder, and the boy didn't even flinch. "I never chose to leave, Ian. And I fought with all that's in me to come back to you as soon as I could. During all that time, I never stopped thinking of you and Simon and your mother."

Ian's blue eyes strayed meaningfully to Abby, standing beside him, and Abramm smiled. "Well, I didn't know about Abby while I was out there, or I surely would have thought of her, too." He grinned at his daughter. "She is so sweet, I could never have stopped thinking of her had I known."

His little girl jumped up on her toes and grinned back at him, then threw her arms about his neck, laughing in delight, too young to have any idea what he was talking about.

"You left!"

A thrill shot through him as he realized Ian had spoken. To him. Bitterly and reproachfully, but he had spoken. Abramm turned back to his son, handing Abby off to Maddie, who had stepped forward to receive her, alert as always to what was going on.

"I know I left," Abramm said quietly, crouching down to face his son. "And I meant to come back much sooner. But I am only a man, Ian. And men don't always get to do what they want. Only Eidon can do that."

"You are going away again."

"You know I do not want to."

Ian wore his reproach on his face and simply stared.

"There are people in our homeland who need me right now. Just as they will need you one day. They have no king. They do not know what to do, and they are very scared and sad. If I do not go, bad men like the ones who came here might come and try to hurt them."

"Does Father Eidon want you to go?"

Abramm held his son's gaze. "Yes, Ian. I believe he does."

"Then he will bring you back."

The confidence in his little boy's voice rocked him to his core. Then, to surprise him beyond anything he could even have imagined, Ian stepped toward him, staring at the scars on his face and finally putting his finger to his father's brow. Transfixed, Abramm watched his son's face as the boy drew his finger down the length of the scars, then met his gaze again and finally threw his arms around Abramm's neck, bursting into tears. "I don't want you to go, Papa."

Abramm held him tightly and whispered, "I know, Ian."

He gathered his son into his arms and stood, carrying him to the end of the dock where the gangplank waited. And when Ian's outburst had ended, he said, "I have brought lots of pigeons with me, and I will send one every day, so you can look for that. If things go as I hope, it won't be long before all of you can come join me there. Would that be all right?"

Ian nodded, and wiped the tears away with his chubby hands. When Abramm put him down, he stood stoutly next to Simon and his thumb stayed down by his side.

And then, at last, it was time to say good-bye to his wife.

He grabbed her and kissed her hard. "I hate this," he said gruffly when he pulled free of her. "You know that, don't you?"

"Well, you shouldn't." She smiled up at him. "It is what Eidon has called you to do, my love. You might as well learn to enjoy it."

He cocked a brow at her. Then she rose up on tiptoe, pressed her hand against the back of his neck, and kissed him just as hard as he had kissed her. "I will miss you worse than ever," she whispered. "Try to get your business done swiftly this time, all right?"

Then there was nothing left but to release her and step across the plank to the deck of the *New Mariner*. But it seemed that all the crewmen were in far too much of a hurry to set sail, and all too soon he was on his way. Back to Kiriath.

It was a bright spring day when King Abramm returned to Kiriath, the land of his heritage. His people turned out in a vast multitude to welcome him home, their vessels filling Kalladorne Bay. Banners of every color fluttered in the breeze beneath the wide blue sky, and as the *New Mariner* turned into the bay's mouth, the fortress cannon on both headlands boomed a welcome.

Slowly his vessel nosed through the mat of boats floating gunwale to gunwale across the bay. People cheered and fluttered hats, cloaks, and even aprons as bands played from the decks. The city bells rang in the distance and fireworks shot off from the shore, exploding overhead in sparkling clouds of thunder. Abramm stood on the quarterdeck, waving and wondering wryly how long it would be before some of them were complaining about him again. Once the thought would have disturbed him. Now he merely recognized it as truth, comfortable in the fact that it wasn't the people who wanted him or didn't want him that had made him king over them again—it was the will of Eidon.

Two years of drought, fires, and flooding had so filled the harbor with silt that deep-drafted sailing ships like *New Mariner* could no longer approach the city itself. Thus the royal barge awaited him halfway, leaders of the interim government arrayed on its deck in their finery to greet him. He saw Seth Harker among them, and his old discipler, Belmir—hardly recognizable without his long Mataian braid and gray robes—but the rest of them were strangers. A new cadre of leaders had moved into the hole created by the loss of the old.

As the *New Mariner* drifted to a stop beside the barge and the crew scurried to make ready for his disembarkation, Abramm surveyed the great crowd that surrounded him on both water and shore. He took in the blackened ruin of Southdock, stark against the new spring greenery of the nicer neighborhoods on the hills above it, all of it overlooked by the royal palace of Whitehill, serene on its high cliffs. His home. Soon to be his kingdom, again, in addition to Chesedh. He had brought the regalia with him, kept safe in a strongbox in the royal cabin.

Eidon had brought it all back to him, just as he'd promised on the walls of Highmount. More than brought it back. And there were moments, like now, when the contemplation of that fact, and the power it had taken to do it, overwhelmed him. For Eidon hadn't just transformed events to bring this about, he'd transformed Abramm himself, and that was the much harder work.

Gratitude flooded him. *Thank you, my Lord. For all that you have done. For taking everything away and all you have shown me through the loss. For making me wait. For all the ways you have protected and provided. . . .* His thoughts danced from wonder to wonder, kindness to kindness—each branching into multiples, and the multiples branching further. . . .

It took his breath away to think the one who could do such things loved him as a father loved a son. That the Creator's very Light dwelt in Abramm's flesh and, more and more now, in his heart. *You have taught me so much, Father . . . and yet it seems I've only begun to know you.*

There was a chuckle. *Do you think it all ends here, then? That I will not continue to teach you until the day that you die? And beyond?*

The men who had lined up in flanking rows between Abramm and the opening in the gunwale now snapped to stiff attention in anticipation of his passage, and silence dropped around them. Beyond the gunwale, the kingdom of Kiriath awaited.

He grinned at Eidon's question. *Of course you will, my Father.*

And with that, he strode through the gauntlet as the trumpets blared in fanfare, and all around the assembled multitude began to roar.